PRAISE FOR DOMINA

"A heady brew of medicine and romance that should appeal to a wide audience. . . . The briskly paced story and attractive characters carry the reader along. Recommended."

—Library Journal

"Domina is fascinating reading . . . it is also a wonderfully frustrating romantic tale. In the end, *Domina* is as captivating as Samantha is herself."
—Detroit Free Press

"*Domina* is an impressively researched and emotionally involving saga of one of the first woman doctors, and a fascination look back into the dark ages of medicine—a century ago. The strong feminine point of view is compelling and passionate . . . A book that inspires."
  —Elizabeth Forsythe Hailey, author of *A Woman of Independent Means*

"A fast-moving tale [with] wide appeal. Wood paces her novel well, peoples it with interesting and often unusual characters, injects the proper amount of bittersweet romance and sets it all against the well-researched and in- triguing background of medicine during an epoch of dramatic change."
—Publishers Weekly

DOMINA

Other Books By
BARBARA WOOD
Virgins of Paradise
The Dreaming
Green City in the Sun
Soul Flame
Vital Signs
The Watch Gods
Childsong
Night Trains
Yesterday's Child
Curse This House
Hounds and Jackals
The Divining

Books By
KATHRYN HARVEY
Butterfly
Stars
Private Entrance

DOMINA

BARBARA WOOD

TURNER

Turner Publishing Company

200 4th Avenue North • Suite 950
Nashville, Tennessee 37219

445 Park Avenue • 9th Floor
New York, NY 10022

www.turnerpublishing.com

Domina

Domina is a work of historical fiction. Although some events and people
in this book are based on historical fact, others are the products of
the author's imagination.

Cover design by Gina Binkley
Interior design by Mike Penticost

Library of Congress Cataloging-in-Publication Data

Wood, Barbara.
Domina / Barbara Wood.
p. cm.
ISBN 978-1-59652-863-5
I. Title.
PS3573.O5877D6 2012
813'.54--dc23
2012006382

Printed in the United States of America
12 13 14 15 16 17 18—0 9 8 7 6 5 4 3 2 1

AUTHOR'S NOTE

Dr. Samantha Hargrave did not exist. She is a composite of several women doctors who lived in the second half of the nineteenth century, and is a product of the author's imagination.

Two women doctors who do appear in this book, Dr. Elizabeth Blackwell and her sister Emily, did live and practice medicine in these years. I have strived to make their dialogue as realistic and close to historical accuracy as is possible, borrowing direct quotes from their journals and letters and creating the rest from what I believe they might have said.

President Grant did have such an accident at an Astor ball, although in another year. All other characters are fictitious; all incidents, medical and nonmedical, are of my own invention, although they were inspired by actual events.

There isn't room to thank everyone who helped me: Harvey Klinger, my agent, who prodded me; Dr. Norman Rubaum, who advised me; and my husband, George, who knows why.

DOMINA

PROLOGUE
NEW YORK 1881

PROLOGUE

*S*HE HAD HAD A STRANGE DREAM. ITS CONTENT WAS GONE NOW, vanished in the bright morning sun streaming through the window. But its dark, unsettling mood lingered. In her sleep she had been terrified of something but could not now recall what. Were dreams prophetic? Did they foretell the future? She shook her head and jumped out of bed. Stuff and nonsense! Dreams were only dreams, nothing more.

Charged with childlike excitement on this special day, Samantha could not resist a quick look out the window before she hurried down the hall to the bathroom. Staying modestly hidden, she pushed the chintz curtains aside and looked out. The street below was bustling with activity, so unusual for sleepy Lucerne! Carriages rattled by, horses clip-clopped over the cobbles, children and dogs ran about, stately men in frock coats and top hats milled around on the sidewalk.

There were no women to be seen.

Samantha backed away from the curtain, frowning.

So. The women were not coming . . .

Two years ago the women of Lucerne had banded together, determined to keep Samantha out; they had refused her lodging, had turned their backs when she walked by and had regarded her with that special righteous contempt reserved for women of questionable morals. Back then, during those first lonely days, Samantha Hargrave had been the object of scorn from the town's women and of prurient speculations among the town's men: What sort of young woman would sit in a classroom full of young men and listen, in their male company, to lectures on subjects not fit for a woman's ears? Clearly, Samantha Hargrave had come to corrupt the morals of their youth.

But that had been two years ago and Samantha had hoped those fears and prejudices had been laid aside. But if the women refused to attend the graduation ceremony today, it would demonstrate their continuing disapproval of her.

Hurt, but deciding not to let the boycott dampen her spirits on this special day, Samantha Hargrave drew upon all the maturity and stoicism of her twenty-one years, took in a long, steadying breath and set about getting herself ready.

As she poured water from the porcelain pitcher into its basin, Samantha paused to study her reflection in the looking glass; she was surprised that no miraculous change had occurred during the night. Strangely, she looked the same. Normally pleased with her fine looks, she now thought in a twist of irony: Too pretty. And then she added: There isn't enough age.

A woman doctor had constantly to fight for acceptance, but a woman doctor who was young and beautiful had almost no chance at all. As though looking at the face of a stranger, Samantha tried to examine objectively the features: the highdomed forehead, narrow nose, arched brows, gentle mouth with a bit of pout to it—all handicaps for a young woman striving to make her way in a man's world. She wondered: Will they ever take me seriously as a physician?

She settled her gaze finally on her eyes. She knew these were her best feature. She had unusual eyes, leaf-shaped, slightly slanted with long black lashes; and the strange, animal-like irises of pale, almost colorless gray rimmed with black made some people think she could see clearer and deeper than most. They were earnest eyes, intense eyes, large and clear and glistening, and when Samantha looked at someone, that person saw a strong and determined spirit shine through.

Samantha went on to her morning bath, bathing the way most women did: standing on a rubber mat, she sponged herself down, from a bowl of water, with a soapy cloth. And, like most women, she did not rinse off. The sit-in bathtub, still a novelty and highly controversial (doctors warned that sitting in water was bad for the health), was found only in the homes of the wealthy and most daring.

Her hands shook slightly as she reached for her corset of cotton twill. She took a minute to steady herself, then cinched herself in, but not so tightly that it made her wince; Samantha was fortunate to have a slender waist (those months of near starvation had done it), for many women required a dose of morphine after the corset was drawn into the fashionable wasp waist. As she stepped into her embroidered pantaloons and drew them up her long shapely legs, a memory was triggered, and it made her smile. Although she had not smiled back then.

Two years before, on her first day at Lucerne Medical College, Samantha had been met by the cruel chanting of her fellow medical students:

> "Venus found herself a goddess
> In a world controlled by gods,
> So she opened up her bodice
> And evened up the odds."

How long ago that seemed! How much she had changed, how much the *world* had changed in two short years! On that day, in October of 1879, a frightened and timid Samantha had meekly entered the first lecture room and wished she could shrink back into the protection of her bonnet, away from the rude stares of the men rising in tiers above her. Oh, the cruel things they had done to her; in retrospect Samantha could hardly believe they had happened! So much had changed since then.

Her hands paused over the buttons of her linen chemise as a pang cut through her heart. How perfect the day would be if *he* came.

Samantha allowed herself a moment to think of him, picture him, savor him, then she resumed her task of buttoning the many buttons, from her breast down to the hem of her chemise, and she sighed with resignation. No, Joshua wouldn't come. Might as well wish for a rainbow.

The dress was unlike any she had ever owned before. Poor all her life, struggling from one week to the next, eking out a penny here, a precious dollar there, Samantha Hargrave had lived spartanly, always with the promise to herself that someday her sacrifices would be rewarded. And today they were. The dressmaker in Canandaigua had created a work of near perfection.

They had chosen dove gray, the color of her eyes, and had gone through the latest fashion magazines for a model to copy. They had picked a creation of Mr. Worth, the most renowned designer of the day, and had altered it to suit Samantha's tall, willowy body. The bustle, which was getting larger in chic European circles, they played down, and also kept the hem of the skirt to the floor instead of revealing her shoes the way shocking Paris society was doing. The jacquard silk was fashioned in a tightly fitting bodice that went below the waist and hugged the hips from where the many yards of gray silk were hung in the front like parlor drapes, drawn up in the rear over a steel mesh bustle. The tight cuffs and high collar ended in crimped Valenciennes lace, and the many buttons, from her throat down to her flat abdomen, were imported from Spitalfields.

Samantha completed her outfit with high-button boots, a little feathered toque which sat on top of the crown of black curls she had swept up and pinned high on her head, and finally a cameo brooch at her throat. All that remained, Samantha realized with an anxious thumping of her heart, was to pull on her gloves and walk through the door.

But she held herself back, closed her eyes, clasped her long, slender hands together and recited to herself a Methodist prayer from her childhood. In passing sadness she thought of her father, wishing he could have lived to see this day, and then thanked God for helping her make it to this moment herself.

That done, and feeling calmer, she picked up her gray suede gloves, checked the back of her neck for straying curls, and, without another glance at the looking glass, walked with resolution to the door.

Today marked a triumph, but it was not going to be easy.

Professor Jones met her in the parlor. He had been waiting for half an hour, pacing like a father before a wedding, and when he turned to see Samantha standing in the doorway, his face beamed like a sunrise.

She smiled; this day was special for him too. All the world was watching this portly man with pink bald head and muttonchop whiskers who had so daringly defied society and convention; for the first time in the history of the school, newspaper reporters were going to attend the graduation exercises. The nervous professor, dean of the Lucerne Medical College, blinked rapidly behind his rimless glasses, unable to speak.

So Samantha spoke for him. "Shall we go, Doctor?"

When they emerged onto the front step, Samantha stopped suddenly and, thinking quickly, drew a hand over her eyes to feign momentary sensitivity to the sun. In truth, she was steeling herself against the stares of the men on the street, all of whom gawked at her. It was reasonable that she should be temporarily blinded: Lake Canandaigua, which stretched out beyond the grassy slopes that rolled down the opposite side of Main Street, shimmered with dazzling whiteness. As Samantha drew her hand away from her eyes, she saw the lake and surrounding countryside in all its springtime glory: the gentle rolling hills around the lake were carpeted with an emerald patchwork of farms and vineyards; the cider-apple trees, growing wild and free around the lake and in the town, were explosions of white blossoms; the sky was a clear blue, the air warm and lazy, riots of blooms filled the little gardens lining Main Street. For a moment Samantha's breath was taken away. Then she saw the men staring at her and she came back to the present.

Putting her hand through Professor Jones's arm, she glided down the steps and off toward the medical school.

I wish the women wouldn't stay away, Samantha thought as she walked beneath the canopy of apple blossoms toward the school's rotunda. Why can't they see that this is their victory as well as mine?

But it was no use. The women would not come; not even little girls were to be seen in the streets.

As she and Dr. Jones stepped onto the little wooden footbridge spanning the stream which separated the grounds of the medical school from the town, Samantha was filled with sudden nostalgia. Today was the last time she would walk this path. As Professor Jones anxiously searched the crowd for a man he did not see, Samantha recalled with sad fondness the first time her eyes had beheld the main hall.

Standing in a clearing carved out of the bosky wilderness just a hundred miles west of the Mohawk frontier and on the site of an old Indian burial ground (which gave rise to talk that the college was haunted), the imposing main building of the medical school looked startlingly garish and out of place against the plain clapboard frontier town. It was a mammoth three-story brick structure with a unique façade of pedimented gable above a wide, recessed porch flanked by Scamozzi columns. Dominated by a gleaming white rotunda, the interior was a maze of lecture rooms, amphitheaters, dissecting labs, library and offices. The building was said to have been designed by Thomas Jefferson, who had a love of the heavy, solid Roman style. Samantha had thought it monstrously pretentious.

Two years before, she had stood at this same place listening to Dr. Jones's account of the Indian legend. Two ill-fated Iroquois lovers had met tragic deaths on this spot, and their spirits were said to roam this patch of ground, calling to one another. Sometimes, working late at night in the anatomy lab, Samantha had heard mysterious sounds which, upon investigation, had remained unexplained.

It was not odd that she should think of ghosts now, for she was surrounded by them. They had all come to witness her triumph today: her father, Samuel Hargrave, the harsh and unforgiving servant of God; her brothers, restless, unhappy spirits; Isaiah Hawksbill; dear Freddy. Was her mother here too? Did Samantha sense in the redolent spring air a sweet, docile presence?

Then she thought of Hannah Mallone, and Samantha experienced a brief saddening of spirit. This is for you, dearest friend, this is our success.

The other students milled restlessly in front of the building, standing in the shade of its enormous porch. Like young horses, barely broken and straining at their reins, the young men had the impulse to romp and whoop and throw their hats into the air but they were held in check by the solemnity of the occasion and the demands of tradition. The professors were assembling, and a few dandyish reporters in checkered jackets and bowler hats mingled with the crowd. Dr. Jones excused himself, muttering something about a Mr. Kent, and Samantha went to join a small knot of medical students who were murmuring quietly among themselves.

Winding through the crowd, poor Dr. Jones wrung his hands and searched this way and that. Where in creation was Simon Kent!

The problem was actually Samantha Hargrave's fault, although she wasn't aware of it. A few weeks ago, one of the professors had brought to Dr. Jones's attention the fact that the usual school diploma would not do at all for Miss Hargrave: the diplomas were engraved in Latin and all terms were in the masculine gender. The graduate's new title was *Domine,* which meant Master. Was there, the other professor had queried, a feminine version? Not a term that meant Mistress, for that was not quite the same thing, but a word that could be taken to mean Female Master? The entire staff had conferred and had finally agreed upon an acceptable substitute. She would be called *Domina.*

The next problem had been the manufacture of such a diploma. The school had had all the sheepskins mass-engraved with a blank space for the graduate's name. What was needed was a local man with a good hand who could draw up an identical diploma with the feminine alterations. Simon Kent, a local farmer, had been commissioned. However, he was supposed to have delivered the diploma to Dr. Jones the day before and he had not yet arrived.

─❦─

It would be worse than embarrassing if Kent didn't show up, it would be devastating! Lucerne Medical College was making history today; the eyes of the world were upon Dr. Henry Jones. (There was even a reporter here all the way from Michigan!) The success or failure of his bold and highly criticized experiment—to allow a female into a male medical college—hinged upon what happened today; his many critics would be only too glad to see him fail miserably. Dr. Jones continued his search for Simon Kent.

"Excuse me! 'Scuse me!"

Samantha turned to see a large burly man with his derby set back on his head push through the crowd toward her. "Miss Hargrave! Can I have a word with you?" He held a pencil in one hand and a pad of paper in the other. "Jack Morley, Baltimore *Sun*. I'd like to ask you a few questions."

"The procession is about to begin, Mr. Morley."

"How does it feel to be the first lady doctor to graduate from a male medical school?"

"I am not the first, sir. Dr. Elizabeth Blackwell preceded me by thirty years."

"Oh, sure, she was the very first, but there haven't been any since. Dr. Blackwell got in on a fluke and after she graduated that school closed its doors to women. I understand you fought like the blazes to get into Harvard."

"I applied to Harvard and was refused."

"May I ask why you had such an ambition? To get into a male school? There are plenty of *female* schools around."

Samantha tipped her chin. "I wished, sir, to obtain the best possible medical education. Since this is a man's world with men holding possession of the best, I deduced therefore that a male college would provide me with that education. Perhaps someday that will change." She turned away.

"You talk like a Lucy Stoner!" he called after her.

The procession was forming; they were to walk into the church in twos. A great deal of discussion had been generated about Samantha's position in the line: where to put her? The consensus had been that she should go at the head, on Dr. Jones's arm, but Samantha had requested she be granted no special consideration for her sex; she was graduating third in the class, she should be third in the procession.

As the others aligned themselves in order of rank, fifty in all, Professor Jones wrung his hands again and swept his eyes once more around the clearing. Oh, *where* was Simon Kent?

Brass horns sounded a sudden chord and Dr. Jones scurried to the front of the line; he gave the signal to begin. The Indians, Senecas in native buckskins and eagle feathers, played a tinny "America" on trumpets, trombones and tuba. The peaceful woodland erupted with life as the parade set off from the steps of the rotunda: wood thrushes and meadowlarks shot up out of leafy elm and maple trees, cottontails scampered through underbrush, and the stately line of black-clad men and one young woman in gray moved forward.

❦

The Presbyterian church, where all community meetings were held, lay at the edge of town about five hundred yards from the rotunda. It took the parade ten minutes to cover the distance and in that time Samantha managed to calm herself. When the enormous crowd of men in front of the church came into view, however, she felt her confidence waver.

There were carriages and buckboards of every type, horses and dogs and small children, reporters and photographers, cameras on tripods; it was like a circus. Largely because one slender, soft-spoken young woman was graduating with the men. One would think she was a freak; they had come from miles around to glimpse this human oddity. A female graduating with men!

The procession paused before mounting the steps in order to give the photographers time to take their pictures. Keeping her head still and face forward, Samantha moved her eyes over the crowd, taking in the gaping expressions of the farmers in their homespun who were witnessing an event they could talk about on winter nights for years to come.

Her heart suddenly leapt. Joshua!

But no . . . The man on the steps turned and she saw that it wasn't Joshua at all, just someone of the same height, the same broad shoulders and dark coloring. How foolish of her to have thought he would come. It had been a year and a half since she had vowed never to see him again.

Samantha squared her shoulders. Over the fierce pounding of her heart she heard the church doors swing open and she thought: If I cannot have him, I don't want any man.

As she waited tensely for the procession to move into the church, Samantha imagined this was what it felt like to be a bride. In a way, she thought, I *am* getting married. I shall enter the church Miss Hargrave and

I shall leave it Dr. Hargrave. This is my wedding day, there will be no other.

Her nerves were so taut, she thought that if the procession did not start up soon she would scream. Samantha felt as if she stood at the edge of a great misty sea and that she had walked hundreds of miles to arrive at this shore, only to discover she must go on. So much had been achieved, so many fights won, so many obstacles overcome, and yet . . .

She felt it up ahead of her, through those doors: her future. New fights, new obstacles, and new (no, she shouldn't think of that) men. This is the end of *that* long road; a new one, going in another direction, opens up. But to where? To what mysterious destiny?

If only the women had come. Why, *why* had they stayed away?

PART ONE

ENGLAND 1860

ONE

THE WOMAN CRIED OUT FOR THE THIRTIETH TIME IN THAT hour. Her last scream tore through the peaceful fabric of the spring night and seemed to cause the foundation of the house to shudder. A black silhouette hunched over her, Mrs. Cadwallader worked a pantomime over the wailing Felicity Hargrave.

"Sumpin's wrong," muttered the midwife. Placing a plump hand on her lower back, she leaned away and gave herself a good stretch. Then she reached for the bottle of cordial, which she had brought along for poor Felicity, and took a healthy swig.

It wasn't going well, this birth, and *him* downstairs wasn't helping any. What man would deny his wife a bit o' cordial to ease her pain? But not Samuel Hargrave, who had expressly forbidden the use of any drugs to aid the delivery. And a sad thing, too, because Mrs. Cadwallader had the best-stocked midwife's kit in London. It contained opium and belladonna; ergot to induce labor and stop the bleeding; an assortment of herbs and folk remedies; and a bottle of the hardiest gin. Corking the cordial bottle and replacing it on the floor, Mrs. Cadwallader leaned forward and stroked her hefty hands down the swollen belly. "Come on," she crooned. "There's a love. Give us it."

Felicity, her hair matted to her face and pillow, grunted and then released a shriek which could be heard, Mrs. Cadwallader was certain, all the way down in Kent.

She sat back and pursed her lips. "Been twenty hours," she muttered to herself. "And this her third. 'S not right." Her generous bosom rose and fell in a sigh. "Ah well, I hates to do it but I gotta give her the quill."

The midwife puffed a little as she reached for her kit and drew out a feather and a bottle. Opening the latter, she dipped the feather fully into the powdered white hellebore, then got up on her knees, reached over the enormous heaving belly, and poked the feather's tip straight up Felicity's nostril. "Take it in, there's a love."

Mrs. Cadwallader quickly sat back down and readied herself for the inevitable result—a sneeze and sudden expulsion of the baby.

Felicity Hargrave, wincing as another severe contraction came on, drew in a deep breath, lifted her body up off the sheets and exploded in a sneeze so violent it ruffled the midwife's hair. At the same time, a little leg popped through the birth canal which, an hour before, Mrs. Cadwallader had greased with goose fat.

The plump woman raised her eyebrows. "So that's the way of it then. T'ain't no more I can do."

Three somber figures sat around the supper table, their hands folded before them, their heads bowed. No platters or mugs cluttered the scrubbed table top now; it was bare except for the sperm lamp which stood in the center casting a sallow glow on the three faces. Samuel Hargrave, Felicity's husband, was praying; Matthew, aged six, gazed at the lamp's flame with eyes like black saucers; and James, aged nine, alternately wrung his fingers and chewed on the inside of his cheek. He looked to his father for reassurance but received none.

Samuel Hargrave, deep in communion with God, clasped his hands so tightly that his knuckles were white; he had held this posture for the past four hours and showed no sign of tiring. So fierce was his concentration that he did not hear Mrs. Cadwallader come down the stairs.

"Father," whispered James, terrified by the grim look on the midwife's face.

Samuel had to struggle out of his thoughts. He raked his heavy gaze from its plane of godly meditation and stared at the face of the midwife.

"Can't be done, sir. Breech it is, and the worst kind, too. One leg down, t'other up 'longside the head."

"Can you not turn the babe round?"

"Not this 'un, sir. I needs to get me whole hand up there and can't on account as yer poor wife hollers and closes up on me. It's a proper doctor she needs, sir."

"No," said Samuel so quickly and forcefully that he startled the old woman. "I'll have no man look upon the modesty of my wife."

Mrs. Cadwallader fixed a keen, beady eye on the man. "If you'll pardon me sayin' so, sir, there's no sin in havin' a *medical* man look at yer wife. Proper gentlemen they are, sir, and completely without *that* sort o' interest, if you read me—"

"No doctor, Mrs. Cadwallader."

The midwife squared her shoulders and snorted contemptuously. "And if I may say so, sir, we've not got the time to be arguin' it, both yer wife and babe are in a serious way. We've a need to hurry, Mr. 'Argrave!"

As Samuel rose up from his chair, his great lanky height seemed to fill the room; little Matthew and James stared up at him. Their father had always had the Records Office "stoop," created by years on a high stool at a desk with ledgers on it, but tonight it seemed his whole back curved beneath an invisible weight. Withdrawing a handkerchief from his pocket, Samuel patted his forehead.

Mrs. Cadwallader waited impatiently. She didn't like Samuel Hargrave—not many people did—what with his Methodist piety and all; she had come only for the sweet Felicity.

Samuel's voice sounded as if it came down from a pulpit: "Mrs. Cadwallader, my wife would be put to mortal shame to have a man trespass upon her Christian modesty. It is her wish as well as mine—"

"Just arsk her now, Mr. 'Argrave, if she don't want no doctor!"

He raised his anguished eyes to the ceiling, and when another cry came from the bedroom above, his face flinched.

Nine-year-old James, gaping at his towering father, who even though in his own parlor was dressed in black frock coat, black trousers, white shirt and starched white cravat, felt his young heart start to race. He had never before seen his father trapped in indecision.

As Mrs. Cadwallader spread her feet apart and put her hands on her hips as if bracing herself for a charging bull, young James slid silently and unseen out of his chair. "I'm tellin' you true, Mr. 'Argrave! yer wife needs a doctor! Now there be a decent man on Tottenham Court Road just that side o' Great Russell Street. A man of honor is Dr. Stone, and no mistake. Many's the time I've seen 'im—"

"No, Mrs. Cadwallader."

While the midwife regarded the towering man with bottled indignation, young James crept on soft feet toward the dark shadows of the hallway. "Really, Mr. 'Argrave, yer wife needs 'elp!"

Samuel snapped his head down and glared at the old woman with such rage that she recoiled. "Then I suggest, my good woman, that you return to your post and help her." He swung away, reaching for his chair. "And *I* shall pray."

As Mrs. Cadwallader marched back up the stairs, and as Samuel bowed his head over folded hands, no one noticed that James had disappeared.

When, some time later, the front door quietly opened, letting in tendrils of late night spring fog and, with them, James, Samuel had been praying so intensely that his face ran with streams of sweat. James stood stock-still, terrified, studying his father's bent head. Then he whispered, "Father."

Samuel struggled to lift his heavy lids and blinked a few times at the boy's abnormally white face. James was heaving, for he had run both ways. "Father, I've fetched help."

Samuel blinked again. "What did you say, James?"

"I've gone for a doctor. He'll be here in a minute."

As comprehension dawned on Samuel, driving away his religious piety and filling him with swelling anger, he slowly drew himself out of his chair. "You sent for a doctor?"

James shrank back. "Y-yes, Father. You seemed not to know what to do—"

He had never known his father to move so fast. Samuel was around the table in an instant and the only thing James saw, before the stars and planets exploded in his head, was the rising of the large hand. He screeched, more in surprise than pain, and immediately cupped his left ear. Samuel reached down, seized the boy by the arm, pulled away the protective hand, and gave him another full-force slap on the side of the head. James tried to wriggle free as again and again the enormous hand delivered the blows until James heard a voice say, "Have I found the Hargrave house?"

The boy lifted his throbbing head and saw through teary eyes the figure of Dr. Stone standing in the hallway.

"We've no need of you, sir," said Samuel flatly.

Dr. Stone's eyes, small and acute behind spectacles, glanced down at James's bleeding ear. "From the look of it, I've come in time."

Samuel looked down at his son and appeared, for the moment, bewildered, then he released the nine-year-old, who instantly scrabbled under the table, and straightened himself up. "This is woman's work, sir. I do not abide a man in the lying-in chamber."

Dr. Stone stepped uninvited into the parlor. He was a small, wiry man in his sixties with a long sharp nose and Dundreary whiskers. He dashed his top hat against his thigh to knock off the dew and said, "The boy says it is breech and Mrs. Cadwallader cannot help."

The midwife, having heard James's screams, now stood at the foot of the stairs. "Good o' yer to come, Dr. Stone," she said. "Been in labor nigh on a day and night, she 'as, and it's her third, which ain't right. Not enough it's breech, but there's the cord around the little 'un's neck and Felicity won't let me turn it. Not that she can 'elp it, poor love."

Dr. Stone pursed his lips. "I'll see what I can do."

"A minute, sir," said Samuel. "I do not want you to attend my wife."

"It's 'im or the Angel o' Death!" said Mrs. Cadwallader.

Dr. Stone's voice was gentle. "I have attended many a childbed, Mr. Hargrave. Believe me, I am a gentleman born and bred and have great sympathy with your sensitivities about your wife's modesty."

"We have the Lord to help us in this house!"

"I serve the Lord, Mr. Hargrave. After all, healing was His profession, was it not?"

Samuel's face took on a haunted look. The moans of his wife upstairs tore at his heart.

"Perhaps," said the doctor comfortingly, "I am the answer to your prayers. Perhaps the good Lord sent me. At least, Mr. Hargrave, let me have a look."

Samuel drew in a shuddering breath. His thoughts, storm-tossed, tried to find a scriptural reference to the situation, but to no avail. "Very well then," he said reluctantly. "Mrs. Cadwallader, will you be certain to—"

"Aye, Mr. 'Argrave, I'll be on 'and, never you mind."

Dr. Stone laid a heavy hand on Samuel's shoulder. "It'll be all right, I assure you. It never fails, not these days, not with the new sleep." He turned to the midwife. "Now then, good woman, shall we?"

Samuel's face darkened. "What did you say? New sleep?"

Dr. Stone held up his black leather bag. "I'm a modern doctor, Mr. Hargrave. I've gone over to the chloroform so that your blessed wife will soon be delivered of her baby in peace."

"What!" Samuel fell back a step.

A small alarm went off in the doctor's head; he had not thought there were many of *this* type left, not since the dear little Queen herself had taken the chloroform seven years before for the birth of the Prince. "It's perfectly safe, Mr. Hargrave. I'll administer the chloroform, your wife will sleep, her body will relax, and I shall be able to turn the baby with ease. It is done everywhere now."

"Not to my wife it isn't!"

"It is the only way it can be done, Mr. Hargrave. In your wife's condition you stand to lose them both."

Samuel's voice grew tremulous. "The pains of childbirth were ordained by the Almighty. Its prevention is sacrilege and your sleeping gas, Doctor, is a decoy of Satan. Birth pain is the curse of God upon womankind for her sin in Eden, and no God-fearing Christian woman would deny herself this righteous punishment which all women have endured since the hour Eve offered the forbidden fruit to Adam!" He raised a shaking finger heavenward. "Unto the woman He said, I will greatly multiply thy sorrow and thy conception; *in sorrow thou shalt bring forth children!*"

Dr. Stone tried to mask his impatience. He had thought this argument, which had once swept London like a raging fibre, was dead and buried. There had been occasions, ten years earlier, when he and his colleagues had been locked in heated debate over the issue of chloroform in childbirth. And it had appeared for a time that Scripture was going to win, but then John Snow had delivered Queen Victoria of Prince Leopold under chloroform and the world had had an instant change of heart. It appeared, however, there were still some pockets of resistance. Dr. Stone said quietly. "And the Lord God caused a deep sleep to fall upon Adam, and he slept: and He took one of his ribs, and closed up the flesh instead thereof.'"

"How dare you utter such impieties in my house, Doctor! To make of Jehovah an operating surgeon and have the absurdity to presume He would need chloroform to put a man to sleep! You forget, Doctor, that the miracle of Adam's rib took place *before* the introduction of pain into this world, during the time of Innocence."

Another cry from above shattered the night silence. The two men looked up.

Samuel continued gravely: "The cries of a woman in labor are music to the Lord's ears. They fill His heart with joy. They are the cries of life and a Christian will to live. No child of mine will slither into this world like a serpent while its mother sleeps unaware of the holy act she has performed. And that, Dr. Stone, is the end of it."

Neville Stone eyed the man before him for a moment, sizing him up, weighing the situation, then reached the conclusion that he would never, after a thousand debates with this man, change the ossified thinking of this

Wesleyan Methodist. So he said, "Very well then," and turned abruptly for the stairs.

The sight that met him caused him a moment's pause: the woman sprawled and gasping on the bed, the heaving belly, the outspread and bloodied legs, and, protruding through the growth of dark curly hair, a tiny white foot. Neville Stone hastily removed his frock coat, handed it to Mrs. Cadwallader, and rolled up his shirt sleeves.

Positioning himself between Felicity's legs, Dr. Stone gently inserted two fingers into her vagina, following the cold, skinny leg that hung down from the neck of the uterus. After a quick exploration, he sat back. "It is as you say, Mrs. Cadwallader."

Dr. Stone opened his bag and lifted out his instruments, placing them handily by Felicity's feet: the obstetrical forceps, designed to clamp around the baby's head and draw it out; a long, curved metal syringe which he had Mrs. Cadwallader fill with water in case he should have to baptize the baby *in utero;* a series of sharpened scalpels, in the event—God forbid!—he should have to perform a Caesarean section; and lastly the crotchet, an instrument for killing, chopping up, and extracting the fetus from the birth canal.

As he worked silently and swiftly, listening to the labored breathing of Felicity, Dr. Stone felt a lacy sweat spring up all over his body. He didn't like this case one bit. One skillful examination had told him the child could not be turned normally, and since Samuel Hargrave had forbidden chloroform, that meant Neville Stone was going to be forced into a decision he did not want to make. There were only two choices: a Caesarean section which would save the infant but kill the mother, or murder the infant and pull it out piece by piece to save the mother.

He felt Mrs. Cadwallader's ponderous presence at his side, her maternal bosom heaving anxiously. He heard Felicity's gasping breaths, felt her thready pulse. He thought of the man downstairs, hands clasped in prayer, and of his own frailty and mortality.

Then Dr. Stone let his gaze travel to his black bag.

Ten years ago there would have been no worrying over it; he would have *had* to choose one of the two horrible paths and would have set to it with all the stoicism of his years of medical experience. How many women had died in childbed before chloroform! But now—damnation!—*today*, there was a simple, lifesaving solution, one which removed from his hands the responsibility for the dreadful decision. A few drops of the miracle liquid and both mother and baby would be saved. . .

In a snap decision (he would face the consequences later), Neville Stone reached into his bag and pulled out a bottle. As Mrs. Cadwallader leaned closer to him, he withdrew a handkerchief from his pocket and rolled it into a cone, like a funnel. As he unscrewed the bottle, he heard Mrs. Cadwallader whisper, "Ye're gonna use the *stuff*, sir?"

He nodded grimly, rose from the bed, and went to Felicity's side. Bending over her and murmuring words of comfort, Dr. Stone delicately placed the broad end of the handkerchief cone over her nose and mouth and proceeded to dribble a few drops of chloroform onto it.

"How's it work then?" whispered the midwife, staring in fascination as sickly sweet fumes suddenly filled the air.

"As the liquid evaporates on the cloth, Felicity will inhale the vapors and they will put her into a deep sleep."

"What d'yer call this sorta thing?"

Neville Stone's voice was mellow and reassuring as Felicity breathed in the first fumes. He spoke more for her comfort than for the midwife's edification. "Four years ago an American gentleman by the name of Oliver Wendell Holmes gave us the word we needed to describe the new sleep. It is called anesthesia."

Mrs. Cadwallader dragged a sleeve under her nose. "Aw, a Yankee, is it? Well, sir, I dunno—"

"Sh." He straightened, leaving the cone on Felicity's face. "She's going under now. As soon as she is sufficiently unconscious I will deliver the baby."

⸺❀⸺

The sweat fell from his forehead and hit the table in great drops; his hands were clasped so tightly they shook. He tapped every reservoir of strength, drained every muscle and nerve, straining to free himself from physical bonds, to turn himself into a purely thinking entity, oblivious of the hard chair he sat upon, of the little boy huddled under the table cupping a bleeding ear, oblivious even of the fact that all sound had suddenly stopped from the bedroom above. He was concentrating on communion with the Lord.

But Samuel's concentration was not as strong as his will, for his prayers were slipping into straying thoughts: how to afford yet another mouth to feed; where to find a trustworthy housekeeper to take care of them while Felicity convalesced; how to meet the tax coming due on the house.

A lump in his throat rose and fell with a difficult swallow. And then the unthinkable: should Felicity die . . .

A sob escaped his throat and Samuel suddenly folded, collapsing onto the table with his arms flung out cruciform, his face flattened on one cheek, eyes firmly closed. His thoughts started to fly. He let them go, too weak to fight to hold on anymore, and his thoughts, unsurprisingly, fled straight to the cause of Samuel Hargrave's torment. He knew he had been fighting it, facing the stark, unbearable truth. He knew he had been immersing himself in prayer not so much for Felicity's salvation as for his *own*; and what he saw plainly now was the stabbing, inescapable reality that he, Samuel Hargrave, was solely responsible for this night of misery.

Now that it was there Samuel no longer tried to run from it. The memory: that night of nine months before which had damned him and Felicity to this night of hell.

In all the years of his manhood, Samuel had never known lust. As a boy, his one and only experiment with masturbation had earned him a severe thrashing from his father. As an adolescent and then as a young clerk in the Records Office he had curtailed involuntary emission at night by tying a string around his penis so that, as he slept, if the traitorous organ became aroused, the stricture of the string would waken him and Samuel could douse himself with cold water. The wedding night with Felicity had been the ultimate test of self-control: he had carried out his marital duty quickly and perfunctorily, never once enjoying the pleasure of the flesh, rejoicing only in knowing he was creating a new Christian for the Lord. And submissive little Felicity, praise be to God, had never been a temptation to Samuel. Only twice had they performed the act and both times, by great fortune, she had gotten pregnant. It seemed so simple a thing to Samuel that he could not understand, could not tolerate other men's carnal cravings.

But then, after nine years of a righteous and moral connubial life, something disastrous had happened.

Felicity had gone into a few weeks of "malaise"; she had become listless, dreamy, forgetful of her chores. Several times had Samuel been wakened during the night by his wife's tossing and turning, her restless sighs, an occasional moan. He had given in and decided the expense of a doctor worth the finding of a cure, but the Harley Street man had only shaken his head and shrugged, at a complete loss to explain Felicity's languor.

Then, one night, just after the midnight hour when respectable Londoners were in their nightcaps and safe beneath their eiderdowns, Samuel had been startled awake. He had opened his eyes to a heavy-lidded, smiling Felicity, the odor of laudanum on her breath. Samuel had tried to speak but she had placed fingertips on his mouth while, with the other hand, she traced electrifying caresses upon his bare chest. Samuel had tried to fight it, to shake her to her senses, but the opium mixture was ruling her brain and the sight of her thick black curls tumbling seductively over her white breasts had stopped the words in his throat.

Samuel remembered little of what happened after that; it came to him in pieces and flashes: the moistness of her lips on his mouth, the sweet tongue forcing its way between his teeth, the explosive touch of her fingers on his erect member, and then a swirling blackness, a dizzying whirlpool, the night rushing in and engulfing them in a frenzy of passion and ecstasy.

The next morning Felicity had returned to her previous self, as though the devils had been exorcised, going peaceably about her mundane chores, patiently tending her two little sons, sitting meekly by the fire with her prayer book, but Samuel had changed. Mortified by what he had done, and comparing himself to the hapless Adam who had been witlessly seduced by Eve into sin, Samuel Hargrave had plunged himself into unparalleled devotion to religion. He started going to the meeting house every night, frequently taking the pulpit. He began writing tracts and distributing them among the poor: sermons on the evils of liquor, of gambling, and of the flesh. He became a stern father to his boys, determined to save them from falling into the same godlessness. And when, a few weeks later, Felicity told him she was pregnant, Samuel had been horrified.

So now the Lord was punishing him. Her delivery should be easy: after the first baby, the rest were hardly an inconvenience. There was no explaining this nightmare other than as the hand of a vengeful God. It might be different for other men, but Jehovah was a stern taskmaster and demanded exemplary behavior from His chosen preachers. A test had been put before him that night nine months earlier and Samuel had failed miserably, so now the punishment was being meted.

Slowly and painfully Samuel raised himself from the table, which was wet with his tears, and massaged his face. And then it struck him: the house was silent.

Mrs. Cadwallader, hands wringing, gazed in wonder at the work the doctor was doing.

Felicity's perineum had finally relaxed and the vagina had yawned so that Neville Stone had been able to reach clear up into the womb and turn the baby around. Without so much as a flicker of Felicity's eyelids! And now the infant was lying on its back between Felicity's legs, its scrawny little body like that of a skinned rat.

Strangely, the baby did not cry.

As Dr. Stone clamped and cut the cord, the midwife lifted the astonishingly light little body off the bed and was about to turn away when Dr. Stone, sweating heavily, said, "Oh, my God!"

Mrs. Cadwallader's eyes flew open at the sight of the blood, bright red and unclotted, rushing from the vagina.

Dr. Stone's hand flew to his bag, fumbling for a clamp, while his other hastily stuffed a towel into the orifice. "It's the placenta, Mrs. Cadwallader! It is misplaced!"

"God blind me!" cried the woman, instinctively drawing the silent baby to her bosom. "She's gonner bleed to death!"

"Not if I can help it." Dr. Stone reached up into the vagina, and with his other hand pressing down in her abdomen, massaged the uterus.

❦

The sound of heavy steps on the stairs brought Samuel out of his disjointed meditation. He came achingly to his feet.

Dr. Stone crossed the parlor, placed himself foursquare before the man and said, "We did everything we could."

For a shooting instant Samuel thought: The baby's dead!

"I'm sorry, Mr. Hargrave, your wife could not be saved."

Samuel stared at the doctor in blank stupefaction as Neville Stone's voice continued gently, "Your wife had an abnormal implantation of the placenta which caused excessive bleeding. But" —he placed a hand on Samuel's arm— "we were able to save the baby."

Samuel blinked dumbly at him. "My Felicity? Gone?"

"Think not of this as misfortune, Mr. Hargrave. Your wife's passing was not for naught. You still have the child."

In a sudden brutish gesture, Samuel flung away the doctor's hand, swept past him and bounded up the stairs. In the bedroom he fell to his knees at Felicity's side.

She looked as if she merely slept, a chaste slumbering angel, her high-domed forehead glowing with perspiration, thick mink lashes resting on pale cheeks as the lids were closed forever over her gray eyes. The pillow seemed to be a halo around her stormy black hair; she looked so peaceful, so perishingly young.

A strangled sound escaped Samuel's lips and he brought up a heavy hand to dash a tear off his cheek. As he drew in a steadying breath, he felt momentarily light-headed, then his nostrils detected a pungent perfume in the room, one which he could not identify. Frowning, Samuel looked at the night table and tried to focus, in the brittle light of the sperm lamp, upon the objects it held. Then he saw them clearly: a bottle of liquid and a handkerchief.

He shot to his feet, his body shaking violently. Dr. Stone said quickly, "It was the only way I could save the baby, Mr. Hargrave. If not for the chloroform, both would have perished and you would not now have the consolation of your new child."

Samuel looked like a statue about to topple. *"You killed her!"*

"I most assuredly did not, sir! In your wife's condition no medical arts in all of Creation could have saved her! Without the anesthesia you would be burying the baby with her!"

Samuel's face darkened menacingly; a crimson tide rose up from his collar and flooded his face to the hair line where the veins in his forehead bulged. Dr. Stone grew alarmed; Samuel Hargrave looked like a man about to have a stroke. But then the redness receded, the tremor abated, and Samuel seemed to deflate. "No," he said lifelessly, "it is not your fault, Doctor. The responsibility for Felicity's death is mine alone. What you are guilty of, Doctor, is defying the Lord's will. They should both have died here tonight, for that was His punishment upon me. The child is the product of my sins. What you have done, Doctor, is saved a child that had no right to live."

"Now see here, sir!" But Mrs. Cadwallader silenced the doctor with a warning hand.

"If it had not been for your meddling, Doctor, my sins would have been purged. But now, because of you and your evil chloroform, I shall have a living reminder of this night . . ."

❦

Dr. Stone stared in horror at the man, then turned to look at the quivering little animal swallowed up by blankets in the midwife's arms. Did it sense the calamity it had entered into, and was that why it had not yet uttered a sound?

"Excuse me, Mr. Hargrave," said the doctor more gently. "But we must settle the matter of the baby's name. It was your wife's final request, it came out with her expiring breath that the baby be named for you. As a physician and a gentleman I have a moral and ethical duty to see that wish honored before I leave here tonight."

Samuel turned away and looked down at the serene white face on the pillow. "Then Samuel it shall be."

"But that is the problem, Mr. Hargrave. Your wife thought the baby was a boy."

When Samuel returned his gaze to the doctor, Neville Stone was stunned by what he saw: the dark eyes were turbulent with hatred and loathing. But for whom? "Then *she* will have my name, Doctor."

"Surely, sir, you cannot mean that! To saddle a girl with a man's name!"

Samuel gave a cry and spun away, dropping to his knees at the bedside; he flung his arms across Felicity's chest and buried his face in her bosom. His arched back rose and fell in silent sobs, causing the doctor and the midwife to withdraw to the dark corner of the room.

"Pity the poor little babe," murmured Mrs. Cadwallader. "First motherless and now fatherless, too."

"He'll come round. I've seen and heard many an oath at the hour of grief that is later forgotten. For now, we must help this poor man and honor his wife's dying wish."

"But what can yer do, sir? The man's a-mournin' and who knows how long it'll be afore he comes round? And the poor little 'un without so much as a name!"

Neville Stone absently scratched his white whiskers while studying the tragic tableau at the bed. And then, like an inspiration, it came to him. "We shall do our Christian duty, my good woman. Please fetch me some fresh water for a christening." He turned away and left the bedroom, leaving Samuel to weep silently over his wife's body, went down the stairs and came into the parlor where there were two forgotten little boys, one standing wide-eyed by the dying fire, the other still cowering like a dog under the table. Dr. Stone went straight to the family Bible and opened the front cover to a page which was decorated with brightly colored swirls and gold-leaf filigree: The Family Record. Dr. Stone found the line beneath the entry dated June 14, 1854, the birth of Matthew Christopher Hargrave, and wrote upon it: *Born to Samuel Hargrove and his blessed wife Felicity {deceased on this day) May 4, 1860, Samantha Hargrave. . .*

TWO

*B*Y THE TIME HER FOURTH BIRTHDAY CAME AROUND, THE GIRL child still had not uttered a word.

It was a dark and silent house she had been born into, her only companions a forbidding man in black who left the house early each morning and returned late each night, two sullen, uncommunicative boys and a dyspeptic housekeeper. The hired woman was uncomfortable around the child, who seemed always to be standing in the shadows, staring up with big animal eyes. She believed the child was retarded and didn't deserve the good looking after a normal one did, so she put the girl on the front steps and out of her way.

St. Agnes Crescent was a blunt strip of arc-shaped street wedged into the angle of Charing Cross and High Holborn, straddling the thin border between Soho and Covent Garden. When Samuel Hargrave first moved here with his bride years before, St. Agnes Crescent had been a decent middle-class neighborhood with terraced houses inhabited by hard-working Protestants like the Hargraves. But then a great population surge had come, bringing an overwhelming tide of potato-starved Irish immigrants who swelled the already overcrowded precincts of Seven Dials and Covent Garden. St. Agnes Crescent, in the path of this great population push, was engulfed by more residents than it could handle, multiplying, like the Dials, as much as five times in population within a few years. As a result, by the time Samantha was put on the stoop by the overworked housekeeper, St. Agnes Crescent was a teeming slum.

At both ends of the street were public houses, the King's Coach and the Iron Lion. In the first-story bay window of the house next door was a faded sign which said, mangling done twopence a go, but which didn't mean anything because the people who owned the mangle had long since moved away and no one had bothered to remove the sign. Across the street was a smoky chophouse where navvies and whores hung out, and all up and down the Crescent were vegetable carts, rag sellers, street arabs, and beggars.

The housekeeper, whose favorite hour of the day was taking tea with a neighboring laundress, would complain what a mystery it was to her that Mr. Hargrave, who made a decent wage at the Records Office, should choose to remain here instead of pulling out, as his old neighbors had done, and move maybe to one of those nice new houses on Brixton Road. But this was just one of the miseries the martyred housekeeper had to deal with; another was the problem of the girl child.

"Keep her clean, he says to me," she reported one day over tea and buttered scones. "And him that acts like she ain't even alive! When I come here to work near four years gone, he give me two orders: that I keeps the girl quiet and outa his way and that she be kept decent. Now the girl, she ain't no trouble to keep quiet on account as she don't talk. Queer in the head, she is. And does she make a body skittish! Sneaks around in the shadows, she does, and yer never know when yer'll turn around and find her standing there, staring up at yer like she was studying yer or something. Don't like having her about, and that's the fact. Now as to keeping her decent, the master is that tight with his money that he don't let me buy no new clothes for her. She ain't got but two frocks and I has to be mending constantly, growing so fast, she is. I've asked him for money to buy some stuff to make her a new one, but that man'd sooner peel a potato in his pocket than share it with you!"

As her friend leaned closer in hungry interest the housekeeper continued. "And there's something else queer about the child. Won't let me touch her hair, she won't. Screams and hollers if I so much as pick up the comb. It's like she knows there's something wrong with her head, she don't like no one to touch it. So I let it go in strings. Now how am I supposed ter keep the kid looking decent on *them* terms?"

Of course she could not, and so when little Samantha grew brave enough to join the wild children in the street, her unkempt appearance granted her immediate membership.

With Matthew and James, now aged ten and thirteen, going off each day to a government school and then spending their evenings over books or in scriptural study with their father, little Samantha found a surrogate family in the streets. She learned quickly. Running mutely at the rear of the pack, following the older, more worldly children, she explored alleys and dustbins, swung from clotheslines and played hunt-the-rabbit or turn-the-trencher. She learned wild, uninhibited freedom; she discovered sunshine and rain, she became an agile acrobat and, although no one knew her name, for she could not speak, quickly earned the admiration of her peers.

Her best friend and protector was a nine-year-old named Freddy, whose mother, an Irish costermonger, had wrapped her newborn in newspaper and left him in a dustbin. An aging cat-flayer, passing by and hearing the tiny cries and thinking he had come upon a good catch, had discovered the abandoned baby, felt sorry for it and took it in. The old man, who made his meager living going out at night with a stick and a sack in search of cats, raised the orphan and taught him his trade. He died of pneumonia when Freddy was seven, leaving the boy to struggle for himself, which he did by sleeping on a sack in a hole he had dug beneath a shed and either begging for or stealing his supper. The nine-year-old, despite malnutrition and missing teeth, was a handsome, cavalier boy who survived by his wits and expert cat-flaying, having learned from the old man how to remove the skin from the cat while it was still alive, for those hides went for the most money; he boasted often of the day he would own his own gin house.

It was Freddy who first got Samantha to talk.

She was their little pet, this mute four-year-old with the enchanting

smile, and she followed the urchins in all their adventures. Late one afternoon, coming back from the Dials after a day of stealing onions and sausages, Samantha and Freddy were wending their way down a twilit alley
when Freddy stopped suddenly and Samantha bumped into him.

"Listen!" he hissed, turning his head this way and that.

Samantha listened and heard, against the background of London noise,
a faint mewling sound.

"It's a cat!" cried Freddy. "Come on, love, we'll catch it an' skin it an' turn
it in fer sixpence. I'll buy you some trotters with it, now thass a treat!"

Baffled, little Samantha followed closely behind as Freddy crept cautiously to a hole in the fence. Dropping to all fours, he peered in. "I was
right! An' already hurt it is, too! Won't 'ave to bother chasin' it and catchin'
it. Can skin it just as it is!"

❧

As he reached into his rope belt for his knife, Samantha knelt low and
peeked into the hole. An old tabby, muddy and scrawny, lay on its side. Its
leg had a gash in it.

When Freddy reached out, Samantha's hand shot forward, seizing his
wrist. The strength of her little grip surprised him. "Whassa matter?"

She shook her head violently, black curls flying.

He tried to pull his hand free. "Come on, love. It means a proper supper
for me."

She opened her mouth and a hoarse sound came out.

He frowned at her. "Whassat?"

It came out as a raspy whisper. "Hurt!"

Freddy's eyebrows shot up. "You can talk!"

"Hurt!" she said again, still holding his wrist, still shaking her head.

"Yeah, love, I know the cat's hurt. Thass what'll make it easy to—"

"Help, Freddy, help . . ."

Now his eyes widened and he leaned back from her. "You want me to
help the shitten cat?"

She nodded vigorously.

"Ye're barmy!"

Tears welled in her eyes. "Help . . . the cat. Please—"

He stared at her pretty little face and felt his stony heart soften at the sight of those beautiful gray and black eyes. "Aw, I dunno. I was just gonna reach in an' give it a good slash. But tryin' to touch it, tryin' to help it, he won't let us and thass for sure. Scratch us good, he will, wounded animals is that way."

She shook her head again and bent low. She smiled at the golden eyes in the darkness and reached in. Old Tabby let her hand stroke his stiff fur.

Freddy rested back on his heels. "Well, if I ain't the Prime Minister . . ."

It took them a week, bringing the cat milk stolen from Samantha's cupboard and coaxing it to eat. She took some moldy bread from a tin which the housekeeper, for some mysterious reason, always kept about and spread the green fuzz into the gash, doing it just as she had once seen the housekeeper do with a cut on Matthew's arm. They met every morning after her father had gone, ran to the alley and doctored the cat. As Tabby would only allow Samantha to touch it (scratching Freddy once when he tried it), Freddy would lean impatiently against the fence while his little friend stroked the cat and fed it and murmured to it in her new-found voice. Until finally the morning came when old Tabby was gone.

It was also Freddy who first warned little Samantha about Isaiah Hawksbill.

There was a dark, silent house near the corner, full of brooding mystery, for although it was boarded up it was inhabited by an old man who lived alone and who fired the children's imaginations with visions of sorcery and witchcraft. No one ever saw old Hawksbill, but those who delivered his meager weekly food ration whispered it about that they had glimpsed him (parcels were to be dropped on the back step, where payment was left in a tin, and a few brave souls, for the notoriety, had hung around to see what they could see) and a horrible sight he was: wizened and gnarled and a face so ugly it would stop the Brighton train. While for the children of St. Agnes Crescent the name Hawksbill struck terror in their hearts (they always crossed the street to the other side when they neared his house), for the adults the name occasioned suspicion and mistrust. There was a story, some years back, about a horrible unspeakable crime Hawksbill had committed against a little girl.

Samantha would stand with Freddy's protective arm about her thin shoulders and gaze across the street at the boarded-up windows while the other children hurled rotten fruit at Hawksbill's door where it clung and dried and would remain until the rain washed it off. And so her days were spent: prowling the Crescent with a pack of wild and homeless children, to come home at night and be fed by the housekeeper and sent to bed, a strange little creature, existing at the periphery of her cold and loveless family.

But then came the day when she noticed her father and he noticed her.

She was six years old, wearing a patched dress too tight for her skinny body and so short as to be immodest; her legs and bare feet were filthy and her hair hung in tangled ropes to her waist. She was sitting on the step of their house, tracing a pattern in the dust on the door, when Samuel, home early because it was the Queen's birthday and the office had closed at noon, came up the steps. He spoke a gruff word to Samantha, thinking her to be a neighbor's child, and made to nudge her out of his way with his shoe when she suddenly looked up and met his eyes. The two of them froze, he tall and dark with his hand on the doorknob, she crouched and dirty at his feet, her face upturned like a sooty sunflower. They stared at one another for a long moment, each discovering the other for the first time, each expressionless and unmoving; and then a passion, long pent up, broke suddenly inside Samuel Hargrave. He was staring down at the face of his precious Felicity.

Feeling his head swim and his body shudder with revulsion, Samuel saw a tiny, dirty hand reach out to touch his pant leg, and he reflexively fell back a step. Spinning around, Samuel burst through the front door, stumbled over the threshold and could be heard booming through the house for the housekeeper. There was a fever-pitch argument:

"She's filthy as a guttersnipe!"

"Why should you care, you don't pay her no mind!"

"I hired you to see after her welfare!"

"At five shitten shillings a week you can't expect me to—"

The housekeeper was sent packing.

A neighbor woman, the mother of twelve, was brought in and given a shilling to give the child a good wash and then half a crown to buy her some clothes and shoes. While Samantha wordlessly suffered the rough scouring and even the hair brushing, she dwelt upon the miracle that had occurred.

He had noticed her. . .

THREE

A NEW HOUSEKEEPER WAS BROUGHT IN AND SAMUEL TOOK IT upon himself, in the evenings, to see to Samantha's religious training. It was there, by the fire in the parlor, that Samantha discovered her profound capacity to love. She regarded the austere man as a savior, as though she were a foundling, for hadn't he taken her in from the streets and now showed concern for her? In a feverish desire to please him, Samantha struggled with her alphabet and Samuel was secretly impressed with her quickness to learn. But he did not show it. He treated the girl like a stranger's child, a foundling indeed, and did his basic Christian duty by her by seeing she was clothed modestly and fed and taught the Scriptures. Her two sulky companions, boys she hardly knew (Freddy was more a brother to her than James or Matthew), took their instruction and then went up to bed without ever acknowledging her existence.

In the daytime Samantha still ran free with her fellow creatures of the wild, learning life and the ways of the streets, but now she left them early to hurry home and wash, change her clothes and anxiously await the return of her father.

Samantha was unique among the urchins of the Crescent in one basic way: she remained uncorrupted. No matter how many mischievous pranks or illegal escapades she participated in, little Samantha managed to retain a simple and uncomplicated sense of honesty. Coupled with this was her innocent trust in the basic goodness of human nature: everyone else saw the surface person, the prostitute, the body snatcher, but the little Hargrave girl, with all the compassion inherited from a gentle mother she never knew, always saw behind the façade a good soul, a woman down on her luck, a man trying to feed his starving family. Samantha simply and firmly believed that people were forced into badness, that no one was evil by nature.

At first Freddy thought her balmy and often told her so, for she felt sorry for the sausage vendors they stole from; Freddy tried to explain to her the simple law of the survival of the fastest. And when she felt sorry for the armless Crimean War veterans begging in Piccadilly Circus and turned over to them what she had stolen that day, Freddy tried to knock it into her that a lot of them were fakes: they hid their arms in their shirts and lived a soft life because of dafties like her. But after a while, seeing she would never change, and seeing that, compared to the unprincipled rowdies he ran with, Samantha was a precious little rarity, Freddy stopped trying to change her.

And if Samantha could see no evil in the wretched inhabitants of the Crescent (she was even secretly unafraid of old man Hawksbill), all the more so did she see her father/savior as the embodiment of the best. To win his approval was all she wanted in the world. However, after weeks of struggling with her alphabet and doing her utmost to elicit some sign of approval from him, none came, so little Samantha sought a way to please him.

She was struggling down the street with a bucket of water from the pump at the end of the Crescent, for her house had no plumbing or water source of its own, when Freddy came up from behind and took hold of the handle. He flashed her a gap-toothed grin. "Don't see yer much no more, Miss 'Igh and Mighty."

Samantha only shrugged as they walked down the dirty street, the bucket sloshing between them; Freddy didn't understand about fathers. When they arrived at the steps of her house, Freddy bragged about a horde of pennies he had recently come by.

"And where's the likes o' you get a fistful o' coppers?" she asked.

"Tanner down the road." He lifted a lazy arm and pointed. "Gives ha'penny a bucket for it. Needs it for 'is tanning work."

"Bucket o' what?"

Freddy gripped his skinny stomach and howled. "Bucket o' what? Whyncha arsk him yerself, Miss 'Igh and Mighty?"

As he ran off down the street laughing, Samantha stood watching and thinking, and it was then the inspiration came to her: with a few pence she could buy something to please her father.

The tanner, it turned out, needed dog droppings for his process, and paid half a penny a bucketful. It was a day's labor to fill a bucket, and since many children did it, the competition was stiff. Struggling with the scuttle and spade the tanner gave her, Samantha foraged the lanes and alleys, taking care to avoid Hawksbill's house even though his unused front steps were rich with mounds, and ended by sundown struggling toward the tanner's place amid a chorus of jeers from her friends: "We 'ave custard on *our* rhubarb!"

Samantha pushed through stoically but gave way to tears when, as the tanner handed her the ha'penny, a ruffian snatched it out of her hand and made off with it. Then the jeering turned to taunting and someone was bold enough to step forward and yank her hair. At that moment a rotten potato flew through the air and scattered the crowd, sending them squealing, and Freddy appeared, grinning.

As he walked her home he listened to her sorrowful account of the day (she was exhausted and filthy and, worse, penniless) and at the foot of the steps stood with his hands on his hips. "Ye're daft, Samantha 'Argrave, fer all yer readin' and writin'. T'others don't work that 'ard at it. Not enough dog stuff to go round. Yer coulda filled the bucket with yer own and raised the level a bit. Tanner don't know no different. Ye're simple-minded, Miss 'Igh and Mighty, can't even sell yer own shit!" And he was bounding off down the street, howling.

Five minutes later Samuel wrinkled his nose at his daughter, inspected the brown smears on her hands and dress and delivered her to the pinch-faced housekeeper, who gave her a severe thrashing and sent her up to bed without supper.

Two days later James left for Rugby.

On the morning of his departure, sixteen-year-old James came down the stairs in his Sunday suit carrying a weather-beaten satchel. After a stilted farewell to his father, James walked down the steps and disappeared.

There were letters in the following year, brief epistles that did little more than convey flat scenarios of James's school life. "I went out for cricket this week past and was put on to bowl; I delivered one ball and was taken off, for the Captain said that if the ball had gone far enough it would have been too wide." Unable to participate in sports owing to his defective hearing, James plunged himself into slavish studying; and he had to work harder at this than the rest of the students because his deaf ear made lectures difficult to follow.

And then, as suddenly as he had gone, James came home. He was a year older and wiser and proudly carried a Certificate in mathematics. Samantha was pleased to have her brother back, for he had grown tall and handsome and looked a lot like Father. But he did not stay long, for soon after his return James set out for Oxford, and this time Father went with him.

On the morning of their departure, heading off to a place they called Paddington Station, Samantha sat on the front steps of her house, chin cupped in her hands. From out of nowhere, as was his style (a talent which kept him out of the clutches of the police), Freddy appeared. He plopped his awkward frame next to her, for he was fourteen now and gangly, and said, "What's the face for?"

"My father and brother 'ave gone off on a train and I wish I coulda gone with 'em."

"Where'd they go?"

"To Oxford, whatever that is."

"What've they gone for?"

"Dunno. They was talking about medicine and studying it. Freddy, 'ow do yer study a bottle o' medicine?"

Her companion smacked his knee, which poked up through the thread-bare fabric of his pants, and howled. "It's not a *bottle* o' medicine yer study, dafty, it's the *science* o' medicine!"

She raised up to face him. "What's it mean then, me dad and brother goin' to Oxford?"

"I 'spect it means yer brother'll be a doctor."

"What's 'e 'ave to go to Oxford for? All a doctor does is spoon nasty stuff into yer mouth."

Freddy leaned close, eyes flashing, his tone conspiratorial. "Ooh, there's more to doctorin' than that! They cut people up, slice 'em like bacon, they do!"

Samantha pushed out her sensuous lower lip. "Do not! My brother'd never do nothing like that!"

"He will if he's gonna be a doctor. They think it's posh!"

"'Ow do you know all this?"

"I'll show yer." Freddy jumped up and grinned down at her. "Coming wi' me, love?"

She eyed him suspiciously. "Where to?"

"Where doctors do their cuttin'!"

FOUR

*S*HE FOLLOWED HIM ACROSS LONDON, ALONG CHARING CROSS Road until it turned into Tottenham Court Road and then down University Street. The four-story North London Hospital stood across from University College and was so awesome it took Samantha's breath away. It was ten o'clock in the morning and the front entrance was a busy place; Freddy beckoned to Samantha as he circled the building and led her to a yard at the rear crowded with carts and carriages.

Some medical students stood near the back door in a tight knot, all straight and handsome and murmuring softly. Freddy whispered, "Them's the same as yer brother, Sam. That's wot James is." Ducking behind a dray, Samantha and Freddy watched the students and saw, a minute later, three young ladies scurry nervously into the yard. When they giggled in a frightened, hysterical way, one young man put his finger to his lips, slid his hand through the arm of one of the girls and escorted her through the door. When they had all gone inside, Samantha and Freddy came out from behind the dray and slipped through the hospital's back door.

When her eyes had adjusted, Samantha found herself in a narrow stone-flagged corridor, on either side of which were double doors. Those on her left were slightly ajar; she gave a quick look in and gasped. Stretched out on a long table, naked and yellowish white, was the corpse of a young man. Four men stood around him, shirt sleeves rolled up, poking into a cavity Samantha could not see. The obvious leader of the little group, a giant of a man with graying red hair and wearing a blood-smeared butcher's apron, was quietly pointing something out.

Close to her ear Freddy whispered, "Wanna go 'ome, fraidy?"

Swallowing painfully, she slowly shook her head and followed him down the hall to a smaller single door into which the medical students had gone. She tiptoed over the flags, trepidly drew open the door and found herself at the foot of dark, narrow stairs. At the top, another door stood open to light and voices.

"We shouldn't be doing this, Freddy," she whispered.

He was behind her, hand on her waist. "I knew yer 'adn't the stomach. Ye're a fraidy, just as I always thought."

"Am not!"

"Shush up or yer'll get us thrown out. Well, if ye're not a-scared, then go on up."

Samantha ascended. At the top she paused and peeked around the door-frame. She found herself on the top tier of an operating theater. The lower three tiers were crowded with medical students, physicians and dressers, shoulder to shoulder, leaning anxiously forward on metal railings with their eyes on the vacant operating table below as if waiting for a performance to begin. On the top tier, farther along, sat the medical students with their nervous, tittering young ladies.

Samantha stayed in the corner, pressed against Freddy's hard body, and saw down below the double doors swing open. Through them strode the giant red-haired man, still wearing the butcher's apron from the post-mortem room. His entry commanded instant silence. This was Mr. Bomsie, professor of clinical surgery. Accompanying him were the three assistants from the autopsy, their hands and arms stained with dark blood, and immediately behind, two porters carried into the operating theater a wicker basket which held the patient.

She was a thin, sparrow-like thing, frightened and trembling; as she was helped onto the table, her eyes darting over the impersonal faces staring down at her and with one of the male assistants unbuttoning her dress, Mr. Bomsie addressed the audience in a bellowing voice: "The patient is female, twenty-five, in otherwise good health, a maid of all work in Notting Hill. She was sent to Dr. Murray by her employer when she complained of acute pain in her right breast. Examination revealed a retracted nipple which bleeds constantly and a lump the size of an apple. Without surgery, she will surely die within the year."

Bomsie nodded to one of his assistants. The young man went to a cupboard against one wall and selected Mr. Bomsie's favorite instruments: two scalpels, a tenaculum, a few Liston clamps, scissors. He spread them out on a tray by the woman's head.

The patient, her chest now bare, begging to be released, was strapped down.

North London Hospital had the rare distinction of being the first hospital in England to administer anesthesia during surgery. This was not to say, however, that the practice was now routine; the question of whether or not to administer chloroform was at the discretion of each surgeon for each case, and Mr. Bomsie chose not to use it. His reason was one shared by many colleagues: too many patients were dying from the inhalation of chloroform and ether. It was not worth the risk—to spare them from a few minutes of pain during the operation—of having them die from the anesthesia. This was Mr. Bomsie's public explanation. His secret reason for discrediting anesthesia, however, lay in his age—he was past sixty—and the fact that he was a preeminent, almost legendary surgeon.

In the days before anesthesia, not long ago, the best operator was the fastest, sparing the patient from as much suffering as possible. In his long and illustrious career, Gerald Bomsie had made a name for himself as one of the swiftest surgeons in England. With the advent of anesthesia, however, and with the patient no longer screaming and fighting against the straps but slumbering peacefully, surgeons could now take their time. The criteria for fame were changing: no longer was it the *fastest* but the most *skillful* who were lauded, and while Gerald Bomsie was legendary in the former, he lacked the latter. Anesthesia was robbing him of his title. And since many of the older surgeons were still performing operations the old way, without anesthesia, no one in the theater on this crisp May morning questioned Mr. Bomsie's method.

Clamping the scalpel between his teeth so that he could run his hands through his leonine hair, and ignoring the terrified pleas of the young woman stretched out before him, Gerald Bomsie spread his fingers over the diseased breast so that the skin was taut, and sliced it open in one clean sweep.

—❁—

Pocket watches came out as everyone in the audience timed him. Samantha heard someone murmur: "Don't blink, he's the swiftest man since Liston! I once saw him take, with one slash of the knife, the patient's leg, testicles, three fingers of his assistant, and the coat-tail of a spectator!"

Samantha's dove-gray eyes grew wide in hypnotic fascination. The breast was being peeled away from the chest wall and rivers of blood were streaming into the sawdust buckets under the table. When the lump of yellow, bloody flesh dropped to the floor, Mr. Bomsie's massive hands rapidly tied ligatures around the bleeding points, poured water over the glistening red muscles, and then drew the skin together with strips of plaster.

Samantha was shaken out of her stupor by the roar of applause. She saw that the patient had mercifully fainted, and so had the medical students' companions.

As the patient was being carried out, Mr. Bomsie washed his hands, something surgeons only ever did *after* an operation, and addressed the audience again. But Freddy and Samantha did not stay to listen. They ducked back down the stairs and hurried out into the corridor to see where the patient was being taken.

As they followed the porters and their basket down the hall, no one paid any attention to the two scruffy children who hurried behind. They came to a lobby busy with doctors and students, patients leaning against walls or slumped to the floor, visitors in top hats and rustling crinolines. Through one of the doors off this lobby the wicker basket was transported.

Freddy grinned wickedly at Samantha. "Ye're lookin' a bit pasty, love. Can't take no more, can yer?"

She had difficulty finding her voice. "I can if you can."

They slipped into the ward unnoticed.

What stopped them first was the stench. Whipping the corner of her shawl up to her nose, Samantha stared at the scene before her: a long room stretching away with a fireplace at one end and a row of beds along each wall. Trying not to be sick, Samantha swept her bewildered eyes over the beds of women: some moaned, some screamed, some were begging for death, a few lay in merciful repose. This was the women's post-surgical ward, and all of them, in various stages of infection, had undergone some form of surgical mutilation.

Near the fireplace was a table at which sat a sister of the All Saints Sisterhood wearing a plain brown holland dress, white cap and apron, and sipping tea. On the wall behind her was a sign: sheets are to be changed once a month whether needed or not. Along the space between the two rows and in between the beds ward maids were busy at their duties: emptying slop pots, turning patients, applying poultices, sweeping the floors. Another sister stood at a cupboard taking inventory and scribbling in a notebook.

Samantha did not know which was worse, the noise or the smell. No torture chamber could deliver up such a pathetic chorus of human suffering. And yet she could not put her hands to her ears, for her nose must be protected; nowhere, not even in the back alleys on a hot summer day, had she ever been assailed by such an overpowering stink. Samantha could see the cause of the foul emanations: the running sores, the draining wounds, the gangrenous flesh, the ribbons of green pus. It was the smell of living bodies rotting away.

Her attention was drawn to the wicker basket, which was now empty, for the pitiable creature, her chest still bare, exposing her one good breast and the oozing red slash of her wound, had been put to bed. At the next bed, Samantha saw a surgeon and three medical students examining a pretty teen-aged girl whose leg had been amputated below the knee, the stump of which was supported on a tray to catch the draining pus. As he lectured, the surgeon removed the girl's dressing—a square of brocade, heavily monogrammed, the charitable donation of an upper-class household. He peeled the rag from the stump, helping it along where it stuck, and dropped the cloth at the foot of the bed. At once a sister retrieved it, carried it to the next bed, where the one-breasted young woman was weeping uncontrollably, and fixed the filthy cloth over her bleeding incision with isinglass plasters.

As two sisters went to help her, one of them sighted the children and shouted, "You there! Be off with you!"

Freddy and Samantha turned and ran, dashing through the busy lobby and down the front steps. They ran with all the speed and agility of their youth and experience, over fences and along gutters until, exhausted, they fell against a wall, heaving.

Freddy began to laugh. "I gotta hand it to yer, Sam, I never woulda thought you coulda done it! Ain't yet seen a female don't faint at the sight o' *that!*"

When her heaving subsided, she grew silent and fixed her eyes on the sooty brick wall across the way. When Freddy also fell quiet, she said softly, "It ain't right, Freddy."

"Aw, come on, Sam, where's yer heart? Everyone does it, sneaking into hospital—"

"That's not what I mean." She turned her wide gray eyes to him, startlingly mature for one so young. "I mean what goes on in there. Doctors are supposed to help, not torture."

"They mean well, Sam. Mebbe they don't know no better."

She swiveled her head away and withdrew into deep, troubled thought.

She was visited by nightmares for weeks afterward and found herself haunted in the day by stark visions of the hospital. But it wasn't fear of the place or being sickened by it that plagued her, as Freddy thought, but a terrible sense of *wrongness.*

When Samantha's preoccupation with the hospital became an unshakable obsession, something happened to lend distraction.

Samuel Hargrave's religious ardor increased with the passing of summer into a winter that blanketed London with a grimy snow. In that year, when not roving the streets with Freddy, Samantha was put to helping her father at night with his divine mission: her job was the sewing of tracts.

No longer content with taking his turn at the pulpit on occasional Sundays, Samuel started taking his sermons into the streets. Armed with biblical tracts which he wrote himself and had printed and had Samantha stitch together by lamplight, Samuel Hargrave imposed himself upon the most salacious of London scenes— Cremorne Gardens, the Haymarket, and Regent Street—thrusting his pamphlets upon prostitutes with an admonition to repent. His fanaticism slowly created a change in him, but it was one which Samantha, in her blind devotion, did not see. And then one night Samuel did a strange thing.

While Samantha was bent over the tracts, her hair falling forward, her cheeks and forehead milky in the lamp's glow, she felt her father's intense gaze upon her. Looking up, she was startled by the wildness in his eyes. Samantha stared back at him for a long time, baffled but unafraid, and then his lips parted and she heard him whisper, "Felicity . . ."

Not knowing what he meant, for Samantha knew no one by that name, she said, "What is it, Father?"

❧

Her small voice seemed to open a door. His face, for the first time in ten years, softened, and a gentle mist came to his eyes. Seeing this, Samantha let out a little cry, jumped up from her chair and ran to him, throwing her arms about his neck and crying into his chest. For an instant he let her hold him, although he did not return the embrace, and she could hear the fearful pounding of his heart. Then Samuel pried his daughter from his body and, composed again, resumed writing his sermon.

Two days later he made the announcement.

It was time, he said in a tone he used when complaining of an undercooked chop, for Samantha to learn the meaning of good Christian labor and the value of a shilling. She was, after all, ten years old and rapidly approaching the threshold of womanhood. There was a gentleman, he explained crisply, who required help around his house, a widower who needed a female to cook and clean. When she wanted to argue that it made no sense to send her out to another household and yet retain a housekeeper for himself, Samantha saw by the firm set of his jaw that to disagree would be futile. She was to go out each morning, he explained, to the house of the man with whom he had made the arrangement, take her dinner and supper there, and return home to sleep in her own bed as the gentleman had no desire for her to live in.

Samantha was to start the next day and the gentleman's name was Isaiah Hawksbill.

FIVE

*T*HE FIRST THING SAMANTHA NOTICED WAS THE GAGGING stench that poured from the open door; the second was the supreme *ugliness* of the man. Gaping up at him, she tried to mask her shock, for Freddy had warned her that once she showed fear to Hawksbill she would be in his power.

"Come in," he said gruffly, "if you're the Hargrave brat."

Samantha swallowed hard, and stepped over the threshold.

They were in the scullery, and once her eyes adjusted to the gloom, Samantha could not help but gasp. It was an astonishing sight, with dirty dishes and pots strewn about, bits of putrid food, filthy mugs and scraps of green bread. "You'll start in here," he said bluntly, speaking, Samantha noticed, either with a speech impediment or the trace of a foreign accent. "I've got no time to bother with this mess, but I haven't a clean spoon to my name and I'm fed up with my own cooking."

His tiny green eyes glinted beneath bushy white brows; Hawksbill's snowy hair grew wild upon his head, badly in need of a cut, and his chin was stubbled from lack of a good shave. He was dressed in a rumpled frock coat, his tie was askew, his white shirt grayish and spotted. All in all, really no more than an untidy old man, but to little Samantha he was truly the monster Freddy had warned of.

She was suddenly gripped with the impulse to turn and flee, but then she remembered that she was here because it was her father's wish (whatever his mysterious reason) and, remembering this, was filled with her undying passion to please him. For her father she would remain.

"Take you all day, this will," came Hawksbill's sour voice. "At noon you'll bring me milk with bread soaked in it. There's a room down that hall and across from the parlor; the door will be locked. You are to put the saucer down and return back here. *Under no circumstances are you to knock.* For supper there's a cold bird in that cupboard. Take a wing for yourself and bring me the rest in a bowl. Put it down in front of the locked door and leave. After you've had your eat, get out. I won't be talking to you again until tomorrow morning. If you've any questions, keep them!"

He lingered a moment to fix a small, malevolent eye on her, running once up and down her thin quaking body, then Isaiah Hawksbill swung around and hobbled out.

The work was tantamount to a herculean labor, but little Samantha set to it with zeal, hoping to receive from Mr. Hawksbill praise which she could offer like a sacrifice to her father. Stoically she cleaned out the shelves, corners, sink and floor, tossing the rancid garbage into the bin out back, then washed and scraped and scoured until her hands were raw. At noon she took the saucer of milk and bread down the long, dark passage, paused before the locked door and listened. From inside came faint, scuffling sounds. Later, at supper, she returned with the stale chicken and found the saucer empty where she had left it. From inside, eerie silence.

The house was dark and dusty, the furniture covered with sheets; the stairs rose up into a forbidding blackness. When night started to descend, Samantha was gripped with a shivering fear so that, having no appetite, she tossed the wing into the bin, slammed the back door, and ran all the way home.

The next morning Isaiah Hawksbill was waiting for her.

"My bed needs changing. Hasn't been touched in nearly a year. You're to strip it, wash the sheets and hang them out. You'll find fresh in a cupboard somewhere. My noon bite will be the same as yesterday, and for supper there's a tin of meat. Spread it thinly—*thinly, mind you*—on some slices of bread and leave it before my door. Have a slice yourself."

He reached out suddenly and seized her arm in a painful grip. "There's one thing you've got to keep in your brat's brain and that is you're never to try to go into the locked room. The rest of the house, I don't give a damn, but that room—" He bent close, his face almost touching hers. "I catch you once, just once, brat, touching the knob of that door, and you'll wish you'd never been born!"

By the end of the week Samantha was near to dropping. The daily chores of Hawksbill's gloomy, two-story row house would have been enough to keep two robust maids going, let alone a skinny girl of ten: lighting the fire in the morning and putting the kettle on to boil; scraping and blacking the grate; shaking the heavy druggets and laying them back down; dusting the potboards; turning out the rubbish drawer; and cleaning the fenders till her arms were black. Hawksbill gave her ninepence and expected her to buy bread with it, and beef pies almost turned, and milk that was seventy percent water. But when he dropped three shillings in her palm (Samantha did not know that most maids of all work earned six or seven) all her weariness dissolved. She would make it a love offering to her father.

"So what's it like then?" asked Freddy, falling into step beside her on her way home.

"It's a house, like any other."

"Does 'e do wicked things?"

She thought of the locked room. "Not as I've seen."

Freddy kicked a stone with his bare foot. He was nearly fifteen, tall and lanky, and starting to show muscles beneath his tight, tattered shirt. "Harry Passwater says the owd man once done a bad thing to a little girl. Nearly 'anged, 'e was, but 'e put a spell on the witnesses so no one could prove nothin'."

"'Arry Passwater shouldn't tell stories."

"Aw, don't come 'igh and mighty with me, Samantha 'Argrave! You may be in service but it ain't to no Member of Parliament!"

⸻❀⸻

At her front steps Freddy spun around and impulsively took Samantha by the shoulders. In a seriousness she had never seen, he said grimly, "If that owd fart ever so much as puts a feather on you, I swear I'll bash his corrupt owd brains in!"

She watched him run off, then hurried into the house. Her father took the shillings without a word.

⸻❀⸻

As summer faded into autumn and then autumn into a dreary wet winter, the days blended into strings of weeks, and a wearisome sameness, with the rare exception of a letter from James at Oxford, settled over Samantha's life. Passing her days within the silent, dreary walls of Hawksbill's gloomy house, and her evenings before a cheerless fire in Bible study, Samantha found a curiosity start to blossom within her.

What did Mr. Hawksbill do behind his locked door?

SIX

*I*SAIAH HAWKSBILL HAD TWO CLOSELY KEPT SECRETS: THE FIRST was buried beneath the floor boards of his entry hall, the other was that he was a Jew.

Born in that bleak strip of land along the western border of Russia known as the Pale, Isaiah Rubinovich was the son of an impoverished peddler and his tubercular wife. He had been forced to flee the ghetto when the "choppers" came prowling one night, searching for Jewish youths to fill the military quota: Tsar Nicholas had ordered that all Jewish boys between twelve and eighteen were to be drafted for twenty-five years of military service. Isaiah had left with a loaf of bread in his pocket and the promise that he would one day, when it was safe, return. That had been forty-five years ago.

Chance and a sharp wit had taken him across Poland into Germany, where Jews enjoyed a greater freedom and where the academic atmosphere was in full flower. After earning his way as an apothecary's apprentice, Isaiah Rubinovich entered the University of Giessen, where he studied pharmacology under the great Baron von Liebig. Yearning often to return some-day to his homeland, the lonely young Isaiah had known this to be a futile dream, for in the years of his absence the Pale had shrunk and most Russian Jews lived on the precipice of starvation and despair. In Western Europe, although lonely and homesick, Isaiah had enjoyed intellectual freedom and the certainty of making his way into a prosperous life.

After distinguishing himself as a scholar and a chemist, receiving ac-colades from the scientific community, Isaiah established a flourishing pharmacy and was held in esteem by many prominent physicians. His quick temper and depths of passion, however, caused him to fall into ill favor with the current powers of government: He came across the Continent to lose himself in the rapidly multiplying masses of London, where he changed his name (taking that of a local tavern) and had been able to establish yet an-other profitable pharmacy, fell in love with and married a beautiful young English Jewess named Rachel, and enjoyed a succession of blissful years un-til the cholera epidemic of 1848 struck.

He closed down his shop, boarded up his house and swore never again to have anything to do with society.

❈

He met Samantha, as was his habit, at the back door precisely at seven. This morning, however, he wore a dusty top hat on his wild hair and an overcoat. "Have to go out, brat. Hate to do it, haven't set foot outside in God knows how long, but it's an errand that has to be run."

Although she fell at once into her chores with all the vigorous determi-nation her skinny body could muster, and although she was used to work-ing alone and roaming the house without the company of another soul, this morning, after Hawksbill's heavy footsteps faded down the path, Samantha could not shake the chilling reality that, for the very first time, she was truly alone in the house.

In an effort to manufacture false courage, she hummed as she dusted, whispered to herself as she swept, walked with clumping steps to spread noise around the house (noticing once that, in the entry hall, the floor boards sounded strangely hollow), and presently, inevitably, found herself standing before the locked room.

She leaned forward as she had done many times and pressed her ear to the wood. Some days she had heard peculiar scraping sounds, occasionally a thump, and only yesterday what sounded like a chain being dragged across the floor. Now all was deathly still.

She leaned away and studied the oak panels.

The proper thing to do was turn around and march away. But indecision immobilized her. Everything her father had taught her about obedience dissipated in the face of her intense child's need to know what was on the other side of that door. Samantha reached out and gingerly touched the knob. To her great shock, the door moved an inch.

Samantha snatched her hand back as if bitten. He had left the room unlocked!

Swallowing for courage, Samantha placed her hand flat on the door and pushed gently; it swung away from her, yawning like a great black maw, revealing nothing more than a formidable darkness on the other side. With her eyes stretched wide Samantha advanced a step. Then another. And another, until she found herself standing on the inside of the forbidden room.

The air was icy. No light shone from any source; she could see thin ribbons of gray morning light between the heavy velvet drapes. But her eyes slowly adjusted until she could make out various objects scattered about.

It was the most cluttered room she had ever seen.

Massive books rose in twisted towers, heaped from floor to ceiling, balanced precariously as if the slightest breeze would topple them; large wooden crates, some with straw stuffing spilling out, stood along the walls; stacks of papers weighed down a table that looked as if it might at any moment collapse beneath the weight; nailed to the walls were charts and diagrams; stuffed owls and falcons were perched on the mantel; inside the fireplace itself was crammed an unopened wooden crate. There was barely any floor space, only a narrow path which Mr. Hawksbill must have burrowed to get around.

Along one wall stood a worktable of some sort, its surface crowded with bottles and jars and all manner of glass objects which Samantha could not identify. There was a high stool, an oil lamp, a quill and inkhorn. Above the table wooden shelves strained beneath the weight of more books and papers and bottles and tins.

And then she saw it. A jar with a little man trapped inside.

✺

Isaiah Hawksbill hurried inside the back door and knocked the raindrops off his shoulders and sleeves. Unwrapping the muffler from around his face, he wiped his feet on the mat inside the door. Under his arm he clutched a paper-wrapped bundle.

Spellbound, Samantha drew nearer the jar, her mouth falling open at the sight of the tiny outstretched arms of the little prisoner. He was trying to get out.

Hawksbill proceeded down the hall, deep in thought, and stopped suddenly when he saw the door standing open.

Samantha rose onto her tiptoes and reached for the jar. Gently taking hold, careful not to hurt the little prisoner, she slid it to the edge of the shelf. But when she started to bring it down, her little fingers barely secure around it, she caught a movement in the corner of her eye.

She turned. He was standing in the doorway. Samantha cried out and dropped the jar. It crashed to the floor in a thousand pieces.

He flew at her like an enormous black bird, his cape flapping. She screamed as his gnarled hands swooped down on her; pain shot through her arms as he seized her. "Please, sir, I only wanted to set him free! I didn't touch anythin' else! Please don't kill me, Mr. 'Awksbill!"

He shook her like a rag doll. "I warned you, brat!"

"He wanted to be let out!" she shrieked. "I was only settin' 'im free!"

"I'll teach you a lesson, brat!"

Samantha managed to wrench an arm free and fling it across her face. *"Please don't kill me, Mr. 'Awksbill!"*

He stopped shaking her and, when Samantha tentatively opened one eye and peeped up at him, she saw his grotesque face twist in confusion.

"What are you talking about? Set who free?"

In a delayed reaction Samantha started to cry. "The little man," she sobbed. "You'd no right to bottle 'im up like that! He was tryin' to get out, I only wanted to help 'im!"

To her immense surprise, Hawksbill released her and straightened up. "Stop that crying," he said flatly.

Samantha sniffed and hiccupped.

"I said stop crying! Now then, what are you talking about?"

"The little man!" She pointed to the broken jar.

Withdrawing a little box from his coat pocket, Hawksbill struck a lucifer match and lit the oil lamp, turning the flame up to its brightest. Then he squatted over the mess on the floor. "My mandrake root," he said in a strangely distant voice. "It's all right, though, it's not damaged." He looked up at Samantha. "Did I hurt you?"

❦

She arched her eyebrows. "N-no, sir."

He looked back down at the jar; his knobbled fingers reached out and gently touched each piece of glass. "I shall have the devil of a time sweeping this up. It was just the right size, I wonder where I shall find another . . ."

Samantha stared down at him, stupefied. She studied the curved back, the bowed shoulders, the pink patch of scalp in the middle of a corona of white hair. Then she said in a small voice, "I'm sorry, Mr. 'Awksbill, truly I am."

He rose to his feet, wincing as his joints cracked. "You can't help your curiosity. Children are like that." His voice softened. "You're sure I didn't hurt you?"

"Not a bit, Mr. 'Awksbill."

"You know, she was just about your age . . ."

❦

"Now the mandrake root is a peculiar thing. It's because it resembles a miniature human that it was believed for centuries to have strange, mystical powers."

They were sitting in the cluttered study, drinking Darjeeling tea. Samantha had swept up the glass and Mr. Hawksbill had found a new jar for his root.

"It was believed that it clung so earnestly to the soil that when it was pulled up it shrieked like a tortured human and that it caused instant death to anyone who heard it. That is why the mandrake root is always pulled up by trained dogs."

Samantha's eyes trailed back to the jar in which the root was imprisoned once again. Now, plainly, it was nothing more than a root. But earlier she could have sworn . . .

"*She* always called it a little man."

"Who?"

"My Ruth. She was about your age when"—he sucked in a steadying breath—"when the cholera took her. I tried everything to save my little girl, but for all my fancy knowledge and pharmacy, I was helpless. That was twenty years and more gone, and still I mourn her passing."

Samantha looked around the jumbled room. "Is this a pharmacy?"

"Oh my, no!" Hawksbill's face creased in an unaccustomed smile. "I gave that up when my Ruth and Rachel died. When I saw how helpless I was, I decided to give it all up."

"Then what is all this?"

"You are a curious one, aren't you? My Ruth was, too, always asking questions . . ." The old man's voice faded away and he fell to staring at Samantha. "Where's your mama, child?"

"Dunno."

"Do you remember her?"

"No."

"Do you . . . say prayers for her?"

"I pray every night for the fallen women on the Haymarket."

"Whatever for?"

"My father says I must."

"And he has never told you to pray for your mama? Have you never wondered about her?"

"I ain't never thought about it and I s'pose that's not right 'cause everyone has a mother, even Freddy. I guess I always thought I never had no mother, but that can't be right, can it?"

"No, that can't be right at all . . ."

It was a new curiosity for Samantha to entertain, for the mystery of Mr. Hawksbill's locked room was solved. He was an herbalist, he said, and was putting together the biggest, best book on organic medicines ever written. It was a large work and required a lot of research and discipline, so he must concentrate all his energies upon it. Knowing now what he did all day long, Samantha turned her questioning mind to her mother.

She found the answer one night in the Bible, on the page entitled Family Record. The next morning she posed the question to Mr. Hawksbill. "What's deceased?"

He had been about to walk out of the scullery. "Why?"

"Because that's what me mother is. It says so next to 'er name."

He sniffed in irritation. "It means dead."

"My mother is dead?"

"That's what it means." He turned away.

"She died on my birthday. How did she die?"

"Why don't you ask your papa?"

"Oh, I can't disturb him."

"Yet you can disturb me!" he shouted.

Samantha shrank back. "I'm sorry, Mr. 'Awks—"

"I'm late to work already! I'm not a young man, you know! Have to keep at it so the blasted book can be published before I am deceased!"

When he spun away on his heel, Samantha said quickly, "Then whyncha hire on help?"

He twirled around, his little green eyes flaring. "What is that, you impertinent brat? First nosing about in my private business and now telling me how to do it! I don't require help at what I do best, you know!"

"But it *is* a big work, Mr. 'Awksbill, you said so yerself. And it would be such a shame if you couldn't finish it afore you decease, and I should think a good strong boy who could lift things and run errands for you—"

"*Himmel*," he muttered, rubbing his stubbled chin. "Brat's got a point."

Samantha, thinking of Freddy, said hastily, "A boy who could go out and get more jars and straighten your books so you could get to them easier and do all the little jobs ye're wasting yerself on when yer could be writing—"

"Don't need a lad," he said curtly. "Why should I spend another farthing when I've already got you?"

Her eyes flew open. "Me, sir?"

SEVEN

*H*E PUT HER TO WORK THAT DAY. THERE WERE JARS TO uncrate and labels to paste and boxes of dried weeds and flower petals and seeds to sort and quills to sharpen and lamps to fill and books to dust; and when the old man discovered she could read, he put her to alphabetizing the stacks of monographs on the natures of hundreds of plants; and when he discovered she could write, he set her to inscribing labels with botanical names because his old hands shook too badly for neatness. And by the end of the first week Isaiah Hawksbill found himself explaining things to Samantha: why licorice was called *Glycyrrhiza glabra,* how the watermelon seed expelled tapeworm, what a wonderful sedative *Centranthus ruber* was, and where in the world snakeroot was found. Her eagerness to learn was compounded with each new fact; the more he taught her, the more inquisitive she became, and when Isaiah Hawksbill would have expected her constant questioning to irritate him, he was astonished to find himself the soul of patience. Indeed, with the child's ever-growing desire to learn, within the petrified spirit of Isaiah Hawksbill was born an intense desire to teach.

And he discovered something else, something about himself he had not, until now, known: that he had been lonely, terribly lonely. . .

They became a team, mentor and pupil; she came less and less to spend her time at menial tasks and more and more to sit at his feet listening, learning, questioning and remembering. When he taught her about the medicinal powers of ginseng tea and discovered she had never heard of China, he drew out an old dusty volume on geography and showed her the lay of the globe. When he discovered that her father had taught her no arithmetic, Hawksbill set about to show her tens and units, sums and subtraction. Her eagerness to learn pleased him; her quickness to grasp inspired him; and her remarkable ability to retain all that he taught made him proud.

As November gave way to December with a snowy January soon following, Isaiah Hawksbill sat with Samantha Hargrave by a roaring fire, in the fireplace that had not been used in years, and imparted to her all his knowledge and wisdom. His obsession with his book of herbals waned; he was finding immense satisfaction in passing along his legacy to this hungry child. To see her grow intellectually was more gratifying than committing his vast knowledge to perishable paper. With the coming of spring and her eleventh birthday, they reached out to new subjects—astronomy, zoology, ancient history—and spent their days exploring the world together.

In all that time Samantha never told her father.

EIGHT

$\mathcal{M}$R. HAWKSBILL HELD UP A MAJOLICA JAR AND TURNED IT slowly in the light. "This is *Smilax officinalis*, Samantha, a prized possession."

She studied the small thorny vines with long slender roots. "Where's it come from?"

"Many places. The gray from Mexico, the brown from Honduras, and this"—he patted the jar lovingly—"the most difficult to come by, is from the western slopes of the Andes."

"What is it?"

"What is it? Why, *Liebchen*, it is a centuries-old remedy for easing the pangs of childbirth. It also cures a chest pain called angina pectoris. And the savages of North America believe it cures impotence."

Samantha tried to pronounce the difficult Latin.

Mr. Hawksbill said, "The Spaniards have an easier name for it, *Liebchen*. They call it sarsaparilla."

The tranquillity of the June morning was shattered by a sudden commotion in the street. Stepping down from his high stool and parting the curtain from the window, Mr. Hawksbill looked out upon a chaotic scene: a runaway dray had thundered down the narrow street, knocking over vegetable carts and scattering people in its path with a frenzied crowd running behind, shouting. Two bold navvies leapt out, managed to seize the reins and wrestled with the frightened mare until she was brought to a whinnying rest directly in front of Hawksbill's house.

Curious, Samantha joined him and peered out. She saw a small knot of people gather at the edge of the mob. "What is it, Mr. 'Awksbill?"

"It looks as though someone is hurt."

She turned her face up to him, "Should we help?"

He let the curtain drop. "No concern of ours."

"But you have all these wonderful medicines!"

"Gave that up years ago."

Samantha looked out again and saw, from down the road, two men running, carrying a door horizontally between them. She spun around, dashed down the hall and out the back door, for the front door was permanently locked, down the alley, around the corner, and came to a breathless halt at the edge of the crowd. The driver of the dray, wringing his hands, was saying, "The lad tried to stop the horse by hisself! I couldna avoid him!"

The crowd parted to allow the men with the door to pass, and when Samantha saw who it was that lay groaning in the gutter, she cried, "Freddy!" and ran to him, falling to her knees. He rolled his head to one side but did not open his eyes.

"Outa the way, miss, gotta get him on this here board." The two men roughly seized the boy by the legs and armpits and dropped him onto the door. Samantha stared spellbound at Freddy's right leg: a compound fracture of both bones had thrust the jagged ends up through his flesh. They glistened with blood and mud in the noon sun.

A shadow fell over her and the crowd drew away; Samantha looked up to see Isaiah Hawksbill standing beside her, "Where are they takin' him, Mr. 'Awksbill?"

He narrowed his eyes at Freddy's mangled leg. "To hospital."

Pictures flashed in her mind, memories of North London Hospital two years before. "They can't!" She whipped around and flung herself across his body.

"Here now," said Hawksbill, reaching down for her.

"No!" she screamed. "Not *that* place! I won't let 'em do it!"

"C'mon, mister," said one of the men with the door. "Get the lass off him. We ain't got all day."

Isaiah Hawksbill stared down at the girl, watched her thin arms embrace the muscular shoulders of the unconscious sixteen-year-old, saw her arched back rise and fall in sobs, her luxuriant black hair streaming over the still body. And he felt an old emotion, one he had thought long dead, stir in his heart. He heard himself say, "I'll take care of the boy. Come with me."

Samantha snapped her head up, her cheeks wet with tears, then she slowly rose and, taking one of Freddy's limp hands in hers, walked alongside as the two men carried the door down the alley to Hawksbill's back door. Inside, they followed the old man through the gloom, their wide eyes turning this way and that, and brought the boy into the front parlor where Hawksbill snapped a dusty sheet off the horsehair sofa. "You can put him here."

The men tipped Freddy off the door as if they were dumping coal and backed out of the parlor. Samantha straightened the lad on the cushions and set about to tending him.

"Don't know if I can help, *Liebchen*," said the old man as he came down the stairs with blankets and sheets. "Here, shred this in long strips. Then fetch me some hot water."

Hawksbill's hands were too arthritic and unsteady to wash the wound properly. When Samantha said, "Here, let me do it," he handed her the cloth and watched as she knelt beside Freddy and tenderly cleansed the raw flesh.

Hawksbill brought in jars from the study, crushed leaves and steeped roots, which Samantha lovingly and delicately applied to the exposed bone and torn muscle. Standing over her and watching her long slender fingers handle the wounded tissue, Isaiah Hawksbill marveled at her unflinching devotion. Most females would be hysterical by now, or in a dead faint. But look how naturally she goes at it, as if it were nothing more than stirring a custard.

Between the two of them, a thin eleven-year-old girl and an arthritic old man, they managed to set the bones, pulling the leg apart and easing it together between two stiff boards; then Samantha, under Hawksbill's direction, drew the flesh together and pressed strips of plaster over the skin. When they were through Hawksbill sank raggedly into a chair with a glass of brandy and Samantha pushed curls off her damp forehead; they noticed it was dark outside and in all that time Freddy had not once regained consciousness.

"We've done all we can, *Liebchen*," said Hawksbill wearily. "It's up to God now."

She was drinking tea. "He'll be all right now, won't he?"

Hawksbill slowly swung his craggy head. "I won't lie to you, child. He's in a bad way. Not many people survive compound fractures."

"Why not? We've set the bones and closed the skin!"

"Because the sepsis will set in and all the world knows there's nothing can be done to fight the sepsis."

"What's sepsis?"

"Poison, *Liebchen,* infection. No one knows what causes it and so no one knows how to fight it." Hawksbill paused. He had heard some talk lately of a young Quaker out of Scotland, Joseph Lister, who claimed to have found a remedy. . . The old man shook his head. He doubted it counted for much, coming out of Scotland and all.

Samantha looked over at the still body on the sofa, the barely rising and falling chest, the chaos of chestnut curls on the pillow, and said softly, "I shall take care of him."

The days that followed were a nightmare. Freddy came down with a burning fever and he tossed and turned in violent delirium. Standing in the shadow of the doorway, Hawksbill watched as Samantha laid her cool fingers on the youth's burning forehead, murmured to him, and seemed, by her mere presence, to quieten him. He watched her handle the pus-filled dressings, insisting on changing them every day, even though Hawksbill saw no point to that. He watched her long, agile fingers daily inspect the wound, apply ointment and mold, palpate the leg for the placement of the bones, all done with such an expert touch that it almost seemed as if the eleven-year-old knew what she was doing.

She stayed late these nights. Not that her father noticed or cared. If Hawksbill had such a beautiful, intelligent daughter he would want her around him all the time to spoil and cosset. Who knew what Samuel Hargrave's insane reasons were? Hawksbill liked having the girl with him. Even if it was only because of that wretched boy in the parlor, burning with infection, the leg swollen to nearly twice its size. The time would soon come, Hawksbill knew, when it would all be over.

Samantha was preparing dripping sandwiches for their supper. In the past few months the old man had opened his fist and allowed Samantha to bring in better food. Now they were regularly eating boiled cabbage and potatoes, fried bangers, baker's bread and jam, unwatered milk, gooseberry cheese and mince pie. "He's been awfully quiet today, Mr. 'Awksbill. It frightens me."

Hawksbill, spreading dried weeds on his workbench, separating comfrey leaves from their stems, murmured, "Maybe it would have been best to send him to hospital. A surgeon's what he needed."

"No," she said softly but firmly. "Hospital's a place of no hope. People only go there to die."

He couldn't argue with that. St. Bartholomew's Hospital, before admitting a patient, demanded a burial fee in advance that would be refunded *if* the patient should recover. Putting down his knife and tweezers, the old man faced her squarely and said, "There's no hope here either, child. The boy can't possibly survive. He hasn't eaten in over a week and we've barely been able to get a bit of water down his throat. He hasn't once regained consciousness, not even for a second—" Hawksbill slumped suddenly, pushing the bones of his old spine against the thin fabric of his frock coat. What was the use in trying to knock it into her head? She was so blamed stubborn. Clinging to this ridiculous fantasy that—

A crash tore the air. Samantha was on her feet and flying into the parlor. Hobbling as fast as he could after her, Hawksbill came to the open doorway and saw Samantha on her knees locked in a wrestling match with Freddy, whose glassy eyes were open and whose arms were flailing wildly. A bottle of water and a glass lay on the carpet in pieces.

"It's all right, Freddy," said the girl, her thin body, so much smaller than his, being thrown painfully about. "I'm here, Freddy. You're gonna be all right."

Spellbound, the old man looked on as the girl managed to calm the delirious youth, push him back on the pillow, and soothe him with a kiss on his forehead. When Freddy was quiet again, Samantha looked up at Hawksbill and whispered with glistening eyes, "He's awake."

Freddy's recovery was a rocky one, but he did eventually get better, sipping broth and undercooked eggs, lying quietly and meekly beneath Samantha's tender care. If Hawksbill marveled at what she had done for the boy, the experience had no less of an impact on Samantha. Every night, lying in her bed until the early morning hours, she went over it and over it: the miracle of restoring her dear friend to health.

A steaming, smoggy summer settled over London, the air foul and yellow with the many curls of smoke that rose from the thousands of chimneys and from the funnels of the packets and penny steamers on the river. It was an unhealthy summer for London's crowded two million; a summer in which the unclean cans of the London milk-women caused an outbreak of typhoid fever in Marylebone, killing thousands before the eyes of the helpless doctors. But as summer waxed into a smoky autumn and as winter frost then gradually washed the sky in crisp blues, Freddy made rapid progress. By November he could bear weight on his leg and could limp up and down the parlor without aid. By this time he had fallen hopelessly in love with Samantha and so, coincidentally, had Isaiah Hawksbill.

NINE

*S*AMANTHA BROUGHT IN A TRAY OF TEA AND SCONES AND A POT of black currant jam and put it down on the table by the fire. Freddy, giving the sea coals a poke, watched out of the corner of his eye as she spooned sugar into the two cups. "Where's the owd man?" he asked offhandedly.

"He's gone to fetch some hyssop. We used it all up on yer leg and so he's gotta restock it." Samantha sat in the easy chair, which had been unsheeted and turned to face the fire weeks ago, and put her feet on a footstool. "Come on, love, stop for tea."

Freddy pushed off the mantel and limped to the other chair. The boards were off his leg now but it was so crooked that he walked with a lurch, like a sailor on a choppy sea. "Best tea this. I never 'ad it so good as when the owd man took me in. I've come to regret all the dog shit I flung at 'is door."

Samantha smiled dreamily and held the cup to her nose so she could inhale the rich aroma.

"Sam, I gotta tell you something."

She continued to gaze into the fire.

"Sam, will you look at me?"

She turned to him. Freddy's handsome, rough face flickered in the fire's glow and his best features stood out: his square jaw, his large straight nose, high cheekbones and deep-set brown eyes. All framed by tousled nut-brown curls that never stayed combed for long. The boy was gone; Freddy was a man now. "What is it, love?"

"Sam, I gotta leave."

She stared at him for a frozen moment, then slowly lowered her cup. "Why?"

"'Cause it's time. I been here five months now and I'm all better and can take care o' meself. It's time I was movin' on."

Her face darkened. "What d'you mean, movin' on?"

"Away from the Crescent, Sam."

"But you can't! There's no need to leave, Freddy, you can stay here as long as you like! Forever, if you want! Mr. 'Awksbill's keen on you!"

"Aye, but I'm not keen on stopping 'ere. It's time I did something wi' meself, Sam."

"Ye're not making sense—"

"Listen, Sam." He slid impulsively to one knee before her, keeping his bad leg straight, and gathered one of her hands into his. "I had a brush with owd man Death, Sam. I stood at his horrible door and saw the other side. Weren't for you, I'd-a gone through. And it made me understand something for the first time. That I gotta make me own way in this world, I gotta *be* something. Sam, I ain't no kid no more. I'm a man and I gotta act like one. Can't go running the streets and stealing apples the rest o' me life. A proper job's what I need, and a proper life."

Her face crumpled and a wall of tears rose in her eyes. "I don't wancha to leave, Freddy! Ye're all I got!"

"Nonsense, Sam. You've got yer dad and Mr. 'Awksbill and yer brother who's gonna be a fancy doctor! And it ain't like I was gonna be gone forever, Sam. I'll come back. Quicker'n you can say Bob's yer uncle!"

The tears spilled over and traced silvery streaks down her cheeks. "Where'll you go?"

"I dunno, but when I find it I'll know it. Aw, Sam." He clumsily caressed the small hand beneath his big fingers and felt that old familiar softening of his hard heart at the sight of her eyes. There was so much more he wanted to say—that he had realized he wasn't good enough for the likes of Samantha, that he wanted her to be proud of him, that he was in love with her and wanted to take care of her the rest of her life—but he hadn't the courage or the way with words to tell her, so it all remained unspoken.

"Listen, Sam, it's a gift you've got, to make the sick well again. Just like that owd tabby. I had dreams of you talkin' to me and I dreamt that you reached yer hand through a suffocatin' mist and pulled me through. I know now them weren't dreams but really happened. You've saved me life, Sam, and I'll never forget that."

She dropped her cup, spilling tea all over Mr. Hawksbill's faded Turkey carpet, and flung her thin arms around Freddy's neck. "Ye're me only friend, Freddy! I shall miss you and I shall pray for you every day that ye're gone from me!"

He held her tightly, feeling strange new stirrings deep in his abdomen; the old brotherly affection had given way to something new and exciting. She wasn't twelve years old yet, but in a few years, after he'd made his fortune and come back a gentleman able to give her a proper life, Samantha Hargrave would be a beauty among beauties and she'd be all his. Freddy buried his face in her thick black hair and murmured, "Wait for me, Sam. Don't never go away from here till I come back for you."

TEN

*I*T WAS TWO DAYS BEFORE EASTER, A DISMAL RAINY MORNING, and Samantha was stamping her feet on the kitchen flags to warm her toes. She blew into her hands and glared at the kettle, urging it to a quick boil.

Isaiah Hawksbill watched her, hidden in the doorway.

In a few weeks she'd be twelve and already the womanly signs were starting: the childhood skinniness was giving way to new curves and flesh. The sight of her made his old heart quake and made his scrawny arms long to hold her. She had let him embrace her once, four months back, when Freddy packed off for parts unknown. Then, Samantha had been inconsolable, crying and carrying on and threatening to follow the boy, but Hawksbill had managed to calm her down by cradling her in his arms and assuring her that Freddy would keep his promise and come back someday.

But that had been four months ago. Since then she had grown quiet and withdrawn and no more physical liberties had been allowed.

"Tea's about ready, Mr. 'Awksbill!" she cried. "Oh, there you are, sir. I didn't see you."

He stepped fully into the kitchen. "Let it steep a bit longer, *Liebchen*, and add half an ounce of camomile to it, I am feeling my joints today."

After he left, Samantha flapped her arms about herself. It was bloody cold in the kitchen (if only her father would buy her a guernsey) to be standing and watching the tea brew, so she decided to nip down the garden to the privy and answer nature's call.

It stood against the back fence at the end of a path, its walls aswarm with brambles and nettles. The stench was not so bad on cold winter days, but in summer Samantha would run with held breath, pop inside, and then run back out gasping. This morning she was a little annoyed to find she hadn't needed to come here after all; back in the kitchen she had felt the urge to move her bowels, but now it was gone. As she stood up from the seat she felt it again, the abdominal rumble that had sent her running here, and as she considered the probable cause—that suet for yesterday's dinner had looked as if it might have "just turned"—she felt a warm wetness between her thighs. Perplexed, Samantha looked down, and there, in the watery light that streamed through the spaces in the boards, she saw on the floor a bright crimson spot of blood.

She ran all the way back, stumbling on the back steps and skinning her knees. She dashed headlong into the study and cried, "I'm dying!"

Startled, Hawksbill got down from his stool. "What happened?"

"I'm dying, Mr. 'Awksbill!" She threw herself against him, flinging her arms about him. "Please don't send me to hospital!"

Stunned, the old man could not for the moment say anything. The sudden contact with her body, the feel of her arms tight around his waist, the rising and falling of her young breast as she sobbed—it was just like four months before . . .

With supreme effort Hawksbill put his hands on her shoulders and drew back a little. "*Liebchen*, what's the matter?"

Her face was blanched to the color of flour. "I'm bleeding."

"You're what?"

"I only just now found it. In the privy. Mr. 'Awksbill, give me a medicine. The papaya seeds, they stop hemorrhage—"

He turned away, groping for the workbench.

"Don't send me to hospital! Don't let me die!"

It wasn't fair, she hadn't had enough childhood yet! His voice came out strangled. "You must go home, *Liebchen*."

"Why?" She was sobbing freely now.

He felt his knees give out. Hawksbill slumped against the bench, gazing at her in sorrow. "You have a housekeeper, have you not? Go and tell her about it at once, *Liebchen*."

"She'll send me to hospital!"

"No, *Liebchen*. Go home, she will know what to do. Trust me, child, you are going to be all right . . ."

It was that humiliating experience that had clapped this degrading stigma upon him. Hawksbill wasn't deaf; he knew what the people of St. Agnes Crescent called him: child molester. A lower animal could not exist, and the problem was, even though it was not true, he couldn't blame them, considering what he had done.

Sitting alone now by the kitchen grate with a shawl over his knees and a bowl of milk and bread untouched in his lap, he recalled that horrifying day of long ago.

He had gone out then, even though still in mourning for his little Ruth and Rachel, he had gone out about London on errands for books and plants. It was spring; he had walked along the Serpentine enjoying the greenness and newness of the world being reborn. It was early morning and Hawksbill was preoccupied with the classification of a puzzling new plant. A young woman in a bonnet and hoop skirt was sitting on a bench engrossed in a book, and a child, no more than eight, was toying at the edge of the water with a beech stick.

He was not able then, nor was he able now years later, to fathom what had happened to him in that instant: the frail thread of sanity had, upon seeing the child, her face familiar, snapped, and Isaiah Hawksbill, then younger and more agile, had cried, "Ruth!" dashed to the little girl, scooped her up in his arms and proceeded to run off with her.

He had no memory of what happened just then; the next thing he knew, a babble of voices and black shapes were gathering about him. A constable was pushing his way through the crowd and the governess was on her knees consoling the wailing child. Bewildered, Hawksbill realized what he had done. Later, in the superintendent's office, frightened but composed, Hawksbill had fabricated a lie: "The child was about to fall into the water and I rescued her, nothing more." The flustered governess, giving testimony beneath the critical eye of her employer, too timid to admit she had been reading and therefore had not actually seen the crime committed, had decided at the last, for her own salvation, to corroborate Hawksbill's story. The case was dropped and would have been forgotten had it not been for the untimely appearance in the park of a resident of St. Agnes Crescent—a sackwoman on her way to the warehouses at Billingsgate—who had perceived the incident differently. The child had not been *that* close to the water, in no danger at all, when Hawksbill came running from out of nowhere, swept the brat up on the run and kept on going and would have got clear to Surrey if it hadn't been for the shout of a passing gentleman.

While the sackwoman, herself guilty of many crimes and preferring to avoid contact with officers of the law, did not come forth and tell the constable what she had seen, nevertheless she spread the story around the Crescent so that by the time Hawksbill came wearily home his neighbors had already passed judgment.

So how could he now in all sanity consider what he was considering?

To ask Samuel Hargrave for his daughter's hand in marriage.

She was gone for five days and in that time the old Jew agonized. He would love her and cherish her, protect her from the evils of the world, and rescue her from the dreary future that stretched before her—years and decades of waiting on her oblivious father, becoming a spinster, a useless faded woman whom, in the end when her father died, no man would want. Isaiah Hawksbill would save her from that curse, give her his name and a home of her own, let her fix it up, bring the sunshine in, buy a pianoforte and teach her to play. There would be cards in the evening by the fire; they would have stimulating talks; he would continue to teach her, unveil the world's mysteries for her. And he would deluge her with the love he so desperately needed to give and which she so desperately hungered for.

When Samantha returned she was subdued, staring down at the carpet as she explained, "You were right, Mr. 'Awksbill, I wasn't sent to hospital. Mrs. Scoggins never said a word but she tore up a bed sheet and tied it round me waist and between me legs. It's over now, but she said it'll come back in a month."

Hawksbill sat awkwardly tapping his fingers on the weed-strewn workbench. "Samantha child, does your father ever receive visitors?"

"Oh no, sir, he's much too busy with his tracts!"

"I should like"—he withdrew a handkerchief and dabbed his upper lip—"to have a word with him."

"Have I done somethin' wrong?"

"Oh, *Liebchen*, no. It is a business matter only, a thing between two gentlemen. I have not spoken with your father in nearly two years, I was only wondering . . . Never mind," he said gently. "I shall find the proper moment to approach him. Now then, what shall we read while we have our tea?" His prehensile fingers reached for a volume on geology.

"Mr. 'Awksbill?"

"Yes, *Liebchen*."

"Explain it to me, please, why I gotta bleed every month."

His hand froze. "Perhaps when you are older."

"Why? If it's happening to my body, ain't I got a right to know?"

He sagged. It was his own fault; he had encouraged her inquisitiveness and had never once refused an answer. "Sit down, child, and I shall try . . ."

When he was through, Hawksbill was frustrated. In 1872 science had not yet been able to unravel the mystery of the female cycle. The many theories were all couched in magic and esoterica, with the most popular belief among doctors being that the moon was directly responsible for triggering menstruation, which, they said, was Nature's way of compensating for the lack of female ejaculation. They suspected it had something to do with childbearing, for its onset signaled fertility and its cessation marked pregnancy, but just how it figured in, no one knew. There were the ovaries, but no one was certain what their function was, and the ovum had only recently been discovered. If the egg played any part in human reproduction, no one had yet been able to deduce just how.

"Why don't men have it?" asked Samantha with a dubious frown.

"Because they, ah, have something else, something similar which takes place during the conception of a child."

"Oh, *that*."

He felt a flush burn up his neck. "That is something you need not concern yourself with for years yet, *Liebchen*, and he added mentally: Possibly never.

Then Hawksbill felt a sharp pang and he thought: There is no fool like an old fool!

What on earth had he been thinking? What temporary madness had gripped him, causing him to seriously believe he could marry this child? Protect her, yes, and shield her and love her, but he could not give her that most precious gift from a husband to his wife—children! He was too old for that; what right had he to deny her the maternity experience? Who was he to say she might never marry? Hawksbill, you old fool!

"Is somethin' wrong, Mr. 'Awksbill?"

He looked sadly into her swimming gray eyes and thought: How could I have been so selfish, pretending I had her welfare at heart? What right have I, in my miserly greed, to lock her away like a china doll too fragile to handle?

When he groaned slightly, she rested her slender hand on his arm. "You're not well today, are you? Feeling the damp a bit? What you need is a nice infusion of acerola berries."

When she left the room Hawksbill did not stir. He was pondering the cruelty of a fate that takes away a man's cherished wife in his prime, hardens his heart against all women, then allows him to fall in love when it is too late.

A single tear fell from eyes that had not cried in over twenty years. The old Jew drew in a shuddering breath and swore a silent vow. He would continue to love her for the rest of his days but, for her sake, he would never speak of it again.

ELEVEN

*N*O ONE SUSPECTED, NOT EVEN MATTHEW HIMSELF, that he was on the verge of a breakdown.

Matthew Christopher Hargrave, eighteen, had worked at his clerical job for almost four years and in all that time not a single day had varied. With the exception of Sunday mornings off for church, Matthew worked seven days a week—seventy-six hours in all—with never a day off for holiday or illness. The routine was almost killing: walking every morning to the river to take the boat taxi down the Thames to the Tower Bridge, from where he walked to the carriage works in Bermondsey. After hanging up his hat and coat in a corner of the stuffy office, Matthew joined the other young male clerks in sweeping the floors, dusting furniture, filling the lamps, whittling the nibs of his pens and, once a week, washing the windows. The office was open thirteen hours a day with half an hour for dinner at noon and half an hour for tea. Those young men who were courting were given one evening off in the week. The use of Spanish cigars, liquor, and the visiting of pool halls and barbershops were reason for dismissal. Bible study was encouraged, and if an employee had an immaculate record for five years running, with not a day of absence or lateness, he was given a pay raise of fivepence per day.

Unlike his fellow clerks who worked diligently and cheerfully and saved every penny toward the day they would marry, Matthew Hargrave, at eighteen, felt stifled and at the end of his tether.

His home life was as dreary as the office; James was away at Oxford, his father was poor company, and his little sister was like a stranger. Matthew had no friends and was frightened to death of females. His sole pleasure in life was his nightly ritual of what his father called self-pollution.

Matthew sensed he was not of a right mind, that he was gradually deteriorating, and knew also that the cause stemmed from masturbation. It was a commonly known fact that with each ejaculation a man lost some of his noble "essence," yet he could not help himself. And accompanying the nightly emission, in order to urge himself to ever more powerful orgasm, Matthew conjured fantasies so debased that afterward he always cursed himself and sobbed himself to sleep.

Underlying this was a crazed jealousy of his older brother.

Matthew toiled like a navvy in that hateful office and turned over every sweated-out penny to his father, who offered not so much as one word of praise, while James, damn him, simply because he was older, had his gentleman's education paid for and got to live on a university campus in the company of good fellows. The jealousy ate away at Matthew's soul like a festering sore. And now that James had graduated from Oxford with a Bachelor of Arts degree and was applying to several medical schools around London, he would be living at home again, a constant perishing reminder that he, and not Matthew, was the sole object of their father's attention.

Though all had eyes and ears in that house, no one saw what was coming, only Mrs. Scoggins the housekeeper, who had taken to bolting her door at night.

It happened on the evening of Guy Fawkes Day.

Neighborhoods all over London were lighting giant bonfires and hanging the infamous subversive in effigy. Everyone turned out to toss something onto the fire and pass the jug. While Samuel was out sermonizing in the Dials and Samantha sat by the fire with a piece of needlework, Matthew stood by the parlor drapes, staring out at the rowdy street.

The mob was wild. Prostitutes freely gave their kisses, navvies danced jigs, firecrackers went off like gunshots, and the jug went round and round. Mesmerized, Matthew was drawn to the front door. Opening it, he stared out. The heat from the flames seemed to boil his blood. He went down the steps, drawn like a moth to the flames, and when the jug was slapped into his hands he drank heartily, he who had never so much as tasted small beer. Amid the laughing and jostling and wild abandon, Matthew soon became drunk.

When Samuel came wearily home, plodding up the steps of his house, he saw a wide-eyed Samantha standing in the open doorway, staring into the crowd around the bonfire. Following her frightened stare, Samuel saw his youngest son in the arms of a whore, his mouth slobbering her dirty neck.

The eighteen-year-old laughed and staggered and drank more ale. Peeling off his dark frock coat, he twirled it over his head and let it fly into the fire. It was then that he saw his father. For an instant he froze in that attitude, arm above his head, lips stretched back in a grin, then Matthew focused on the damning black eyes of Samuel. The street sounds receded, the heat from the flames cooled, the dancing shadows on the house fronts disappeared. Everything fell away until all Matthew was aware of were two hellfire black eyes.

He felt a cold metal coil, like the spring of a clock, start to wind up inside him; it grew tighter and tighter until, snapping, it catapulted him toward those hateful, accusing eyes.

Someone other than Matthew Hargrave flew up the steps that night, pushing his father aside, crashing blindly into the parlor; and hands that were not his seized the heavy volume off its stand and carried it back down to the street. Muffled, garbled sounds tried to penetrate Matthew's ears; a shocked white face, arms reaching out, the accusing eyes now frenzied—oh, the *power* of it! Matthew threw back his head and howled like an animal in pain as the Bible sailed up out of his hands, high into the air, and vanished into the yellow flames.

Samuel, picking himself up from the steps, flung himself at his son, knocked him aside and plunged into the fire. As panicked hands seized him and tried to pull him back, Samuel saw the beloved book blacken and char and curl and disappear into the bowels of the bonfire.

The laughter stopped. Those who had danced now ran after the delirious Matthew, who dashed a zigzag pattern through the crowd. It took four men to hold him, and when he finally fell, Matthew writhed on the cobblestones, foam spilling from his mouth. Oblivious of the critical burns on his hands and face, insensitive to the intense pain, Samuel tottered to where his son lay. With bleeding, blistered lips he spoke, and against the silence of the mob and the crackling of the fire, his words rang through the night: "You are damned to hell for all time, Matthew Christopher, and from this night forward you are no longer my son."

Samuel swooned to the cobbles and was carried up to his bed, where a doctor took one look at his burns and predicted he would not live through the night. Samantha stayed at his side, nursing him, washing him, spooning tea between his lips and applying plasters of triturated comfrey leaves to his raw wounds. James, having started to walk the wards of North London Hospital, took over some of the care. Although not much could be done for the wounds, which, after a week, started to run with green pus, James could relieve his father's pain and mental anguish with frequent administrations of morphia. In the evenings, while Samuel tossed beneath his counterpane, Samantha sat beside his bed reading Mr. Hawksbill's pharmacy books by a farthing dip. At night she slept on a mattress at the foot of the bed; by day she washed and dressed his wounds, fed him broth, emptied his bed pot, changed his sheets; and prayed over him.

It was not until spring that Samuel, weak and requiring assistance, could stand up out of bed. His recovery had been slow and uncertain, taking him to death's door several times but always bringing him back, and although there was no longer any doubt that he would live, Samuel Hargrave was mutilated beyond recognition.

If his body mended, his mind did not. Samuel no longer cared about God. His tracts and sermons ceased. He sat every day, all day, in his room, his head pulled down to his chest by thick bands of white scar tissue so that he could not button his collar, his bottom lip dragged down so that he drooled perpetually, and he stared vacantly, often not even acknowledging Samantha's entry. To protect him from further anguish, she did not tell him about James.

After a short stint at North London Hospital James had been expelled and from there had gone to Guy's. After a rocky six months there, he had been ousted and had moved on to St. Bartholomew's, which was where he was now. But far worse than his baffling school record was a shocking new life of gambling and drinking and the company of whores.

Samantha's heart was breaking. Her family was rapidly slipping away from her, and she suspected she would never hear from Freddy again. The only person she had left was Isaiah Hawksbill.

TWELVE

IT WAS AN AUTUMN MORNING, WITH EARLY FROST ON THE EAVES, when Samantha found Mr. Hawksbill in bed, unable to move.

She had been shocked to come in the back door and find the house cold and dark; in the four and a half years she had worked for him, Mr. Hawksbill had always been up and ready for her. Standing in the scullery, she heard a groan and, following it, went upstairs to find the old Jew in bed, still in nightcap and nightshirt, curled up on his side and panting like a dog.

He managed a few words. "A doctor, *Liebchen,* I need . . ."

There was a medical man two streets over, a Dr. Pringle. Samantha ran all the way. In dressing gown and slippers, he listened to Samantha's breathless account of Mr. Hawksbill's condition, then said he would come by after breakfast.

Dr. Pringle appeared two hours later, in which time Isaiah Hawksbill had gotten worse. He had wakened, he haltingly told the doctor, with a severe pain in his lower right abdomen and had been unable to get out of bed. Now he had a high fever; his green eyes sparkled like chips of peridot.

Dr. Pringle drew down the blanket and gently probed Hawksbill's abdomen. He shook his head and said, "You have the iliac passion, sir, an inflammation of a small appendage on the intestine. I shall do what I can."

Samantha stood at the foot of the bed and watched with mounting anxiety as the doctor withdrew a jar of leeches from his bag, hiked up Mr. Hawksbill's nightshirt and dropped the slimy black creatures onto his white skin. While they gorged until they dropped off, leaving little red marks, Dr. Pringle mixed up a dose of strychnine and forced it between Hawksbill's lips. Almost immediately the old Jew began vomiting violently; Samantha held a basin by his head to catch the vomit. This therapy was repeated all day long, bleeding and purging, with intermittent bouts of explosive diarrhea, until the old man wailed for mercy. By six o'clock Dr. Pringle announced there was nothing more he could do.

Isaiah Hawksbill was a shocking sight: dehydrated, wizened, stinking of his emissions, his skin a deathly pallor but with the crests of his cheeks an unhealthy bright red.

"I am dying, *Liebchen*," he whispered.

She sat on the edge of the bed holding a cloth to his forehead. "No, ye're not, sir. Don't say that!"

"I haven't much . . . time. I felt it go, I felt it burst. The poisons have me now, *Liebchen*. There is something I must tell you."

"Save yer strength, Mr. 'Awksbill. We can talk in the morning."

"Won't be a . . . morning for me . . ."

She tried to speak but her throat closed up. It wasn't fair, cried her mind. The doctor should have been able to help. He was no good. He only made him suffer more!

Isaiah tried feebly to lift a hand to touch her cheek but was unable to. "I have to tell you something." His chest rattled with each breath. "I want you to be taken care of in life. I don't want you at the mercy of your . . . family. You must be your own woman, Samantha . . ."

He rolled his head from side to side in agony. His mouth was so dry his tongue stuck to his palate. "Take it," he whispered hoarsely. "It's yours now. Can't let them find it, it will go to the Crown. You are all I have in the world, child . . ."

Samantha dug a fist into her eye. "Please don't die!"

His pupils were so dilated that no green iris showed. Hawksbill looked for a moment like a madman; he cried, "My books! My plants!" then closed his eyes and peacefully breathed his last.

Samantha continued to sit beside him long into the night, torn between rage and sorrow. Then she stood silently by as two men in a black carriage carried his blanket-wrapped body to the street.

The old Jew's house stood empty for several years until it was purchased from the Crown and converted into a tavern. Forty years after Hawksbill's death, when a fire swept St. Agnes Crescent and gutted all the houses, the floor boards of his entry hall fell through, revealing a charred strongbox. When it was pried open it was found to contain a secret cache of money, reduced now to black ash by the intense heat. The sum had been Hawksbill's life fortune—nearly fifty thousand pounds—and it would have made Samantha, had he had time to tell her of it, a very wealthy woman.

The second tragedy followed so closely upon the first that Samantha had little time to mourn for her lost friend.

One week before Guy Fawkes Day, 1874, the second anniversary of Matthew's rampage, Samuel Hargrave stopped eating. No amount of coaxing from Mrs. Scoggins and Samantha could dissuade him from his determined course. Having not eaten or spoken a word in over seven days, he contracted pneumonia, and on the night of the holiday, with the lights of the bonfires shining through his window, he died.

Samantha and James sat solemnly in the parlor while the agent from Welby & Welby spoke in a soft modulated voice. Their father, they learned, had not died without a will. James, as sole heir (since Matthew had run away and could not be found), was to receive a yearly allowance for the duration of his medical education, at the end of which time, upon passing the qualifying exams and putting out his own brass plaque, the remainder of the inheritance would be turned over to him. Also, the house and all it contained reverted to James's ownership, with the provision that it could not be sold until he was set up in his medical practice.

And Samantha was to go to Playell's Academy for Young Ladies in Kent.

THIRTEEN

*S*HE WAS NUMB.

Dressed in her Sunday frock with black lace hastily sewn on the borders, she rode the train out of London in silence, staring at but not seeing the beautiful wooded parkland that was painted in the reds and golds of autumn. It was Mrs. Scoggins, not James (who had begun his studies at Middlesex Hospital), who had seen her off at Victoria Station, giving the girl a sterile embrace and a handkerchief bundle of bread and cheese for the journey.

She was met at Chislehurst station by a fly handled by a dour old man named Humphrey. They rode unspeaking down country lanes with the late afternoon sun flitting in and out of the overhead branches. There was a loamy smell to the area, the scent of rich dirt and thick green grass and crackly brown leaves; on either side of the lane Samantha glimpsed stately mansions set far from the road and fronted by long drives and clusters of willows. Into one of these circular gravel drives Humphrey presently guided the fly, and Samantha saw a magnificent Tudor mansion loom before her.

With the feeling that a hundred unseen eyes peered down from the mullioned windows, Samantha stepped down from the fly and was met by a tall, prim, forty-ish woman in black bombazine. This was Mrs. Steptoe, matron of the academy, and the withering look in her narrow eyes made Samantha wonder what she had done, so soon, to earn this formidable woman's disapproval.

Mrs. Steptoe, Samantha learned later, found displeasure with everybody. A widow lady at the tender age of twenty-two and left unprovided for by her young husband, Mrs. Steptoe had been forced into the unpleasant and demeaning situation of having to earn her way through life. She had come to Playell's as an instructress long before and, by cunning and politicking over the years, had achieved the supreme post of matron. The Playells were long dead, the academy was operated on a trust fund and the fees paid by the students; Mrs. Steptoe had total and absolute power here.

"Follow me," she said to Samantha, turning on an unseen heel and gliding with such smoothness over the parquet floor that Samantha wondered if the woman rolled on wheels.

The house had been built in the time of Elizabeth; its layout was in the shape of an E. There was a central hall with sitting rooms, reception rooms, library and an awesome stairway which curved up to the second floor where, in the north and south wings, were the classrooms and dormitory. Mrs. Steptoe led her to a regal old bedroom with dark paneling, rich carpets and a massive gray stone fireplace. It contained four beds, two desks, two chairs, a wardrobe, and a wash table with pitcher and basin. Astonished to discover that this was to be her home for the next few years, Samantha dropped her battered satchel and ran to the window to look out.

The cuff on the back of her head made her squeal. Rubbing her scalp, Samantha looked up into the chilling eyes of Mrs. Steptoe and heard her dry voice explain that it was a rule of the academy always to walk in a ladylike manner and to give proper respect to the staff. The punishment for three infractions of the academy rules was to clean the privies for a week.

In the days that followed, Samantha cleaned the privies often and in that time grew to detest the academy and, even more so, Mrs. Steptoe. By early spring Samantha was planning her escape.

Because she was rough and baseborn and spoke in a funny way, Samantha was an outcast among the refined girls and so never shared in the nightly gossip and whisperings that went on after the gas jets were turned down. But she listened. Her three roommates invariably turned the hushed conversation to the same topic.

There was only one male teacher at Playell's, Mr. Roderick Newcastle, and he had arrived just two months before Samantha. All the girls were desperately in love with the short, bald mathematics teacher, and he enjoyed the singular status of sitting with Mrs. Steptoe at her table on the platform in the cavernous dining hall. One afternoon Miss Tomlinson, the plump hygiene teacher, gave the girls a lecture on preparing for marriage and referred to something called The Duty.

"Remember, young ladies, that no virtuous woman finds The Duty pleasant, but the virtuous wife submits nonetheless. Since men have certain drives that we do not have, we cannot possibly understand them, and so we must deliver ourselves into our husband's care, trusting that he is the wiser judge in this sacred matter, and derive pleasure not from the act itself but from knowing we are pleasing our husbands and bringing a new Briton into the world. Duty to husband and country, young ladies, always remember that. If you find the experience too unpleasant, close your eyes and think of England."

After the jets were turned down the girls whispered from their beds. "I shouldn't mind submitting to Mr. Newcastle!"

"Then you'll have a baby growing in your stomach."

"How does it get out?"

"Your navel opens up and the baby pops out."

Samantha listened and could have laughed. You didn't live on the Crescent and not know what sex was all about.

The oldest girl, seventeen, settled the discussion by stating matter-of-factly, "It's nothing. It's rather like getting poked with a stick."

The girls grew silent and Samantha rolled over to entertain her favorite fantasy: running away.

She would leave tomorrow, taking the train to Liverpool, and go in search of Freddy. They would buy a beautiful house and get married and live happily ever after. Or she would wait until James received his certificate and then go live with him on Harley Street and help him with his patients for the rest of her life. But her favorite was the comforting vision of Freddy riding up to the academy in a fine carriage, wearing a top hat and silver-tipped cane, and announcing to Mrs. Steptoe and all the girls that he had come to take her away to his country manor in Cheshire.

There was a rumble, like distant thunder, followed by a cry and then a crash. Samantha bolted up in bed.

"What was that!" said one of her roommates.

Bare feet pounded down the hall.

Samantha was the first out of bed and at the door. Looking out, she saw all the girls in their long flannel nightgowns leaning out their doors and peering toward the east end of the dark hall. Plump Miss Tomlinson was padding by with her dressing gown and braids flapping.

The girls whispered and waited, and when Miss Tomlinson shrieked and thudded to the floor, a few of the bolder girls ran to her, Samantha among them.

Miss Tomlinson had fainted at the head of the stairs, from where one could see, down at the bottom, in the dim light of the night jets, the crumpled form of Mrs. Steptoe. And the scarlet stain spreading on her skirt.

Another girl joined Miss Tomlinson on the floor in a delicate swoon and the others had to steady themselves on the newel. Samantha flew down the stairs and arrived at the unconscious matron at the same time as Miss Whittaker, the stitchery instructress. Without thinking, Samantha fell to her knees and took hold of Mrs. Steptoe's wrist between her thumb and fingers as she had seen James do. "She's alive," she murmured, and Miss Whittaker started to sob.

"A doctor!" someone called out.

Now more girls were grouped at the top of the stairs where Miss Tomlinson was rousing. Then Roderick Newcastle, in shirt sleeves and suspenders, pushed through. He looked down at Matron, blanched to the color of a peeled potato, and said, "Oh, my God."

Someone wakened Humphrey and sent him to Chislehurst for the doctor. Mr. Newcastle and Miss Whittaker carried Mrs. Steptoe the short distance down the hall to her quarters on the first floor and carefully laid her down on the half-tester bed. As Miss Whittaker sank into a chair and Mr. Newcastle mopped his head, Samantha removed Mrs. Steptoe's boots and covered her with the counterpane.

The doctor was a long time coming. Derry Newcastle started a fire in the grate and Miss Whittaker made tea. Samantha stayed by the bed and continually checked Mrs. Steptoe's pulse and respiration. Once she lifted the counterpane and saw that the bloodstain had spread.

There was a staccato rap on the door and Miss Whittaker opened it to a short, fiftyish woman and Humphrey anxiously twisting his cap behind her. Miss Whittaker looked bewildered.

The woman glided past, drew off her cape and came to the bedside.

"Who are you?" demanded Derry Newcastle.

"This is no place for a gentleman, sir," the woman replied smartly, her back to him. She took hold of Mrs. Steptoe's limp wrist the way Samantha had.

As Mr. Newcastle left the room uncertainly, closing the door behind him, the woman lifted the counterpane, studied the stain for a moment, then said, "I shall need hot water and sheets torn up." She raised her eyes and looked directly at Samantha. "I shall also need help with this."

Miss Whittaker dashed to the door. "I'll fetch the water and sheets!" Then she was gone.

The woman stared at Samantha across the bed, their faces illuminated by oil lamps. "It appears you've been elected. Can you take it?"

Samantha realized her heart was racing. "Yes, ma'am, I've had some experience."

"Good. Roll up your sleeves, we're in for a time."

As Samantha tucked her long black braids down the back of her night-gown and pushed up her sleeves, she kept her eyes on the woman opposite. About fifty years old with graying blond hair parted at the top and swept back over the ears in old-fashioned wings, she was small and compact and gave an impression of robust health and youthful vigor. Samantha watched in fascination as she rolled up the white lace cuffs of her blue serge gown, lifted each of Mrs. Steptoe's eyelids, and bent low to inspect the recumbent face. "I am Dr. Blackwell, what's your name?" she asked without looking up.

Samantha's eyes flew open. "Samantha Hargrave, ma'am." Her cheeks instantly flushed. "I mean Mrs. Blackwell. I mean Doctress—"

Elizabeth Blackwell tossed her a brief smile. "Doctor will do fine, dear. Help me with her gown."

⚜

As they undid the many buttons and gently lifted Mrs. Steptoe out of the bodice, Dr. Blackwell spoke in a soft voice, her accent strange; Samantha had never heard one like it before. "I was in Chislehurst visiting an old friend. When your man came flying into the inn, looking for the town doctor, I offered to come. Poor man, he didn't know what to do. 'A doctor is what I came for,' he said. 'Not a midwife!'"

They untied the bands of Mrs. Steptoe's many petticoats, all blood-soaked, and drew them off her legs. "It's not as bad as it looks, Samantha," the doctor said in a soothing tone. "Spread around, it always looks more than it is."

Samantha kept her wide, unblinking eyes on Dr. Blackwell as she went to the washstand, poured water into the basin and gave her hands a good scrubbing. Returning to the bed while drying her hands on a towel, Dr. Blackwell said, "Most doctors only wash their hands afterward. I say it can't hurt to do it before. Now then, let's see what we've got here."

Her small clean hands first moved over Mrs. Steptoe's abdomen, pressing down in places, then gently parted the milky thighs and did a deep, inner exploration. Dr. Blackwell's handsome square face remained in a concentrated, unreadable expression; her deep-set eyes stared at a point above the bedstead. When she was through she wiped her hand on the towel and said, "I'm afraid the poor woman has miscarried."

Samantha gasped. "Mrs. Steptoe's pregnant?"

Dr. Blackwell reached for her bag. "*Was*, my dear. The fall caused a miscarriage. She was almost four months along, judging by the size of the uterus."

Samantha looked down at the pale, sleeping face and thought that, for the first time, Matron looked at peace. "I wonder how it happened," Samantha said distantly. "She's been up and down them stairs a thousand times . . ."

Tossing the girl a sharp look, Dr. Blackwell said, "We have to get to work now. Please bring that lamp over and place it between her legs."

Miss Whittaker tiptoed in, deposited the water and sheet strips by the bed and left without a word. When Samantha had the lamp on the bed, she helped Dr. Blackwell part Matron's legs as far as they would go, drew up her knees and then held them in place. "What're you gonna do?"

"The baby cannot be saved. Our job now is to complete the process the fall down the stairs started. It is the poor woman's only chance." Dr. Blackwell withdrew from her bag a silver instrument that looked to Samantha like the bill of a duck. Repositioning the oil lamp for better light, the doctor added: "Watch her face, Samantha. If she shows any sign of waking, let me know and I shall stop at once. Now I must work quickly. Her fainting state will allow me to work without having to resort to anesthesia, which can be dangerous. Please try to keep her legs steady."

Samantha was stretched across Matron's body, her hands having to continually push on the uncooperative knees. She snapped her eyes back and forth: from Matron's peaceful face to Dr. Blackwell's rapidly moving hands, back to Matron's face. Dr. Blackwell placed a basin beneath the grooved speculum, then picked up a strange instrument. It was a porcupine quill fitted at one end with a sharp-edged silver disc.

"What's that for?" whispered Samantha.

"It is a curette." Dr. Blackwell gently guided the silver disc up past the speculum and closed her eyes for a moment, watching its path with her mind. "I have to be certain I am in the uterus and have not entered the abdominal cavity instead."

Samantha held her breath as she watched the tiny hand manipulate the quill, inserting it far up until only a few inches showed. "There," whispered Dr. Blackwell, opening her eyes. "It's seated. Look at her face, Samantha. Any signs?"

"No, she's still out. An' her chest is rising and falling nicely."

Dr. Blackwell regarded the girl in a moment of surprise, then she commenced with the curettage.

In fascination Samantha heard, against the still night, a curiously muffled scraping sound and saw, beneath her outstretched arm, the slight undulations of Mrs. Steptoe's abdomen as the curette did its work. Samantha opened her mouth to speak, then clamped it shut and swiveled her head away.

"How is she?" asked Dr. Blackwell.

Samantha's voice came out as a squeak. "Fine—"

"Are you all right?"

"Yes—"

"What I am doing, Samantha, is removing the rest of the fetal tissue from the womb. If this is not done, if she is not scraped clean, she will have complications. Hemorrhage, infection, pain. This *must* be done. Do you understand that, Samantha?"

"Yes, ma'am." Samantha swung her head back around and regarded the austere face of the doctor, her handsome, robust features clearly chiseled in the lamp's yellow glow.

"There." Dr. Blackwell laid the curette aside and picked up a long silver forceps with a ring at the end and tucked a wad of sheet strip into it. "The uterus is clean. Now we mop up. Any signs yet?"

"Her eyelids are fluttering."

"Good . . . almost done."

After the ring went in a few times, with the sponges coming out cleaner and cleaner, Dr. Blackwell inserted the styptic, another porcupine quill dipped in alum paste. "This will stop any minor bleeding." Lastly she packed Mrs. Steptoe's vagina with sheet strips.

Half an hour later they were drinking Oolong tea by the fire. As they were washing her, Mrs. Steptoe had wakened and drunk a dose of laudanum; now she slept peacefully between fresh sheets.

"Will she be all right, d'you think, Doctor ma'am?"

"I believe so. You did very well, Samantha. I would have had a much harder time without your help."

Samantha gazed shyly into her cup, watching a few vagrant tea leaves swirl on its surface. Feeling exhausted and yet strangely exhilarated at the same time, Samantha was trying to analyze the queer euphoria that filled her. What she had done, working closely with Dr. Blackwell, had left her feeling oddly and awkwardly intimate with this woman. It was nothing she could put into words, this nebulous emotion, but for the first time in her life Samantha experienced comradeship with another female. And praise from this woman, whom she had known only two hours, suddenly meant everything in the world to her.

Dr. Blackwell studied her silent companion and thought her a unique combination of rare beauty and humbleness. The doctor could not remember having ever met a girl so enchantingly lovely and yet seemingly unaware of her good looks. Elizabeth Blackwell was curious about her: the rough speech, the lack of airs, the graceless way she held her cup in both hands and slurped her tea. What was this slum child doing in a place like Playell's among all the fine young ladies of the upper crust? An analogy came to the doctor's mind: Samantha Hargrave was a rough, uncut diamond in a collection of polished rhinestones.

"Do you like it here, Samantha?"

"No, Doctor ma'am."

"Why not?"

"I don't know what I'm doing here. I ain't got no friends. They all hate me. I get cuffed a lot. An' in the mornings I'm always stuck with the last wash when the water's gone all dingy."

"Your parents must have a good reason for sending you here," said the doctor gently.

"Ain't got none. Mum died when I was born, and me dad—" Her voice caught.

"What are you going to do with your life after Playell's? Have you thought about it?"

Elizabeth Blackwell had a strangely comforting effect, her voice so compelling, her manner almost maternal. Samantha knew instinctively this was a woman she could confide in. "Truth is, Doctor ma'am, I been plottin' to run away."

"Where would you go?"

"Dunno."

"You know, Samantha," came Dr. Blackwell's careful tone, "you seem to be quite at ease around sick people. You quite impressed me tonight. You've done it before, I suspect."

Samantha's face brightened. "Oh yes, Doctor ma'am. I took care o' Freddy, you see, and then me dad when he was burned bad."

"I see . . ." The doctor considered something, then said, "Have you ever thought of devoting your life to that sort of work?"

"You mean be a nurse, like them new Nightingales?"

The sudden sparkle in the girl's eye was not lost on Dr. Blackwell. "Possibly, only I was thinking more of the medical profession. Why not become a doctor?"

Samantha lowered her teacup. "A doctor? Women can't be doctors!"

"Of course they can. Look at me!"

"But . . . you ain't a *real* doctor, are you?"

Dr. Blackwell laughed merrily. "I most certainly am! And as good as any man, I might add!"

"But don't doctors cut up bodies? That ain't ladylike."

"My dear, there exists nothing repulsive or *unladylike* in the study of nature: each muscle and tendon and bone is like a stanza of poetry."

Samantha gazed at her earnestly. "What's it like to be a lady doctor?"

"I will show you by example. The other day a man came to me with an ailment which I was able to cure. When, afterward, I told him the fee, he responded with: 'For that money I could have had a *real* doctor!'"

Samantha turned inward at this. "A woman bein' a doctor. Fancy that . . ." She leaned forward in her chair. "'Ow d'you get to be one?"

"First you must have the desire, which I believe you do. And next you must have a good education. Finally you must work to refine yourself and turn yourself into a proper lady."

Samantha frowned. "You mean I gotta stay on here and learn which hand to hold me teacup in and which for me cake?"

"Something like that. To get into medical school you need a Bachelor's degree, which you can get at this academy if you don't run away. Learning to speak properly is also important."

"I've always 'ad trouble speaking. Freddy said I never uttered a word till he tried to take a knife to an owd tabby. I was four years old then, and now whenever I meet someone new I'm *that* speechless for ever so long!"

"Then you must overcome that, for doctors have to be the best of talkers!"

As the fourteen-year-old sank deeper into private thought, Dr. Blackwell stood and retrieved her small beaded bag. From it she withdrew an engraved calling card and handed it to Samantha. "I should love for you to come and visit me sometime. Here is my address in London. Think about what you did here tonight, and if you should want to talk, my door is always open."

Samantha lay in bed too tense to sleep, her body charged with a strange new vitality, her mind racing in circles. As she listened to the soft respirations of her slumbering roommates, a parade of visions marched before her eyes: Mrs. Steptoe crumpled at the foot of the stairs, Samantha's unthinking flight down to her side, the arrival of the strange doctor, the quills, the blood, Dr. Blackwell's commanding presence. Samantha tried to understand it all. Frightened out of her wits, she had been no less panicky than Miss Whittaker and would have loved to run from the scene. Yet she had not. Why? What had propelled her down those stairs when the others fainted? What had kept her grimly positioned over Matron's legs when Miss Whittaker fled?

Am I really so different?

There were many threads to untangle, straighten out and reweave into a recognizable fabric. Yes, Samantha knew she was different. But how? Was it as simple as Dr. Blackwell had put it, that she was "at ease with sick people"? More scenarios marched by: the stiff fur of an old tabby, Freddy's mangled leg, her father lying helpless.

Was that it? Possibly, yes . . . the elusive answer she had tried since Dr. Blackwell's departure to grasp. Aside from the wonderful new emotion she felt toward that remarkable woman, Samantha was also suffused with another vague emotion, hauntingly familiar. Now she knew what it was. Working over Mrs. Steptoe's unconscious body, Samantha had been filled with a blinding sense of purpose. And it was familiar because she had felt it before, not as strongly as tonight, but there nonetheless: tending Freddy's leg, slowly nurturing him back to health; and then her father, taking command of his poor burnt body, bringing him along the road to recovery; and . . . earlier, dimly remembered, the intense need to see a worthless tabby restored to health . . .

Samantha filled her lungs as far as they would go and held her breath so long that pains shot through her chest.

A doctor! cried her mind. To be like *her!* To do what *she* did tonight!

Samantha stretched her eyes wider and wider, searching for a hidden truth in the black ceiling overhead. Her body tingled; every nerve was stretched to breaking. She dug her fingers into the mattress to keep herself from shooting off the bed and dashing headlong through the stars.

Earlier today I was nobody, going nowhere. Now I know who I am and where I am going . . .

FOURTEEN

*M*RS. STEPTOE RAPIDLY RECOVERED AND THE SCHOOL RE-
turned to its normal routine. But some things were
different. Derry Newcastle had vanished in the night and
a new mathematics teacher was brought in; Matron grew quiet and subdued, no longer the formidable tyrant whose mere presence used to make
the girls tremble; and Samantha Hargrave was transformed. She plunged
wholeheartedly into the academic curriculum, which Samantha discovered
was not taxing, for the instructresses all held to the popular belief that too
much studying withered a girl's reproductive organs. Emphasis was upon
belles-lettres, elocution, and music. There was French and German, rudi-
mentary Latin and Greek; the smattering of science—botany, chemistry,
and zoology—was easy for Samantha because of her years with Hawksbill.
She worked hard at improving herself socially and, with the aid of Dr. Blackwell, whom she visited in London as often as she could, soon smoothed out
the roughness. As the months passed and a gem emerged from the crude
slum child who had first come to Playell's, the other girls gradually came to

forget their initial scorn of Samantha and eventually included her in their friendships.

She went home, over the next three years, several times, and sometimes James was there, drunk and belligerent, complaining about his studies, gambling away his pocket money, but more often he was absent. During her third Christmas home, while she was getting ready to have dinner with Dr. Blackwell, James stumbled in with the news that he had been booted out of Westminster Hospital.

One week before her seventeenth birthday, Samantha received a notice that James had been arrested and tried for murder and was awaiting execution at Newgate Prison.

<hr/>

He begged her to come.

On the night before his hanging, Samantha took the train to Victoria Station, hired a cab and arrived, in the evening, at Newgate. Asking the driver to wait, she stepped down.

The formidable gray stone edifice momentarily cowed her; then she resolutely picked up her skirts and marched over the murky pavement to the unassuming little entrance. She would have to pay many bribes, James had told her in his hasty letter, and so she did: a succession of guards, terrifyingly seedy and reeking of gin, leered at Samantha as they accepted her coins and led her along damp stone passages, their massive keyrings jangling. It was like descending into hell: the rank odors, the slime on the walls, the interminable gloom. As she followed close behind the jailer and his swaying lantern, Samantha heard the scrape of heavy chains and the shouts of men as she passed: "Hey, lovey, hike up yer skirts and give us a glimpse o' paradise!" One sweep of the guard's stick sent them falling back from the bars.

Presently the jailer stopped, at the lowest level, where the air was difficult to breathe and the only light came from flickering torches, and said with fetid breath, "This here's a condemned man and I ain't supposed ter be allowing 'im no visitors. It could get me into a heap o' trouble."

Samantha reached into her reticule and dropped several shiny shillings into his filthy hand. "Five minutes," he said gruffly and turned away.

Before her stood the bars of a cell, and beyond them, impenetrable blackness. Cautiously, as though approaching a wild animal's cage, Samantha moved toward it. There was the sudden rattle of a chain, then a phantom face rose before her.

"Sam," whispered James coarsely. "You've come."

She was stunned. Could this scruffy, skeletal wretch be her handsome brother? She went to the bars and reached out a hand.

"Don't do that," said James softly. "The bastard'll think you're passing me something and he'll toss you out. We haven't much time and I've so much to say."

He brought his face close to the bars; James had aged incredibly. "They're topping me in the morning, Sam."

With difficulty she found her voice. "What happened, James?"

"I went to the Iron Lion for a tot of gin and while I was drinking he came at me, all of a sudden like, a big stinking Irishman that's been hot for my Molly, and as he surprised me—I didn't hear him coming on account of my deaf ear—I let him have my best fist, which sent his nose up into his brain. I swear, Sam, if I'd heard him coming I'd have pulled my punch. It was self-defense, but Paddy had too many friends and they all testified against me."

Samantha took hold of the bars; they blackened her gloves.

"You never knew, did you, Sam? What gave me my deaf ear? I'll tell you."

She listened to his soft, emotionless account of the night of her birth. He ended with, "Isn't it ironical? The thing that I did to save *your* life has come through the years to snuff out mine! All my life has been a misery because of you. My ear kept me out of sports and I had to study twice as hard because I missed a lot of the lecture. And because of that I had no social life at all. Sometimes I wondered if you were worth all that, Sam."

She heard herself murmur, "I'm so sorry . . ."

"It was bound to happen, I suppose. We were all doomed from that night on. Look at Matthew, wherever he is. D'you know why I did so much drinking after Oxford? Why I changed? It was because of Father. I worked and slaved at my studies to earn a bit of approval from him, to get some sign he'd forgiven me for fetching that doctor, but when I got my degree and he never came nor even gave me so much as a handshake, something inside me snapped. I said to blazes with him and decided to make up for the boyhood I never had." James bowed his head and pressed his rich black curls against the bars. "He always hated us, Sam, because we killed our mum. We're bound together in ruin, little sister. We received our sentences seventeen years ago, and mine will be fulfilled tomorrow. But mark me, Sam, your turn will come."

She closed her eyes as a cold wind swept her soul.

James raised his face; tears streaked his dirty cheeks. "I've an appointment with Jack Ketch in the morning, Sam. Pray for me."

"Here, you!" came a bellow from the shadows.

Samantha spun around.

"Yer time's up!" The jailer lumbered toward her like a bear on its hind legs and sent his stick crashing against the bars.

"But it hasn't been five minutes!"

"It has if I say it has, now move along."

"Give him more money, Sam!" cried James.

"But I haven't any more money!"

"You ain't got the money, you don't get no more time."

"Please, sir, just one more minute. I haven't anything more to give you."

The guard's face spread in a piggy grin. "Oh, haven't yer?" His porcine eyes went up and down her body.

James shouted, "Get out, Sam! Run for it!"

She backed away from the jailer, slipping on the slimy floor. He remained before James's cell, rocking back and forth on his heels, filling the stony chamber with his evil laughter; Samantha fled.

The next morning, her hands and face bitten with cold, her eyes swollen from a night of weeping, Samantha pleaded with the governor of the prison, but he would not release James's body to her, for her brother had willed himself to the medical school for dissection. And so, without the solace of a funeral, she returned to the empty house on the Crescent.

FIFTEEN

*I*T WAS MAY 1878, AND ALL THE WORLD WAS IN COLORFUL bloom. Mrs. Steptoe, in the familiar black mourning gown she had worn since her husband's death twenty years before, cut a stark contrast against the rainbows of spring. She was by the fire in her parlor with her feet on a stool; on a small table by her hand stood a teapot and a plate of buttered scones. As she sipped from her cup, she gazed out the window at the garden; there was the familiar rolling lawn, the rose trees, the hollyhocks and marigolds, the brand-new Michaelmas daisies. So pleasant to sit here and watch the world go through its seasons.

Mrs. Steptoe was thinking of the day, four years before, when a skinny little girl with hair like rattails had stepped down from Humphrey's carriage and looked up at her with great, frightened eyes. Mrs. Steptoe had not liked Samantha then. Had it not been for the persistence of Mr. Welby, the girl's solicitor, she would not have taken her in. The girl had been crude, came from a deplorable background and God only knew what sort of blood. But that had been almost four years ago. Last week a lovely and refined Samantha Hargrave had received her Bachelor of Arts degree.

Mrs. Steptoe looked around the office that had not changed in nearly twenty years: at the straddle clock on the mantel; the Wardian vases of dried flowers; a faded Chinese fan; the glazed Staffordshire dogs; and the papier-mache tables cluttered with the many photographs of girls who had passed through the academy. She had been fond of them all, but none had been as special to her as Samantha. Samantha, who had been with her on that fateful night and who had then stayed by her bedside until she was well. Dear Samantha, who had been so gentle and understanding, never passing judgment, keeping Mrs. Steptoe's precious secret firmly to herself. But not even Samantha knew the deepest secret of all—that, rejected by Derry Newcastle, she had flung herself down those stairs with the intention of ending her life. Afterward, restored to health and looking back on the folly of her actions, Mrs. Steptoe had blessed Samantha for having helped save her life that night, and although, in the ensuing three years, Mrs. Steptoe had withdrawn into herself, shutting everyone else out, she had admitted Samantha into her heart. And now she dreaded to see her leave.

But Mrs. Steptoe had a plan. She knew of Samantha's ambition to become a doctor; however, Mrs. Steptoe thought she could dissuade her. After all, she had some considerable influence over the girl. She would offer her a choice plum she could not refuse: Matron's post at Playell's.

Mrs. Steptoe wouldn't mind abdicating to Samantha if it would keep the girl here. And it would have to be a price that high, because she knew Samantha to be a young woman of high goals; nothing less would do. How could Samantha refuse such an offer, a golden opportunity that came into few women's lives? Once told, she would abandon her medical plans and stay on here as Matron, with her dear friend Mrs. Steptoe living in semi-retirement, helping her run the academy . . .

There was a soft knock at the door. Alice, the maid, poked her head in and said, "Mrs. Steptoe? There's someone here to see Samantha Hargrave."

Matron put down her cup. "I beg your pardon?" In her nearly four years at Playell's Samantha had never had a visitor.

"A man it is, and he's asking to see Miss Hargrave."

Mrs. Steptoe stiffened. Samantha was in London for the day visiting Dr.

Blackwell again. "Bring him in to me, please, Alice."

A minute later his bulk was filling the doorway: a big, strapping young man with coarse, handsome features, a head of wild chestnut curls, and wearing the uniform of the merchant navy.

"Please come in," said Mrs. Steptoe primly.

He was twisting a knitted watchman's hat in his huge hands and walked toward her with an odd lurch. "Thank you, ma'am. I'd like to see Samantha if I might. Tell her Freddy's here."

SIXTEEN

I CAN'T SEEM TO MAKE THE DECISION, DR. BLACKWELL."

Elizabeth smiled. In three and a half years she still had not been able to convince her young friend to call her by her first name. "I can only advise you, my dear; ultimately it is up to you."

Upon receiving her certificate from Playell's Samantha had had to face the decision about where to go next. While she would have preferred to stay on in London and study here, prospects for a woman to get into medical school, as pointed out by Dr. Blackwell, were almost impossible. Dr. Blackwell's advice was to go to another country. But here were all her friends, a city she loved and knew so well, and then there was Freddy.

Samantha had rented out the house on the Crescent and had left instructions with the people to give Playell's address to anyone who came asking for her. If she were to leave England, she would have to sell the house and her traces would be lost.

Or possibly that was a hopeless hope anyway. Freddy was probably married, or in Australia, possibly in jail or even dead. After all, it had been nearly seven years. He had made his promise to her when he was an impetuous youth; surely he'd forgotten her by now.

But the trouble was, Samantha had not forgotten him.

Dr. Blackwell poured the tea and handed a cup to Samantha. "I almost envy you, my dear, starting out now. Medicine is on the brink of a grand revolution and I fear I shall not live to see its wonderful victories. But you, Samantha, will be part of that revolution."

Samantha smiled in gratitude for the change of subject.

"There is a new man at King's College," Dr. Blackwell went on, "who is causing quite a stir. Mr. Lister claims to have worked miracles at the Royal Infirmary in Edinburgh. He says that wounds he has dressed, wounds that should have become gangrenous and killed the patient, healed in a few weeks because he washed them in carbolic acid.

"One startling case that has been reported to me was of a ten-year-old boy whose arm was badly crushed in a turner's factory. The arm was so mangled that the only course of treatment open to the medical staff was amputation at the shoulder. But Joseph Lister stepped in and said he would experiment. He did something that has never been done before. He set the bones, stitched the wound back together and wrapped the whole perishing mess in a plaster of carbolic solution. Everyone said he had done a foolhardy thing, for with immediate amputation the boy had had a chance to live, whereas this way he was sure to die of gangrene. But a miracle occurred. Mr. Lister removed the dressings and found that the arm had healed. Seven weeks after the accident the lad was sent home with a perfectly functioning arm."

"But how is that possible? You have always told me that fresh air is the only way a wound can heal and that to wrap it traps in the foul air."

"Possibly I was wrong. In France Mr. Pasteur has examined diseased wine and milk under a microscope and claims to have found tiny organisms, not visible to the unaided eye, that cause the spoilage. And in Germany Dr. Koch claims to have discovered the microscopic animal that causes anthrax. Mr. Lister calls them bacteria, insists *they* cause wound infection, not foul air, and claims that his carbolic solution destroys them, thereby allowing the flesh to heal properly and without pus."

"I have never heard of such a thing! A wound must have pus in order to heal."

"Possibly we have been wrong all these years." With a rustling of her skirts, Dr. Blackwell rose from her chair and went to stand before the fireplace. The silver streaks in her blond hair cast off highlights of afternoon sun streaming through the parlor window. "Medicine is changing, my dear. And I firmly believe that a large part of that change will be the future increase of women doctors. There aren't many of us right now, Samantha. Today Dr. Garrett and I are the only two women on Britain's Medical Register, and we got in on legal loopholes which have since been closed. But the men will not keep up the fight for much longer, I feel sure. The medical schools are closed to us here for now, but someday soon those doors must come down."

She drew in a deep breath, causing the whalebones of her corset to creak. "And I am afraid the new nursing is not helping our cause either!"

None of this was new to Samantha, she had heard it all before. How Florence Nightingale's revolutionary new nursing was attracting women who might otherwise have put up the fight to get into medicine. The Nightingale School at St. Thomas's was the first experiment in educating single women for a profession and it was proving immensely popular; it was also highly controversial and had to be constantly on guard against its many critics.

Considering what she had done to upset the medical establishment and shock Victorian sensibilities, one might label Florence Nightingale a feminist. She was not. Firmly believing in women's inferiority to men, she advocated meekness and total subservience in her nurses, frowned upon "unladylike" behavior and was firmly opposed to women becoming doctors, insisting that those who succeeded had only "ended up third-rate men." Besides, the great lady said, there was no need for women in medicine.

Samantha had met Florence Nightingale. Dr. Blackwell had taken her, the summer before, to visit St. Thomas' Hospital on the Albert Embankment opposite the new Houses of Parliament, and there Samantha had observed the mortal shame many women felt at having to submit to an intimate physical examination by male doctors. It was here that Samantha learned, from Dr. Blackwell, that many women preferred to stay at home and suffer from their female afflictions rather than submit to such embarrassment.

From St. Thomas' they had gone to the house of the famous "Chief" herself who, reduced to invalidism because of her exertions in the Crimea, was unable to leave her bed. She granted her dear friend and young protegee an audience like a queen dispensing favors. Samantha had found Florence Nightingale a woman of contradictions: small and diminutive in appearance, a full-force gale in personality. They had heartily debated through the afternoon the issue of women entering medicine and Samantha had not been too shy to voice her opinion. At the end of it Miss Nightingale had sent them home with a cake.

Dr. Blackwell stirred from her introspection and looked long at her young companion. "Your decision must be made soon, my dear, for you cannot stay at the academy any longer."

Samantha heaved a weighty sigh. "I have thought over everything you have said, Dr. Blackwell, and even though I am sure America holds the best promise for me, I do so hate to leave London."

Elizabeth Blackwell had studied medicine in America (which accounted for her strange accent) and was firmly convinced that was the best road for Samantha. The doctor's beautiful deep-set eyes, one of which had been blinded while treating a diseased baby, settled upon the young woman thoughtfully. After some mental deliberation, she said gently, "Is it a man who holds you here, my dear?"

Samantha regarded her in surprise.

The doctor laughed softly. "I have seen the look before, Samantha. In my own looking glass. My dear—" Dr. Blackwell came to sit next to her on the sofa and said in a rush, "I am going to tell you something I have never told a living soul. When I was young I did not have the burning desire to be a doctor. Indeed, I reached the decision quite intellectually, and that decision sprang from my problem with men."

Samantha's eyes widened.

"You see, my dear, I have always been very susceptible to men. I have, all my life, been perpetually in love with one or another of the opposite sex at all times, and I saw early that this could be my downfall, how easily I could be manipulated by a man if I did not provide myself with armor. I knew the instinctive dependence I have on men, that if I were to succumb I would forever be the slave of men."

Samantha saw in her mind the faces of men she had loved and lost: her father, her brother, Hawksbill, Freddy . . .

Elizabeth's voice went on, "I needed a strong barrier to protect me, to permit me to be my own woman. I decided to refute marriage and abstain from men entirely, much like the alcoholic who must turn away from that first drink, for there could be no halfway measures with me and men. I needed something to engross my thoughts, some object in life which would fill that vacuum and prevent a sad wearing away of my heart. If I could not find satisfaction in a husband or children, then I must seek it elsewhere. I chose well in the study of medicine, Samantha, for no man wants a woman doctor for his wife."

"Can that be true?"

"In America, which is a vast continent thousands of miles across, there are under five hundred female physicians, and of them only a small percentage are married. Those who are, are married to doctors."

"Why is that?"

"Insurmountable prejudice, my dear. We live in an age of male dominance. Females threaten their kingship. Someone called it 'storming the citadel,' as if we were battling their defenses. Why they are afraid of us I cannot say, only that in my thirty years of practicing medicine I have yet to meet a man who does not exhibit some form of this fear of us. They mock us, Samantha. One great surgeon once said that the world is divided into three groups: men, women, and women doctors. You will hear us called 'hen medics.' They do not know how to classify us, neither lady nor tramp but some grotesque mutation in between. As a consequence, my dear, in order for you to be accepted as an equal among them, you must do better than they, and once you have superseded them, what man will want you for a wife? To make the decision to practice medicine, Samantha, is tantamount to deciding for a life of spinsterhood."

Samantha sank back into the sofa and stared for a very long time into her cold tea.

Mrs. Steptoe could barely keep her hands from twisting the arms off her chair. She tried hard to hide her rage. How dare he! she thought in thinly contained fury. How dare this crude beast come in here and presume to take my Samantha away!

"So that is it, Mr. Hawksbill. As I said, Samantha left the academy a week ago and gave no forwarding address."

Freddy's roughened hands continued to work over the watchman's cap. He sat on the edge of the brocaded chair as if aware his coarse clothes would defile it. "And she ain't coming back?"

Certainly not to you; Samantha belongs to me. "I highly doubt it, Mr. Hawksbill. She spoke of visiting France."

"But surely she'll write to you!"

Mrs. Steptoe compressed her thin lips into a white line and thought: Get out of here, you uncouth creature! "There is a possibility she will write."

Freddy reached into the pocket of his pea jacket and pulled out a sealed envelope. Handing it to her, he said, "If you do hear from her, will you pass this on? It tells her the address where I'm staying in London. I've got me a job working on the docks and I'll be there six months. Tell her I'll be waitin' for her."

Mrs. Steptoe gingerly took the letter and rose stiffly.

Taking the signal, Freddy Hawksbill, who had taken the surname of the man who had saved his life, rose awkwardly and touched a finger to his forehead. "Thanks, ma'am. I mightily appreciate yer help."

After the door closed behind him and she saw his hulk lurch down the path in that repulsive limp, Mrs. Steptoe turned smoothly about, glided to the fireplace and tossed the letter into the flames.

SEVENTEEN

*T*HE CARRIAGE ROLLED GENTLY FROM SIDE TO SIDE AND THE clip-clopping of Humphrey's horse was hypnotic, but Samantha did not doze as she usually did on her way back from the Chislehurst station. Her mind was in torment.

The decision had to be made: where to go?

Voices echoed in her head: Freddy, so long ago. "Wait for me, Sam. I'll come back for yer, I promise."

Dr. Blackwell: "I wanted to be my own woman."

"We're bound together in ruin," came James from the grave. "Mark me, your turn will come."

She screwed her eyes shut tight. Bound together in ruin . . . Yes, Father, you would like that, wouldn't you? First Matthew, then James, now me. After eighteen years you would have your revenge.

But you won't. I intend to make my way in this world, and without the help of men. Freddy's gone, he's forgotten me. I shall go it alone. In America . . .

PART TWO

NEW YORK 1878

ONE

"*D*ON'T BREAK THE CIRCLE," SAID LOUISA IN A THROATY VOICE, her head flung back dramatically. "And don't open your eyes. We must concentrate. We must open our consciousness to the spirit world. We must all be receptive. Concentrate, ladies, concentrate . . ."

Samantha resisted the impulse to open her eyes and look around. She knew what she would see. Five young women sitting around the dining-room table holding hands, eyes firmly shut, their solemn faces illuminated by the flicker of the candle at the center. And beyond them: darkness.

Earlier, they had been sitting in Mrs. Chatham's finely appointed parlor using their one evening off in the week to catch up on mending, letter writing or reading the latest sensational news in Frank Leslie's *Illustrated Newspaper*. All five girls worked long hours, as many as fourteen a day in Louisa's case. Pale Helen worked in the library; the Wertz sisters were salesclerks on Fifth Avenue; plump Naomi was a milliner's apprentice; and beautiful, green-eyed Louisa had the most prestigious job of all: she was a typewriter at the new Bell Company.

Samantha felt Louisa's hand twitch in hers and heard her sing-songy voice call out, "I can feel the Way opening . . . The barriers are dissolving, the spirits are approaching . . ."

Half an hour earlier, Louisa had tossed aside her fashion magazine in boredom and had suggested they hold a séance, informing Samantha that only last month the group had raised the spirit of Joan of Arc. Louisa's contagious energy and flashing malachite eyes had made it difficult to refuse. Only now, holding hands in the darkness and listening to Louisa's chanting, Samantha frowned: the last thing she wanted to do in her new country was contact the dead.

"I feel a Presence!" cried Louisa. One of the girls gasped and Samantha felt Naomi's moist fingers tighten around her hand. Louisa's voice came out in long syllables: "Who is there? Who has come among us? Give us a sign . . ."

Despite herself, Samantha felt her heart race.

Two days before, she had arrived on the Cunard liner *Servia* and had not, thanks to Dr. Blackwell's advice that she travel second class, had to submit to the humiliating quarantine and "disinfection" to which the steerage immigrants were subjected. It had cost a lot of money—nearly half the proceeds from the sale of the house on the Crescent—but it had been worth it. A perfunctory inspection of her baggage on the dock by a polite customs officer, a quick look at her papers, and Samantha had been released. But on the other side of the fence she had seen the teeming mass of immigrants, most of them carrying their worldly possessions in paper bundles, being herded along like cattle: Germans in lederhosen and Dutchmen wearing sabots mingled with Connemara cloaks in a babble of tongues. The quarantine process, Samantha had heard, took hours, sometimes days. All because of the cost of one's ticket.

From the Battery Samantha had come to this section of town, between Greenwich Village and the Lower East Side, recommended by Elizabeth Blackwell as being clean and respectable but not expensive, and after a short walk down Houston Street, she had come upon the sign in Mrs. Chatham's window: ROOM FOR RENT, NO JEWS OR ITALIANS NEED APPLY.

The three-story brownstone was occupied by Mrs. Chatham, a bosomy widow in her sixties, a simple-minded girl of thirteen hired to do the cleaning, and five young boarders. Samantha had been given a room to share with a girl her own age named Louisa Binford.

That had been Friday. Samantha had quietly eaten a supper of roast chicken in egg sauce with Mrs. Chatham and the other girls, then had slipped wearily into bed. Unable to sleep, she had listened to the irregular knock of the radiator and the distant rumble of something called the El, and had choked back the tears of homesickness.

At breakfast the next morning the other girls in their long dark skirts and white blouses had introduced themselves, asked a few impersonal questions, then grabbed their hats and shawls and hurried off to their various places of employment. After a morning of reading New York newspapers in the parlor, Samantha had taken a walk to find the New York Infirmary, which turned out to be not far away on Second Avenue, and had made an appointment for Monday to be interviewed by Dr. Emily Blackwell, Elizabeth's sister.

Everywhere she went Samantha had been painfully reminded that she was a stranger in a strange land, self-exiled from the England she loved. With each new sight in this awesome city, with each syllable of American drawl, with each new custom she encountered (the carriages went down the wrong side of the street), Samantha felt her initial courage and determination wane. Had she done the right thing? Or was this wild, untamed new land going to be her downfall?

"Who are you?" moaned Louisa. "Who has come among us?"

The silence in the dining room was profound; Samantha imagined she could hear the combined beating of six anxious hearts. Preposterous! she thought as her fingers reflexively tightened around Louisa's hand. The dead can't be raised . . .

"The spirit has come to talk to one of us. It is trying to contact someone sitting at this table."

Samantha felt her breathing quicken.

Louisa's voice grew shrill. "Give us a sign, O visitor from Beyond! Whom do you wish to communicate with?"

Samantha heard a soft groaning. She tilted her head back and lifted her eyelids a little. Across the table she saw a strange illusion. It was a glow, softly incandescent, hovering in the blackness of the wall opposite. She gasped.

"What is it!" cried Louisa, her slender body swaying. "Whom have you come for? Speak to us, O spirit from the World of No Return—"

There was a sudden wail, then a crash.

Snapping her head forward and her eyes open, Samantha saw Edith Wertz bent over, gaping at something on the floor. The halo glow was gone.

Now they were all springing to their feet. Louisa hastily lit the gas jets while Samantha ran around the table. Fragile Helen lay sprawled on the floor, her chair on its side, her fluffy platinum hair creating a cloud about her head. Samantha's "phantom."

"She's fainted. Get Mrs. Chatham's smelling salts."

A few minutes later Helen was stretched out on the red velvet sofa with a damp handkerchief pressed to her temples. She looked at the faces hovering over her with frightened eyes. "What happened?"

"The spirit was trying to communicate with *you!*" said Louisa, sitting on the edge of the sofa. "But you weren't strong enough to allow it in."

Studying Helen's ashen face, her pinpointed pupils, the peculiar coloring of her lips, Samantha suspected another cause for Helen's fainting spell.

Louisa stood up and straightened her skirt, fussing with the folds gathered over her bustle. "Well, I guess the spell has been broken. No use trying to reconnect the circle."

"Perhaps next week," said Naomi, whose eyes glittered with excitement and whose dress showed half-moons under the plump arms. "I wonder who could have been trying to reach you, Helen dear!"

The girl rolled her head from side to side. "I don't know any dead people . . ."

Samantha helped Helen up to her room and sat with her while her strength returned. Helen boiled some water on the spirit lamp Mrs. Chatham allowed her boarders to have and sparingly spooned a bit of tea into her chipped pot. "It'll be weak," she said shyly, "but there's enough for two."

Samantha settled back in the one easy chair in the small room and looked around. Mrs. Chatham prided herself on providing her boarders with pleasant surroundings; Helen's room was like all the others, with a single brass bed and chenille spread, a mahogany wardrobe and dresser with ceramic pitcher and bowl, a colorful hooked rug, Currier & Ives lithographs of the Hudson and Mississippi rivers and frilly curtains that hid a view of the brick wall outside the window.

Helen sat on the edge of her bed nervously twisting her fingers. "That's the second time this week I've fainted. I was putting books back on the shelves, and the next minute I was lying on the floor looking up at the ceiling. Mr. Grant, the librarian, was furious. He thought I was faking. I've been dragging my feet, he said, and he accused me of malingering."

Samantha waited patiently while Helen plucked at the fabric of her skirt. "I don't want to lose my job at the library. I was lucky to get it. I can't do anything else. There aren't enough jobs to go around in New York. There are a hundred girls waiting to step into mine. And I can't go back to my father because he . . . he . . ." She bowed her head.

When the water boiled, Samantha made the tea. It was horribly weak and she wished she could have added a pinch of her own, but she sipped it politely.

Helen regarded Samantha with doe eyes. "I haven't any savings. I've only been in Manhattan for three months. If books are found damaged, the money is taken out of my salary. I'm expected to dress nicely every day, and you know how expensive clothes are."

Samantha studied the milky face and noticed a twitch at the corners of her mouth. After a few minutes Samantha said gently, "What's the matter, Helen?"

She looked down at her tea, at the cup which didn't match its cracked saucer, and dumbly shook her head.

"You don't have to tell me, of course, but sometimes it helps."

More minutes stretched by; outside, metal carriage wheels whined over the pavement. In the distance, from the direction of the slums, came the faint, tinny notes of a German street band.

Finally Helen looked up, her eyes wide with fear. "I have this . . . this *problem*," she said softly.

"A female problem?"

Helen blushed and nodded.

"What is it?"

She pressed her lips together. The back of her neck was red with embarrassment. "It won't stop," she whispered. "It keeps on."

Samantha put her cup to one side and came to sit next to the girl on the bed. "How long has it been?"

"Two weeks now. It's normally four days at the most. But this time it won't stop."

"Is it heavy?"

"Yes."

Samantha kept her eyes on the frayed cuffs of Helen's plain blouse. "What are you doing about it?"

The girl leaned forward and withdrew a bottle from behind the hurricane lamp by her bed. Samantha read the label: *Mrs. Lydia E. Pinkham's Vegetable Compound.*

"It says on the bottle," said Helen defensively, "that this will cure any female ailment."

"How long have you been taking it?"

"Over a week, but so far it hasn't helped."

Samantha put the bottle down. "Helen, you must see a doctor."

"No!"

Her reaction was so quick, so loud, it startled Samantha. "Why not?"

"I couldn't *bear* it! I mean, a man . . . I'd be so ashamed . . ."

"But doctors aren't like ordinary men, Helen, they're trained in this—"

She shook her head violently. "I don't care how much training they've had, it's not normal. A man is a man, and it's not right that he should discuss a young lady's private problems and not think *something!*"

"Then perhaps you can find a woman doctor."

Helen regarded her blankly. "Why would I want to do that?"

"If you're embarrassed to talk to a man—"

Helen shook her head again. "I wouldn't trust a woman doctor. Most of them are quacks."

Samantha leaned away and rubbed her hand over the back of her neck. She was extremely tired; the ten-day boat journey was catching up with her.

"Can *you* help me?" whispered Helen.

"Me? I'm not a doctor." Samantha had not told her fellow boarders why she had come to America. "But what is happening to you is abnormal, Helen, you need professional help. That bottle isn't going to do it for you."

"It promises on the label!"

"Helen, labels can say anything they please, you know that. You're only fooling yourself."

"Then it'll go away by itself. It's just been the strain. On my feet twelve hours a day with only fifteen minutes for lunch. And it takes me an hour each way to get to the library, and that's on a horse-bus hanging onto a strap. It's bound to upset my delicate female system!"

"Helen, you're not helping—"

"I won't go to a doctor, Samantha, and that's that."

Louisa was already in bed, propped up by pillows, her green eyes hungrily devouring a romantic novel. Samantha languidly bathed at the basin, then slipped her nightgown over her head.

"Is she all right?" asked Louisa, putting her book down.

Samantha slid between the cool, clean sheets. "Yes."

Louisa stared for a long moment at the girl in the next bed; so far, Samantha Hargrave was a mystery. "Are you homesick?" she ventured.

Samantha bunched a pillow behind her back and nodded. But there was more to it than that. There were the cold fears starting to infiltrate her self-confidence. Eighteen years old, all alone in an overwhelming city, with no friends or relatives, her money severely limited: what madness had possessed her!

"It's the same for everyone at first," came Louisa's quiet voice. "I left Cincinnati a year ago and I trembled like a sparrow under my bedclothes every night for a month!"

Samantha turned to look at her. Louisa was what one would call fetching. Her face had a mischievous appeal: a pixie-like beauty framed by honey-gold curls. Her green eyes were always glinting in private amusement. "But after a while I discovered what a wonderful adventure this is! No stern father to lower his eyebrows at me, no strait-laced mother clucking her tongue. Just myself, all on my own!"

Samantha felt herself smile. Louisa Binford liked to think of herself as "fast." She had once played tennis on Long Island and openly bragged about it.

"Listen, Samantha, we're all of us here on our own, away from home, making our way in the world. Doesn't that excite you?"

It had amazed her, Samantha had to admit, to find upon first arriving at Mrs. Chatham's a boardinghouse full of young females all on their own, respectable, earning their own wages, without a father or husband or other male relative dominating them. Such a phenomenon was almost unheard of in England, where a woman on her own was either labeled a spinster or questions were raised about her virtue. Although she felt out of place among these brave young women, Samantha admired their ambition and sense of independence.

Louisa chattered on: "Still, New York isn't the place for *every* girl. An awful lot of them would do better staying at home."

"Why?"

"Because terrible, *unspeakable* things befall girls who aren't careful. Their money runs out quicker than they realize and before they know it they're forced into the lascivious demi-monde where they suffer all sorts of horrible fates! The *Police Gazette* is full of such sad tales. Now me"—she gave a coquettish toss of her curls—"I'm a survivor. I'm going to marry a rich man and have a carriage with four perfectly matched horses and satin upholstery the color of my hair."

Samantha studied the faded ribbon threaded through the cuff of her old nightgown, deep in thought.

Louisa was silent for a moment, then she said, "Why did you come to New York?"

"To go to school."

"And study what?"

"I'm going to be a doctor."

There was a split second of silence, then Louisa blurted, "A doctor! How positively *delicious!*"

Samantha frowned as Louisa went breathlessly on: "There's a *terrible* fight going on! They're trying to force Harvard University to take in female medical students and it's in *all* the papers. Why, you'll be right in the middle of it!"

Samantha smiled apologetically. "I'm afraid I'm not going to apply to

Harvard. I expect to go to school at the New York Infirmary on Second Avenue."

Louisa's smile fell. "Oh."

"What's wrong with that?"

"I thought you meant you were going to become a regular doctor."

"What do you mean?"

"Well, not everyone thinks the graduates of the Infirmary are regular doctors. Legally, I suppose they are."

"I don't understand."

"Maybe it's different in England, Samantha, but here in America there are two kinds of doctor: the regular and the irregular. You see, in America anyone can call himself a doctor, anyone can hang out a shingle. It doesn't require a medical diploma. Homeopaths, water-methodists, Grahamists, Mesmerists and the magneticists all call themselves 'doctor.' They have their tubs of water, their magnets, their electrical belts, Mr. Graham has his cure-all crackers; and then on the other hand there are the *regular* doctors, the ones who went to real medical schools and are doctors such as you and I think of. But they're all in competition together, the regulars and irregulars, and it causes such a confusion!"

"But surely a patient would want one of the regulars!"

"True, but how is one to know ahead of time? You go to a man who calls himself a doctor and halfway through the treatment you realize you're being swindled. Now, add to that *women* doctors and you see what I mean."

"But just because they're women doesn't mean they are irregular."

"Doesn't matter. People just assume they are."

"Even if they carry diplomas from a regular school?"

"Not possible. Women aren't admitted to regular schools. I just told you about the fight at Harvard."

"But Dr. Blackwell told me there are plenty of schools in America that admit women."

"Sure, but they're all *female* colleges. And people automatically assume that, if you graduated from one of those, then you can't be very good, because it means you settled for second best. And therefore *you* are second best."

"I see . . ."

"But don't take my word for it, Samantha. I'm sure you will do very well at the Infirmary. It does have a good reputation. Now *me,* I can't imagine working with sick people. I do so love my own job!"

She went on to tell Samantha how she had ingeniously managed to secure a position as a typewriter at the brand-new telephone exchange on Nassau Street. "They had advertised for a young man and were quite shocked to see me in the crowd. There were a lot of them applying. About sixty, I'd say, just for the one job. Anyway, they were shocked to see me come for an application and tried to drive me off. The supervisor actually told me I couldn't be a very virtuous woman if I wanted to work at a typewriter!"

"Then how did you get the job?"

"Oh, I just charmed the old goat. I pointed out that the four telephone operators were men, the filing clerk was a man, the secretary was a man, and so was the messenger boy. Think how nice it would be, I said, flashing my eyes, to have the female touch in the office. The others were scandalized, of course, thinking that my presence would cause their *downfall,* but old Mr. Rutgers seemed to weaken. And then, when I offered to work for less than they were advertising, that I'd take the job for half the salary, he jumped at it. That was six months ago, and since then I have learned to typewrite and even talk over a telephone!"

Samantha nodded absently at her roommate, then turned away, returning to her own thoughts. Louisa had introduced some new, unexpected complications. This business about the Infirmary, *female colleges.* Was it true? Were women doctors considered *irregular?* Elizabeth Blackwell had said nothing about that. And then this problem with money and employment. Samantha had expected that, if the Infirmary couldn't take her right away, she could find a job somewhere and support herself in the interim. But what if I cannot find a job? What if my money runs out . . .

TWO

O UR SCHOOL SPRANG FROM A NEED, MISS HARGRAVE. FOR every one or two women who manage to get into a men's college there are hundreds who are refused. My sister established this Infirmary in 1855, and in 1864 legislation was passed granting us the right to confer the M.D. degree. Nine years ago we held our first commencement and had five graduates."

They were sitting in Dr. Emily's cramped office. The woman was very much like her sister, handsome and compact, an efficient little machine of femininity and strength. Dr. Emily had graciously taken the time to show Samantha around the premises—two adjoining brownstones on Second Avenue which had been converted into a hospital complete with wards, surgery, pharmacy, dispensary, and classrooms. Samantha had visited the spotless wards and had met the nurses, female doctors, and medical students, all bustling to meet the demands of a heavy patient load.

"The Infirmary was started out of a need to give medical care to impoverished women and to give care to women for whom the prospect of being exposed to a male doctor is unbearable. In our first year, Miss Hargrave, we treated three thousand patients. That was twenty-three years ago. Now we are seeing ten times that number."

Dr. Emily smiled proudly. "It followed, therefore, that we should establish a school where we could train women to work here. Our students see the patients in the dispensary, counsel them, and send them home with medication and instructions on hygiene and health. We are in an immigrant neighborhood, Miss Hargrave, and many of these women have peculiar ideas about cleanliness. So we have a visiting program in which our nurses go out and see to the sick in their homes and, if possible, teach them about sanitation. As you can see, our students have received thorough, clinical experience."

Samantha voiced her concern about the female diploma.

"I will not deny that there is strong prejudice against us and that those few women physicians armed with diplomas from male medical colleges fare better, but I feel that, in time, when we have proven our worth, we will be accepted. Despite what people say of us, Miss Hargrave, we *are* a regular school."

Samantha came away in a state of indecision. The Infirmary had impressed her, and to be a member of such a progressive institution, to work at the side of brilliant practitioners like the famous Dr. Mary Putnam Jacobi, was an opportunity not to be scorned. And yet the woman she most admired, Dr. Elizabeth Blackwell, had attended a male college.

Unfortunately, Samantha would have ample time to make her decision: the school was currently full and could not accommodate any more students for six months. However, Dr. Emily assured her of admission in the coming January, adding that, in the meantime, it was highly advisable Samantha secure an apprenticeship with a regular practicing physician. Samantha agreed, for Dr. Elizabeth had served an apprenticeship before attending college (it was a common road for most medical students), and gratefully took the list of recommended doctors Dr. Emily proffered.

In the next few days, however, Samantha's optimism turned into anxiety; none of Dr. Emily's physicians came through. A few already had apprentices and others hadn't a practice large enough to take on an assistant.

Late at night, alone in her room, Samantha counted her money by the light of a solitary oil lamp and estimated that, with frugal spending and self-denial, it would last three months. After that . . .

The first thing she did was go through all the newspapers, circle the notices for physicians advertising for apprentices, then knock on doors the breadth and width of Manhattan. The reactions varied from undisguised amusement to blustering indignation: most were shocked by her proposal, calling it immoral; a few laughed good-naturedly, certain she was not serious; three made improper overtures; and one made an offer of marriage.

She started in the fashionable thirties on the avenues and gradually worked her way down, with some reluctance, into the Tenth Ward, also known as the Pig Market or Typhus Ward—the most crowded slum in Manhattan. She walked the filthy sidewalks of Little Italy, where the cries of children and the hurdy-gurdy of the organ grinder mingled with the shouts of street vendors. She walked with black-hatted rabbis down Orchard and Hester streets, dodging garbage strewn in the gutters, deafened by the hawking of bearded used-clothing peddlers. Immigrants of all ages approached her for handouts, brazen children and shy young women clutching their shawls modestly over the bulge of pregnancy. Physicians were fewer here and those whom she did manage to see either spoke no English or gave her an Old World lecture about going home to her mama where she belonged.

It took a week, seven days of walking, climbing steps, reciting her proposal, receiving a variety of rebuffs, coming home exhausted, soaking her feet and feeling, each night, the weighty mantle of disappointment. Yet Samantha remained dauntless. With each rejection her determination grew. Somewhere in this city of golden opportunities was a physician who would take her in.

THREE

*I*T WAS ON THE CORNER OF EIGHTH STREET AND SECOND Avenue that the accident occurred. Samantha had been about to step off the curb when a young man, nattily dressed in a cycling uniform, came wheeling through the traffic on his flashy Columbia high-wheel ordinary. Seeing her, he grinned and doffed his fashionable blue polo cap. As he sped by he looked back over his shoulder, still grinning, still pedaling. Samantha saw the carriage whip around the corner and opened her mouth to shout a warning. She froze as the cyclist turned around too late. The horses reared and shrieked, the carriage gave a sickening lurch. Samantha gaped in shock as the cyclist and his shiny ordinary collided with the phaeton in an eruption of screams and the jangling of harnesses. The horses bucked wildly, thrashed in their rigging and sent the carriage crashing onto its side. An unoccupied hansom, unable to stop in time, received the full impact of the phaeton, catapulting the driver through the air.

It was over in seconds. The intersection was a chaotic scene of twisted wreckage; the horses lay squealing on their sides, struggling to get up;

wheels still turned on broken axles; other carriages jolted and careered, creating a deafening jam of traffic. People were running to the accident scene; Samantha was the first there.

In a quick sweep her eyes took in the state of the victims. The hansom driver was dead, his head flattened against a telegraph pole; the four occupants of the phaeton were strewn on the pavement, one unconscious, two groaning, the fourth trying to get up; their driver was crawling out from under the carriage, dazed and cut. But it was to the cyclist Samantha turned her attention, for he was pinned under the cab, his right arm caught at a grotesque angle between the steel spokes of his Columbia.

While several men tried to heave the heavy carriage off the youth, Samantha reached into the phaeton, seized a white silk scarf, and hurriedly but skillfully tied it tightly around the boy's upper arm. As the hansom shifted, so did the bicycle, causing the cyclist to let out a howl. The street was now a roar of moans and sobs, horses whinnying, people shouting. Samantha hastily checked the boy for other injuries, took a quick look at his pupils and did a short count of his rapid pulse; his wound, despite the makeshift tourniquet, was losing a constant stream of blood.

"An ambulance!" she cried. "Someone fetch an ambulance!"

There appeared to be a lot of ineffectual milling about; a mob had gathered and now ringed the scene. A young lady had fainted on the sidewalk and was being fanned by two gentlemen. Several other men were trying to hoist the phaeton passengers to their feet. The cyclist was sweating badly; he slipped into merciful unconsciousness.

When the hansom finally creaked upright and crashed down on its wheels, two men started pulling at the bicycle.

"No!" cried Samantha. "Do it slowly! He'll lose his arm that way!"

"Listen, lady—"

"Has someone gone for an ambulance?"

"I guess so. Who are you?"

The youth groaned and sank deeper. Samantha murmured quietly over him, her cool hand on his forehead; a steady ribbon of blood flowed from the scarf to the pavement.

A man in black frock coat and top hat was making his way through the wreckage, stooping over each victim and giving them a hasty check. Then he was at Samantha's side. He dropped to one knee and leaned over the cyclist, examining first the arm and then head and neck. When he opened the black bag he was carrying and withdrew a binaural stethoscope, Samantha studied him in curiosity.

The profile beneath the black top hat was striking: coal-black eyes beneath heavy brows, a large straight nose, thin mouth, sharply chiseled cheeks and a square, firm jaw. A hint of gray above the ears put him in his early forties.

When he leaned back and thrust the stethoscope into his bag, Samantha said, "The others—"

"They're all right. Their injuries can wait until the ambulance arrives. This boy cannot. He must be seen to immediately."

A policeman pushed through the crowd. "St. Brigid's is sending a wagon, Dr. Masefield."

"I have to get this boy to my office. I'll need help carrying him."

"Hey, you two!" bellowed the policeman. "Come here!"

The stranger finally looked at Samantha. His face, though grave, was startlingly handsome. "Hold his arm while I pull on the wheel. If you feel the bone ends shift, tell me at once."

"Yes—" she said breathlessly.

The policeman also dropped down and seized the rim of the wheel. While he and the doctor exerted a gentle pull, Samantha held the boy's arm fast. He moaned softly but did not waken. Beneath the silk scarf she felt the warm blood and knotted muscles; her strong, slender fingers managed to keep the broken bone ends immobile as the wheel gradually drew away.

The doctor shot to his feet. "Be careful how you carry him. One bad jolt and the jagged bone ends will sever whatever nerves and vessels are still intact. With luck we can save the arm."

As the two men gently lifted the cyclist and started forward, Samantha rose stiffly to her feet and brushed straying curls off her damp forehead. Dr. Masefield started to walk away, then paused, turned to her and said abruptly, "Are you coming?"

His office was only a short distance away. They were led through an entry hall into a carbolic-smelling surgery. As the men carefully laid the boy on the table, Dr. Masefield snapped orders at Samantha. "You'll find ligatures in that cupboard. I'll need gut as well as silk. Run them through the acid first. You'll find an apron behind that door."

As Samantha, her heart racing, fumbled with the spools of suture, having not the slightest idea what to do, Dr. Masefield removed his frock coat and top hat and started rolling up his sleeves. "Pour some carbolic into that basin."

Samantha quickly scanned the shelves and found a large brown bottle labeled "Carbolic Solution, 5%." She grabbed it, uncorked it and clumsily slopped some into the enamel basin. Then she returned to the sutures. Two years before, she had been visiting Dr. Blackwell when an injured chimney sweep had been brought in. Dr. Blackwell had cut strands of silk about twenty-four inches long. Using scissors from the cupboard, Samantha proceeded with trembling fingers to snip similar lengths.

"Bring me that tray," came the doctor's curt voice.

She turned questioning eyes to him.

"Up there," he indicated with a nod. "They've been in the acid. Put it here, by my right hand."

She reached up and drew down the tray. Dr. Masefield, having dipped his hands in the carbolic solution and dried them on a towel, set about to peel the sodden scarf off the arm.

"You can stop that now and come help me. Drop the sutures in the basin."

She did as told, then whipped the apron off its hook and hastily tied it behind her.

"Did you do this?" he asked, lifting the scarf off and dropping it into a bucket.

"Yes," she whispered.

"You probably saved his arm. Okay, bring that lamp over here and hold it so it shines right into the wound."

They worked for nearly an hour. Dr. Masefield sat on a stool, like a jeweler, cleaning the wound, scarifying the edges and tying off vessels. Samantha helped him set the bone, ran to the cupboard for whatever he demanded, moved the light whenever he shifted his position, and soaked the final bandages in the acid. In all that time Dr. Masefield did not once look at her.

"There," he said, leaning back and wiping his bloody hands on a towel. "Now the ambulance can have him."

Samantha hovered uncertainly, plucking at the bloodstained apron.

Dr. Masefield stood and leaned over the boy. As he felt the neck pulse and lifted each eyelid, he murmured, "Pull that bell rope."

Samantha turned around. It hung in the corner. She gave it a tug and almost instantaneously an elderly lady in maroon bombazine appeared in the doorway, her fleecy white hair contained in a mobcap. "Yes, Dr. Masefield?"

"Mrs. Wiggen, would you please send the Horowitz boy to St. Brigid's for an ambulance? And then please put water on for tea." He straightened up and finally looked at Samantha. "Or would you prefer coffee?"

Her eyes flew open. "Oh. Tea is fine, yes—"

The housekeeper turned primly away and Dr. Masefield heaved a great sigh. "Well, I think he'll be all right. These cyclists are a hazard to traffic."

Not knowing what to say, Samantha stared at the supine body, his once fancy uniform of white flannel shirt and blue knickerbockers now tattered and filthy.

Dr. Masefield went to the basin and washed his hands. "It's lucky for him you were at the scene," he said with his back to her. "You did a good job back there. May I ask where you got your training?"

Samantha shifted uncomfortably. "Well, I . . ."

He turned around, drying his hands. "Forgive me, I haven't introduced myself. Joshua Masefield."

She felt faintly absurd, standing there in a bloody apron with her hat sitting at an angle on her hair. "Samantha Hargrave."

He didn't smile; his mouth appeared unused to that gesture. His brooding black eyes continued to stare at her.

Samantha fumbled with the ties of her apron. "I'm afraid I've soiled this."

"Mrs. Wiggen will take care of it. Just drop it down and she'll pick it up with the rest of this mess. You look as if you need a few minutes off your feet."

She followed him across the hall to a parlor that was tastefully furnished with velvet sofa and matching easy chairs, engravings on the walls, a large Boston fern in the window, dried flowers on the mantel. But it had an air, Samantha could not help thinking, of being seldom used.

She sat on the sofa while he remained standing. Beyond the window, on the busy street, traffic had resumed its noisy flow. And from somewhere at the back of the house came sounds of dishes and running water. Samantha folded her hands in her lap and discovered with dismay a large bloodstain on her skirt at the level of her knees.

"Mrs. Wiggen will take care of that for you," said Dr. Masefield, leaning on the mantel. Despite the fact that the calamity had passed, his air of gravity did not lift, and Samantha began to wonder if it ever did.

"Oh no," she said faintly, "I can take care of it."

"Nonsense. Mrs. Wiggen deals with that sort of thing all the time. She's an old hand at it. Surely you cannot expect to go out into the street like that."

Samantha bowed her head, unable to meet his gaze. Her childhood affliction, the sudden inability to talk, which she thought she had conquered long ago at Playell's, now came back to plague her.

"You're from England, aren't you?"

"Yes."

"How long have you been here?"

"Ten days."

"Then you received your training over there. In London?"

Samantha could neither conquer her maddening shyness nor free her tongue. Annoyed with herself, she said without looking up, "What do you mean, sir, training?"

"Where did you study medicine?"

Surprised, she raised her head. "I haven't studied medicine at all."

Although his expression didn't change, the astonishment was clearly seen in his eyes. "But surely you've had some education in it! As a ward sister at least!"

She mutely shook her head.

"Great heavens," he said quietly, studying her with increased interest. "When I saw how you conducted yourself out there, giving orders, taking the wounds by priority, I assumed you were a doctor, or a nurse at the very least. I certainly would not have had you come back here with me had I known, and I certainly would not have put you through *that*." He waved in the direction of the surgery. "Great heavens," he repeated softly. "What must you think of me . . ."

They stared at one another across the room, their eyes locked, and all sounds of the morning seemed to fade away. For a moment Samantha heard only the thumping of her heart, then the creaky voice of Mrs. Wiggen in the doorway shattered the spell. "Tea's ready, Doctor."

"We'll have it in here, Mrs. Wiggen."

The old woman registered fleeting surprise and cast a critical glance at Samantha. As she shuffled away, Dr. Masefield said, "I'm afraid I get so few visitors that Mrs. Wiggen sometimes forgets herself."

After the tea was set down, Mrs. Wiggen brought a skirt from downstairs. Samantha changed into it in the surgery, handing her own to the housekeeper, who sniffed disapprovingly. The replacement skirt, of good-quality wool, had a small waist; it couldn't belong to plump Mrs. Wiggen. Whose then?

"You must forgive my improbable behavior, Miss Hargrave," said Dr. Masefield when she rejoined him. "And you must believe me when I say that, had I known you were acting out of charity and not medical training, I never would have pressed you into service! I am appalled at my shocking lack of judgment!"

Samantha kept her eyes on her teacup. Now that he sat opposite her and a little closer she could not bring herself to look at him. "Actually, Dr. Masefield," she said in a breathy voice, "you were not entirely wrong."

Briefly she recounted her experiences in England, her friendship with Dr. Blackwell, and ended with her reason for coming to New York. Joshua Masefield listened with acute interest, and when she had finished he appeared visibly relieved. He sat silently studying her, Samantha uncomfortable beneath his bold gaze, until the clatter of horses in front of the house intruded upon the silence. Footsteps hurried up to the door, followed by a staccato rap.

The wagon from St. Brigid's. Dr. Masefield helped the attendant carry the boy out by stretcher while Samantha remained in the parlor, awkwardly sipping her tea. When he returned and resumed his seat, she tried very hard to command her voice. "I expect my skirt must be done by now."

"Never rush an artist. Mrs. Wiggen will have it stretched over a jar and is deluging it with a magic brew from her secret cupboard. It's a process she has perfected after ruining too many skirts."

"Is Mrs. Wiggen your assistant?"

"After a fashion. She isn't trained, but she keeps the patients orderly in the waiting room and cleans up afterward. Once in a while I use her help, as I would have today if it hadn't been for you."

Samantha forced herself to look at him. "Have you thought of taking on an apprentice?"

"As a matter of fact, I have."

The cup rattled in its saucer; she deposited them on the table. What was wrong with her! All week she had presented herself with poise and confidence to countless physicians. Why did this one disconcert her so?

"And he's to start next week."

"Who?"

"The medical student I've hired."

She stared at him for an instant, then quickly looked away. Hopes raised and dashed in the span of one minute!

"Have I said something, Miss Hargrave?"

Haltingly she described her seven days of searching for just such a position, reluctantly adding that she seemed now to be at the end of the road.

"So you're going to attend the Blackwells' Infirmary in January. Then that's probably the reason why you were turned down everywhere. Few physicians can be bothered with a six-month apprentice. A year is the standard term."

Samantha smiled in gratitude but shook her head. "Somehow, Dr. Masefield, I don't think that's why I was rejected. But it's kind of you to say so."

Mrs. Wiggen's bulk filled the doorway; she held Samantha's skirt in her hands. "It's still damp but the stain's out."

Samantha changed back into it in the surgery and noticed that, in the meantime, everything had been cleaned up. She also noticed that the instruments Dr. Masefield had used were now soaking in the basin of carbolic acid.

Back in the parlor, straightening her hat and tucking up loose strands of hair, she said, "You Americans seem very progressive. That's the first application of Listerism I've seen."

Dr. Masefield rose. "I'm afraid it's not all Americans, Miss Hargrave, but a dismal handful of us. I read about it in the journals and did some experimenting on my own. I was instantly convinced. The majority of American physicians, I fear, still fight the microbial theory."

"Yes, well . . ." She ran her hands down her skirt and fumbled with her cuffs. Joshua Masefield strode past her toward the front door.

"Shall I call you a cab?"

"No, thank you, I'm not far. Just on Houston, at Mrs. Chatham's. Thank you for the tea."

"Thank you for your help. I believe that boy owes you his life."

She squinted at the bright sunlight flooding through the open door. "Hardly, it was really your . . . oh dear."

"What's the matter?"

"My gloves. I took them off at the scene of the accident. I have lost them now for sure. And they were the only pair I had."

He stood silently by the door, holding it open.

She smiled shyly up at him, murmured, "Good day, Dr. Masefield," and hurried down the steps.

That night he gave her no peace. As she lay in the darkness listening to Louisa's gentle respirations, Joshua Masefield invaded Samantha's thoughts. What was it about him that intrigued her so? His arresting appearance, to be sure: the stormy black hair with a touch of gray, broad shoulders, and back so straight he reminded her of a military officer. But there was something else, a mystique; Joshua Masefield seemed cloaked in melancholy, his black eyes held depths of sadness. Hadn't his manner struck her as a little stilted, as though he were not showing his true self but hiding something beneath? And then there was that little parlor, so touchingly ready for visitors who never came.

This last thought made Samantha curl up on her side and blink at the dark wall inches from her face. Had she imagined it or had Joshua Masefield seemed awkward in that parlor, unsure of himself, as if the innocent ritual of visiting with a caller were something alien to him? But how could that be? Surely a man like Joshua Masefield had many friends, must entertain frequently.

Samantha reluctantly forced him from her thoughts. There was so much else to worry over: where to turn next, how to make her money last . . .

FOUR

*I*T WAS FOUR DAYS LATER WHEN THE MESSENGER BOY ARRIVED. As Samantha was out looking for a job Mrs. Chatham took the package and put it in Samantha's room; when she came home that evening after a dispiriting day, Samantha found the box and, curious, hurriedly tore off the wrapping. Inside the nest of tissue paper lay a pair of dove-gray suede gloves and a note which read: "You cannot expect to make a good impression without gloves. For your excellent services." It was signed J.M.

She told herself she had forgotten him, but she had not, and as she walked up the steps to his door the next morning she chided herself for being nervous. She would be polite but brief, maybe she could even hand over the box to Mrs. Wiggen without having to see him and leave the message that, while Dr. Masefield's generosity was appreciated, she could not possibly accept the gift.

To her dismay the entry hall was congested with patients and Mrs. Wiggen was nowhere in sight.

Feeling self-conscious beneath the open stares, for Samantha's clothes were better than everyone else's, she tried to find a place to sit. Two long benches lined the walls; it was a system used in all doctors' offices: when the patient currently with the doctor came out, the one seated nearest the door got up and went in. Then everybody would slide down the bench and those standing would fill the end vacancy in order of arrival. It was an honor system that rarely went awry.

Samantha remained standing with two men and a little boy. For a room so crowded it was curiously quiet. One flush-cheeked woman fanned herself with a handkerchief. A young mother fretted over a baby squirming in her arms. An old lady with a black shawl over her head and a heavy crucifix on her bosom stared with glassy eyes.

When the surgery door opened all heads turned and Samantha's heart leapt. Joshua Masefield, in his shirt sleeves, leaned out and said, "Signor Giovanni," and gestured to one of the men standing. The immigrant whipped off his cap and hurried through, the door closing firmly behind him. If Dr. Masefield had seen Samantha he gave no indication.

The minutes dragged. Muffled voices came from the other side of the door. Those waiting seemed unconcerned. Samantha shifted nervously, turning the little box over and over in her hands.

When the door opened again she started. The Italian emerged with his arm around a young woman who was weeping silently into her hands. As they passed through the front door, Samantha's eyes met Dr. Masefield's. They stared at one another for an instant, then he said, "Next, please," and turned back inside. When a young man with a bandaged wrist stood up and went in, the door closing behind him, Samantha felt her nervousness turn to annoyance.

Everyone slid down the bench, leaving a space. The man with the little boy who was ahead of her pointed shyly to the bench and murmured something in a foreign tongue. Samantha smiled uncertainly and sat down.

More long minutes stretched by. Samantha found herself tapping her foot. Occasionally someone would glance at her in disinterest and then turn away.

When the door opened again, Samantha checked the impulse to shoot to her feet. She watched as the young man shook Dr. Masefield's hand, put his worker's cap on his head and hurried out. There was another brisk "Next," and the old lady with the crucifix hobbled in. Samantha slid along the bench and felt her annoyance wax into indignation.

She was beginning to wonder if she should get up and leave when the sound of rustling skirts came from down the hall. Mrs. Wiggen glided up to Samantha and said, "Will you come with me, please."

Samantha was taken into a room that adjoined the surgery. Like the parlor across the hall, it fronted the street and had a fine marble fireplace. But there the similarity ended. Joshua Masefield's private study had not a hint of pretension and was obviously well lived in. There was a horsehair sofa with deeply buttoned velvet upholstery; a carved oak bookcase filled to overflowing; matching armchairs with well-worn squab cushions; a heavily draped loo table in the window supporting an overgrown plant; and finally a mahogany roll-top desk cluttered with papers, books, magazines, a stained inkhorn and a few small pieces of dusty statuary. The wallpaper was faded but had a lovely repeating theme of spring flowers against an ecru background; the Turkey carpet was old and thready but obviously had once been of good quality; and on a papier-mache pedestal table in the corner stood a crystal service of a brandy-filled decanter and glasses. The atmosphere was homey and stamped with the personality of a man who cherished his privacy and solitude. But there were no photographs anywhere and that was very odd.

"What can I do for you, Miss Hargrave?"

She spun around. Joshua Masefield was coming through the door that led to the surgery; before it closed Samantha glimpsed behind him Mrs. Wiggen helping the old lady off the examining table.

"I came to return these," she said, holding the box out to him.

His brows rose slightly but he made no move to take it.

"I cannot possibly accept the gloves," she said in a rush. "I am not in the habit of taking gifts from gentlemen I hardly know."

His eyes remained on her face, his expression maddeningly noncommittal.

"So you must take them back." She looked around, then dropped the box on the cluttered desk. "I'm sorry if I've disturbed you. Good day, sir." She turned to go.

"I am afraid you flatter yourself, Miss Hargrave."

Samantha stopped and turned around. "How so?"

"The gloves weren't a gift, they were payment for your help. When I visited the cyclist in the hospital his father gave me a check for our services. Since I knew you badly needed a pair of gloves, I took the liberty of purchasing them for you instead of sending the money. If you are going to be a doctor, Miss Hargrave, you are going to have to learn to accept payment in goods; your patients will not always have ready cash."

Her fingers twisted the handle of her knitted purse. "Oh dear, I thought—"

"I know what you thought, Miss Hargrave. Now here." He picked up the box and held it out to her. "Take them. Frame them if you wish as your very first payment for medical services."

Samantha took the box and fabricated a smile. "I feel such a fool."

The door behind him opened and Mrs. Wiggen's mobcap poked through. "Doctor? Mrs. Solomon is waiting."

"A moment, Mrs. Wiggen."

After the door clicked shut Samantha said, "She doesn't like me, does she?"

The corners of his mouth jerked a little, as if in a smile. "Mrs. Wiggen is overly protective of me, like a hen. Tell me, Miss Hargrave, have you had any success in finding a position?"

She had not, nor had Dr. Emily been able to give her much hope. "I am afraid circumstances force me to look for other, nonmedical employment until the Infirmary can take me."

"That will not be easy. There are hundreds of young women in your predicament. I have been thinking, Miss Hargrave. The young man whom I have hired is going to attend Cornell University. He comes from a well-to-do family and has excellent references. He would have no trouble at all finding an apprenticeship with any physician in Manhattan. So it had occurred to me, Miss Hargrave, that I should take you on instead. After all, you're much more in need of this job than he is, you have already proven your ability to me, and your friendship with the Blackwells counts for a lot. It also came to me that a female assistant would be of great help with many of my female patients, who often are very uncomfortable with me. Would you consider it, Miss Hargrave?"

She gazed at him in disbelief.

"I do, however"—Dr. Masefield turned away and walked to the corner pedestal table where he paused, like an orator, and rested his fingertips on the inlaid surface— "have other, personal motives which I must voice, for I've no doubt they will influence your decision."

Samantha waited upon his next word.

"I have in mind for you to assist me in a private matter, Miss Hargrave. It concerns, you see"—he averted his eyes—"my wife."

He stopped speaking for a moment and the noise from the street rushed in. Samantha waited.

"Mrs. Masefield is an invalid, bedridden, and sometimes requires such attention as Mrs. Wiggen is ill equipped to handle. I had thought of hiring a private nurse, but the job is not demanding enough for round-the-clock care. Mrs. Masefield is only . . . *incapacitated* at times."

He finally turned to look at her. "For most of the time my wife is quite capable of caring for herself. But she has . . . relapses. That would be when I could use your help. But I hasten to add, Miss Hargrave, that such occasions are not frequent and that for the rest of the time you would be working here with me."

She continued to gaze at him long after he had finished speaking. Samantha felt herself strangely moved. His words had come out with such effort, so painfully, his manner so awkward, that it was as if he had made a great, secret confession to her.

"You will want time to consider it, of course—"

How incongruous, this magnificent man, normally so self-possessed, so in command, stumbling over his words like a timid lover.

"I need no time, Dr. Masefield. I should be honored to accept."

FIVE

*S*HE MOVED IN THAT AFTERNOON WITH LOUISA'S HELP. Samantha's room was on the third floor next to Mrs. Wiggen's; together they shared the newly installed bathroom at the head of the stairs. Samantha's excitement was tempered by a nagging uncertainty: she had made a snap decision and what, after all, did she know about this man?

It did not take long to put her room in order; Samantha was soon primping before her looking glass and getting ready for tea. To her great disappointment, however, she learned she was to take all her meals in the kitchen with the dour Mrs. Wiggen and Filomena, a young Italian girl who came in three days a week to clean. The Masefields, she was told crisply by Mrs. Wiggen, who did not disguise her contempt for the newcomer, always took their meals in their own rooms. She would be permitted use of the parlor to take callers, but the doctor's study was never to be entered, nor was she to be disturbing Mrs. Masefield except when called upon. Sundays were her days off.

Dr. Masefield was to remain, Samantha soon found, a private and securely locked man. She was not to experience any further intimacy with him; the few questions he had asked the day they met were to be the only ones. Joshua Masefield came downstairs promptly at eight o'clock each morning, spoke a cordial "Good morning," then had Mrs. Wiggen send the first patient in. He remained stiff and professional always, never inquiring after Samantha's night's sleep or if she was wanting anything; Mrs. Wiggen, it was assumed, would see to all that. Nor could Samantha find a way in: only once did she inquire innocently after Mrs. Masefield (whom she had yet to meet) and received a polite but cool rebuff. At first Samantha wondered if she would be able to stand it, with the dyspeptic housekeeper and the distant Dr. Masefield, but she did have her wonderful Sunday outings with Louisa and Dr. Masefield's practice was so busy that, after a while, Samantha had little time to worry about anything else.

She would stand by and watch as he examined each patient, asked questions, diagnosed and prescribed, reassured them in a gentle tone, and sent them away with something from his pharmacy cupboard. While he washed his hands he would explain each case afterward to Samantha: "Rabies can be inflicted by the bite of any animal, even a household pet such as poor Willie's cat. The child you just saw, Miss Hargrave, will suffer every torture imaginable. He will choke, have difficulty breathing and, worst of all, will suffer a hellish thirst which cannot be relieved, for the very sight of a glass of water or cup of tea will drive the boy to fits of hysteria. Bleeding and opium are the standard treatment, but they don't work."

"There is no cure?"

"None. Rabies is more dreaded than the plague, for no one survives. They say the disease lurks in the saliva of the animal, and I understand Mr. Pasteur is searching this very moment for a cure, but it will not come soon enough for poor Willie."

With female patients he was exceptionally gentle and kind, never rushing them, sympathetic with their modesty. In deference to their sensitivities he always resorted to the long Laennec stethoscope to avoid embarrassing them with his nearness, and he exhibited the remarkable ability to ask very intimate questions without appearing to do so. As physical examination was out of the question with women, Dr. Masefield would take more time, patiently rooting out the problem without the benefit of seeing it for himself, then prescribe, advise, and give comfort.

"Mrs. Higginbotham suffers from severe cramps," he told Samantha. "For the woman's monthly illness there are many forms of temporary relief but no cure, for she will be afflicted with it every month until the menses cease. I routinely prescribe a dose of arrowroot and laudanum. For pregnant women with morning sickness, calumba root and peppermint four times daily can help."

And then there were those ailments Joshua Masefield could not or would not correct. "Miss Sloan asked me for a cycle restorer. Although she did not admit it, I suspect she is pregnant. She asked me to restore her menses."

"But that would mean—"

"An unwanted pregnancy is a sad thing, Miss Hargrave. Remedies abound, but I doubt they do any good. A tea made of the mistletoe berry. Chrysanthemum flowers sometimes work, or a drink of pennyroyal or slippery elm. Some midwives, I understand, ply a lucrative trade in abortion."

"What do you do with such patients?"

"I advised Miss Sloan, if that is her real name, to see her priest, but no doubt she will stop at DeWinter's Drug Store and purchase one of his patent medicines."

"Can that be done?"

"Female regulators are big business, Miss Hargrave, although they do not work. James Clark's Pills. Ford's Regulator. Dr. Kilmer's Female Remedy. Any woman with fifty cents can purchase a bottle of false hope."

Dr. Masefield knew enough words in the neighboring languages to ask basic questions of the immigrants who came to him. Filomena was frequently brought in to translate, and Samantha's French occasionally helped. With children Dr. Masefield was profoundly patient, stroking their hot little foreheads and telling them stories while mending cuts and scrapes. Samantha never ceased to marvel at the transformation: alone with her or Mrs. Wiggen, Joshua Masefield was rigidly formal, keeping the mask always in place. But with the patients he changed, softened, became friend and confidant.

Alone in her room at night, after a tiring day of observing, memorizing, cutting bandages, and after a cheerless supper with the unspeaking Mrs. Wiggen, Samantha would sit by her little fire and think about him, wonder about him, try to solve the mystery of why a marvelous practitioner like Joshua Masefield, so skillful, so able to put the most anxious patient at ease, was not more than he was—an unknown neighborhood doctor. Further, Joshua Masefield clearly had no friends or social life. Other than patients, Filomena and the young man who made the weekly deliveries from DeWinter's Drug Store, no one ever came to the front door. Samantha wondered why he did it, a man so brilliant, so handsome, so elegantly cut, why he retired each night to his study, closing the door against the world (except for going out on house calls), with not even an occasional evening at a gentlemen's club. Why did he make of himself an exile in that gloomy house?

Perhaps it had something to do with the unseen Mrs. Masefield.

"What's wrong with her?" asked Louisa as they ate lunch in Macy's new tearoom.

"I don't know." Samantha didn't like talking about the Masefields, honored their wish for privacy, but Louisa could be very persuasive.

It was a warm summer day and the two girls were planning after lunch to go to the Elysian Fields in Hoboken to see the New York Knickerbockers play baseball against the Cincinnati Red Stockings. In the month she had been working for Dr. Masefield Samantha had started exploring New York with Louisa. They always had merry excursions, but unfortunately Louisa could not curb her intense curiosity about the Masefields.

"You mean you're supposed to take care of her and he hasn't even told you yet why?" Louisa's green eyes glinted. "Samantha Hargrave, how can you stand it!"

Samantha glanced around at the other tables, fearful that Louisa's voice had carried. "He will tell me when he's ready."

"What if it's something positively *dreadful!*"

"You read too many novels, Louisa."

"But isn't it romantic? He's so handsome and so *suffering*."

"Come now, Louisa!" Samantha hated to admit it but Louisa had put her own private feelings into words. There *was* something tragic about him . . . But Samantha would not be drawn into an exchange of gossip with her friend. Dr. Masefield had a right to his privacy, and besides, Samantha owed him a great debt: he had rescued her from possibly dire circumstances, given her an enviable post (eight dollars a week on top of room and board), and was giving her the best medical education she could hope to receive anywhere. It was going to be a shame to leave him in five months.

"How do you know there even *is* a Mrs. Masefield?"

Samantha's sandwich stopped at her lips. "I beg your pardon?"

Louisa leaned across the table and said with Sen-Sen breath, "After all, it's highly improper for a young lady to be living under the same roof as her male employer. What would his patients think? So he made up a perfect cover, he invented a wife."

"Louisa Binford, you shock me! Dr. Masefield is the very soul of propriety. And besides, Mrs. Wiggen is also in that house."

"Who probably sleeps like the dead once she closes her eyes." Louisa leaned back and tilted her head. "I've seen him, Samantha, and I think it's all a disguise, that coldness. He's simply a man, living alone. And there you are, so pretty, so innocent, how can he resist?"

"Louisa Binford, what are you saying?"

"That one of these nights he'll come knocking at your door. Mark my words."

SIX

*H*E DID JUST THAT, SIX DAYS LATER. IT WAS LATE SATURDAY
night and Samantha was composing a letter to Dr. Blackwell
in London. Although it was nearly midnight he was dressed in
a charcoal-gray frock coat and trousers, as if ready to go out. His expression
was intense. "Will you come with me, please, Miss Hargrave."

Draping a shawl about her shoulders, Samantha picked up a lamp and
wordlessly followed him down the stairs. He paused before a door, his features cast in austerity by the lamp's glow. "I must go out and my wife requires
bedside vigilance. This has always been Mrs. Wiggen's job, but she has a
habit of nodding off. I trust you will remain alert."

Samantha was not prepared for the sight that met her on the other side.
Mrs. Masefield's bedroom was as elegant as if it were inside a Fifth Avenue
mansion and a dazzling contrast to the rest of the somber house. The polished ebony, gilt cherubs and filigree, the Berlin-wool-work fire screen, the
exquisite Louis Quatorze chairs, the pre-Raphaelite scenes from Greek and
Roman mythology, and glittering crystal all made Samantha think she had

stepped into a fairyland. A hot fire crackled in its fireplace of Derbyshire marble, casting reflections off bronze marquetry and porcelain plaques, and pale blue Wedgwood vases held bouquets of summer blossoms.

Samantha's attention was drawn to the bed where Dr. Masefield was bending over its unseen occupant: velvet and satin topaz draperies hung from the canopy in festoons of tassels and fringe. She held back a moment, too spellbound to move.

"Miss Hargrave."

Samantha drew near, holding the lamp high, and received a second shock. Estelle Masefield was the most beautiful woman she had ever seen.

A corona of corn-silk hair spilled over the satin pillow, rippling like liquid with each motion of the delicate head. Her skin was pale as an infant's, her cheeks crested with crimson: roses on snow. When her saffron lashes fluttered, Samantha glimpsed eyes the color of violets, sprinkled with gold flecks. Her nose was narrow and classical, the heart-shaped face tapered to a perfect chin; altogether the image of the goddesses in the painting over the fireplace.

Dr. Masefield was holding a bird wrist in his fingers. "She has a high fever. I want it kept down. Use this, the temperature must not go above one hundred and two." He picked up a thermometer from the nightstand; it was metal and ten inches long and was to be held in the patient's armpit for five minutes.

Mrs. Masefield groaned and rolled her head from side to side.

"She will have periods of clarity. Tell her who you are—she already knows about you—and that I've gone to deliver a baby on Mulberry Street. If the temperature goes above one hundred and two, bathe her in this." He indicated a bottle of alcohol on the table. "From head to foot. Remove all blankets and her nightgown. Continue the sponging until the temperature is down. I shall try not to be gone long."

He started to turn away, then paused. "My wife has leukemia, Miss Hargrave. Her blood is so thin that she is susceptible to frequent infections, which can easily lead to pneumonia if unchecked. She has already suffered several bouts of pneumonia and now has so many adhesions on the pleura and pericardium that she is in constant pain and her circulation and respiration are so poor that the barest exertion debilitates her. You are not to leave her side for even a moment. If you must, pull that rope. It rings in Mrs. Wiggen's room."

He turned abruptly and, without another word or glance at the woman in the bed, walked out.

Samantha had only just pulled a chair up to the bedside when there came a soft knocking at the door. Mrs. Wiggen's head came through and she whispered, "How is she?"

"She's asleep."

The housekeeper came all the way in, clutching a wool shawl around her shoulders, and shuffled to the foot of the bed. Her lumpy face softened as she sadly shook her head. "Poor man, as if he hadn't enough with the rest of Manhattan to look after." She turned a pitying smile to Samantha. "I had her all last night. I expect that's why he called you in, wanted me to get a bit of sleep. But how could I sleep with my angel suffering so? You can go to bed, Miss Hargrave. I'll see to her now."

"Dr. Masefield asked me, Mrs. Wiggen, and I gave him my word not to leave her."

For a moment the housekeeper's little currant eyes flared and her lipless mouth worked in and out over false teeth. Then her shoulders drooped and she said, "Ah well, I suppose you're right. I'll fetch us some tea, as it'll be a long night."

While Mrs. Wiggen was gone Samantha took Mrs. Masefield's temperature and was relieved to see it was only a hundred. She sat on the edge of her chair and studied the delicate profile, the blond lashes resting on the flushed cheeks, the childlike transparency of her skin, with a tracery of blue veins beneath. Estelle Masefield couldn't yet be thirty years old.

Mrs. Wiggen came back with a tray of tea and Scottish shortbread, placing it all on a low ivory-inlaid table between two Queen Anne chairs before the fire. "Come along, Miss Hargrave, it's not necessary to sit right on top of her."

Hesitantly, Samantha joined the housekeeper, but shifted her chair around so that she could keep an eye on Mrs. Masefield's face. As Mrs. Wiggen poured, she said, "Sad turn of events."

"Has she had it long?"

"No, stricken early last year, she was. Only twenty-eight years old. They didn't know what it was at first. She started getting weak after just a little exercise, and then there were the fainting spells. We all thought she was pregnant, which would have been so nice since they were desperate for children. They've only been married three years, you know. But then they found these lumps in her neck and Dr. Washington was doing some fancy experimenting with a microscope and took a look at some drops of her blood. Now I don't understand it like Dr. Masefield does, but it has something to do with things going funny in her blood."

Samantha looked over at the wraithlike creature lying beneath the satin coverlet; Estelle Masefield looked barely more than a child.

"It wasn't long after that Dr. Masefield decided to bring her to New York."

Samantha blinked at Mrs. Wiggen. "Where did they come from?"

"Why, Philadelphia, of course! And what a life *that* was! They had a grand house on Rittenhouse Square and mingled with only the very best society. There were parties and balls, never a quiet moment in that house because my little angel was so full of life and loved to be surrounded by people all the time. And Dr. Masefield, why, he was one of the most prominent physicians in that city. Lectured at the university, he did, and only the best families were his patients. Not like now." Mrs. Wiggen heaved a ragged sigh and sipped her tea. "Oh my, but those were the days . . ."

"Why did they leave?"

The housekeeper's face darkened, her voice dropped, mindful of the third occupant in the room. "Leukemia's a funny thing, Miss Hargrave. It's one of those illnesses people don't like to be around, although for the life of me I can't imagine why. Some think it's catching, I guess. You know how people are about cancer. Right away her friends fell off, all making excuses. And because of getting tired so easily, and then the pneumonia problem, Estelle was confined to the house and that was like putting a bird in a box. She started to waste away, like a flower needing the sun. Poor Dr. Masefield, he was beside himself. Many's the night I heard him crying all by himself—"

Mrs. Wiggen, suddenly remembering herself, cast a quick glance at

Samantha. "Oh well, that's all in the past now. And I guess if he hasn't told you any of it, then it's not my place to be telling you."

"But about the illness," she urged gently. "You can tell me about that, if I'm to take proper care of her."

"I only know as much as Dr. Masefield has told me, and what I've seen with my own eyes. Leukemia takes different people different ways. Some die right off, others linger and linger, like my poor angel there. Some days she's like her old self, happy as a little lark and fit to go for a carriage ride, and the next she's weak as a newborn kitten and I have to do for her."

Samantha kept her eyes on the golden head on the pillow. "What is the prognosis?"

"What's the what?"

"The probable outcome. Will she ever get well?"

Mrs. Wiggen bowed her head. "That's the tragedy of it. She's never going to get well, my poor little angel. She's only going to get worse. And that's all the future they've got, Dr. Masefield and his wife. There's no hope for children now." Mrs. Wiggen raised her head and tears tumbled freely down her cheeks. "You see, Miss Hargrave, that's why he brought her to Manhattan. *To die here.*"

Samantha touched the housekeeper's arm. "But why would he do that?"

"Because being near their friends but having no one come by was more than he could bear. I once overheard him begging—" Mrs. Wiggen pulled a handkerchief out of her apron and blew noisily into it. "He didn't want Estelle to die knowing her friends had abandoned her. So he made up a story, said he *had* to come here for professional reasons, and she doesn't know the truth."

"Surely not all abandoned her!"

"No, there were a few young ladies who kept coming by, but it was after the doctor they were! Dr. Masefield's a handsome man; they were thinking he's going to be a widower soon and—" Remembering herself again, Mrs. Wiggen waved a pudgy hand. "It's time to check her temperature."

He came home just before dawn. After looking in on his wife and seeing that her temperature had dropped and she was sleeping peacefully, like Mrs. Wiggen in her chair, Dr. Masefield went down to the study and poured himself a glass of brandy. Samantha followed.

"She had a quiet night, Dr. Masefield," she said, folding her arms into the warmth of her shawl.

"Thank you."

"Did you have a boy or a girl?"

"Boy."

The parlor was dark, but the first pale wash of dawn could be seen in the crack between the curtains. "Tell me about your wife's illness, Dr. Masefield," Samantha said softly.

He downed the brandy and poured himself a second. He didn't look at her as he said, "Leukemia is thought to be a form of cancer: cause unknown. It can strike anyone at any age in life, rich or poor, is sometimes fatal within days, sometimes will not lead to death for three or more years. Symptoms are: weakness, anemia, and hemorrhaging. Complications are: pneumonia and tumors. There is no cure and no one survives."

"I'm sorry," she whispered.

He raised his head and stared at her for a long moment. Then he said with great weariness, "Go to bed, Miss Hargrave, you look done in."

Samantha eased herself between the sheets and lay perfectly still, troubled by thoughts. The fabulous house on Rittenhouse Square, the glittering society, the whirl of parties and balls, fame and prominence in medicine. Joshua Masefield had given all that up because of his wife's illness . . .

Samantha stared at the ceiling, at the ribbon of sunlight breaking through the curtains. It wasn't right. It didn't follow. Something was wrong; a piece was missing from the puzzle. His ailing wife couldn't be the only reason for leaving that fabulous life. Hidden somewhere beneath the protective layers, Samantha was certain, was another answer, possibly the real answer to Joshua Masefield's sudden desire to withdraw and cut himself off from all contact with the world. And whatever it was, he was using his wife's illness as the excuse . . .

SEVEN

A SLUGGISH SUMMER ROLLED OVER NEW YORK AND A FEW record-high temperatures caused outbreaks of violence in the Bowery and rampant fevers which not even the famous Croton water could curb. Growler gangs kept the Metropolitan Police busy. President Hayes and his teetotaling wife "Lemonade Lucy" retired to the summer White House in Spiegel Grove, Ohio, and Joshua Masefield's office was busier than ever.

Samantha was able to observe the entire spectrum of ailments known to mankind; she watched and listened and committed to memory. Dr. Masefield taught her the uses and proper handling of his many tools: bone-handled scalpels and amputation saws; lancets for bleeding; German aneurysm needles; French catheters; stone crushers; anal and vaginal specula; silver tongue depressors, and tonsil guillotines.

His collection lacked nothing. Joshua Masefield had a brand-new Helmholz ophthalmoscope; copper enema syringes; trocars and tourniquets; medicine cups and porcelain pap boats; folding lorgnettes and quizzing glasses. There was even an apparatus for administering ether.

His pharmacy was just as impressive; Samantha read the labels, recognizing a few from her days with Hawksbill, and tried to memorize the purpose and correct dosage of each: white, yellow and gray powders; red and blue liquids; pastes and pills; jellies and ointments; shelves upon shelves of bottles and tins and boxes. Dr. Masefield's cupboard was so well stocked he rarely had to write out a recipe for a patient to carry to a drugstore.

The swollen patient load forced Samantha to give up her status as mere observer; once a patient was seen, Dr. Masefield would have Samantha apply the poultice or change the dressing or inject the pain reliever while he moved on to the next patient. Their days were hectic with rarely a break for lunch. The entry hall was constantly packed with crying babies and rash-covered children, old men with hacking coughs, and laborers with weepy eyes. At night the house was always silent with Samantha reading in her room or sitting with Estelle Masefield while the doctor retired to his study or went out on a house call. Even Sundays saw patients during this burden-some summer, but Joshua insisted Samantha continue to take her regular Sundays off. She introduced Louisa to Luther Arndt, the affable blond youth who made the weekly deliveries from DeWinter's Drug Store, and the three of them began sharing weekly adventures.

Samantha came to know Manhattan as well as any native. They rode arch-roofed buses down Fifth Avenue, marveling at the stately mansions that flanked the narrow cobblestoned street. They passed brownstones and Gothic churches and the new St. Luke's Hospital, counting off the street numbers that rose higher and higher as they went north, Fifty-fifth, Fifty-sixth, until they came to the edge of the city and the beginning of wilderness. The gay threesome explored Central Park with its shanties and squatters' farms, laughed at the new monstrosity called the Dakota (so called for its distance from the city), and visited the isolated Museum of Natural History. Walking a rural lane, Luther Arndt showed his two companions the farm on the corner of Seventy-first and Madison where he had first lived after coming from Germany.

They bought sausages and apples and had picnics on the grassy banks overlooking the Hudson River, watching side-wheelers and square-riggers go by. They visited Madison Square and climbed up inside a giant bronze arm that stood on display—an arm big enough to hold people and which, Luther explained, was one day going to be part of an enormous statue that was going to stand in the bay. They went to Macy's and Tiffany's, watched the elegant carriage crowd pull up to Delmonico's; they rode the El and went to see the first span of the not yet completed bridge to Brooklyn. They roamed the sidewalks and byways of New York, listening to street musicians, buying food from vendors and tossing an occasional coin to beggar children, and usually ended, by late afternoon, back in their own neighborhood at DeWinter's Drug Store where Luther worked.

In all that time, Samantha never stopped thinking about Joshua Masefield.

DeWinter's Drug Store never ceased to amaze Samantha. So unlike a chemist's shop back home, it had shining plate-glass windows displaying hernia trusses and uterine pessaries, Dr. Scott's Genuine Electrical Belts, corsets, and breast enlargers. Inside the store, on shelves and beneath glass counters, stood bottles of nostrums and elixirs, tonics and purifiers, compounds and liniments, patent medicine curealls whose labels promised everything: the "bottles of false hope" Dr. Masefield had spoken of. On the tops of the counters were colognes and powders, confections and greeting cards; and along one wall stood the newest touch: the soda fountain.

After his two companions were seated at one of the little tables Mr. DeWinter had installed, Luther would go around the marble-topped counter and draw up three glasses of brown fizzy liquid. It was a new drink made up of carbonic acid and coca juice which many people ingested to calm their nerves.

After joining the young ladies, Luther was not beyond gossiping about the store's customers.

"Do you see that one?" he murmured when a majestic lady with an enormous bustle glided through the door. "That's Mrs. Bowditch, comes in here once a week for a bottle of Bowker's Stomach Bitters."

Samantha and Louisa watched the woman exchange a few words with the portly Mr. DeWinter, then take her wrapped package and leave.

"Mrs. Bowditch," Luther said in a low voice, "is president of the local temperance league. She claims she drinks Bowker's for her indigestion. Every morning and night like clockwork." He emitted a dry laugh. "Bowker's Stomach Bitters is forty-two percent alcohol!"

Luther Arndt was a witty, charming escort who never failed to make Samantha and Louisa laugh. Every Wednesday morning he came by Dr. Masefield's office with the order that had been sent the night before and always had a few words to spare for Samantha. On Sundays, dressed in his best suit and new high-crowned bowler, he would call for her and Louisa and take them around the town. It was not lost on Samantha that he and Louisa were smitten.

"He says he's going to own his own drugstore one day," said Louisa as she and Samantha enjoyed a late afternoon stroll around Washington Square. This was the hour when fashionable society ladies came out in their carriages to be seen; the two eighteen-year-olds loved to stare at the beautiful gowns and parasols. "Luther studied pharmacology in Germany, you know. He says it's only a matter of time before old Mr. DeWinter makes him a partner. And when he does, Luther will be very well off."

"Why, Louisa Binford, you've only known him two months and already you're going to marry him."

"I knew I was going to marry him the instant you introduced us! He's positively *nifty!*" Louisa delicately lifted up her skirts as they stepped off the curb. "A girl has to look out for things like that, Samantha. You aren't going to be single all your life, you know, and you aren't going to be *young* all your life either. Once you pass a certain age, no man is going to want you! It's never too early to start looking for a prospective husband." She cast a sideways glance at her friend. "I don't suppose you have anyone in mind yet?"

"No, no one at all."

Samantha had argued with herself many times, hotly denying the thoughts that crept insidiously into her head during the day while working at his side, or at night as she lay in bed unable to sleep. How could she be falling in love with a man like Joshua Masefield, a man more than twice her age, married, unreachable, untouchable? After three months as his assistant she still knew nothing more about him than she had that first day. The few scraps Mrs. Wiggen occasionally uttered were hardly enough to fill the picture. All Samantha knew was the surface man; Joshua Masefield underneath remained a total stranger.

Samantha was intrigued by him, puzzled by him, but surely not falling in love with him. Especially considering Estelle.

After that first night, Samantha had helped more and more often with Mrs. Masefield, supporting her in the arduous walk from bed to chair, helping her dress, eat, reading to her, reporting what she had seen in Washington Square. "The bustle is getting bigger and little jackets are coming in." Estelle Masefield, so young to be confined to bed, was hungry for news of the social world. Samantha would read to her from the *Register*, citing the impressive lists of names attending Mrs. Astor's famous balls, or who was in Newport this summer. Although they had little in common, Estelle and Samantha formed a gentle friendship. Samantha often looked forward to her afternoons or evenings in that elegant room listening to the soft voice of Estelle reminisce about the grand days in Philadelphia; and Estelle quickly formed a strong attachment to this quiet young woman from England who would listen patiently, who would offer a feminine ear, who would share her views on hemlines and hats and romantic novels.

Although this should have been enough to dispel any thoughts of intimacy with Joshua Masefield, there was more. There was Joshua's attitude toward his wife, and Samantha had witnessed it enough times to know beyond a doubt that Joshua Masefield was desperately in love with Estelle. The gentle way he approached her, the touching devotion in his manner, the love that filled his eyes, and then, later, the way he silently suffered, having been reminded again of the brevity of their life together.

And so, considering all of this, how could Samantha possibly fall in love with him?

EIGHT

*E*ARLY AUTUMN FROST WAS A HARBINGER OF THE FIERCE WINTER TO come and was also a painful reminder to Samantha that, in three months, she would be leaving.

Although the heavy summer load had slackened, Samantha continued to be entrusted with the care of certain patients—women and children—and in October she accompanied Dr. Masefield on her first house visit.

A ragamuffin child had been sent. Joshua picked up his bag and top hat and rapped on Samantha's door. "It's a sick baby and it was a neighbor, not the family, who sent for me. I expect resistance. It might help if I have a woman with me."

They walked streets Samantha wouldn't normally venture into at night, but Dr. Masefield was a familiar figure, a man who was well loved and respected and so could move through the area in safety. This was the section of Manhattan the Bureau of Vital Statistics called the Suicide Ward: Hester Street and Mulberry Bend. People sat on stoops or leaned against lamp-posts, hailing the doctor and his pretty assistant as they passed; Samantha picked her way through garbage and dog dirt and heard shouts and laughter and an occasional song drift down through open windows. For an instant she felt a pang of nostalgia: how like the Crescent this neighborhood was!

The raggedy child met them and led them to a tenement where they had to climb four flights of rickety stairs. On the top landing they came upon an anxious woman who wrung her hands and prattled in Italian. Joshua and Samantha followed her down the hall and came to an open doorway.

It was hard to tell whether this was all one family or several families sharing one dingy flat; whatever, there were a lot of them and they eyed the intruders with suspicion. Samantha stayed close to Dr. Masefield as a large, brutish man in undershirt and suspenders stepped forward. "We don' need no *dottore* here. We take-a care of our own."

From a back room came the fitful mewls of an infant. "I might be able to help," said Joshua softly.

The family drew close as if by herding instinct. Samantha had seen them before, their type, in Dr. Masefield's office, and even farther back, on the Crescent: children with skinny limbs that never saw sunlight, young women worn out before their time, old men with pigeon chests and missing teeth. Every single moment a life of despair.

"Get out," said the big man.

Dr. Masefield removed his top hat. "I'd like to talk with the mother if I may."

A thin young thing with a worried expression stepped around the door. Samantha saw her brown-stained hands and knew she was a cigar roller, one of society's most pitiable creatures, who worked seventeen hours a day seven days a week for a few pennies. And if she missed so much as an hour of work, she would be dismissed and another wretch would eagerly take her place.

The frail thing put a tentative arm on her husband's shoulder. His coarse Sicilian features twisted in misery.

An old woman hobbled forward. "I take-a you," she rasped.

Samantha followed Joshua into the bedroom where they had to step over straw mattresses spread on the floor. In an orange crate beneath the window lay a quiet baby.

"She no eat," crackled the old woman as Joshua knelt by the crate. "She no cry. She no move."

Joshua placed a hand on the infant's cold, clammy skin. "How long has she been like this?"

"Two, three day."

He looked up at Samantha. "*Trismus nascentium*. Infant lockjaw. And they caused it themselves." Very gently he gathered the baby into his arms and cradled it against his chest. As Samantha knelt next to him, he took her hand and delicately placed it on the back of the baby's head. "Do you feel that slight indentation? They lay the infant on its back so that it sleeps with pressure on the occiput. A newborn's skull is soft and malleable, the occipital bone presses against the brain and cuts off circulation to a vital area. The baby soon develops gaspy breathing, is unable to take nourishment and has violent spasms in which the arms and legs go rigid. They call it the nine-day fits because that's as long as the infant can last before it dies. Caught early, it can be saved. Left too long, there is no cure."

Samantha, leaning against him, whispered, "Can you do anything for it?"

"If she's telling the truth, that it's only been two or three days, yes, we can help. All we have to do is lay the baby on its side. That will restore circulation and body functions."

He gently deposited the little thing back in the crate and supported its back by balling up a blanket. Then he stood and Samantha rose with him. They turned to find the entire family clustered in the doorway. "Keep your baby on her side. See that she doesn't roll onto her back and in a few hours she should be all right." They regarded him blankly, so he turned to the old woman. "Do you understand?"

"*Si, si!*" She bobbed up and down. "*Capisco, capisco! Mille grazie, Signor Dottore!*"

He placed his hand lightly on Samantha's arm and guided her through the flat and out into the street. As they walked in and out of the glows of gas lamps, Dr. Masefield said, "Some cases are easy. It's only a matter of basic education. If they do what I said, the baby will be fine tomorrow and able to eat."

She had to walk fast to keep up with his long stride. Samantha didn't speak. She was thinking about how it had felt when he took hold of her hand and placed it against the baby's head. The feel of his hand around hers . . .

—❧—

Dr. Masefield's office saw many prostitutes. For the majority, their story was the same: ignorant girls who, believing the lies of the shipping lines that in America they didn't need money and would be taken care of, had turned over every penny of their savings to buy passage, only to discover the harsh truth at the other end— that American streets were not paved with gold. At the docks they would be met by young Jewish men, charming and smooth ("cadets," they were called, and they made up the majority of pimps in New York), who would invite the girls to a social evening with their own ethnic groups; friends who would help them out with lodging and work. Unable to speak English, trusting and guileless, the girls would seize the invitation, only to find themselves that night the hapless victims of a bordello. With virtue gone after the "initiation," penniless and scared, they rarely tried to escape. And after a while they would come shyly to Dr. Masefield for abortifacients or cures for venereal disease.

The prostitutes were not the only ones who presented ailments related to sex. Overworked immigrant women, for whom a rest from pregnancy would be a blessing, timidly requested contraceptive advice.

"The tragedy is, Miss Hargrave, if their husbands ever found out they would be beaten black and blue. Unfortunately, there is nothing I can prescribe. It is up to the husband to take precautions against conception, for they alone have the one reliable device."

Samantha was asked to leave the room one morning when an anxious young couple, married less than a year, came to Joshua Masefield for advice. Later, after they had gone, he spoke in a clinical tone, as if he were discussing a lanced boil. "The marriage act is painful for the young woman and so it is rarely consummated. She suffers from vaginismus, a contraction of the vaginal muscles during intercourse.

They requested that I go to their home one night and administer ether to the young bride so that the husband may dispense his duty. They desperately want children. Of course their request is out of the question, but I did prescribe a bromide for the young lady to relax her nerves. Ninety percent of vaginismus cases are mentally caused, few have physiological origins."

"Mentally caused?"

"The young lady is either frightened to death of the act or intensely dislikes it, hence she closes up. Rarely will you encounter a case that can be treated surgically or with medication."

Samantha tried to hide her discomfiture. *How queer to speak of such a forbidden subject with a man who is little more than a stranger to me! A subject never mentioned even between husbands and wives! And how am I to respond, I who know nothing of the act other than its mechanics? What does it feel like? Why do some women fear it while others can't seem to get enough of it? What would it be like with him . . .*

Every day they came to him, some women begging for contraceptive advice, others pleading for a way to get pregnant. Motherhood—to some the Devil's own curse; to the rest, God's blessing. Mrs. Malloy, a woman in her late thirties who had never had children and had long since given up, came in one afternoon to proudly show Dr. Masefield the bulge in her abdomen. While Samantha stood at a discreet distance, Joshua Masefield asked the delicate questions: "When was your last menses?" ("A month ago.") "When did you last permit intimacy with your husband?" ("I don't remember.") "Is your bust tender?" ("No.") He went so far as to inspect her wrists and ankles for swelling, but no further. Beaming, blissful, Mrs. Malloy answered all his questions and even permitted a delicate probing of her abdomen through her skirts. When he recommended she get a second opinion from one of the fine surgeons at Woman's Hospital, Mrs. Malloy airily refused. "That won't be necessary, Doctor. I only wanted to confirm my suspicion. I have never seen Mr. Malloy so *happy.* He's painting the nursery right now."

Joshua Masefield had Samantha pour the woman a glass of brandy and then explained as gently as he could that it was not a baby growing in her abdomen but a tumor. Samantha had to dodge the flying glass and later wiped the brandy off the wall, but not until she had spent half an hour helping Joshua calm the woman down and accompany her home.

They rarely drank coffee together, but this afternoon they did, sitting in his study and watching the late autumn shadows gradually lengthen across the carpet. "If Mrs. Malloy were better educated she would have known that a month is not enough time for a pregnancy to show. But, sadly, women are kept ignorant about their bodies and often learn the truth too late."

"What can be done for her?"

"If she is lucky it is nothing more than an ovarian tumor that can be amputated through the smallest incision. Or possibly a fibroid on the uterus. The men at Woman's Hospital have learned to get into the abdomen quickly, excise the mass and close with minimal bleeding."

"And if it is something other than that?"

"Nothing can be done. There are experiments in abdominal surgery being conducted in Germany right now, but so far no one has had any success. There is a man in England who is working on trying to excise the ruptured appendix, but to date all of his patients have died. I have no doubt, Miss Hargrave, that the day will come when abdominal surgery will be routine, but for now, with etherization so dangerous and bleeding uncontrollable, even the most adventuresome surgeon will attempt only the quickest foray into the peritoneal cavity."

Did he always have to speak so? Was he never curious about her; was there no doorway through that professional façade? Samantha had frequently to console herself with a reminder that she was learning more from Joshua Masefield than could be found in a number of college classrooms.

One afternoon Dr. Masefield gave priority to a young Polish garment worker who had run her hand through a sewing machine. Crying and clutching a bloody handkerchief, she was helped into the surgery by one of her co-workers, another thin blond girl no more than sixteen who spoke soothingly in Polish but who then had to hurry back to her own machine.

"Sad cases, these," murmured Dr. Masefield as he gently unwrapped the hand. "She will not be able to work for a few days and so she will lose her job. Then she will lose her small space in a crowded tenement room and will end up with a cadet taking care of her."

Samantha kept an arm around the girl's thin shoulders and saw how pale she was, milky skin that didn't know the sun, and how frayed her blouse and skirt, no doubt the girl's only outfit. From what sort of life in Poland had she fled to come to this? "But there are no factories near here, Dr. Masefield."

He didn't look up from his work. "Most sweatshop work is done in tenements rather than in factories because then the laws governing factory work can't touch them. They are getting away with genocide." He dropped the bloody handkerchief into a bucket. "These poor creatures slave away for twelve hours a day, eat bad food, breathe foul air, sleep with vermin and try to preserve their dignity. In many cases, they were better off in the old country. Here are the wounds."

As he tried to pry open the girl's fingers she shrieked. "Six minims of Magendie's, Miss Hargrave."

He had taught her how to administer narcotics. Samantha measured the morphine in a sweet syrup and gave it to the girl on a spoon.

Dr. Masefield next "froze" the back of her hand with a spray of ether. When the skin was numb, he carefully dropped into each puncture nitric acid, which at once crackled and sent little spirals of smoke up out of the flesh.

The girl screamed and raved in Polish and tried to jump up and run out, but Samantha held her fast. After the little wounds were explored for any fragments of sewing needle, Samantha bandaged the hand and Dr. Masefield gave the girl a small bottle of Magendie's morphine and a piece of paper on which he had written the only Polish he knew: "One teaspoon whenever in pain." To Samantha he said, "We'll dispense with the two-dollar fee."

NINE

*L*ATE ONE EVENING IN THE MIDDLE OF A CRISP NOVEMBER Samantha sat by the fire in her room with a blanket over her legs and a magazine lying forgotten in her lap. That afternoon she had received a note from Dr. Emily informing her she could take up residence at the Infirmary the first week in January. As Samantha listened to the silent house and the lonely wind beyond the curtains, she felt none of the excitement the letter should have generated. In six weeks she would be leaving the Masefields for good.

She gave her head a little shake and picked up the magazine, the latest issue of the *Boston Medical and Surgical Journal.* The first article was titled, "The Woman Question: Or, the Lesser Physician."

The author, a Dr. Charles Gage, made clear his intentions from the outset: he was going to outline *scientific* proof of why women should not become doctors. "No woman, *by her nature,*" the article read, "is fitted to withstand the anxiety, the nervous strain, and shocks of the practice of medicine. Woman, *by nature,* lacks the courage and daring necessary for the making of difficult and oft dangerous decisions incumbent upon the physician. In addition, women are not, *by nature,* free agents but rather prisoners of their own biology: specifically the monthly illness. It is as if the Almighty, in creating the female sex, had taken the uterus and built up a woman around it; what she is in health and character, mind and soul is contingent upon her womb alone. What patient would trust his life in the hands of one whose equilibrium resembled that of a maniac—varying from week to week, now up, now down? The periodic infirmity of woman influences her mental state, she suffers a time in which she is temporarily insane; indeed, on such occasions the woman herself is more in need of medical aid than able to administer it!

"Since it is an accepted fact that the female is inferior to the male and that in the population at large the lower status is to the female, the higher to the male, it is only logical to assume therefore that a profession deluged with females will be lowered in prestige. What society needs women doctors in an age of too much bad piano playing and too little cooking and sewing?"

Samantha closed the journal and recalled an incident just the week before, when Dr. Masefield had been suturing a scalp wound. She had said, "Next, please," and a great bear of a man had lumbered into the study, workman's cap clutched in his meaty hands. When Samantha had asked him his problem, the Irishman had said, "If ya don't mind, miss, Oi'll wait for the doc." Explaining Dr. Masefield's temporary unavailability, Samantha had tried to reassure the man she might be able to help him. To her great astonishment, the Irishman had jumped to his feet, outraged and red-faced, shouted at the indecency of her suggestion, and stormed out. Later, Dr. Masefield had explained: "That would be Roddy O'Dare. He suffers chronically from swelling of the testicles. I quite understand his mortification. From now on, Miss Hargrave, leave the men to me."

Samantha had been annoyed then, just as she was now with the *Boston Journal* in her lap: a woman was expected to discuss with a strange man her most intimate problems, and yet the mere suggestion that the reverse should be done was a moral outrage.

Samantha had started subscribing to a publication called the *Woman's Journal,* edited in Boston by Lucy Stone, and while she did not agree with its overall militant feminism, Samantha saw that the *Journal* championed the cause of women doctors. "Let men not feel too sure that they alone hold the key that unlocks the door to medical science. They bolt and bar the doors of hospitals in Boston against all women medical students and heap upon them undeserving ridicule. Men hold up to the world women's constitutional weakness as if they themselves had no weaknesses whatever. But, aided or unaided, the day is not far distant when women will compel medical men to know that as physicians they are equals."

Recalling Dr. Elizabeth's words of long ago, "They are afraid of us and I don't know why," Samantha wondered about Joshua Masefield. She had encountered no outward prejudice from him; indeed, she suspected he was treating her the same way he would have treated that Cornell student whom she replaced. But what about after she was a practicing physician? Might his attitude change?

The fact that she was going to encounter obstacles in her career Samantha was prepared for. But was she going to start off with a beginning strike against her by graduating from a female college? Would she be considered a quack, as both Louisa and Luther had insisted would happen?

The quandary kept her up all night until, in the hour before dawn, stiff and achy and cold, Samantha unfolded herself from the chair and came to a scary decision.

For the sake of her future she would try to obtain a diploma from one of the recognized male medical colleges. The fact that this meant she would stay on with Dr. Masefield for another nine months had not the slightest influence, Samantha was certain, on her decision.

She was nervous about approaching him. Her biggest dread—that he would try to persuade her to go to the Infirmary and thus leave in five weeks—brought on her old speech problem: each time she worked up the courage to tell him, her tongue failed her.

The first day of December saw a heavy snowfall and by midnight the drifts were so high that the fetlocks of horses were bandaged heavily in calico and few pedestrians were abroad. Samantha could not sleep. Dr. Masefield had gone out after supper to see a child with a high fever and had not yet, by one o'clock, returned. Hearing the snores of Mrs. Wiggen in the next room, Samantha wrapped her dressing gown tightly about herself, picked up a candle and went down the stairs where she looked in on Estelle. Mrs. Masefield slumbered like a child. Trembling with the cold, Samantha descended to the bottom landing, for she intended to go to the kitchen and warm some milk, but was startled by the sudden opening of the front door. An arctic gust blew in, raising her long black hair off her shoulders and extinguishing the candle's flame. Joshua Masefield had to push the door closed with his shoulder, then hurriedly removed his top hat and muffler.

Knocking snowflakes off his arms, he stopped suddenly and looked up. "Miss Hargrave," he said softly.

"I was just going to make some hot milk. How is the child?"

Dr. Masefield finished removing his ulster and hung it on a peg. "Scarlet fever. He won't last another day."

Rubbing his hands together, Joshua strode into the dark study. Samantha heard him strike a match, then saw a glow in the doorway. "Miss Hargrave," he called, "come here by the fire."

Forgetting that she was in her nightclothes, Samantha followed, holding the candle high despite its lack of flame. Dr. Masefield's broad back was bent over the fireplace where he poked at the embers and dropped new coals on them. "It's a hellish night. Come here and warm yourself."

She glided to his side, deposited the candle on the mantel, and when he straightened, Joshua Masefield looked directly at her. He stared down at her for an instant, his black eyes cast in shadow, then he turned abruptly and went to the pedestal table in the corner. "A bit of brandy will help you sleep, Miss Hargrave."

She watched him pour into two glasses and bring them back to the struggling fire. When she took her glass, their fingertips accidentally brushed.

"How is my wife?" he asked quietly, taking a sip.

"She's sleeping comfortably."

He continued to gaze down at her with piercing eyes. "And why couldn't you sleep, Miss Hargrave?"

"I . . ." She fought to command her unwilling voice. "I have something on my mind."

"I suspected so. These last few days you have seemed distracted."

"I hadn't meant it to interfere with my work—"

"It did not. Your work was beyond reproach as usual."

Her thin brows rose. This was the first time, in all their weeks together, he had praised her.

Joshua's handsome features were etched in dark planes; the chiaroscuro heightened his mystique. His nearness, the uncharacteristic softness of his voice, suffused the moment with unexpected intimacy. "Is it something you wanted to discuss with me, Miss Hargrave?"

"Yes . . ." she whispered. Was it her imagination or were his eyes, in their black recesses, now smoldering with passion? She had to look away. "I have been thinking, Dr. Masefield, that I might possibly be making a mistake going to the Infirmary."

When he said nothing, she put her glass on the mantel and walked a few steps away. Out from under the spell of his mesmerizing stare, Samantha felt freer to talk. "I had thought I might do better to attend a regular male college, as Dr. Blackwell did, for such a diploma would serve me well in the face of possible future adversity. I wish to be the best possible doctor."

To her immense surprise, he said, "I agree."

She swung around. "You do?"

"But you will have the devil of a time finding such a school."

"I'm prepared for that," she said in a rush. "I can only do my best effort and, if I fail, then I will go to the Infirmary. But I cannot go straight there without at least trying."

"How do you propose going about getting into such a school?"

"I was hoping that you would help me . . ."

"Then I shall." Joshua drained his glass and strode back to the pedestal table. "We will draw up a list of likely schools and I shall draft a letter of recommendation. I am not without some influence in the medical field."

Samantha gazed at him in disbelief. "Then it is all right if I stay on here?"

"Of course. We will aim for next September, in which time you will have completed one year of apprenticeship."

"Dr. Masefield, I don't know how to thank—"

He kept his back to her. "I am acting out of selfish motives, Miss Hargrave. I will have your excellent assistance for another nine months and

Estelle will continue to have your company, which she so cherishes. And now"—he finally turned around—"it is late."

Samantha blinked a few times; she suddenly had a picture of how she must look—standing there in her dressing gown with her long black hair hanging in disarray down to her waist. Instantly embarrassed, she hurried to the door. "Good night, Dr. Masefield, and thank you so much."

He stood for a very long time staring after her, listening to her footsteps fade at the top of the stairs, ending with the closing of her door. Then he looked down at the glass in his hand and saw that his fingers clutched it so tightly that his whole arm shook.

TEN

*E*STELLE ENJOYED A SPELL OF WHAT APPEARED TO BE A STEP TO-ward recovery: during February and March, despite the penetrating damp and biting cold, she was able to rise out of bed on her own and take little walks around the room. These were interludes of joy for Samantha, seeing the color of peaches return to that pallid complexion. But Joshua Masefield refused to be lured into false hope and so was not as devastated as Samantha when Estelle's relapse hit harder and more cruelly than ever. This was a few days before Memorial Day.

It was a new holiday recently established to honor the Civil War dead, and secret plans had been spun between Samantha and Estelle to ride in a carriage to Fifth Avenue and watch the parade. There would be brass bands, firemen pulling their pumping engines, splendid ranks of Civil War veterans in their blue uniforms, followed by veterans of the Mexican War and even a few old-timers from the War of 1812. Then they were going to cajole Joshua into taking them to Central Park for a picnic of fried chicken and homemade pickles and angel food cake. But a week before the event Estelle caught a draft and collapsed in a fever so merciless they all feared they were going to lose her.

It hurt Samantha to see the life rapidly fade from the angelic face. It pained her even more to watch Joshua spend endless hours at the bedside. Her love for them both drove Samantha to question, for the first time in her life, the so-called justice and compassion of the Almighty.

Louisa's pragmatic attitude nettled Samantha. "Grieving isn't going to cure her. Face it, the woman is dying. And when she's gone he'll be free to marry."

In a glib moment, back in March, they had sat by a roaring fire cutting out Easterchicky decals for boiled eggs that were going to the children of Bellevue Hospital (in honor of yet another new national holiday declared by President Hayes), and the two friends had shared a few moments of feminine intimacy. Louisa had voiced her suspicion that Luther now reciprocated her deep affection, and Samantha, in return, had finally confessed her tender feelings for Joshua Masefield.

Now she regretted that candid moment and wished she had kept her secret locked in her heart, for Louisa was once again putting into words the dark hopes that Samantha feared to admit to herself. "Estelle won't die soon, Louisa. A person can live with leukemia for as long as ten years. By then I shall be gone from here."

But Louisa's elfin eyes glinted knowingly and she gave that toss of her honey-gold curls which always meant: We all know better than that, don't we?

❈

In June the responses to Samantha's applications to twenty-six medical schools started to come in.

"Madam," read one from a prominent upstate college. "Do yourself and society a favor by abandoning this insanity and returning to the teachings you learned at your mother's knee. Only a young lady of questionable moral character would make application into a male medical school."

Another read, "I urge you to remember, Miss Hargrave, the Creation: women were an afterthought."

Although she had been prepared for rejection, Samantha was surprised and dismayed at the strong tone; judging by the vitriolic content of a few, she had, for some reason, aroused masculine indignation. As more letters came in, ranging from polite rejections to out-and-out condemnation of her actions, Samantha became angered. The letter from Harvard University brought her to the decision that she must make a move to defend herself.

June 10, 1879

My dear Madam:

While I personally found your application into our medical school exemplary and beyond fault, and while I found nothing in the School's statutes denying women the right to attend lectures, I was nonetheless prevailed upon by my colleagues to present your petition to the Student Body for the final vote. The following is their response.

"Resolved, that no woman of true delicacy would be willing in the presence of men to listen to the discussions of subjects that necessarily come under the consideration of the student of medicine.

"Resolved, that we object to having the company of any female forced upon us, who is disposed to unsex herself and to sacrifice her modesty by appearing with men in the lecture room."

The consensus, therefore, Miss Hargrave, among the Student Body and Faculty was to deny your application. I sincerely wish you luck elsewhere.

The letter was signed by Oliver Wendell Holmes, dean of the Harvard Medical School.

"Sixteen rejections, Dr. Masefield, and not one of them offering a reason other than that I am a woman. I cannot stand by and let them debase me so, merely because of the accident of birth."

"What do you intend to do?"

She looked at the letter in her hand. "I will go to Boston."

She had gathered from the tone of his letter that Dr. Holmes was a reasonable man; Samantha felt confident that if she could appear in person and present her case and demonstrate her worthiness, *show* them that she wasn't "just a female" but a serious student of medicine, he would use his influence to sway the students' vote.

She was gone for two days, and when Dr. Masefield met her at the train station in a hired carriage, he saw at once that she had failed.

They rode home in silence. Entering the house, Samantha handed her bonnet and cape to a solicitous Mrs. Wiggen, then sank into one of the chairs in the parlor. Joshua Masefield stood by the fireplace. "Tell me what happened."

Samantha rested her head back and stared at the ceiling. "I had an interview with Dr. Holmes and, although he was very kind, he couldn't open himself, as he put it, to abuse and criticism. It is not only the university, he said, that would disapprove, but the Massachusetts Medical Society as well. He said that they had voted to keep me out so that they may preserve the dignity of the school. He said that my presence would undermine their prestige."

Joshua arched one eyebrow.

"I told him that I was willing to enter into any agreement and accept any conditions they cared to impose upon me, providing I still received the diploma in the end. But there was the rub. Four faculty members were impressed with my presenting qualifications, which exceed, they said, the qualifications of many of the male students, and these four were willing even to instruct me, but they would not, because I am a woman, approve of my being granted the Harvard degree. It might degrade their diploma, they said."

Samantha looked at Joshua. "Do you know what else Dr. Holmes said? That the students regarded a woman's presence in the classroom as socially repulsive." She brought a fist to her eyes. "Dear God, socially repulsive . . ."

Dr. Masefield pushed away from the mantel and sat in the next chair. "Did he offer any recommendation?"

"Yes." She brought her hands down. "He said that the University of Michigan is now accepting women students into their medical school and he would gladly write a letter of recommendation for me."

Joshua's eyes flickered. "Michigan," he murmured. "So far away . . ."

"Is it so hopeless, Dr. Masefield? Must I surrender before there has even been a fight? I have no weapons. My qualifications count for nothing when they see that I am a woman!"

He gazed at her a moment longer and then, unspeaking, got up and left the parlor. Samantha remained seated, wringing her hands, water rising in her eyes as frustration turned to disappointment. She did not at first see what he held out to her, had to blink away the tears, then she heard him say, "These came while you were gone. I took the liberty of opening them."

Samantha took the two envelopes without looking up at him. The first was from the University of Pennsylvania School of Medicine; an apology to Dr. Masefield for not being able to accommodate his fine apprentice "as we have not the proper facilities to accommodate female students." Samantha tossed it to the floor. With a sense of fatalism, she read the second:

June 14, 1879

Dear Miss Hargrave:

As your petition for entrance into our School came to us unprecedented, and as our statutes make no provisions for such an instance, we of the Lucerne Faculty put your application before the general Student Body for a vote. Their response is as follows.

"Resolved, that one of the radical principles of a Republican Government is the universal education of both sexes; that to every branch of scientific education the door should be open equally to all; that the application of Samantha Hargrave to become a member of our class meets our entire approbation; and in extending our unanimous invitation we pledge ourselves that no conduct of ours shall cause her to regret her attendance at this institution."

You are advised, Miss Hargrave, to take up lodging within the week prior to the start of the new term, which is the last Monday in September, and to report to my office on the morning of that day.

Yours Respectfully,
Henry Jones, M.D.
Dean, Lucerne Medical College

Samantha was held for a frozen instant, poised at the edge of her seat, eyes still fixed to the letter, then she looked up and whispered, "They want me?"

"Congratulations."

Samantha sprang up from her chair and impulsively threw her arms around his neck. "They want me, Dr. Masefield, they want me!"

Stunned, Joshua stumbled back a step. Samantha twirled away from him, pressing the letter to her breast, and danced around the room. He watched her pirouette like a ballet dancer in and but of the golden sunlight coming through the window, her face glowing. Then Joshua Masefield turned away, unable to watch any longer.

ELEVEN

*I*T WAS A STILTED FAREWELL BENEATH THE STRIPED AWNINGS OF the new Grand Central Terminal. Dr. Masefield, having seen to Samantha's tickets and luggage, gave her gloved hand a perfunctory squeeze and returned to his cab, leaving her to stand and watch him ride away down Forty-second Street.

As the train lurched and pulled out a few minutes later, Samantha was reminded of departures and farewells in her past and thought that surely this had been the most painful. At the last moment she had questioned the wisdom of this move: attending the Blackwells' Infirmary would have kept her close to him. And then two more acceptances had come in, both from colleges closer to home. But Dr. Masefield knew of Lucerne's excellent reputation and insisted Samantha seize the opportunity. After that there had been the painful good-by to Estelle, whose violet eyes had held the unspoken fear that she would not, in all probability, be alive to see Samantha return. Even Mrs. Wiggen had embraced Samantha, and both Louisa and Luther, with misty eyes, had heartily promised to send many letters.

Sad though the departure was, Samantha had one consolation: in nine months she would be back.

-❦-

It was a long and wearisome journey. The town of Lucerne, located three hundred miles from Manhattan on the northern tip of Canandaigua (the "thumb" of the Finger Lakes), was reached by traveling first to Albany, then transferring to the train bound for Rochester, following the Mohawk River, switching over at Newark to a local which passed through Geneva on Seneca Lake, and from there hiring a carriage to go the last sixteen miles. In all it took Samantha two days and a night, bringing her to the steps of Lucerne's one hotel late the second evening.

Samantha knew nothing of the place that was to be her home for the next nine months, knew nothing of the narrow, provincial minds that were soon to bring anger and frustration. For now, it looked a peaceful town on the edge of a peaceful lake. Tomorrow she would register at school, find a place to live, and next week start classes. It was all going very well.

-❦-

"*Who* did you say you are?"

A little taken aback by the man's reaction, Samantha primly repeated herself.

He seemed to bluster a little behind his spectacles, then Dr. Jones occupied himself with shuffling papers on his desk. "I see. Yes. Hargrave. You petitioned us last June."

Samantha shifted uneasily in her chair. The dean's manner sent off small alarms in her head. "I trust everything is in order, Dr. Jones. I have come at the right time, haven't I? Your letter said—"

"Yes, yes." He waved a pudgy hand. "I know what my letter said. It's just that . . ." His words fell off and he stared at her owlishly. "Well, to be frank, Miss Hargrave, you are not at all as I imagined you. *Not at all!*"

She raised her eyebrows. "Am I offensive in some way?"

"Dear heavens, no! Quite the contrary, Miss Hargrave!" His face went the color of a radish. "I mean, we had been expecting someone . . . *older.*"

"I'm not disqualified, am I?"

He shook his head and rubbed his whiskers in dismay. "Ah well. You're here now, aren't you? Dear heavens, but this *will* cause a stir." He fussed with the paper a bit more and withdrew a printed sheet of foolscap. "You'll have to fill this out. Statistics for our records. Return it to my secretary any time this week."

Samantha carefully folded the paper and put it in her reticule. "Dr. Jones, I was wondering if you could help me find residence. I am currently at the hotel and it's frightfully expensive—"

"We have a few boarding houses here, Miss Hargrave, but all the young men fill them up. A female student, you know, is highly irregular."

Samantha frowned. Dr. Jones had written the letter of acceptance; why did he now seem to be trying to discourage her?

She rose smoothly. "Thank you, Dr. Jones. When do I report for class?"

"Monday, eight o'clock sharp."

"And where?"

"Report to my office first."

Finding a place to live turned out to be impossible. Word had spread so rapidly through the small town that Samantha soon found herself already known to landladies and being turned down before she could even knock on the door. By late afternoon she had visited nine boardinghouses and had received nine flat refusals.

There was a tearoom in the hotel for ladies only where no smoking or strong drink was allowed. Samantha took a table by the window and ordered a cucumber sandwich. Resting her chin in her hands, she gazed out at the pleasant afternoon and fought the cloud of depression that was threatening to descend.

In her day of walking she had found Lucerne to be a quiet town of tree-lined streets and white clapboard colonial houses. Samantha had delighted in the changing colors of the elms and oaks, the ripe apples hanging from their branches, the grassy pastures of buttercups and goldenrod. She had paused to watch red-shouldered hawks soar against the clear sky and to observe little boys dangle their fishing lines into the lake's edge, their baskets filled with trout and perch. Butterflies, lady beetles and mosquitoes congested the early autumn air and an occasional cool gust rippled the glassy surface of the lake to remind everyone that summer was ending.

But it hadn't been enough. The tranquillity of the town, the polite nods and smiles from passers-by, the lazy pace so inviting after hectic Manhattan—none of these had been able to shake from Samantha a feeling of alienation and utter dejection.

Samantha heard a throaty voice declare, "So here you are, and it's disappointed I am!"

Startled, she looked up. The woman stood with her hands on her wide hips, her head tilted to one side. Her thick red hair was piled on top of her head and her freckled face was molded in amusement. "I beg your pardon?" said Samantha.

"I'd been hopin' you had two heads, for all they've been sayin' about you. And so I come all the way here to catch a look at you, and what a disappointment you are!"

Samantha stared at the woman in bewilderment.

"Hannah Mallone's the name and it's pleased to meet you I am!" The woman thrust out a gloved hand, which Samantha accepted.

Hannah Mallone drew the opposite chair out and sat, uninvited, with a creaking of corset stays. She was an ample-figured woman with a large bosom and an even larger bustle and a lusty voice that was thick with Irish brogue. "I've heard about your trouble, darlin', and I don't mind sayin' it gets me temper up!"

"I've had nine doors slammed in my face today. Can you tell me why?"

"It's no one wants a freak in their home, darlin'!"

"Freak?"

Hannah's amber eyes softened, turned to honey, and her voice smoothed to velvet. "Ah, you poor darlin'. It's me whole sympathy you've got, and that's for sure. When I heard only an hour ago down at Mr. Kendall's Dry Goods about this brazen young tart that was walkin' our streets in broad daylight and thinkin' she could find lodgin' in one of our fine houses and all the chicken-chatter about how you've no shame and what's the world comin' to when women like you can come a-waltzing into Lucerne like as you please—"

"Women like me?"

"It's you're a fallen woman they're thinkin'."

Samantha drew back, stunned.

"You poor darlin', you had no idea? There's minds in this town so narrow you couldn't pass a thread through them. They don't want no female medical student and that's the fact of it. Some o' those places you went had plenty of rooms to let but not to the likes of a woman they'll be callin' scarlet. I can sympathize with you, darlin', because I've had me share o' that prejudice here, too."

Samantha frowned. "I received letters from medical schools telling me I had no morals for wanting to become a doctor, that no *decent* woman would have such an ambition." She turned her head and squinted through the lace curtain, recalling Dr. Jones's odd behavior. "Now I'm beginning to wonder why *this* school accepted me . . ."

"Sure and that's nothing to worry about now. It's a place to live you need."

Samantha brought her head about. "Can you help me?"

"It's a big house I've got and what with my husband gone for most of the time I get an awful loneliness! It'd be nice to have some company."

Samantha liked Hannah Mallone's face. It was square and honest and the amber eyes sparkled with vitality. "That's very kind of you, Mrs. Mallone."

"And you'll start by callin' me Hannah!"

The Mallone house was indeed a large one, a two-story colonial set on a large tract of grassy land near the edge of town. When Sean Mallone and his new wife had come to Lucerne fifteen years before, it had been with the intention of raising a large family. Now, however, most of the upstairs rooms stood empty.

"We're not far from the suspender factory," said Hannah over tea that evening. "Sean worked there awhile before he went a-trappin'."

Samantha looked around the oversized living room. "It's such a large place, Hannah. Why don't you let some rooms on a regular basis?"

"Sean wouldn't have it. Black Irish he is, just as I'm red. Got pride stiffer than pokers, have the black Irish, and Sean is the worst of them! Don't want the town to think we need the money. It's a good living Sean earns, and when the day comes we've enough, Sean'll hang up his gear and stay with me for good."

"What did you say your husband does?"

Hannah pushed herself out of her easy chair and went to a drum table by the window. She was dressed now in a flouncy green gown with deep sleeves and ruffles. Hannah despised the confinements of women's dress—the painful corsets, the pounds of skirt, the hems dragging through the dirt—and always rebelled in her own home.

She picked up a daguerreotype and brought it back to Samantha. "That's my Sean. Got the blood of ancient Irish kings in him, he has."

Samantha was impressed. Leaning casually on his wheel-lock rifle with a rakish smile on his handsome face, Sean Mallone was dressed in buckskins and furs with the pelt of an animal spread before his feet.

"When I first met Sean sixteen years ago he was workin' at the brick kilns at Haverstraw. But it was the outdoors and freedom he yearned for, not slavin' like a navvy to an early death. He come to Manhattan to look at prospects and that was where we met. I was twenty-four years old then. I'd come to America on one o' them sailin' ships that rescued the Irish from the famine. By the time I met Sean I'd been here four years . . ."

Samantha looked up from the daguerreotype. Hannah's voice grew distant. "Sure and it was a harsh life for a twenty-year-old girl whose ma and da had died on board and whose poke had been stolen by other thievin' Irish. I landed on American shores without a penny. Just me flamin' red hair and me pride . . ."

She shook her head. "But *that's* in the past now. Sean saved me from a killin', he did. I was bein' beaten bad in an alley and so severe that I knew all the saints couldn't help me. And then this big brainless bear of a County Cork man came out o' nowhere and bashed the bastard's brains over a barrel!

"Sean didn't care about me past, that I wasn't no Virgin Mary, he loved me just for me. He'd heard there was a bounty up here, twenty dollars on panthers, thirty on timber wolves. So we come to Lucerne. The game's gettin' scarcer, so he has to go farther north. He's gone most o' the year now, but he comes back with a good poke and sometimes a nice beaver pelt to make me a muff. It's a good life we've got, I only regret I didn't give him no kids."

"There's time yet," said Samantha gently.

"God bless ya, girl, but it ain't so! I'm forty years old. After sixteen years o' tryin'—" Hannah tossed back her head and let out a lusty laugh. "Jesus, Joseph and Mary how we tried!" She smiled at Samantha. "That's one thing about the man I married. He don't hold it against me I'm barren."

Hannah clapped her hands together. "Well now, darlin', it's weary to the bones you must be. I'll stop me spoutin' and let you be off. I've a notion you'll be needin' your strength in the days to come!"

It wasn't only strength Samantha needed but a deaf ear and a blind eye as well. At first it shocked her, the attitude of the citizens of Lucerne, but her surprise quickly waxed into anger. As if she had a disease, the women would cross the street so as not to share the sidewalk with her, whispering behind their parasols and shaking their heads. Children jeered and taunted, following behind and chanting: "Doctor, Doctor in petticoats, do you cure corns or do you cure throats?" The men no longer doffed their hats and she felt curtains move away from windows she passed.

Having filled out Dr. Jones's statistical sheet, she returned it one afternoon to the school. A few students, with nothing to do, loitered against the pillars of the ostentatious Roman porch; they fell silent as she passed, stared rudely, then erupted in laughter behind her back. Dr. Jones's secretary, a young man suffering from *rigor mortis,* gingerly took the sheet without a word and deposited it on the dean's desk. The professor was nowhere about.

"I wonder if I'm up to it, Hannah. Two years of this, I don't know," she said that evening as they prepared supper together.

"Sure you are, darlin'." Hannah was stirring a custard in a shallow brass preserving pan; she had dropped ten marbles in it to prevent the mixture from sticking. "It'll pass, you'll see. You're a novelty now, but in time they'll get bored with you and look for someone else to crucify. D'you think it was easy for me and Sean, a couple o' scruffy Irish in a pointy-nosed Protestant town? But they've gotten used to us now, as they will to you."

Samantha forced a smile and ran her sleeve across her forehead. Perhaps Hannah was right: it would be difficult for a while, but then everything would eventually be all right.

TWELVE

*A*GAIN THAT ODD BEHAVIOR. AS THOUGH HE HAD HOPED SHE would somehow vanish. On the first Monday morning of classes Samantha presented herself at Dr. Jones's office. He seemed a jumble of surprise, dismay, and annoyance. After a few distracted words to her about ladylike deportment, the roly-poly dean led her upstairs to the first lecture theater.

He didn't take her through the main door. Instead, Samantha was escorted into a small anteroom which, Dr. Jones explained, was used for patients and lecturers waiting to take the stage. He insisted she sit. Then, with a ceremonious straightening of his waistcoat, the professor entered the theater.

Samantha had heard, through the closed door, a thunderous rumble of stamping feet, hooting and howling; but as soon as the dean appeared, the theater fell silent.

Both Dr. Masefield and Emily Blackwell had warned her of this: the accepted rowdiness of a medical class. Medical students had the universal reputation of being wild young men who expelled their energies in the classroom; even the great Dr. Lister, speaking at University College in London, had barely been heard above the rude catcalls and stamping feet of the students. Perhaps this was the cause of Dr. Jones's nervousness: what mayhem might result from the intrusion of a beautiful young *female* student?

He was addressing the class. Samantha did not wonder at their unexpected politeness; they were probably very curious to hear what he had to say. His voice was muffled. She couldn't catch one word,

When the door opened, she started. "Miss Hargrave?"

She rose gracefully and followed Dr. Jones into the theater.

Bright morning sunlight pierced the high windows and flooded the room. The transition from the dark antechamber made Samantha wince. To her left, as she crossed the platform, was a wall covered with anatomical charts and blackboards; to her right, rising in horseshoe tiers up to the windows, were silent, staring young men. The only sound in the still morning air was the whisper of her skirts across the floor boards. Dr. Jones escorted her to a special desk, at the edge of the platform and separate from all the others, and Samantha sat, her back to the class. She removed her hat and slid it under her seat. Then she opened the notebook she had brought, dipped her pen in the inkhorn and gazed expectantly at the lecturer.

Both men stood like a daguerreotype. Portly Dr. Jones and tall and lanky Dr. Page. Behind her, a hundred and nineteen young men sat like statues.

Then, remembering himself, Dr. Jones suddenly cleared his throat, nodded curtly at the perplexed Dr. Page and walked out as quickly as his short legs would allow.

Blinking, Dr. Page adjusted his spectacles, sniffed a little, then reached for his notes and said in an uncertain voice, "The circulation of the coronary arteries, the aortic arch, and the four chambers of the heart."

Behind her, over the pounding of her own heart, Samantha heard a collective sigh followed by the rustling of notebooks and the shifting of feet.

For two hours Dr. Page spoke. Uninterrupted. Unchallenged. Every so often he paused and looked at the new student, her head bent, her pen scratching across paper, and he would blink in bafflement. In all his years of teaching he had never had so quiet a class. The young men were actually taking notes!

At the end of the lecture Dr. Jones appeared in the doorway across the platform. Samantha gathered up her things, walked over to him and disappeared into the antechamber. The instant the door closed behind her, the theater burst into whoops and thundering feet.

"I'm to do that every day for two years," she said to Hannah that evening by the fire.

"You don't sound pleased with your first day, darlin'."

"I don't know if I am or not. I had five lectures today. For each one I had to wait in that silly little room and come out on a signal. Take my special seat and feel all those eyes burning my back."

"Still, it's a victory. And it sounds like you're goin' to be tamin' them devils." Hannah tied a knot in her thread and bit the rest off. "I heard once about a school that literally picked up a woman student and threw her out."

Samantha nodded pensively. Dr. Elizabeth had told her that story, and others, more horrible. Just getting accepted wasn't guarantee of a woman making it through medical school: there were the students to contend with. But then, weren't these the very ones responsible for her being accepted? They had all voted, the letter said, and unanimously agreed to take her in.

Samantha felt vaguely uneasy now, sitting in the fire's glow with an unfinished letter to Louisa in her lap. It had been nagging her all week, this nebulous feeling that something was wrong, that things were not as they seemed. And now it gave her a chill, despite the fire.

Samantha was soon to have her answer.

The next morning's first lecture was on contagions, and the class, once Samantha entered and took her seat, remained politely quiet and dutifully took notes. However, halfway through the lecture a paper dart came sailing down from one of the upper tiers and landed on her sleeve. Although her cheeks burned, Samantha did not acknowledge the dart but left it where it was. A few minutes later another paper missile hit the back of her head.

When the class was over she very calmly gathered up her things and exited, looking neither right nor left, chin held high.

During the afternoon lecture on nervous disorders, Samantha felt a little scratchiness at the back of her throat. She coughed lightly. Behind her, one hundred and nineteen students coughed in unison. Toward the end of the lecture she accidentally dropped her pen. A hundred and nineteen pens fell to the floor. The lecturer, Mr. Watkins, turned red and stuttered but continued speaking. At the end, Samantha exited as serenely as she could.

After a lonely walk back home, trying to ignore the stares of people she passed, Samantha sank into a chair, close to tears.

"This is what they want to see, darlin'. Don't give 'em that satisfaction."

"I shan't be able to keep it up, Hannah! I am on trial, they are watching me for my first mistake. I am so nervous that I can't concentrate on what the lecturer is saying. And now I'm too upset to study! Why are they doing this to me? Why can't I be allowed the same consideration as any male student? Is it such a sin to be born a woman?"

"Can't you talk to Dr. Jones about it?"

"I have a feeling he'd be more than pleased to tell me that if I can't take it I should go back to Manhattan. I just don't understand, Hannah. I thought they wanted me here. Now they are trying to drive me off. Medical school is difficult enough without spending each day in a bundle of nerves. It's as though I must walk a high wire!"

"Don't buckle to it, darlin'. It's a fight they're after, so give it to 'em!"

It came the next morning. She sat in the anteroom listening to the boisterous cacophony on the other side of the door, and when Dr. Page appeared, the class fell silent. Samantha walked rigidly across the platform, feeling every hostile eye on her, and tried to keep herself from shaking. When she reached her desk, she removed her hat and started to sit down. She stopped herself in time. In the center of her seat was a puddle of black ink.

Something inside her snapped. Gazing down at the pool of ink, Samantha felt rage and indignation rise in her soul. Very slowly, to keep her trembling from being seen, she turned on the spot and for the first time faced the class. Five tiers of black suits and blurry faces rose up before her. There was a snicker; a suppressed chuckle.

With her hands curled into fists at her sides, Samantha took three steps forward, holding herself stiffly, and stood before the students at the end of the first row. Two of them looked away, one smiled up sheepishly, and the fourth grinned flatly.

In a voice that startled even her, Samantha said loudly and crisply, "Excuse me, sir, have you a handkerchief?"

The grin evaporated. "Huh?"

She held out a hand. "Have you a handkerchief?"

"Uh, yeah. I mean, yes, ma'am." He fumbled in his pocket and, frowning, handed her a clean, starched square of linen.

"Thank you." Samantha glided back to her seat and mopped up the ink.

Returning to the stunned young man, as the class watched with one held breath, she extended the sodden handkerchief and said in a voice that rang out: "Thank you so much. You're very kind."

There was only a moment's hesitation, then the entire classroom erupted in deafening applause. Startled, Samantha looked up and saw, surrounding her and towering over her, smiling, beaming faces. They smacked their palms together and hammered their boots on the floor; they shouted and called out and clapped one another on the back. Even the young man whose handkerchief was ruined gave a little shamefaced smile and rapped his knuckles on his desk top.

Samantha had passed her first test.

THIRTEEN

"THEY'RE NOT BAD BOYS, MISS HARGRAVE. MANY ARE SIMPLE farm boys from around here. They meant no harm."

"But I don't understand, Dr. Jones. They were the ones who voted for my acceptance. Why did my arrival seem to come as a surprise to everyone?"

They were sitting in his office drinking tea. A feeble fire burned in the corner stove and through the window, through the leafy branches of the chestnuts outside, came a bit of wan sunlight. Dr. Jones added another lump of sugar to his tea. "This is rather awkward, Miss Hargrave," he said without looking at her. "You see . . . your petition for admittance was considered something of a joke."

The cup stopped at her lips.

"Not by the staff it wasn't," he hastened to add. "We all knew it was a genuine petition, but some of the students suspected I was playing a prank on them . . ."

"Please go on, Dr. Jones."

He lifted his eyes and faced her squarely. "The truth of it is, Miss Hargrave, when your letter came across my desk, I was put in a dilemma. While your presenting qualifications were excellent—better, I might add, than most of your fellow students'—I did not want a female student. I was and still am opposed to your being here. Back in June the school was having a fund-raising campaign and we were falling short of our goal. Your connection with the Blackwells and Dr. Masefield caused me to fear that, should I outright reject you, they might use their influence to dry up certain sources of our funding. However, it came to me that if it was the *students* who rejected you, then I and the school would be free of blame. Unfortunately"—he bowed his head and a bit of sunlight glimmered off his shiny scalp—"my brilliant scheme backfired."

"How so?"

"I presented your petition before the class, certain they would out and out reject it. Much to my surprise, they said they wanted to put it to a vote. As there ensued a hot debate, I absented myself to allow the young men to speak more freely, but the proceedings were reported to me afterward."

He removed his spectacles and made a display of polishing them with his handkerchief. Anything to avoid meeting her eyes. "You see, Miss Hargrave, I'm not well liked here. The students will do anything to counter my wishes. Since they knew I would be opposed to a female student, they purposely voted *for* you just to enrage me. The majority of the vote was planned as revenge against me; a few thought it would be a lark to have a female in the class, and the rest simply suspected a trick on my part."

"I see," said Samantha coolly. "And I was naive enough to think I had been accepted on my merit. Now I find I have been used to make a buffoon of you."

"Don't hold it against them, Miss Hargrave. After all, you have now been completely and unconditionally accepted into their ranks. I believe they are now glad you're here."

"However, none of what you have said explains the reception I received. Why was everyone so surprised to see me?"

He seated his spectacles back on his little knob of a nose. "Miss Hargrave, no one expected you to show up. We were certain that before the term started you would see the folly of your ambition, that your family and friends would talk you out of it—as happens with so many women who express a desire to go to medical school— or possibly even that you might get married. And then when we heard from Mr. Rutledge, the hotel owner, that the female student had arrived that evening . . ." Dr. Jones hoisted his shoulders. "And then you walked into my office, well, surely you can understand."

"Dr. Jones, what are you saying?"

A red tide rose up from his detachable collar. "Miss Hargrave, we had all expected you'd be six feet tall, talk in low G, and sport a mustache!"

Samantha stared at him for a second, then quickly brought up a gloved hand to stifle a laugh.

Flustered, he returned to his tea, tossing in another lump. "But now you are here, Miss Hargrave, and I suppose we'll have to make do. You have the students on your side now and some of the faculty. But you have not yet proven yourself to me. I will be frank: I do not approve of women in the medical profession."

"But, Dr. Jones, woman by her nature is the *natural* doctor. In her capacity as mother she must tend bodies, keep a stock of remedies, nurse the sick, pull splinters, cleanse wounds, bandage, mend, fix, and even set broken bones. Mothers all through history, while their men have been away, have been physicians in their own tiny hospitals—their homes. Where then, sir, did it come about that God intended only men to be doctors?"

His voice grew chilly. "It came about, Miss Hargrave, when medicine advanced from home remedies to *science*. It follows, therefore, that with the elevation of medicine's status the study of it should fall to the superior intellect, that of man."

"But surely women have a place there. At the Blackwells' Infirmary the female physicians—"

He raised a hand. "Save your breath to cool your porridge, Miss Hargrave, I will not debate with you. In case you were unaware of it, this region of New York is a veritable hotbed of certain Amazons who call themselves feminists and who plague us with their squawks about women's rights and *liberation*. I have heard that lame argument before: women helping women, and I have never before heard such a preposterous notion! A dog in distress does not go to another dog for help, does he? Nor does a child seek aid from another child? Of course not. That responsibility falls to the *master*. And man, in his innate superiority over woman, is the divinely appointed guardian of her well-being. Now I will discuss the issue no further. As I said, you are here and so we shall have to make the best of it. I'm a busy man, Miss Hargrave, I can't be at this all day. I want to apprise you of a few standards I expect you to uphold."

Samantha, to maintain composure, had to put her cup down on the desk and clamp her hands together in her lap.

"Aside from the expected rules, you will at all times conduct yourself in a ladylike manner and will not fraternize with the male students or any faculty member—"

"Fraternize, Dr. Jones? I don't understand. They are my fellow students. We must study together, discuss the day's lectures—"

"Miss Hargrave." Dr. Jones folded his arms on the desk and leaned on them to punctuate his point. "We have the reputation of this school to protect. Any socializing with the students or a faculty member outside of the classroom will be cause for immediate dismissal. Is that clear?"

She nodded.

He sat back. "Further, there are certain lectures you will not attend. Those which are not suited to a woman's delicacy. Specifically, any discussions involving the generative organs and the diseases thereof."

"You can't mean that, sir!"

"Nor will you be admitted to the dissection lab."

She stared at him in dumfoundment. "Dr. Jones, how can I possibly have a good knowledge of anatomy if—"

"Nor will you be permitted to examine any male patient except from the neck up."

The words caught in her throat; her voice failed her.

"And now, Miss Hargrave"—Dr. Jones stood, pushing his chair back—"I believe that is everything."

FOURTEEN

*W*HEN THE DAY CAME, IN NOVEMBER, FOR THE ANATOMY LAB
to start, Samantha had to make a decision.

"Don't go against his wishes, darlin'." Hannah warned as they
strolled along the lake's edge, arms linked, parasols opened to keep leaves
from falling on them. "It's madness. He's hoping you'll defy him and then
you'll be out."

Samantha watched a cottontail dart into the tall grass; to her left the
placid lake mirrored the autumn sky. If only she could talk to Dr. Masefield. But here it was her seventh week in Lucerne, and still no letter from
him. "I wouldn't be able to call myself much of a doctor without training in
anatomy, Hannah. That lab is the very core of my course here."

"What're you thinking then?"

Samantha had decided to put Dr. Jones's orders to the test. Her hope was
that, if she attended the first session and proved herself a worthy student, he
would ease his unfair restriction. And to guard against the signs of female
weakness they would all be closely watching her for, Samantha had a plan.

Dr. Elizabeth Blackwell had once recounted to Samantha one of her own medical school experiences. "They were constantly watching me," she had said, "for the slightest slip so they could criticize me. While I knew I was as up to dissection as any man, I knew my body could betray me with the one reflex over which I had no control—the blush. So I devised a plan. In the weeks preceding the commencement of cadaver dissection I did everything I could to control that traitorous reflex. I practiced, late at night, standing before my looking glass, trying to conjure the most shocking, improper and embarrassing situations I could think of, anything to make myself blush. And then I tried to counter the instant reddening by sheer force of will. I also embarked on a near starvation diet, abstaining from meat, and also denied myself any wine or medicine, even when I had a headache or cramps, for these properties dilate the facial vessels and lend floridness to the complexion. Finally I lightly dusted my face with talc every morning. My big test came when we were to study the male reproductive organs. There lay our cadaver, and while our lecturer spoke, pointing with his pointer, I concentrated so hard, for the full hour, on not blushing that when I came away from the lab I realized I had heard not one word of his discourse!"

For three weeks Samantha had been preparing herself: the spartan diet, the denials, the abstentions, the practicing before her looking glass. And this morning she had lightly dusted her cheeks with alum. But it was all to be for nothing. When, at ten o'clock, she arrived at the dissection lab on the third floor, Samantha found the door locked and the students milling about in the hall. Mr. Monks, the anatomy speaker, would lead no class at which a female was in attendance.

The next day, the same thing happened. The door was locked, the students turned away.

She appealed to Dr. Jones. "Surely you cannot mean for this to go on all year, sir! At least let the others in, if not me."

"Miss Hargrave, it is up to Mr. Monks. He knows you plan to attend and it so shocks his sense of decency that he prefers not to hold lab at all."

"The others are suffering because of me," she told Hannah that evening, pacing before the fire. "They'll grow to resent me. Such a dilemma, Hannah! It is a matter of being damned either way I go. If I insist on attending, the door will continue to be locked and the other students will soon want to throw me out of the school. If I acquiesce and stay away from the lab, then I will have failed myself and will graduate under false pretenses! A doctor who has never studied anatomy! Such madness!"

Hannah continued to calmly drive her needle down into the linen stretched over the hoop, her full bosom rising and falling gently. After a while she said softly, "'Tis an easy problem to solve, darlin'."

Samantha stopped where she was. "What do you mean?"

Hannah looked up with a glint in her eye. "Sure and it's surprised I am that a smarty like yourself hasn't thought of it." She let her embroidery fall to her lap. "You can satisfy yourself *and* your Dr. Jones *and* the other students as well."

Samantha blinked at her. "How?"

⁂

She stopped by his office on her way to the first lecture and said as she shook autumn raindrops off her coat, "You can tell Mr. Monks that I won't try to get into his lab any more."

Dr. Jones eyed her skeptically.

"You have my word on it, sir. My conscience has been bothering me. My stubbornness should not be the cause of keeping the rest of the students from the dissection. Mr. Monks can keep his door unlocked, I shan't go in."

And she didn't. But what Samantha did do was get a chair from one of the nearby lecture theaters and place it outside the door of the lab after the dissection had begun. Although the door was closed, she was able to lean over and listen at the keyhole. She took notes on all she heard.

One of the students, who had overslept, came hurrying down the hall and stopped short when he saw her. "What are you doing out here, Miss Hargrave?"

She told him. He thought about it a moment, then turned away and disappeared into the neighboring classroom. When he emerged a moment later with a chair, and then sat down opposite her and proceeded to take notes on what he heard through the keyhole, Samantha sat back in amazement.

Dr. Jones, curious to see if the first session of the dissection lab was going well, happened upon the scene a few minutes later. After demanding of Samantha and her companion what they were up to, he exploded over her explanation and banished them from the hallway.

That night Samantha scowled at Hannah and told her she didn't think it had been such a good idea after all. "I could have been expelled. And I had no right to put that poor young man in such a precarious situation!"

But Hannah only smiled. "Give it another try, darlin'. You're underestimatin' your fellow students. Take it from a woman who knows what makes a man tick. Do the same tomorrow as you did today, and I'll be blown if you don't get some results."

The next day, to Samantha's great astonishment, when she mounted the stairs to the floor of the dissection lab, she found the hallway congested with chairs and desks, all taken from the lecture theaters and all occupied by her fellow students. Speechless, she could only stand and stare. One of them, a chosen spokesman, timidly stood and explained what they were doing. The first young man, he said, who had joined her yesterday, had told them of the incident and they had all decided that, if the hallway was good enough for their Miss Hargrave, then it was good enough for them.

She tried to fight back the tears (another bodily reflex over which she had no control) and tried even harder to be "their Miss Hargrave" when both Dr. Jones and Mr. Monks appeared, demanding an accounting of this outrage. The hallway confrontation was unpleasant—with expulsion threatened for all—but the outcome was a final relenting on the part of Mr. Monks (who, seeing Samantha for the first time, decided he wouldn't mind her in his room after all) and a menacing glare from Dr. Jones, who gave grudging approval and marched away.

Traditionally, dissection begins on the arm. In the weeks that followed, however, as snow fell over Lucerne and the students in their unheated classrooms shivered, the anatomy lecture gradually moved to the more delicate parts of the body, and Samantha's rigid self-training in preparation for this moment failed.

She blushed.

FIFTEEN

"Couldn't you stay with me, darlin'? Sean won't be home till spring."

Samantha did not break her rhythm of fluffing, folding and packing; nor did she look up at Hannah, who leaned against the doorframe.

"It's lonely I shall be without you."

Samantha finally paused and looked up. "I'm sorry, Hannah, truly I am, but my friends at home miss me." Which was partially true. Louisa's most recent letter had implored Samantha to come home for Christmas, but there still had been no word from the Masefields. This alarmed Samantha, who feared Estelle had succumbed to the inevitable.

Hannah continued to lean in the doorway with her arms folded, watching her young friend resume packing. She had a few solid opinions of Samantha Hargrave, opinions which would never be voiced, one of which was on this outlandish notion the girl had about becoming a doctor. Samantha should be breaking young men's hearts, not learning how to mend them. It wasn't natural, a pretty young thing like that surrounded daily by gallant young men and not the barest flicker of amorous interest. Not to fault the young men; there were a few, Hannah had noticed in amusement during their evening walks, who would bow deeply and sweep their hats off their heads and whose eyes held a special longing when they fell upon Samantha. No, there was nothing wrong with the young men, it was the girl, something not quite right there.

Hannah knew nothing about Joshua Masefield. Samantha had made vague mention of him back in September and had never spoken of him again. But Hannah had seen how eagerly Samantha went through the afternoon mail and how disappointed she always was. Who was it she so desperately wanted a letter from? A man it had to be, and one so special that he could make Samantha blind to the attentions of those charming medical students. But who? And why should she keep it such a secret?

Hannah shook her head and pushed away from the door. "I'll be fetchin' you a carriage then."

When they parted, Hannah surprised Samantha with a Christmas gift of an otter muff. Touched, Samantha could only say, "I've nothing for you."

Their breath came out in little steam jets as they embraced in the snow. "It's an impoverished student you are now, darlin', but comes the day you're a grand lady I shall expect the favor to be returned. Now be off with you and have a cheery Christmas with your friends."

No one met her at Grand Central Station, but she hadn't expected them to. As the hansom creaked down Bleecker Street, Samantha felt her pulse race in anticipation. It had been almost four months, how would he receive her?

There were a few patients in the entry hall; those who knew her smiled. Leaving her carpetbag by the door, Samantha removed her hat and coat, hung them up and went in search of Mrs. Wiggen.

The housekeeper was in the kitchen wiping breakfast dishes and putting them away. Her face spread in a wide smile when she saw Samantha and she held out her arms for an embrace.

"I was so glad to read your letter saying you were coming for the holiday!" said the old lady as she stemmed a rise of tears with the corner of her apron.

"How is Estelle?"

"Not good, poor thing. The cold hits her bad. She has these awful pains and a difficult time breathing. Dr. Masefield said something about her lungs sticking to the lining of her chest."

"And how is he?"

"Same as always. He's with Mrs. Creighton right now."

As she checked her hair for straying curls and smoothed down her dress, Samantha had to catch the impulse to hurry out of the kitchen.

She rapped lightly on the door of the examing room and heard his voice say, "Come in, Mrs. Wiggen!"

Samantha slipped in and closed the door. She hesitated, watching how, with his back to her, he tapped Mrs. Creighton's knees with a little mahogany mallet.

"It's the arthritis, isn't it, Dr. Masefield?" asked the middle-aged woman, still wearing bonnet and gloves.

Dr. Masefield straightened up. "You have every symptom, Mrs. Creighton. But don't worry, I think I have something that can help. Mrs. Wiggen, will you please hand me those special tablets for Mrs. Creighton?"

Samantha went to the cupboard, withdrew the bottle and brought it back, dropping it in his outstretched hand. He murmured, "Thank you," looked away, then snapped his head back. "Miss Hargrave!"

She smiled self-consciously. "I'm back for the holidays, Dr. Masefield."

His expression remained severe. "You're thin."

Samantha looked down at herself and saw how her dress hung on her, the result of all those weeks of semistarvation to curb the blush.

"Is there something wrong at school that prevents you from eating properly?"

"I . . ." His angry tone confounded her; Samantha felt like a scolded child. "No, Dr. Masefield, nothing wrong. I only . . ."

He turned away from her. "One pill each evening before you retire, Mrs. Creighton. Be certain not to increase the dose or to skip a night. That is very important."

"Yes, Doctor." As the small kid-gloved hand accepted the bottle, Samantha quietly retreated from the examining room.

Upstairs, unpacking her bag, she quivered, not from cold but from mortification. If he had not wanted her here over Christmas he should have sent a telegram. Samantha wanted only to be where she was appreciated and now regretted having abandoned Hannah Mallone's warm hearth.

But Louisa and Luther, the next day, made everything better. As the three rode a sleigh through Central Park, calling out to skaters and sharing a basket of pastries, Samantha felt her soul lighten: she should not judge Joshua so harshly—he had little reason for cheer with Estelle slipping away from him like a slowly fading tintype. She would talk to Mrs. Wiggen about putting up a tree in the unused parlor and lighting candles on it.

⚬

The old routine resumed: Samantha assisted him with patients and accompanied him on nearby house calls. But he never asked about school, never inquired about her new friends, never expressed interest in how she lived or studied. Joshua Masefield remained as distant as ever.

Which was why, two weeks before Christmas, on a Saturday evening deep and cold, when he came to Samantha's door to ask a favor, she was stunned.

"If I may speak to you for a few minutes, Miss Hargrave. It is a matter of some importance."

She stepped back as he entered, closed the door and remained there, uncertain. Dr. Masefield hovered for an instant by the fire, then sat in one of the two chairs facing it. "I have a very large favor to ask of you, Miss Hargrave, and am at a loss as to how to go about it." Dr. Masefield kept his profile to her as he spoke; Samantha saw a tightness about his mouth and jaw. "I should not even be asking it, but I am in something of a bind."

He fell silent, staring into the fire. Samantha took this as her cue to urge him on. Joining him in the next chair, she said, "Please go on, Dr. Masefield."

"Are you aware, Miss Hargrave, that there exists in the city of New York not a single hospital that will take cancer patients?"

"I wasn't aware."

"People fear that cancer is contagious, and while doctors know it is not, we cannot convince the public otherwise. If any hospital were to admit a single cancer patient, its wards would empty at once and the hospital would have to close. As a result, cancer patients like my wife must be treated either at home or in private clinics which are expensive and remotely situated. Because of this, many have no treatment or care whatever and suffer lingering and solitary deaths."

He raised his eyes to hers. "There is a movement afoot to erect a special cancer pavilion at Woman's Hospital. It is a cause of the highest ideal, for it would mean proper care for many women who are suffering alone without solace or help."

Samantha had heard of Woman's Hospital, a highly esteemed facility founded by the great Dr. Marion Sims, who, even though he was still alive, was rapidly becoming a legend.

"There is to be a charity ball on Christmas Eve at the house of Mrs. Astor for the raising of funds for that pavilion. And I have received an invitation."

He fell silent again and returned to staring into the fire. Samantha waited for him to speak, listening to the silence around them as New York slumbered beneath a mantle of gently falling snow.

"My problem, Miss Hargrave," he said after a length, his voice sounding distant, "is this. I have never told anyone of my wife's illness, no one in Manhattan knows. I am assuming that, by now, Mrs. Wiggen has told you all about Philadelphia, and that Estelle and I came to New York last year. So. It is Estelle's wish that no one know about her illness and so I must put up a pretense to protect her feelings. Those few people with whom I am acquainted here in New York have never met Estelle but they believe that she is perfectly well. I have even, on rare occasion, fabricated a few innocent stories about Estelle's active social life. Unfortunately, Mrs. Masefield is now being called upon to make an appearance."

"Surely that's not possible."

"Of course it's not possible. However, I am pressed for a solution. I must attend. To refuse an Astor invitation is unthinkable. But, more so, I ardently wish to be a part of the pavilion project."

"You could say Estelle is ill with something temporary."

He sprang to his feet. "In the time I have been in New York I have attended four social functions. On each occasion I used that excuse—a headache one time, a chest cold another. I cannot use it yet again and hope for my veracity to go unquestioned. Mrs. Astor will be offended, thinking my wife is antisocial."

"Then tell the truth."

He turned away from her, casting shadows which danced on the walls. "I cannot. For Estelle's sake . . ."

"Then what can you do?"

His shoulders and back tensed for a moment, then Joshua slowly turned to face her. "Miss Hargrave, would you consider accompanying me to the Astor ball as my wife?"

Samantha's eyes flew open.

Joshua added in a rush: "It is a subterfuge, I know, and I am asking you to aid me in deception. But it is a harmless charade, no one will be hurt by it. Indeed, all will benefit. Estelle's reputation will be saved and I shall have the satisfaction of having aided this noble cause."

"But what will Estelle think of this?"

"It was her idea."

Samantha had to pull herself away from his gaze. "Can it work?"

Visibly relieved, Joshua Masefield returned to his seat. "No one has ever seen Estelle. Very little would be required of you, Miss Hargrave. I shall see to it you are not taxed. We would stay a respectable length of time and then leave."

Samantha's mind was in a turmoil. The other women at the ball, in their imported gowns from Worth's of Paris or Lucile's of London. The names she had often read to Estelle from the *Social Register:* Stuyvesant, Belmont, Roosevelt. Joshua cutting a dashing figure in top hat and opera cape. And Samantha being his wife for one evening . . . "The Astor mansion," she said. "I have nothing to wear!"

"Then you will help me?"

Samantha smiled. "Yes, Dr. Masefield, I will help you . . ."

SIXTEEN

HER IDEA WAS TO RENT A GOWN FOR THE EVENING, BUT Joshua flatly rejected it, saying that his wife would not appear at an Astor ball in a rented gown. So Samantha turned to Estelle for help. Estelle wouldn't hear of Samantha borrowing a gown, she must have one of her own, and so she gave her the address of a draper on Fifth Avenue and the name of a dressmaker of excellent reputation.

"There isn't enough time," fretted Samantha.

Estelle, propped up on satin pillows, said in a breathy voice, "Mrs. Simmons is used to rush orders, especially at this time of the year. She can work miracles. And when you tell her it's for the Astor ball she will put her seamstresses on it night and day." Estelle added wistfully: "Truly, I wish I could go, but I'm glad you can go in my place, Samantha, for Joshua's sake. The pavilion means so much to him. A harmless little masquerade, it's so kind of you to do it for him . . ."

Samantha went with some trepidation to the draper and selected several yards of charcoal taffeta with a bit of black velvet for trim. Lace and bows and other adornments she rejected as too costly. To Mrs. Simmons, who was as impressed and solicitous as Estelle had predicted, Samantha stressed conservatism in the design: not too full in the skirt, a modest bustle, very little shoulder revealed, no flamboyance whatever.

When the dress arrived, five days before Christmas, Joshua Masefield exploded.

In the presence of the timorous delivery boy, he dashed the gown back into its box and said, "What the devil were you thinking, Miss Hargrave, to order something like *this!*"

Samantha, startled, could not reply. Five minutes earlier, she and Dr. Masefield had brought the package into the parlor to inspect the garment before the delivery boy got away. After the string was cut and the lid lifted, Joshua had stared at the dress in blank confusion. Then he had accused the boy of delivering the wrong gown. Samantha had interjected that it was indeed the gown she had ordered, and Joshua Masefield had exploded.

"Whatever possessed you, Miss Hargrave! If you have no taste in clothes, then you should have asked Mrs. Simmons' advice!"

"What's wrong with it? I thought—"

"What's wrong with it? It's hideous! It's the dress of a common working girl! Did you actually expect to appear in public, at my side, as my wife, in *that!*"

Samantha's eyes flickered in the direction of the delivery boy. "Really, Dr. Masefield," she began breathlessly. "I was only trying to—"

He turned his back to her, gathered up the box and wrappings and thrust the lot against the boy's chest. "Take it back. We don't want it."

Stupefied, the youth fumbled to catch it all in his arms.

"Really, Dr. Masefield, that is not necessary. I can make some alterations, add some trim if you wish. Mrs. Wiggen can help me—"

He spun around. There was a queer coloring about his lips and nostrils; his pupils were strangely pinpointed. "The only thing that will help that monstrosity, Miss Hargrave, is fire!"

She fell back a step.

Behind, the delivery boy shifted nervously. Joshua Masefield glowered at Samantha another moment, then waved an arm. "Get that thing out of here. Tell Mrs. Simmons to send me the bill."

The boy dashed out and slammed the front door behind himself. In the parlor, Samantha and Joshua continued to glare at one another.

Joshua said, "We'll have to come up with something else now. Five days is not much time."

Samantha's voice was glacial. "If you had given me some idea beforehand, instead of leaving it entirely up to me—"

"Confound it, Miss Hargrave! I didn't think that was necessary! Ordering a simple dress, for God's sake!"

"What was wrong with it?"

"It was *ugly!* No wife of mine is going to appear in public dressed in a rag!"

"It was not a rag and I am not your wife! I was only trying to—"

"I suppose I should be thankful you are not my wife."

"And may I *please* just once finish a sentence?"

He fell silent, his lips compressed into a white line.

"You act as though I did this to you on purpose, Dr. Masefield, to make you angry, to humiliate you. When I ordered the gown, I was in fact thinking of you. I was trying to save you money."

His eyebrows arched. "Surely you are joking."

"I am not."

"Do you think I'm *poor*, Miss Hargrave?"

"Dr. Masefield, I was raised to respect the saving of—"

"I don't give a hang how you were raised, Miss Hargrave!"

She blinked at him in astonishment, then said in a barely controlled voice, "I see no call for you to speak to me thus."

Joshua glared at her a moment longer, his black eyes stormy, then he turned on his heel and stalked from the room.

Unable to move, unable even to take a breath for fear it would cause her to break down and weep, Samantha remained standing rigidly in the parlor. A moment later she heard the front door slam and saw, through the bay window, in overcoat and muffler, Joshua Masefield march down the icy steps and plunge into the swirling snowfall.

The incident was not mentioned again, nor was there any more word of the party. He came back late that evening, ate a solitary supper in his study and retired early to his bedroom, which adjoined Estelle's. The next morning Samantha did not attempt any false civility with him. After a subdued breakfast with Mrs. Wiggen, Samantha called the first of several patients into the examining room and assisted Dr. Masefield in stony silence.

On the day before Christmas Dr. Masefield was called away to deliver a baby. Samantha sat anxiously by the parlor fire and mentally urged the hours to hurry by. In her lap lay a card which had just arrived: two rosy-cheeked children crouched at the feet of a slender Father Christmas. Inside, in a neat copperplate, was a cheery greeting from Hannah Mallone.

It was early evening when Dr. Masefield returned. Samantha was up in her room writing letters by the fire when she heard the front door open and close, then his boots stamp off snow. She heard his footsteps mount the stairs to the first floor where his and Estelle's bedrooms were, but to Samantha's surprise he mounted the next flight. When his steps stopped at her door, she sucked in her breath.

He knocked.

Carefully laying aside her stationery and inkhorn, and hastily checking her hair to be sure it was neatly tied up, Samantha opened the door.

A scowling Joshua Masefield stood on the other side holding a large parcel. "We haven't much time," he said, extending the package to her. "The carriage will be here in one hour."

Puzzled, Samantha took the box, found it very heavy, and said, "What is this?"

"Your gown, Miss Hargrave. I was to have picked it up from Mrs. Simmons earlier but the Levy baby did not cooperate." He turned to go.

"I don't understand. What gown?"

He turned back around, clearly impatient. "The one that you are to wear tonight," he said as if talking to a child.

"What do you mean? I hadn't thought I was going."

His irritation turned to mild surprise. "Indeed? And why not?"

"Why not? Dr. Masefield, must I remind you of that outrageous scene in the parlor five days ago?"

His look was one of complete innocence. "What of it?"

"I took your anger to imply I was not going tonight."

"My anger? For God's sake, Miss Hargrave, I was angry at the blasted dress, not at you!"

"You humiliated me in front of the delivery boy! You railed insults upon me! And now you expect me to blithely accompany you to that . . . that *blasted* ball!"

His face broadened in disbelief. "You're angry with me, Miss Hargrave."

"Yes, I am!"

"And I had thought you such a mouse."

She glared at him, her chest rising and falling dramatically. "I have been waiting for your apology."

"I see. And is that what it will take for you to accompany me to the ball? An apology?"

She met his eyes boldly. "Yes."

"Then I apologize. Now, can you be ready in an hour?"

SEVENTEEN

AMANTHA FELT AS IF SHE FLOATED DOWN THE STAIRS ON A cloud. Never in her life had she worn a gown so beautiful. It was made of peacock-blue satin and Mrs. Simmons, in her rush, had indeed worked miracles to match Samantha's measurements. The small waist was snugly fitted, her breasts roundly emphasized. The skirts, heavy and layered in front like window drapes, were gathered up into a bustle and cascaded down the back in a train. A mist of ice-blue tulle embroidered with silver flowers and arabesques settled around her bare shoulders, which, like the soft swell of her bosom, were daringly revealed by a low déolletage. An extra touch was a pair of elbow-high evening gloves of Lyon silk and a lace fan.

Samantha moved as if in a dream, but when she saw Joshua waiting for her at the foot of the stairs, gazing up at her as if he saw an apparition, Samantha was brought back to reality. It is Estelle he sees, she thought, not I.

Over one arm he carried a heavy wrap which he now shook out and held for Samantha to step into. She gasped. The outer cloth of the hooded cape was merino wool but the lining was chinchilla and Samantha shivered as the luxuriant fur engulfed her bare arms and shoulders.

"It is Estelle's. She insisted you wear it."

Samantha caressed the smoky fur as if it were alive as Joshua stood behind her and laid the heavy cape across her shoulders. As he reached around to fasten the clasp Samantha imagined she felt the warmth of his body through the cape, and when his hands drew back they lingered a moment on her shoulders. "You are lovely tonight, Samantha."

"Thank you, Dr. Masefield."

He stepped away from her. "You must remember to call me Joshua this evening."

Samantha turned to face him; his features were cloaked in shadow. Of course, the charade.

Joshua helped her down the icy steps and into the waiting carriage. Inside, he sat close to her and brought the heavy blankets up over their legs. During the long ride not one word was spoken.

❈

When she saw the parade of carriages in front of 350 Fifth Avenue Samantha felt her courage falter. The Astor mansion was ablaze with lights, every window a pane of gold. Even more dazzling were the people who stepped from their carriages—the gentlemen in their black opera capes, the ladies swathed in jewels and furs. Seeing them, Samantha suddenly felt very out of place. A mouse indeed . . .

She was gripped by a feeling of panic. How could she possibly hope to keep up the pretense! What madness had driven her to believe she could go through with this! Their carriage lurched forward in line. She turned to her companion. "Dr. Masefield—"

"My Christian name, please." When their carriage door opened, he added, "And do not forget that you are my wife."

They joined the procession up the steps and into the inviting glow of the house. With her hand linked through Joshua's arm, Samantha held her head high and glided with self-assurance toward their hostess, who, standing alone beneath the portrait of herself done by Carolus Duran, greeted each arriving guest as if she were a queen receiving homage.

Mrs. William Astor, who preferred to be known simply as Mrs. Astor, was a short plump woman so weighted down by clothes and jewels that she could not bend and only hardly move; the effect was a regal posture she did not really possess and a bearing which made people meeting her for the first time terrified. Samantha tried not to stare, but the Redfern gown was a monument all by itself: purple velvet trimmed with pale blue satin and embroidered with gold paillettes. The front and back were so heavily encrusted with beading and jewels that the gown appeared to have been built around her. The corsage of orchids, so rare in December, was the most conservative of her adornment: around her neck Mrs. Astor wore a triple necklace of diamonds, on her bosom an enormous diamond brooch said to have belonged to Marie Antoinette, her wrists and fingers were awash with diamonds, and interwoven into the raven wig she wore (her own hair being too thin even for a comb) was a network of diamond stars topped off by a queenly coronet.

Samantha, having watched how the women preceding her greeted Mrs. Astor, checked the impulse to curtsy. When Joshua introduced himself and his "wife," Mrs. Astor graciously acknowledged them, bestowed a courtly smile upon Samantha and thanked them for helping her with this noble effort. Then a blue-liveried footman took their capes and Joshua's hat and cane and the couple followed the procession along the Aubusson carpet toward the ballroom.

As the palatial room opened before her, Samantha's breath was taken away.

This was the famous Astor gallery where the paintings were hung museum style, one above the other up to the towering ceiling: works by Jean François Millet, Constant Troyon, and other painters of the Barbizon school. A thousand glittering lights emanated from massive candelabra from Italy; eleven thousand dollars' worth of flowers and potted plants from Klinder's transformed the snowy night into a summer's eve. Servants in blue livery, exact copies of the uniforms worn at Windsor Castle, moved among the crowd with trays of champagne and delicacies. There were over six hundred guests in the ballroom.

"Would you care for something to eat?" asked Joshua.

"No, thank you! I couldn't possibly eat!"

"Some champagne, then." He escorted her to one side where chairs had been arranged around palm trees and little tables decorated with Gloire de Paris roses, then he turned and made his way back through the crowd. Nervously twirling her fan, Samantha kept an eye on Joshua and thought he walked rather stiffly; and when he had disappeared and she could no longer see him, Samantha worked up the courage to look around.

The women were incredible; so different from her, a species apart. She wondered what they did with themselves, how they lived. All of them, regardless of age or size, seemed to be trying to achieve the popular eighteen-inch waist and so all were painfully corseted, with the displaced flesh rising up and out into the fashionable full bosom. Estelle had once told Samantha that a typical summer wardrobe for one of these women would consist of ninety gowns with matching parasols, hats, and elbow-length kid gloves.

She saw Joshua coming back through the crowd with two glasses. He was limping.

They sipped in silence for a few minutes—Joshua seemed disinclined to conversation—and when the balcony orchestra, hidden by sprays of flowers, struck up "The Blue Danube" and couples moved out into the center of the dance floor, Samantha felt her heart race with hope. Surely Joshua would ask her to dance at least once.

As the orchestra moved from one waltz to another and as more and more couples twirled around the dance floor, however, Samantha realized there would be no invitation from her silent partner; it appeared this was to be their evening, to sit and watch. "I think I should like something to eat after all," she said, laying aside her empty glass and feeling the first effects of the champagne. "Would it be all right if I fetched it myself? I would so like to see the table."

To her surprise, he didn't protest but merely nodded, and Samantha wondered fleetingly if he welcomed the chance to be alone.

The table, which ran the length of one wall, was something out of a fantasy; Samantha could identify only less than half of the selections and had no idea how one was to properly eat the rest. Mrs. Astor was famous for her chefs: there was tortue claire; mousse aux jambon; terrapin; filet de boeuf with truffles; riz de veau à la Toulouse; pâté de foie gras en Bellevue with artichoke sauce barigoule; maraschino sorbet; Camembert cheese with biscuits; and pudding Nesselrode. Samantha didn't know where to begin.

"May I recommend the steak?" came a deep voice next to her.

She looked up into a charming smile and soft brown eyes. "I beg your pardon?"

The gentleman, tall and lean, around thirty years old, inclined himself toward the steaming platter of filet de boeuf. "I'm afraid I recommend it because it is the only thing I recognize."

Samantha swept her eyes again over the vast spread. "I do hope all this food gets eaten."

"It won't. It isn't fashionable to stuff oneself at these functions. But don't worry, all leftover food and flowers will be taken to Bellevue Hospital."

She looked up at him. "Indeed?"

The handsome gentleman gazed down at this nameless young lady, intrigued by her fox-silver eyes, so wide and questioning, and mystified by her obvious newness to society. Who the devil was she and where was her escort? "Every time Mrs. Astor gives a ball, the patients of Bellevue Hospital fall to their knees in gratitude. Normally, you see, they eat their slop directly from the table top, as they have no utensils. And it is slop indeed."

"You can't be serious!"

"I couldn't be more serious. A committee recently investigated conditions at Bellevue and found not only the appalling practice of having the patients eat with their fingers directly off the table surface, they also could not find a single bar of soap on the premises."

Samantha put down the china plate she had been holding. "I don't think I am hungry after all."

"Forgive me, I have spoiled your appetite. And I have also forgotten my manners. As there is no one around to do the honors, permit me to introduce myself. Mark Rawlins."

"How do you do. Are you Society?"

He stared at her for an instant, then threw back his head and laughed. "Great heavens, no!"

Samantha wasn't sure she liked being laughed at. She looked across the room for Joshua but could not see him. Her companion said, "I'm here as a token. I am one of the poor overworked, underpaid, and unappreciated medical men whom Mrs. Astor invited to this charitable event."

By his appearance, the smart cut of his frock coat and striped trousers, Dr. Rawlins didn't appear underpaid or overworked, and it occurred to Samantha that he was mocking her. "You are a doctor, sir?"

He bowed slightly. "A surgeon. And now that I have had the shocking audacity to introduce myself to you, may I be so bold as to ask you for a dance?"

She frowned in indecision. "It is kind of you to ask, sir, but I am here with someone."

"You have a gentleman escort? Then I must again beg your forgiveness! I had thought—" Confound it, what was she doing then, fetching her own plate? Mark Rawlins gazed down at her; she seemed in no hurry to rejoin her escort. So he ventured carefully, "Do you think he would object to just one dance?"

Samantha tried again to find Joshua through the crowd but could not. She looked up into Mark Rawlins' smiling face and felt the temptation make the decision for her. She did so want to dance and Joshua clearly was not going to ask her. "Perhaps it would be all right . . ."

Before she knew it he was twirling her over the parquet floor, one hand pressed at the small of her back, the other cradling her hand. Samantha felt as if she had suddenly come alive: the music, the freedom, the room spinning around her, and Mark Rawlins' charming smile beaming down at her.

"You haven't told me your name."

"Sam—" she started. "Estelle Masefield. *Mrs.* Estelle Masefield."

Dr. Rawlins' expression didn't change. "Joshua Masefield's wife?"

Her breath caught. "Yes—"

His grin deepened. "I must say, you are looking greatly improved since the last time I saw you, Mrs. Masefield."

Samantha faltered and stepped on his foot. They came to a halt. "Oh, I'm sorry—" Other couples artfully steered around them as Samantha, flustered, stared up at the man who still held her.

"You haven't injured me," he said gallantly. "I can still dance." They started up again, joining the flow, and Samantha realized they would soon be dancing in front of Joshua.

"You're very red," said Mark Rawlins. "You won't faint on me, will you?"

"I don't know what to say."

Dr. Rawlins gazed down at her bowed head, at the flush along her slender neck, and wondered what mysterious connection she had with Joshua Masefield. She was a young woman a man could easily fall in love with; had Joshua succumbed? "So you are here with Joshua? It will be good to see him again."

Samantha raised her large gray eyes. "Do you know him?"

"We were friends back in Philadelphia. I was with Joshua when he received the verdict from Dr. Washington." They glided effortlessly across the floor, guided by the spell of many violins. "I am curious about your charade . . ."

"Estelle is too ill to attend, and Dr. Masefield didn't want to make excuses for her. It seemed harmless, pretending to be his wife for one evening."

Harmless, thought Mark Rawlins, and just a bit thrilling? How much does she know, I wonder, about Joshua? Surely he hasn't told her everything . . . "Now tell me," he said aloud, "where does Joshua know you from?"

She told him and suddenly Dr. Rawlins was looking at her differently. "A medical student. I *am* impressed. Forgive my saying, but one would never guess by looking at you."

Samantha opened her mouth but no voice came out, for just over Dr. Rawlins' shoulder she glimpsed the grave countenance of Joshua Masefield. He was slowly rising to his feet, his face oddly pale, and his black eyes were fixed on Samantha.

Mark Rawlins spun her around, obscuring her view, and when she was able to see again, Joshua was gone.

The music stopped and Samantha wafted herself with her fan. "Dr. Rawlins, would you be so kind as to fetch me some champagne?"

He saw first that she was seated among the palms, then hurried back through the crowd. Samantha's anxiety started to mount as she searched frantically for Joshua. "Your champagne, Mrs. Masefield."

She looked up, startled, at Dr. Rawlins holding a glass. "Thank you . . ."

He sat in the chair next to her and sipped. "So where is Josh tonight? I don't see him."

She stretched her neck and shifted in her chair, looking this way and that, unaware of Dr. Rawlins' admiring eyes on her. "He was here a minute ago."

A dark thought crossed Mark Rawlins' mind: I know where he is. But out loud he said with forced flippance, "He'll be back soon enough. Can't imagine what got into Josh, leaving a beautiful young lady on her own."

Samantha tasted her champagne and tried to control the nervous fluttering of her fan.

"How do you find medical school? Have you encountered problems because you are a woman?"

Glad of the diversion, Samantha related to Mark Rawlins her first weeks at Lucerne. As he was an attentive listener and obviously interested, and as the champagne worked its relaxing magic through her body, Samantha felt her nervousness subside; she soon became animated. "There is one old crane, Dr. Page, who did not approve of me at first. He is so tall and thin that, during lectures, I half expect him at any minute to raise a leg and stand on one foot!"

Rawlins laughed and reached for two more glasses from a passing tray.

"I feel as though I am constantly on trial, as though the slightest mistake will be cause to send me packing." Samantha fanned herself; she was starting to feel giddy. "I quite thought those first days were also to be my last, everyone resented me so."

Mark Rawlins silently studied his companion, the sparkle in her smoky eyes, the enchanting way a few black locks had tumbled and now teased the back of her neck. "I am sure," he said softly, "they are now quite in love with you."

Samantha laid aside her empty glass. "The affection is brotherly, I assure you."

Mark Rawlins surveyed the room. "It appears Joshua is engaged elsewhere. Shall we dance again?"

They did, two more times, until Samantha was breathless and laughing and clutching Dr. Rawlins' arm. It was near the midnight hour and the party was at its peak. Seven hundred guests, the very cream of New York society, danced and drank and courted one another's favors. Mark Rawlins escorted Samantha around the room, telling her bits of gossip about the people they passed, eavesdropping on conversations and introducing her to those whom he knew. For a man who was "underpaid and overworked," Mark Rawlins was on comfortable acquaintance with many of New York's aristocracy.

They came to a halt at the edge of a knot of people. "Who is it?" asked Samantha, trying to peer over their heads.

"We'll see in a moment."

They were surrounded by fame and wealth. To Samantha's left stood Mrs. Astor's daughter and her new husband James Roosevelt; to her right, the much-talked-about Ellin Dynley Prince, who had the distinction of being married to the only Jew admitted to New York society. The snatches of conversation swirling around Samantha might as well have been in a foreign language: summering in Newport; taking the sun at Bailey's Beach; soirees at Beechwood, Mrs. Astor's Newport summer mansion; trying tennis at the Casino without one's corset; the nerve of some *nouveau riche* trying to get into Newport when everyone knew you had to start at Bar Harbor. And of course, the favorite topic of gossip: where was William Astor while his wife was giving this grand event?

Mark Rawlins bent his head and said quietly to Samantha, "Mrs. Astor's husband is down in Florida right now enjoying close companionship on his yacht. They say he has donated money to the governor of Florida to finance a company of mercenaries to search for hostile Seminoles in the Everglades."

A commotion suddenly erupted in the nucleus of the small group. Someone in the center, hidden by gowns and evening tails, was sputtering and gasping and calling for water. An anxious murmur rippled through the crowd; they were calling for a doctor. Rawlins immediately pushed his way through with Samantha in tow. They found a short, bearded gentleman gulping water and a husky woman at his side holding ready another glass.

"What happened?" asked Rawlins, kneeling next to the seated man.

"His cigar," said the woman who, Samantha saw, had an artificial eye that did not move with her other one. "He accidentally put the lighted end in his mouth."

While the encircling crowd appeared solicitous and concerned, Samantha noticed the winks and suppressed smiles. Mark Rawlins got the man to stop drinking long enough to examine his mouth. "It'll be all right, sir, you'll raise a blister, that's all."

The bearded gentleman mopped his handsome, square face with a handkerchief and waved away the second glass of water. "I prefer whiskey, Julia, my dear."

From behind, Samantha heard someone murmur, "You'd think he's had enough of *that*."

Ulysses S. Grant was a marvel of a man and when Samantha realized who this was, recognizing him from portraits she had seen, she was awestruck. Mark Rawlins' medical attention earned for him and his companion an introduction to the man who, only two years before, had been president of the United States.

Rawlins offered Mr. Grant a few words of advice on the care of his small wound and, while he did so, Samantha noticed that each time the man took a sip of whiskey he winced slightly. She attributed it to the burn on his lip, not knowing, as even Grant himself did not yet know, that the famous Civil War hero was suffering from cancer of the throat and would in five years be dead.

Rawlins led Samantha away to allow others to come forward and pay their respects; at the same time, a footman approached and informed Mr. Grant that the orchestra leader would be honored to take a musical request.

"Now there's irony," said Rawlins close to Samantha's ear as he guided her by the elbow through the congestion. "Mr. Grant is so unmusical that he once said he only knew two songs: one was 'Yankee Doodle' and the other wasn't."

Samantha laughed behind her fan but her eyes were once again searching for Joshua; it had been hours since she had seen him.

"Would you care to dance again?"

"If you don't mind, Dr. Rawlins, I prefer to sit."

They returned to their original table, picking up along the way two more glasses of champagne. "Do you know," said Rawlins as they sat, "you still haven't told me your real name."

A voice behind them said, "She is Estelle Masefield."

They spun around and saw Joshua standing behind a potted palm. "Josh!" cried Mark Rawlins, jumping up. "How good to see you again! We've been looking for you!"

Joshua held his granite eyes on Samantha. "Have you?"

"Won't you join us? I mean, do you mind if I stay on with you and your lovely companion?" Rawlins clapped Joshua on the back. "How long has it been, Josh? I'm at St. Luke's now. Been there six months."

At first Joshua showed no sign of joining them but continued to stare darkly at Samantha; then he came around and took the vacant chair. As he did so, Samantha saw that a film of perspiration covered his upper lip.

"I really would like to know the young lady's true identity," said Rawlins.

"She is my wife."

Mark Rawlins stared for a moment, smile still fixed on his face, then he cleared his throat and shifted his chair so that it made a loud scraping noise. "I quite understand the reason for your charade, Josh. The young lady explained it all to me."

"Did you, my dear? It did not take you long to forget our agreement."

"Don't blame her, Josh. I practically tortured her until she told the truth. But I still don't know her real name."

"Nor will you."

Dr. Rawlins shifted again in his chair, acutely aware of the undercurrent flowing between his two companions as they stared at one another. Had he wondered earlier if Josh were enchanted with her? Well, now it seemed the young lady was as much under Joshua's spell as he was under hers. A peculiar relationship, this. She seemed drawn to him and at the same time afraid of him . . .

"I was telling the young lady earlier that she doesn't look like a medical student."

As if suddenly remembering herself, Samantha snapped to life. She pulled away from Joshua's imprisoning gaze and turned, with a fluttering of her fan, to Dr. Rawlins. "I have even been told, sir, that as a medical student I should be older and fatter. That was when they tried to bar me from dissection."

Rawlins tried to ignore Joshua's oblique stare. "You aren't allowed in dissection?"

"I am now, but I had to fight to get in." As she described the hallway confrontation, Samantha was acutely aware of Joshua's burning eyes. "We have since divided into groups of five and work at nights on our own. Sometimes the others in my group prefer to go to a tavern and so I am left alone, which I deplore, for the school makes me nervous at night."

Mark Rawlins only half paid attention to her rapid speech. The transformation was remarkable: the mere presence of Joshua Masefield made her edgy. What strange hold did he have over her?

"They say the medical school is haunted."

He blinked at her. "I beg your pardon?"

"It comes from an Indian legend . . ." Samantha's voice grew distant as she told the tale of the two ill-fated lovers who met a tragic end on the site where the rotunda was built. "A youth in the Wolf clan was in love with a girl of the same clan, and she with him. But the girl's mother had already arranged for her to marry a young man of the Turtle clan. The night before the wedding, the youth from the Wolf clan stole the girl away; they ran off and consummated their love in the forest. The offended Turtle clan youth found them, killed the girl and castrated the youth. In the eyes of the Wolf clan the lovers had committed incest and so the clan was shamed; the youth was ostracized and, with nowhere to go, lay down beside the girl's body and after many days died. The legend goes that the spirits of the lovers roam the halls of the medical school, calling out to one another, but because they are cursed they can never be reunited."

When Samantha fell silent, the music from the hidden orchestra sounded suddenly rude and harsh. Mark Rawlins stared at the floor, deep in thought; it was Joshua who broke the spell. "Love, it seems, never brings anything but sorrow."

"It can bring happiness," said Samantha quietly, "if one would but allow."

And then everything came suddenly clear to Mark Rawlins. "I say!" he said loudly, straightening. "There's old Doc Barnes and his horsey-faced wife. Why, I haven't seen Barnesy since med school days." Mark Rawlins stood and extended a hand to Joshua. "Sorry to run off like this but I have a score to settle with Barnesy. You know where I am, Josh, at St. Luke's. Let's not be strangers?" They shook hands. Then he turned to Samantha. "It has been a pleasure, Mystery Lady. I hope we will run into each other again. And have no fear," he added significantly. "Your secret is safe with me."

He started to go, then stopped and said, as if in afterthought, "You know, Josh, your little masquerade is a success, but it might appear odd to some that a man doesn't dance at least once with his own wife. Good evening."

They watched him go, weaving through the crowd and ultimately out the main door. Samantha opened and closed her fan, sharply aware of the silent man at her side. He startled her by saying, "Shall we dance?"

Samantha would have liked to refuse; Mark Rawlins had almost shamed Joshua into it. "Yes, I would love to."

As they walked onto the dance floor Samantha again noticed the limp. "Have you hurt yourself, Dr. Masefield?"

"It is nothing." He extended his arm out straight so that he stood well away from her and lightly rested his hand on her waist. On the downbeat they swung away and fell in with the current; but it was not at all like dancing with Mark Rawlins, for Joshua moved mechanically, as if executing some tiresome chore, and he didn't look down at Samantha, but kept his eyes fixed firmly above her head.

"I was worried about you, Dr. Masefield," she ventured after several minutes. "You were gone so long."

"But you weren't lonely in my absence."

Samantha wondered if it had something to do with the scattered lighting overhead, but Joshua's coloring was odd. "Dr. Rawlins said you and he were old friends. I should have thought you would have had more to say to one another."

Joshua didn't respond. Still gazing intently at a point beyond his dance partner, he appeared to be trying very hard to concentrate. A fine lace of perspiration had sprouted now on his forehead.

"Dr. Rawlins seems a nice man."

Joshua finally looked down at her. "Are you going to see him again?"

"Whatever for?"

"He would be perfect for you. Mark has an impeccable reputation, he has a good income and a large practice, he has no vices, he is a decent-looking fellow, and he is smitten with you."

Samantha stared up at him.

The waltz reached a crescendo. As they did a turn, Joshua drew her closer to him. She said breathlessly, "Surely you are mistaken about *that!*"

"I have known Mark for a long time and I have never seen him look at a woman the way he looked at you. It's not an idle thought, Samantha. Whom you marry will have a great bearing on the success of your medical career. Mark, I believe, would be supportive."

"I don't wish to think of marriage right now—"

He fell out of step and seemed about to lose his balance.

"Dr. Masefield, are you all right?"

He sagged a little, leaning his weight on Samantha. "Perhaps we should sit down for a moment . . ."

They separated from the rest of the dancers and headed toward some vacant chairs. The limp was more noticeable and he openly mopped his face with his handkerchief.

"Can I get you something, Dr. Masefield?"

He waved a hand. "I haven't been feeling well all day. It must be the start of a winter cold. I think it best we leave, just as soon as my strength returns . . ."

Ten minutes later she was helping him down the slippery steps. The footman, thinking the doctor had tasted too much champagne, put an arm around Joshua and helped him into their carriage. Samantha climbed in behind and hastily pulled the blanket over his knees. Joshua's face had gone shockingly white.

During the slow ride home, as the horse picked its way over glassy cobbles and around snowdrifts, Joshua shivered and sweated beneath the blanket. But he refused her assistance going up the front steps, insisting that the cold air had revived him and that she go straight up to bed. Then Dr. Masefield hurried into his study and closed the door.

As Samantha mounted the stairs, undoing the clasp of her chinchilla cape, she decided that over all the evening had been a success. Although a little sad to see it end, she smiled at the wonderful memories she had collected and even conceded, when she reached the first landing, that it would be nice to see Mark Rawlins again.

There was a light under Estelle's door. Samantha suspected she was waiting up to hear news and gossip and to see the gown; but when Samantha tapped lightly and entered, she found Mrs. Wiggen bent over the bed. "What is it?" she asked, hurrying to the bedside.

Estelle's eyes fluttered open. "Ah, Samantha dear . . ." she whispered. "I can't seem to get enough breath. Oh, the dress is *beautiful,* how clever of you to choose that color, it makes your eyes look sky blue."

Joshua chose the color, not I, thought Samantha as she laid the cape across the foot of the bed and sat down to take hold of Estelle's cold hands.

"How was the ball? Tell me about it . . ."

Forcing a gay mood, Samantha recited the names, described the gowns, recounted the amusing incident with President Grant, and tried her best to bring the Astor ball into this pathetic bedroom. But the more she spoke and the faster her words tumbled over one another, the more the pain deepened in her heart. She left out Joshua's disappearance, his rudeness to an old friend, the way he had stared at her, their premature departure, and much, much more . . .

Estelle closed her eyes and smiled dreamily, recalling her own days as Philadelphia's grand hostess. "And Joshua, did he enjoy himself? Did you dance with him many times, Samantha? Joshua does so love to dance . . ."

Samantha turned away, fearful of Estelle seeing her tears. "I had to pull him away from the ball. I had had quite enough and was ready to drop, but Joshua could have gone on all night—" Lies and deception!

"That's Joshua. He was always the most popular man at the party, with the ladies always crowding around him hoping for one dance. I can see him now, at the Astor ball, the center of attraction. Thank you, Samantha, for giving him that again . . ."

She fled from the room and stumbled blindly up the stairs and into her own room, where she fell to her knees by the bed.

For the first time in her life Samantha had trouble praying; what frantic words she could manage brought no solace. She recited the rote words of her childhood, praying as her father had taught her, and Samantha felt a chill creep into her soul. She imagined God to look like her father—remote and vengeful—dressed in a preacher's black clothes and clutching a Bible in one hand. She imagined Him to be saying from His high place: For whom do you pray, Samantha Hargrave, that poor woman downstairs or yourself?

For Estelle! cried her guilt-ridden soul. She spread out her arms and pressed her face into the counterpane, suppressing deep sobs. I am praying for Estelle! I do *truly* want her to get better!

But the grim face of Samuel/God was molded in condemnation and Samantha felt a petrifying of her spirit. It was no use; no matter how frantically she prayed, how frequently she told herself she wanted Estelle to live, *He* heard the awful truth murmuring in her heart, and He passed His awful judgment on her: You cannot absolve your sin by praying for that poor woman. There is only one way to cleanse yourself of the sin of adultery you have committed with your heart—

There was a crash downstairs.

Samantha jerked her head up and listened. Someone was moving around in the rooms on the first floor.

She picked up the lamp by her bed, lighted earlier by Mrs. Wiggen, and stole quietly into the hall. Seeing that no light shone under the housekeeper's door, Samantha crept softly down the stairs and paused at the next landing. Both bedrooms were dark and silent; the Masefields were asleep. She leaned over the bannister and saw, below, a light under the door of the examining room. With held breath, Samantha continued down and stopped at the bottom to listen. Someone was riffling through the supplies, carelessly knocking bottles and tins about.

She considered her next move. This must be a patient, desperate for medication but unable to pay for it. It happened to other doctors, Samantha had heard, patients breaking in and stealing, but rarely did it happen to Joshua, for it was commonly known that if one could not afford something he gave it freely. Whoever it was, Samantha was sure she could reason with him.

She turned the knob slowly and, without making a sound, silently swung the door inward.

She gasped.

Joshua Masefield, standing in the center of the mess he had created, spun around and said through clenched teeth, *"Where is it, Miss Hargrave?"*

Samantha was too stunned to speak. Joshua had torn wildly through the supply cupboards and had mindlessly scattered things about. A bottle of quinine lay shattered at his feet.

"The morphine! Where is it?" Joshua held in one hand a hypodermic syringe; the sleeve of his other arm was rolled up. "There was a bottle of Magendie's here this morning. Where is it?"

Samantha's words rushed out. "The Evans boy. This afternoon. He cut his head playing hockey. I had to suture it. It was while you were out. I gave him an injection—"

"All of it?"

"The needle frightened him. He struck out at my hand and I dropped the syringe. Then he knocked over the bottle. A lot was spilled."

"Do you mean there is *none left?"*

"I . . . I don't understand, Dr. Masefield."

"Hell and damnation, woman! D'you mean you used the last of the morphine and didn't tell me?"

"I didn't think it was nec—"

"Tomorrow's Christmas!" he shouted, stepping closer. "How will I re-fill it?" Samantha saw that his pupils were abnormally dilated, that his eyes watered and that he perspired heavily. Thinking quickly, she put the lamp down and closed the door. "If you're in pain, Dr. Masefield, we have oral compounds you can take."

He swung away from her, limping back to the cupboard.

"Have you hurt your leg, Doctor?"

"Need the injectible," he muttered, pushing bottles around on the shelf. When Joshua's hand accidentally knocked over the carbolic solution, Samantha darted forward but was too late; it smashed to the floor, spattering her ball gown and suddenly filling the air with a dizzying pungency.

"What is it, Dr. Masefield? How did you hurt yourself?"

"Damn it, woman! Do I have to spell it out for you? Haven't you learned *anything* in the past year and a half? I didn't *hurt* myself, I'm a morphine addict!"

Samantha's jaw went slack. Before her, Joshua glared like a madman, his hair disheveled, his eyes made blacker by the dilated pupils. He was panting, as if he had been running, and his shirt clung to him in spots.

They stared at one another for a long, hollow moment, then Samantha, her nostrils stung by the carbolic vapors, calmly swept past him and came to stand before the cupboard. She had to clasp her hands tightly together to keep them from shaking and her voice was tremulous as she said, "There must be something in here, Dr. Masefield, that you can take for now. Tomorrow I will go to DeWinter's—"

"It won't be enough," he said behind her, now oddly subdued. "I'm up to three grains a day."

Samantha saw the cupboard swim through a rising wall of tears. Everything was suddenly, brutishly clear: the real reason for leaving Philadelphia, the real reason for his reclusive way of life, the *real* tragedy in this house . . . She reached out and blindly closed her fingers around a bottle. "Morphine is a derivative of opium, is it not?"

"Laudanum won't help. I need three grains *by vein!*"

Fighting to compose herself, she calmly turned around and held the bottle out to him. "It will at least allay the worst of your symptoms. I will call on Mr. DeWinter in the morning. If he is not at home, I shall go on to Dr. Newman's house. Christmas or not, emergencies must be taken care of."

He beheld her for a long moment with eyes that were heavy with sorrow and shame, then he meekly took the bottle from her and turned away.

Dr. Masefield went into his study and quietly closed the door. Heedless of the ruin she was making of her elegant satin gown, Samantha knelt and very patiently cleaned the examining-room floor.

Ten minutes later she was standing in the doorway, watching him. Joshua was slumped in his easy chair and staring into the cold fireplace; one hand held the empty bottle. Then he finally said without looking up, "I'm sorry for all that in there." His voice was dull, as if all the life had gone out of him. "And for the things I said to you. You can't imagine the panic I felt when . . . God," he groaned, "the awful panic . . ."

Samantha came into the study and drew up a footstool. Sitting by his side, resting her elbows on the arm of his chair, she said softly, "Are you feeling any better?"

He nodded. "It helped a little. The crisis . . . has passed. But in the morning—"

"It's all right, Dr. Masefield, at first light I shall go to DeWinter's."

"I can't ask that of you."

"You will be in no condition to do it yourself, Dr. Masefield. It will be just one more lesson for me in handling medical emergencies."

He was finally able to bring himself to look at her. Joshua's pupils were back to normal size, his skin was dry, but he was still ashen. "How you must despise me now."

"You insult me, Dr. Masefield, to suggest I would judge you so. If you have no faith in yourself, then at least have faith in my loyalty to you."

Her words seemed to cause him pain, for he winced and averted his head. "Admirably spoken," he said dryly. "To regard me as simply another medical problem, very admirable indeed. But I am a wretch, Miss Hargrave, and whether or not you will admit it to yourself, there is no more despicable man alive than one who is slave to the narcotic habit."

Samantha reached out and touched his sleeve. "How did it happen?" she asked gently.

Joshua stared into the cavernous fireplace. His voice was flat and distant. "It happened almost twenty years ago, at the First Battle of Bull Run. When the War of the Rebellion broke out, I signed up to serve in the Union Army as a field surgeon. The war was only two months old and we under General McDowell were certain we'd rout the Rebs and that would be the end of the conflict. But . . . it all went wrong. Beauregard's Confederate troops were reinforced by Jackson, who rightfully earned the nickname 'Stonewall' at that battle by putting the Union to shame. I caught a Confederate bullet in my thigh."

He drew in a ragged sigh and laid a hand over Samantha's. "It shattered the femur. Five big men had to hold me down while the surgeon poured fuming nitric acid into my exploded flesh. I mercifully passed out before he went after the bullet, for in those days we didn't have anesthesia in the field. How I survived I shall never know. The weeks that followed were pure hell and I often begged for death. Fever and pain created a madman of me; they dosed me with morphine to give me relief. No one knew anything about the addictive properties of narcotics in those days. It was given freely, and many men came away from the war with the habit. The 'soldier's disease,' they call it."

He paused to lick his lips. "I suppose I should count myself lucky. For one thing, they managed to save my leg. For another, when the army moved, I went with it. Bull Run occurred before the Union had organized field hospitals and nurses. Those who were critically wounded and could not walk were left behind on the battlefield when we retreated, but because I was a surgeon I was valuable to them and so they carried me along. I moved with the troops, alternating between intense pain and dulled senses. I eventually recovered and lived to see Gettysburg, the turning point of the war, and joined Sherman in his march to the sea. But by then I was hopelessly addicted."

Finally he turned to look at her. "You have no idea the nightmare I live every day of my life."

Samantha looked down at the large, strong hand clasping hers. She was not as ignorant of drug addiction as he thought. She had seen what slaves opium and morphine could make of innocent users; two instructresses at Playell's had been opium users, both addicted to Dr. Richter's Nerve Tonic. It always started the same way: innocently going to the chemist's for relief from menstrual cramps. One purchased commercial compounds in fancy bottles with labels that guaranteed relief "or money cheerfully refunded." Relief always came, for the compounds were heavily laced with narcotics, although there was never any mention of that on the bottle. A few teaspoons a day and the consumer felt worlds better. But then came the inevitable day when she tried to stop and discovered to her shock she could not. Samantha, lying in her bed at Playell's, had heard the late night cries of the instructress who had unwittingly let her supply run out. The sweats, the violent shakes, the vomiting and agonizing pain. Then the desperate rush early the next morning to the chemist's in town, the grasping of the bottle, the eager guzzling in the privacy of the carriage, the killing realization that she was now a prisoner of the stuff, and the damning humiliation of it.

Samantha whispered, "Can you not take a cure?"

He emitted a short, bitter laugh. "A cure? For the soldier's disease? There is no cure but cold abstinence, and believe me, Samantha"—Joshua rolled his head to the side so that their faces were inches apart—"I have tried that. Oh, God, how I have tried, and prayed, and stayed away from the drug until I have again prayed for death." His words came out in gaspy breaths. "Do you have any idea what it means to give up a morphine addiction, Samantha? The first stage is almost bearable: irritability, watery eyes, yawning. But this quickly passes into a sublime form of torture. Every nerve feels as if it is flayed and exposed to the air. There are muscle spasms that make a tooth pulling seem perfect ease. Every pore drips sweat. There are incapacitating abdominal cramps. At the same time, the mind and soul are in mortal battle, for while the mind knows it must abstain from the drug, the soul cries out for it, as a starving man would for food. The brain feels as if it is being squeezed in a vise, like an orange for its juice, until the final stage, insanity. Believe me, Samantha, *I have tried to quit.*"

She regarded him steadily, clutching his hand in hers. "Is that what you were doing this evening? Trying to quit?"

He snatched his hand away and shot to his feet. "Yes."

"But why?"

"I had my reasons."

Samantha remained as she was, crouched on the footstool, as Joshua, no longer limping, paced back and forth behind her. "The last time I tried to give up the habit was two years ago. I failed then but I thought, somehow, that this time would be different because of—" He stopped and looked down at her. "You have guessed by now the real reason why I had to leave Philadelphia. The addiction had become obvious to some of my friends. If my patients had ever found out . . ." He shook his head. "You cannot imagine the strain of constantly holding myself in check. I have so little control over my body and emotions, every waking minute of my life is a battle to maintain equilibrium. I had to get away, before I broke down. Estelle was a perfect excuse." He turned impulsively and strode across the room.

When Samantha saw that he was filling a glass with brandy she struggled to her feet. Hampered by skirts and petticoats, she stumbled across the room. "Don't drink that!"

He downed it in one toss.

"Joshua!" she cried. "Not on top of opium!"

He gave her a self-deprecating smile. "Why not? My body can stand it."

"Don't be so hard on yourself, Joshua. It isn't your fault."

He gazed at her for the space of one breath, then looked away. His voice was suddenly full of contrition. "I . . . want to apologize for the episode with the gown. I was being unreasonable."

"No, you weren't," she said gently. "I should have realized you would want people to see how well you dress your wife. I had been thinking only of money—"

"Confound it, Samantha!" he shouted, startling her. "It had nothing to do with impressing people with how my wife dresses! I did it to show *you* off! You always dress like a mouse, hiding yourself. You've a good figure . . ." He swung away and clumsily reached for the decanter. "You should show it off. I wanted to see you just once as you should be seen." He sloshed more brandy into his glass. "You don't stick a rose in a tin can, do you?"

Stupefied, Samantha could do no more than gape at him.

This time he drank the brandy slowly, and after the first sips said quietly, as if to himself, "It was a year and a half ago that a very proud young lady came into this room to return a pair of gloves. She pretended to have been offended by the gift, but the way her cheeks blazed . . ."

Joshua turned around and regarded her with turbulent eyes. Then he took a step toward her and reached up to brush her cheek with his fingertips. "It's Christmas, Samantha."

She closed her eyes, certain his fingers had left a mark.

"I've never told you," he began awkwardly, "how proud I am of you. I will admit, I had my doubts when you first came to work for me. You seemed so young, so unarmed. But look how you've changed, how you've grown, so confident, so sure of what you want. Lucerne has done a good job on you."

"It wasn't Lucerne," she said softly. "It was you, Joshua. I love you."

His face twisted. "You mustn't say that."

"It is true, nonetheless."

He struggled, a tremor racked his body, his handsome features rippled in indecision; then he snapped loose, as if catapulted, flung his arms around her and pulled her hard against him. "I love you, too," he murmured into her hair. "I have for so long . . ."

Samantha wanted to cry and laugh at the same time, but instead remained quiet and unmoving in his arms, savoring the moment. This was the embrace she had so long dreamed of, and because she had experienced it countless times in fantasy she now had to work to convince herself it was real. Samantha hung upon each tactile sensation to give realness to the moment: Joshua's masculine smell, the deep resonance of his voice against her ear, the warmth coming through his clothing, the rhythmic throb of his heart against her breast.

In the next instant his mouth was covering hers and it so startled her, the sudden *realness* of it, the sudden taste of his lips and tongue, more sensations she had for so long tried to imagine but which had fallen far short of reality, that she held her breath until the room started to sway. She was falling, tumbling down the dark void, and nothing existed but Joshua's tempestuous kiss, the feverish working of his tongue, the tickly feeling deep in her abdomen as his male hardness pressed urgently against her skirts . . .

And then he suddenly pulled away. "No, I cannot do this! I have no right. I will not drag you down with me." He wrenched away from her, leaving her suddenly cold and abandoned.

Joshua groped for the wall, laid his palms flat on it, braced himself upright with arms outstretched and elbows locked, and bowed his head between his shoulders, looking at the floor. "I have no right. Such joy is not mine to have. I love you too much, Samantha, to bring you down to my depths."

She laid her hands beseechingly on his broad back and felt the muscles that had tensed to marble hardness. "Joshua, Joshua, it is not to depths you take me but to heights!"

"You don't understand," he groaned. "My dear, dearest Samantha, you don't understand." With great effort Joshua pushed away from the wall and turned volcanic eyes upon her. "Samantha, you are no ordinary woman. You are special, more so than you think you are. You were born for a great purpose, you were born to a unique destiny. I have seen that for a long time now, and it has been my one bit of joy in life to know that I am helping you toward that end. But it has changed now. In my weakness I have robbed myself of that reward."

Her eyes rapidly searched his face. "Joshua, I don't understand."

"If we succumb tonight, then we shall be lovers. And I know where that road will lead, where it must lead. To obsession. To self-loathing. Right now, Samantha, you are consumed with your dream to become a doctor, but as your lover I shall replace that dream. Your career will no longer be the focus of your life, I will."

"And would that be so bad?"

"If you were an ordinary woman, no. But you are not. I have no right, in my selfish greed to gratify my desire, to rob you of your true purpose in life."

"I can continue my studies and love you at the same time."

"Can you?" His mouth lifted in an ugly way. "I know what energies the study of medicine requires, what singleness of purpose, how clear the mind must be. How free will your mind be when you sit by my wife's sickbed during the day and then come into my arms at night? Will you be able to divorce the guilt, all thought of me, from your mind so that there is room only for your studies? And after you graduate, can you go on with your training, can you pursue the meritorious career that awaits you while saddled with a hopeless drug addict? Before you came into my life, my existence was one long road of hopelessness, at the end of which was waiting for me the final needle that would end my misery. But then you came and I was given new hope through you. If there was no chance of my being saved, at least I had the satisfaction of watching *you* become something, watching you grow and transform into a woman who is going to make an indelible mark upon the world. My joy was knowing that I was instrumental in helping you succeed. But now, if we pursue this madness, all will be lost—you will follow *my* wretched path, and I shall have to bear the knowledge that it was I who diverted you. Oh, Samantha . . ." Tears rose in his eyes as he drew in a rattling breath.

She glided into his arms as automatically and easily as if she had done it a thousand times. "I love you, Joshua."

"If you truly did, then you would leave this house and never come back." But even as he said it his embrace tightened and his body moved against hers and his lips worked along her hair, down her cheek and at last found their place on her mouth.

Everything he had said vanished, all the guilt, remorse and portents of a disastrous future dissipated before the great flood of passion suddenly unleashed, no longer held in check; two hungers fed upon one another, forgetting in an instant all the wiseness of his words and the folly of what they were about to do. Oblivious of everything but their mutual desperation, they sank to the carpet; in the back of her mind Samantha marveled at her frenzy, but she was unaware of making such an observation. Her soul and body were conscious now only of Joshua, of banishing his loneliness and replacing it with searing love, as if to brand herself upon him, to make him forever hers, and her forever his.

In all her dreams and fantasies she had never suspected it could be like this, both pain and ecstasy, the filling of a cup that could never be full, the reaching up, the yearning, the aching, the scream held in her throat, the delirious feel of him inside her, his weight smothering her, glimpses from under her lashes of his rapturous face, and finally the unexpected explosion at the end that both shattered and melted her body. And afterward, the sweet cradling in each other's arms, oblivious of the smell of carpet dust and of the feel of the coarse weave against her bare back, with Joshua's head resting on her naked breast, the delicious satisfaction, the overwhelming sense of peace.

When they had recovered a little they went up to her room where they would not be heard and where they spent the last few hours before the cold Christmas dawn living only for each other, exploring, experimenting, gratifying, all beneath the concealing cover of night. But when the first pale wash of blue light came through the curtains and Samantha slumbered, her hair fanned out on the snowy pillow, Joshua peeled himself up and crept out of the room. And later, drinking the cocoa Mrs. Wiggen had brought up and feeling immensely satisfied with herself, Samantha found the note.

"As you read this, dearest Samantha, I am walking the streets in search of morphine; when I return I shall be interested only in my injection—nothing more. Estelle is in pain this morning, the pleural lining has been made more adhesive by the sharp cold air; while you and I abandoned ourselves to our selfish wants, my wife lay in bed, alone and suffering. What was done, dearest Samantha, was done, but we can never repeat it. If you truly love me, and if you hold dear the destiny that awaits you, you will go away from this house today. Grant me, in my wretchedness, one last thread of self-respect."

EIGHTEEN

S HE WALKED THE WINTER LANES OF LUCERNE ALONE, plodding over drifts of snow so high that she could reach up and touch telegraph wires, listening to the crunch of each bootfall, the only sound to disturb the pristine January stillness. She walked for miles, her face bitten and raw with the cold, the hems of her skirts making sodden, icy slaps against her legs, her fingertips growing numb even in the womb of her otter muff. Occasionally the distant tinkling of sleigh bells worked through to her awareness, but Samantha made it a point to avoid the roads that had been cleared of snow and the areas of the lake where skaters glided and twirled; her steps carried her to the lonely fringes of Lucerne where she stood no risk of encountering anyone, where she wouldn't be suddenly called upon to muster a greeting, a smile, even a glance in their direction. She needed to be alone.

Back in the warm house Hannah would occasionally part the curtains and look out, hoping to glimpse the dark-caped figure against the white world, then she would shake her head and let the curtain drop and return to her baking or basting, mystified, but convinced, in her basic uncomplicated way, that whatever it was that disturbed the girl, whatever had happened over Christmas, would in time fade, as did all things, good and bad, and that she would come around and be her old self again.

That Samantha would never be her "old self again" didn't cross Hannah's mind; she who never felt the need to delve into the mysteries and intricacies of the psyche firmly believed that the only real change a person underwent was death. After all, wasn't she still the same life-loving girl who had grown up along the Shannon years ago? Hannah believed she had never changed, but if she had ever once stopped and done some inner exploration as Samantha now did out in the snow she would have found some surprising and most likely dismaying truths about herself. And possibly that was why Hannah Mallone never did dabble in delving, left that to priests and philosophers; she knew who she was, what she wanted and where she was going, no need to go upsetting comfortable applecarts by digging around. As Samantha was doing now. Ah well, if it is what the girl needs, then let her be. In time she'll come around and it'll all be forgotten.

From the moment she returned Samantha felt no compulsion to explain to Hannah. She had arrived unexpectedly on her doorstep two days after Christmas, face pinchy and bloodless, and had delivered herself into the enveloping glow and warmth and homey protection of Hannah's comfortable little world. A few words, nothing more, and she had settled down to a quiet routine of surface living, going through motions, eating but not tasting, sleeping but not resting, and striking off each morning swaddled in her cape to go in search of something she could not identify.

Samantha had some vague sense of having come to the end of a phase in her life, that something—she didn't yet know what—was closed forever; she would step out of the house into the glassy air, survey the fresh blanket of snow covering the world, and think: My future begins today.

She thought it odd, because generally one could only see the stages of one's life in retrospect, with time and distance giving an objective view. A woman of forty, like Hannah, could look back and say, "That was the day my life took a turn," but she could see it only from a twenty-year vantage point. Was it possible, therefore, for a nineteen-year-old to see the demarcation while she was going through it? Especially since she had no idea just what she was moving *from*?

Samantha stood at the edge of the lake and let the cold wind lift the hood off her head. Before her, like a looking glass on its back, lay the frozen lake, its surface milky, dark in spots where the ice was dangerously thin. She stood and wrestled with her thoughts until her skin cried out in pain, reminding her that even in her spiritual struggle the flesh must still be taken care of. She would scan that vast stretch of pure whiteness for the thing she sought. What was it she tried to seize upon that was so maddeningly elusive? That it had come to an end she knew, but what was "it"? Sometimes, coming upon a white hare and startling it so that it sat up, frozen, whiskers twitching, Samantha thought she could almost grasp what she sought. But then the rabbit would dart and the thought, like a feather just beyond fingertip reach, would flutter away.

In time Samantha would come to know, but it wouldn't be for a long time, not until years and distance brought her to a point where she could look back and say, "Yes, that was the day my life took a turn. That was the day my innocence ended."

The winter gave way to a drizzly, muddy spring, and then to a fragrant, reborn spring that brought back the wood thrush and ruffed grouse and splashed the meadows with Queen Anne's lace and devil's paintbrush. In late May, Sean Mallone came home and Hannah underwent a miraculous transformation. The years seemed to peel away from her as she bustled about with new youthful energy, bringing back the Shannon girl Hannah always fancied herself. Her amber eyes glowed like the windows of the Astor mansion, her cheeks flushed with peaches and roses; she worried over her hair, laid in stores of Sean's favorite foods and whiskey, and filled the house with nosegays of strawberry blossoms and black-eyed Susan.

Happy for her friend, Samantha retreated to give them room. Sean's return did not intrude upon her life: Samantha kept rigidly, for self-preservation, to her routine of going to classes, studying late into the nights, spending the weekends in solitary walks, and occasionally gathering wild berries to help Hannah put up jams and jellies. There was survival in routine.

It was during the last week of school that she found the glade.

The medical students were wild beyond toleration, and the citizens of Lucerne, as they did every year at this time, turned to one another and grumbled that they *knew* they never should have permitted a medical school to be built here. Four students went too far: one drunken night they hauled their dissection cadaver, seamed along the arms and legs with long rows of clumsy stitching where dissection had been done, and sat it up on the horse statue in the town square, lashing its arms around the long-forgotten general's waist; then they hid in the bushes, giggling, to wait for dawn to see the townspeople's expressions. But instead they passed out and were found peacefully asleep on the lawn and they were expelled that day.

To disassociate herself from her rambunctious colleagues, Samantha celebrated the end of school by taking long walks around the countryside. She stumbled into the glade by accident, deep in thought, and stood in its center slowly turning. It was like a little room: tall poplars and birches were the walls; their outspread branches met overhead to form a ceiling through which bits of blue showed; the floor was hard-packed earth and carpeted with leaves; an old log, felled long ago by lightning, created a perfect little bench. Samantha sat on it and wondered if anyone ever came here; it didn't appear so, since the blackberries hung lush in their briar vines, unplucked even by birds, some lying rotten on the ground.

Samantha, to whom that most sacred of mysteries—the human body—was no longer a mystery, needed a little mysticism in her life, and she began to think her glade enchanted, magical. She found an Indian arrowhead and wondered if, long ago when they were still pure and savage, the Indians used this as a place of worship. They revered practical spirits, gods who lived in corn and trees and water, gods you could touch and taste and *commune* with, not like the remote, faceless God of Samuel Hargrave; with its rich smells of loamy earth and decaying leaves, the pungency of rotting berries, the glade was like a church of the senses, its very air a heady sacramental wine that made one feel the old gods were still there. At the least, it was a quiet spot perfect for contemplation, and Samantha, just turned twenty, fell beneath its languorous summer spell: she fancied the glade had been waiting for her . . .

It was the perfect place for sorting things out, for straightening the muddle her life had reached at Christmas. She would come with a picnic basket of cold ham and biscuits and a flask of lemon tea, wearing a cotton frock and starched sunbonnet, and she would let the enchantment do its work. Frequently, after their noon dinner of jointed rabbit or roast fowl and potatoes in gravy with apple pie, Samantha would catch the lazy look in Sean's eye and the dreamy way he reached out to touch Hannah's arm and Samantha would invent an excuse to go out—she needed a card of thread or a tin of talc—and she would strike off first to have a look at the lake to satisfy herself that it was still there; then she would tread the familiar path to the glade and deliver herself into its soothing sanctuary; often, the mere act of stepping beneath its leafy boughs brought instant solace. (Samantha had tried once, months ago, attending Lucerne's Presbyterian church but had come away feeling as if she had just left a huge feast still hungry. Since there was no local Catholic church, Hannah said a rosary every Sunday morning and Samantha, to please her friend, learned it and recited along, but it also gave her no satisfaction. The glade filled a primal need.)

Samantha never minded being excluded from Sean's and Hannah's relationship, her need to be alone was as great as theirs to be together, and she would occasionally gently reflect on what they were doing at that moment, taking a small vicarious satisfaction in their afternoon love-making, happy for them for having known a little of it herself, and then she would urge her mind along to give them privacy.

At first it was almost always Joshua. But each day she felt a little more healed, a little freer of him. Had it truly been love? She was no longer sure. She had nothing previous to compare it to. Once, a long time ago, there had been Freddy and it seemed to Samantha she had loved him, but that emotion was old and fuzzy now, too out of focus to recall precisely, like a tintype in which someone has moved. Perhaps there were different kinds of love. For Joshua she had felt something more like idol worship, love nonetheless but not the sort of love that naturally leads to a sexual embrace. This last

Samantha pondered most of all, for, curiously, with the sex act her love for Joshua had changed.

As the summer days came one by one, none more remarkable than the rest, Samantha came to a revelation in the glade: Joshua was a symbol. He was like the flower you press between book pages, you don't love the flower but what it stands for, a moment you cherish. Joshua stood for something, he represented the turning point from her girlhood to womanhood, and for that Samantha held him most dear, for she would never pass that way again. You can only have your first time once; she was glad it had been with Joshua.

With the help of her glade and its ancient spirits Samantha was finally able to place Joshua in a little room in her heart where he would always reside and where, occasionally, she would visit him. With the drawing near of autumn and the new school year, she came to accept the fact that she would never see or hear from him again.

With Joshua taken care of, Samantha was able to swivel her thoughts around one hundred and eighty degrees, from pondering the past to now looking at the future. Another revelation came to her that at first struck her as peculiar, but the more she examined it, the more she began to feel comfortable with it and accept it as a truism: she had indeed been born to study medicine. Going back, back, she saw the moments in her life that stood out in stark relief, beginning with an old injured alley cat, and then taking care of Freddy, and her burned father, and finally Mrs. Steptoe; those were the times when she had felt most *herself*, the most in harmony with what she was. Mr. Hawksbill had seen it, Dr. Blackwell had seen it, Joshua had seen it, and now Samantha was seeing it. And seeing it, accepting it, feeling *right* with it, Samantha decided in her little glade that her course was set and that she would never, no matter what, allow herself to be diverted from it again.

In August she received the jubilant news from Louisa that she and Luther were going to Cincinnati to be married, and Samantha, dipping into her small and growing smaller savings, sent off a teapot and matching cups from Kendall's Dry Goods. Fall came rapidly to Lucerne, draping the town and countryside in a mantle of reds and golds and browns, and a new school year was suddenly, busily in session. Because it was the second year, the work load was increased—this was when many students fell out—and Samantha, free from involvements and preoccupations, just as Joshua had wanted her to be, plunged wholly and with true dedication into her studies and the pursuit of her destiny.

Sean returned to the mountains in October, leaving the house curiously hollow and echoing, and with the onset of November rains Hannah took to wondering again about Samantha. She hated to admit it, but the girl had, after all, somehow changed.

Hannah didn't care for analyzing other people, her homespun mind was uncomfortable with speculation and abstracts, but this time she could not help herself; sitting in the cozy circle of the fire with a pot of steaming tea at her elbow and listening to the rain pelt the windows beyond the heavy draperies, Hannah would occasionally look up from her mending, consider the young head bowed over a medical book—open to an indecent illustration—and wonder why, unlike any other woman in the good Lord's creation, Samantha Hargrave never once opened up.

It was only natural, two women sharing a house, ensconced in the fire's glow with a pot of tea and the rainy night ticking away on the clock, it was only female-natural for them to feel compelled to share little intimacies, to confess woman problems, to seek comfort from a sister sympathizer. Women never tired of exchanging, like recipes, their most personal confidences. Nights like these always brought out things that remained private all other times: remedies for menstrual cramps, peculiar dreams of late, the delicious, risque novel under the pillow, an unsettling notice of the new man at Kendall's Dry Goods . . .

Hannah studied a stitch and tried to help things along, firmly convinced that a good confession, like a laxative, would set Samantha right again; she would murmur a private worry, dream or observation and wait for the traditional reciprocation. But none ever came. Samantha would utter a polite response ("I know what you mean, Hannah, I too always dream more vividly during my monthly days; I don't think it's anything to worry about") and then she would draw the door closed.

It wasn't right, especially in light of what the girl was studying. A most *unprivate* occupation to say the least, Hannah thought, inspecting the most secretive nooks of a person's body. Nothing was held back from the doctor, no crevice or orifice or inner clockwork escaped his inspection; he saw people's nakedness and heard more intimacies confessed probably than any priest ever did, and Samantha was learning to be just such a person, a person before whom all that is human is revealed—how then could she herself remain so closed?

Ah well, thought Hannah, maybe that was the answer, plain and simple. Maybe when you have every human and bodily thing blatantly revealed to you, maybe you start to yearn for a last outpost of privacy. Maybe your basic nature thinks it's unnatural to have such a clear view and, without knowing it, you long to hold onto that last reservoir of privacy and sanctity—yourself. Come to think of it, Hannah decided as she resumed her stitching, old Doc Shaughnessey was a mighty closed-up-tight man, knew everything about everyone in the village but himself remained an enigma. Were they all like that, doctors? Maybe so. Samantha Hargrave was certainly heading that way.

Hannah stirred and sighed and glanced over again at her companion, thankful that the offensive page had been turned and the illustration out of sight, studied the cameo profile—the long slender neck, classical nose and chin, thick fur lashes, finely drawn brows, and that stunning high-domed forehead—gave her one more minute's consideration (oh well, still waters, they say), then Hannah shrugged it all off, thinking herself unsuccessful in her clumsy attempt at analysis.

The truth was, Hannah had hit it right on.

NINETEEN

I HAVE NEVER BEEN SO HUMILIATED IN ALL MY LIFE," SAID Samantha as she darned a hole in one of her stockings. "I'll be glad when school is finished and I have my diploma. Then I shall be a doctor and won't be subjected to any more indignities."

Hannah cast a sideways glance at her friend, a look which said: Don't count on it, darlin'. But she kept her silence. Hannah Mallone had other things to think about right now.

It was a pewter-gray January afternoon and the heat from the cast-iron stove seemed no match against the arctic drafts whispering through the house. Samantha's hands were chilled and her anger did little to keep the needle under control. She felt restless, confined; she needed her little glade now but it was buried under snow.

Hannah had her back to Samantha, dicing carrots into neat little cubes to be dropped into the bubbling rabbit stew. "So why did they make you sit behind a screen, darlin'?"

The memory of it made the anger rise again so that she couldn't speak.

The special lecturer from out of town, the intimate subject of his talk, the righteous indignation at discovering a *female* in the class, his pompous refusal to go on with the lecture, Dr. Jones's plea with Samantha to absent herself "just this once," her own obstinacy, the showdown, and the ultimate compromise that the man would deliver his talk if the female student was put out of his sight so as not to offend him. They erected a screen in a corner and Samantha was put behind it where she could listen to his discourse on human sexuality and not give the gentleman apoplexy by reminding him of her presence. Once, during the section on how to conduct a vaginal exam, Samantha had sneezed and the distinguished gentleman had had to sit down to recover.

"Normally the students snicker and guffaw and make lewd remarks during that lecture," Dr. Jones had explained to her after the first of five sessions. "But because they know you are in the room, albeit hidden, they hold themselves in check."

For the first time Samantha was annoyed with her fellow students; Dr. Miller had admonished the young men to be certain to maintain an air of total disinterest during a vaginal exam, to choose some object in the room upon which to fix one's gaze and to conduct the exam under the lady's clothes and *never* insert more than one finger at a time.

A student had giggled and another had quickly coughed to camouflage it, but Samantha had heard.

Hannah now said without interrupting the rhythm of her slicing, "I have to agree with the professor. I don't approve of you sittin' in on somethin' like that. 'Tain't respectable."

"A doctor must learn those things."

"It's the job of a husband to teach his wife about sex. No *proper* lady'd sit with a bunch o' men and hear about them things. You won't go to your marriage bed innocent, and there's not many men as would like that."

"You weren't innocent, Hannah, and it didn't bother Sean."

Hannah shrugged. Her case was different.

Samantha put down her mending. She was recalling the last of Dr. Miller's lectures. "Remember, gentlemen, since most female complaints are incurable anyway, it is the role of the physician merely to humor the lady.

You will find that most of your female patients will come to you with trifling reasons about which they groan mightily. To quote the esteemed Dr. Oliver Wendell Holmes, 'Woman is a constipated biped with a backache.'"

Hannah bent over and opened the oven to inspect the two big potatoes browning in their jackets. Normally she found joy in cooking; today she was distracted. Not lucky enough, like Samantha, to have been gifted with an orderly mind, Hannah's thoughts were all a-jumble. Men, it had to do with men.

Her undisciplined mind rolled back to Christmas Day, just three weeks gone, and the sorry failure *that* had been. It would be nice, she had thought, to invite one of Samantha's student friends to share Christmas dinner with them. One who had no home and family to go to for the holidays, a proper gentlemanly one, and one who would appreciate the opportunity to spend an afternoon with Samantha. Well, there certainly were enough in *that* category.

The young man had shown up wearing a forest-green frock coat and charcoal trousers of such excellent cut and fabric that Hannah was certain he was rich and therefore a good catch for Samantha. In the living room where a fire burned hotly and pine boughs gave off a rich scent, he had shyly given his hostesses each a present: for Hannah, a lavender sachet, for Samantha a copy of *Ben-Hur,* just written by the governor of the Territory of New Mexico. While Hannah had invented excuses to spend most of the time in the kitchen, the two young people had sat in the parlor.

Hannah had eavesdropped on their conversation: "There is word going around, Miss Hargrave, of a Polish surgeon in Vienna who is experimenting with wearing sterile linen gloves in surgery. The other students laugh, but I think there might be some merit to it. What do you think, Miss Hargrave?"

"It is entirely possible, Mr. Goodman, that wounds become infected by the surgeon's hands. It has to do with whether or not one advocates the microbial theory. If there are indeed such things as *germs,* then it would follow that germs on the surgeon's hands could cause infections. However, it would seem the surgeon would lose his sense of touch if he wore gloves."

The young man, in an awkward attempt to steer the conversation to something more personable, had ventured to say, "I do hope you enjoy this book, Miss Hargrave, it is a rather excellent rendering of the life of Christ."

"Sadly, I've little time for novels, Mr. Goodman. But speaking of reading, only the other day in the *Boston Journal* I read of a Dr. Tait in England who has successfully removed an appendix and the patient lived. He did the most remarkable thing, Mr. Goodman. He *sterilized* his instruments beforehand . . ."

Hannah had had to fight the impulse to rush in and give Samantha a good shaking. Damn and blast ya, girl! she had thought. You don't know how good you've got it! Open yer heart and let the lad love ya! It's spinsterhood ye're headed for and that's a fact!

Hannah now scooped up the carrots and turnips and plopped them into the simmering gravy. Then she ran the back of her hand across her forehead; what on earth was wrong with her today? She had the disposition of a broody hen. She paused before the stove. Her face darkened. Hannah Mallone knew very well what was wrong with her; pretending she didn't wasn't going to make it go away. The problem was, what was she to do about it? Well, that frightening decision had been made weeks ago; it was just a matter of screwing up the courage to approach Samantha with the dreadful proposition . . .

Although they were in the same room they were in different worlds. Hannah was bedeviled by her powerful problem and Samantha had another preoccupation. Louisa's letters of late had taken on a disturbing tone. Samantha couldn't pinpoint it, no matter how many times she read them, but there was definitely trouble.

Hannah washed her hands, dried them on her apron and pulled out a chair at the table. "I'm all done in. I've got to sit down."

"Are you feeling all right, Hannah?"

The woman didn't answer. She lifted the cozy off the teapot, poured herself a cup and spooned in two dollops of wild honey. She cradled the cup between her hands as if to warm them even though she looked flushed and hot.

Now that Samantha thought about it, as she bundled up her mending and put it in her basket, Hannah's appetite hadn't been good the last couple of weeks. On the table between them were the remnants of a cold meat pie they had had for breakfast; Samantha lifted the cloth, broke off a piece of crust and popped it into her mouth. "I think you need a tonic, Hannah. Some people's blood thins in winter."

Hannah thought a moment. "Perhaps you're right, darlin'." With uncharacteristic weariness she rose, went to the cupboard and pulled down a bottle of Sean's Irish whiskey. Returning to her chair, she uncorked it and decanted some into her tea. Then she held the bottle suspended and looked questioningly at Samantha.

Then Samantha saw something in her friend's eyes—she had seen it once before, when a patient had been presented for class inspection and Dr. Page had announced in his professorial tone that Miss Bates had cancer. Miss Bates had had the look in *her* eyes—a flicker of bleakness, as if for one fraction of a breath her soul had given up. And then it was gone and Hannah was only looking at her with a tired expression. "Thank you, Hannah. I could do with a bit of bracing myself."

They sipped in silence for a few minutes; little bubbly sounds came from the stove, and occasionally a pack of snow broke away from the eaves and fell to the ground with a *whump.* The longer the silence stretched, the more Samantha came to realize there was something wrong.

"I've somethin' on me mind," said Hannah finally.

Samantha waited.

"I suppose you've noticed the new"—Hannah lifted her cup an inch off the saucer and with her other hand started turning the saucer in circles—"the new . . . gentleman at Kendall's?"

Yes, Samantha knew him, although she wouldn't call him a gentleman. No one knew much about him. He had appeared in town one day in October and Mr. Kendall had given him a day's work to earn his supper; but the man had proven such a willing and agreeable and efficient worker that Mr. Kendall had kept him on. All Samantha knew about him was that his name was Oliver and that she didn't like the way he looked at her when Mr. Kendall wasn't around. "What about him, Hannah?"

"Well, darlin' . . ." Round and round went the saucer, making a scraping sound on the scrubbed table top. "He sorta took a fancy to me, you see, and he's been very kind to me, seein' I get a few pennies off a yard of cloth.

You know how tight Mr. Kendall can be, but when he ain't around Oliver's always fair to me. He's even carried my parcels all the way home for me, and I've had him in for a cuppa."

Samantha kept her eyes on the steadily turning saucer.

"Well, one afternoon, it was while you were taking that important exam . . ."

Back at the end of November. Samantha had come home so distracted she hadn't noticed Hannah's queer silence over supper. Looking back, she saw it now.

The saucer stopped, the cup rattled back into its indentation. "He stayed all afternoon." Samantha felt Hannah's intense shame across the table invade her own body. "And it wasn't just the once."

Samantha looked up. Hannah's amber eyes were wide and clear. Her voice sounded as if she should have tears but there were none. "I'm scared, Samantha."

"That Sean will find out? How can he?"

Hannah shook her head. "It was all done so secret, there's no way of Sean knowin.'"

"Is it . . . over?"

"Bless me, girl, it lasted two weeks and then I put a stop to it!"

"Then what are you worried about?"

"I'm pregnant."

Samantha stared. "Are you sure? Have you been to a doctor?"

"I don't need no doctor to tell me what it means when I skip my monthly days and throw up in the mornings and my ankles are swelling like melons! I've seen enough of this condition in other women to know what's up!"

"Oh, Hannah . . ."

The woman tipped her chin and set her jaw firmly. "That's why I'm tellin' you all this, Samantha. I want you to help me."

"What can I do?"

"Get rid of it for me."

Samantha blinked as if she'd been slapped.

Seeing the look on her face, Hannah had to turn away. She got up and went to the stove, lifted the lid and gave the rabbit a poke. "You've got to be wonderin," she said in a faraway voice, "why I did it. Why, when I've got a man like Sean Mallone in me bed five months of the year, why I would muck with another man, a man the likes of Oliver at that."

Samantha gazed up at her friend but made no reply.

"Well, darlin', maybe right now you wouldn't understand. You're twenty years old and slender, and your skin is like cream, with the kind of freshness that makes men hungry. I was like that once, too. Years ago . . ." Hannah moved around the kitchen, touching things as if to keep a hold on the ordinary. "These last few years I've been lookin' at myself in the mirror and I've been seein' the lines comin' and my waist thickenin' out and gray comin' into my fine hair that was once my pride. And I got to thinkin', late at night, that maybe Sean loved me because I was a habit with him and comfortable and he was used to me. And then I got to thinkin' that I didn't appeal to men any longer like I used to."

She swung around and looked down at Samantha. "And then I got to lookin' at the years ahead. Me growin' fatter and grayer and maybe one mornin' Sean wakin' up and takin' a good look at me and finally seein' me for what I really was. It wouldn't be half so bad, Samantha"—her voice grew tight—"if there'd been children. If you've got kids, it don't matter that you grow old and fat. You've got some-thin' to be proud of. Some proof that you was once a desirable and useful woman. But me, what've I got? I'm tellin' you, girl, I got scared."

She returned to her chair and refilled her cup with whiskey. "I wasn't in love with Oliver, I didn't even feel no real passion for him, but he made me feel young again with his flirtin' and callin' me *Miss* Mallone, and when he touched me it was like I was twenty again and he made my spirit come back to life like Sean hasn't been able to do in a long time." Hannah took a long, invigorating drink. "And then after two weeks the feeling died and I was simply an old woman makin' a fool of herself with a younger man and so I sent him off and told him not to come back . . ."

Samantha's hand inched across the table and curled around Hannah's wrist.

"You know what to do, girl. You've learned all about these things. You know what to do to get me out of this perishing mess. Something to drink, maybe—"

"Hannah," whispered Samantha. "Do you really want that?"

"No, I don't really, but I have to and that's the reality of it." Tears finally filled the topaz eyes. "Lord knows how badly I've wanted a baby. There's been times I prayed so long to the Virgin that my knees bled. And now to think . . ." Hannah gazed down at her abdomen in wonder. "To think the blessed little darlin's in there at last, all curled up and asleep, waitin' to come Irish-kicking into the world—" Her face clouded. "I love this baby of mine, Samantha, but I love Sean more. So I've got to get rid of it."

"But you don't have to choose! You can have both. Tell Sean the man forced his way in, threatened you. Sean is a compassionate and understanding man, he'll keep the baby and raise it as his own—"

"That's not the point, girl. It's not for *me* I'm doin' it, it's not *my* reputation I'm worried about, it's *Sean's*. Oh, darlin', don't you see? All these years it's me we've thought was the cause of our childlessness. But *this,* this would mean it's Sean, that he can't father children, and it would strip the manhood from him. I've no right to do that to him. You've got to help me preserve Sean's self-respect."

Samantha searched the room for an answer. "Have you told Oliver?"

"No."

"He has a right to know."

"He's got no rights. What was comin' to him he got upstairs. We're all paid up, I don't owe him nothing." Hannah leaned across the table, anxious. "It don't have to be quick and painless, I'm not askin' that. I 'spect the Lord'll want me to suffer for it. I only want you to promise me it'll be thorough!"

Samantha started to tremble. If only she didn't know, didn't have the awesome knowledge of how to prepare the concoction that would do the job, then the decision would not be hers, but she did have the knowledge, the answer was at her lips, it would be so simple—an infusion of cottonseed tea or a dose of slippery elm; even oil of tansy could be gotten at the town's pharmacy—and Hannah would be free by morning. "Hannah," she whispered. "Are you *sure?*"

"Oh, darlin', d'you think I haven't gone over and over this for the last ten nights, d'you really think I don't know what I'm askin' yer? D'you think it ain't killin' me to be doin' the askin'?" Hannah rose, trying to maintain dignity, but by now the tears were streaking down her face and landing in large stains on her dress. "It's me punishment for what I've done. I'd no right to go diddlin' with another man. It's the good Lord's judgment on me, it is. I'll never go to heaven, girl, it's eternal hellfire for me, but . . ." Hannah teetered and groped for the back of the chair. "I'll do it to spare Sean the pain o' knowin' the truth about himself!"

Samantha was instantly out of her chair and taking the weeping Hannah into her arms. She felt her own tears start to rise but fought them back.

"Set things right for me, I'm beggin'!" sobbed Hannah into her hands. "Back to the way they used to be, and I'll take all the blame onto meself. I know it ain't fair to drop this on yer, but there ain't no one else I can turn to." Her voice dropped to a whisper. "I'm all alone in this . . ."

"No, you're not, Hannah. You have me. We're in it together." Samantha gently stroked the red hair. "Hannah, are you sure there's no way we can keep it? We could maybe go away somewhere together, and when we come back, tell Sean it's mine."

Hannah sniffed loudly and hiccuped. "Bless ya, girl, you'd do that for me? But you'd have to quit school and yer reputation would be spoilt and then maybe you'd never get that diploma, and I wouldn't want *that* on me conscience. And we couldn't say it was anyone else's because its flamin' red hair would tell everyone it's mine. No, darlin', I've thought of every possible solution and this one's the only way."

Samantha fixed her gaze on the row of crockery above the stove; her voice was bowstring-taut. "Hannah, the preservation of life is my deepest conviction. It is what I have dedicated myself to. I can't . . . kill a baby . . ."

Hannah drew her hands away from her face and regarded Samantha with swimming eyes. "And what do you think *my* convictions are? I'm committin' a mortal sin. I shall go to hell for this. And d'you think I don't love the little life inside o' me?"

"I'm sorry, Hannah, I didn't mean it to sound like that. I think I know what you're going through. I only wanted you to understand why . . . why I have to think about it. I'm confused, Hannah. Give me some time. It can wait till tomorrow, and by then I'll think of something."

Hannah's large bosom rose and fell in a decisive sigh. She pulled herself out of Samantha's embrace and brought up her apron to wipe her eyes. "I'm suddenly bone-weary, darlin'. I think I'll go upstairs for a lie-down." She untied her apron and carefully hung it on its hook.

"Hannah, I really will try to think of something."

"Of course, darlin'. Mind you, I don't want to put it off too long. If you can't see yer way to doin' it for me, I shall have to see Widow Dorset and she's twenty miles away."

"Widow Dorset?"

Hannah's lips tried a brave smile. "A discreet old lady who don't ask questions and who's as safe as pumpkin pie. Sure and I'm surprised you ain't heard of her. Best midwife in the county. Don't let the rabbit go too long."

Samantha did not eat. After setting the stew on a trivet, she wrapped the hardening biscuits in moist cheesecloth and set the milk on the windowsill. Then she went up to her room.

The hours fled by at an astonishing rate; she wasn't even aware of their passing. It had been dark when she first came up, but now it was blackest black out and bone-snapping cold. Wrapped in her shawl, Samantha paced in front of the fire, forcing her body through an endless circuit as if physical exertion would make the answer come more easily.

Samantha was angry. She didn't know at whom: certainly not Hannah, for whom she felt only deep and miserable sorrow; maybe she was angry at the smug Oliver, like a fat cat who's stolen the cream and gotten off free. It was even possible she was angry at herself, at her inability to take hold of the situation, to take a firm stand; Samantha detested being helpless. She also experienced tremors of guilt, guilt for an act another woman had committed; and mixed with these were feelings of having somehow let her friend down.

Samantha wrestled with herself all night, trying to sort out the twisted threads of her thoughts, but always she came back to the same conclusion: she had to help Hannah.

It was really very simple, once she understood it; Hannah was in trouble and she needed help. Just as I once needed help, Samantha thought as she came to a standstill after hours of pacing. No one would give me a room, every door in town was closed against me, but Hannah was good and kind enough to take me in. What would I have done if she hadn't?

But it went even deeper than friendship and returning a favor. It had to do with Hannah being a woman in trouble, with a problem only a woman can have, and turning to another woman for help. How many thousands of times had this very drama been played out, down through the centuries, a woman frightened and alone, turning to a friend/sister/Widow Dorset for help? It was a ritual as ancient as womankind.

Samantha stood in the center of her room, her tall shadow dancing on the carpet, and she realized there was nothing more to think about. Once, the thought passed through her mind: Have I the right to take the life of an unborn child? And she had answered it: Have I the right to deny the knowledge to Hannah that should be hers as well as mine? Deciding that time for deliberation was over, Samantha left her room and went to Hannah's door where she knocked softly.

She was not surprised to receive no answer. The raw iciness of the hallway told her it was very deep into night, probably even near dawn, and Hannah would be asleep.

She knocked again, louder. Then she tried the knob and the door swung away. Hannah's room was cold and dark, like a cavern, and Hannah was not there. Hurrying down the stairs, she called out her friend's name, poking her head into each cold and silent room, then Samantha went to the entry hall where she quickly pulled on her boots and gloves, wrapped a woolen muffler around her neck and settled her heavy cape around her shoulders. When she opened the front door the frigid air stood like a wall of glass before her.

There had been a snowfall during the night and a fresh blanket lay over the world. The trail leading away from the house was sharply distinct, as after a finger has been drawn through whipped cream: Hannah's plodding footprints and the wide sweep of her skirt had made a path across the snow; it was like an arrow pointing the way.

Drawing her hood tight around her head and clutching it at her throat,

Samantha set out into the ghostly world. She kept her eyes fixed on the trail, breathing slowly and shallowly, for the arctic air hurt her lungs; she tried to ignore the eerie shapes looming around her, twisted black trees and grotesquely hunched bushes—such a delight to the eye in the day but at night strangely sinister and threatening. The trail led along the edge of the wood and down to the lake. Picking her way carefully down the perilous slope, hearing only her sharp respirations exaggerated inside her hood, Samantha realized in dawning horror that Hannah's footsteps continued onto the frozen surface of the lake.

Cupping her hands around her mouth, Samantha called out her friend's name. Her voice sounded rude and obscene in the glacial stillness. She called again. The light was poor; the lake was a fantastical landscape of white on white ringed by towering black guardians. Samantha searched frantically for some movement, held her breath to catch a sound, but it was as if the world had been captured on a tintype and held there frozen, soundless and lifeless.

The cold went beyond making the flesh shiver; it was not a cold that made your nose and fingers feel bitten and raised bumps on your skin, it was a knife that sliced right to your deepest core and chilled you from the inside out. Samantha couldn't feel her hands or toes. She tried to move, to flap her arms and stamp her feet, but some strange spell was working to make her a permanent inhabitant of the winter photograph.

Then she heard it. Faint, distant, like a wishbone snapping. She swung her head in its direction. Yes, there, out on the ice, movement.

"Hannah!" she called. Samantha plunged out onto the ice and tried to walk quickly on the slick surface. When she fell she was sure every bone in her body would snap. She struggled to get back to her feet, still breathlessly calling Hannah's name. Samantha gingerly picked her way over the ice, holding her arms out for balance. She stopped every few feet to look up and make sure of her direction. To her left the sky behind the trees was weakening; a queer pastel light spilled over the forest and onto the lake. She saw Hannah clearly now. Her friend stood strangely still, staring at something, oblivious of her name ringing out to the sky.

"Don't move!" cried Samantha. "The ice is breaking! Oh, God—"
She lurched forward and back, her arms describing little circles in the

air. Samantha tried to hurry. All around, little splintering sounds warned menacingly.

When she was close enough, Samantha saw that Hannah wobbled; absurdly, she had her wooden skates on. "Hannah . . ." she called breathlessly. "Don't move . . ."

But Hannah mustn't have heard because she took a step and in the next instant was gone.

Samantha blinked. She rubbed frozen fists into her eyes. Then she tried to run, felt her feet fly out from under her and crashed to her knees. Samantha scrambled on all fours, feeling the ice sway sickeningly beneath her. She reached the black hole and screamed, *"Hannah! Hannah!"* Part of a cloak still lay on the ice, trailing into the churning water; Samantha blindly lunged for it and tried to pull with all her strength. Then she heard more crunching, like walnuts beneath a heel, and she felt the ice beneath her knees buckle, rise up, and then suddenly drop away.

The water was too cold to be felt; it enveloped her in a peculiar lack of sensation. Samantha gasped and the water filled her lungs. She thrashed her arms and legs but her skirt and cape pulled her down. Beneath the surface her feet bumped something solid. Groping frantically for the edge of the ice, which came away beneath her hand, Samantha dashed her other hand under the water and latched onto a hank of hair. But she couldn't pull Hannah up. Samantha went down like a stone, blackness covering her head.

This is it, she thought with unexpected calm. And all because I hesitated . . .

In the next instant, absurdly, she was lying on her back gasping and staring up at the paling sky. Then she felt two painful grips under her armpits and realized she was being dragged backward over the ice.

In between bouts of delirium she had lucid moments and heard snatches of conversation. Mr. Kendall's gravelly voice: "What were they doing skating at that hour?" Dr. Jones: "Dissolve half a teaspoon of this powder in warm water and force-feed it every four hours. It'll keep the fever down." Motherly Mrs. Kendall: "The poor woman. It's a blessing it was quick. She never knew what happened."

When she slept it was not a peaceful sleep, for she was tormented by nightmares. Ghosts rose up from the swirling mists: Freddy, his coarse handsome face as sharp as if he stood before her; James stretched out on a dissecting table, his neck discolored by the hangman's rope; the hideously mutilated Samuel; and old Mr. Hawksbill trapped in a jar trying to get out. Samantha woke often to find her nightgown drenched with sweat and Mrs. Kendall bending over her, cooing maternally.

Finally, when Mrs. Kendall's diligent nursing care and Dr. Jones's doctoring brought her out of the worst of it, at the end of February when Samantha discovered to her astonishment that she had lain in fever and near death for six weeks, she learned it was farmer McKinney and his son who had pulled her out of the water. For Hannah, they were sad to report, they had been too late.

-✦-

Dr. Jones sat by the bed delicately holding her wrist as he stared at his pocket watch. Then, satisfied, he snapped the watch closed, returned it to his vest pocket and gently deposited Samantha's arm by her side. "Well, young lady, it looks as if you're going to make it," he said with an effusive smile. "You've a mighty strong constitution, Miss Hargrave. I've seen very few recover from the degree of pneumonia you had."

She gazed at him dully.

"Now don't you worry about a thing. Mrs. Kendall's giving you this room for the rest of the term, and Mr. Kendall has brought all your things over from Mrs. Mallone's. As far as school is concerned, you're such an excellent student I've no doubt you'll have no trouble making up the work. At any rate, allowances will be made."

Her lips were dry and cracked. She tried to lick them before whispering, "And . . . Sean . . ."

Dr. Jones's face clouded. "He'll be told as soon as he can be located. Now you rest, my dear. You've been through a terrible ordeal. Another few seconds in that water and you would have frozen to death."

At the first hint of thaw Hannah Mallone was buried. It was a busy week for Reverend Patterson, who had to preside over the funeral services of everyone who had died during the winter; because the ground was frozen too hard to dig graves, the bodies were kept in the church basement, and Reverend Patterson, in his morbid aversion to the dead, was only too relieved to see them interred. Hannah had a simple marker and a simpler ceremony. It was one of those late March days when winter couldn't make up its mind to leave or not; even as the dirt was hitting the lid of Hannah's plain pine box, snowflakes started to drift down.

Dr. Jones had hotly denied Samantha permission to attend, she was still very weak, but Samantha would have crawled on her hands and knees if she had to, so he had relented and offered to be her support, but strangely, Samantha had asked Mrs. Kendall to stand by her. And so they circled the grave, a tiny, silent group, while Reverend Patterson did his best to add a Catholic flair to his Protestant prayers.

They all stared down, heads solemnly bowed, each following private thoughts. Mr. Kendall was sorry to see a good customer go, Mrs. Kendall was worrying about the suet simmering on the stove, Dr. Jones watched Samantha's chalky face in curiosity (Really, what *had* they been thinking, going skating at that hour?), and Samantha, leaning heavily on Mrs. Kendall, was noticing how meticulously some graves were kept clear of snow by devoted relatives, as if it made any difference to the dust and bones below.

But as the weather started to warm and she was able to visit the grave alone, Samantha found herself tenderly planting seeds in the soft mound, pulling young weeds, and caring for the little plot as dearly as if she were tending Hannah herself.

Her glade was habitable again but Samantha found herself drawn inexorably to the graveside. She went there every day looking for answers. What happened, Hannah? You knew I was going to help you, why did you do it? Was it the way I so clumsily handled it? Did my hesitation, my words about the sanctity of life, hold up your sin before you in a way that you did not need? I was no help to you, dear friend, I made you feel ashamed. I let you down. There is no Widow Dorset, is there? You said that only to give me a guilt-free exit from a decision I was ill-equipped to make. And the skates, too, were for my sake, weren't they? To protect me from having to explain your death. I was not prepared, Hannah; they teach me blood and bones but there is a glaring absence in the classroom of the study of the human *soul*. There are no books to teach me how to repair the injured spirit.

A cold spring gust rose up from the muddy ground and it carried Hannah's ghostly whisper: "Don't worry yerself about it, darlin'. It's me punishment. I'd no right to go diddlin' with another man. It's the Lord's judgment for what I did."

Samantha's soul flared. Then where is Oliver's punishment, Hannah? He'd no right to diddle with *you*. Where's the Lord's judgment on *him*?

As the days rolled by, Samantha began to draw strength and dawning comprehension from her daily conversations with Hannah; the deep sorrow waxed gradually into anger, and with the anger Samantha felt a fortifying of her spirit. They have no idea, the men, of what really happened here, not an inkling of the staggering significance of Hannah's action, and if they did, if they came dangerously close to understanding it, they would quickly turn away, fearful of the truth they saw there. The truth that *they are not what they think they are*. Men are wrong in believing themselves to be the masters, the God-ordained guardians of life and death on earth. They only *think* they hold the daily verdicts of life and death in their hands because women permit them that illusion, to keep them satisfied; the very primary decisions in life and death abide solely with women, that mystic sisterhood of secret-keepers—Hannah has proven that. Down through the centuries, the secret meetings, the scrapings and flushings, the recipes whispered from mother to daughter, a life snuffed before it has begun, like the little life buried here with Hannah, and the menfolk never knowing, never knowing . . .

Oh, the awesome power we women have, Hannah. No wonder the men fear us so.

It was on a blustery April day when goldenrod was in the air and Samantha had to wrestle with the wind for possession of her cape that she experienced an astonishing revelation. As though it was Hannah whispering from the grave, Samantha heard the pronouncement that was going to change her life forever: "Because they fear us men keep us enslaved, but only with our consent; they are our jailers but we are their wardens."

Samantha fell to her knees and recited the Hail Mary Hannah had taught her. Then she said to the mound of serene green grass, "I will make it up to you, Hannah, I promise, somehow. I cannot bring you back, I cannot right my wrong, but I can make you a solemn vow. I promise you, Hannah Mallone, dearest friend, that I will keep you with me always, your soul will find immortality in me, your death will not have been for nothing, for out of it has come my new strength. Never again will I let them rule me; I am my own master. I shall carry your counsel with me always, dear friend, so that along my future path, when I encounter other such unfortunate sisters as you, I shall know what to do; and I promise you, dear Hannah, that because of you I shall never, *never* hesitate again . . ."

TWENTY

OUTWARDLY SHE APPEARED CALM, BUT INSIDE SAMANTHA WAS tense, anxious. The graduation procession had halted before the steps of the church in order to give the photographers time to take pictures, and as she stood with her head held proudly, Samantha could not shake the gloomy cloud that had invaded her soul. First the elusive dream last night, prophetic and ominous but out of the grasp of memory, and now the boycott of the women.

Why, oh, why after two years had they done this to her? She knew they still maintained some prejudice against her; kindly Mrs. Kendall had made no secret of the fact that she thought Samantha was seriously jeopardizing her reputation by attending a male medical school, and a few stubborn women still refused her society, crossing the street if they saw her coming, but Samantha had thought that, in two years, surely the majority of the women had come to accept her, had discovered she wasn't a woman of loose morals after all, and that her attendance at the school hadn't brought scandal upon the town. This was a terrible blow. Hannah, if she were alive, would be here . . .

During the annual Apple Blossom Festival Sean Mallone had come home. When he returned to the oversized house near the suspender factory he was wild with grief, but Samantha had kept her terrible secret, allowing Sean the solace, at least, of thinking his wife's death an accident, and in time Sean had been able to collect himself, consign Hannah's soul to the Legion of Saints, sell the house, and return forever to the mountains.

With Hannah's spirit and her own troubled conscience finally laid to rest, Samantha had devoted the last month of the school year to such intense study that she had brought herself up, to everyone's surprise, from the twentieth place in class (due to her weeks of illness) to the third. The photographers and reporters took special note of this, marveling that someone so young and pretty could have distinguished herself so. A freak indeed.

The Indians stepped to one side, struck up "America" again and the procession started forward. As Samantha glided into the dim interior of the church she was startled by the rustling of silks and a chorus of whispers as bonnets and feathered hats swiveled to face her.

The women!

They filled the pews and crowded the galleries overhead; a sea of bright colors and elaborate hairdos; fans fluttered and jewels glittered; the women were decked in their finest to honor her. *To honor her.* Samantha's heart swelled; two giant tears rose in her eyes. The women had not abandoned her after all.

As the graduates filed into the front pews, the menfolk now crowded into the church to squeeze into every available space and line the walls. The air was charged, like the prelude before a summer lightning storm; it was a big day for a small town. Dr. Jones hurried up to the dais that had been constructed before the altar and donned his velvet cap of office. As his voice rang out over the congregation, reciting the speech he gave every year (and mentally cursing the tardy Simon Kent and his blasted handwritten diploma), Samantha received a second shock. Up on the dais, sitting with the rest of the professors and facing the audience, was Dr. Mark Rawlins.

Samantha couldn't help staring. Why hadn't she noticed it before? Mark Rawlins was an exceedingly handsome man. She saw now what her obsession with Joshua Masefield had caused her to miss at the Astor ball: the thick brown hair that was daringly long, ending in little curls that teased his coat collar, fashionable for artists and actors but unusual for a doctor; the soft brown eyes, large straight nose and square jaw. He was tall and lean, but something in the way he sat, the way the fabric of his trousers strained over his thighs, hinted at a tight musculature beneath, as though he were an athlete and not a man who divided his hours between a desk and a hospital ward.

Mark Rawlins casually glanced her way. Their eyes met and held for a second; he smiled briefly, lifting one corner of his mouth where, Samantha noticed for the first time, there was a small white scar, a flaw. Then they both returned their attention to Dr. Jones.

Dr. Rawlins, it turned out, was the guest speaker for the commencement, and Dr. Jones now introduced him. Samantha watched him slowly rise from his chair, towering over little Henry Jones, and walk with long, self-assured strides to the podium. Samantha recalled how it had felt to dance with him.

Mark Rawlins spoke with ease and confidence; his fluid gestures and Bostonian drawl made one think he chatted by a hearth in the company of a small circle of friends. He held his audience rapt, and as he spoke, Samantha tried to remember some of the things he had told her about himself. But it was no use. In her preoccupation with Joshua Masefield, Samantha had barely heard a word Mark Rawlins uttered that night at the ball. It was as though a total stranger stood before her.

After Dr. Rawlins returned to his seat, Dr. Jones bustled back up to the podium, then, deciding he could stall no longer to give Kent time to show up with Miss Hargrave's special diploma, started calling out the graduates' names.

He called them alphabetically. When *Domine* Gower and then *Domine* Jarvis were called, Samantha decided he must be saving her for last. It seemed to take forever. One by one they went up to the podium, took the sheepskin and shook the dean's hand. No one noticed how nervous Dr. Jones was, or that the pile of diplomas was short by one. The graduates tried to keep from shifting and Samantha had to fight the impulse to look again at Dr. Rawlins.

There was a slight stir down the side aisle. A man was hurrying unobtrusively along one wall. When he reached the front pew he bent down, whispered something to the usher, handed him an object, then stood back in the shadows. The usher rose slightly, stretched forward and laid the object on Dr. Jones's table just as the dean called *Domine* Young. Henry Jones heaved a barely perceptible sigh of relief, picked up the diploma, which was the last on the table, and called out proudly, *"Domina* Hargrave . . ."

They tried to keep the procession leaving the church as sedate as possible, but once they were outside the new doctors flung their hats in the air and whooped and hollered like little boys let out of school. The church grounds were chaos: parents embracing sons, gentlemen shaking hands, ladies dabbing handkerchiefs to their eyes, children dodging in and out of legs, reporters bumping into one another, dogs yapping. Samantha searched the crowd. Dr. Rawlins had disappeared.

"Miss Hargrave." It was the boorish reporter from the Baltimore *Sun.* "How are people supposed to address you now? Is it Miss Doctor? Doctress?"

She pretended not to have heard and looked around. How had so many people managed to fit inside the church? Mrs. Kendall, crying, came up and chattered breathlessly about how beautiful it all was and how lovely Samantha looked in her dress. Then Dr. Jones came up with chest puffed out like a bantam cock, saying something about Samantha being the pride of the school and making sure the reporter heard. More people came up with smiles and well-wishes; she was the star of the day. They shook her hand and mouthed words of praise, women who before would not deign to speak to her now acted like old friends. Other graduates, the professors, more reporters, all gathered around Samantha. She summoned up polite smiles and only barely heard what they had to say. Where had Mark Rawlins gone?

A voice, deep and cultured, said quietly, "Dr. Hargrave, may we offer you our sincerest congratulations?"

She turned. Standing before her were two women she had never seen before. The one who had spoken was a woman in her sixties who, although dressed in black bombazine and with her gray-streaked hair drawn back in a severe bun, was strikingly handsome. Her deep-set eyes, hollowed cheeks and chiseled jaw gave her a formidable countenance, but when she extended her hand and smiled, she radiated warmth and charm. "I am Miss Anthony, and this is my friend Mrs. Stanton."

Samantha accepted the firm handshake. "How do you do."

The other lady was the antithesis of her somber companion. Dressed in a gown of rose-pink satin with many ruffles and lace, Mrs. Stanton was incredibly short and plump with a moonface surrounded by a mass of white curls.

Miss Anthony spoke. "We came here today to witness your achievement and to extend to you the warmest felicitations of your sisters everywhere. What you have done, Dr. Hargrave, is no mean accomplishment. Nor is it going unrecognized. You have struck a vital blow for the cause of women everywhere."

Samantha frowned slightly.

"Perhaps you are not aware," said Miss Anthony, turning so that she stood almost in profile, "of who we are or the cause we represent, but that does not matter right now. We are not here to crusade or recruit, merely to thank you."

"Thank me? For what?"

"For what you have done here today. The fact is, Dr. Hargrave, the women of this nation are in chains, and their servitude is all the more debasing because they do not realize it. What you have done, Dr. Hargrave, is take a step to compel them to see and feel, to give them the courage and conscience to speak and act for their own freedom."

Samantha was curious about the peculiar way Miss Anthony held herself: always maintaining a profile. Susan B. Anthony had a physical defect— one eye was off center. An inept surgeon had once tried to correct it, turning the eye far in the other direction. As Miss Anthony was acutely sensitive to it, she tried always to maintain a profile, especially in portraits.

Mrs. Stanton laid a hand on Samantha's arm and said quietly, "Dr. Hargrave, you are the new generation. Miss Anthony and I are old, we started the fight and we fought it to the best of our ability. We now entrust the finish of that battle to the next generation of women."

Perplexed, Samantha watched the two walk away, unaware that Jack

Morley of the Baltimore *Sun* had sauntered up. "Friends of yours?"

She turned to him, saw the pencil poised over the notepad and said pleasantly, "Excuse me, sir, but I really must join the others."

Following her tall and slender figure with his eyes as she walked away, the reporter touched the tip of his pencil to his tongue and jotted on his pad what he would later telegraph to his editor: "The lovely Doctress Hargrave should confine her practice to ailments of the heart!"

He was standing on the steps of the church engaged in a quiet conversation with Dr. Page. Samantha paused at a short distance and watched. The sight of Mark Rawlins brought back so much that she had not thought about in a long time: the Astor ball, the giddy waltzes, the champagne, Joshua's kiss, their night of lovemaking. Seeing him now standing at complete ease, his hands moving lazily as he emphasized a point, Samantha remembered other things long forgotten: the awkward scene with Joshua in front of Dr. Rawlins, Mark Rawlins' obvious ill ease, his shaming Joshua into dancing with her; and then, later, Joshua's words that had hurt and confused her so. "I have known Mark for a long time and I have never seen him look at a woman the way he looked at you . . . he is smitten with you. He would be perfect for you."

Painful words soon dismissed. But now, looking at Mark Rawlins for the first time really, she wondered if Joshua had been right. At the time, perhaps; fine music and champagne can make any man look at a woman in a special way. But it had been a year and a half; did Dr. Rawlins remember that night, did he indeed remember *her* and was his presence here today possibly more than a coincidence?

He glanced her way, as if he had known she was there, and again their eyes met briefly. Then he turned back to Dr. Page, murmured some polite parting words and came down the steps. "Dr. Hargrave," he said with a glowing smile, "allow me to offer my congratulations."

"Thank you, sir. Do you recall that we have met before?"

"Of course! Did you think I had forgotten?" Mark Rawlins stared down at Samantha, who, although tall herself, was a head shorter than he, and the look in his brown eyes intensified. "Little did I know, as I spent those hours in your charming company, that I was in the presence of a young lady who was going to make history."

Samantha stood immobile for the space of one heartbeat—he remembered her!—and then the spell was broken. "Ah, here you are," called Dr. Jones behind her.

He was perspiring heavily and his face looked like a cherry. "Forgive me for ignoring you, Dr. Rawlins, I was literally cornered by a fellow from the *Boston Journal!*" Dr. Jones seized Mark Rawlins' hand and pumped it vigorously. "I cannot thank you enough for coming today, sir! You added a touch of prestige to our little commencement. But, I say, didn't Mrs. Rawlins accompany you?"

"I'm afraid she wasn't up to the trip."

"Nothing serious, I hope?"

"Not at all, just a mild indisposition."

Tuning out their voices, Samantha thought: He has a wife!

". . . will be at four o'clock," Dr. Jones was saying. "You can't miss it. It's the big white house on the corner with yellow shutters."

Dr. Jones tipped his hat to both of them and hurried off. Mark Rawlins turned to Samantha. "Will you be there at the celebration dinner?"

"Certainly. My residence is at Mrs. Kendall's."

"Then if you will kindly excuse me, Dr. Hargrave. I have something to see to at my hotel." He smiled hesitantly, as if considering saying something further, then Dr. Rawlins doffed his top hat, bowed slightly and said, "I shall see you at four o'clock."

Mrs. Kendall had outdone herself. The table literally groaned beneath the weight of the bounty; the silver and china dazzled; and the fragrance of rose blossoms mingled with the aromas rising from steaming dishes. She had spent the last four days preparing the feast and now sat beaming at one end of the table as the guests were overwhelmed by savory course after savory course. Mr. Kendall, from his seat at the opposite end of the table, nodded approvingly as the guests heartily devoured the oyster cream soup, baked ham in raisin sauce, veal cutlets, tomato pie, pickled celery and cabbage, and heavily buttered saffron bread, all accompanied by generous servings of wine from Lake Canandaigua's own vineyards; and waiting in the kitchen, chestnut pudding, plum jelly turnovers and brandied peaches.

Samantha sat in the center of one side of the long table, between Dr. Jones and his wife. On either side of them were Dr. and Mrs. Page; across the table were the Reverend Patterson and his wife, the man from the *Boston Journal*, Mr. Collins, Lucerne's own local newspaperman, and finally, directly opposite Samantha, Mark Rawlins.

Everyone was engaged in conversation. While Samantha listened to Mrs. Jones's tales of her grandchildren, her husband, on the other side of Samantha, engaged Mark Rawlins in an animated dialogue.

"Is your father also a physician, sir?"

Dr. Rawlins turned his charming smile to Henry Jones. "My father is a lawyer, sir, as was his father before him. Both were Harvard graduates, and my great-grandfather had the honor of serving George Washington as an adviser."

"Indeed? Coming from a line of legal minds, one wonders why you didn't follow their example."

"That, sir, is precisely why I did not. I shall be candid with you, Doctor: I chose to enter the study of medicine merely to confound my father, who is something of a despot over our family. At the age of eighteen there is little a young man can do to challenge his father's authority, outside, of course, of acts of immorality and social rebellion. It was not my desire to defy society, only my father. And I wanted to do it in a respectable way. He commanded I should become a lawyer. I became a doctor instead."

Dr. Jones laughed into his napkin. "Well, I confess, sir, you *are* candid. But then, is medicine nothing more to you than something to flaunt in your father's face?"

"It was at first. But when I entered Cornell I discovered to my delight that I had a natural penchant for medicine. I have since come privately to thank my father for having driven me to it."

"How does he feel now?"

"The day I announced my intention to enter medicine, which was the day of my eighteenth birthday, he disinherited me. That was thirteen years ago and we have not exchanged a single word since."

Dr. Jones settled back in his chair. "Oh, that *is* a pity!"

"Not at all, sir. My three brothers are at this moment ruled by my tyrannical father and they are miserable. I, on the other hand, am a free man."

"But at such a price! To be cut off from your inheritance!"

"It was difficult at first, I will admit, but I am quite comfortable now. One does not have a practice on Fifth Avenue and remain impoverished."

"Might I have heard of your father?"

"You might. He is Nicholas Rawlins."

"The Ice King? Indeed I have heard of him! I had wondered if you were related, but I'd no idea you might be his son! I should be most fascinated to hear his story, sir, for I understand it is quite remarkable."

Mark Rawlins glanced at Samantha; she only picked at her food and, although she appeared to be paying attention to Mrs. Jones's grandchildren stories, her eyes betrayed mental distraction. Samantha's mind was far away and Mark Rawlins wondered where. "My father's story, sir, is indeed an interesting one . . ." Nicholas Rawlins, in his youth, had once made the observation that the winter ice on a nearby lake could be sold, like a crop. In a gamble that was as daring as the spirit of the man behind it, young Nicholas plunged ten thousand dollars into a "crop" of ice and personally accompanied the 130-ton shipment to the sultry island of Martinique, where he boasted to the proprietor of the famous Tivoli Garden that he could produce ice cream cheaply and quickly. Instantaneously, the ice cream became the rage of the island; by the end of six weeks the ice was all gone and Nicholas had incurred a loss of four thousand dollars. But the people of Martinique were convinced they could never again live without ice cream.

In Havana Nicholas sold chilled drinks for the same price as unchilled so that the preference for ice in one's drink was craftily cultivated. When competitors brought in ice shipments from New England Nicholas sold his ice at a penny a pound until the competitors' ice melted at the dock. He was unprincipled and unscrupulous, but he came away, in the end, with legal monopolies in the ice trade and the exclusive rights to build icehouses from Charleston to St. Croix. He then raised his prices, soon making back his tremendous losses, and before his thirtieth birthday people from New Orleans to Tortola were ingesting the water of New England.

"I suppose," said Dr. Jones, "that your father has no objection to being called the Ice King?"

"Hardly, sir!" Mark picked up his wine, tasted it and was surprised, when he glanced away from Dr. Jones, to find Samantha openly staring at him.

Mrs. Jones had shifted around to exchange grandchildren anecdotes with Mrs. Page; Dr. Jones turned his attention to Mr. Collins opposite him; the rest chatted with whoever was handiest. Only Samantha and Mark were silent, and they regarded one another across the table.

After a minute Mark reached for a slice of pumpkin bread and generously buttered it. "Tell me, Dr. Hargrave, what are your plans after Lucerne?"

"I have in mind, sir, a small neighborhood practice."

Mark could not help thinking: You mean like Joshua's practice.

"You see, Dr. Rawlins, I want to go where there is a need. I have done a little research into statistics, and it would seem there is a shocking imbalance in the dispersion of physicians in New York. Paradoxically, where the population is thickest, there are the fewest doctors."

Then Mark Rawlins saw something in Samantha's eyes that had not been there a year and a half ago; without a doubt Samantha Hargrave had undergone some sort of change. Outwardly she was the same, enchantingly beautiful, although perhaps now she carried herself with a little more confidence; but in her eyes there shone an inner strength that had not been evident in the uncertain young woman he had rescued at the Astor ball. A year and a half ago Samantha Hargrave had been a trifle nervous and girlishly awed by the extravagances of society. Sitting before him now was an evolved Samantha Hargrave: secure, confident, determined. No longer a girl, a woman.

"Tell me, Dr. Rawlins. How are the Masefields?"

He stirred, brought himself out of his reflection. "I am sorry to report, Dr. Hargrave, that Mrs. Masefield succumbed to her illness some time ago. We had a fierce January in Manhattan and the poor woman hadn't the strength to make it through."

Samantha murmured, "Oh . . . I'm so sorry . . ." It all rushed back, flooding her as if a sluice gate had broken, old passions, memories once laid to rest, conflicting, clashing: her grief to hear of Estelle's passing—her joy to hear of Joshua's sudden freedom. No, she had promised him, promised herself, that it was all over, finished . . .

"I say," came Dr. Jones's voice nearby, "do I gather correctly that you two know one another?"

There was a strain in Mark Rawlins' voice as he said, "We met through a mutual friend."

"I see! Then Miss Hargrave is the acquaintance you referred to in your letter."

Samantha turned. "I beg your pardon, Dr. Jones?"

"Dr. Rawlins wrote me some time ago to ask the date of our commencement exercises. He and Mrs. Rawlins were planning to attend, he said, as an acquaintance was in the graduating class."

Samantha looked at Mark. "Is that true? You are here because of me? Then it is not a coincidence after all."

Dr. Rawlins opened his mouth but it was Dr. Jones who spoke. "I did some rapid thinking when I read that letter. Since most of our students are local boys, the sons of farmers, we are rarely honored by the attendance of a gentleman of such esteem as Dr. Rawlins, and so I summoned up the audacity to write back and ask him to deliver our guest address. But I had no idea, Miss Hargrave, that *you* were that acquaintance."

She regarded Dr. Rawlins steadily. "I am flattered, sir, that you came all this way just because of me."

A look of discomfort rippled across his handsome features again, and this time Samantha saw it. Dr. Rawlins was growing increasingly distressed and she wondered why.

They both returned to their meal and finished it in silence. When the hired girls cleared away the dishes, Mr. Kendall stood and invited the gentlemen to join him in the drawing room for brandy and cigars. Mrs. Kendall, anxious to loosen her corset, ordered coffee for the ladies. Samantha rose to follow the women into Mrs. Kendall's gaudily appointed parlor, but she was stayed by Dr. Rawlins. "May I have a word with you?" he asked quietly. "In private?"

"Certainly." Assuring her hostess she would join them in a moment, Samantha closed the dining-room door after everyone had left and turned to Dr. Rawlins.

"Dr. Hargrave, I asked for a moment alone with you because I've something to tell you. And to give you."

She waited, her back against the door, as Dr. Rawlins reached inside his coat and withdrew an envelope. He turned it over in his hands a few times, frowning down at it, before he finally faced her squarely and said, "Dr. Hargrave, my motives for coming here today are not what you think. It was not my idea that I attend the commencement but Joshua's."

She caught her breath and held it.

"And this is from Joshua. He asked me to deliver it to you."

Samantha looked at the buff envelope being held out to her and she hesitated, for a fraction of a second, before taking it. "Thank you, sir."

She tried to slit it open without doing damage, but her hands shook and the envelope shredded. Unfolding the single sheet inside, she saw that the letter was not in Joshua's hand. It began: "My dear Dr. Hargrave. I address you in this manner for I have instructed Mark to give you this letter only after you graduate; as you read these words you are at last a doctor—and my dearest wish has been fulfilled. I am sorry that I am not able to attend the occasion in person, sending instead Mark, but as I dictate these words the life is leaving my body, and as you read them I am already dead."

She kept her head bent, her eyes fixed on the last word; vaguely, in the background, Samantha heard Mr. Kendall's booming voice come from the study, followed by a chorus of masculine laughter. The letter suddenly blurred and swam before her eyes. She whispered, "You must excuse me, Dr. Rawlins, but I cannot read this here . . ."

He murmured his understanding as she reached blindly for the doorknob, flung open the door and dashed into the hall. It was an automatic gesture, reaching for her cape, as she had no idea of the weather outside; she hurried down the steps, the letter clutched in her hand, and headed in the direction of the lake.

The sun was setting when she reached her glade; shadows were long and inky, the sky salmon pink. She sank onto the log where she had come to so many important decisions in the past year and tried to read, in the fading light, the rest of Joshua's letter.

"Mark Rawlins has diagnosed my condition as congestive heart failure; the left ventricle is not emptying all the way before expanding again. I make it to be endocarditis. Mr. Pasteur in Paris would say it was caused by bacteria on the hypodermic needle. He might be right. Who is to say what is right in medicine any more? We have been making unforgivable mistakes in our ignorance. Remember, Samantha, it was medical ignorance that got me hooked on the morphine habit; had physicians known twenty years ago what we know today, I should not be in this wretched state. It has to change. Doctors have a sacred duty to do only the right thing. Medicine, my dear, is still in the Dark Ages and we are little more than charlatans.

"I write this letter, dear Dr. Hargrave, to extract a promise from you. And I know that, in the name of what we once shared, you will carry out my last wish. I want you to work hard, Samantha, to bring light into the medical darkness. Fight for what is right; do not, I beg, bury yourself in a mediocre practice, as I was forced to do; any second-rate physician can do what I have been doing, it was meant for you to do greater things. I know what you are capable of, Samantha. Use your knowledge and skill to improve the science of medicine; go on from here, do not be satisfied merely with your diploma. Allow me to die knowing that I bequeathed to the world a doctor who will make changes.

"I leave to you my surgical instruments, dear Samantha. Mark will see that you get them. I entrust them to you in the safe knowledge that you will put them to better use than I did.

"It was never meant to be for us, my love, from the start we were doomed. I have no breath left in me to tell you what remains. My heart is failing with each beat. Mark will tell you the rest. He knows what to say. Farewell, my love."

There was a scrawl at the bottom; it barely resembled Joshua's signature.

She read the letter again, even though by now the light was gone and she could barely see the words. Tears rose in her eyes and tumbled to the paper, spreading the ink; Samantha didn't sob or blubber, her weeping was gentle, whisperlike, the tears streaked her cheeks without reddening her eyes. When she heard a twig snap, she raised her head and looked up into the shadowy face of Mark Rawlins.

She opened her mouth. One word came out. "When?"

"Six weeks ago."

Absurdly, as if it meant something, Samantha tried frantically to recall what she had been doing six weeks ago; it was important to know what she had been doing, what she had been thinking at the hour of Joshua's death.

"It was quick and painless," said Mark quietly. "When he realized he was ill, he sent for me. I found him in distress but he would allow me to do no more than administer digitalis by vein. Just enough to give him an hour to dictate this letter. He wanted to die."

She kept her face upturned to him, the tears gently rising and tumbling. "Why?" she whispered. "Why did he want to die?"

Dr. Rawlins walked over the carpet of brittle leaves—he was a shadow passing before her eyes—and sat next to her on the log. Thin columns of moonlight streamed down through the branches overhead, casting Samantha's glistening face in a pale glow. Mark Rawlins thought she was the most beautiful woman he had ever seen. "I argued with him. He wanted me to tell you something, but I saw no purpose to it. He insisted, saying you must know. And that you would know why he had me tell you." Mark's voice was subdued, sounding in the night as if it came from far away. "Estelle didn't die from her illness. Joshua killed her."

Samantha didn't move, gave no sign she had heard him. Sitting close to Dr. Rawlins in the sylvan darkness, their arms touching, she gazed steadily at him.

He went on: "Estelle was suffering terribly. The infections attacked her one after another; she was in constant pain; she grew weaker and weaker; she was so thin she looked like a skeleton. She begged him—" Ironically, Samantha reached out and rested her hand on Mark's, as though he were the one in need of consolation. "He gave her an overdose of the very morphine that sustained him, and as she breathed her last, free of pain, she thanked him . . ."

Yes, Joshua, Samantha thought sadly. I know why you wanted me to know this. There are no simple and clear-cut decisions in medicine, nothing in black and white. To kill an unborn baby to save a woman's life, to kill a woman to end her suffering. Sometimes doctors must decide for death in order to preserve life, sometimes they must ask themselves: Which is more important, the quantity of life or the quality? Not all answers are in textbooks, the physician must search for some within himself—that is what you intended by having Mark tell me the truth about Estelle; even in your final confession, Joshua, you have left me a precious legacy. It is this rare quality that distinguishes the great doctors from the mediocre . . .

He knew that, Samantha's mind whispered as she leaned, suddenly very tired, against Mark Rawlins. Joshua knew that I have that quality. Even in death he guides me . . .

"Dr. Rawlins," she murmured, "will you please leave me now?"

"Here?" He looked around the forest room, barely illuminated by moonglow. "Is it safe?"

"I shall be all right. No harm can come to me here."

"But—"

"Please. There is something I have to think about and here is the only place I can do it. I shan't be long. Please make my excuses to Mrs. Kendall."

Long after Dr. Rawlins had gone Samantha continued to sit motionless on the log, staring into the night, listening to the familiar wood sounds that had accompanied so many of her decisions and revelations in the past. Samantha sensed gentile presences all around her: the gods who dwelt in the trees and vines, the spirits of the Indians who had visited this glade long ago, and dear friends, Hannah and Joshua, to help her come to an understanding about herself.

A frightening, perilous road stretched before her, one that no woman had ever walked before. And Samantha saw now, more clearly than she had seen before, that that was the way she intended to go. With the help of God and those she had passed along the way and those she would encounter in the future, Samantha Hargrave was going to fight to bring light to the medical darkness.

PART THREE
NEW YORK 1881

ONE

*S*AMANTHA KNEW WHAT DR. PRINCE WAS UP TO, SHE SAW through his plan: ever since she had gotten into St. Brigid's on a legal loophole four weeks before, he had been trying to find a way to get rid of her. Now he had set a trap; but Dr. Prince, in his scheming, had made one vital mistake. He had underestimated Samantha Hargrave. She had a plan of her own.

What she was going to do tonight no woman in history had ever done, and although she was confident she would succeed, Samantha was edgy. Pacing the limits of her small room, she clasped and unclasped her hands, waiting impatiently for the inevitable ringing of the ambulance bell.

She had not wanted to resort to trickery tonight, just as she had not wanted to four weeks earlier, but desperation forced her to it, just as it had back then. Immediately upon her return to Manhattan from Lucerne, Samantha had set about applying at every hospital that had an intern program. It was the only way, Dr. Jones had assured her, that she could possibly elevate herself in the medical world; any doctor could have a diploma, it was a certificate of internship that marked the first-rate physician. So she had set her mind to obtaining an internship only to discover that not a single hospital in New York would admit a female doctor.

She was rejected at every one of them; the instant she walked in the door, the hospital officials took one look at her and, without bothering to examine her credentials, told her their programs were full. After two weeks of rejections Samantha saw the pattern and knew that, before her list of prospects was totally exhausted, she would have to change her tactics. To the last four hospitals, instead of applying in person, she wrote letters, enclosing a summary of her excellent educational record and copies of letters of recommendation from Dr. Jones and Dr. Page. She signed the letters S. Hargrave, M.D.

The wait for the responses had been agonizing but profitable. All four had immediately written to Dr. Jones for verification and had received glowing reports; all four had sent letters to S. Hargrave accepting her into their intern programs.

She chose St. Brigid's for two reasons: it was a large institution with four hundred beds and it offered a surgical training program. Samantha was immensely pleased with herself, Dr. Silas Prince was not. When she presented herself in his office and he realized, after a few confusing moments, that *she* was S. Hargrave, the sixty-year-old chief of staff informed her, with barely contained indignation, that they could not possibly, after all, admit her to their program. But Samantha had been prepared for this reception and in a poised, cultured manner had informed Dr. Prince that his change of mind was a legal breach of contract and that she would be forced to secure an attorney.

It had been a bluff, of course, for Samantha had little money left; but Dr. Prince had taken her at her word and had sent her off, saying he had to take the matter to the administrators.

What it had ultimately boiled down to was that the Hargrave woman did, because of Dr. Prince's carelessness, have a strong legal case: she had the letter of acceptance with Prince's signature on it, and also, ironically, the hospital's own support in that nowhere in its charter did it specifically prohibit women doctors. Well, the debate went, no one had thought it necessary to specifically exclude women doctors in the charter's wording since it was simply assumed no woman would have the brazenness to apply. The lawyers would have a heyday with this one, and so would the feminists and liberal presses. Samantha Hargrave's suit against St. Brigid's would generate unfavorable publicity—a big-city hospital picking on a defenseless woman—and certain financial backers of the hospital would frown.

"All right, Dr. Prince, we are forced to let her in. In the meantime, the charter will be rewritten to guard against future such situations, and we assume you will be more careful in the future screening of applicants. Further, you are to keep quiet the fact that we have a woman doctor on our staff. We wouldn't want to start a trend, would we?"

"But surely, gentlemen, this cannot be tolerated! She is a female. How can I accommodate a woman to my staff, examining patients in the company of men, living in the interns' quarters, using their facilities—"

"That is precisely what we want, Dr. Prince. The woman will expect special treatment because of her sex. Well, she has a surprise coming. You will see to it, Dr. Prince, that Dr. Hargrave takes part in *all* aspects of the intern program and that she is to be considered the equal of any man. That will soon send her packing."

A great underestimation. For one thing, Samantha was pleased that she would be granted no special allowances because she was a woman; and, for another, perhaps for a woman of a more genteel background the living situation might be too radical for her sensitivities, but for an old Crescent girl, having a room on a floor where only men resided, having to share their one bathroom at the end of the hall, and overhearing ribald stories and the clink of whiskey glasses late at night cowed her not the least bit.

But it wasn't going to be easy. Dr. Prince had been humiliated; he was going to get revenge.

The chief of staff was not the only one who resented her presence. Aside from the other interns, who felt their evening hours of masculine pleasures were going to be cramped by the interloping female, the nurses were appalled that they should be expected to take orders from her (Samantha upset their sense of place; doctors were their superiors, women were their equals—but what did you do with a woman doctor?), and most disapproving of all was Mrs. Knight, the senior matron.

Aside from supervising the underpaid, ill-bred and barely educated nurses (the Nightingale system had yet to reach St. Brigid's), it was also Mrs. Knight's responsibility to oversee the interns' living quarters. And when she settled Samantha into the vacant room at the end of the hall, Mrs. Knight took no pains to hide her displeasure.

"I'll have the janitor install a lock on the bathroom door," she said, jangling the ring of keys that hung from her belt. "Until then, you must sing loudly to prevent an embarrassing situation. You are to keep your door locked at night, and under no circumstances are you to go out into the hall other than fully dressed. The staff dining room is on the third floor, meals are to be taken on time or they are missed. I protested that you should eat with the nurses, but Dr. Prince insists that as a member of the medical staff you are to join them." Mrs. Knight was an obese woman with iron-gray hair; she reminded Samantha of Ursula the Pig Woman in Ben Jonson's *Bartholomew Fair*. She clasped her hands over her enormous bosom and sniffed disapprovingly. "I want you to know, Dr. Hargrave, that I am very much against your being here. This experiment was tried once before, at Pennsylvania Hospital back in '69. Those so-called women doctors didn't last the first day. They had tobacco quids spat at them. Women are not meant to be doctors, they haven't the capacity for that sort of responsibility. I give you a month."

She jangled her keys again to remind Samantha of her authority. "One last thing. You must remember to absent yourself during your monthly days. The nurses aren't allowed on the wards then, and neither are you. We can't have an unstable woman around the patients."

It was a mean little room with a window so sooty that one could barely see out, a dresser that leaned and a bed that sagged, but to Samantha it was a palace. And the work proved hard and the hours long, but Samantha's enthusiasm and determination gave her the needed strength to meet the rigors of internship (much to everyone's surprise). Her one regret was that the other interns refused to accept her. There were nine in the program, seven after Samantha was admitted, for two left, refusing to tolerate the insult; those remaining greatly resented her presence, believing she had lowered the prestige of the institution and made them a laughingstock. All complained to Dr. Prince and all were assured that the female couldn't last long. They treated her as if she didn't exist: no one sat with her at meals, she was excluded from discussions, and in the evenings, when the interns relaxed after their exhausting day, sounds of laughter and banjo music floated down the hall but there was never a knock at her door.

For Dr. Prince Samantha was a constant reminder of the mistake he had made and the day came, after four weeks, for him to exact his revenge.

This was his plan: Samantha Hargrave had weasled her way into the hospital on a legal hitch, she would be gotten rid of the same way.

First, it was written in the hospital rules that all female employees must conduct themselves properly at all times, they were not to use tobacco, strong language or alcohol, and their appearance must at all times reflect the propriety of the institution: dresses were to cover the ankles, wrists and neck. Any woman found in offensive or indecent attire would be dismissed at once.

Second, all interns had to put in a certain number of hours in each of the specialty rotations—Accident Ward, Maternity, Ambulance Call. No exceptions. Not even for the female intern who could not possibly fulfill that last duty, Ambulance Call, because of the restrictiveness of her clothing. In her dresses, there was no way Dr. Hargrave could swing herself up onto the back of the ambulance without either splitting her skirt or falling flat on her face. And since she could not be permitted to wear trousers (they came under the heading of "indecent" for a woman), then it did not seem to Dr. Prince that Samantha Hargrave could possibly fulfill her ambulance rotation. Hence: quick, quiet and legal dismissal.

But Samantha had anticipated him. When, one week earlier, she had seen her name on the ambulance roster and realized that she had one week in which to think of something, she had gone at once to a tailor on nearby Fiftieth Street with a most unusual request.

In order to pay for the costume, Samantha had had to pawn the beautiful, silver-belled binaural stethoscope Dr. Jones had given her as a graduation present; but the old Jew had refused her money. The costume was a challenge, he had told her, and good advertising. As long as she told everyone she had gotten it from Rabinowitz, she could have the outfit for free.

A week later, unbeknownst to anyone at the hospital, Samantha returned to Mr. Rabinowitz's shop.

The outfit was a clever deception. Short enough for safety yet long enough for modesty, rugged but still acceptably feminine, the uniform was made of navy-blue serge with a form-fitting jacket and a skirt that was a marvel of illusion: it was divided like billowy pantaloons but still had the appearance of a skirt. Dr. Prince could not say she was indecently dressed, and she could hop on and off the ambulance with ease. The final touches were plentiful pockets with button-down flaps and the name of St. Brigid's embroidered on the sleeves in gold.

Tonight was the test and so Samantha paced.

Most interns tried to get some sleep while they were on ambulance call, for the bell could be heard up in their third-floor quarters and they knew they could jump into their clothes and be down at the ambulance house in the required three minutes. But this was too monumental a night for Samantha to sleep through; everyone would be watching her to see what she would do. And Dr. Prince, who rarely spent the night at the hospital, had given up his comfortable Park Avenue bedroom in order to be on hand for the victory.

Samantha, as she paced, was not concerned about everyone's reaction to her special costume: whether it was rejected or accepted didn't matter now. It was the keen anticipation of her first emergency case. What would it be, would she be able to handle it? She had earlier gone down to the ambulance house to familiarize herself with the bus and driver and had run back up to her room, timing herself. How much more prepared could she be?

She stopped suddenly and swung around. Outside, coming down the hall, were familiar footsteps and they made her instantly angry. Not you again! she thought. And tonight of all nights!

On the first night of her arrival, four weeks earlier, Samantha had wakened out of a light sleep to the sound of footsteps coming down the hall. At first they had not concerned her, but as they drew close and she remembered that the bathroom was at the other end of the hall (this end only had a fire escape) she became alert. The footsteps stopped outside her door. Samantha lay taut, holding her breath, and wondered who was out there, listening; she had the prickly feeling the person was peeking through her keyhole. After a minute, however, the footsteps had turned away and faded back down the hall, and Samantha had thought: Nosy Parker, and drifted off to sleep.

But the footsteps had come again and again, usually three times a week, always late at night, alway pausing for a minute, as if listening to her or trying to look in. Samantha had considered complaining to Mrs. Knight, but decided that the senior matron would only tell Samantha she had brought it on herself. Whoever it was seemed intent on no harm and was probably only curious about the female doctor, so Samantha had chosen to ignore it.

But this time she was angry. Hearing the footsteps draw near, Samantha seized an atomizer of cologne off her dresser and stationed herself next to the door. When the footsteps stopped and she was certain the spy was peeking in, Samantha swung around with the atomizer, thrust the nozzle into the keyhole and gave it a few hefty squeezes. On the other side of the door there came a surprised cry and then a thud, as of someone falling onto his buttocks. A moment later the footsteps thudded away down the hall.

She leaned against the wall and angrily threw the cologne onto the bed. In the next instant the still night air was disrupted by the rude clanging of a bell. It came from the ambulance house.

-❈-

The horses were quivering in their harnesses. Jake, the night driver, jumped down to help her up, but Samantha waved him back to his post. Somewhere hidden and watching, she suspected, was Dr. Prince. Samantha seized the rail and pulled herself up with such a surge of strength that she nearly fell headfirst into the ambulance. Before she could regain her balance, the omnibus jolted forward and tore out of the ambulance house, throwing Samantha to her knees.

As they swung down Fiftieth Street, bells clanging, Samantha hung on with both hands, thankful now for all her pockets, which held her medical supplies. It was early evening and quite a few pedestrians were abroad; those who noticed that the doctor wobbling on the tailboard seat of the ambulance was a woman stopped and pointed. Samantha saw only a tableau whiz by: statues on the sidewalk with their mouths hanging open. Her heart thrashed with the rhythm of the clanging bell. She had no idea where she was going.

Near the East River, they pulled up in front of a brightly lit brownstone that had a red lantern over the door. A crowd had chased the ambulance and now clustered around, curious to glimpse the female doctor, and when Samantha pushed through, ragged little boys chanted, "Get a man, get a man!"

Samantha and Jake were met by a narrow-faced woman in severe gray bombazine who led them upstairs. Hanging about in scant clothing were women of all ages and types, some sobbing, others ogling in morbid fascination.

"She hasn't been well these last few days," said the dour proprietress as Samantha pushed into the room.

On the bed lay a girl of no more than fourteen, her spare body clad only in a lacy peignoir. She appeared to be asleep, her hands folded across her stomach. The instant Samantha saw the bluish tinge around the lips and nostrils, she said, "What did she take?"

The woman pointed to an empty bottle by the bed. Dr. Hansen's Elixir. "All my girls take it now and then. It says on the label that it's perfectly safe. I don't see how this happened."

Samantha lifted the victim's eyelids and found pinpointed pupils. She was barely breathing but her pulse was still good. "It's an opium overdose, Jake. We'll have to get her back to the hospital fast."

As they laid the girl on a stretcher and hurried down the stairs with her, the prim woman followed, saying, "This isn't my fault, you know. I run a clean establishment. None of my girls has ever—"

As the ambulance swung away Samantha sat anxiously over the girl, rubbing her ice-cold hands and mentally pleading, *Don't die! Please don't die . . .*

The accident ward was deserted; after they had the girl on the examining table, Samantha sent Jake for help. By now the child was quite blue.

Samantha attempted a stomach wash first; but as the tube brought up little of the "elixir," she knew it was too late for that. She had now to resort to "heroic" measures. Dr. Page's voice rang up from the past: "Restore the breathing artificially, flick the abdomen with a wet towel, warm the hands and feet, give black coffee, walk the patient . . ."

When Jake returned Samantha was pumping the girl's flaccid arms—up over her head, down onto her abdomen, press; up over her head, down onto her abdomen, press. Behind Jake, still buttoning his celluloid collar, was one of the senior residents. He strode to the table, placed fingertips to the girl's neck, took one look at the blue face and said, "My dear, you are working on a corpse."

Samantha paused long enough to search for a pulse in the wrist. Certain she felt one, she resumed artificial resuscitation. "I need help, Doctor. Until she breathes spontaneously we must do it for her."

He shook his head. "You are wasting your time, Miss Hargrave. You are trying to resurrect a dead child. I suggest you pronounce her and go to bed. Judging by what I guess to be her profession, she is better off dead anyway."

After he left Samantha hissed at Jake, "Get me anyone!"

The exertion required for the resuscitation had Samantha near to collapse when Jake returned with Mrs. Knight. Without a word, the senior matron moved into Samantha's place and took up the pumping without breaking the rhythm. But Samantha did not sit down. From what she knew of overdose victims, she knew they were in for a night. Removing her hat and jacket, she periodically listened to the girl's struggling heart through her stethoscope. At fifteen-minute intervals she and Mrs. Knight, who still spoke not a word, changed places.

Around midnight, when the two women were still laboring in the deserted accident ward, one of the young interns appeared in the doorway. He watched them silently for a few minutes, then hastily removed his jacket and stepped in to relieve Mrs. Knight. Jake, from his corner, watched in fascination. Clearly the whore was a goner, but that Dr. Hargrave was a feisty little cat, you had to allow her that.

The intern, less enthusiastic in his pumping, said, "She's cashed in, Doctor. I think you should pronounce her."

"Not while there's still a pulse, no matter how faint. If you are tired, Doctor, I can take over."

But he kept on. They continued this way for two more hours, pumping, listening for the heartbeat, massaging the blue hands and feet, until finally, when a fine perspiration glistened on the intern's forehead, the girl's color began to change. Slowly the blue faded and her cheeks began to pink, like night giving way to dawn, and then finally the girl drew in a long shuddering breath and coughed.

The intern ceased pumping, and while he and Mrs. Knight looked on, Samantha picked up a towel she had had soaking in ice water, parted the peignoir to reveal a bare abdomen, and proceeded to administer stinging slaps. With each ice-cold smack the girl gasped and rolled her head. When her eyelids fluttered, Samantha said, "Mrs. Knight, we shall need a lot of black coffee."

Soon they had the girl on her feet, supporting her under each arm, and paced her back and forth, pouring copious amounts of coffee down her throat.

It was nearly dawn when Samantha deemed the girl fit to be sent to a ward bed. As she wearily picked up her cap and jacket, Samantha found her way blocked by the intern. He was holding out his hand. "You've won me, Dr. Hargrave. You're all right in my book."

The breakfast talk was all about the attempted assassination of President Garfield, which had aroused a deeper public sentiment than had Lincoln's sixteen years before. By the time Lincoln was shot the public had suffered four years of killings and atrocities; Lincoln was merely one more casualty of war. But James Garfield had come in a time of peace, was a symbol of prosperity, and therefore generated great public fervor. President Garfield now lay in the White House dying a little each day. His wound was probed and poked for the missing bullet, sometimes with a metal catheter, sometimes with a doctor's unwashed finger. Professor Alexander Graham Bell had designed a contraption to locate buried metal; however, the bedsprings confounded the device and made it click no matter where it passed over the President's body. The esteemed physicians who hovered over him round the clock had absolutely no idea what to do. It was a favorite breakfast topic for the staff of St. Brigid's.

"The Democrats are behind it!" announced one old surgeon as he tucked into his bacon and eggs.

"I tell you, sirs," came another voice over buttered toast and coffee, "it is folly to attempt to open the abdomen. It doesn't matter that the bullet is still lodged within him. To open the abdomen is sure death."

Samantha walked in just then and the dining room fell silent; all heads turned to stare (including one abashed young intern whose eyes were red and puffy and weepy from the spray of cologne). Dr. Prince rose from his table and came slowly toward her, holding in his hand the morning edition of the *Tribune*. The chief's eyes burned coldly and his white muttonchop whiskers seemed to bristle. "Have you seen this, Dr. Hargrave?" he asked, holding the newspaper out to her.

She had. Someone had left one before her door and she had found it on her way to the bathroom that morning. There was a small item on the front page about Samantha's heroism during the night.

"I do not approve of this sort of thing, Dr. Hargrave. The man responsible is the ambulance driver, Jake, who apparently earned himself a bit of notoriety by boasting about the night's adventure to a reporter who happened into the ambulance house. Now there are six reporters down there, all asking for stories about the *doctress*. I have reprimanded the man Jake; he has been put on report. And I advise you, Dr. Hargrave, to see that you are discreet and avoid seeking cheap renown for yourself. St. Brigid's is not a side show."

She held her head high, her eyes gazed at him steadily. Her voice was the only sound to be heard in the still and silent room. "Yes, Dr. Prince."

His cold eyes narrowed; Dr. Prince was clearly dissatisfied with her small victory. This woman was fox-cunning, he would not underestimate her again. "And one more thing, Dr. Hargrave. To take all night on one worthless prostitute is evidence of your poor medical judgment. The effort has exhausted you for rounds this morning, you caused the hospital unnecessary expense by tying up our senior matron and another intern, and you were not available in case another hurry call came through. You are going to have to learn discrimination in your medical excesses, Dr. Hargrave."

"Yes, Dr. Prince."

He seemed to consider briefly saying something further, but then he turned abruptly and marched out of the room. Stiff with anger, Samantha walked to her usual seat at an empty table, and with slow and deliberate motions took her place. When the serving girl came by with tea and honeyed biscuits, Samantha tried to pretend that twenty pairs of eyes were not staring at her.

And then softly, like the beginning patter of a spring rain, the intern at the next table started clapping his hands.

Startled, Samantha looked up.

The others joined in. For a moment, the medical staff dining room thundered with applause, and Samantha, looking in bewilderment at the smiles and approving faces, could not swallow her tea.

TWO

*S*AMANTHA WAS STUNNED BY HOW MUCH HER FRIEND HAD changed. It wasn't just the outward appearance—the extra pounds, the untidy hair, the puffy face—something in Louisa's manner had altered as well; her gestures betrayed a nervous undercurrent, her green eyes were never still, and her voice rose frequently to an edge. Not at all typical of an eight months' pregnant woman. Samantha was dismayed. Could one year of marriage do this?

When Louisa put her hand to her lower back, hoisted herself off the sofa with a grunt and waddled out of the room, Samantha took the opportunity to look around the parlor.

Luther was making good money now as Mr. DeWinter's new partner; in the corner stood a brand-new musical sewing machine, a monument to the Arndts' middle-class prosperity: as the treadle worked the machine it also turned rollers which produced tunes. Unfortunately, the machine was covered with a patina of dust, as was the Rogers group that sat on it. Louisa had always been a little careless in keeping her things in order, but this dusty, littered parlor showed plain neglect, a reflection of the woman who spent all her days here, a woman who seemed to have given up caring.

"Garfield, Garfield, Garfield," Louisa sighed, returning to the sofa with a tray bearing two glasses of brown liquid, slices of poppyseed cake and something new that Samantha had never heard of before—oleomargarine (Louisa still had a penchant for the most modern things at the expense of good taste). "It's called root beer," said Louisa, "and it's very new." Samantha reached for a glass. "No, that one's mine," said Louisa, taking it from her. Samantha noticed that the foam was not as high on that one.

Louisa pulled her swollen feet up onto the sofa, knocking a Montgomery Ward's mail-order wish book to the floor. "They are calling this the Summer of the President. Garfield is all anyone talks about. I'm sick of it."

Samantha tried to keep her disappointment from showing; she had looked forward to being reunited with Louisa after so long. When she had finally managed a day off from the hospital, she had put on her best dress and gotten on the Fifth Avenue bus, full of excitement; but the Louisa she had expected to answer the door—the Louisa with the perfect honey-gold curls who had once tried to raise the spirit of Joan of Arc—never appeared.

Although there had been joy in Louisa's welcome, embracing her friend so tightly that Samantha had felt a little unseen foot kick her stomach, after fifteen minutes of animated reminiscing about the past Louisa seemed to grow bored, as though Samantha were a new toy whose novelty had worn off, and now she lay stretched out on the sofa, bloated and uncomfortable, her green eyes shifting from side to side.

Samantha wanted to say: What's wrong? but feared to hurt her friend's feelings. "How is Luther?"

"Fine," came the vague response.

"You must be very pleased about the partnership."

Louisa's busy green eyes found a place to settle; she gazed absently at the fern growing wild and dusty in the window. "He spends all his time at the pharmacy now. They're going to sell ice cream. In a drugstore."

There must be something that interested Louisa; if her husband didn't turn the trick—although after just one year of marriage there should be a little more spark than that—then surely the baby would do it. "You must be busy with the nursery."

Louisa gave Samantha a flat, dumb stare.

"Is it ready? I should so like to see it."

Louisa shrugged and pushed herself to her feet. Following her up the stairs, Samantha wondered if pregnancy did this to all women; maybe eight months of waiting for an event that it seemed would never arrive dulled one's interest in everything else. After the baby, Louisa should be all right again.

Samantha said, "Oh," and wished she hadn't asked to see the nursery. It was upstairs next to the master bedroom, where Samantha saw an unmade bed, and it was bare except for a half-painted crib and some rolls of wallpaper lying on the bare floor. "Well, you've still got time."

Again Louisa gave her the flat, blank stare and Samantha thought: This isn't going well at all.

She deliberated all the way down the stairs and finally, back in the parlor, said, "What's wrong, Louisa?"

To her surprise, her friend said passionately, "Just everything, Samantha," and her face finally showed life. "I don't want to pour my miseries on you but I have to tell someone. I've been cooped up in this house for so long that I think I'm going mad. It isn't fair, Samantha, that pregnant women have to be confined. People are such hypocrites. They love babies but they don't want to be reminded where they come from. It makes me feel as if I should be ashamed. Society insists you get married and have children, but as soon as one is on the way, society shames you into staying hidden. If I went outside people would look at me and they would know at once what I've done. Well, Luther's done it, too, but he can still go outside and no one would ever know he's done it. Women are marked after intercourse, but on men it never shows. It isn't fair!"

It isn't just the pregnancy then, Samantha thought, hearing a message other than the one Louisa's words were speaking. The tone of her letters had started changing back before she was pregnant; Louisa's problem went deeper than she was admitting, as though she wanted to express it but couldn't find the right path to it. Samantha helped by asking gently, "Are you having problems in the marriage bed?"

Louisa picked at the ruffled cuff of her peignoir and nodded mutely. "You don't know what it's like, Samantha, you're not married."

With a pang Samantha thought of Joshua and then immediately, to her surprise, of Mark Rawlins. She hadn't seen him since that evening at Mrs. Kendall's. He had given her his address in Manhattan and had invited her to come and collect Joshua's instruments any time; but Samantha had been putting it off, telling herself that there was nowhere to store the instruments in her little room, that she didn't need them yet, that they were safer at Dr. Rawlins' house, anything to put off having to see him again. For the past two months Samantha had been telling herself that it was because he reminded her of Joshua, but now, in Louisa's stuffy little parlor, the truth came crystal clear: it was because of the unwanted feelings he aroused in her . . .

Louisa raised her mossy green eyes. "I don't know what I expected, Samantha. But I thought somehow it would be clean and pure. I was shocked on our wedding night. Luther kept telling me it was all right, that that was how it was done. I cried every time he did it. Samantha, it nauseated me! He wouldn't stop. He said it was natural for me not to like it, that only men are supposed to like it. I was so relieved when I found out I was pregnant because then Luther left me alone."

Louisa wasn't telling the truth. The fact was, on her wedding night Louisa had been thrilled and ignited by what Luther was doing but she had felt instantly shocked and ashamed to discover such base feelings inside her; Louisa quickly became revolted with herself and despised Luther for having stirred such disgusting thoughts and desires. She hated herself for lusting after him, cried to discover that she looked forward to going to bed with him, and came to believe that she must be a wretched, degenerate woman. But as Louisa was not one to be comfortable with self-dislike, she managed, over the months, to transfer her self-loathing to Luther, telling herself nightly that no such feelings existed within her, that it was Luther who made her imagine them, and so in time had come to transfer that loathing onto Luther and had successfully convinced herself, after a year, that she had not, after all, enjoyed sex, but found it repulsive, as she should.

"Luther does unspeakable things to me. He doesn't even have the decency to let me undress and put on my nightgown and get under the covers before he comes into the bedroom. He insists on removing my . . . unwhisperables. And with the lights on!" She shuddered. "He makes me look at him, and touch him. Oh, even to recall it brings back the nausea!"

Samantha felt sorry for her two friends. How remarkable that the same act performed by different people produced such different results. "Have you told Luther how you feel?"

Louisa's eyes stretched. "You mean . . . discuss it with him? Samantha, such a suggestion!"

"But surely at some time you've exchanged words—"

"Oh yes, words! Do you want to hear something really revolting? When Luther makes love to me he *talks*. He says words in my ear, horrible words. Some of them I don't even know the meaning of . . ."

"Louisa," said Samantha gently, "maybe Luther doesn't realize how much you dislike it. A lot of brides cry at first and then they get used to it and even to like it. Maybe Luther thinks you'll get over it. Louisa, you will drive yourself into a nervous condition if you don't get it straightened out."

"I can't talk about it with Luther and that's that! You're the only person in the whole world I can say these things to, Samantha, because you're my best friend and you're a doctor. And you're easy to talk to. You're understanding. I never get the feeling that while I'm talking to you you're thinking: Silly cow!"

"Do others make you feel that way?"

"Dr. McMahan! He's an odious little man who treats me like a child. When I complain about how uncomfortable I am he pats me on the head and chuckles. I can tell by his eyes that he hasn't the slightest bit of sympathy for me. He says I should feel beautiful because I'm performing a sacred function. Look at me, Samantha! Look at this body! If men could get pregnant they would soon stop thinking it was 'beautiful!'"

Samantha frowned. Why was Louisa doing this? A pregnant woman *could* be beautiful, radiant even; it was almost as if Louisa's neglect of herself and this house were on purpose, a planned act of rebellion.

"Samantha," came her suddenly subdued voice, "I'm going to tell you something I haven't told a single other soul. I resent the baby. I resent what it's done to my figure and how it's kept me a prisoner in this house. Samantha, I feel so terrible! I don't want the baby! I have no *feelings* for it. It's like a little parasite that's invaded my body and is feeding off me. If it weren't for the baby, I'd go outside, I could go shopping, I could still be working at the Bell Company."

Samantha had tried to boost her friend's spirits by making a show of enjoying their snack, but the warm root beer did little to help the cake and oleomargarine go down. Brushing crumbs off her lap, Samantha said, "Then you should go out, Louisa! You should get exercise and fresh air. It would be good for you."

Louisa was plainly shocked. "Samantha Hargrave, being a doctor has turned you all back to front! I can't go out like this! What would people think?"

"Louisa, pregnancy isn't an illness, there's no reason an expectant mother can't take exercise and fresh air. We could have a day just like old times. Lunch at Macy's and then we could go to the Hotel Everett to see Mr. Edison's new incandescent lamps, a hundred and one in all. You would like that, Louisa, they are a positive marvel!"

She seemed a little interested. "When?"

"When? Well, I don't know. I have every other Sunday off but then I have washing and mending to do—"

"It doesn't matter, Samantha. I couldn't go out like this anyway. Maybe after the baby's born . . ." Louisa's face collapsed and her eyes turned the darkest green as a thought came to her mind, one she had entertained frequently of late: I can't go anywhere and I have no friends. No one has time for a pregnant woman. But if the baby died I'd get a lot of sympathy and people would come around and treat me extra special. Or if Luther got killed in an accident I would be a widow and everyone would treat me kindly and I would never again be expected to marry and have children.

Unaware that she was doing so, Louisa's thoughts segued into spoken words. "Well, I won't go through this again. Luther will have to learn to live without it. Or if he has to satisfy his disgusting animal lust, there are plenty of women who—"

The sound of her own voice startled her, and when she met Samantha's eyes, Louisa felt instantly ashamed. There was an awkward moment of rapidly blinking green eyes and a few stuttering sounds, then Samantha said, "It really is a warm day, dear. I think I shall freshen up. Where is the littlest room?"

With eyes that mutely pleaded: *Don't hate me,* Louisa pointed down the hall to the back of the house. Seeing that Louisa's glass was drained and the cake gone, Samantha picked up the tray and carried it along to the kitchen.

Lucky Louisa had all the gadgets and modern conveniences a woman could wish for, but here again clutter and neglect spoiled the effect. Depositing the tray by the sink, Samantha saw the two empty bottles of Levis & Hires Root Beer and, next to them, one of those fancy new "automatic" can openers. Picking it up and absently toying with the cutting wheel, Samantha stared at the third bottle by the sink. Dr. Poole's Soothing Syrup for Expectant Mothers. Samantha uncorked it and sniffed. A sickly sweet odor filled her nostrils but did not quite do the cover-up it was meant to: Dr. Poole's elixir contained a drug—she couldn't identify it—and Louisa was taking it.

A moment later Samantha stood in the newly furbished bathroom (the Arndts even had a new pull-chain flush toilet) pressing a cold cloth to the back of her neck. Next to Luther's shaving mug stood a bottle of Dr. Raphael's Cordial Invigorant for the Wonderful Prolongation of the Attributes of Manhood.

What was happening here? Samantha recalled the two merry young people she had spent her Sundays with, Louisa flirtatious and energetic, Luther proud and generous. Samantha saw them now as little more than strangers. She and Louisa had not one thing in common; their dialogues were filled with ever widening silences. Louisa needed other friends, married friends, women with children.

Samantha neatly folded the washcloth and hung it back on its hook. *Our ways are parting, Louisa. Do you see it? Is that why you are angry with me, with the world? After the baby, the gap will be so wide we shall never be able to bridge it. Do you blame that on Luther also?*

In the distance she heard the front door. Making a final check of herself in the mirror, Samantha went down the hall and received Luther's insistent handclasp. He hadn't changed a bit: still tall and straight, his platinum hair fashionably parted in the middle and plastered down, his pale blue eyes warm with friendship. When he bent to kiss his wife, Louisa offered her cheek, and when he asked how she was feeling, she complained of a backache. And Samantha thought: She is punishing him.

They sat in the parlor attempting a pretense of normalcy. "I understand you're very busy at the pharmacy now, Luther."

While he spoke, his eyes went continually to his wife. "It is a lot of work and responsibility, but I welcome it. Mr. DeWinter is old and old-fashioned; he intends someday to leave the pharmacy entirely to me. I am trying to bring him up to date, but Mr. DeWinter occasionally fights me."

Louisa let out a loud cow yawn, not bothering to cover her mouth.

Luther leaned forward, hands earnestly clasped between his knees. "I wish to bring the pharmacy into modern times, you know? You will appreciate this, Samantha. There is a new wonder drug coming out of my homeland. It is a white crystalline powder that cures all pain and lowers fever and has no bad effects whatever on the body. It is called salicylic acid and the Bayer Company in Berlin plans to make it into tablets and put it out under the brand name Aspirin. And do you know? Mr. DeWinter will have none of it!"

Samantha glanced covertly at Louisa; while Luther was trying too hard, Louisa wasn't trying hard enough, and it created a palpable imbalance in the air. "It sounds like something we could use at the hospital. Aspirin, you say?"

Luther rubbed his hands together. "Louisa, my love, have we plans for dinner?"

"You were supposed to bring it home."

He flushed right up to his transparent eyebrows. "Of course, I had forgotten. Perhaps we could invite Samantha . . ."

"I would love to stay, if you're up to it, Louisa."

"Oh yes—"

"Excellent!" Luther got up and went to the sideboard to pour them all small glasses of cordial. Samantha said to Louisa quietly, "Perhaps we can talk later, would you like that?"

Louisa smiled. "Yes, Samantha. I'd like that very much."

Later, after dinner and much talking, Luther walked Samantha to the front door. In a low voice, so that Louisa in the parlor couldn't hear, he said, "It is a bad time for her, Samantha. We must be patient."

"I understand. After the baby everything will be all right."

"Samantha, I am worried about Louisa. She is so afraid."

"Of what?"

"Of the birth of the child. She is convinced she will die. She does not want to go through with it, Samantha. She becomes hysterical at the thought of it."

Samantha looked long and consideringly in the direction of the parlor. "When her time comes, Luther, send for me."

THREE

*I*T WAS A TORRID SEPTEMBER AFTERNOON IN WHICH NO AIR circulated to sweep away the foul hospital miasmas. The eight interns under the supervision of one of the staff doctors shifted and continually ran their fingers under their celluloid collars as they tried to pay attention to the bedside lecture. "And so, Doctors, the diagnosis for this patient is asthma. What would be the course of treatment, Dr. Weston?"

A young intern said, "Marijuana, three times daily."

"Precisely. Next we have a woman who—" He was interrupted by a sudden commotion a few beds down.

Sitting up against the iron bedstead and clutching her covers up to her chin was a plump woman in her forties. She was staring in horror at a frock-coated gentleman bending over her; they were arguing.

"Really, madam," he said in extreme exasperation. "How do you expect me to help you if you do not cooperate?"

"You ain't touching me!"

The physician, Dr. Miles, threw out his hands and looked up at the ceiling. Then he took another step toward her and the woman shrieked.

"Confound it, you silly creature!" he boomed. "You'll either do as I say or I shall have you discharged from this institution!"

The woman burst into tears and buried her face in her blanket.

As snickers rippled through the knot of interns, Samantha disengaged herself from them and hurried to the bedside. Sitting on its edge, she put an arm around the heaving shoulders. "There, there."

"Don't let him touch me!" wailed the woman into the blanket. "I would die of shame!"

Samantha looked up at Dr. Miles. "What is her problem?"

"How should I know? The silly creature won't let me examine her—"

"No!" The woman jerked her head up and glared at him. "You think just because I ain't paying to be here that I got no self-respect. Well, I do, and you ain't touching me!"

Samantha continued to pat the woman's shoulders and croon gently to her. This scene was repeated so many times in the women's wards that Samantha needed no more information to know what was wrong.

Finally, calming a little, the woman turned her moonface to Samantha. "You understand, don't you?"

"Of course I do." It was a problem with most female patients. In a society that dictated a woman must guard her modesty at all costs, and in an age where the sight of a female ankle could rouse men's passions, most women preferred to suffer with their intimate ailments rather than submit to the examination of a male physician.

"She came in during the night with severe abdominal pains," said Dr. Miles irritably. "They might be labor pains, but the silly cow is so fat she doesn't know if she's pregnant or not."

Samantha said gently to the woman, "Do you think you might be in labor?"

"I don't know."

"Have you any children?"

"Nine living."

Samantha thought a moment. "You need to be examined to see what your problem is—"

"No! I won't let no strange man touch me!"

"I'm a doctor. How about if I examine you?"

The woman's eyes widened. "You're a doctor?"

"Now see here—"

Samantha looked up at Dr. Miles. "I believe the patient will submit to me, Doctor. If you will but permit, I can discover her trouble in minimal time."

The woman whispered, "But not with him around!"

"Could we have some privacy, please?"

Indignant, Dr. Miles muttered something about *pestis mulieribis* and marched a few paces away.

"What'll you do?" asked the woman, seizing Samantha's hand.

"I shall do a hasty check under the covers. You shan't be exposed, I promise. Now if you will just relax . . ."

A moment later Samantha joined Dr. Miles. "She has a prolapsed uterus, sir."

"Hmph. No doubt from her corset. Silly cow was laced tight as Dick's hatband!"

"Dr. Hargrave." She looked up to see Dr. Prince standing in the doorway at the end of the ward. "May I speak with you in the hall?"

Outside, he turned to her and said, "You had no right to interfere with that patient. She is not one of ours."

"She needed help and Dr. Miles was getting nowhere."

"What do you expect when the creature's hysterical?"

"Shouting at her did no good."

"That is often the only way to handle such women. One must be stern, show them who is master. We cannot mollycoddle them, Dr. Hargrave. Really, I don't know what gets into the silly cows! We are, after all, doctors!"

Samantha compressed her lips to maintain silence. She wanted to ask him how he would like to have his testicles examined by a woman doctor.

"You are not to interfere again, Dr. Hargrave. You can be thankful Dr. Miles is a forgiving man." He turned to go but Samantha said, "Excuse me, sir, now that I have your ear I should like to discuss a matter of great importance with you."

He turned back but his manner was one of barely constrained impatience, as though any second he would dash away. It was a trick he used to get the person to hurry up and speak quickly, stumble over his words and thereby be put in a position of supplicant. It usually worked; Dr. Prince won most arguments with this tactic. But Samantha refused to be manipulated. She spoke slowly and confidently, and it irritated him. "My name is not on this month's surgical list, Dr. Prince. I have been here eight weeks now, I have gone through all the services and find that I am back in Maternity, which is where I started. It is my turn for surgery, sir, has there been some oversight?"

"It is no oversight, Dr. Hargrave. You will not be admitted into the surgical program."

She had been prepared for this and so was able to conceal her anger. "Dr. Prince, surely that is unfair. Why am I barred from the operating room?"

"Because the operating room is no place for a woman except in the capacity of a maid. The nurses wash the floors and windows and empty the blood buckets and that is all. Surgery, Dr. Hargrave, is a man's province. Women are not physically fit for the practice of surgery."

"If I may be allowed to disagree—"

"I will not stand here, Dr. Hargrave, and debate so immutable a truth with you! I'd sooner argue the color of the sky! Woman's monthly instability *naturally* precludes her participation in anything so life-and-death critical as the operating room. I will grant you that some exceptional women have the necessary courage and insight for surgery; however, once a month they are rendered as infirm as the patients they care for! It is inconceivable that a person who is prone to monthly fits of instability and lapses in good judgment be allowed to train as a surgeon! Even you, Dr. Hargrave, cannot dispute that."

"I was given to understand, Dr. Prince, that I was expected to fulfill all the required services of the intern program and that I was to be granted no special considerations because of my sex."

"You are being granted no special considerations, Dr. Hargrave. It is not for your sake that you are to be kept out of the operating room, it is concern for the patients' safety."

Dr. Prince loved to punctuate sentences with dramatic gestures; it was his way of reminding everyone of his superiority. Since he knew the Hargrave woman capable of a healthy and prolonged debate, he chose this moment to put a period to his sentence with a snap-turning of his body and to leave her glaring at his back as he strode away.

Samantha took a moment to calm herself before returning to the patients. Yes, she had been expecting this, the minute she had seen that her name was omitted from the surgical roster. But Dr. Prince was not going to have his way; somehow, she wasn't sure yet how, Samantha was going to find a way through the jealously guarded doors of the operating room.

She turned to go and then stopped short. At the end of the hall, rounding the corner from the direction of the entrance foyer, were two people whose elegance and refinement cut a stunning contrast against the hospital's dreary interior. The gentleman was tall and walked with a combination of military straightness and loose-jointed ease, the confident walk of the aristocracy. He wore an excellently cut frock coat which showed his broad shoulders and trim waist to their best advantage; and when he lifted his black top hat from his head he revealed waves and curls that were unconventionally long, resting on his coat collar and free of Macassar oil. The lady was his match. Slender and graceful, beautifully dressed in a midnight-blue silk dress which matched the blue of her eyes and set off the silver blond of her upswept hair, she was perhaps twenty-two, twenty-three years old, laughed in a way that sounded like little bells, and appeared comfortably at home on the gentleman's arm.

Samantha could not help but stare; her imagination had been unfair to Mrs. Rawlins. The woman was breathtaking.

Dr. Rawlins glanced her way and the smile froze on his face. When their eyes met Samantha felt an old reaction, one she had thought she had gotten over, take place deep inside, and for an instant she was trapped in indecision. Wanting to avoid Dr. Rawlins but at the same time magnetically attracted to him, by the time she decided to duck back into the ward he had recognized her.

His companion, seeing his expression, followed the line of his gaze. Her smile also froze, but in a different way: it hardened, solidified, and as she and Dr. Rawlins drew near, the hardness had reached her eyes. In that moment, for reasons she would understand only later, Janelle took an instant dislike to Samantha Hargrave.

"Dr. Hargrave," he said softly, inclining from the waist.

"How do you do, Dr. Rawlins? What a pleasant surprise." Samantha was suddenly, maddeningly aware of a frayed spot on the hem of her dress. She turned slightly to hide it.

"I am afraid, Dr. Hargrave, I have you at an advantage. Finding you here is no surprise. In fact, I had half expected to run into you."

"Indeed, sir! How is it you knew I was at St. Brigid's?"

He laughed warmly, contrasting the chill that emanated from his silent companion. "My dear Dr. Hargrave, all the city's a-buzz about the female doctor who stormed the defenses of St. Brigid's! I have heard you described alternately as an Amazon and a sorceress, either way something less than a lady!"

"I had no idea!"

"And because of you, every hospital in the city is being besieged by female doctors and their lawyers. You have caused quite a stir, Dr. Hargrave!"

They laughed together and when his companion's grip tightened on his arm Dr. Rawlins said, "I have forgotten my manners, forgive me. Janelle, allow me to present the audacious Dr. Samantha Hargrave."

Janelle did not share in the humor; her eyes remained cobalt-hard as she murmured, "How do you do?"

"I am pleased to meet you, Mrs. Rawlins."

Mark looked perplexed for an instant, then said, "Mrs. Rawlins! Great heavens, Janelle is not my wife! How I have mishandled this. Dr. Hargrave, this is Miss MacPherson, an old and dear friend."

Was it Samantha's imagination or did those black pupils flare at the word "old"? "Please forgive my blunder, Miss MacPherson. I just assumed you were Dr. Rawlins' wife."

Janelle remained silent, clearly unamused by the error; to be mistaken for his wife was precisely her ambition. But Mark's eyes twinkled; he seemed to be enjoying himself hugely. "Now where did you get the notion I had a wife?"

"Haven't you?"

"Not when I last looked."

"Then I *am* embarrassed, sir. In Lucerne, after the commencement, Dr. Jones inquired after Mrs. Rawlins."

"Ah yes. My mother. She had expected to accompany me but a periodic attack of arthritis kept her home." His compelling brown eyes gleamed down into her face. "So you thought I was married . . ."

"It was my pleasure to have met you, Dr. Hargrave," came a frosty voice. "Mark, darling, we shall be late."

He absently patted the gloved hand on his arm. "One more minute, Janelle, I pray. Dr. Hargrave, I've been expecting you to claim your inheritance."

One quick appraisal of the cold, ivory face of Janelle MacPherson told Samantha everything she needed to know about this "old and dear friend." Like a cat guarding a mouse, Miss MacPherson seemed to be challenging Samantha to try to steal what was hers. You aren't his wife yet, Samantha thought briefly, but you wish to be. Marrying the son of the Ice King would make you the Ice Princess. Apt.

"I've had little time for excursions outside the hospital, Dr. Rawlins. But I shall certainly make the effort when an opportunity arises. I trust it is not an inconvenience for you to store Joshua's things for me."

"Not at all. Tell me, how do you find the hospital drudgery?"

Dr. Prince flashed into her mind. "It is at the same time tiring and stimulating."

"How long have you to go?"

"Thirteen more months."

"I could hardly believe it when I heard of your riding the ambulance!"

"Without Jake's kindness I don't know what I would have done. He has been driving the ambulance for years, and he is my most valuable teacher at times. He taught me how to swing up to the tailboard without flying across to the other side, and has the most uncanny eye for diagnosing those emergencies which require breakneck speed back to the hospital and those which can allow us a saner pace."

"I have read of your adventures. Remarkable."

Unfortunately, because of Jake's boasting, the whole city was reading of St. Brigid's daring "doctress." "I am afraid Dr. Prince is at sixes and sevens. He tried to silence Jake, but certain of our financial backers, it seems, approve of the notoriety. Certainly St. Brigid's is no longer considered a backwater hospital!"

His smiling eyes considered her cryptically. "How thrilling your life must be."

"In a way, yes, in another way, no," she replied and said no more on the subject. Samantha would not concede to Mark Rawlins that the price she had to pay for her notoriety and exceptional medical training was loneliness. Even though her fellow interns had come around to accepting her, many even to admiring her "pluck," she continued to remain outside their circle. Owing to an acute sensitivity to the uniqueness (and sometimes questionable propriety) of the situation, after working hours the interns went to extremes to respect Samantha's privacy lest she be offended. They were gentlemanly to a fault, radically polite and exaggeratedly proper, all in an effort to be certain that no social conventions were being overstepped. Many evenings Samantha would hear, as she sat over a book or mending, female giggles through the walls and the popping of corks. It was an unfair twist of irony, this price she must pay for her career, for although Samantha had obtained exclusive female membership in an all-male world, and although she might be envied by other women for her constant society with men, surrounded by them, working, eating, residing with them, she remained more apart from them than did ordinary females. At times Samantha ached for the intimate attention of a man.

There was a rustling of cool silk as Janelle reminded them of her presence. "Forgive me, my dear," said Dr. Rawlins. "You're quite right, we must be getting along. Dr. Hargrave, Miss MacPherson is president of the Madison Avenue Ladies' Charity League. St. Brigid's is one of the recipients of their noble and worthy deeds. And as I am on the staff of this hospital, I have been invited to sit in on their meeting this afternoon."

Samantha nodded in polite interest, trying to conceal the effect eight of his words had upon her. "Indeed? You are on the staff of St. Brigid's? I have never seen you about."

"St. Brigid's is out of the way for most of my patients and therefore I do most of my work at St. Luke's. But occasionally I bring a surgical patient here, for the operating facility is excellent. Haven't you found it so?"

"I have not had that opportunity yet, sir, but I shall. And now if you will excuse me, I am late for rounds. Dr. Rawlins, Miss MacPherson, good day to you both."

FOUR

*S*AMANTHA STARED AT THE SMALL WATCH IN HER PALM, AND when the sweep hand reached the twelve, she put it down and picked up the scalpel. Speed was vital; even though the patient was anesthetized, he still ran a high risk of shock. Three clean slices, then Samantha dropped the scalpel and reached for the saw. This was the tricky part.

She fumbled for the retractor; it slipped from her hand and clattered to the floor. Samantha whispered, "Damn," and flung the pillow angrily back onto the bed.

She stood for a moment, her feet and back aching, and thought of giving up for the night. But then her eyes settled on the case standing open on the floor, with its shelves and drawers opened out and the name engraved on the silver plate: Joshua Masefield M.D. And she thought: All right, Samantha, try one more time.

It wasn't going at all smoothly but Samantha was determined to make it work. After sending Jake to Dr. Rawlins' house on Madison Avenue for

Joshua's instruments, Samantha had purchased the best surgical text, familiarized herself with each instrument and the anatomy it related to, and proceeded on a course, self-taught, on surgery. Her only aids were the instruments, the book and a pillow that had been slashed and stitched so many times it was no longer comfortable to sleep on.

She stationed herself over the pillow again and set to work. Through the transom over her door Samantha could hear male laughter dotted frequently by one high-pitched female squeal. That would be Amy Templeton, junior nurse, entertaining the interns again. Every so often they smuggled her in, bribed her with baubles and then had their way with her, all seven of them.

Samantha was confident she could master surgery. Really, anyone with a bit of training could perform the operations that were being done; most of the work was on arms and legs. President Garfield had recently died because no one had had the courage to open him up and retrieve the bullet. Only one abdominal operation was being done with any success at all, and that was the ovariotomy—a quick foray through a tiny opening. No one had ever opened an abdomen to try to remove a bullet; and so the President had died. At his trial the assassin Guiteau had declared: "It was the doctors that *killed* him, I simply shot him."

As Samantha pretended to saw the "bone," she thought: How wonderful it would be if a way could be found into the abdomen. All those lives saved, all those tragedies averted: uterine problems, ectopic pregnancies, a whole world lay below an inch of flesh and it was as myterious to them all as the starry cosmos.

A knock at her door startled her. She held her breath and looked up at the transom. "Yes?"

"Dr. Hargrave," came Mrs. Knight's voice, "Dr. Prince wants to see you in his office."

"Now?"

"Immediately."

Taking a minute to put away her instruments and slide the case under her bed in the event anyone should accidentally come into her room, Samantha thought: *Now* what?

—❊—

It never ceased to amaze Samantha that the medical profession attracted so many ill-tempered men. She knew it was only a façade with most ("Always maintain a stern and serious countenance," they taught in medical school. "No one trusts a cheery doctor"). But with Dr. Prince she suspected this was his true nature. She stood before him (he never invited her to sit) while he deliberately delayed acknowledging her presence; then he finished shuffling papers and fixed a cold eye on her. "Dr. Hargrave, each year the members of a certain charity group hold a benefit for several of New York's hospitals. The purpose of this event is to determine which hospital will be that year's recipient of the money the charity group has raised. It has been the misfortune of St. Brigid's not to have been chosen for many years, but this year we stand a good chance of receiving the gift. It is a soiree of some special notice and so as a rule interns do not attend, but this year St. Brigid's has been requested to produce its newest addition to the intern program. You are to attend the soiree, Dr. Hargrave."

He looked at her expectantly; she offered no comment.

"Certain influential members of the group have long wanted to see women doctors admitted to hospital staffs. They are rather outspoken ladies of high rank who call themselves feminists. They have asked that you attend and that they be given the opportunity to acquaint themselves with you. I assured them you would be there. It is a week from tomorrow night and Dr. Weston will be your escort. I expect you to make a good impression, Dr. Hargrave. The finances of this institution depend upon your conduct that night."

You old fraud, she thought. So, all of a sudden I'm worth something to you, am I? Well, perhaps a trade can be worked out . . .

As she turned to go, Dr. Prince said, "Dr. Hargrave, I cannot stress sufficiently the importance of your attendance at the soiree." His cold eyes spoke muted threats. "You are to arrive on time, Dr. Hargrave, and you are to see to it the ladies are favorably impressed."

⁂

As she buttoned the many buttons of her gray silk graduation gown, Samantha smiled at her reflection in the looking glass; she knew exactly what she was going to do. If Prince wanted her cooperation, he was going to have to give something in return.

She glanced out the window. The gaslights on the street were coming on, looking like fleecy dandelions in the evening fog. "Yes, Mrs. Stuyvesant," she said out loud, practicing what she was going to say. "I am happy at St. Brigid's. It *was* charitable of them to grant me the opportunity to take part in their intern program. But, alas, I still find myself the victim of unfair male prejudice, for, you see, I wish to train in surgery. And yet I am forbidden—"

There came a sharp knock on her door. "Who is it?"

"Someone to see you in the foyer, Dr. Hargrave," came Nurse Amy's young voice.

Samantha glanced at the fob watch pinned to her bodice. Dr. Weston would be calling for her soon. "Who?"

"Says he's Mr. Arnold and it's an emergency."

Luther!

He paced the foyer, his face potato-white. It was Louisa, he said. She was in labor and screaming for Samantha. Yes, there was a midwife with her but Louisa wouldn't let the woman touch her.

Samantha ran back up to her room, left a note on her door for Dr. Weston—he was to go ahead alone, she would catch up with him later—and then she seized her cape and bag, took Luther's arm and struck out into the foggy night.

⁂

Initially, Samantha saw no reason why Louisa had sent for her. An examination showed a normal birth process, no complications, and the midwife looked a respectable lady with clean linens and scrubbed-pink hands. But then Samantha saw the raw fear in Louisa's eyes and knew why she was there.

"You're going to be fine, Louisa. It's a normal presentation, everything is going exactly as it should. You've nothing to worry about."

"Samantha!" Louisa's plump fingers attached themselves to her friend's wrists. "I'm going to die! I know it! I've had dreams, I won't make it!"

Samantha tried to conceal her concern. "I'll be right back, Louisa. Mrs. Marchand is with you." She pried herself out of Louisa's grasp and went downstairs. Luther was sitting in the messy kitchen, looking lost and bereft. He lifted bleak eyes. "She doesn't want the baby, Samantha. She hates the baby."

"Louisa's just frightened, Luther." Samantha sat next to him and placed a hand on his arm. "Once the baby is born she'll see things differently."

He shook his head. "After this she will hate the baby even more. And she will hate me."

Samantha stared at him and thought: He might be right.

"Samantha," came his softly accented voice, "let me be with her. She shouldn't have to go through this alone. It is our baby, we must do this together."

Samantha hesitated. In rural areas husbands frequently attended their wives' deliveries and not a single eyebrow was raised; but city men were somehow not credited with the same constitutions. It was highly indecent, everyone cried. Even male doctors were strongly resisted; in the neighborhoods around St. Brigid's many an intern had had a door slammed indignantly in his face. This was woman's work; men had no business interfering.

Samantha thought of Dr. Prince and the soiree. Then she thought of Mrs. Marchand upstairs. A staunch old member of the jealously guarded sorority of midwives, she would never allow Luther in the room. Suddenly Samantha knew what she had to do.

※

When Mrs. Marchand saw Luther come in behind Samantha she shot to her feet and started to protest, but Samantha said quietly, "Mr. Arndt is going to help."

As he took his place by Louisa's side, dropping to his knees and stroking her damp forehead, the midwife narrowed her eyes and pursed her lips in supreme disapproval. First they call a *doctor,* and now the husband wants to meddle. Well, the Arndts could bank on calling another midwife next time.

The labor went fairly easily once Louisa was comforted by Luther. Mrs. Marchand remained at Samantha's request (although *why* was beyond her) and sat in the corner over her knitting, casting occasional sideways glances at the fancy woman doctor in her fancy silk dress.

When the contractions grew stronger Louisa started to scream. "Don't let me die! It's killing me!"

When the baby's head finally crowned, Samantha said, "Your baby is coming, Luther. Come and sit here, and put your hands here . . ."

As another contraction came on Louisa groaned and her face flushed crimson. "There," said Samantha quietly. "The top of your baby's head."

Luther blinked; in an instant his shirt collar was soaked with sweat.

"All right, Luther, this will be it now." Samantha reached for his hands and positioned them, one above, one below. She stayed close.

The little head protruded, then receded; protruded again, then receded again, like a tide, and with each contraction Louisa pushed down. Spellbound, Luther held his hands where Samantha had placed them, and when the head suddenly popped out, he moved quickly. His lower hand raised up to cradle the face while the one on top delicately protected the soft skull as it slowly rotated.

Luther's face was a mask of fascination, like that of a man enchanted, under a spell, and his hands seemed to move of their own will, instinctively, as though performing a task they had always known. He didn't pull on the head, as Samantha had feared he might; instead he waited patiently for the rotation to stop and the next contraction to come, his hands outstretched. Then, when Louisa's next push thrust out a little shoulder, Luther leaned forward protectively, flattened his lower hand like a shelf, and received the little body as it slithered from its mother.

Samantha opened her mouth to speak but Luther moved before she could say anything. Rapidly he wiped the nose and mouth with the corner of a towel, then instinctively he gently patted the little back. There came a gasp, then a tiny wail.

"Is it a boy?" cried Louisa.

Samantha now pushed in, hastily tying the midwife's strings around the cord and cutting, and as soon as she was finished Luther bundled the little thing in a blanket, cradled it lovingly against his chest, got shakily to his feet and went around to the side of the bed. As he knelt, delivering the bundle into Louisa's outstretched arms, he whispered, "Yes, Louisa, we have a little boy."

"A boy! A *boy!*" Louisa drew the baby close to her face, with wonder-struck eyes took in its pruny features and sighed. "Oh, Luther, he looks just like you . . ."

Samantha sat back as some of their rapture reached into and expanded her soul. Then she looked over at the clock on the dresser and was stunned: it was three o'clock in the morning.

Luther insisted on seeing her home. Although it was the hour before dawn, they were able to find a cab and ride, in the heavy mist, through the deserted streets of Manhattan.

"She is already in love with that baby, Samantha," said Luther in wonder as the carriage creaked and swayed and the horses' hoofs echoed off the sleeping buildings. "And now I believe she is in love with me too."

"She always has been," Samantha said with a weary smile. She wasn't sure which was the miracle tonight, but it didn't matter. Deep down she knew everything was going to be all right for Luther and Louisa from now on. It was only when the formidable stony façade of St. Brigid's came into view that Samantha started really to think of herself.

Asking the cabby to wait, Luther went up the steps with Samantha. She turned at the door. "I shall be all right from here, Luther. Thank you for bringing me back."

"We shall never be able to repay you, Samantha."

"Just go back to your family, Luther. Mrs. Marchand will want to get home."

On an impulse Luther threw his arms around Samantha and held her in a tight embrace. She returned it by wrapping her arms around him in a sisterly hug.

On the other side of the massive oak door a man crossed the dimly lit foyer with heavy steps. He'd been called in during the night to resuture a wound and he was anxious to get home to have a few minutes' rest before returning for a morning operation.

Mark Rawlins pushed open the door and stopped short. It took only seconds for the scene in front of him to be stamped on his memory—Samantha Hargrave in the feverish embrace of a young man. Mark ducked back, let the door swing silently closed and chose an alternative route by which to leave the hospital.

Silas Prince was so furious that any thought of discretion or ceremony was swept aside. When Samantha came into the staff dining room he shot to his feet, nearly sending his chair over backward, strode up to her, planted himself in her path and said, "Where were you last night, Dr. Hargrave!"

His outburst so stunned her that for an instant Samantha did not reply, resenting the rudeness and the stares from all tables.

Dr. Prince repeated the question, his body stiff and trembling, and Samantha, shocked that he should demand that she account for herself before an audience, could only stare back in mute dismay.

Behind her, from the table he was sharing with two other men, Mark Rawlins, mistaking her silence for a stall during which to invent an excuse, spoke up. "She was with me, sir."

All heads swiveled toward Rawlins. Silas Prince's eyebrows rose up nearly to his hairline as he sputtered, "She . . . what?"

Samantha swung around as Mark rose to his feet and strolled over, hoping with his manner to ease the tension in the charged atmosphere. "It's all my fault, sir. Dr. Hargrave tried to tell me we wouldn't be back in time, but I was pigheaded and coerced her into joining my mother and me in a drive around Long Island. Before we knew it the fog had quite impeded us."

Samantha gazed at him in astonishment, then said, "Excuse me, Dr. Rawlins. You need not fabricate a story in my defense. I'm quite capable of speaking for myself. Dr. Prince," she said, turning away from Mark, "I was delivering a baby last night. I can provide you with the name and address if you wish verification."

Silas Prince's face went through a series of baffled expressions, glancing once in confusion at Mark Rawlins. "You could have sent someone else, Dr. Hargrave. You weren't on call."

"The patient is a personal friend. I had promised to deliver her."

"Was there no midwife available?"

"There was one in attendance."

"Then why did you go? Was there a complication?"

"Not at all."

"Then why"—his voice rose again—"why were you there and not at the Vanderbilt house?"

"As I said, Dr. Prince, I had promised my friend."

"Dr. Hargrave." Silas Prince was clearly wrestling for control over his rage. "You embarrassed me last night. You embarrassed this institution. We awaited you all evening. I had no idea what to say to the ladies. I felt the fool. Dr. Weston said you had been called away. Our hostesses were most disappointed." He drew in a breath. "You realize what you have done, Dr. Hargrave. You have lost St. Brigid's only chance for that money this year. Money that could have bought badly needed beds and mattresses, additional nurses, quinine—" He stopped, tethering the outburst that was sure to come, and said in a constrained tone, "The primary rule of this institution, Dr. Hargrave, is obedience. We cannot tolerate blatant disregard for authority. You are to pack your things and be gone before this day is out."

"Surely, sir, there must be exceptions! Consideration for the patient must override the most hard and fast rule."

His cold glare shot like an arrow through her. "Was the patient's life in danger, Doctor?"

"No, but—"

"Was her safety, or the baby's safety, threatened in any way?"

"No."

"Was she without help?"

Samantha sighed. "She was not."

"Then what you did is inexcusable. You will please effect a hasty departure from this hospital."

Samantha remained standing in the center of the room after Silas Prince stalked out and after, by ones and twos, the rest of the staff, embarrassed and uncomfortable, also left, until she stood alone with Mark Rawlins. Turning now to him, Samantha said, "I appreciate your desire to help me, sir, but I cannot fathom why you should think I needed it."

Dr. Rawlins looked around the dining room to be certain they were truly alone, then he said in a low voice, "I was on my way out of the hospital early this morning when I happened upon your leave-taking on the steps."

She frowned. "I don't understand."

"I realized you could hardly tell Prince you missed the soiree because you were with a gentleman."

"With a gentleman! Oh, you mean Luther. He is the husband of the woman whose baby I delivered." Samantha's eyes widened in sudden comprehension. "And you thought—I'm flattered, Dr. Rawlins, but it was not what it seemed! And I appreciate your chivalry, but I assure you I needed no rescuing. I am perfectly capable of taking care of myself."

"Are you indeed? I fear your honesty, Dr. Hargrave, has gotten you ousted from this hospital."

"Yes," she said sadly. "It appears so."

"What will you do?"

"I don't know. I had not expected he would deal so harshly with me."

"Will you permit another act of chivalry?"

Samantha regarded his smile and thought for an instant that he was mocking her; but then she saw the genuine concern in his eyes. "What do you propose?"

"The director of St. Luke's owes me a favor—"

"Thank you, Dr. Rawlins, but I should not feel comfortable with a post that was gotten on an obligation."

He stared down at her, at her beautiful face that was tipped so proudly yet showed, just below the surface, a fetching vulnerability. "Please do not be so hasty to reject my assistance. It is not a sign of weakness to ask help of a friend."

She gazed up at him, reading the sincerity in his intense brown eyes; his closeness momentarily immobilized her. She was aware of a compelling masculine smell about him, a mixture of broadcloth, cologne and traces of cheroot tobacco. Mark Rawlins had the astonishing ability to make her feel as no other man did—utterly feminine. And, at this moment, helpless. "I am afraid you're right, Doctor. Right now I need all the help I can find."

"Shall I speak to Prince on your behalf?"

"I wouldn't want to give him that satisfaction, for I am certain he would still refuse you."

"Then the director of St. Luke's?"

Samantha continued to be held by his gaze, and even though she was aware he stood unconventionally close to her, she could not break away.

"St. Luke's is a good hospital, Samantha. You could do worse."

Finally she smiled and said, "I am grateful for your interest, Dr. Rawlins. I don't know just yet what I shall do, but if I should change my mind . . ."

"You have my address. Please feel free to call upon me at any hour. I am totally at your service."

—⚬—

The last of her things were packed and Samantha sat by the window, counting her money once again in hopes the amount would come out higher. It did not. She had exactly $29.47.

Hearing a knock at her door, she opened it to find Dr. Prince's secretary. "Dr. Hargrave," said the young man, "I have been sent to inform you that you are to stay on at St. Brigid's for the completion of your internship."

Samantha stared at him, deliberating. "Please tell Dr. Prince I should like to hear that from him in person, or else I shall depart as planned."

Five minutes later she received a summons.

"There, I have said it to you in person," he said, standing at the window with his back to her.

"Why have you changed your mind about dismissing me?"

Dr. Prince turned, fixing a resentful eye on her. "St. Brigid's is receiving the charity's money, Dr. Hargrave, but it has been donated in your name."

"But why?"

"Thanks to the press, the ladies feel they already know you. The decision, it appears, was made even before the soiree, and your attendance there was merely a formality." He came around the desk and faced her squarely. "Dr. Hargrave, for the sake of this institution I will make concessions, even sacrifice personal principles. But I warn you now, Dr. Hargrave, and take heed: I stand firm on my continued disapproval of your attendance at this hospital. Because of St. Brigid's great financial need, I tolerate you, but I hasten to assure you, Doctor, that I have my limits. This incident will not go forgotten. I advise you to step very carefully from now on . . ."

FIVE

A COLD, DAMP AUTUMN EVOLVED INTO A FRIGID, BITING winter. All available blankets were heaped on the patients, and the stoves in the wards kept the air smoky. Winter also closed Samantha off from the rest of the world: the snows were often too deep for her to venture out to visit Louisa, and victims of carriage accidents and pneumonia kept her busy on the wards.

She encountered Mark Rawlins seldom, but on occasion she had the feeling that he had gone out of his way to be where she was. It was usually in the dining room and she would catch his eye across the room, staring at her even though he was in a conversation with someone at his own table. And once in a great while he would smile, intimately, knowingly, as if they shared a secret.

Janelle MacPherson was seen frequently on the wards, sweeping through in her ermine coat and hat, followed by a queenly entourage of well-meaning but bored young ladies who brought blankets and Bibles to the patients and who congratulated themselves on their good deeds at a yearly banquet. Whenever Samantha encountered Miss MacPherson, their exchange was formal, with barely a flicker of recognition.

Samantha often encountered Letitia MacPherson, Janelle's pretty and personable younger sister, a girl with an easy laugh and hair the color of a sunrise who seemed to have genuine compassion for the patients. She was also, of the group, the only one who ever paused to offer a word of cheer to the drably dressed female doctor.

Samantha's evenings continued to be spent in her secret, solitary pursuit of learning surgery. It was a lonely ambition, made all the lonelier by the merry sounds of holiday celebration down the hall, but she was determined, more so than ever. She had come finally to know everything there was to know in theory—the book was memorized, the instruments comfortable in her hands, the stitching mastered. All that remained now was to begin to put it all together in action.

<hr />

The first bell startled her out of a deep sleep, but by the second bell she was running down the hall in her billowy costume and hastily pinning her hospital-issued ambulance cap to her hair. Jake was flapping his arms and pacing by the horses. "Rotten bad night, Doc!" he said, helping her up.

"What is it this time, Jake?"

"Accident at the Meadowland. Don't know the details."

Samantha clung to the rail as the ambulance swung out into the snowy night; she could feel the icy metal through her two layers of gloves. The Meadowland. No doubt an injured trapezist. It happened all the time at those dance halls: the performers took terrific risks in order to pack the audiences in.

As house fronts flitted by, their windows ablaze with candles, Samantha realized that it was Christmas Eve. Not that she minded. In order to let the other interns join their families, Samantha had volunteered to take ambulance call tonight. The Arndts had invited her for dinner, but they didn't need her, having eyes only for bouncy little Johann; Samantha convinced herself it was just another night of the year.

The façade of the Meadowland was itself like a Christmas tree, all lights and colorful playbills. Fashionable patrons in gowns and opera capes picked their way across the icy sidewalk from their carriages to the entrance, and a few heads turned as the ambulance drew up. Then a nervous little man came rushing up. "Doctress," he said frantically, eyes darting this way and that, "backstage. Quietly, please. No one knows."

Samantha and Jake followed the manager through a back door, up a flight of stairs and through a jungle of ropes and props and people in outrageous costumes. From beyond the closed curtain came the strains of an orchestra tuning up and the low rumble of an excited audience.

"Such a night she chooses!" said the nervous little man when they reached a door with a glittery star glued on. "We're packed to the rafters! Christmas Eve, people get restless, and then *she* has to go and do this!"

The door swung open upon a cluttered dressing room brightly ablaze with gas jets. Of its two occupants—one lying on a chaise and the other kneeling next to her—only the one who knelt turned in the direction of the visitors.

"It's the doctress from St. Brigid's," said the manager.

The woman, dressed in a sequined leotard and ostrich feathers, got to her feet and stepped aside as Samantha moved to the chaise. "What happened?"

The sequined woman glanced at the two men and said quietly, "She had an accident with a knitting needle."

As she dropped to her knees and reached for the blanket covering the supine woman, Samantha tossed a look over her shoulder at the two gawking men; they read the signal and hastily retreated. Then Samantha drew back the blanket. "When did she do it?" she asked, raising the unconscious woman's skirt with one hand while with the other she felt for a pulse.

"I dunno. 'Bout half an hour ago, I guess. She was supposed to go on. She's the Golden Nightingale, you know. Anyway, just before she goes on, *he* comes backstage . . ."

While she listened Samantha examined the damage the woman had inflicted upon herself and felt rage shoot through her own body. What desperation women can be driven to!

"They had a terrible row. We heard it all over the theater. She tells him she's in a family way and he says it ain't his and then he calls her a whore and then she begs him not to leave her, so Mr. Martinelli, he's the manager, he sends me in here after the lout leaves to make sure she goes on tonight and I catch her doing it with a knitting needle and I'm too late to stop her 'cause there's this *awful* rush of blood—"

"Get my man in here," said Samantha, pulling the dress down and rapidly tucking the blanket around the legs.

"The towel was my idea," said the woman as she hurried to the door. "Was that all right, Doctress?"

"You probably saved her life."

❧

Bent over her unconscious patient as the ambulance swayed and skidded over the ice, bell clanging, Samantha's face looked chiseled from marble, as though she hadn't a thought in her head; but behind her heavy gray eyes rapid deliberation was going on. The woman had done herself a great deal of injury, perforating her uterus, peritoneum, and possibly the bowel beyond. Samantha knew how her chances stood: nil. Unless the woman had surgery at once.

Samantha's mind galloped ahead. There was a Christmas party at Dr. Prince's house and nearly all the staff were there; five of the interns had been allowed to go home. Samantha was left on ambulance call and young Dr. Weston on the wards.

Samantha measured the time it would take to fetch one of the surgeons from Dr. Prince's against how long this patient had and she felt a lump gather in her throat. There was too little time . . .

As Jake carried the woman in his arms through the foyer, Samantha ran on ahead. Dr. Weston was warming his buttocks before the stove in the deserted accident ward when Samantha rushed up, whipping off her cape. "Is there anyone else in the house besides us, Doctor?"

He shook his head and looked past her. "What happened?"

"Attempted abortion. I think there's internal damage. She's bleeding out, Dr. Weston. She needs immediate surgery. Can you do it?"

He shook his head again. "I only just started my rotation. I wouldn't have a clue. Better send Jake for someone."

Samantha spun around. "Jake, get someone, anyone, whoever's closest. But first take her up to the operating room."

"What—" Dr. Weston started to say.

She turned back around. "We'll have to start, Doctor. This woman is critical, she hasn't much time left."

"But we can't perform surgery without a staff man!"

"We can start it, Doctor. Do you know how to give anesthesia?"

"But, Dr. Hargrave, you haven't had—"

"Jake, get going! Come along, Doctor. We're wasting time."

Mrs. Knight, who had heard the ambulance bell, met them on the stairs, her great and formidable bulk blocking the way. "What is going on, Dr. Hargrave?"

"We're taking this woman up to surgery. Will you help us, please?"

As Samantha pushed by, Mrs. Knight said, "But who will operate?"

Samantha continued to hurry up the stairs. "I will."

She moved swiftly but methodically; she was tense and a little frightened, but weeks of training on the wards kept her mind and body moving—this was no time for panic. While she searched the cupboards for what she needed (Samantha had never before been in an operating room) Mrs. Knight lit the gas jets and Dr. Weston strapped the patient to the table.

As ether fumes started to fill the air, Samantha carried her armload of instruments to a basin and said, "Mrs. Knight, will you please pour carbolic into this basin."

"Over the instruments?" A look of bafflement crossed Matron's face, then she did as told.

Samantha ignored the bloody butcher's aprons hanging on pegs and chose instead to pin a clean towel to the front of her dress. Then she did something that surprised the others in the room: before proceeding she dipped her hands into the carbolic solution. Samantha's voice was steady as she said, "Mrs. Knight, will you please support the patient's legs?" but her mind cried: Oh, Jake, *hurry!*

The hemorrhaging had abated but that wasn't necessarily a good sign;

there could be bleeding internally. And the light was outrageous—as a rule surgery was done only in the mornings when the best light came through the windows; clouds canceled operations and surgery was rarely attempted at night. Samantha's mouth went painfully dry and her pulse thundered in her ears. "Mrs. Knight, I need more light, please. A lamp, possibly . . ."

The ether fumes made her momentarily dizzy. "Dr. Weston, that should be enough for now. A few drops every few minutes if you please . . ."

Samantha picked up a tenaculum out of the basin, struggled to steady her hand and gently inserted it. She saw the textbook illustration before her and then, in the next instant, Elizabeth Blackwell's capable hands working on Mrs. Steptoe. Seating the teeth of the instrument into the cervix, Samantha manipulated the uterus and, by the light from the lamp Mrs. Knight had placed on the operating table, was able to see the perforation.

Samantha thought the night was dragging eternally but knew in reality only minutes had passed. While she mentally prayed for Jake to return with help Samantha's voice came out calm. "What is her pulse, Dr. Weston?"

"About ninety and steady."

"Will you please monitor it while I work? Check it every few minutes." *Please God, give me strength. And don't let me lose her . . .*

Long minutes stretched by, filled with deep and hollow silence; the air in the room was deplorably cold. Dr. Weston shivered. The patient's chest rose and fell in gentle slumber; Samantha worked wordlessly, her mouth set grimly while Mrs. Knight stood opposite, a loyal sentinel.

Samantha's fingers felt stiff and uncooperative, she continually fought down rising panic, and while she executed each step memorized from the textbook, she waged an argument with herself: I shouldn't have started, I shouldn't have gotten into this. Yes, I should have, it was the only course open. She would be dead now, waiting for a surgeon. She's still alive, barely, but alive. But how long can I keep her alive? God, I'm going to lose her. I shouldn't have started—

The double doors burst open and Mark Rawlins, still in his snow-decked top hat and overcoat, said, "How is she?"

Samantha was overcome with relief. "Still alive, Doctor. But only barely."

In the next instant he was at the table replacing Mrs. Knight and doing a quick assessment of Samantha's work. "Here," he said, taking the tenaculum and repositioning it. "Like this. Better exposure, see?"

"Yes . . ." she said breathily.

"Now take this clamp, Doctor . . ." Mark's hands guided hers, gently, firmly, while his deep voice filled the room. "Make more use of your sponges. Keep your field clear at all times. Mrs. Knight, this light is deplorable. Dr. Weston, the patient is feeling it. More ether."

Instead of simply taking over, as Samantha had thought he would, Mark joined her, working with her, instructing, leading. "You have made the correct approach, Doctor, but this retractor will be more to your advantage if placed here." His hand curled around hers. "Not too much tension or you will tear the tissues. Are your sutures ready?"

"Yes. The gut is soaking in the carbolic."

He looked up from the wound. Samantha's head was bowed and he saw on the crown of jet curls the tiny diamond drops where snowflakes had melted. Mark opened his mouth to say something, then changed his mind. When Samantha grasped the needle holder he gently changed the placement of her fingers, and when she tremblingly tied the knot, he seated the scissors in her hand and guided her through the correct way to snip.

Samantha never once looked up. Her concentration on the job appeared so intense that Mark was certain she was barely aware of his presence. But in truth Samantha was acutely aware of him, of his nearness directly opposite, of the feel of his hands, firm but gentle, over hers, and she drew from his strong, comforting presence a reassurance that soon calmed her and returned command of her hands to her.

Samantha worked rapidly, deftly, never having to be shown more than once. Mark threaded the curved needles for her and watched as she drew the torn tissues neatly together and tied secure knots as skillfully and unhesitatingly as if she had done this many times. Mark glanced over at the instruments in the basin, all correctly chosen, at the proper lengths of suture, and then he considered her boldness in starting the case alone and unaided.

"You saved this woman's life, Doctor," he said softly.

Now Samantha raised her head. She lifted her face up to his, her skin like ivory in the lamp's glow, her eyes cast in deep, dark shadow, and she whispered, "Without you I would have lost her."

He stared back into those long-lashed silver eyes that showed so much strength and determination and he saw, thinly glazing them, like the frost on the windowpanes, her frailty and uncertainty. "You have done everything perfectly, Doctor."

When he reached across and squeezed her hand, Samantha cast her eyes down. In that fraction of an instant, as his warmth and vigor passed through her fingers, Samantha experienced one of the happiest moments of her life. She had saved a doomed patient, she had taken the bold step into surgery, and she knew she had fallen in love with Mark Rawlins.

"She must be closely watched for the next five days, Dr. Hargrave," he said, releasing her hand and reaching for a clean towel from Mrs. Knight. "Her chances of peritonitis and septicemia are great. Auscultate her abdomen at least three times daily and monitor her temperature closely."

Samantha smiled up at him. "Yes, Dr. Rawlins."

Lifting the butcher's apron over his head and striding to the door to hang it up, Mark took out his pocket watch and clicked it open. "It's Christmas, Dr. Hargrave."

She glanced at the lacy curtain of snowflakes on the other side of the windows. "So it is," she murmured.

He came back to the table and again took her hands in his. He stood close, regardless of the stares from Dr. Weston and Mrs. Knight, and gazed solemnly down at Samantha. "You have won my undying admiration, Dr. Hargrave. I shall never forget tonight."

Samantha was worried. She had performed surgery; Dr. Prince would have his revenge at last. Would Mark's support be enough to save her from dismissal? It was impossible to swallow much of the Christmas dinner she shared with Louisa and Luther, or to sleep well the next night. After twenty-four hours had come and gone, and then another unsettled day and night with still no outburst from Dr. Prince, Samantha was convinced he was preparing his case against her. This would be no rash act on his part; she had foiled him too many times. While Samantha did not regret what she had done for the Meadowland singer (who was convalescing) she did start to have doubts about the haste of her actions.

The summons came two days later.

When Samantha entered the office she was met by a grim-faced Silas Prince, who stood behind his desk with all the dignity of a tombstone, and, to her mild surprise, by a stranger whom Samantha had never seen before.

"Dr. Hargrave," said Dr. Prince crisply, "may I present Dr. Landon Fremont? Dr. Fremont, Dr. Samantha Hargrave."

She nodded warily toward the stranger, thinking that his name was somehow familiar, and noticed that his smile reached his eyes. She also saw, in a quick appraisal, that he was in his early thirties (although a receding hairline aged him slightly) with a tendency toward plumpness, was well dressed, and that he stared at her in patent surprise.

"Please be seated, Doctors," said Dr. Prince, sitting ceremoniously like a judge at his bench. "Dr. Hargrave, Dr. Fremont would like to have a few words with you."

The stranger seemed a little uncertain of himself and cleared his throat to cover his embarrassment. "Please forgive me, Dr. Hargrave, but I had not expected you to look so . . . Well, I had expected a more *mature* woman. You see, I have heard so much about you, and read of you in the press, that I, ah, well—" He waved smooth, plump hands. "I shan't detain you long, Doctor. I want only to ask a few questions, if you will permit. You see, Dr. Hargrave, I have been told about your experience in the operating room the other night and I would like to discuss it with you."

Perplexed, Samantha assented.

Dr. Fremont seemed to search the room for a place to start, lingered over a stitched sampler behind Dr. Prince's desk that read "nihil humanum MIHI alienum est" and presently brought himself back to Samantha, his small eyes betraying a keen and lively interest in her. "Dr. Hargrave, Dr. Rawlins told me that you washed your instruments and your hands in carbolic solution before commencing the operation. May I ask why you did that?"

"My former mentor, Dr. Joshua Masefield, practiced antisepsis and taught it to me."

"Then you advocate the germ theory?"

"I'm not certain, but in case germs do exist, the carbolic destroys them and lowers the chance of wound infection. If, on the other hand, bacteria do not exist, then no harm has been done."

Dr. Fremont nodded thoughtfully. "For years I have used wine to wash wounds, for it contains a polyphenol even stronger than carbolic, and for years my colleagues have laughed. But fewer of my patients died from infection than did theirs, and now that Mr. Pasteur is on the verge of proving what has until now only been speculation, my colleagues are less quick to laugh." His little eyes flickered toward Silas Prince. "I also understand, Dr. Hargrave, that you asked Dr. Weston to monitor the patient's pulse during the operation. May I ask why?"

"With so many patients dying on the operating table from the ether inhalation and for reasons unknown to us, I had thought perhaps sudden death during surgery could be averted if the vital signs were watched more closely."

"I have never heard of such a practice. Where did you learn it?"

"Nowhere, Doctor. It was my own idea."

"And where did you learn surgery?"

"From books. I taught myself."

"You had no formal training?"

"No. May I ask, sir, why you are asking me these questions?"

Dr. Prince leaned forward, webbing his hands on his desk before him. "Landon Fremont is a new addition to our staff, Dr. Hargrave. St. Brigid's has received a grant to open a new specialty, gynecology, and it will be housed on the first floor of the east wing. Dr. Fremont will head the service and he is to be allotted one intern to train under him."

Samantha looked back at Dr. Fremont, who said quickly, "Please forgive my rush of questions, Dr. Hargrave, but when Dr. Rawlins told me of your performance in the operating room . . ."

For a moment Samantha relived that magical hour with Mark, the way he had stood with her, by her, supported her; his closeness in the mellow light, the reassurance of his deep voice, his hands guiding hers, his power and strength, the intimacy of the moment . . . Samantha knew that no matter where they might go from there, where their separate destinies might carry them, she and Mark Rawlins would always be joined by that special hour.

"And so, Dr. Hargrave . . ." She stared at Landon Fremont. He had gone on talking and she hadn't heard. "It would be an honor to have you work with me in this new service . . ."

"Dr. Fremont, I hardly know what to say!" She glanced at Silas Prince; his face was set stonily. "And, Dr. Fremont, the honor is all mine. I accept your proposal most eagerly and give you my word, sir, that you shall have no cause to regret this decision."

Dr. Fremont rose and extended a hand to Samantha. Then Silas Prince surprised her by standing also and offering his hand. As if he had called a brief armistice, he said, "I wish you luck, Doctor," and for the sparest instant his cold eyes thawed and a little admiration shone through.

But it was to Mark Rawlins that Samantha wanted to express her deepest appreciation. She had not seen him since Christmas but had no doubt that she would encounter him again, and soon.

SIX

ENEATH THE FOUNDATION OF ST. BRIGID'S LAY THE BONES OF suicides who, in the eighteenth century, were buried along the public highway with stakes through their hearts. On this twilit summer evening, as Samantha moved down the ward lighting the gas jets against the encroaching night, she turned to see one of those restless spirits gliding toward her, arms outstretched, long hair flowing wildly. She took the woman's elbow and said gently, "Come along, Mrs. Franchimoni, you mustn't be out of bed."

The woman's eyes were windows into a bleak landscape. "My baby. Have you seen my baby?"

Samantha guided her back to bed and tucked her in. "We can't have you walking around, Mrs. Franchimoni. You need to mend after your ordeal."

"And my little one?"

"Sleep is what you need now. There, sleep . . ." Samantha stayed by the bed until the woman closed her eyes and finally delivered herself into the welcome embrace of oblivion; then Samantha smoothed the blankets, straightened and looked around the ward. Typical of June twilights, night had fallen like a curtain while her back was turned and the gynecological ward was dark, blessed every few feet with the frail halo light of a gas jet. The women slept, they were at peace for a while, like Mrs. Franchimoni, who did not yet know that her baby had not survived. When was Landon going to tell her? When was it ever a good time to tell a mother her baby was dead?

Sighing, Samantha turned away and went to the end of the ward where a solitary nurse sat at the desk rolling bandages. One of Landon Fremont's radical innovations in his new ward was to bring in nurses trained in the new Nightingale way; unlike the rest of the nurses at St. Brigid's, Landon Fremont's nurses were educated, clean, honest, and dedicated. Mildred raised her young face to Samantha and smiled. "Maybe we'll have a quiet night for a change, Doctor."

Samantha settled into the other chair with the wearines of an old woman—she had been in the operating room all day—and laughed softly. Such a thing to hope for, a quiet night! Samantha didn't let her expectations get too high, the gynecological ward never stayed peaceful for long. "Mildred, why don't you fetch us some tea?"

"Yes, Doctor!" She jumped up and was gone.

Samantha sighed again and pulled out a little footstool from under the desk. Propping her feet on it, she decided she was too tired even for sleep. Not that she minded. These past six months had been worth the fatigue; and the remaining four until she received her final certificate were going to be equally so. Working under Landon Fremont had been such a joy, such a treasured time, that Samantha knew she was going to hate to see it end.

The one cloud in these past six months was Mark's absence.

Shortly after Christmas Nicholas Rawlins had suffered a massive heart attack and had died in his gloomy mansion on Beacon Hill. Samantha had seen Mark only once then, briefly, when he had come in to arrange for Dr. Miles to take over his patients. She had encountered him on the ward and he had been distracted, clearly upset; Samantha had barely had time to offer condolences and he was gone. In the following months she had continually watched for him, listening for news, overhearing once that he was still up in Boston trying to straighten out his father's complex estate, and as the weeks and months passed Samantha began to despair of ever seeing him again.

To heighten her anxiety, Janelle MacPherson had also vanished.

A moan from the shadows brought Samantha instantly to her feet. She was at the woman's bedside at once, bending over her, stroking the burning forehead and murmuring soothingly. This was one of the tragic cases.

The young woman, eighteen years old, had been brought in that afternoon by her distraught husband; she had a severe pain low in her abdomen and was running a fever. Dr. Fremont had first diagnosed it as appendicitis, but then an onset of bright red bleeding had told them it was in fact a tubal pregnancy. Landon and Samantha had done what they could, which had amounted to little more than going through hopeless motions: flushing the uterus and tubes with saline in hopes of dislodging the fetus before the tube ruptured. They had been unsuccessful; such flushings rarely worked, and now the unconscious woman lay dying in this hospital bed while her helpless doctor stood by in silent rage.

One thing above all that Samantha had learned from Landon Fremont these past six months was that the practice of gynecology brought more frustration than satisfaction, that more cases were lost than saved, and that gynecology was, in the end, little more than a science of half-truths, speculations and mystery. Not even the brilliant Landon Fremont, who was making medical history with his surgical innovations, could find a way to get into the abdomen without killing the patient, and until such a way could be discovered, countless women would suffer automatic death sentences from such simple complications as a tubal pregnancy.

Samantha turned at the sound of footsteps and saw Mildred setting out cups. Joining her, Samantha saw that the nurse had also brought a plate of buttered poundcake and she was reminded that today was Saturday, the day charity ladies visited the hospital.

Returning to her chair and picking up her tea, Samantha thought again about Janelle MacPherson and the fact that she had not, since Christmas, been seen in the wards with her usual retinue, even though her sun-haired sister Letitia had. And this led Samantha down a darker path of thought, with the cup poised at her lips; for, of late, Letitia MacPherson had begun to trouble Samantha.

From the start Samantha had liked Janelle's vivacious younger sister and had always appreciated Letitia's care to spare a few words for all. Most charity ladies glided through as if on another plane, never venturing too close to the patients, and treating the nurses and Samantha little better than servants. But Letitia, despite her obvious breeding and expensive gowns and superior status, observed no barriers between herself and the hard-working nurses, nor did she find it distasteful to exchange a few words with Dr. Hargrave. Letitia MacPherson's smile always had sunbeams in it.

But then—when was it?—one day last month Samantha had been bent over a patient changing a dressing; she had reached for the scissors and had happened to glance in the direction of the doors at the end of the ward. There she had seen Letitia in what appeared to be an improperly intimate conversation with Dr. Weston, who, from the width of his grin, was obviously quite taken with the young lady's attention. Samantha had dismissed the incident from her mind and wouldn't have given it another thought if she hadn't observed Letitia, again by chance, the very next week in a similar tête-à-tête with Dr. Sitwell.

After that Samantha had paid closer attention to Miss MacPherson when she came through with her weekly gifts of cakes and flowers and had noticed that, each time, Letitia managed to dawdle at the rear, catch the eye of whatever physician happened to be in attendance and proceed to work her charms on him. That Letitia delighted in the effect she had on men was apparent, but did the girl know what fire she toyed with? Society sheltered such princesses: from the hour of her birth Letitia MacPherson would never have known a minute out of the severe eye of a constant chaperone. Obviously these weekly hospital rounds were her one opportunity to dabble in a game which intrigued her but whose rules she knew nothing of. Samantha had read the intention in Dr. Sitwell's eyes; Letitia clearly had not.

"What's wrong with Mrs. Mason, Doctor?" Samantha looked at Mildred. "I beg your pardon?" "Bed Ten. Brought in this morning. What's wrong with her?"

Samantha turned her head and tried to see the bed, but the far end of the ward was in shadow. "She has yellow skin, itching all over, and occasional sharp pains in her upper right abdomen. We have several choices for a diagnosis, but I think the rule of the Four Fs will be our guide here."

"The Four Fs, Doctor?"

"Fair, fat, female, and forty. If your patient has those four qualifications, Mildred, you can be almost certain she has gallbladder disease. And Mrs. Mason is fair, fat, female, and forty."

"Can she be helped, Doctor?"

Samantha was about to say, "No," when, at the far dark end of the ward, the door opened and standing there, with the light in the hallway making him a silhouette, was a man in a top hat and opera cape.

He stood far away, he could have been any man; but Samantha knew. Slowly rising and replacing her cup on the desk, she felt herself move down the rows of beds, gliding, floating toward the man in the doorway. When she reached him she held out her hand and murmured, "Dr. Rawlins . . ."

He took her hand in a warm clasp. "I'm glad I found you up. It's so late."

His voice brought everything back in a rush. The six months vanished: she stood with him again over the operating table in a union new in its intimacy, and she felt strongly again what she had pushed to the periphery of her mind—how very much in love she was with Mark Rawlins.

"It's my night to sit on the ward," she heard herself say. "How are you, Dr. Rawlins? We all missed you terribly."

"I missed you too. I'm afraid I have been out of touch with the world, Dr. Hargrave. I have spent these past months like a prisoner in my ancestral home trying to make sense of the perishing mess my father left."

"I'm so sorry . . ."

His voice softened; it was barely more than a whisper. "Don't be. He was a ruthless old despot who had had his way with the world long enough. No tears were shed, I assure you."

"Then all the greater the tragedy." Samantha looked down at the strong hand holding hers and wondered if every time she encountered him she would wish the moment would never end.

"I've only just got back," he said. "Now I shall have to straighten out the mess my absence has created!"

"Will you have some tea with us, Doctor?"

He moved slightly to see past her shoulder and the motion brought his face into the light. Samantha could barely keep from crying out: had Mark Rawlins always been this handsome? Or had love distorted her vision? Even the flaw, the little scar that tilted his mouth, was precious beyond enduring.

"I unfortunately cannot linger, my dear Dr. Hargrave. I've only come to invite you to have dinner with me and my family a week from tomorrow night."

"Dinner? I would love to."

He continued to gaze down at her, smiling cryptically; for a man who could not linger, Mark Rawlins seemed in no hurry to go. "How do you like working for Landon?"

"It's a dream fulfilled. And I have you to thank for it, Dr. Rawlins."

"Nonsense. You earned it," he said softly. His eyes, hidden in shadow, continued to gaze down at her, and Samantha felt her legs go weak. On those late nights when April rain had pelted her window and the interns' hall had rung with laughter, Samantha had lain awake in bed, staring up at the darkness, wondering, fantasizing, a willing prisoner of his spell. And now, when she had begun to fear she would never see him again, here he stood, close, overpowering, that familiar electrifying current passing from his hand into hers.

"I'm afraid I must go," he said quietly, the tone intimate. "The carriage will call for you at eight." Giving her hand a final squeeze, Mark added, "You've no idea how I look forward to it."

SEVEN

*S*AMANTHA HAD KNOWN MARK RAWLINS' FAMILY HAD MONEY, but she had never thought much about it. Yet the Rawlins mansion on Madison Avenue could rival the Astor mansion: high ceilings, blazing chandeliers, paintings, Turkey carpets, handsome furniture, gold satin drapes and potted palms—all might belong to a monarchy. And the people inside, like nobility, suited the scene so well that, when the butler led her through the double doors of the grand parlor, Samantha feared she could never belong.

Then she saw Mark standing by the fireplace in animated conversation with Janelle and Samantha resolved at once that she did indeed belong.

The young man at the piano glanced up and ceased his lively polonaise. All heads turned, and when the butler announced her name in a ringing voice, Samantha felt as if she'd made a stage entrance. Mark was suddenly striding toward her and the seated gentlemen in the room were instantly on their feet.

"Dr. Hargrave! We were wondering what had happened to you!" Mark took her arm and led her into the room.

"Forgive me, Dr. Rawlins. At the last minute I had to see to a patient. I hope I haven't inconvenienced anyone."

"Not at all," drawled the young man at the piano, rising and walking toward her with a lazy gait. "Punctuality is such a bore."

"Dr. Hargrave, may I present my brother Stephen?"

The resemblance was there, but vague. Stephen suffered perhaps from too much perfection—no sweet scar to distort his lip—and Samantha detected a strain of vanity in his smile. When he took her gloved hand and kissed it, clicking his heels together, Mark said, "Stephen has just come back from Europe."

Henry and Joseph Rawlins were introduced next, both younger than Mark but older than Stephen, so that Samantha placed them in their late twenties; congenial young men, good-looking but lacking that special something that set Mark apart, and when they smiled Samantha thought she detected something empty in their welcome. Their wives looked like ordinary women whose waistlines were already showing the result of children and an easy life, and they gave Samantha the impression of being in constant competition.

Lastly came Letitia, curiously dressed in a red velvet gown which did not suit her, and Janelle in ice-blue satin, which did.

"We are waiting upon Mother," said Mark, offering Samantha a seat on the brocaded sofa. "The privilege of making the last entrance always goes to her."

A maid came in with a tray of canapés and Samantha took one, uncertain of what it was, and accepted a glass of champagne. After an awkward silence, conversations resumed: Joseph and Henry took up where they had left off debating a point of law while their wives resumed their contest of witty baby stories, and Letitia took over at the piano to plink out a modern tune whose lyrics, which Samantha had once overheard, were too risqué to be sung here. When Mark went to the sideboard to refill Janelle's glass, Stephen stole the opportunity to sit down next to Samantha.

"Mother won't allow the New York *Herald* in this house, Dr. Hargrave, she thinks it is too sensational. But I've managed to read it all the same, and not a few times have I been entertained by reading about your astonishing exploits."

"I fear those reports are greatly exaggerated, Mr. Rawlins."

"Not according to the way Mark talks! Why, I had quite expected you to be ten feet tall and carrying a spear and shield!"

Samantha looked up at Mark, who had resumed his place by Janelle; they must be involved in a serious dialogue, for there was not the trace of a smile on Mark's lips, and Janelle was speaking quietly, earnestly, her head inclined toward him, her dark blue eyes grave.

The double doors opened then and Clair Rawlins entered. The piano stopped as if it were connected to a mechanism in the door, and the four brothers snapped to attention like puppets on strings. There was no mistaking that here was a woman to reckon with.

Dressed entirely in black, from high on her throat to her wrists and down to the hem sweeping the carpet, and with her silver hair combed into a queenly crown, Clair Rawlins was tall and slender, moved with astonishing fluidity for one of her years, and observed the gathered company through a rose-tinted lorgnette which glinted beneath the chandelier in diamond facets.

"Good evening, everyone," she said imperiously. Her eyes seemed to settle long and measuringly on Samantha, then Mark stepped forward and said, "Mother, may I present Dr. Samantha Hargrave? Dr. Hargrave, my mother, Mrs. Rawlins."

The lorgnette came down and Samantha was surprised to be staring into a pair of gentle brown eyes. Mark's eyes, they were, soft and feeling, evidence of a kind and sympathetic spirit, the eyes of a woman who has loved and suffered deeply. "It is a pleasure to meet you, Mrs. Rawlins."

Clair nodded imperceptibly, as though she had sought something in her proud young guest and had, to her satisfaction, found it. "I am pleased you could join us tonight, Miss Hargrave. Mark so rarely treats us to the company of his colleagues."

"Mother, can I tempt you with a glass of champagne?"

She waved her arm; diamonds flashed on her wrist. "It depresses the appetite. I wish to acquaint myself with our guest."

Her tone was one of dismissal and all obeyed. Letitia returned to the piano, choosing to soothe the atmosphere with "Liebestraum" while the others picked up where they had been before—even, Samantha noticed, Mark and Janelle in their serious talk.

"You are a great curiosity to me, Miss Hargrave. How and why did you choose the study of medicine?"

It had come out as a command, not a request, and while Samantha spoke, reciting the life story she told most people, she felt a growing doubt that her usual explanation for her career was going to satisfy this woman. Clair Rawlins was after more, and it made Samantha think: I am on trial.

When the dinner bell rang Samantha followed the others to the dining room on Stephen's arm and found that she was to sit at Clair Rawlins' right. Mark, who seemed annoyed at the seating arrangement, was at the opposite end of the very long table with Janelle and Letitia on either side.

The dinner was sumptuous beyond belief, but Samantha took it in stride, acting as if she were used to twelve courses with unpronounceable names, all eaten with many utensils arrayed around her plate, and served by a steady parade of servants. Two years of fighting for survival in medical school had taught Samantha the gracious stall: if she took a sip of water each time before starting a new dish, she was able to see which fork or spoon the others picked up.

"Tell me, Miss Hargrave, don't you find your sense of delicacy and propriety offended by the work you do?"

Samantha picked up what she supposed was the proper fork and sliced into her crimped cod. "When one has the satisfaction of having saved a life, Mrs. Rawlins, propriety seems terribly insignificant."

Stephen, sitting opposite, said, "I do believe, Mother, that Miss Hargrave prefers the address of doctor."

Clair tossed her head, an admonishing gesture to a little boy who's been naughty. "Nonsense. Miss Hargrave is a woman first, a doctor second, and therefore prefers to be addressed like a lady. Don't you, my dear?"

"Actually, Mrs. Rawlins, your son is right. I prefer to be called Doctor."

Clair made a display of putting down her fork and giving Samantha a frankly surprised look. "How irregular!"

"I am *first* a doctor, Mrs. Rawlins. I have, after all, earned the title."

"But how will people know your marital status if you are addressed as Dr. Hargrave?"

"I presume that, if they really wish to know, they will ask."

"My dear Miss Hargrave," said Clair in the way she often addressed her daughters-in-law ("My dear Elaine, you will have twelve at your dinner party and you will serve pheasant"). "No gentleman of breeding would dare think of asking you outright whether you are married or single. Many will assume you are married and then good prospects will pass you by. How do you expect to catch a husband?"

As it happened, this, of course, was the moment when all conversations fell silent and Samantha found herself the object of everyone's attention.

"Mother," came Mark from his end of the table, "you are embarrassing Dr. Hargrave."

Samantha offered him a gracious smile and said, "It's quite all right, Dr. Rawlins. I don't mind." She turned to Clair. "I appreciate your concern for my situation, Mrs. Rawlins, but I assure you I have not compromised my chances of marriage or my femininity with my profession. Should I ever marry, the man will have to be very special. I'm sure you'll agree, ours cannot be a conventional relationship. It is my sincere hope that, should such a unique man present himself in my future and find me a desirable marriage partner, he would be forthright and honest enough to ask me outright my marital status. I would regard such directness as a sign of character, Mrs. Rawlins, not a lack of breeding."

Everyone blinked at her for a moment, then they managed to find their spoons, forks, while Samantha and Mrs. Rawlins were locked in each other's gaze. Only Mark did not move; he was mesmerized. No one, not even his father, had ever challenged his mother.

Finally Clair said dryly, "What sort of man would marry a lady doctor?"

Before Samantha could reply, Mark spoke up from his end of the table. "Why, another doctor, of course."

As Clair regarded her favorite son with a hard expression, she did not fail to catch a special exchange pass briefly between Samantha and Mark. Nor did Janelle MacPherson, who stirred with a rustling of ice-blue silk.

The awkward silence was ended by Stephen, who, with a flirtatious grin, inclined himself toward Samantha and said, "I shouldn't mind marrying a lady doctor."

Samantha laughed softly and reached for her wine glass. "When your supper is burnt once too often because your wife has been called away on a medical emergency you might change your mind."

As the glazed duck was brought out, the conversation changed. Opinions were voiced on the new transition from Impressionistic art into something even more "preposterous," as was best illustrated in Cézanne's (they all agreed) ghastly *L'Estaque,* and when that subject was exhausted, coinciding with the sugared raspberries, a general dialogue was enjoyed by all on Henry James's new novel, *The Portrait of a Lady.* While she divided her attention between Stephen, who was anxious to please her, and Clair, who clearly was not, Samantha occasionally turned her head to the left and a few times found Mark watching her.

"I think," said Joseph Rawlins, sitting at Samantha's right, "that the basic question James is propounding is one of free will. A young girl of high intelligence is given free choice to live her life the way she wishes but she makes a fatal error for which she must pay the rest of her life."

"Then what you are saying, Joseph dear," said Clair, "is that there is a lesson to be learned from this book." She turned to Samantha. "Have you read it, Miss Hargrave?"

"I'm afraid I've little time for nonmedical reading, Mrs. Rawlins."

Clair's brows rose in an exaggerated arch. "Pity."

Samantha bowed her head as she dipped her spoon into her raspberries and glanced surreptitiously at Mark. Having expected to receive one of his secretive smiles, she was surprised to see him grinning handsomely at Janelle, who appeared to have captivated him in an engaging story. When she smiled, she dazzled, like the diamond choker around her throat, and when she laughed, she pressed her hand to her bosom, drawing attention to her low-cut decolletage.

"Miss Hargrave," came Clair's crisp voice. "I trust this is not one of those nights you warned about when you will be called away on a medical errand?"

Samantha looked up. "I beg your pardon?"

"Letitia is going to recite for us while we have our coffee. She gives a very moving rendition of *Annabel Lee*. But afterward, Miss Hargrave, I should like to have a few minutes with you alone. If that is agreeable with you."

"Certainly, Mrs. Rawlins."

"Actually, that is why I asked you here tonight. I've something important I wish to discuss with you. In private."

Samantha stared at Clair for a moment, then she snapped her head to the right. Mark was laughing heartily with his head thrown back and Janelle was beaming at him.

Confused, Samantha returned to her raspberries. So, it wasn't Mark who had wanted her here tonight, but Clair. Clair who seemed to disapprove of everything about Samantha and who didn't think it necessary to hide that disapproval. Something important to discuss in private . . .

Clair was right, Letitia did recite *Annabel Lee* most touchingly and Samantha would have been quite moved had she not been mentally distracted. As they all sat in the parlor with cups of brandied coffee watching Letitia emote dramatically in the dim light (the lamps had been turned down for effect) Samantha could not help puzzling over her reason for being here tonight. Nor could she help feeling disappointed. Clearly, she must have misread Mark's intentions.

But when Letitia cried most movingly, with her hands clasped over her bosom, "'I was a child and she was a child, In this kingdom by the sea, But we loved with a love that was more than love—'" Samantha turned her gaze in the direction of Mark where he sat across the room, his legs stretched before him and crossed at the ankles in a casual posture, and she found him staring intently back at her. His face was in shadow, his expression hidden, but Samantha felt an intensity emanate from him, as though he were trying to reach out and touch her. Samantha's cup stopped at her lips. She couldn't swallow. As if the words of Mr. Poe had transformed him, a different Mark Rawlins gazed at her across the dim room. The façade was stripped away, no cultured gentleman idly watched her now; she sensed his power, his maleness, felt him invade her and take possession. His mouth was thin, severe; his body appeared at ease but she sensed tension, determination. Samantha was held, the moment seemed to last forever.

Then the sound of polite applause brought her back to reality. Stephen was turning up the lamps and everyone praised Letitia for her performance, and when Samantha looked again at Mark she found him still staring. But now that his face was in light she saw the gravity of his expression and a brooding depth in his eyes. She trembled. Mark said softly, for only her to hear, "Did you like the poem, Samantha?"

"Yes."

"But it was so tragic."

"There can be beauty in tragedy."

Everyone was now standing and making moves to adjourn to other rooms—the men to their cigars, the ladies to their footstools—but Mark and Samantha made no move. "What is your favorite poem, Samantha?"

She thought a moment. *"The Prisoner of Chillon."*

"Byron. More tragedy."

"And yours?"

His lips started to lift in a smile. And then Clair's imperious voice suddenly filled the room. "Miss Hargrave, might I have those few minutes alone with you now?"

Samantha took a seat in a handsome leather chair that smelled of lemon oil and watched Clair decant brandy into two crystal glasses. They were in the Rawlins library, surrounded by four walls of cases containing a wealth of human knowledge, two women alone beneath the impersonal marble gazes of Julius Caesar, Voltaire, Napoleon Bonaparte and, from his gilt frame over the fireplace, Nicholas Rawlins, Ice King.

Clair handed Samantha a glass and took the chair next to her. "I have friends in the Temperance League who roundly denounce my little liquor habit while at the same time they gulp bottles of drugstore tonics that contain enough alcohol to knock out a horse. Even Nicholas, God rest him, disapproved."

Clair gazed up at the towering portrait. Her voice softened. "He was not an easy man to love, Miss Hargrave, but because I had to fight constantly to keep him, I cherished him all the more."

"I was sorry to hear of his passing."

"It was swift. Now then, Miss Hargrave, let me get to the reason why I asked you here. I do not approve of professional women. Lady doctors, lawyers, judges, photographers—their sacrifice is too great, it embarrasses me for them. I loathe to see a woman unsexed. And yet—and here you will think me a hypocrite—I find myself forced to turn to you for the very thing you are. Miss Hargrave, I need a woman doctor right now. The concession has been a difficult one for me to make."

Clair sipped her brandy, swirled it in the glass for a thoughtful moment, then continued: "I have always been a robust woman, in excellent health, have always found exercise and a good diet to be the best remedy for most ills. I could never countenance those frail, vaporous ladies our society has created. A woman can be equal to a man in body as well as mind and still retain her femininity. I never used my monthly days, as so many women do, as an excuse for retiring from responsibility. And I have never once, Miss Hargrave, in all my life, turned to a physician for anything."

Samantha could easily believe that, for she could see the years of hardening, of toughening, of layering herself with an intractable mettle that would keep her standing against the forces of society and husband. But through the soft brown eyes, through the hard and self-sufficient façade, Samantha saw another woman look out: a hidden, tender woman who looked out through gentle eyes, like a prisoner peering through the bars of a cell, as if yearning to be free.

"I was worried that you would not be what I was looking for, Miss Hargrave. I feared you would be like so many doctors, very good at the artful dodge and the couched lies, and quick to flatter. But I saw this evening that you are strong and honest and that you will tell me the truth."

"The truth about what, Mrs. Rawlins?"

"How long I have to live."

Samantha stared at her. Before she could speak Clair said, "I want you to examine me. How is that best done?"

"What do you wish me to examine?"

"My breast."

Samantha put her glass down and stood. "On the couch would be best. I cannot do it through your clothing—"

Clair waved an arm. "I'm not squeamish. Just be frank, that is all I want."

A few minutes later Samantha asked, "How long have you had this lump, Mrs. Rawlins?"

"Four months."

"Why didn't you go to a doctor then?"

"Miss Hargrave, I have never in all my life exposed myself to a man other than my husband."

"That is foolish and dangerous pride."

"I am aware of that, Miss Hargrave. I had also thought the lump would go away. What is your verdict?"

The lump was the size of a tangerine, rock-hard, movable, clearly defined, and the nipple was retracted. Samantha dabbed her handkerchief to it and came away with a brown spot. And there were lumps in the armpit. "A few months, no more."

"That is not enough time, not so soon after my husband's death. My family cannot do without me yet. I need a year."

"It is not mine to give." As Samantha helped Clair with the straps of her camisole she was reminded of a saying among soldiers of the Civil War: *There's little difference between dying today and dying tomorrow but we all prefer tomorrow.* "If you had gone at once to a doctor, Mrs. Rawlins, he could have removed the breast—"

"I will not end my days as anything less than a whole woman, Miss Hargrave. My sister died of breast cancer, so I knew what was in store for me. She had a mastectomy and, yes, she lived a little longer but they had removed all her muscles so that one arm dangled uselessly and her shoulder was pulled forward almost to her breastbone. She was hideously mutilated and in constant pain. After the operation she never saw the sun again, and admitted only her family into her room, no friends. Yes, Miss Hargrave, my life might have had length added to it, but would it have had *quality?*"

Samantha helped Clair button her dress. "Does Mark know?"

She waved a hand as if they were discussing nothing more than a luncheon menu. On the surface she was hard and unmoved by her death sentence, but the woman trapped inside the tough shell was crying. "If I had gone to Mark he would have been too emotional. He and I share a . . . special relationship. This is a difficult enough pronouncement to hear without having it come from the trembling lips of one's beloved son. And he is not to know, Miss Hargrave, for it would devastate him. None of them are to know. I wish it kept a secret until the very last."

They returned to their chairs and Clair picked up her glass. "Brumaire," she said quietly. "My husband's favorite brandy. Nicholas was an unloved tyrant, you know. No one cried when he died. I even fear Joseph and Henry are secretly glad he's gone. He shan't be missed, that is for certain. And now I wonder how *my* death will be received." Clair turned glistening eyes to Samantha. "I'm not afraid of death, Miss Hargrave. I'm just not ready—" Her voice broke.

As Samantha reached out and placed her hand over Clair's, she thought: I am looking in a mirror into the future. When I am fifty-two, will I be like Clair Rawlins, still fighting for my dignity when all odds seem against me? What have you sacrificed, Mrs. Rawlins, to stand on your own as a woman in your own right? How were you able to give yourself to the man you love and yet keep your identity and uniqueness?

Clair sniffed and patted Samantha's hand. "I would appreciate it if you would sit with me for a while, Miss Hargrave."

"Of course."

"Tell me, will I have much pain at the end?"

⁂

Mark sat opposite Samantha in the gently swaying carriage, watching her face as it was illuminated by passing street lamps. Since coming out of the library she had been quiet and distracted; he was disturbed, for he knew what his mother could be like. He was also puzzled: what on earth had gone on behind those doors?

Although Mark enjoyed a special relationship with his mother, for she admired his strength and courage in fighting for what he thought right at any sacrifice (the day Mark walked out of his father's house fourteen years before Clair had decided she loved this son above the others), and although she turned to Mark in moments when she needed guidance and advice, Clair Rawlins, on this particular occasion, had chosen not to confide in her son. She had heard about the new woman doctor at St. Brigid's, had made inquiries of Mark and had finally asked him to bring Miss Hargrave to dinner.

"Now that you have had the singular honor of meeting my mother," he said, as the carriage merged with the late evening traffic on Broadway, "what do you think of her?"

Samantha forced a smile. "She's a remarkable woman."

"What did you two talk about for such a long time?"

"Things."

"Secret things?"

"Woman things."

He regarded her in seriousness. "Is she ill?"

Samantha returned his gaze with a steadiness she did not feel. "She asked me to repeat our conversation to no one and I gave her my word."

"I see." Mark lifted his cane, casually examined the ornate silver handle, then put it back down. "Has she a medical problem?"

"I can't tell you."

"I have a right to know," he said softly.

In that instant Samantha suddenly felt sorry for, not Clair, who would face her death stoically, but Mark, who would soon be grieving. She wanted desperately to tell him, to allow him the dignity of preparing himself, but Clair had forbidden it. Samantha struggled with her ethics. In her love for Mark she wanted to tell him, to help ease his pain; but she could not betray a patient's confidence. True to herself or true to her profession, Samantha had never thought the two could come in conflict.

"She asked my advice and I gave it. That's all I can tell you."

He considered this, then, accepting it, nodded. "I'm glad you joined us tonight. You made the evening special."

Samantha had to look away. Mentally she urged the horses to a faster pace. Mark sat so close, her desire for him was so great, that she feared she couldn't maintain equilibrium much longer. She wanted to cry. Not for Clair but for Mark. That wretched promise. If only she could tell him . . .

"Do you know this one, Samantha?" came his voice, deep and intimate. "'The lady sleeps. Oh, may her sleep, which is enduring, so be deep. Heaven have her in its sacred keep. I pray to God that she may lie forever with un-opened eye, while the pale sheeted ghosts go by—' Samantha!"

"I'm sorry—" She dashed the tear off her cheek.

In an instant he was at her side, an arm about her shoulders. "Forgive me," he murmured, pulling out a handkerchief. "I've upset you."

She pressed the handkerchief to her eyes. It smelled faintly of his co-logne. "I'm sorry," she said again, drawing in a steadying breath. "It's not your fault, Mark. I'm tired."

"No doubt Landon is overworking you."

She lifted her head to smile apologetically up at him and found his face inches from hers. Through her cape she felt the warmth of his body; his arm held her close to him, protectively. Once again his eyes had taken on that dark, veiled quality that had been inspired by *Annabel Lee*. His gaze was intense, his expression grave, and again Samantha puzzled over it. She had never known a man like Mark Rawlins, a man who, on the surface, cut a debonair figure, the witty, cultured gentleman she had met at the Astor ball, but who was underneath a mystery of power and virility. Twice she had glimpsed this other Mark Rawlins and he excited her. Samantha closed her eyes and savored his nearness; for once she didn't feel like being strong, like fighting for control, she wanted to give in to weakness and let Mark be her shelter.

He held her close for the rest of the ride, comforting her with his strength and stability, silent and involved. For, if Samantha marveled at the effect Mark Rawlins had on her, Mark was no less amazed by the effect she had on him. How could a woman be so strong and independent, yet fragile and vulnerable? How could she make him admire her courage and fortitude and see her as a woman standing firmly on her own, yet at the same time make him feel fiercely protective of her? The almost violent sexual arousal he had experienced during Letitia's recital, as he stared at Samantha, had astonished him. No woman had ever had such power over him, dominating his thoughts, confounding him, making him a slave to his desire. She was as much a perplexity to him as he was to her, a complex woman who continu-ally revealed some new aspect to him. Each time, as Mark thought he finally knew her, Samantha Hargrave surprised him again.

He wanted the ride to go on forever—the lights, the scented summer air, the smell of the carriage leather, the feel of Samantha under his arm—and was disappointed to see St. Brigid's draw up too soon.

Mark walked her into the gaslit foyer where a sleepy porter kept vagrants out and stopped to take her by the shoulders. "Are you sure you're all right now?" he asked gently, looking down into her face.

Samantha nodded.

Mark waited. There was so much he wanted to say, a hundred words stood at his lips, but for some reason his usual glibness eluded him now. So he said simply, "Good night, Samantha."

And Samantha, having no experience with men and love and words, whispered, "Good night, Mark," and turned away.

Although it was late, there was a party going on in Dr. Weston's room: female giggles accompanied banjo plucking. Samantha rushed by, down to the quiet end of the hall, where she fell inside her own room and rested against the closed door, struggling for control.

Love wasn't supposed to hurt.

Then heavy footsteps came down the hall, followed by a sharp rap on her door; thinking it was a drunken colleague deciding at last that she should join them, she flung open the door to find Mark standing before her. He pushed his way in, angrily slammed the door, seized her by both arms and said, "Damn it, Samantha. I love you!"

He pulled her hard against him, and she melted into his embrace, and when he covered her mouth with his, a groan escaped from her throat. It startled him, the passion of her response. He pulled back, looking down at her with stormy eyes, and said huskily, "God, I love you, Samantha. I love you . . ."

Mark now marveled at other things: how small she felt in his arms, yet voluptuous; how clear and incredibly deep her eyes were—a man could drown in them; how she made him surge with desire and suddenly want to run out and slay dragons for her. He had wanted her for a long time, had thought and thought about her, but *this*, this was unexpected. This sudden release of passions he had no idea she harbored.

Mark was also surprised to hear himself speaking the word "love" for the first time in his life. There had been women in his past, but love had never entered into it, not even with Janelle. Love was something alien to Mark, for it had never been displayed between his parents, he had known only a cold and loveless youth, had always thought himself incapable of such feelings. And yet here he was, spilling out the word as though he had meant all along to say it, and to his further surprise it felt right, sounded right. He meant it . . .

This staggering revelation took place in the fraction of a moment. He drew away from her, bewildered, slowly realizing what he had done. "Forgive me," he whispered hoarsely. "Forcing my way into your room, grabbing you . . ."

Her voice, barely more than a whisper, reached him from across the dark space, for no lights were lit in the room. "Do you regret it?"

"No," he said simply. "I want you to marry me, Samantha."

He heard her gasp and realized it was her turn to be surprised. He used her brief unbalance to his advantage. "I do not expect an immediate answer," he said in a rush, "only that you will grant me the honor of considering it. We can have a good life together, Samantha, a family. Our shared profession, working side by side . . ." Good God, where were these words coming from?

A cool hand reached for his; she drew him close to her again and rose up on her toes to kiss his mouth. His arms went around her, feeling as though they were coming home, and he did nothing to hide his sexual arousal, knowing that she wanted it. And when he started undoing the buttons of her gown, she helped him.

In all his life Mark Rawlins had only been dedicated to two things: defying his father and practicing good medicine. To those he now added a third: he would dedicate the rest of his life to loving Samantha Hargrave.

EIGHT

*T*HERE MUST BE A WAY, LANDON," SAID SAMANTHA, PUSHING
away her plate of toast and bacon. "I refuse to stand by and
watch any more patients die uselessly."

He didn't reply; they had this discussion every week. When the patients
came in with tubal pregnancies, they died. It was a fact of life. Why couldn't
she accept it?

Samantha tapped her spoon on the table top. "A small incision, a quick
ligation of the tube, pluck out the fetus and sew the patient up! Why can't it
be done?"

He stared at her in mute response. She knew very well why: because the
patient always bled to death.

"Landon, come now, think! There must be a way to control hemorrhage!
If we could but find the way, think of the thousands of abdominal operations
we could safely perform! Appendectomies, gallbladders, hysterectomies—"

The dining-room door opened and Mark Rawlins stepped in. And it never
failed, Samantha blushed; they had been secret lovers for three months now.

He looked around, said good morning to the few doctors at the other tables, then made his way to where Samantha and Landon sat. "Good morning, Doctors, am I interrupting anything?"

"Just the same old thing, Mark," said Landon, pulling out his pocket watch and clicking it open. "Abdomens."

"Mm. We'll do it someday, I'm sure. Halsted claims to be having some success with his new clamp."

"I observed one of his theatrical operations. Gallbladder. There must have been fifty clamps sticking out of the wound. Halsted had no room to work in. Took him over an hour."

Mark raised his eyebrows. "A whole hour for an operation?"

Landon clicked his watch closed and replaced it in his pocket. "Better be seeing to Mrs. O'Riley. She's been in labor for nearly two days now. Looks like a Caesarean section."

"I shall be along as soon as I finish my tea," said Samantha.

He nodded absently and wandered away from the table. Mark turned to Samantha, eyes twinkling. "How are you this morning, Dr. Hargrave?"

"Just fine, Doctor, and you?" Three months ago they had argued about this charade: Mark had wanted to climb to the top of St. Patrick's Cathedral and shout about their engagement, but Samantha had insisted they keep it a secret. St. Brigid's had very clear-cut rules about their female employees and Samantha didn't want to jeopardize her certificate of internship now, only a month away. The rules were explicit: female employees could not be married, they could not be engaged, they could not "court" while working at St. Brigid's. And Samantha, in the eyes of Silas Prince, was a female employee. Mark thought her fears groundless, Samantha disagreed. At any rate, she didn't care to put their theories to the test. Only a few weeks ago a very efficient and dedicated nurse had been dismissed when it was discovered that she was engaged.

After that first night, in her bed, they took no more risks; they met discreetly once a week at Mark's apartment on Fifty-seventh Street, and for the sake of protecting her until that precious certificate was in her hands, he had reluctantly agreed to tell no one about their engagement, not even his mother. And not even, to the point of creating some awkward moments, Janelle.

They fell silent when the serving girl came up with Mark's coffee. He ordered eggs and asked what fresh fruit was available. While he spoke, Samantha sipped her tea and observed him through her thick lashes.

She was thinking of his body. Specifically, his chest. It was a wonderful chest, muscular and matted with hair; and his arms, sinewy and knotted; and his shoulders and hard back; his strong thighs—

The girl went away and Mark turned to Samantha. "Why, Dr. Hargrave, your face is red."

What incredible discoveries they had made in each other's arms; what delirium and lunacy! It seemed as though they had been created for one another, body and soul. They knew no embarrassment, no limits to their lovemaking. And when they were not engaged in physical love they solemnly planned their future together, deciding where Samantha would open her practice, which hospital she would affiliate with, where they would live, how the children would be raised. Joshua had been uncannily accurate: Mark Rawlins was going to be a perfect husband for Samantha.

When his egg was brought, Samantha said, "How is your mother, Dr. Rawlins?"

"She's fine. Why do you ask?"

Samantha had seen Clair several times in the last three months and each time their friendship had deepened. Over their brandy, which was becoming a tradition, Clair would speak of the past, of the challenge of living with and holding onto a man of such boundless energies as Nicholas Rawlins, of trying to raise four sons to be their own men and succeeding with only one, of the fragile balance between fighting to be accepted as an individual with rights of her own and yet retaining her femininity. Samantha had tried to illustrate to Clair that she was in fact describing those very professional women she condemned, but Clair refused to see it. "There is only one career that is natural for a woman—wife and mother. I am speaking of a woman maintaining her individualism within that sphere, not to step out of it, as you describe, and compete with men. A woman's place is at a man's side, not opposite him." They debated endlessly, and enjoyed it. Several times Samantha had come close to disclosing her secret, but it was too risky—Silas Prince would finally have his weapon.

It is only one more month, Samantha thought as Mark finished his breakfast. In four weeks I shall have my certificate.

She watched him push his plate away and dab his mouth with a napkin (she was thinking what it was like to be kissed by that little scar and wondered if other women were similarly afflicted with constant thoughts of intimacy with the men they loved). But when he lifted his eyes to hers and she saw the gravity in them, her playful smile vanished. "What is it, Mark?"

"I'm afraid I've a bit of bad news, Samantha. I've been trying to think of a way to tell you. I'm going to have to go to London next week—"

She stared at him, then quickly recovered, remembering where they were.

"St. Luke's is sending me. I'm to represent them at an American congress there."

"Can't someone else go?"

"It's important for me as well as the hospital. Right now I'm still just one of the staff men. Politically, this can get me my own service."

Samantha nodded. Already their careers had intruded upon their private lives; it was something they were going to have to be reconciled to, if their future was to be harmonious. "I understand, my love," she said very quietly. "How long will you be gone?"

"It's only for a week. My passage has been booked. I shall be sailing on the *Excalibur* to Bristol. Weather permitting, I shall be back the last week in October. Four days, in fact, before the certification ceremony."

"My heart goes with you."

"And mine remains here with you."

"Four weeks."

"An eternity."

"How shall I survive?"

"Samantha." Mark's hand started across the table, then he pulled it back. "Let's get married now. Before I go."

She thought a moment, then shook her head. "It would kill your mother. She so looks forward to the day you marry, she plans a wedding party to rival anything Mrs. Astor can do. We can't rob her of it, Mark."

"Oh, Mother can weather any disappointment. She's a tough old bird. She'll get over it."

"No, Mark. It's only four weeks. Then we'll be free."

They fell to staring at one another. It was on her lips to stand up and shout, "Damn you all!" and kiss Mark boldly in front of them. Then they could have a hasty civil wedding, a few days of honeymoon before he went; maybe she could even go with him, see London again after all these years, Dr. Blackwell, a nostalgic look at the Crescent. She could show Mark the places she had explored as a little girl, it would be a chapter out of Paradise . . .

But no. That certificate was too vital; Prince would seize upon anything to keep it from her. And also Clair would be robbed of her final dream before departing this world.

"How lucky I am," said Mark softly, solemnly. "I wonder if someday I shall wake up and find you've only been a dream."

Samantha forced a flippancy she did not feel. "I'd best be seeing what Landon's up to. We've got four in labor this morning! If you will excuse me, Dr. Rawlins."

He looked at her, a little sadly. "Tonight?"

She thought. It had been a week, Landon would give her time off. "Tonight," she whispered and hurried out.

❦

"Good morning, Dr. Hargrave!"

Samantha looked up from her stethoscope to see Letitia's sunny smile beaming down at her. A basket of roses was cradled in her arms, no doubt from last night's dinner table, and behind her stood a housemaid carrying what looked like an arm-load of sheets.

"Hello, Letitia," said Samantha, pulling the covers back over the patient's chest.

"I've brought linens for bandages. Mama got tired of them but they're in good condition."

"Thank your mother for us. Pearl, would you please give them to the nurse at the desk?"

"And who should be the recipient of these today?"

Samantha looked at the blossoms, which were very fresh and then scanned the ward. The September sun streamed over neat little beds; golden motes, like sundust, floated on the beams. Samantha rested her eye on Mrs. Murphy and couldn't resist a smile.

Grandma Murphy had come in the previous week with severe stomach pains and chronic vomiting. An old woman of the Old World, she had never before seen a stethoscope; when Samantha applied the silver bell to her chest, Mrs. Murphy, mistaking the stethoscope for some fancy modern treatment, had sighed heavily and said, "Sure and I feel better already!"

"Mrs. Murphy over there will be kind to them, Letitia. She's the one wrapping her hair in rag curls."

Letitia turned spritely away and hurried to Bed Seven, leaving Samantha to stand and look thoughtfully after her. Of late, Letitia MacPherson had become a real concern.

Samantha was thinking of the last time she had had dinner at Clair's house. Samantha had gone back to the kitchens to fetch some milk with which Clair could take a morphine powder, and, traveling the maze of carpeted halls, she had passed by a door slightly ajar, from which she thought she had heard a moan. Her medical instinct made her stop and listen. Pushing the door open a few inches, she peered in. The room was dark; Samantha could only barely make out the silhouettes of heavy furniture and massive plants: an extra sitting room for the comfort of exhausted ladies when Clair Rawlins gave one of her extravagant balls. It was deserted now except for someone hidden in the shadows and clearly in distress.

Thinking that a maid, come in to clean, had fallen and was hurt, Samantha started to go all the way in, but then a low rumbling laugh stopped her. She froze and listened, then, startled, she recognized the sighs and moans of passion and hastily withdrew.

After obtaining some warm milk in the main kitchen from an assistant cook who was shocked to see a guest come in, Samantha started back to the library. She had to quickly duck into a recess when she reached the dark sitting room, for its door was opening. Out stepped Stephen Rawlins, smoothing down his hair. A voice called out after him. It was Letitia.

Samantha had told Mark about it and he had then had a talk with Stephen, but that did nothing to help Letitia, whom Samantha suspected of courting the favors of more than one man.

Samantha pondered now as she watched the girl sweetly tie the rags on Mrs. Murphy's head. Lately Letitia had been coming to the hospital in the company of only a maid. Samantha wondered why.

Dr. Weston chose that moment to enter the ward. When he saw Letitia, his stride broke slightly, and when Letitia looked up, her face pinked. He continued by and she kept up her chatter with Mrs. Murphy, but Samantha had seen the brief communication and it sent a jolt through her: Do Mark and I betray ourselves in thousands of such insignificant ways?

When Letitia returned, Samantha was shaking down a thermometer and placing it under a patient's armpit. I should talk to her, Samantha thought. Letitia has no idea the fire she's playing with.

⚜

In fact, Letitia MacPherson knew very well what danger she courted. She had discovered at a very early age the joy of a certain solitary activity; and a few years later, in the garden gazebo of their summer house, Letitia had her first real sexual adventure: her accomplice had been a cousin named Will. Since then Letitia had decided that no occupation would ever satisfy her as much: she played an ordinary piano, plied a mundane needle, painted mediocre pictures, but in concert with a male body she was a prima donna.

She had also discovered that half the thrill of sex was the danger of discovery. Being married and sleeping with the same man every night did not seem anywhere near as delicious to anticipate as a different partner each time; the supreme pleasure in sex came from variety, and from the threat of being caught at it. As for pregnancy, Letitia had gone, on a friend's recommendation, to a lady in Greenwich Village. She sold Letitia a bottle of "protective" solution and a sponge which, soaked in the liquid, was to be inserted just before intercourse.

Samantha knew none of this. To look at, Letitia MacPherson was a blushing girl, as fresh and innocent as a primrose; the fact that she loved sex was not known, least of all by the various men who, enchanted by the girlish smile and naive manner, each thought himself to be her first.

"We're all going to the Wild West Show this Saturday, Dr. Hargrave. They say they have *real* Indians!"

Samantha smiled and withdrew the thermometer from the patient's armpit. As she read it she thought: I worry too much. Letitia's too sweet and sensible a girl to let a man get too far with his advances.

"Dr. Hargrave!"

She looked up. Dr. Weston stood at the end of the hall holding the door open and waving his arm. "Can you come at once? You are needed."

When she got there, Samantha saw that the accident ward was chaos: bodies on litters, nurses running about, doctors turning up their sleeves. There had been an accident in a nearby intersection, caused by a runaway horse; several pedestrians had been killed and carriage drivers lay critically injured on the examining tables.

"Over here, Doc!" called Jake. He was helping a policeman control a raving man whose leg had been run over by a carriage wheel.

Samantha ordered his coat removed, then gave him an injection of morphine. As he quieted, Samantha was able to inspect his injury. The leg had been neatly severed at the knee, and the policeman, a quick-thinking man, had bundled some rags against the stump to stanch the bleeding and had held them in place the whole time. Now he let go as Samantha stepped in; she gently pulled the bloody cloths from the stump and was shocked to find them icy cold. In the center of the bundle was something hard, like a rock.

Seeing her puzzled expression, the policeman said, "It's a trick I learned as an orderly in the Union Army. One of the vehicles in the accident was an ice truck. I helped myself."

Samantha gazed down at the man's severed leg and saw that there had been remarkably little bleeding. But, as the warmth of the room met the wound, the vessels dilated and the flesh began to pink. She knew already he would heal nicely with little infection. And he'd lost so little blood.

Ice, she thought with a thrill. Ice . . .

NINE

*I*T WAS THE KIND OF OCTOBER DAY WHEN CATS' FUR STOOD ON end and petticoats crackled. Leaves littered the sidewalks, red and gold, looking as if paint from the sunset had been spattered; the air was charged. It was dry and cold; the doorway to winter was inching open.

Samantha washed her hands at the end of the ward and sighed heavily. It had been a busy day, she was tired, but as the setting sun heralded evening and thus the end of her shift, Samantha felt a new vitality surge through her: a letter, she had been informed, was waiting for her upstairs. From Mark!

She smiled, all alone, by herself, at no one and at nothing. She just smiled. Yesterday the *Excalibur* had left Bristol and Mark would be home in a week.

Mildred's face emerged around the door. "Dr. Hargrave? I'm awfully sorry, but Dr. Weston thinks he has a gynecological case for you."

Samantha smiled wearily. "I'll be right there, Mildred."

Dr. Weston was bent over a young lady seated in a chair, trying delicately not to get too close with his stethoscope. Times like this, he wished he could afford one of those new binaural stethoscopes like Dr. Hargrave's instead of using this old wooden tube that brought his face too close to a young girl's breast.

He straightened when he heard Dr. Hargrave enter and she was surprised to see his face blanched to a terrible whiteness. "What is it, Dr. Weston?"

He turned away from the patient and, taking Samantha's elbow, steered her to a discreet distance. "Her family says it's her appendix," he murmured. "But I don't think so."

Samantha did not miss the nervous twitch of his mouth. "Why?"

"She has vaginal bleeding."

Samantha pushed past him and stopped short before the patient. It was Letitia MacPherson.

Her head was lolled to one side, her eyes closed, her cheeks crested feverishly. "Let's get her onto the table, Dr. Weston. Was she unconscious when her family brought her in?" Samantha gently lifted the girl's skirts and palpated the abdomen.

"Yes," said Dr. Weston, licking dry lips. "They said she complained all day of feeling nauseated and then shortly past noon she said she had a sharp pain in her pelvis and collapsed. They put her to bed and called in their family physician, and it was he who recommended she be brought here."

"Where is he?"

"In the foyer with the mother and sister."

Samantha glanced at Dr. Weston and read an entire story on his ashen face. So, Letitia *had* allowed more than a few harmless liberties; if she's pregnant you're afraid you're to blame.

Samantha's long tapered fingers found the small mass beneath the skin; she gently felt around it and probed the soft uterus, all the while studying the queer little red marks on Letitia's white skin. The entire time, Mrs. Knight and Dr. Weston stood by silently, anxiously, and when Samantha spoke they almost jumped. "It's a tubal pregnancy," she said finally, "and it has just ruptured."

Mrs. Knight shook her head sadly and crossed herself, her pragmatic mind already doing a quick review of the shroud cupboard, hoping they had one left.

"Mrs. Knight," said Samantha, pulling down Letitia's skirt, "get the operating room ready. I shall need all the light you can put your hands to."

Matron's eyes widened. "You're going to operate, Doctor?"

"Yes. And is there ice available in the kitchen?"

The woman nodded uncertainly and turned away to carry out her orders.

"Surgery!" said Dr. Weston, who had slumped into a chair. "You can't be serious!"

"I'll want you on ether, Doctor. And please send someone to Dr. Fremont's house. I shall want his assistance."

Samantha drew in a breath, girding herself, then went through the doors that led to the foyer. Janelle MacPherson shot to her feet, but the frail, older woman with her remained seated.

Samantha clasped her hands tightly in front of her as she stood before Janelle. "Can we sit down, Miss MacPherson?" she said as gently as she could. "I'm afraid I've some unpleasant news for you."

"I prefer to stand, Dr. Hargrave. What is wrong with my sister?"

"Letitia requires emergency surgery."

Janelle paled to the whiteness of her platinum hair. "Surgery? Since when are appendixes operated on?"

"Please, let's sit down."

After they were seated on the bench, Samantha tried to break the news as easily as she could. "Letitia hasn't appendicitis, Miss MacPherson, she has a pregnancy outside her uterus; it requires immediate removal."

Chilly autumn drafts found their way up the steps and through the cracks in the main doors, sweeping through the foyer like malicious whispers. Janelle MacPherson's dark blue eyes hardened to slate. "What did you say?"

Samantha reached out to touch her arm but Janelle moved away. "Letitia is pregnant. I'm sorry. The fetus is lodged in one of the tubes leading to her womb and the tube has ruptured. She has little time left."

"How dare you."

"I beg your pardon?"

"How dare you make such an accusation against my sister!"

"It is not an accusation, Miss MacPherson, I assure you. And if I do not operate at once—"

"You are not operating on my sister!"

"Now see here," intervened a deep baritone. Samantha looked up at the gentleman who had been standing by Janelle's mother. He was very old and looked very distinguished and his joints creaked when he walked. "I made the diagnosis myself. That girl has appendicitis."

Samantha did a quick sizing up. Retained by the family for more decades than he could remember, Dr. Grimes's idea of practicing medicine clearly was holding hands and dispensing sugar pills, listening to the imagined ills of Fifth Avenue matrons and debutantes, making impressive-sounding pronouncements through a monocle and raking in enormous fees. "I'm afraid I must differ with your diagnosis, Doctor," said Samantha guardedly. "Appendicitis would not produce the hemorrhaging."

"The girl is obviously having her menses."

"But the mass is clearly palpable, sir, and the pain is on the *left* side."

"That is still no indication of pregnancy, madam."

"That is true. However, the greater percentage lies with pregnancy and that is my diagnosis."

"Even so, madam, surgery is no recourse."

"Neither are leeches, sir."

His old eyes flickered and Samantha read in them the cold fear of a man who realizes that the world has moved on without him. Dr. Grimes was a relic, a dinosaur, and he knew it.

Samantha returned to Janelle, saying more gently, "Miss MacPherson, I know how terrible this must be for you, but the fact is, Letitia has a dangerous condition that increases with each minute. If we do not attempt surgery at once, she will not live through the night."

"Dr. Hargrave," said Janelle, visibly straining to hold herself together, "there is no possible way in God's creation that my little sister could be pregnant. What you are implying is monstrous. To sully the reputation of an innocent child for the aggrandizement of your own career—" Janelle drew her voice down to a controllable level. "You will not use my sister as a stage prop. If you need a flamboyant gesture for the newspapers, find someone else."

Samantha looked over at the sad little woman behind Janelle. Mrs. MacPherson had not been as lucky as Clair Rawlins, had not had it in her to stand up beside her own husband and fight for her right to be a person. Mrs. MacPherson looked old and worn out before her time, a mere shadow of her Wall Street spouse, a vehicle for producing his offspring and nothing more. But the unhappy eyes that met Samantha's tried, for an instant, to recapture her old strength from years back. Mrs. MacPherson clearly knew the truth, suspected what dangerous games her daughter had been playing, and almost, just almost, came to the point of saying so to Samantha. But she hadn't the strength, she was unused to voicing an opinion all her own, especially against her domineering daughter who, after her husband forgot her existence and ceased to bully her, had taken over as head of the household. And so Mrs. MacPherson gave up and looked back down at her hands.

"Do not lay a finger on my sister, Dr. Hargrave. For if you do I shall bring criminal charges against you."

❧

Samantha came back into the accident ward. Dr. Weston was taking Letitia's pulse again.

"Is Landon here yet?" asked Samantha, coming up to the table.

He shook his head. Then, putting his watch away, he looked up. "She's shocky, Dr. Hargrave. What did her family say?"

"They've refused me permission to operate."

"Hm. It's just as well. She's inoperable anyway."

Samantha shot him a hard look. "I disagree, Doctor."

"Really, Dr. Hargrave, it hasn't been done! Opening her up for a tubal pregnancy is tantamount to killing her!"

As Samantha was about to reply, Letitia groaned and rolled her head. When her eyes fluttered open, it took her a moment to focus, then she whispered, "Dr. Hargrave . . ."

"Hello, Letitia," said Samantha, taking the girl's hand and squeezing it.

"Where . . . am I . . ."

"St. Brigid's. And you're going to be all right."

Letitia licked her dry lips, then rolled her head away to look at Dr. Weston. "I'm dying," she said.

"No, you're not," came his choked reply.

"Letitia," said Samantha, bringing the girl's wandering attention back, "do you know what is wrong with you?"

"No . . ."

"You need an operation, Letitia. And I want to do it. I think I can help you." Samantha bent close. "But Janelle won't give me permission. Letitia?"

"Save me . . ." breathed the girl. "Oh, God . . . save me . . ."

"Listen, Letitia. You stand a chance if I operate on you. Do you understand me? Letitia?"

"Yes," whispered the girl. "Do . . . what you must, Dr. Hargrave. Operate, please . . . save me . . ."

Samantha straightened and stared at Dr. Weston. He swallowed painfully.

❦

Up in the chilly operating room Samantha was instructing Mrs. Knight to have plenty of ice on hand when Landon Fremont came in. "What's this all about, Samantha?"

As she described Letitia's symptoms Dr. Fremont went to the table and looked at the girl. "You can't be serious."

"I'm going to do it, Landon."

"You'll kill her."

"And she'll die if we don't do something. I have a plan that I think will work. This ice, Landon—"

"Samantha," he said, turning and regarding her gravely, "the girl will die either way, so it's out of our hands. What is important, Samantha, is *where* the girl dies. If it's in a ward bed we can't be held responsible. But if it's up here, they'll say we murdered her."

"Landon, listen to me. No great step in medicine is taken without risks. I have done with standing by and watching these women die! I think I have a way to control the bleeding, with this ice. If it works, we can save her life. But we'll never know unless we try!"

"And what if you open her up and find your diagnosis was wrong? What if it is her appendix or some other bowel problem? We don't know how to repair any of those conditions, she will die, and in the meantime you have compromised your position here at St. Brigid's and have brought scandal to her family by claiming she was pregnant!"

Samantha inspected her instruments. "I am right in my diagnosis, Landon, and I know we can save her. But I need your help, I cannot do it alone."

He studied her long and hard, seeing the rigidity in her back and shoulders, the determined set of her head. Then he suddenly thought: If I'd wanted to stay safe I could have been an insurance clerk. "All right," he said finally. "We've come this far together, it would be a mockery of what we've worked for if I didn't stand by you now."

She smiled and said, "Thank you, Landon," but she thought: Oh, Mark, my love, if only you were here now! This is where we belong, working together. This is our future . . .

Getting to work, Samantha said to Dr. Weston, "A few drops at a time, please. No heavy pouring."

He nodded earnestly. One thing was certain, they weren't going to lose this patient because of *him*.

Under the gaslight Landon Fremont studied Samantha's features. This is either going to be the end of us or the start of us. I wish I had your courage, my girl.

She spread her fingers over Letitia's abdomen to make the skin taut, then brought down the scalpel.

There were moments when Landon thought sure the patient was lost— her pulse couldn't be found and bleeding was excessive—but Samantha pushed on, her lips compressed into a thin line. They continually packed ice into the wound, and as it melted, the sodden towels were removed and more ice applied. Remarkably, the bleeding abated. And Landon thought:

Of course . . .

"There," said Samantha softly. "The ruptured tube with the placenta protruding through. Now I shall tie the broad ligament . . ."

TEN

"WE'RE IN A HELL OF A LOT OF TROUBLE," SAID LANDON UN- happily.

Samantha nodded wearily; she hadn't slept all night, and the biting October dawn had not revitalized her. Letitia was still alive, but only barely so, and just a while ago the MacPhersons' attorney had joined Dr. Prince in his locked office. It didn't look good. It didn't look good at all. "I'm sorry, Landon, for getting you into this. But I had to go ahead, you know that."

He nodded as he looked around the staff dining room, thankful it was deserted at this early hour. "In hindsight, yes, I agree with you. But I still think that at the time you acted rashly. Experimental surgery like that must only be performed under ideal conditions."

"The girl is alive. That is all that matters."

"And we are being sued."

"We did nothing wrong," she said quietly. "Letitia gave me permission."

"It's your word against theirs, and as long as that girl lies in a coma, you haven't a chance."

"Dr. Weston is my witness."

Landon thought of saying something about that, about the fact that Weston was so afraid of Prince she shouldn't count on him; but he kept his silence.

The far door opened an inch and Dr. Weston peeked in. Seeing that the room was empty, he came all the way in and joined them at their table. He laid his folded newspaper to one side, rubbed his stubbled chin and said, "We're in for it now! What do you suppose they'll do to us?"

"You have nothing to worry about," said Landon. "You were only following orders."

Dr. Weston brightened briefly, then his face collapsed again. That was not what he was worried about. When Letitia MacPherson regained consciousness she was going to name the man responsible for her pregnancy, and Dr. Weston believed that his charms were the only ones Letitia had surrendered to.

"How is she doing?" he asked.

"Still in a coma."

"But alive, thank God." He looked hopefully at Samantha. "They won't prosecute once they learn from Letitia herself that she gave permission."

The tension in Samantha's soul invaded her hands; she absently picked at the edges of Dr. Weston's newspaper, thinking: I doubt it is as simple as that. Samantha knew something her two companions did not, that this issue had roots far below the surface, and that the cause of Janelle MacPherson's anger lay not so much with anything so vital as life and death or so grandiose as legal acrobatics but with a very primitive, age-old conflict: two women vying for the love of one man.

Dr. Prince's secretary materialized in the doorway and summoned Dr. Weston. After he left, Samantha tried to reassure Landon that he was in no danger, for she intended to take the brunt of Janelle's attack upon herself. But when Dr. Weston returned a few minutes later, Samantha betrayed her underlying nervousness. Her cup clattered back into its saucer. "That was fast. I suppose they hadn't many questions of you?"

"They didn't ask me any. They've gone. It was most peculiar. There they were, Miss MacPherson, that quack doctor of hers, two fancy lawyers, and

Dr. Prince. I had just sat down when Miss MacPherson gave out a sudden cry and fainted cold on the floor. They put her on Dr. Prince's couch and when she came to she claimed she couldn't go on and insisted on being taken home."

"What was the cause?"

"Near as I can tell, when I walked in the lady had been leaning forward looking at a newspaper on Prince's desk. That was when she cried out."

Landon picked up Dr. Weston's folded newspaper, opened it and exlaimed, "Good God!"

"What is it?"

"A ship is down!" He flattened the paper for the others to see and the sensational headline jumped out.

Samantha's heart stopped in her breast.

"'Ocean Liner Down at Sea,'" Weston read aloud. "It's the *Excalibur!*" He scanned the article below, muttering, "Hit an iceberg . . . all hands and passengers lost . . . no survivors—" He snapped his head up. "The *Excalibur!* Wasn't Mark Rawlins—"

The room started to spin. Muffled voices barely came through to her consciousness. Samantha groped for the edge of the table; she felt the cold, merciless waters of the Atlantic wash over her head and engulf her. The *Excalibur* gone, Mark gone, all in an instant; all in the time it takes to draw in a breath . . .

There were arms around her shoulders and then her nose drew in the acrid fumes of ammonia, her head cleared and all was in sharp focus again. She was still at the table and Landon was kneeling next to her, holding a bottle of smelling salts to her face. "There, there, old girl," he murmured. "Don't quit on us now."

She blinked at the two faces peering intently at her and mumbled, "He missed the boat, he's still alive . . ."

"Come on, old girl," said Landon, helping her to her feet. "You need some rest. You've been under a terrible strain these last twelve hours. Let me take you to your room."

Shakily, Letitia MacPherson clung to life. All the arts of modern medicine and one brave doctor had been used on her, it was now up to the girl herself. Samantha stayed at the patient's bedside almost around the clock, her staring gray eyes never leaving the sleeping face. She ate only when Mildred brought in a tray and forced food on her. Everyone assumed Samantha's silence to be due to the legal ax hanging over her; nothing was being done yet, everyone was waiting to see whether the girl lived. Only Silas Prince had made a step: he had given Samantha her formal dismissal notice. Officially she was no longer on the staff of St. Brigid's; however, she continued to sit by her patient and allowed herself occasionally to be sent upstairs to sleep. All the rest—the legal action and forcibly moving Samantha out of the interns' quarters—waited in suspension until something definite happened with Letitia.

The real tragedy lay not in Samantha's being persecuted for doing what she had believed in but in the injustice of her having to grieve in loneliness and solitude over the loss of the man she loved. Outwardly Samantha could only voice the usual regrets upon hearing of a colleague's death; internally she grieved to such a degree that she felt she, too, had drowned in those arctic waters. The frail hope that Mark might have missed the boat or that the imperfect news report had overlooked a few survivors died with each passing day. Deep in her soul she knew he was dead, just as she knew a part of her was dead.

The tragedy became all the greater when something she had only suspected became finally confirmed: Samantha was pregnant.

And she could tell no one. Louisa and Luther had taken Johann to meet his grandparents in Ohio; Landon Fremont was too distraught by the lawsuit to be a receptive ear. Twice Samantha had tried to see Clair but had been turned away by a stony-faced butler who informed her the family was in mourning and receiving no visitors. It was Janelle, dressed in black and supported by friends when she came to see the unconscious Letitia, who received the sympathy and kindness that rightfully belonged to Samantha. It wasn't fair; she had never in all her life felt so desolate, so alone.

Paradoxically, however, Mark's death saved her. Had the *Excalibur* not gone down, Janelle MacPherson would have gone ahead with her lawsuit regardless of Letitia's recovery, and she would have won (for, as it turned out, Letitia had no memory of asking Samantha to operate). But Mark's death halted her attack on Samantha long enough to give Letitia time to recover fully and be out of danger.

It was a miracle, everyone said: the staff of St. Brigid's roundly praised Samantha for what she had done. The issue of the lawsuit was quietly dropped and the girl was taken home to convalesce. No more words were exchanged between Samantha and the MacPhersons. It was as if she no longer existed and as if the incident had never taken place.

Only Silas Prince remained vindictive.

On the day of Letitia's dismissal from the hospital, Samantha received a written notice from the chief of staff that she might be granted reinstatement if she publicly apologized to him for the scandal she had caused.

ELEVEN

*H*ER IMPULSE WAS TO IGNORE THE KNOCK ON HER DOOR. The last of her things were packed; she was anxious to leave.

It had been painful, but Samantha had laid aside her pride and gone to Dr. Prince with an apology, for the sake of the certificate. She had found, however, that the reinstatement was conditional. Silas Prince, a man to savor victory (and wishing to dim some of the light on Samantha's success), had informed her that her term of internship had been extended. She wasn't ready, he had said pompously, to take on the responsibilities of a fully accredited surgeon; there was the matter of loyalty and obedience. She could have the certificate in six months.

Landon Fremont, seeing nothing objectionable about Prince's proposal, had tried to persuade Samantha to agree to it; but to no avail. She couldn't stay, was all she had said, she must leave, even if it meant giving up the precious certificate. And now she stood among her suitcases waiting for the carriage she had hired.

The knock on her door persisted, so Samantha went to answer it. Janelle MacPherson stood on the other side.

They regarded one another across the threshold and a hundred communications passed silently between them. Samantha stepped back, holding the door open, and Janelle walked in. Seeing the suitcases, she said, "You are leaving?"

"Yes."

"Why?"

Samantha was torn. Janelle seemed only a former enemy now, belonging to a battle that no longer raged; what they had fought over no longer existed, now she was simply another woman. Still, Samantha could not drop her guard. The wounds went too deep. She could not tell Janelle about Prince's decision and that she could not accept it because of her pregnancy. So she said simply, "I just wish to leave."

Janelle thrust her hand into her reticule and drew out a piece of paper, which she handed to Samantha. "I thought you should see this. It's a telegram from the steamship company confirming Mark's name on the passenger list and his death at sea."

Samantha tried to read it but the words blurred. She raised her head. "Why have you brought this to me?"

"In case you harbored any false hopes that he was still alive. I did." Janelle's voice broke.

Samantha handed back the telegram. "Thank you."

"I know you loved him, Dr. Hargrave. We both did. And I suspect there was more between you and Mark than a professional relationship. I even feared he was falling in love with you and . . . in my jealousy I hated you."

Samantha gazed at her with misted eyes.

Janelle tipped her chin proudly. "I suppose I never had a chance with him once you came along. You gave him something I could not. Sharing all this . . ." She waved an arm around the room, a gesture meant to encompass the hospital and the practice of medicine. "I'm afraid, Dr. Hargrave, I owe you an apology. And that is the other reason I have come. You saved Letitia's life. Now I understand everything. She has told me about . . . about her indiscretions. Thank you for saving her life, Dr. Hargrave."

Janelle reached again into her reticule and withdrew a small bundle, pressing it into Samantha's hand. "Letitia asked me to give this to you. It meant a great deal to her. It's the best way she knows of thanking you."

Samantha opened her hand. A hard object was nestled in a tissue wrap, and when she parted the paper, she found a blue-green stone about the size of a silver dollar.

"Letitia bought it years ago from Gypsies in a circus. They told her it was centuries old and that it would bring good luck to the bearer. There's a superstition attached to turquoise. Apparently the stone can change color. The legend goes that if the stone fades, one's luck has been drawn on it and the stone must be passed along to someone else. Letitia had it in her purse the night you operated on her."

The stone was a highly polished turquoise, the color of a robin's egg, with a curious veining down the center. A backing of yellow metal embraced it, as if the stone had once hung on a necklace.

Janelle added, "Letitia insists the stone is pale now. I do not see it, but my sister is very superstitious . . ."

Samantha curled her fingers around it, the tissue crackling. "Please thank her for me. I shall treasure it."

Janelle looked away, at the suitcases. "Where will you go?"

"Just . . . away." *To California. And a new life. There is nothing left for me here except painful memories. Out West there is hope for a new start.*

"Can I help in any way?"

Samantha thought a moment, then said, "Yes, please." She reached for an envelope that lay on her nightstand; it was sealed and addressed and awaiting a stamp. "Would you please give this to Mrs. Rawlins? I was afraid that if I mailed it she might not get it. I've tried to see her but she's receiving no one."

"Mrs. Rawlins has gone back up to Boston. Mark's death hit her harder than expected. She took ill and is now confined to bed. I'll gladly give her your letter, Doctor, and if there is anything else I can do . . ."

"You've done enough just by coming here."

They embraced briefly and in that moment Samantha felt a kinship with this woman who had once been her opponent; they held each other in deeply felt sympathy, for each suspected the other's pain as no one else could. And Samantha thought fleetingly how ironic it was that the long-awaited consoling embrace should finally come from her old enemy.

After Janelle had gone, Samantha pulled on her gloves and gave a last look around the room. She didn't know what awaited her in California, where her path would lead, for she had chosen that distant shore because it was so far away; Samantha knew only that she had to go, she had to find a place where her wounds would heal. And a place where the little life inside her, Mark's baby, could be born.

We shall start a new life together and part of Mark will be with me always . . .

PART FOUR
SAN FRANCISCO 1886

ONE

*S*AMANTHA DROPPED A PENNY INTO THE BOX, PICKED UP A taper candle, touched its wick to the flame of another candle, and fitted it firmly on a vacant prong. Then she rested her elbows on the prayer rail and, with her hands folded beneath her chin, gazed up into the sublime eyes of Mother Mary. Although she wasn't a Catholic, she had long ago discovered the peace and tranquillity of the Mission; two years ago the kindly priests had comforted her when her little daughter, Clair, had died in the diphtheria epidemic. Today was little Clair's birthday; she would have been three years old.

Tears filled Samantha's eyes as she gazed up into the sweet face of the Madonna. The flames from the many candles at the statue's feet broke into facets, shimmering through the prism of Samantha's tears. She was sad, she would never stop mourning the deaths of her baby and Mark, but the solace of this little chapel made the pain more bearable.

Beneath her dress, lying reassuringly upon her breast, was the strange stone Letitia had given her. When Samantha had looked closely at it, she had found it to be a most curious object.

It was not perfectly round, was encased in yellow metal, and had an inscription on the back in a foreign language. And there was a date, no longer decipherable because the engraving was so worn, and some unrecognizable symbols. The rusty veining down the face of the stone, when looked at one way, resembled the figure of a woman with her arms outstretched; another way, it looked like two snakes coiling up a tree. When Samantha had been able to afford it, she had gone to a jeweler to have a chain made for the stone. He had said it was very old and of some real value (he speculated it might have come from a region of the Sinai). He had also remarked on the rich color, a vivid blue.

It was Samantha's only tactile link with the past and frequently, when alone, she brought it out from under her clothing and caressed the smooth surface, an action which had a curiously tranquillizing effect.

In the early days after her arrival in San Francisco, Samantha had felt sharply alone and desolate, and she had found that a quiet hour of reflection and reminiscing brought, if not comfort, at least an easing of pain. Her fingers would gently stroke the polished face of the stone. As if the lingering energy of hundreds of hands down through the centuries caressing the stone imbued her with a special mind sight, Samantha would then relive in remarkable realism and vivid detail memories from her past.

She would close her eyes and be back on the Crescent again, under the brotherly protection of Freddy, and his voice would come through as if he were in the room with her ("If that owd fart ever so much as puts a feather to you I'll bash his corrupt owd brains in!"). From there her thoughts would travel other happy paths: her first days as Joshua's assistant, the idyllic months in medical school, delivering Louisa's baby, her nights in Mark's arms . . .

She took to standing back and surveying her life as if she were a geographer, and she saw now, from the vantage point of years and miles, that while her life until now had been remarkably full, there was one thing glaringly absent. And if she had not considered it before, she now dwelt upon it almost daily: *I am completely alone in the world. I can have friends, companions, even lovers, but I am not truly connected, blood-connected, to anyone.*

Samantha knew that it was the nature of her profession that was generating these thoughts; every day she had to deal in some way with family—with birth, mothers and babies, with siblings and offspring, with *family*. And every day brought sharp reminders that there was no one on earth to whom she could point and say: We sprang from the same font. The Hargraves were all gone now (even baby Clair) and of her mother's family Samantha knew nothing. In her years of growing up in the gloomy house on the Crescent she had never heard mention of Uncle So-and-so; no prying aunt or grandparent had come up the steps. It was as if Samantha Hargrave had sprung from a void. *I stand alone.*

A shifting at her side caused Samantha to look down at the child kneeling next to her, hands folded in imitation, face turned up to the Virgin, and Samantha smiled in loving sadness. *No, not entirely alone.* The Lord taketh and the Lord giveth, thought Samantha, as her heart went out to the little girl at her side.

It had been a year ago this very day, when Samantha had been on her way back home from her annual visit to the Mission, that she had been called off the street to help a woman in one of the tenements behind the Opera House. Samantha had hurried up the stairs in time to see an old Irish midwife pull a lifeless baby from its dying mother; she lay on newspapers, and rats darted out from under the floor boards to drag the placenta off. In the corner stood a skinny little girl, with eyes too big for her head, looking mutely upon the wretched scene, sucking all the fingers of one hand. The poor woman died then and the old midwife complained that she would have to take in the half-wit brat; it had no father or relatives to look after it.

Despite severe malnutrition and a coating of filth, there was something enchanting about the child's Gypsy face, something in the way she looked up at Samantha, that had stirred the maternal yearnings which had not died with little Clair. "Touched by the fairies, that one is," the midwife had grumbled, already stitching the shroud. "The only one of Megan's brats to live and it don't talk. Just stares and stares, making folks nervous."

Samantha never learned how old the child was, but guessed eight years; her name was Jennifer. So Samantha had taken the child home, adopted her and given her the name of Hargrave. *If we must be alone, then we shall be alone together . . .*

A brown hem and leather sandals whispered over the tile floor as Brother Dominic came to a halt in the nearby shadows. He smiled benevolently at the two at Mary's altar. The doctress had been coming here for almost four years now—he recalled when she first appeared, clearly pregnant, lighting a candle for her husband drowned at sea. And he had hoped, in those four years, to convert her officially to Catholicism. But the doctress seemed a little afraid of a formal declaration, preferring to come instead when the soul hungered. She worshiped in her own fashion. Well, Brother Dominic didn't press it. The look on her face told him she truly loved the Blessed Virgin and the serenity she derived from these visits told him the Virgin was answering.

Little Jennifer shifted on the hard wooden kneeler and Samantha stroked the child's thick black curls. Jennifer was deaf and couldn't talk and so Samantha had never been able to explain to her the meaning of this ritual; but the child patiently joined in because she saw something that no one else did: that the face of the statue was identical to that of the lady kneeling next to her. Little Jenny, in a peculiar wisdom, knew that Samantha came here in part to talk to her own mother.

"We have to go now, Jenny," murmured Samantha; she always spoke to the girl even though she couldn't hear.

Samantha hated to leave the Mission; she loved the incense, the seventeenth-century statues, the carved altars from Mexico. But she knew there would be patients waiting for her. Samantha rarely closed her office, rarely did anything for herself, but these visits were essential to her peace of mind—when she grew afraid or lonely or yearning for the past, she would come here and be comforted. But an hour was all she could spare.

As a physician among the working classes of San Francisco, at first Samantha had had a hard time: the city on the Golden Gate could be hard on a woman on her own, especially a pregnant one. But she had rented a flat on Kearny Street, and the slow business of starting a medical practice had begun. They were suspicious of her at first, since the majority of San Francisco's female "doctors" were abortionists, but gradually word spread and they came to her, mostly working women and some prostitutes, some paying, many not. At times Samantha had suffered desolate, grieving nights.

Then she had found the Mission and her old spirit had returned. Her practice grew and she became more financially comfortable. She delivered her own baby all alone in her upstairs bedroom and saw at once that the baby had Mark's big brown eyes. And then when little Clair, barely a year old, had fallen victim to the diphtheria epidemic, Samantha had operated on her little throat to let her breathe but it had been too late. The baby was buried in a cemetery on a hill overlooking the ocean, but Samantha never visited the grave. Little Clair wasn't there, she was here, in the loving care of the Mother of Heaven.

They left the Mission by way of the garden, for it was summer and the whitewashed adobe walls were ablaze with purple and scarlet bougainvillea; clustered around the ancient gravestones were bursts of fuchsias and hibiscus; and along the pebbled paths were poinsettias and ferns and mosses. Just a last reminder, as one left the Mission, of God's promise of life.

As Samantha headed for Market Street with Jenny's little hand in hers, she felt her soul expand in the summer sun. After the early trials and tribulations, her old optimism and enthusiasm had come back. Although at first she had been homesick, Samantha had never thought of returning to New York; going "back" was not a solution, she must keep pressing forward to her destiny and better days. Although they had corresponded frequently at first, her letters from Landon Fremont dwindled, and when he went to Vienna to live and teach, they stopped coming altogether. Coincidentally, Luther took Louisa and Johann and baby Gretchen back to Germany where he opened a pharmacy in Munich. The ties eventually broke down until there was no longer a link with New York.

Samantha was content to be severed from that part of her life, filled with such struggle and painful memories; and she had grown fond of San Francisco. Only on rare occasions did she look back—on milestone days when she would look at the calendar and think: Today is Mark's birthday, he would have been thirty-three; or, Today the *Excalibur* went down, I shall take Jenny to light a candle. Mark was allowed into her late night thoughts and into her dreams, but he was kept apart from the demanding daily routine, for always his memory stole a little of her strength and rendered her vulnerable. Samantha would never stop loving him, mourning him, but the business of living had to have first consideration.

The July sun was warm and invigorating, the bustling city an inspiration; Samantha always enjoyed their walk to and from the Mission. Today, however, as she picked her way along the wooden sidewalk with little Jenny in tow, she felt her usual after-Mission jubilation cloud a little. Of late she had discovered, to her mild alarm, a growing restlessness of spirit.

As they passed the new Crocker Woolworth Building, listening to the clang of the Market Street trolley, Samantha considered this curious new restlessness and wondered what its cause might be.

Was it possibly yearning for a man? She thought not. Her days of passionate love were over, they had ended with Mark's death. And besides, she certainly wasn't lacking for male attention. Even though she was twenty-six and past the bloom of her youth, Samantha still received declarations of affection and proposals of marriage—some from grateful patients (she'd learned that a man will sometimes mistake gratitude for relief from pain as love), some from men in the neighborhood (Mr. Finch, the widower pharmacist, nearly fell over his counter every time she came in). She had received one proposal from the kindly policeman on the beat (Derry McDonough, who had once defended her against a charge of running an abortion business). They had all insisted that Samantha couldn't possibly survive on her own, that she needed a man.

No, it wasn't want of a man that made Samantha's soul restless. It had to be something else, something that had nothing to do with earning a living, with making a comfortable home, companionship, friends, for Samantha had all these things. What, then, could possibly be missing?

At first San Francisco had bewildered and overwhelmed her. A city of bizarre little communities, from Chinatown with its strange little men in dishpan hats, pigtails and floppy blue pajamas to the rum-crazed sailors on the Barbary Coast, from the wedding-cake mansions up on Nob Hill down to the houses of prostitution near Portsmouth Square where as many as four hundred girls were crammed into cribs like caged animals, San Francisco had been like stepping into a foreign country. And so Samantha had had to struggle to survive. Then she had had to struggle for acceptance and respectability; then the fight for baby Clair's life, and later the challenge of finding a pathway of communication to Jennifer. All four years had been filled with constant strife and struggle. But now it was over; she was accepted, she was comfortable.

Perhaps, Samantha thought, I am *too* comfortable.

They made their way along the crowded Kearny Street sidewalk, with Samantha hoping Mrs. Keller would be sober enough to cook supper, when she became aware of a commotion up ahead. A fine carriage was parked along the curb and a small crowd of children had gathered to gawk.

Samantha thought: I suppose Miss Seagram has an eminent visitor today.

When she rented the flat four years before, she had been pleased to see that her adjoining neighbor was a lady daguerreotypist who apparently had a prosperous business, judging by her clothes and the quality of the oval portraits displayed in her bay window; but as time went by Samantha had noticed that Miss Seagram's customers were all men, that they stayed a long time (sometimes overnight), and that none of them were ever seen leaving the establishment with pictures under their arms.

When Samantha drew up to the foot of her steps she was surprised to find a lady's maid awaiting her at the top, and then learned that the carriage was not there for Miss Seagram at all but had brought a mysterious patient in search of medical help.

TWO

ESPITE THE WARM JULY WEATHER THE WOMAN WAS COVERED from head to foot in a luxurious wool cape, the hood of which fell forward and hid her face. As she was helped from the carriage and then climbed laboriously up the steps, as though in great pain, it was impossible to guess her age; but one thing was certain, the mysterious woman was very wealthy.

Samantha took her into the little parlor off the examining room where she frequently interviewed patients: the lace curtains and vases of fresh-cut flowers often put the most anxious woman at ease. This curious woman now took a seat on a little brocaded chair, sitting gingerly, and Samantha knew at once why she had come.

She closed the door and sat on the other chair while the woman's maid stood behind her mistress. Then a voice came from under the hood, cultured and refined, and Samantha was surprised at its youthfulness. "Are you Dr. Hargrave?"

"I am."

Gloved hands appeared from under the cape; they untied the cord and drew the cape off her shoulders, revealing an exquisite day gown of powder-blue satin with mother-of-pearl buttons. The hood fell back to disclose a lovely face, young and smooth, but spoiled by signs of pain and exhaustion; premature lines, violet smudges under the blue eyes, and a paleness that was not becoming indicated how very ill this young woman was.

"Dr. Hargrave, I have an intimate problem and I have been to several doctors who say I cannot be helped. My personal maid told me about you. She suffered terribly from cramps, to the point at times of being unable to get out of bed, and when I sent her to my own physician, he told her she was imagining it. She had heard of you, Doctor, from one of my seamstresses and so she came to you and you cured her. Her name is Elsie Withers."

Samantha recalled the case. A simple scraping of the uterus had relieved much of the problem and Samantha had added a regimen of exercise and daily doses of camomile tea.

"She spoke very highly of you, Doctor, and so I . . ."

Samantha spoke gently, for the woman was clearly under great strain. "If you will permit me to examine you, I can tell whether or not I can help."

"Yes . . . of course . . ."

At St. Brigid's Samantha had seen many sufferers with this condition, and until Landon Fremont joined the staff and introduced the perfected Sims technique, the poor creatures had been sentenced to suffer the agonies of hell for the rest of their lives. It was called the vesicovaginal fistula, a little passageway between the bladder and vagina usually caused by a difficult childbirth, and it was one of the worst calamities that could befall a woman. A hole in the vaginal wall allowed a constant dribble of urine into the vagina, causing unbearable inflammation which could not be cured; soon, pustulous eruptions developed which gave off a powerful odor and which no amount of cleansing could get rid of. As a result, the poor victim dared not go outside, for her petticoats would soon be soaked and the odor would drive people away from her. Sufferers from the vesicovaginal fistula ultimately were restricted to their beds, for they could not even sit on a chair for long without getting the seat wet, and in bed their sheets were soon soaked with urine. They developed sores all over their delicate parts, pain and constant drainage created a torture that no one could imagine; no one would visit the poor woman, for to be in the room was soon unbearable, and the worst tragedy was that she knew she was doomed to suffer like this the rest of her life—an invalid, isolated from friends and family, loathsome even to herself. Many such cases ended in suicide.

When Samantha saw to what extent the erosion had gone in this poor young woman, she wanted to cry; back in the parlor after they resumed their seats she gently asked a few questions. "When did it happen?"

"It happened a year last Christmas while I was giving birth to my daughter. It was the fault of the forceps; they tore me."

Samantha nodded in understanding, masking an instant flare of anger. So many male obstetricians were taking to employing forceps to hurry up deliveries, not content to wait and let nature do its job, anxious to meddle and thus earn their fee. This poor woman was not the only victim of such unnecessary intervention. "How old are you?"

"Twenty-four."

"Have you other children?"

Tears rose in the delicate blue eyes, the lips trembled. "Merry was my first. And she will be my last—"

"You say you have seen other physicians?"

"They told me I couldn't be helped." She leaned forward, her voice earnest. "Dr. Hargrave, you have no idea the nightmare my life has become. I spend all my days in my room, for I cannot go outside, nor even into the other rooms of our house in case I should soil the furniture. My husband has taken another bedroom and we have stopped having relations. Elsie is my only companion, I refuse to allow my friends in, for I know how offensive I am. I must change my skirt several times a day and all the bathing and douching cannot cleanse me of this odor. And the burning, Doctor! The burning keeps me awake at night until I think I shall go insane or kill myself!"

Samantha studied the intense face, the desperate eyes, and her heart went out to her. "I believe I can help," she said quietly. "But it will require surgery."

"Surgery . . ." The smooth forehead gathered in a frown. "I would rather not go into a hospital, Doctor, but if that is the only way . . ."

"I will do it here, in my office."

The relief was palpable in the air. "Can you truly, Doctor? And what is the surgery?"

Briefly Samantha described the procedure she had learned from Dr. Fremont, who had been taught by the great Dr. Sims, its inventor. Because it was so new and revolutionary an operation and because Sims was unpopular with the conservative medical establishment, his procedures were having slow acceptance across the country, which accounted for why the other doctors this woman had seen had not thought to attempt it. Either they were unaware of its existence or had not been trained in it.

"However, I cannot guarantee success. The erosion has progressed to a critical stage. There is even a possibility I could make the condition worse."

"I will take that chance, Doctor. How soon can you do it?"

"Since it will require ether and since the sutures are so delicate, you will have to convalesce here. Ten days, I should say. Is that all right?"

"I will tell my husband I have to visit my sister in Sacramento."

Reading Samantha's puzzled expression, the young woman looked down at her hands. "Dr. Hargrave, I must confess something to you. My husband does not know I am here. And if he were to find out he would be furious. He thinks women doctors are quacks and that you would butcher me."

"And what do you think?"

She raised her head and gazed steadily at Samantha. "I believe you can help me."

"Then come back when you are ready. And please bring Elsie with you. My daughter Jenny will also help."

⁂

Her name was Hilary Gant and her final words to Samantha before Elsie placed the ether cone over her face were, "If anything should happen to me, my maid has instructions. You will not be implicated, Doctor, no blame will come to your doorstep, I promise."

Samantha smiled and kept a hand on Mrs. Gant's shoulder until she was asleep. Don't worry about me, she thought, keeping an eye on Elsie and the ether. I have weathered such gales before. Let us worry about you and getting you well again. "Just a few drops, Elsie. Stop now and watch her eyelids. If they flutter, dribble a little more on."

Elsie was pale-faced and trembling, but Samantha's calmness gave her confidence. She smiled bravely and held the bottle next to Hilary's face; her mistress wasn't going to suffer another second of pain.

Jennifer obediently held the vaginal retractors while Samantha worked. The mute girl was used to helping in the office; she needed be shown only once and she never forgot. Unquestioning, uncurious, Jenny never flagged at any task set before her, but kept to it diligently and devotedly, as she did now, standing until her legs hurt and her fingers grew cramped around the retractors. Her big eyes watched as Samantha's hands moved deftly and swiftly.

Samantha worked with great care, making sure the edges of the wound were drawn together precisely and that the silver sutures, when quilled, did not tear the delicate tissue. Finally, she inserted one of the new self-retaining catheters and sat back with a sigh, saying, "We've done all we can here, ladies. She's in God's hands now."

She and Elsie carried the unconscious woman into the downstairs bedroom and laid her gently on the fresh sheets. It was a pleasant room, outfitted with thought for the mending of the spirit as well as the body: fresh flowers, pretty pictures and a colorful counterpane were as essential to healing, Samantha thought, as basins and bandages and stethoscope. For the first two nights Samantha slept on a cot brought into the room; after that Elsie slept there, vigilant, for the sutures were delicate and easily dislodged.

Hilary Gant lay in Samantha's guest bedroom for nine days, a docile and uncomplaining patient. She was fed, bathed and cared for by Elsie and silently suffered Samantha's thrice-daily examination. There was little communication between doctor and patient; the few minutes they spent together were subdued and professional. In the meantime, Samantha continued to see patients in her office and make house calls, and at the end of the ninth day Samantha removed the silver sutures; on the tenth day she declared Hilary Gant cured and sent her home.

It was a week later when the note arrived, written on exquisite stationery, an invitation to tea. The address was California Street, Nob Hill.

THREE

*S*AMANTHA HAD SEEN THE MANSION FROM THE STREET DURING one of her walks around the city and had paused to stare at the square palace that rose up from green lawns; she had wondered about the people who dwelt there. But now, driving through the wrought-iron gate in the Gants' carriage, Samantha could see close up the towering gables and turrets and gaudy decoration around the many windows and eaves, and she was filled with a feeling she was calling on royalty.

In a way she was. The Gants of California Street belonged to one of the oldest and wealthiest families in San Francisco.

She was led by a Chinese houseboy down a hall of stained glass windows, gilt mirrors, imported dark woods, oriental carpets, ferns and statuary; and then the sliding doors of the drawing room opened to reveal an incredible display of opulence and extravagance.

Four massive bay windows, their panes so clear as to appear nonexistent, allowed the afternoon sun to fill the room to every corner, spotlighting the crystal chandelier, the polished tops of mosaic-inlaid tables, silver and gold objects, glazed Chinese ceramics, red velvet drapes, gold upholstery, sprays of roses and lilacs. It was a showcase of ostentation and snobbery, the handiwork of people who cared not so much how they displayed their wealth but simply that they did.

In the center of it all, like a queen in her throne room, Hilary Gant rose gracefully with a rustling of twenty yards of silk. For an instant Samantha didn't recognize her. During her ten-day stay with Samantha, Mrs. Gant had made not the slightest show of her social and financial standing; she had arrived plainly dressed and had lain in bed in a simple nightgown. But here, surrounded by palatial splendor, Hilary Gant dazzled the eye with her rich auburn hair swept atop her head and fixed with diamond pins, her cinnamon silk day gown catching and tossing off summer sunlight, and diamonds at her ears and fingers, winking like stars. She glided toward Samantha with her hands held out, came to rest before her and smiled speechlessly with mist in her eyes. As Samantha offered her hands and they clasped, Hilary whispered, "Dr. Hargrave . . ."

They gazed at one another for a moment; they could have been two women anywhere, in the middle of a laundry room, on the prairie grass of a farmstead, for they had no differences, united in a basic mutual regard that observed no social barriers. The unspoken gratitude glowing in Hilary's blue eyes reminded Samantha that that was exactly what she lived for: she could wish for nothing better.

"I am *so* glad you could come," Hilary murmured.

"The honor and pleasure are all mine, Mrs. Gant."

The sapphire eyes continued to gaze at Samantha, speaking more than words ever could, and through her gloves Samantha felt the warmth and firmness of Hilary's grasp. "For what you did for me, Dr. Hargrave, I should go down on my knees before you."

"You are embarrassing me, Mrs. Gant."

Hilary indulged herself in a final squeeze of Samantha's hands, then stepped back. "Please have a seat, Doctor, and take tea with me."

"I'm afraid I can't stay long, Mrs. Gant. I've left my daughter in the care of the lady next door, and if Miss Seagram should have an unexpected customer, Jenny will have to go out."

The tea was served from a silver samovar so highly polished that the whole room was reflected in it in miniature. Samantha sat on an antique Biedermeier chair and accepted the cup of Sevres china.

"Your daughter," said Mrs. Gant wonderingly. "You must have had her at a very early age, Doctor!"

Samantha laughed. "You flatter me, for I assure you I am old enough to have a nine-year-old. But she is adopted, and has been with me for a year, I had a little girl, once, but she died in the diphtheria epidemic . . ."

"Oh, I am sorry. I understand how you must feel. My own little Merry Christmas is the most precious thing to me in the world. I don't know what . . ."

She fell silent, her gaze settling on the surface of her tea so that, for a moment, the only sound in the room was the ticking of the clock as both women reflected fleetingly upon babies and life and loss. Then Hilary, the gracious hostess, artfully lightened the moment. "My joy in seeing you again, dear Dr. Hargrave, has made me forget my purpose for inviting you here." She picked up an envelope which was embossed with a crest and handed it over. Samantha put down her cup, took the envelope and opened it. Inside was a check for one thousand dollars.

Stunned, she stared at the piece of paper. Her fee for the operation had been fifty dollars. In the fraction it takes to blink, Samantha considered refusing the check and then she remembered the tuition needed for the School for the Deaf in Berkeley that would take Jenny next year. Samantha murmured, "Thank you, Mrs. Gant," and carefully folded the envelope into her reticule.

"It is not enough, Doctor. If I could give you a million dollars I would, and still it would not be enough. You saved my life. And you saved my marriage." The blue eyes glistened. "Mr. Gant has moved back into my bedroom . . ."

Samantha turned her gaze to the bay windows and looked out at the breathtaking view of the sweep of San Francisco Bay. Over gabled rooftops she saw an expanse of blue water, dots of boats with little wakes, and on the other side, olive-green hills rolling up to a blue sky. We think these gods and goddesses in their hilltop palaces haven't a worry in the world, but after all they are human and burdened with the same afflictions as the humblest woman . . .

The sliding doors opened and a prim nanny in a crisp uniform brought in a toddler with a head of reddish curls. Samantha's heart experienced a pang: little Merry Christmas wasn't much older than Clair had been when she died.

Hilary got up and gathered the cherub into her arms, chattering baby talk, while Samantha smiled and recalled the day, a year ago, when she had brought the mute Jenny home. She had been a marvel from the start. Once washed, the child's natural beauty had come forth like a spring moon. Her hair sat on her head like a fluffy cap of lamb's wool; her skin was dusky and unblemished; her face exotic. Her docile nature both intrigued and perplexed Samantha, for as a rule slum children grew up wild; Jenny was meek and submissive, and she never smiled.

At Christmas the girl hadn't known what to do with the doll Samantha gave her, and in April she had received the chocolate Easter egg with total passivity. Once, Samantha had taken Jenny to the ocean; they rode the horse-omnibus all the way out to Seal Point and watched the waves crash on the rocks beneath the Cliff House; Jenny had not been moved. But her eyes, sharp and curious, had taken it all in—the seals, the gulls, the spray of the ocean—and when Samantha took her hand to go home, Jenny had meekly turned away and walked to the horse-bus without looking back.

She was a strange, withdrawn child, protected by a silent barrier, trusting and lamblike, but watching, always watching. Suspecting she was intelligent and not retarded, Samantha had tried to teach Jenny the alphabet and simple arithmetic but had failed, nor had she found the doorway into the child's heart. Jenny was like a blank slate waiting to be written upon.

Merry Christmas started to cry and startled Samantha from her thoughts. The nanny took the child from Hilary's arms, there was a fuss of kissing and cooing, and when they were gone, Hilary sat back down and laughed merrily. "My, but children are exhausting!"

There was a moment of silence as they sipped their tea, both women comfortable with each other, and at peace, and in that pause Samantha visualized faces from the past—Elizabeth Blackwell, Louisa, Estelle Masefield,

Hannah—and she felt her soul rock a little, as she had twice felt the city of San Francisco move; a tremor, a small quake of the heart, as she recalled with affection those dear friends who had walked the road with her part of the way, joining her for a while and then leaving. And now Samantha found herself suddenly yearning once more for companionship along that road. She studied the gentle features of Hilary Gant, a woman who, despite her trappings of wealth, was free of affectations and snobbery, a fresh and honest young woman who seemed unencumbered by a need to remind the world of her position. Samantha was suddenly curious about her, suddenly wanting to know everything about her, and found herself, in that instant, wanting to be Hilary's friend.

To protect herself after Mark's death and the incidents at St. Brigid's, Samantha had learned to hold herself at a distance, opening up rarely. But now, for the first time in four years, she felt herself reaching out, a soul yearning, a heart hungering; and by the miracle of coincidence, she had chosen well, for Hilary Gant, a little in awe of this woman doctor in the plain dress, was wanting the same thing.

But since it is hard to say, "Please be my friend," small steps first were taken. Hilary cleared her throat and said, "I think the worst part of my affliction this past year, Dr. Hargrave, has been the mortal shame of having to expose myself to scornful male physicians. They had no sympathy whatsoever. It was they who damaged me in the first place and then they abandoned me."

Spoken without bitterness, a simple statement. Samantha wondered at the compassion of this young woman who could suffer so in body and spirit and yet hold no rancor in her heart. "Elsie told me about you months ago, Dr. Hargrave, and it took me all that time to decide to see you. I have never known a woman doctor before and the only one I have heard of in this city has, well, a *questionable* practice. To be frank, I was afraid of you. Then I reached the bottom; I could not stand one more of Dr. Roberts' treatments. He had been applying leeches to my vagina, leaving them on until I begged for mercy. I decided then that I would rather die than let him touch me ever again. Elsie finally convinced me to go to you. And you worked a miracle."

"My only miracle, Mrs. Gant, is that I am a woman."

"To be able to do what you do, Doctor, is a profound gift. When I was younger, before I married Mr. Gant, I longed to accomplish such as what you have, but it had to remain only a dream, for in my world there was but one path open to me." The touch of sadness in Hilary's voice suffused the moment with intimacy; Samantha sensed she was confessing something she had told no one else. "Please do not mistake me, Doctor, I love my husband very much and I have a wonderful, fulfilled life. But sometimes, when I sit and watch the fog roll into the bay, I wonder . . ."

The shadows on the carpet were growing long; Samantha glanced at the clock that chimed on the mantel.

Hilary caught the gesture. "I am keeping you, Doctor."

"It's my daughter I'm concerned about. The woman I have left her with could only promise an hour and Jenny cannot take care of herself. I truly wish I could stay longer. Indeed, I feel I could sit endless hours with you, Mrs. Gant!"

Hilary's eyes smiled in gratitude. "Then we shall do just that. And from now on I shall send all my friends to you. I know of one who suffers abominably because she refuses to be seen by a male physician. I believe, Dr. Hargrave, she would be comfortable with you." Hilary added quietly, "As I was."

They rose and Hilary said anxiously, "Can you come for dinner Sunday? I told my husband about you and what you did for me and he has asked to meet you."

"I should love to."

Hilary walked her to the front door where they clasped hands again, standing among the potted palms and dark wood and smiling at one another in silent confirmation of what had happened and, most important, what they sensed was yet to come.

Thus it began. The next day Kearny Street was treated to yet another stunning coach-and-four, as an elegant lady in wine velvet hurried up the steps to Samantha's office, her face discreetly veiled.

Dahlia Mason was twenty-eight years old and, after seven years of marriage, still childless. Every prominent physician in San Francisco had interviewed her and then pronounced her barren, the result of which had been a cooling of her husband's ardor and a straining of her own nerves. She had been leery of this woman doctor, fearful of quackery, but Hilary's cure was so stupendous that Dahlia Mason had screwed up the courage to come.

The first thing Samantha learned was that none of the physicians had examined her physically; another was Mrs. Mason's total ignorance of the mechanics of conception. After examining her and discovering that Mrs. Mason had a tipped uterus—a condition the other doctors could not have known about without having examined her—Samantha then drew a simple diagram and delicately explained how the abnormal tilt of the womb prohibited conception. Her advice was simple and easy to follow: "Remain on your back for at least half an hour after relations with your husband and do not douche as is your habit. I cannot guarantee this will make you pregnant, for your infertility might be the result of other causes unrevealed to me, but if this is your only problem, then there is no reason why you cannot have children."

Dahlia Mason left in uncertainty, for Dr. Hargrave had given her no pills, no bitter medicine, nothing to make her feel she had done anything tangible, and the idea that so serious a condition could be cured by so simple a solution had Dahlia Mason half convinced the visit had been a waste of time. But she did try Samantha's advice the next time she had relations with her husband, thinking she had nothing to lose, and then each time after that until she learned she was pregnant.

The news made the society columns and Samantha Hargrave found herself a celebrity again.

But it was not the humble miracle she had worked on Dahlia Mason that catapulted Samantha, almost overnight, into San Francisco society; rather, it was her friendship with Hilary Gant. Drawn to one another in a mutual need and attraction that could not be denied, they each filled an absence in the other's life, so Samantha found herself a frequent guest at the house on Nob Hill where she became familiar with San Francisco's peculiar aristocracy.

Lacking inbred finesse and polish, their show of wealth was gaudy, mimicking a social stratum they knew nothing about. San Francisco's "society" was nouveau riche, enthusiastic and resilient, mobile and future-looking, and proud of their mean beginnings. Darius Gant, Hilary's husband, was their best example: a big, rough-edged, lovable bear of a man who had made his fortune in the Con-Virginia shaft and at the faro-bank table. Hilary's father, a forty-niner who had come over on the S.S. *California* and was one of the founders of San Francisco's aristocracy, had had high hopes for his eldest daughter, but when she fell in love with this bombastic, earthy millionaire, the old snob had given in, grudgingly admiring the down-home honesty of the man. And Samantha liked him, too, from the start. Darius had financial interests in every facet of the California boom: wine, cigars, oysters, railroads and, of late, oranges from Los Angeles. He was an intriguing, colorful and generous man, a supporter of the arts and anxious to show off his taste for the latest fads. But at heart Darius Gant remained a poor country boy who had come to California with a dream: he still laughed out loud during *The Marriage of Figaro.*

Samantha managed to spare time every week to spend with Hilary, in a leisure she had not known since her days of roaming the Crescent with Freddy; and she was exposed to a San Francisco she had not known existed. Hilary could not do enough for her new friend: they went to see Mr. Isaac Magnin and ordered a new wardrobe for Samantha, then to the City of Paris for accessories and "unmentionables"; but when they went to Gump's for a set of china and to Shreve and Company for a "fountain" pen, Samantha finally put a stop to the extravagant spending. Hilary took Samantha horseback riding in Golden Gate Park where they alternated sidesaddles—one with a right, the other with a left pommel—in order to maintain symmetrical muscular development, after which Samantha was introduced to the new popular sport of archery, Hilary's passion. And since new friends are often like new lovers, the two were soon spending every Monday together, their day culminating in a late luncheon at a discreet Montgomery Street restaurant that catered to unescorted ladies.

It was at Chez Pierre that Samantha learned to open up to her new friend and give voice to her inner life and professional concerns.

"Your friends, Hilary," she said as they munched cucumber sandwiches and sipped Oolong tea. "They are harassing me to move my office. They claim they don't like coming down into that neighborhood. I suppose I don't blame them, but if I move, then how will my working-class patients get to me? If I take an office uptown they will have to spend trolley fare to get to me. I am close to them now, convenient. I maintain that it is easier for your friends to come to me than it would be for my poorer patients to come to a new office."

"Then don't move," said Hilary simply.

"That's not the only problem. My patient load is getting so large I can hardly handle it. I have to turn away many major operations. Minor surgery I can handle, but the more involved cases I must send to someone else because I don't have a certificate, and I deplore that."

Hilary nodded. She knew all about Samantha not receiving her certificate from St. Brigid's, and why. It seemed a silly technicality to her, keeping a marvelous surgeon out of San Francisco's hospitals. While they ate and talked, Hilary was formulating an idea.

Samantha went on: "And the epidemic of ignorance among my patients is appalling! Not just among the lower-class women, Hilary, but among your friends as well. You would be surprised how many of your friends believe that wearing a necklace of garlic will keep them from having a baby! I know one woman who thinks if she lies perfectly still during intercourse and doesn't enjoy it she won't conceive!" Samantha took a sip of her tea but didn't taste it. "I don't know, Hilary, if only there were some way I could teach them. Right now I am so hurried, it is all I can do to examine and prescribe. I don't have time to sit and talk to each individual woman as I would like."

Hilary took another bite of her sandwich, and said, "My dear Samantha, the solution is so obvious, so perishingly plain, that it is plainer than the nose on your face."

"And what is that solution?"

"Open your own hospital."

Samantha blinked at her. "Do what?"

Thrilled that she had come up with an idea that suddenly sounded brilliant, Hilary spoke quickly. "A hospital. *For* women, operated *by* women. You could do all the surgery you wanted, hire on a staff and have time to counsel women. It's really so simple, darling. I'm surprised we haven't thought of it before!"

Samantha stared at Hilary's smiling face and suddenly it all came clear, like clouds parting to reveal the sun: the restlessness she had experienced on her way home from the Mission. This was what was missing from her life—a new step, a new challenge to give focus to her days.

"My own hospital!"

"You could make your own rules, hire anyone you wish—"

"An intern program, nurses' training, free inoculations, counseling. Oh, Hilary, can we do it?"

"Of course we can!"

Their hands clasped across the table. The current that passed between them jolted them both, and in that instant Samantha and Hilary knew why their paths had converged into one; this was their mutual purpose, their reason for being, and in that split moment they both saw the vision and both knew, without having to say so, that the plan would succeed, that *they* would succeed.

FOUR

*Y*OU'LL NEVER DO IT, DR. HARGRAVE. THE ENTIRE PLAN IS SIMPLY not feasible." Samantha stared at the man who spoke. LeGrand Mason, Dahlia's banker husband, was a stocky, barrel-shaped man who liked to make pronouncements with a finality that suggested he was the end authority in all things. But it was not his manner that disturbed Samantha just now, it was the fact that he was repeating what she had already heard, first from Darius and then from the Gants' attorney, Stanton Weatherby. These three financial experts had separately examined her proposed plan and had flatly pronounced it impossible.

Samantha rose from her chair, crossed the room and went to the bay window. The hour was late, the city swathed in fog; through the mist, from its unseen source, came the mournful lowing of the Fort Point foghorn. By listening carefully for a minute, one could tell by the duration of the bleats the position and location of the fogbank. Samantha shivered and rubbed her arms, even though the Gants' parlor was warmed by a blazing fire.

Her chill, she knew, came from within. From the cold fear that her dream, so recently born, was about to perish.

From the moment of its conception at Chez Pierre, the hospital had been struggling for survival. Samantha and Hilary had researched the structure and operation of various hospitals around the country and then had drafted a projected financial plan of their own. But the sheet, it turned out, was sadly unbalanced: too much outgo and very little income. LeGrand Mason had worked out on paper the discouraging projection that, in less than six months' time, the San Francisco Infirmary for Women and Children would be bankrupt.

"No one is going to invest in a losing venture," he said now behind her. "If you charge each patient a fee, then you'll have all the investors you need."

She turned. "Mr. Mason, it is ludicrous to expect a charity hospital to turn a profit. Our financial backers, sir, will not be investors but *donors*."

❧

"It can't be done. Granted, you'll get the Crockers and the Stanfords to give monetary gifts for the founding of the hospital, but you cannot expect them to regularly pour money into it. A charity hospital is a *drain*, Doctor. You must aim for profit."

"The profit, Mr. Mason, will be human life."

He looked for support to Darius, who said, "Samantha, you might raise enough money to get the hospital started, but you'll never keep it going. And then you won't even have the profit of human life."

"It can be done, Darius. I'll manage the money."

"How?"

"Hilary and I have some ideas. Charity bazaars, raffles, pledge drives. And, of course, we plan to ask the state for a grant."

"That will cover one month's operating expense."

"Fine, then all we have to worry about are the other eleven."

Darius shook his head and returned to staring into the fire. He liked Samantha Hargrave, admired her spirit and optimism (privately he gave her his highest compliment: she was as good as a man), but her stubbornness annoyed him. And it had infected his wife. Ever since the two had become friends Hilary was a little headstrong herself.

Silence filled the room as the five occupants sat deep in thought, listening to the distant foghorns warn ships off the rocks in the bay. LeGrand Mason stood at the fireplace impatiently drumming his fingers on the mantel. He was not opposed to the idea of the Infirmary—in fact, ever since Dr. Hargrave had worked the miracle of Dahlia's pregnancy, LeGrand couldn't do enough to aid her in her wonderful work. But the problem was, Samantha was not going about it the right way. *He* was the banker, the expert here; she should listen to him. Charity hospital indeed. Already the Stanfords and the Crockers had paths beaten to their doors by every charity in San Francisco—shelters for animals, homes for old sailors, orphanages—and now here was one more. If only he could convince her to charge a fee for each patient . . .

The third gentleman in the room was thoroughly enchanted with Samantha Hargrave. Stanton Weatherby, the Gants' attorney, was a polished, charming widower of fifty who had been convinced upon his wife's death fifteen years before that there could never be another woman for him. And then he had met young Dr. Hargrave a few weeks ago and had had to reevaluate that conviction.

"Anyway," said Darius, stirring, "we still haven't even found a site for the Infirmary yet, and until one is found, all discussion of money is moot."

"Oh," said Hilary brightly, "but we *have* found one."

The three men turned to her. She glanced first at Samantha, a little nervously (they had both steeled themselves against this moment), then she went on in a rush. "In fact, we haven't found just a site but a *building* that is so perfect one would think it had been built with the Infirmary in mind. And it is in a good location, close to cable car lines, right in the heart of the city so that patients will have easy access."

"Where is it?" asked LeGrand.

"It's on Kearny Street."

The three men waited, then Darius said, "*Where* on Kearny?"

"Not far from Portsmouth Square."

His brows shot up. "What is the building?"

She clasped her hands tightly in her lap. "It's the Gilded Cage."

"The Gilded—" sputtered Darius, jumping to his feet. "Great God, you aren't serious!"

LeGrand, thinking the ladies were having a joke on them, chuckled; then his face fell. *They were serious.*

"Madam," boomed Darius, "have you taken leave of your senses?"

"Please don't shout, dear. The Gilded Cage is a perfect house for our hospital," she said calmly. "Samantha and I did a careful inspection. The top floor is perfect for the nurses' quarters, and there are dumbwaiters to carry food up from the kitchen—"

"Mrs. Gant!" he cried. "Do you mean to say you have stepped foot *inside* the place?"

"We had an escort, Darius."

"Who?"

"The real estate agent."

He slammed a fist on the mantel, causing the ormolu clock to jangle. "Are you raving mad, madam?"

LeGrand put a restraining hand on Darius's arm and said calmly, "Wait a moment. Let me see if I understand you ladies correctly. The Gilded Cage is up for sale and the two of you, accompanied by the agent, went in to see it?"

"Yes."

"But, my dear ladies, do you realize—"

"Mr. Mason," said Samantha quietly, "we know what the Gilded Cage is, but we cannot let our thinking be influenced by that. The fact is, the building is for sale and it is perfect for the Infirmary."

"No," said Darius.

Everyone looked at him.

He turned slowly. His face was set. "It is out of the question."

"But, Darius dear—"

"The subject is closed, madam."

Samantha kept herself perfectly still in her chair, knowing that her slightest movement would betray her annoyance. She and Hilary had suspected this might happen. In fact, they had held off telling the men, who were to be the Infirmary's trustees, until a good moment arose. But the problem was, it was never a good moment to break news like this. Even Hilary, just a week ago, over lunch at Chez Pierre, had been shocked at Samantha's suggestion that they convert a notorious whorehouse into their hospital. But Hilary had come around. These men clearly would not.

Samantha was getting used to shocked expressions. When they had gone to the agent's office and told him they wished to inspect the place: dumb shock from him, his partners, and their male secretary. Then the coach driver who had taken them there and had helped the ladies down. And then the doorman (for the Gilded Cage was still in full operation); the men at the gambling tables; the bartenders; the piano player; finally, "Choppy" Johnson, the owner.

Samantha and Hilary had been ill at ease beneath the rude stares (had everyone thought they were prospective "hostesses"?) but Choppy Johnson, despite his reputation and sinister connections, was a gentleman and endeavored to keep the meeting businesslike. The tour had not been thorough, since many of the rooms were in use, but Samantha had been able to look at it all with a medical eye. The rooms the girls now inhabited would be perfect for the nurses and resident doctors; the storeroom on the top floor, jumbled with roulette wheels, faded nude paintings and broken chairs, would make an excellent operating room. The Gilded Cage was no mean establishment; Choppy Johnson had had the comforts and convenience of his clients foremost in mind: there was the latest indoor plumbing, gas lighting throughout, the finest nickel-paneled stove range in the kitchen, and a tank for hot running water. When Samantha's eyes went this way and that, they didn't see the women in spangles and fishnet stockings, the mahogany and brass bar, the red velvet hangings, the men who gawked at her; she saw instead rows of neat beds, crisp nurses, rolling carts of supplies. Renovation would be fairly easy. A team of cleaning ladies armed with buckets and Bon Ami cleanser—

"What's the price?" asked LeGrand. "I didn't know Choppy Johnson was selling."

"He's asking twenty thousand."

LeGrand's quick analytical mind did a hasty assessment. "That sounds steep."

Samantha smiled. "He's including the 'business' with it."

"Of course. Choppy can guarantee a loyal following."

"Confound it!" snapped Darius. "I will not stand here and discuss such an establishment with ladies!"

"Think of it as a hospital, dear," said Hilary.

When her husband fixed a correcting eye on her, Hilary reddened. She had overstepped her bounds and could expect a lecture after the guests were gone.

"A hospital should be out where there is fresh air," said LeGrand. "I had thought you might choose a site in the Richmond district."

"Mr. Mason," said Samantha, "a hospital should be where the patients can get to it. Many of the women who come to my office cannot afford trolley fair, much less the time off work for the long trip. That is why the Gilded Cage is so perfect."

"She's right, Darius."

Everyone turned to Stanton Weatherby, who, until now, had not spoken. He smiled graciously at Samantha. "I think your proposal is quite reasonable, Doctor."

She smiled back. "Thank you, sir. Now, if you could convince these other gentleman at least to look at—"

"Absolutely not!" said Darius.

"I wonder why Choppy is selling?" said LeGrand.

"He told us he wants to retire. He's going to live with his brother in Arizona."

"Retire? Choppy Johnson isn't a day over fifty."

Samantha had had the same thought until Choppy moved into the light coming through his office windows and she had seen the shocking pallor of his complexion, the circles under his eyes, the sunken cheeks, the way he absently rubbed his stomach. Choppy Johnson was a very sick man.

"You'll never raise twenty thousand," said LeGrand.

"I think I can get him down to eighteen."

"I don't see why. There are plenty of, ah, businessmen in this town who would gladly give him twenty for it. Why should he sell it for less to someone who intends to close it down?"

Samantha had thoughts on that, too. On Mr. Johnson's roll-top desk Samantha had glimpsed several tracts calling sinners to repent. She suspected that his close brush with illness and therefore with his Maker might be prompting repentance. She said, "When we told him our intentions, he said he would hold off considering other offers for a week."

"And come down to eighteen thousand?"

"Well, he didn't exactly agree to that."

"Hmm."

"It is pointless to discuss this," said Darius. "I refuse to have dealings with a man like Choppy Johnson, even in the name of a good cause, or to see my good money go into corrupt pockets!"

"You're being bullheaded," said Stanton. "It sounds like a worthy investment to me. And I think the least we can do is take a look at the place."

"Oh, it'll be easily converted into a hospital all right," said LeGrand, and then he instantly blushed and hastily added, "That is, according to what the ladies have told us about the place."

When the meeting broke up a few minutes later, Stanton Weatherby offered Samantha a lift in his carriage. As the coach inched its way through the fog, Samantha slipped into singular reflection, causing her companion to study her. Each time he saw her, Stanton decided, he admired her a little more.

Stanton Weatherby, looking younger than his fifty years, was stylishly dressed and handsome in his meticulous beard and mustache. He was also a man of great charm and wit. Now, he spoke.

"There is an old saying, Dr. Hargrave, that a committee is a group of men who individually can do nothing, but collectively meet and decide that nothing can be done."

She brought her attention back to him. "I beg your pardon? Oh, I am sorry, Mr. Weatherby. I had so hoped this evening would go better. I cannot stress too strongly how ideal the Gilded Cage would be for our purpose."

His eyes twinkled merrily. Such determination was attractive in one so young and pretty. She positively captivated him. "Fear not, dear lady. I shall speak to Darius. And in the meantime I suggest you go ahead and try to get the money together."

"Thank you, I shall do just that." And she added with a smile, "I do thank you for your support."

He returned her smile, thinking: Why the devil isn't she married? Then he cleared his throat and said offhandedly, "Might I be so presumptuous as to ask if you have yet seen the Victoria Regina in Golden Gate Park? They say it is the largest flower in the world, measuring five feet in diameter."

"I'm afraid I haven't had the opportunity, Mr. Weatherby."

"Then perhaps you would do me the honor of allowing me to escort you some afternoon, say, a Sunday perhaps?"

"Unfortunately, sir, Sunday is my busiest day. Since many of my patients are working women, I must see them during their free hours."

"I see. Yes, well." He tugged at his kid gloves. "At any rate, Dr. Hargrave, please don't worry about the Gilded Cage. I can practically guarantee that Darius will come around."

Darius didn't budge. He lectured Hilary sternly and ended by forbidding her to have anything to do with the plan to purchase the Gilded Cage. As a result, as the two women paused on the sidewalk in front of the imposing James Flood brownstone mansion, Hilary was defying Darius. It was the second time in her life she had contradicted his orders; she felt it wasn't going to be the last.

"Well," said Samantha, crossing the Floods off the list in her little book. "We are still far short."

Hilary frowned. In three days they had paid calls on most of the aristocracy of Nob Hill and so far the majority would have nothing to do with the purchase of one of San Francisco's most notorious establishments. Even though they were Hilary's friends, they could not condone her plan; the fifty-year reputation of the Gilded Cage would carry over and taint the Infirmary, they said, and the neighborhood it was in was a bad one, most of the patients would no doubt be women of questionable morals. No self-respecting woman, they declared, no matter how poor or ill, would go to the Infirmary.

Hilary was angry. "In three days Mr. Johnson will sell to someone else. I wish I had my own money, Samantha. My father left me such a grand inheritance but it's all in Darius' name."

"We can't give up yet, Hilary. Now then, shall we pay a call on Mrs. Elliott?"

Hilary gazed across the street at the turreted castle-like palace that stood behind a thirty-foot fence. The Elliott mansion was the first and oldest on Nob Hill, crowning California Street like a medieval fortress. But it stood in mystery and silence. This was the one house Hilary had never entered; nor, for that matter, had very many of San Francisco's society. The lone inhabitant was a very old woman, Mrs. Lydia Elliott, who had come to San Francisco from Boston decades before as the wife of an illiterate gold prospector. James Elliott, a San Francisco legend, had died twenty-five years before in a duel on the shore of Lake Merced, but not without having left his widow and son a legacy of railroad stock. On the day of the duel Mrs. Elliott had hung a black wreath on the front door and had never come out again. Of the only son, there were vague rumors but no one knew what had happened to him.

"I doubt she'll receive us, Samantha. They say she doesn't like visitors."

"We can only try."

As they trudged up the steep drive—two elegant young ladies in shoulder capes of nutria fur and long, straight skirts narrowly cinched at the waist—Samantha and Hilary experienced the eerie feeling of being watched. But the draperies, drawn over the windows twenty-five years ago, didn't move, and the house had a strangely deserted air. No gardeners, no carriages, even the birds seemed to stay away.

"She might not even still be alive," murmured Hilary.

Samantha raised the great knocker and let it fall. Dust from the old wreath showered to the threshold. As Hilary turned to whisper, "Let's go," the door swung open and, to their immense surprise, standing before them was a very regal and impeccably dressed butler. "Yes?"

Hilary briefly explained the purpose of their visit and then handed him her engraved calling card. As they took a seat in the vast hallway, watching the butler walk away with the card on a silver tray, Samantha and Hilary looked around with enormous eyes.

"It's . . . beautiful," whispered Hilary. "And so *clean*."

Samantha stared at the polished chandeliers, table tops, mirrors and vases.

The butler returned and, to their further surprise, led them into a small but lavishly and tastefully furnished morning room. They took seats and waited; a few minutes later Mrs. Elliott appeared.

She walked with the aid of a cane, bent over, and her face was a map of fine lines; she looked unaccountably old but her eyes betrayed a keen and lively mind. Her white hair was meticulously parted and combed down over her ears and into a knot at the back and she creaked as she crossed the room, not because of her joints but because of the crinoline beneath her black gown. Like her hair style, the dress was old-fashioned, a style that hadn't been worn since the Civil War, but it was clearly recently made, as though Mrs. Elliott were defying time, trying to make it stand still.

After introductions (the little eyes flickered at the address of "Doctor") Mrs. Elliott said, "I rarely receive visitors, you know, but that is because so few call these days. My man tells me you've come about a charity hospital?"

Hilary spoke and Mrs. Elliott seemed to listen with interest; but then Hilary came to the part about purchasing the Gilded Cage, and the old woman turned pale. "Stop," she said. "Go no further. I wish you to leave now. Charnley will see you out."

"But, Mrs. Elliott—" started Hilary as the woman rose.

"Young lady," said their hostess, banging her cane on the floor, "how dare you come into my house and speak of that place! When Charnley informed me of the purpose of your visit, I opened my home to you. You have betrayed that trust. I wish you to leave at once."

"Mrs. Elliott," said Samantha quickly, "I'm sorry if we offended you, but the Gilded Cage is so perfect for our—"

"Offended me?" cried the old woman. "You have torn open a wound and poured salt into it!"

Samantha and Hilary stared at her.

"There!" she cried tremulously, pointing to a portrait above the fireplace. "My husband. Shot down by the owner of just such an establishment as the Gilded Cage.

Those were the days of the vigilantes, but they never brought the man to justice. It was a duel, they said, on the field of honor!"

"I'm sorry, Mrs. Elliott."

"Sorry? That won't bring back my poor husband. Nor my son. Now please leave, at once."

Hilary started to go, but Samantha held back. "What happened to your son, Mrs. Elliott?" she asked gently.

Tears rose in the lively eyes and the old woman sank back into her chair. Her voice came from far away. "He used to go there. I never knew it. It wasn't easy raising a son on my own, after James had gone. Philip went there almost every night. And then he met that hussy and she turned his poor naive head."

Samantha and Hilary stood silent, unmoving.

"The Gilded Cage killed my Philip," she went on distantly. "He was a good boy, but easily led astray. They taught him gambling and drinking. Then one of those women told him she was having his child. Philip did the honorable thing and married her. But there was no child. She spent his money, and then went off with another man. Philip shot himself."

Samantha and Hilary stared for a moment, then Hilary said softly, "We're sorry, Mrs. Elliott, to have disturbed you."

"Mrs. Elliott," said Samantha, "here is your chance to vindicate Philip."

The old woman raised her head and said wearily, "Please go. What's done is done. Nothing can change the past."

"I know that, Mrs. Elliott, but if we purchase the Gilded Cage and convert it into a hospital, we can prevent such tragedies from happening in the future."

"I will have nothing to do with that despicable place. I will not give money to the man who owns it." Composed, she stood and hobbled to the bell rope. Giving it a tug, she said, "You have exhumed painful memories and brought back unhappy ghosts. In the future I shall be more careful about whom I allow into my house."

"Mrs. Elliott," said Samantha almost pleadingly, "if we don't purchase the Gilded Cage, another Choppy Johnson will, and then future Philip Elliotts will suffer as your son did. Here is your chance to rid San Francisco of an evil that has plagued it for too long. What better justice than to take a house where women are abused and turn it into a place to heal them?"

Mrs. Elliott's eyes went hard. "Leave my house at once."

As they walked down the driveway toward the street Hilary said, "We shouldn't have done that, Samantha. The poor old thing might have had a stroke."

Samantha was trembling, causing the long egret feather on her hat to quiver. She stopped at the gate, her face set to the wind, gazing at but not seeing the whitecapped water of the bay and the fleecy clouds crowning the green hills of Marin. "There must be a way to make them see reason."

"Samantha, let's give up on the Gilded Cage. We'll find another building. Perhaps we should do as LeGrand suggests and build in the Richmond district."

But Samantha was reluctant to let go of what was right. The moment she entered the dance hall she had seen the obstetrical ward; in the kitchen she had seen the hundreds of meals; in the rooms above, the tidy furnishings of the medical staff. And outside, instead of a glaring marquee advertising the most beautiful and compliant "hostesses" in the city, a modest plaque declaring this to be the San Francisco Infirmary for Women and Children. She had felt it too strongly, it had felt too right for her to give up now.

"Mrs. Gant!" came a voice behind.

Hilary and Samantha turned to see a maid in cap and apron hurrying down the drive. She drew up, panting, and held out an envelope. "The madam sent me to give you this."

Hilary opened the envelope. It contained two things: a check for ten thousand dollars, and a note which, in shaky copperplate, requested that a floor of the Infirmary be named the Philip Elliott Ward.

※

With the money from Mrs. Elliott they were able to buy the building, but they still needed funds for furnishings, equipment and staff.

They sat down with LeGrand Mason and Stanton Weatherby (Darius was down in Los Angeles rescuing a crop of oranges that was rotting in a derailed railroad car). They drew up a projected financial plan: ten thousand, it was agreed, would be needed to cover all initial costs and to keep the Infirmary running for twelve months, at which time solicitation would have to begin again. Of that ten thousand, they had four.

Samantha and Hilary set to with great energy and determination to raise the remaining six thousand, and since society still, for the most part, disapproved of their purchase of the Gilded Cage, they decided to go to the people for help.

Dahlia Mason, although in confinement, wanted to help. When it was discovered that she had a talent for painting exquisite violets in a quick hand, she was set to the task of drawing and inscribing thank-you cards to be presented to anyone making a donation, whether in goods or money (a local butcher promised a dozen plucked turkeys). These cards soon became fashionable possessions. They came to be found all over the city, proudly displayed in parlors (especially since the card did not designate the size or nature of the donation), so that it became fashionable to have made a gift to the new Infirmary (a clock, a worn gown, fifty pounds of used linen), and to display one of Dahlia Mason's cards.

When the flood of gifts slowed to a trickle, Samantha arranged to use the unsold space in a local newspaper for the listing of names of contributors, large or small, so that the tide of donations increased again as people were motivated to see their names in print. For monetary donations of a hundred dollars or more, a wall in the newly partitioned foyer (where once customers had deposited their hats and canes) was set aside, and a stonemason, working for free, engraved the names. Some of the most appreciated gifts, however, were those considered luxuries, items that would have been nice to have but which would never have been part of the Infirmary's budget: hooked rugs for the sitting rooms, flower vases for the nurses' quarters, books for the library, and, from Stanton Weatherby, a beautiful grand piano for the common room.

As workmen and cleaning crews labored day and night to give the

Gilded Cage a new look of respectability, small crowds gathered on the sidewalk to watch and comment, and Hilary never missed the opportunity to pass a plate around. And as all evidence of the former whorehouse gradually disappeared, society started to come around.

Then Hilary devised another money-raising plan—the idea of "Support A Bed": a person could finance for one year the care of patients occupying a particular bed. LeGrand broke down the operating costs: he estimated it would cost thirty cents to do a year's laundry for one bed, forty-eight dollars for meals, twelve cents per day for nursing duties, and so on. Added to that were estimated drug and surgical expenses. Finally it was decided that the cost of supporting one bed for a year should be set at seventy-five dollars. Dahlia Mason, using her most exquisite calligraphy and gold paint, inscribed placards to be fixed above each bedstead, stating the name of the sponsor. The idea caught on: before the new beds even had mattresses on them, all fifty had sponsors.

Hilary and Samantha spent long hours over plans. Aside from organizing her Ladies' Committee, which would be an elite group and which would be responsible for many vital functions, Hilary was also busy planning an extravagant ball to commemorate the Infirmary's opening. Samantha, meanwhile, was down at the Infirmary at almost any hour, overseeing work crews, arguing with the architect (he insisted the postmortem room be attached to the operating room, as it had been for centuries, and Samantha insisted he put it in the basement). She was also busy interviewing applicants.

Her first hired employee was a former resident of the Gilded Cage, a woman in her forties who had been kept on by Choppy for sentimental reasons but who now couldn't find employment elsewhere. Samantha hired her to work in the kitchen. Her second employee was Charity Ziegler ("Sent from heaven, I'd swear," Samantha had told Hilary), who had recently come to San Francisco with her husband. Mrs. Ziegler had been a senior nurse at the Buffalo General Hospital for six years and was not only expert in overseeing a nursing staff and training probationers, she had also learned "sick cookery" and was able to take over menu planning. To the valuable Charity Ziegler went the astronomical salary of six hundred dollars a year.

Samantha's first intern was Willella Canby, a short, plump young woman who had recently graduated from Toland Medical College of the University of California. She had come highly recommended, was bright and eager and didn't balk at the idea of working without pay, with room and board.

Slowly, gradually, the Infirmary took shape. Hilary formed her Ladies' Committee, Stanton Weatherby drew up the charter, city and state licenses were granted, Samantha had her complete staff and, by July 1887, nearly one year from the day the idea had been born at Chez Pierre, the San Francisco Infirmary for Women and Children was ready to open.

All they needed now were patients.

—❀—

The last workman had gone, the last bucket and brush were out of sight; the rooms all smelled of fresh paint and furniture oil. There was a coal stove on each floor (Samantha had wanted to install steam heat but that would have cost another five thousand dollars). There was a nurse's bell rope by each bed and, running through the building, an ingenious network of speaking tubes, like those on a ship. The staff quarters upstairs were ready to be lived in: each room contained two beds, a rug, washstand, dresser and writing desk. These rooms would soon be occupied by fifteen nurses and probation-ers, Dr. Willella Canby, Dr. Mary Bradshaw of Cooper Medical College, and Dr. Hortense Lovejoy from the Women's Medical College of Pennsylvania, the resident physicians. Downstairs, the kitchen was scrubbed and stocked. In the common room, for the convalescent patients who could walk, there were the piano, comfortable chairs, a fireplace, and shelves of books. Down the hall were the examining rooms, the Accident Clinic, and Samantha's private office. Lastly, in the foyer, above the desk of the admitting nurse, a large sign, freshly painted, forbade smoking by male physicians and visitors in any part of the hospital.

The Infirmary stood empty, waiting. Samantha also stood waiting. Hav-ing inspected everything one last time before locking the front doors to go home and dress for Hilary's ball, she paused in the foyer. It was early evening, sounds of traffic came through the open door. Samantha slowly turned, taking in the polished benches, the flowers, the box requesting donations, and was filled with a sense of wonder, excitement, and a little fear. They had come this far, achieved this remarkable goal, but there was no guaranteeing success. Had she done the right thing? Would women be able to forget this was once the Gilded Cage, would they come to her?

She ran her hand along the polished surface of the desk and thought of Mark. If only he could be here now.

Hearing a sound behind, Samantha turned and saw a small woman standing in the doorway, timidly clearing her throat. She was plainly dressed, weary-looking, clutching a shawl over her head. "Are you the doctor?" she asked.

Samantha went over to her. "The hospital opens tomorrow. Can I do something for you?"

"Are you the doctress? I work at the flower market. I couldn't come sooner."

"Have you a problem?"

"I get these awful headaches. I've had 'em for a month."

"How frequent are they?"

"Once a day. Always at noon."

Samantha said gently, "The hospital opens tomorrow. If you come back then and tell the nurse your problem, she'll take you to a doctor."

The woman returned the smile, uncertainly, bobbed a bit of a curtsy and turned away.

Samantha put her hand on the doorknob and closed her eyes. Tomorrow . . .

FIVE

*I*F ONE COULD PART THE EARTH'S ATMOSPHERE TO LOOK AT THE sky one would see the stars as they really are: fixed, untwinkling dots of cold light; quite possibly a lot of their mystique and appeal would be stripped away. This was how little Jennifer saw life, with a soul pure and unsullied by prejudice, fears, lies, or illusions. Jennifer, who had never heard an untruth, a phrase of false flattery, words of deceit or conceit, had no idea that people used their mouths to hide behind. And so, when Dahlia Mason came up to the nursery to fuss once more over the hapless little Robert who wanted only to be left alone and sleep, Jenny, from her spot in the corner, did not know that the lady's mouth said one thing while her eyes said another. The nanny heard, "What a lovely room! I wish my little Robert were as fortunate as Merry Gant!" but Mrs. Mason's squinty eyes declared: You'll never catch my Robert so blatantly overindulged!

The mouth was the focus of the guise, it drew attention away from the truth-telling eyes and other little revealing signs; the fast talker, the smooth talker, the flatterer, the liar were all seen by much of the world as they wished to be seen, through voice and volume and clever turn of phrase. Jennifer Hargrave had never learned to be lured by the mouth, she saw people as they really were, and very often didn't like what she saw. Dahlia Mason was one, but Jenny knew she was innocuous, no threat. But there were others, dangerous ones, and they frightened her. Tonight there was one in particular downstairs and Jenny had to think about him.

When Megan O'Hanrahan had given birth ten years ago, she took one look at her listless baby and instantly rejected her. As a result, Jenny had been fed by whoever thought to do it, touched only to be pushed aside. She was seen as being simple-minded and so no one ever tried to communicate with her. Then she grew filthy, and filthy objects often become objects of scorn. Jenny never learned what love was, for, if children learn by imitation, they learn also by reciprocation: nothing was given to or expected from Jenny. But if she knew nothing of love, she also knew nothing of sorrow, and when her mother had died nearly two years before, Jenny was unmoved.

And then from out of nowhere the Lady had come and taken her away.

Jenny had studied her new surroundings with sharp eyes, unafraid, and most of all she had watched the Lady, a beautiful woman who looked like the pretty ladies in the pictures that had hung on the grimy walls of her other home—ladies who held crosses and flowers and who had suffered in some horrible way. This Lady must also be suffering because she frequently fell to staring at Jenny with great sadness in her eyes.

Jenny didn't love her Lady, for that sentiment was yet a bud within her; nonetheless, Jenny had her instincts, and was governed by two that held powerful rein over her: loyalty and a sense of danger. She might not love her Lady but she was consumed with a dogged loyalty, like an animal that has been rescued and fed. And her sense of danger had been sharply honed in the tenement jungle. Tonight the two instincts rose up in that small body.

The nanny had taken the girls part way down the stairs to peek at the party below and Jenny had seen the silver-haired man whose eyes followed her Lady around the room. Jenny mistrusted him instinctively.

❈

Samantha greeted a late-arriving guest at the doorway of the ballroom: Mrs. Beauchamp, a widow in her fifties and a patient of Samantha. Dressed in black, even though her husband had died twenty years ago, Mrs. Beauchamp pumped Samantha's hand. "My dear, you have no idea the pleasure it gives me to be here tonight!"

Samantha smiled. She had shaken three hundred hands so far but was as fresh as if Mrs. Beauchamp were the first. By all rights Samantha should have been exhausted, but she was imbued with that special vigor drawn from a heightened spirit. They were all here tonight to honor the opening of the hospital; it was beyond thinking that Samantha could possibly be tired.

She glanced past Mrs. Beauchamp at Hilary across the vast ballroom and had to smile at the energy of her friend. Four months pregnant and shocking society by not trying to hide it, Hilary supervised this grand extravaganza as if it were nothing more than a tea party. Cool and efficient in her white satin gown trimmed with ermine (ostentatious, but Darius's choice), Hilary gave signals to chefs, oversaw the army of servants and managed to pay graceful attention to each of her guests, mingling as comfortably with the Princess of Hawaii as with her old school friends. She was at the peak of her glory, a gracious queen with flushed cheeks but not a curl out of place, and when she looked across the room and her eyes met Samantha's, she smiled secretively, knowingly, flashing her friend a private message. This was their night.

Mrs. Beauchamp was saying something about the color of the nurses' uniforms—oughtn't they be a more somber color befitting a nurse instead of that impractical pale blue?—and Samantha countered gently: "A hospital is a dreary enough place, Mrs. Beauchamp, without adding to it. Bright colors can cheer people up, and when the spirit is cheered, then the body heals more readily. Wouldn't you agree?"

"Why, yes. Yes, of course!" Mrs. Beauchamp's eyes darted about, looking for the promised celebrities; Samantha realized that the woman had taken a healthy dose of Dr. Morton's before coming here. Mrs. Beauchamp had come to Samantha for treatment of varicose veins, and although she generally took Samantha's advice, on the issue of Dr. Morton's Mrs. Beauchamp had stood firm. It helped her get through "bilious" days, she exclaimed, and she denied that it could possibly be as harmful as Samantha averred. After all, it was available in the best drugstores; they wouldn't sell anything that could be harmful, would they? Samantha had tried to explain that the elixir was heavily laced with opium and that Mrs. Beauchamp was fast becoming an addict, but this had greatly offended the woman, who believed that drug addiction could be found only among the lower classes of society. When a laundress took a tablespoon of Dr. Morton's a day it was an addiction, but when a society lady did the same, it was necessary medication.

Mr. and Mrs. Charles Havens came next, exuberantly declaring their hopes for the success of the Infirmary; they had financed the operating room. Rosemary Havens was also a patient of Samantha. She had been for years an arsenic eater, taking daily doses of Fowler's Solution to add luster to her complexion. However, unlike Mrs. Beauchamp, Rosemary Havens had heeded Samantha's warning, had given up Fowler's and was now treating her complexion instead to daily washings of her face in cucumber juice.

As the Havenses moved on to be presented to Princess Liliuoka-lani of Hawaii, Samantha wondered if she might steal an opportunity to retreat a little for some air.

This event was on a par with the Astor ball; San Francisco's nobility, forgetting their initial resistance of a year ago, were honoring Samantha's and Hilary's achievement. Sprinkled among the foreign dignitaries, politicians and famous names in the arts were the Crockers, the Stanfords, and the De Youngs. They sipped Mumm's champagne and discussed silver mining and cockfights in Marin. Men wore swallowtail coats and ladies were festooned in duchesse and Smyrna lace. But the difference between this ball and the ball of eight Christmases ago was that Samantha was tonight the guest of honor: all were here because of her. And, at that other ball, Mark Rawlins had been present.

It was July and the Gants' garden was redolent with new blossoms and freshly cut grass. A few guests also sought the evening air, murmuring beneath the glow of garden lamps and helping themselves from passing trays. For this gala occasion Hilary had hired San Francisco's finest chefs, providing the three hundred guests with tripe a la mode de Caen, green turtle steaks, ragout of spring duck, jellied shrimp, and crab legs in creamed sherry sauce; trays of caviar, smoked salmon, assorted cheeses, fruits and nuts were in constant circulation and, typical of San Francisco society, only California wines were served from the crystal carafes. A maid approached Samantha with a tray of champagne and Samantha shook her head with a smile. She had not touched champagne since her last dinner at Mark's house five years before and she never would again; some things had to remain special, reserved for the treasured past.

She came to a secluded marble bench and sat down; her thoughts were not on the hospital or the gala celebration going on behind her, but rather, overcome by a feeling of immense satisfaction and accomplishment, Samantha rewarded herself with a rare indulgence: she thought of Mark.

He should be here with her . . .

"Excuse me, Dr. Hargrave."

She looked up.

"I have been waiting for the right moment. Have I chosen poorly?"

"The right moment for what, sir?"

"To pay you my respects. When I arrived earlier such a crowd was pressed about you. I prefer solitary audiences. Warren Dunwich at your service, madam."

She stared up at him, intrigued. He was too elegant, too refined to be a San Franciscan and yet his accent was without doubt from the West Coast. In his early fifties, she judged, but youthful; the beautiful silver hair did not age him, rather it seemed to sharpen an impression of strength and vigor.

"How do you do, Mr. Dunwich. Are you new to San Francisco?"

He smiled a strangely cold smile. Handsome in a severe, almost harsh way, his jaw line, hollowed cheeks, narrow aquiline nose bespoke old European aristocracy and Samantha fleetingly imagined him as the master of a crumbling castle, surrounded by the slow decay of ancient nobility. "I am new to San Francisco every year, madam, even though I call the city my home. I must travel a great deal."

Warren Dunwich had incredibly blue eyes. They were sharp and intense, as indeed was his entire bearing, for he held himself rigidly, bowing from the waist. Samantha felt as if she was being attended by a count. "May I fetch you something from the table, Doctor?"

"No, thank you, Mr. Dunwich. I should return to my guests."

"May I escort you then?"

She threaded her arm through his. "What is your business, sir, that it takes you away so much?"

"I have my hand in many enterprises, madam. But I should very much like to hear about this remarkable hospital and even more so about its founder."

Hilary was engaged in a conversation with Lily Hitchcock Coit, the legendary mascot of Knickerbocker Hose No. 5, when she glanced across the room. Her brows arched slightly to see Samantha enter on the arm of a stranger, and laughing, as though she were quite comfortable with him.

Hilary pursed her lips. What *was* his name? A member of Darius's private gentlemen's club, the courtly stranger struck both a positive and negative note with Hilary: he was exceedingly handsome and she believed he was rich, and unattached; but there was something else, something cold and stilted about his manner, that put her off.

She excused herself and wove through the crowd toward them. Along the way she caught snatches of conversation and was not surprised that the controversy still raged: whether or not to admit women of questionable morals as patients. Hilary had to smile. They could argue all they wanted, Samantha stood firm. Some of the contributions had carried the condition that the Infirmary admit no prostitutes or cases of venereal disease, others that no Chinese or Mexicans be treated, and Samantha had returned the money: the Infirmary was to be open to *all* women.

"Why, Samantha Hargrave, I do believe you are in the company of the one person in this room whom *you* know and *I* do not!"

Samantha introduced him, catching a special glint in her friend's eye. Hilary spoke right up. "I believe you are a member of Mr. Gant's club, sir. It is a pleasure to meet you. And will I be meeting Mrs. Dunwich here tonight?"

Samantha flashed a chastising look but Hilary ignored it. They had had more than one discussion on this issue: Samantha's being unmarried. Hilary, a born matchmaker, insisted Samantha needed a man in her life and Samantha quietly declared that she did not. "My wife is deceased, madam," said Mr. Dunwich. "For eight years now."

"Do you make San Francisco your home, Mr. Dunwich?"

"I reside in Marin, but I am frequently in the city."

"Well then, you *must* come to dinner some—"

"Hilary dear, I believe Darius is looking for you."

"Oh?" Hilary turned and looked over her shoulder.

In that moment Samantha was struck by sudden vertigo. And so, coincidentally, was Hilary. As the two quickly raised their hands to their foreheads, a low rumble, like thunder rolling over the bay, rose up from the earth and in the next instant the air was filled with the tinkling of crystal. The orchestra stopped playing, all conversations fell silent. The tremor passed quickly, leaving an eerie silence behind; not one of the three hundred guests moved or spoke. Then there was a collective sigh of relief, followed by nervous laughter. As conversations started to resume, Hilary turned to Samantha. "Gracious, that was a strong—"

The crash that next jolted the house nearly sent her to her knees. This time the roar was deafening and people no longer stood staring up at the swaying chandeliers; they dashed for whatever cover they could find. Samantha teetered but was kept on her feet by Mr. Dunwich, who had her firmly about the waist. It seemed to last forever but was in fact a brief quake: samovars toppled from the buffet tables, champagne buckets spilled to the floor, ladies cried out or swooned.

When it was over no one moved, no one breathed, as if feeling the air for a sign; and then, in that instinct peculiar to San Franciscans, the guests roused themselves, knowing the quake was over.

Warren Dunwich, still holding Samantha, opened his mouth to ask if she was all right but, to his mild surprise, she inquired first of him, then quickly scanned the crowd. From overhead came a sudden wail. "The children!" Samantha cried, and hurried away.

Several people clambered up the stairs to the nursery but Samantha was the first in. Merry Christmas was screeching in the nanny's arms while a lustily bawling Robert was swept up to his mother's bosom. Jennifer was sitting in the corner, eyes wide, face expressionless.

Samantha dropped to her knees and inspected the girl's face. Out of habit she asked, "Are you all right, darling?" She checked Jenny's pupils, her color, searched for signs of shock or fear, but there were none, as though nothing had happened.

What no one could know was that Jenny, in her silent world, shared those same acute instincts as the Gants' now baying hounds; she had felt the quake coming and was not taken by surprise. Samantha ran her hand over Jenny's thick curls. "Everything's all right, dear, it was just a tremor."

In that moment Jenny raised her head and her pupils flared as she stared at something above her Lady's head. Now reading fear on the child's face, Samantha turned her head and looked up. Warren Dunwich had just walked in and stood behind her, staring down at Jenny. Samantha shifted her gaze and saw with horror a monstrous crack cleaving the ceiling of the nursery.

"It's all right, darling," she said, gathering the child into her arms. "The ceiling won't come down, I promise."

But it wasn't the crack that had suddenly frightened the girl, and as she now stood passively in her Lady's embrace, Jennifer gazed up at Warren Dunwich with big, wary eyes and he, also a sensitive being, gazed back down and knew what the child had seen.

SIX

"THERE'S SOMETHING WRONG, DOCTOR. SHE ISN'T TAKING IT."
Samantha left the sterilizer and came to stand by the patient's
head. "Try a little more," she said, watching carefully as the nurse
dribbled ether onto the mask. The patient stirred beneath the sheets, then
quietened. "That should do it," said Samantha, and returned to the sterilizer.

It was a device of her own invention. Most surgeons, if they practiced
asepsis at all, used carbolic, but Samantha had found the acid irritating to
patients' sensitive tissues. She had read of a new sterilizing technique being
tried—steam—and after experimenting on her own, Samantha had engi-
neered her own sterilizer. It was the first of its kind she knew of and it caused
a lot of comment. Especially noted was that the Infirmary's infection rate
was lower than the national average.

As she lifted the hot instruments out and placed them in a basin, Samantha noticed that the glass doors of the cupboard next to the sterilizer
steamed up. Making a mental note to have the machine moved, she picked
up a towel and gently wiped the glass. This was a special cupboard.

On its shelves lay Joshua's instruments. They hadn't been used in a long time and probably would never be used again, for they were out of date; but Samantha kept them nonetheless. Those handsome old instruments represented to Samantha the Future and Progress. They reminded her that this was a New Age. In the sterilizer were the instruments she had ordered specially and which all her surgeons now used: the new all-metal, smooth instruments that surgeons all over the country were switching to. As the germ theory gained rapid acceptance, it became apparent that the old-fashioned bone- and wooden-handled filigreed instruments would have to be done away with, for they could not be sterilized. Those exquisite works of art, ornately carved in a day when the quality of a surgical instalment was determined by how well it pleased the eye rather than by its function—they were now obsolete. Samantha could have sold them, but she preferred to keep them, to remind herself that all things must go forward, and of a promise she had once made.

From somewhere on the floors below, distantly and sweetly, came the strains of "Silent Night" as the Ladies' Committee moved through the wards with fruitcake and eggnog and led the patients in carols. It was the day before Christmas, a brisk, sunny day, and the Infirmary was a beehive of activity. Not, thought Samantha with a weary smile, that the hospital had known one slow day since its opening five months before. They had feared no patients would come, but on the morning after the grand ball she and her new doctors had arrived to find a small crowd quietly waiting at the doors, and since that day not a single bed had been empty.

But the Infirmary's success was proving, paradoxically, to be its own undoing: the heavy patient load was making LeGrand Mason's prediction come true—after only five months the money for operating expenses was nearly gone.

"Dr. Hargrave!"

She snapped her head up. Nurse Collins was struggling with the patient beneath the ether cone. Samantha hurried to the table, pinned down the bucking shoulders and said, "More ether, Nurse!"

"But I'm already reaching the lethal dose, Doctor!"

"Well, clearly it isn't having an effect! Give her more!"

The pale-faced young woman shakily complied and in another minute the patient was sleeping peacefully again.

At that moment Dr. Canby came into the room, pinning a cap to her hair. "I'm sorry I'm late, Doctor. I got called to a house visit—Oh, you haven't started yet."

"The patient isn't taking the ether. Will you watch her for a moment, please?" Samantha picked up the chart that hung on a hook at the foot of the table and reread Mrs. Cruikshank's history and the results of her physical. Perplexed, Samantha found nothing in the woman's background or current health status to explain why she was not taking the ether.

When the patient started bucking again, with Dr. Canby trying to hold her down, Samantha said, "All right. We'll have to postpone the surgery until we can find out what's wrong."

"How extraordinary," said Dr. Canby. "I've never seen anything like it!"

"I have," said Samantha, frowning. "Once. It was back in New York. We were to do an amputation on a longshoreman and no amount of ether would keep him under long enough to do the surgery. Questioning afterward revealed that he was an extremely heavy smoker of cigarettes. There was clearly no exchange of gases in his lungs."

Dr. Canby looked down at Mrs. Cruikshank, a middle-aged woman who was to be operated on for an ovarian cyst. "That can't be her reason, can it?"

"I think it's highly unlikely. Anyway, Nurse Collins, please watch her carefully until she is fully awake and then walk her back to her bed. I shall talk to her later."

Dr. Canby left the operating room with Samantha. "You must go down to the Children's Ward, Dr. Hargrave, and see the tree the Ladies' Committee has put up!"

"Whatever would we do without the Committee?" murmured Samantha, hurrying down the stairs. "I'll look in later."

Dr. Canby, staying behind, shook her head. In her five months at the Infirmary she had not once seen Dr. Hargrave move slowly. Their directress was an inspiration to them all—who could flag in her duties when Dr. Hargrave kept at it after going all night without sleep? But Willella did wish, for Samantha's sake, that she would take it a bit easy now and then.

Willella had just returned from a home visit. It had been a nasty one: a poor old invalid woman had been neglected in her bed and had developed bedsores. What was worse, the family didn't care and had barely listened to Dr. Canby's instructions. Willella decided to stop now in her room and freshen up.

No one complained about the cramped living quarters. The nurses, grateful to have been chosen (of over a hundred applicants, only fifteen had been accepted), gladly doubled up in rooms barely large enough for one person, and the three resident doctors, all of whom had been turned down by other hospitals because of their sex, thought their small suite down the hall from the operating room a luxury. The largest of the two rooms contained three beds, and as their shifts were staggered, there was always someone asleep; adjoining it was a sitting room with a coal stove, easy chairs, rug, books, and a spirit lamp for making tea. Because it was Christmas, the suite was empty: Dr. Bradshaw had gone to visit her family in Oakland and Dr. Lovejoy was on the wards. Dr. Canby went to the washbasin.

In the looking glass she inspected her hair. Dr. Hargrave had hard and fast rules on the staff's appearance: more than one nurse had been sent off the ward for a stray lock of hair. Dr. Canby then looked long at her face.

Willella was heir to that natural plumpness that, in early years, is called "baby fat" and later "bonnie," and which no amount of exercise or diet would ever reduce. Her cheeks were full, her face round and pretty like a china doll's; she was short and sturdy and didn't need to wear a bustle. Dr. Canby's manner and personality matched her appearance: she was pragmatic, honest, and forthright. The staff liked her, the patients adored her, and Dr. Hargrave hoped that, after the completion of her internship, Dr. Canby would stay on at the Infirmary.

But the truth was, beneath the dependable and down-to-earth exterior there existed another Willella: romantic, idealistic, and desperate to fall in love. Hidden beneath her pillow was *The Life of Napoleon*, by Sara Mitchell, complete with dashing engravings, and Willella Canby was certain that, from the way it was written, Miss Mitchell was in love with the Little Corporal, as Willella secretly was.

And here lay the focus of her dilemma. Although Willella was glad she had become a doctor (since her earliest childhood she couldn't recall ever wanting to be anything else) and although she enjoyed the Infirmary and was grateful to be studying under Samantha Hargrave and would like to stay on afterward, Dr. Canby was a young woman yearning for romance, a husband, and children. But as the days and weeks passed within these walls, and she treated women patients and worked with an all-female staff, Dr. Canby began to see herself as living the life of a cloistered nun. There were no men in her life; she saw none on her horizon. She was twenty-five years old, already a spinster, and beginning to fear that her hopes were dissolving into an empty dream.

She thought of Dr. Hargrave, whom she admired but also envied; the directress seemed to have no lack of male admirers, especially the amusing Mr. Weatherby, who was forever punning, and the marvelously aristocratic Mr. Dunwich. Lucky Samantha Hargrave! Being a doctor didn't seem to get in the way of *her* chance for romance, and no doubt soon she would be getting married. But what chance had Willella? Short, plump and a doctor—there wasn't a man in San Francisco who'd think twice about her!

Well, she wouldn't give up hope (Josephine was thirty-two when she met Bonaparte). Pinching her cheeks to give them color, Dr. Canby did a final inspection of her uniform and marched stoically out.

-&-

Whatever would we do without the Ladies' Committee? thought Samantha again as she entered the general ward. The carolers were just leaving, stylish young women in leg o' mutton blouses, long slim skirts and little fur capes that matched their hats. They were Hilary's friends, a small army of energy and ideas, so unlike Janelle MacPherson's group back at St. Brigid's. Hilary's Ladies' Committee, fast becoming famous in the city, was more than a group of idle women coming around once a week with flowers and Bibles; these ladies, despite the fact that they were handed down from fine carriages and cosseted by the males around them, were a force to be reckoned with. Their services went beyond flowers and cakes, and beyond, even, their valuable fund raising (which, at the moment, was their most vital function). The Ladies' Committee took care of babies abandoned on the Infirmary's steps or orphaned by mothers who died in childbirth and saw that they were adopted into good homes. They found destitute cases around the city and reported them to Samantha so she could send a visiting nurse. They sat at bedsides and read; they listened to the frightened, counseled the troubled, and held the hands of the dying. The San Francisco Infirmary for Women and Children was rapidly gaining a reputation for being more than a hospital—it was a harbor of feminine compassion and solace, women helping women through the crises of life, and Hilary's Ladies' Committee played a large part.

Well, thought Samantha as she paused at a bed to check a patient's dressing, they shall have their work cut out for them in the New Year.

Funds were dropping so low that already Samantha was buying coal and wood on credit. By the end of the month the butcher would have to be put off. Hilary, as always, had come up with some solutions, but because of her confinement (she was due to have her baby in a week) she was unable to take an active part in the Committee. But after her recovery, she promised, she was going to call the ladies together and plan some fund-raising events. One was going to be a "Calendar Fair." Each booth would represent one month of the year so that one could stroll through the seasons and purchase Valentines, June-bride gifts, handmade autumn centerpieces, and so on. Her other idea for a money raiser was a ladies' bicycle marathon through Golden Gate Park.

Samantha missed Hilary very much. Because of her condition, their weekly luncheons had been suspended, archery was out of the question, and even the cup of tea in Samantha's office whenever Hilary dropped by couldn't be hoped for. Samantha did manage to get away from the Infirmary and up to the house on California Street, but their conversations invariably revolved around the hospital and money.

At the next bed Samantha smiled and exchanged a few words with the patient, a bright young woman who was sitting up drinking eggnog. Two weeks before, she had been brought in unconscious and feverish with a ruptured appendix; Samantha and Willella Canby had operated and now the girl was completely recovered. As Samantha examined the healthy pink scar, she recalled the many appendix cases in the past, going all the way back to Isaiah Hawksbill, all of which had died. Now, even though it was a risky operation, the patient at least stood a chance.

When the door at the end of the ward opened and a nurse came through with an armload of sheets, Samantha caught the brief aroma of roast goose. For those patients who could tolerate it, there was to be a Christmas dinner of goose with stuffing, yams and giblet gravy, mince pie, and lemon tea. And thinking of it, Samantha realized she was hungry. It was afternoon and she had eaten neither breakfast nor lunch, she had been so busy. But tonight would make up for it. Tonight she was going to Coppa's with Warren Dunwich.

Her few evenings off, when they weren't spent with Jennifer, were divided between Stanton Weatherby and Warren Dunwich, both of whom were paying diligent court to her. Hilary had had high hopes at first, gently urging Samantha toward matrimony, but she had finally given up. Samantha and Hilary had long ago learned to speak freely with one another, confessing things they kept secret from everyone else, and when Hilary frankly asked Samantha about her relationships with the two men, Samantha had candidly replied, "They are nice, but there is no spark."

Although there was no spark, she looked forward to the evening. Warren Dunwich was a congenial companion, a nice diversion from the hectic pace of the Infirmary. He was courtly, chivalrous in the extreme and ever anxious to please her. When Samantha expressed a desire to "do the Monkey Block," Warren had promptly complied.

The Monkey Block was San Francisco's bohemian quarter where artists and writers congregated. A neighborhood of colorful types and Basque and French cooking, it had become a chic haunt for the upper class to visit after an evening at the opera. Warren in his silk top hat and red-satin-lined opera cape would escort Samantha to Coppa's where they would dine in a cramped and smoky atmosphere on Coppa's famous chicken Portola—disjointed chicken, browned bacon, peppers, onions, corn, tomatoes, coconut shreds, and spicy "secret" sauce all sealed inside a coconut and stewed for an hour. To accompany the meal, a bottle of Clos Vougeot, which commanded a whopping four dollars.

They would talk; Warren would ask about the hospital and listen with genuine interest, he would tell her about his lumber business up in Seattle, and he would flatter her with his Continental attentiveness. But then Samantha would finally become conscious of the time, of Jenny at home with the housekeeper, of early morning duties at the hospital, and she would ask Warren to take her home. So it always went. Warren Dunwich, with his patrician good looks and air of nobility, would never strike that needed spark.

Stanton Weatherby, on the other hand, had true San Francisco character. His quick wit and sense of humor always made her laugh, he took her to imaginative places—Woodward's Amusement Park and dinner at the Poodle Dog. He was forever making puns and quoting comic sayings ("A fishing rod is a stick with a hook at one end and a fool at the other"). And, like Warren, he was always anxious to please. But again, no spark.

Samantha liked both men but when away from them she hardly thought about them, and when with them she could not help comparing them to Mark.

Mark Rawlins was and always would be her one love. She was reminded of him by a hundred little things all through the day, every day. A patient coming in and Samantha thinking, Mark would prescribe such and such. In surgery, picking up the tenaculum and thinking, He taught me to hold it this way. A visiting physician: Mark wore just such a coat, but on him it sat so much better . . . And at night, the last thing, as she lay her head on her pillow, Samantha never failed to think of him, to conjure up his image, to make love with him again, bringing him back to life, his warmth, his fine strong body, the lingering way he kissed. Sometimes the fantasies sustained her, she was grateful for what had once been; but sometimes she would cry, sad for what could never be again.

"Dr. Hargrave?"

She looked up, drawing the patient's blanket back up. Nurse Hampton, today on admitting duty, was standing at the foot of the bed. "There is a new patient waiting to see you."

"Thank you. I shall be there in a minute." To the patient in the bed she said, "You shall be having Christmas dinner with your family tomorrow, Martha." She gave the girl's hand a squeeze and walked away.

Moving toward the doors, Samantha did an inspection, as she always did, and, as always, gave orders along the way. "Please put a tent over Mrs. Mayer's feet. She has gout, remember. Mrs. Farber cannot reach her bell pull. The lady in Bed Six is having trouble breathing. Please put another pillow at her back."

So much to do, to think of, to oversee. Samantha had had no idea, when the Infirmary first opened, what would be the extent of her duties. She had envisioned only patients; but there was more to being directress than diagnosing and treating. Charity Ziegler came with reports on her nurses; Mrs. Polanski was having trouble with her laundry assistant; Mr. Buchanan, the porter, was intoxicated again; and there was evidence of mice in the basement.

Before going into the examining room, Samantha glanced at her fob watch. It was getting late and she wanted to spend some time with Jenny before Warren came for her.

The night before, Samantha had shown Jenny a Christmas tree and how to trim it. The girl, in perfect imitation, had tied on the bows and strings of popcorn, her big eyes watching, her nimble fingers making no mistakes; but Jennifer, as always, showed no curiosity, no wonder, and when the tree was done and the candles lighted, had only gazed expressionlessly at it.

Samantha had decided months before against sending Jenny to the School for the Deaf in Berkeley; she wanted her at home, hoping to find a way to reach this special child. But, as Hilary and Darius had pointed out, Samantha didn't have the time necessary for such an ambition; finding a way to communicate with Jennifer was a full-time job. So Samantha had compromised. After the first of the year a tutor was to move in, a Mr. Adam Wolff, highly recommended by the school as an excellent teacher for deaf children. Even though he could speak, he was deaf himself.

Once Samantha had made that decision, her thinking went a step further. Wanting only the best for Jenny, it had occurred to Samantha that, now that her patients were seeing her at the hospital and no longer came to the house on Kearny Street, it might be wise to find another place to live. After all, Kearny was a busy street, the traffic dangerous and some of the local element unhealthy. Also, the house was really too small for herself and the child, the live-in housekeeper and, soon, Mr. Wolff. Darius had recommended Pacific Heights, a quiet neighborhood with houses not too large but large enough, and each with a bit of ground. A back yard would be nice for Jenny, and Samantha would like a study in her home. Maybe, after the holidays, she would let Darius find her something.

She pushed open the door of the examining room and said, "Hello, I'm Dr. Hargrave."

The young woman, no more than seventeen, jumped to her feet. Before going to the basin to wash her hands, Samantha took in, with a quick glance, the fingers that nervously twisted the fringe of the shawl, the unusually pale skin, the stiff and edgy manner. "It's Christmas Eve," said Samantha, smiling as she dried her hands. "I can think of a hundred places I'd rather be than in a hospital, can't you?"

"Yes, Doctor . . ."

Samantha invited the girl to sit, then, taking the chair opposite, asked gently, "What is your problem?"

She had skipped her monthly days twice now and was sick in the mornings, the girl haltingly explained. While she listened, Samantha again noted the girl's jerky manner, her clothing, which suggested she was a working girl, and knew there was something amiss. Girls in the working class rarely went to a doctor to have a pregnancy confirmed; they learned basic facts at an early age and often lived in a large family where there was always a mother or an aunt to advise. Nonetheless, Samantha examined her and said, "Congratulations, Mrs. Montgomery, you're pregnant."

The girl's reaction didn't surprise her. "It's *Miss* Montgomery and congratulations aren't what I came for. I already knew I was in the family way."

"Then why did you come here?"

Miss Montgomery avoided looking directly at Samantha. "I don't want it."

"The baby?"

"It was a mistake, y'see. Well, I'd had some gin and this fellah, he offered to walk me home. It's not like I tumble easy, Doctor, but he'd done it before I knew it and it's not like I'll ever see him again, so it was all a *mistake.*"

"And what do you want from us?" Samantha already knew, these requests were common, but she wanted to hear it from the girl herself.

Miss Montgomery looked down at the floor. "I want you to get rid of it for me."

"Why don't you want to keep it?"

The girl lifted her head, her eyes were full of fear. "It's not like I can stay home and take care of it. I support my paw and kid brothers. I'm the only one bringing in money, and if I don't they'll starve."

"Where do you work?"

"At the Union Laundry on Mission Street. I'd last as long as it didn't show"— tears sprang to her eyes—"and then Mr. Barnes'd toss me out and then my paw and brothers'd go hungry and we'd all be out on our ears. Listen, Doctor, I'm sorry for what I done, but I can't let it go on."

Samantha nodded, deep in thought. After a minute she said, "Miss Montgomery, I do believe you are the answer to a prayer."

"How's that?"

"I know a woman, a very dear lady, who has tried for years to have a child, but she cannot. Only recently she and her husband decided to adopt a baby, but you see, Miss Montgomery, there is a problem. The lady wants the baby to look as much like her as possible, and the only orphans we have had lately have been Mexican and Oriental. But now here you sit, Miss Montgomery, with the very coloring and features of the lady herself. I call it an answer to prayers."

The girl frowned. "But I didn't ask to get rid of it after it's born. I mean *now*."

"I know you did, Miss Montgomery, but I was thinking of the lady and her husband and how happy they would be to take your child. They are good people, I assure you, and have a comfortable home. Your baby would be raised in—"

The girl leaned forward, pleadingly. "But I *can't* have it! How can I go to the laundry with my belly out to here?"

"Yes," Samantha said. "You can't do that. I have an idea. As it happens, I am desperately in need of help in the hospital laundry. Only this morning Mrs. Polanski was asking me to hire someone. Now what do you think, Miss Montgomery, of leaving your job at Union and coming to work here? You could stay until your confinement, I would make sure the work was easy, and then afterward you could keep the job if you like. We wouldn't turn you out. What do you think?"

Miss Montgomery wiped the tears off her cheeks. "I dunno . . ."

"We'll pay you what you make at the Union." Samantha's mind moved rapidly. She'd have to cut costs somewhere else to make up the salary. And she would have to explain to Mrs. Polanski why she was getting yet another assistant.

"D'you mean it?"

"Of course I do. And you can start right away."

The girl's face brightened; she shrugged her shoulders as if someone had lifted a heavy bundle from them. "All right, Doctor! I'd rather work here anyway!"

Samantha rose and went to the door. "Report the day after Christmas. Mrs. Polanski will get you started."

"Thank you, Doctor!"

"Oh, and Miss Montgomery. You are not obligated to give up the baby. If, after it's born, you should decide to keep it . . ."

"That's all right, Doctor. I'd rather the nice lady took it. Thank you again, and bless you!"

As she went down the hall toward her office, Samantha withdrew a notepad and pencil from her pocket and wrote: *Find someone to adopt Miss Montgomery's baby.*

"Doctor! Dr. Hargrave!"

Samantha stopped and looked up. Nurse Hampton was running toward her, one hand holding up her skirts, the other waving. "Doctor! A delivery! Outside! We can't get her out of the carriage!"

Samantha dashed past.

Parked at the curb in front of the hospital was a hansom cab, the horse jittery in its harness, the driver holding the door open and raving in rapid-fire Italian. When Samantha pushed past him, he said, "Doc, you gotta get her outa there! She gonna ruin my upholstery!"

Ignoring him, she climbed inside and knelt next to the woman who lay on the seat, clutching her swollen abdomen. "I'm Dr. Hargrave," said Samantha. "Let me help you into the hospital."

The woman's face twisted in pain, her teeth clenched, veins at her temples rising; then she said in a half-gasp, "I can't! It's coming! Oh, God!"

"We'll carry you."

The woman cried out, "No!" and rolled from side to side.

Samantha turned and said over her shoulder, "Nurse, get me my stethoscope, a blanket, towels and the obstetrical instruments. And a lantern!"

"Hey!" shouted the driver. "She can't have her kid in my cab!"

"Will you please close the door and give this lady some privacy!"

After doing a quick check of the woman's vital signs, Samantha lifted her heavy velvet skirt. "I'm going to check your baby now. It won't hurt."

The woman, Samantha knew, was in too much pain to care—the contractions were two minutes apart and she shrieked with each one.

Samantha felt for the baby's head: it was still up in the cervix, which was dilated to ten centimeters. When the carriage door opened and her stethoscope was handed through, Samantha listened for the fetal heartbeat. Outside, Nurse Hampton and a policeman kept a crowd from gathering. Samantha listened. She looked at her watch. Only a hundred beats per minute.

The baby was in trouble.

Rapidly opening the bundle of instruments the nurse had brought, Samantha said, "Okay, I'm going to break the membrane now. You won't feel it. If you could just hold still for one minute . . ."

Steadily guiding the forceps and scissors in the light cast by the lantern between the woman's legs, Samantha snipped the membrane and studied the fluid that escaped.

Her worst fear was confirmed. The normally clear amniotic fluid was stained greenish brown, which meant it contained meconium, fecal material from the baby that indicated it was in distress.

Samantha listened to the heartbeat again. It had dropped to ninety.

A split-second decision had to be made: whether to take the time and move the woman up to the operating room for a Caesarean section or attempt the delivery here.

Samantha made her decision: there was no time to move her.

In the instrument pack was a set of French obstetrical forceps; she deplored them as a regular practice, but in emergencies they could be lifesavers.

The head was crowning now but the baby made no further progress. The mother screamed with each contraction.

Not knowing if she heard or not, Samantha said, "I'm going to deliver your baby now. When you feel me tug, I want you to bear down as hard as you can."

"Let me rest!" she cried. "Oh, God, stop the pain! Put me to sleep!"

"I can't. I need you to help me. You're going to have to work hard now."

As Samantha gently guided the blades of the forceps up the canal, she closed her eyes and felt with the fingers of her other hand the baby's head and face. The forceps had to be seated in a way that wouldn't hurt the skull: just before the ears, on the jaw. When they were situated, she said, "All right now, let's get him out. Push!"

Samantha tugged, then relaxed, then tugged again, imitating the natural birth process, and when the head came halfway through the opening, she removed the forceps and took the soft little skull gently in her hands.

"Oh, Jesus!" wailed the woman. "Stop it!"

"Push again! It's almost over. Push!"

Samantha rotated the head and then eased the shoulder out. This was the hardest part, the most damaging to the mother. To prevent tearing, Samantha firmly seated her fingertips against the perineum, lifted the baby and eased the other shoulder out. The rest of the little body came through in a rush.

Normally the cord would not be cut now; the baby would be wrapped up with its mother and carried into the hospital for a safer, cleaner delivery of the placenta. But there was no time for that now.

The baby wasn't breathing.

Samantha held it up by its ankles and flicked the soles of its feet sharply. No reaction. She pinched its buttocks. Then she gave it a slap.

Moving quickly, Samantha worked to open the clogged nose and mouth with a rubber syringe. The infant was cold and white. But its little heart continued to beat feebly.

Fortunately, the mother had passed out. She never saw Dr. Hargrave place her mouth over the baby's face and puff into its lungs. She didn't see the whiteness of the doctor's face as she frantically tried to blow life into the moribund baby. Or the tears that sprang to her eyes.

Live, pleaded Samantha's mind. *Please live!*

She puffed, watched the chest rise and fall, puffed again. Then she paused, waiting for him to breathe on his own.

But as the little body grew colder and, finally, the pulse ceased, Samantha knew it was no use. She gathered the baby close to her, bent her head over it, and silently wept.

SEVEN

*T*HE COACH WAS TOO ELEGANT FOR HER, BUT SAMANTHA HAD been unable to refuse. Mrs. Bethenia Taylor, wife of the railroad magnate, had suffered for years with a femoral hernia and Samantha had repaired it with a technique learned from Landon Fremont. In gratitude, the woman had made a gift of an elegant brougham with square kerosene lamps of silver and beveled glass and hard rubber tires that made the ride luxuriously smooth. Samantha had wanted to sell it but Hilary wouldn't hear of it. A doctor needed a carriage, she had said, it wasn't right that Samantha went on house calls on the cable cars. Still, Samantha felt self-conscious every time she pulled up in it and was only too glad to see it go into its rented garage across the street.

She mounted the steps wearily, having lost all desire to go out with Warren Dunwich tonight; all she wanted was an evening alone with Jenny, her daughter, her baby . . .

In her three years of having Jennifer with her, Samantha had never given up the hope that one day the girl would come running with an embrace when Samantha came home. But this evening, as Samantha paused in the doorway to listen for the sound of running feet, all she heard was Miss Seagram's piano next door playing Christmas carols and the clatter and jangle of the busy holiday traffic on the street.

Samantha sighed and closed the door.

Miss Peoples, the live-in housekeeper, came out, wiping her hands on her apron. "Dr. Hargrave, are you all right? You don't look well."

"I'm tired, Miss Peoples. We had a ghastly day."

The housekeeper's eyes, which had learned to read her mistress' face, took in the strain, the paleness, the grief. And she thought: Lost another one. "I'm sorry to tell you this," she said quietly, taking Samantha's coat and bag. "Mr. Dunwich is here."

"What? But he's hours early!"

The housekeeper held out her hands helplessly.

"Oh, all right, Miss Peoples. Offer him a brandy and tell him I'll join him in a few minutes."

Samantha went up the stairs, wondering about Mr. Dunwich's unexpected early arrival, so out of character, and she was a little annoyed. She needed desperately to rest and to think.

Why? Why had the baby died? So much progress in medicine these days and still so many babies died. It wasn't fair!

But the death of this nameless baby was not the only reason for Samantha's mood on this Christmas Eve; there were other things on her mind, not the least of which was the problem of Mrs. Cruikshank.

After sitting alone for a while in her office to recover from the tragedy, Samantha had gone out onto the ward to have a talk with the woman.

After explaining why the surgery had been canceled—"We can't risk it; the ether didn't put you out"—Samantha asked a few questions that had not been asked before. But nothing new was revealed. No, the woman didn't smoke; no, she did not take alcohol, not even an occasional glass of wine; no, there was no family history of respiratory problems. Samantha was utterly confounded until the woman said, "I've been healthy as a horse all my life, Doctor, except for this cyst. And, of course, the anemia."

"Anemia?"

"I had it years ago. But it was cured, that's why I didn't bother mentioning it. My blood is wonderfully healthy now."

"How was your anemia cured, Mrs. Cruikshank?"

"My doctor told me to take a blood restorer. I went to a pharmacist and he recommended Johnston's Blood Tonic. Sure enough, soon as I started taking it, I felt better."

"How long ago was that?"

"Seventeen, eighteen years."

Samantha shook her head. No connection there.

"Of course," Mrs. Cruikshank went on, "since it warned on the label that stopping the tonic would bring the anemia back, I kept it up."

"You've been drinking Johnston's Tonic for eighteen years?"

"Regular as clockwork." The woman reached into the little locker that stood between her bed and the next and pulled out a bottle. "I don't go anywhere without it. I carry it in my purse."

Samantha took the bottle and read the label. It promised everything from hair restoration to curing impotence, but its main charge was that it "thickened and invigorated the blood." No mention was made of ingredients.

"How much do you take, Mrs. Cruikshank?"

"Well, Doctor, eighteen years ago a tablespoon in the morning and one at night was enough, but after a while I felt a need to increase the dose. I suppose one can build up a tolerance to medicine. Now I take a glass in the morning, one at noon, one with supper, and one at bedtime."

"But, Mrs. Cruikshank, that would be the whole bottle."

"A bottle a day, that's about it, Doctor. But it's good medicine. It truly keeps me in top form. If ever I let my supply run out, I can feel how bad my blood really is. I get weak and shaky and *very* out of sorts."

Samantha uncorked the bottle and sniffed. The smell of alcohol was so strong it was like inhaling whiskey. There was the problem; one other condition besides smoking made anesthesia difficult: alcoholism. Mrs. Cruikshank was an alcoholic and didn't know it.

As Samantha now sat before her dresser and took down her hair to give it a vigorous brushing, she felt her frustration rise. While the Infirmary had brought boundless satisfaction and gratification, it had also brought frustration. One could build the best hospital and employ the most skilled staff in the world, but in the end the initial problem remained: ignorance. Clearly, Samantha was beginning to realize, it wasn't enough to provide medical care after the fact, women needed to be educated beforehand, before the accidents, addictions, and unsanitary conditions could get started.

But it wasn't easy. Not only must public ignorance be overcome, but the prejudice of the educated as well. Only the week before, an editorial in the *Chronicle* had criticized the Infirmary's practice of dispensing sterilized milk. "All the goodness is being boiled out of it," the opinion read. "One might as well feed the baby water." Mr. Pasteur's new process for purifying milk and wine was having slow acceptance in America, and until the germ theory could be proven beyond a doubt, *pasteurization* would be considered so much quackery.

Where did a doctor's responsibility lie and what were her limits? The hundreds of cases passing through the Infirmary had awakened Samantha to the fact that many of those cases went beyond simple medical issues: they involved moral and social judgments as well. How far should she, as a doctor, extend herself?

It had begun with intimate problems, women seeking advice on how to make the sex act bearable so they wouldn't have to turn their husbands away. Then came the wives who could not or would not tolerate another pregnancy (locking their bedroom doors against their husbands), requesting birth control advice. Then the Infirmary saw prostitutes, the women to whom the rejected husbands turned. This was where the cases went beyond merely medical and became social issues. Unfortunately, although Samantha saw the cause, she had no remedy. A major quest among her patients was anticonception: if they could surrender to their husbands without fear of pregnancy, it would help them be more loving, more willing, and thus keep their husbands home. There would be fewer babies abandoned on the Infirmary steps, fewer attempted abortions, fewer women dying at the age of thirty because of the twelfth pregnancy, and quite possibly a lot less vice in the city of San Francisco. But the law was clear: dispensing anticonception devices was illegal.

Samantha was appalled at how little most women knew about their bodies and basic health. Like Mrs. Cruikshank, who innocently drank the equivalent of a pint of whiskey a day and was addicted. Women who washed their dishes in the same water that had been the family's Saturday night bath. Women who believed the "safe" days were those in the middle of their cycle, or who thought that urination immediately after intercourse prevented pregnancy, or that a bracelet of cloves provided effective contraception. From upper-class women who corseted themselves too tightly and thus deformed their rib cages to working mothers who dosed their crying babies with Winslow's Soothing Syrup, not knowing it contained morphine—every day Samantha saw afflictions that could have been prevented with a little knowledge, a little awareness.

She realized she was staring at her reflection in the mirror, the hairbrush forgotten in her hand. Miss Peoples was right, she didn't look well.

Every woman's death diminishes me. And every baby's . . .

She felt tears burn her eyes. They lost so many, so many. Infants born with heart and lung deformities, babies born blind, babies born crippled—so many birth defects due to improper care during pregnancy because the mother simply didn't know better. It wasn't fair. All the pale little bodies that came into the world, struggling for survival and not having a chance. The Infirmary had a lower infant mortality rate than the national average, but it wasn't enough. There were still too many deaths in the delivery room and, later, toddlers just learning to talk and grasp life dying from diseases that crept about the city on invisible feet.

Samantha bowed her head and rested it on her hands.

A soft knock at her door brought her back. Samantha looked at her watch. Where had the time gone? She had been home for an hour. Mr. Dunwich!

The housekeeper opened the door and put her head in. "There you are, Doctor. I thought you might be taking a nap."

"I'm sorry, Miss Peoples. I lost track of the time. I do hope Mr. Dunwich isn't distressed."

"He's sitting quietly in the parlor with his brandy. I explained as how you needed to change and all. He's very understanding, is Mr. Dunwich."

"Yes, he is. I shall hurry."

"I wanted to ask you, Doctor, about Miss Jenny." The housekeeper came all the way in, bringing with her, by the wrist, Jennifer. "Shall I give her her supper now?"

Instantly Samantha's anxieties and frustrations melted away; this was *her* baby. Dropping to her knees, Samantha held out her arms and said, "Come here, darling."

With a push from Miss Peoples Jenny went passively into Samantha's embrace. "I'm afraid Mr. Dunwich's early arrival has upset things," she said to the housekeeper, stroking the girl's hair. "I shan't have much time with her."

Jenny was eleven years old but still small. Her little body felt frail in Samantha's arms. "I'm so sorry, darling," murmured Samantha. "But I promise you I'll make it up. Tomorrow will be all ours. After we open our presents we shall take a lovely carriage ride . . ."

Miss Peoples, an elderly lady with a soft heart, looked on sadly. It nearly moved her to tears the way the dear doctor talked to the child, as if she were normal. Why couldn't she just accept the girl for what she was?

The previous summer, when Samantha had decided against sending Jenny to the special school in Berkeley, she had decided to investigate the child's background to see if she could find the cause of her deafness. But the poor doctor, Miss Peoples knew, had gone back to that slum neighborhood only to find the tenement torn down for a new warehouse and the Irish all dispersed. There was an old priest at the Catholic church who remembered the O'Hanrahans and their queer daughter, but all he could tell Samantha was that he thought he recalled a scarlet fever epidemic some years back, about the time the child was around two years old. If that was true, and if Jennifer had had scarlet fever, then that would account for her deafness. But it would not explain her muteness, nor her strange, withdrawn behavior.

Samantha held Jenny for a long time, waiting for the return hug that never came, then got back to her feet. "Please tell Mr. Dunwich I'll be down in five minutes," Samantha said, and turned to her dressing table.

As Miss Peoples led Jenny from the room, neither the housekeeper nor Samantha saw the way the girl looked back, with longing, at the beautiful Lady whose black hair cascaded down her back.

Warren Dunwich looked at the straddle clock on the mantel and compared it to his pocket watch. There was a three-minute discrepancy. He clicked his watchcase closed and slid it back into his vest pocket. The one on the mantel was off; if there was anything Warren Dunwich prided himself on, it was his keen sense of time. Coming here early tonight had been a great step out of character, but it had been necessary. Having deliberated for days, Mr. Dunwich had decided that tonight would be perfect for his important question, and for that he wanted to be alone with Samantha.

He ran a critical eye around the parlor. It was deplorable that a woman of Samantha Hargrave's prestige and social standing should have such a residence. It was clean, tasteful and neat, but so lacking in fashion and polish. She had spoken of late of looking at houses in better neighborhoods. Well, Warren Dunwich had a better idea. He was going to purchase the old Harrold mansion and he was going to ask Samantha to share it with him, as his wife.

This was not to say that Warren Dunwich was in love with Samantha, for, being a cold man, he was incapable of that gentle sentiment. What Warren felt for Samantha was unutterable fascination, an almost obsessive involvement with her mystique.

Five months before, Warren Dunwich had accepted the invitation to the celebration ball only to renew old acquaintances, since his frequent business trips kept him out of touch with the social world, and he had expected to stay only a short time. But then he had caught sight of that enchanting creature, the Dr. Hargrave whom he had expected to find repulsively mannish, and he had been at once captivated. Nothing interested Warren Dunwich more than a mysterious woman; he would single one out and then commence to explore her like a dark continent until, thoroughly familiar with her, he would cast her aside and search for a new challenge. Only one woman in his past had not been easily grasped, and she had so piqued him that he had ended up marrying her, for he would not give up his delving until the lady was totally revealed to him. Of that woman, the first Mrs. Dunwich, Warren had soon tired and their marriage had turned into a polite dialogue between two strangers. Now he had found a new mystery, and in all his womanizing years, Warren Dunwich declared, of them all, Samantha Hargrave was the most deliriously puzzling.

He had set himself immediately to exploring her, to finding out everything he could, only to discover to his immense surprise and heightened curiosity that she kept herself a carefully guarded secret. As though guessing his intention, Samantha had erected intriguing barriers, allowing him only tantalizing glimpses of her true self. Rather than discouraging him, this had only intensified his interest.

It had gradually occurred to Warren that all the casual courting in the world would never fully reveal Samantha to him—an occasional evening at the opera, a stroll through Golden Gate Park. What was necessary for the achievement of his goal was a drastic step. Warren did not regard marriage, as some men did, as a sacrifice but as a means to reach a desired end, and although a cold man, he was not without passions: marriage with Samantha Hargrave would not only allow him to explore her fully, but the promise of the marriage bed was a further incentive.

"Mr. Dunwich, do forgive me."

He rose and went to meet her in the middle of the room. "It is I who should be begging forgiveness, madam. My early arrival has no doubt upset your routine. But I assure you, dear Dr. Hargrave, that it was not an impulsive action."

Warren Dunwich was without a doubt pleasing to the eye: the beautiful silver hair, combed back over his sleek head, shone in the firelight; his hollowed cheeks and sharp jaw were chiseled planes. If only his personality matched his dashing good looks! "Please have a seat, Mr. Dunwich. May I refill your glass?"

When Samantha went to the service cart that stood in the curve of the bay window, she saw that the street outside glistened in the dusk. She was surprised. The day had been so sunny, but now heavy clouds rolled in from the ocean and a light drizzle forewarned of a storm to come.

They sat in the two wing-backed chairs facing the fire. "How is the Infirmary, Doctor?" he asked, as he always did.

She hesitated. "Busy, but well, thank you. And the lumber business?"

"Prospering." He sipped his brandy. "And how is Jenny?"

"She continues to be both my joy and my heartache."

"Your care of the girl is admirable, dear lady, considering she is not your child."

Samantha glanced sharply at him and then away, reminding herself that not everyone shared her philosophy of the universality of the Child. She also reminded herself that, despite five months of earnest trying (Warren always brought little gifts for Jenny), he had not been able to win the child over. Jenny made no outward gesture, of course, no facial expression, but Samantha sensed her fear and mistrust of Mr. Dunwich, and it puzzled her.

"She is eleven now, in a few years she will be a young woman. I am afraid for her, Mr. Dunwich. She is not armed, she is like a kitten, utterly defenseless."

Although he remained silent, Warren disagreed. Those big black eyes had gazed at him enough times for him to detect currents: the child was not as helpless as Samantha thought. And she was smart—too smart. He felt she saw right through him and Warren didn't like that one bit.

"Perhaps you should reconsider the special school."

"No, I have definitely decided against sending Jenny away. Mr. Wolff, the special tutor I have hired, is said to have had some remarkable successes."

"Did you not say he is also deaf?"

"He lost his hearing in an accident of some sort, but he can speak normally."

"When does he arrive?"

"Next month. He shall have the downstairs bedroom and I have converted what was once my examining room into a little schoolroom for them. I am praying Jenny takes to him."

Warren was disappointed Samantha would not be persuaded to send the girl away, but that just added to his fascination with her—Samantha's refusal to be dominated.

"Jenny is going to be a beautiful young woman," Samantha went on. "Even now, men stare at her. I will not always be around to protect her. If Mr. Wolff can teach her even the most basic communication, then I shall be grateful indeed."

"It seems, dear lady, the child needs a protector."

"She has me. And when I am not here, Miss Peoples."

"I mean someone more substantial and reliable than a housekeeper. The girl needs a father."

"Sadly, Jenny's father is unknown, Mr. Dunwich."

"I was referring, madam, to myself."

She turned to regard him. "What are you saying, Mr. Dunwich? Are you proposing marriage?"

"I am."

Samantha didn't know why, but she suddenly felt sad. "You're very kind, Mr. Dunwich, to be so concerned for Jenny—"

"My concern is for you as well, my dear."

"Do you think I too need a protector?"

"Not in the least. I had been thinking of companionship."

She looked away. Her sadness increased. "But I'm not in love with you, Mr. Dunwich."

"Nor I with you. But surely a sound marriage can be based on other things. Mutual respect, a sharing of interests."

"There have been other men in my life."

"My dear Dr. Hargrave, I am a man of fifty-two years. I have few illusions."

She gazed into the fire, recalling another proposal, so long ago—Mark bursting into her room, seizing her, their kiss, the passion, the intensity of it. And here was Mr. Dunwich making the same proposal, speaking offhandedly, as if about the rain now pelting the windows.

"Great heavens," he said quietly. "I fear I've upset you."

"I must confess that you have, Mr. Dunwich, but the fault is not yours. I did not come home in the best of moods, for we had a death today at the Infirmary. A baby."

"I'm so sorry."

"And then your proposal brought back a memory, from long ago . . ."

He could barely contain his excitement. So, the indomitable Dr. Hargrave had tender places! "I have blundered," he said, reaching for her hand. "In my growing admiration for you, madam, I became filled with the mad hope that you returned the regard. I fear now I was mistaken."

"Mr. Dunwich, please do not chastise yourself. If I led you to believe my intentions were of a more serious nature, then I apologize."

He squeezed her hand then released it. "Please do not refuse me at once, dear lady, but grant me the consideration of at least thinking it over."

"Mr. Dunwich, I had never thought to marry. It is not you; I am too devoted to my work, I would not give you the time and devotion you deserve from a wife."

"My dear Dr. Hargrave, I am aware of your great responsibilities as a doctor and would not dream of stealing you away from them for one minute! Ours would not be the usual union of domesticity, but rather of sharing and companionship and of friendship. And if you should so desire, although I promise I would never press my husbandly right in that delicate sphere, to have children someday . . ."

Samantha pushed herself up from the chair, hesitated before the fire, then turned away. She went to the service cart and poured herself a small glass of brandy, noticing as she did so that the rain was now coming down heavily.

Warren Dunwich had unknowingly touched a sensitive spot. As Samantha gazed at the rain-slick horses and carriages on the street, she recalled another stormy night, four years before, the night Clair had been born.

The contractions had come on suddenly and Samantha had been unable to fetch a midwife. Alone in the upstairs bed, she had brought Clair into the world. Then she had cut the cord herself and lifted the baby up to her breast to await the delivery of the placenta. It had been the most wonderful moment of her life.

To have another baby again . . .

Samantha sipped the brandy and felt it warm her as it went down.

Warren's proposal hadn't come as a great surprise, just as she suspected Stanton Weatherby was also leading up to the same question. On the surface there appeared to be nothing to consider: she didn't love either man, she was devoted to her career, she didn't need to marry. So many women entered into loveless marriages to escape the stigma of spinsterhood; many married out of loneliness. These were not considerations for Samantha.

The glass paused at her lips. *Or,* whispered her mind, *am I lonely?* The answer gave her a chill: *Yes . . . sometimes.* But is that a reason to marry?

Samantha studied her reflection in the glass and, beyond, Mr. Dunwich, elegant but uninspiring, sitting before the fire, waiting patiently for her answer.

There was no reason in the world to think of marrying him!

Samantha's fingers tightened around the glass. *Then why do I not refuse him right here and now? Why do I hesitate?*

How wonderful to have another baby . . .

Then she thought of Mark and suddenly she wanted desperately to be alone.

—❦—

Out in the hall, Miss Peoples was pushing Jennifer along and, like most people, spoke to the girl out of habit. "All right then, missy. We'll say good night to your mama and then put you to bed. St. Nick comes down the chimney tonight."

When they got to the parlor door Miss Peoples had expected to knock but, finding it open, went ahead and gave Jenny a gentle push through. She was about to make the announcement when she saw Mr. Dunwich, unaware of the two in the doorway, suddenly rise up from his chair, stride to the window where Dr. Hargrave stood, put his hands on her shoulders and turn her to face him. Realizing she had blundered, the housekeeper pulled the child back.

But, to her surprise, Jenny resisted. Standing rigidly, the girl stared at the man with the silver hair who was holding her Lady's shoulders and moving his lips rapidly.

Her Lady had a distressed look on her face.

When Warren bent his head and placed his mouth on Samantha's, Jennifer broke free. Shrieking, she flew at him. Startled, Warren spun around. Jennifer howled, beat at him with small fists, then flung her arms around Samantha's waist.

"What the devil!" he cried.

Stunned, Samantha tried to pry the girl's arms loose, but Jenny clung with astonishing strength. An eerie keening sound came from her throat.

Miss Peoples rushed in. "I'm sorry, Doctor! We came to say good night. The door was open. I had no idea we were interrupting—"

"Jenny?" said Samantha, looking down at the head buried against her skirt. Gently, Samantha worked the girl's hands free, then slid down to her knees so that she was at eye level with Jenny. Samantha was startled to see the huge eyes wide with fear, the lips quivering, the stark emotion on the pale face. "Jenny," murmured Samantha wonderingly, stroking her hair.

"What the devil?" Warren demanded.

"She thought you were hurting me," said Samantha quietly. Tears rose in her eyes. "She *does* feel after all. And look, she's trying to talk."

Jenny's jaw moved awkwardly, working up and down; her eyes now stared intently at Samantha's mouth as she tried to imitate speech.

"You need voice too, darling," said Samantha gently. "Oh, Jenny, how can I reach you?" The tears fell and tumbled down Samantha's cheeks. "Look how she's moving her mouth. She doesn't know. Dear God, please give her a voice!"

From where he stood, towering over them, Warren watched as a small hand reached up and touched Samantha's cheek. Jenny's fingertips traced the path of the tear, then they came away and traced the same path on her own cheek.

"She wants to cry," said Samantha softly. "Go ahead, Jenny. Cry."

More tears rose in her eyes and again the girl took them onto her fingertips and transferred them to her own cheek.

"I wish," said Samantha tightly, "I wish I knew how to reach you. I wish I could get into your little locked prison. How can I reach you, Jenny?"

"Samantha."

She looked up. Warren was gazing dispassionately down at her. "I think you'd better go, Warren," she said.

He opened his mouth to speak, then, changing his mind, strode to the table where his hat and gloves lay.

"Mr. Dunwich," said Samantha, "Jenny is clearly afraid of you. I think it best we not see each other again."

He nodded curtly, too proud to show his indignation. But as Miss Peoples showed Warren to the front door, his anger was turning to annoyance; and within a few minutes, riding off in his carriage, he was thinking about his dinner.

Samantha struggled to her feet, asked Miss Peoples to make some tea, then guided Jennifer to the fire. Sitting down and stationing the girl in front of her, Samantha searched the anxious face, watching the jaw move up and down.

"Sweet child," murmured Samantha, "I was right and everyone else was wrong. You do have feelings, and you can make sounds. But how can I get you to release them? Does it take fear? The threat of danger? Jenny, oh, Jenny. How can I reach you?"

Jennifer's fingertips touched Samantha's lips, then touched her own. Samantha took the girl's hand and placed it on her throat. "There, do you feel that? You must make sound, Jenny. You have vocal cords. There is no reason why you can't talk."

The large eyes blinked wonderingly. Jenny drew her hand away and placed it over her own throat. Her lips formed oh and ah and ee, but it was no use, she simply didn't understand.

"Jenny, it's started. You've taken the first step. How can I make you go further? Imitation isn't enough, you just don't *understand*. Dear God, please help me get through to her."

When the doorbell sounded Samantha thought Warren had come back. Since Miss Peoples was back in the kitchen, Samantha went to the door herself; she would be firm with him. It was all over between them. She could not think of seeing a man who frightened her daughter.

But instead of Warren, Samantha found on her doorstep, standing in the downpour and holding a dripping carpetbag, a young man whose long hair was plastered to his skull and whose suit was several sizes too small for his slender frame.

He blinked the rain from his eyes and said awkwardly, "Dr. Hargrave? I'm Adam Wolff from the School for the Deaf. Have I come on time?"

PART FIVE

SAN FRANCISCO 1895

ONE

*H*OLDING BACK TEARS, HILARY KISSED EACH CHILD ON THE forehead and then scooted them off to the waiting nanny. Merry Christmas, now eleven, received the kiss without the slobbery reciprocation of her brothers and sisters; she was a proper young lady now and proper young ladies, even though yearning in their hearts to make overt gestures of affection, kept themselves in restraint. She coolly received her mother's kiss, then turned away. Eve, on the other hand, at age eight, still threw her arms around her mother's neck and pasted a wet kiss on her cheek. Julius came next, a serious little boy of seven. He thought it more dignified to shake his mother's hand but at the last minute, as always, hugged her desperately in that curious son's love that smacked of master and lover.

The tears that Hilary held in check were not for these three, for these were Hilary's pride, they had been conceived and brought into the world in joy. It was for the next ones in line that she wanted to weep: homely little Myrtle, who had been an unpleasant pregnancy and a difficult birth; four-year-old Peony, whose conception had not been intended, for after Myrtle

Hilary had tried to restrict herself and Darius to "safe" days; and lastly two-year-old Cornelius on wobbly legs, whose conception had come as a shock since Hilary had been secretly practicing birth control.

As the children marched off to their beds, Hilary straightened, placed her hands on her abdomen and felt, once again, tears coming, threateningly close to breaking. Six children in nine years, she thought bleakly. And now a seventh on the way...

"Be sure to sterilize Cornelius's bottle, Griselda," she said to the starched old nurse who gathered up the baby.

"Yes, ma'am." Griselda, in her sixties, privately thought this new germ mania sweeping the nation a lot of nonsense. In her forty years as a nanny she'd never had to put up with the silly fears and fetishes that Mrs. Gant now demanded of her. And it wasn't just the Gants. When Griselda spent her one afternoon a week off with a knot of fellow nannies, they all complained about this new antigerm fad that was making a drudge of their lives. Why, a few years ago no one even knew what a germ was, and now all of a sudden everyone was screaming, "Bacteria!" And nurses and maids countrywide were being nagged to sterilize the house. The nannies clucked their tongues and agreed on the superiority of the good old days. When Griselda, her sherry glass empty, suddenly shrieked, "Look! A germ!" and then stamped her foot on the carpet, her cohorts burst into laughter.

Hilary made her way down the hall and paused at one point to listen to the vast stillness of the house. Choking back a sob—the servants mustn't see her like this—she thought of Darius spending a weekend on a friend's new boat (another fashionable new fad, sailing), and she was filled instantly with resentment. For the first time in their fifteen years of marriage Hilary resented Darius for being a man and for being free, and then she resented him for making her resent him.

Reading her twisted thoughts, Hilary finally did sob and hurried the rest of the way down the hall. Falling into the bedroom and slamming the door, Hilary let the tears come. I hate you, Darius Gant, for doing this to me again. And I hate you for making me not want this baby!

Oh, it was all so confused, so convoluted! Hilary loved Darius as much as she had on the day of their wedding, but the razor's edge was easily crossed.

When the tears subsided she dried her face with a handkerchief and started the weary process of undressing. Normally, Elsie would help her, but of late Hilary had begun to resist having every little thing done for her. In all her thirty-three years she had never questioned the service constantly attendant upon her; but in the last few months Hilary had found herself growing impatient with butlers opening doors, men helping her up steps, maids dressing and undressing her.

She paused. Her temples had started to throb. Two months along and she was already as miserable with this pregnancy as she had been carrying Myrtle. Seven more months of nausea, pain, lethargy. And that deplorable bloating. Hilary went into the adjoining bathroom, opened a cupboard and took out a bottle. Farmer's Female Friend. Dahlia Mason had recommended it because *her* second and third pregnancies had been unpleasant. "It really works wonders," she had told Hilary. Hilary had taken it during the last pregnancy and had kept on with it occasionally since, for it did relieve backaches and monthly cramps. The label claimed the tonic to be specifically and "scientifically" formulated for the expectant woman. "If you suffer from any of these symptoms," it read, "lethargy, languor, listlessness, nausea, bad taste in mouth, impaired general health, dry skin, frequent urination, tender bust, a feeling of dread, a feeling of impending evil, sparks before the eyes, throbbing temples, poor sleep, palpitations, depression, or any of the symptoms which naturally accompany the state of pregnancy, Farmer's Female Friend will absolutely and certainly cure all of them instantly or your money back."

Some of the symptoms didn't plague Hilary, but others most definitely did. Primarily depression and listlessness. And the medicine did work; it had never failed to stave off impending blues.

She swallowed a tablespoonful, waited a moment, then took another.

It wasn't just the pregnancy; not this time. Of late, Hilary had started to become restless and bored, burdened with a sense of purposelessness. Her work at the Infirmary had been fulfilling these past seven years, but it had only been part time because of almost constant pregnancy. After Cornelius, she had hoped to be free from that imprisoning state and thrust herself full time into the Ladies' Committee. Now that hope was dashed.

The week before, facing the next seven months gloomily, Hilary had thought that perhaps if she could be more useful in the management of the house, perhaps share in the responsibility, it would give her a feeling of being needed. She had asked Darius to explain their finances and he had simply laughed; when she had asked to see the checkbook he had looked at her quizzically; and when she had inquired into their personal debts and assets, Darius had gotten indignant and ordered her to stop this nonsense.

It was then that Hilary had a chilling revelation: I am unnecessary!

Now, sitting before her dressing table and waiting for the medicine to work, she felt as if the threads of her life were coming apart, as if she were losing control.

What Hilary needed was to talk to Samantha. But Samantha, these days, was not easily available.

The hospital had grown bigger than either had anticipated; two years ago a second building had been added and renovated, fifty more beds moved in, and the nursing school moved to a house across the street. New equipment, more staff, budget juggling, and a rash of new medical discoveries had robbed Samantha of much of her private time. Except for meetings concerning the Ladies' Committee and fund-raising, Samantha seemed unable to spare time for her friend. It had been six weeks since their last luncheon at Chez Pierre.

Hilary debated. She needed to talk to Samantha. She looked at the clock by her bed and wondered where Samantha might be at this hour—at home or, more likely, at the Infirmary. Hilary had called at the hospital that morning only to learn that Samantha was in surgery; she had then gone to Dahlia Mason's house, to be told her friend was horseback riding.

They're free and I'm not.

Hilary returned to her reflection in the mirror, thinking that she looked older than she was; and she suddenly felt very alone.

She reached down and opened a drawer. From it she withdrew a lacquered Chinese jewel box which, when opened, played "Fur Elise" on a hidden mechanism. In it was a plain little cardboard box that looked as if it contained a gewgaw from Chinatown. Darius, if he ever accidentally looked in the jewelry box, would think this little carton of no account.

But in fact it contained an instrument of life and death.

—❧—

Samantha leaned back and lifted the spectacles off her nose; they were feeling inordinately heavy tonight. But she knew it wasn't really the glasses that were heavy but the legal case that lay spread out before her: Dr. Willella Canby had been charged with performing an illegal operation—an abortion—in the Infirmary.

Samantha looked up from her desk and was surprised to see that it was dark out. When she had sat down it was still daylight. She got up to turn on the electric light, then she walked toward the french doors and saw in the glass a tall and graceful woman glide toward her from the other side. She looked younger than thirty-five, although the glasses might add a bit of age, and not much changed from the uncertain young woman who had sought to find her dream among San Francisco's hills thirteen years ago. Her reflection looked as if she was taking a stroll in the September evening; Samantha wished she could do that right now, indulge herself a little, but this case was coming up tomorrow and she had to be prepared.

Willella was badly shaken. The patient had used an old trick on her: she had bought a live chicken, cut its throat and soaked a rag in its blood, then, with the rag stuffed in her underwear, she had staggered up the hospital steps to claim she was having a miscarriage. Standard procedure was to take the girl up to surgery. Technically, Willella had performed an abortion; ethically, she had only done a routine surgical procedure.

Continuing to gaze out through the french doors, Samantha listened to the silence in the house. Darius and Hilary had bought Samantha an Edison Standard Phonograph, one of the first in the city, to counter the unnatural silence that perpetually filled the house, but Samantha never used it. She had become accustomed to the constant quiet, grown even to appreciate it.

She glanced at the small watch on her wrist (another modern gadget, a gift from Darius) and realized the children must be asleep.

This thought never failed to bring a smile to Samantha's lips. She might be old enough to be Jenny's mother, but she certainly was not old enough to be Adam's. Still, she couldn't help fondly thinking of them both as her children. Ever since that rainy Christmas Eve when he had stood on her doorstep, drenched and lost-looking, Samantha had regarded Adam Wolff as a son. Even though he was only six years younger than she.

The lure of the garden was too much. Samantha decided to indulge herself in a walk before returning to her desk.

The three-story house on Jackson Street in Pacific Heights was a perfect haven away from the hustle and bustle of the Infirmary. When Samantha had gone looking, seven years before, she had had in mind to buy a house that was in the city, convenient and close to friends and the hospital; a house not too large, like Hilary's, but large enough for individual freedom and privacy; a house, preferably, with a view of the bay and a bit of grass around it. She had found just such a house almost the first time out. It stood on the crest of a hill, not far from Divisadero, looking down on the Marina, Alcatraz Island, and the Golden Gate itself. It was not a big house—just large enough for Samantha to have her own suite of rooms and a study off the garden, for Adam and Jenny to have their own rooms and a schoolroom, and quarters upstairs for the two maids and Miss Peoples. The front steps touched the sidewalk, but on one side of the house there was a strip of lawn to separate them from the neighbors, on the other, a carriage house for her brougham and two horses, and in the back a terraced garden with a gazebo.

Samantha held her face into the breeze, taking in the tangy salt air and delighting in the lights twinkling far below at the wharfside. Such demand was made on her time nowadays that when she stole an occasional moment for herself, she relished it in full.

And during these stolen moments she never ceased to marvel at the turn her life had taken. She felt many of her dreams had been achieved, she felt professionally accomplished; her hospital was flourishing; she had dear and wonderful friends; she lived comfortably and contentedly; and she had her two "children."

The miracle of that Christmas, seven years ago, continued to work to this day. It was as if that night had been fated: Jenny's sudden breaking free from her bonds and Adam's coincidental arrival. Yes, as if indeed it was meant to be.

Adam Wolff, Samantha firmly believed, had been God-sent. Within an hour of his arrival he had established the unique and special bond with

Jenny that had strengthened with each passing year, that had borne such miraculous fruit, that had won him everyone's admiration and praise so that, today, those who loved him did not see his ugliness.

Adam Wolff might have been a handsome young man. The accident had happened in 1876, when he was ten years old and working with his father on a demolition crew that was blasting Telegraph Hill for its rock quarry. Young Adam, a handsome, robust boy who earned ten cents a day at the wheelbarrows, had been too close to the explosion. He had lost his hearing, his face had been badly disfigured and his father had been killed. It was through the brothers at the Mission that he had been taken in at the School for the Deaf as a pauper student where, for six years, he had learned the manual alphabet of the deaf and lip reading; for the remaining five years he had been a teacher there.

The arrangement with Dr. Hargrave had initially been short-term. Adam Wolff was to stay only for as long as it took to teach Jenny basic communication skills; but something magical had happened. At some time, while patiently instructing the girl in the finger alphabet, Adam Wolff had unwittingly unlocked and set free the beautiful, ethereal spirit of Jennifer Hargrave.

It hadn't happened all at once, but gradually, until one day everyone forgot that the boy was supposed to leave. He stayed on, became a member of the family and found, after his heart had been hardened on the day of the explosion, a capacity to love once again.

Samantha had wondered at first if there was something that could be done for the boy's looks. But the scarring, she found on close examination, was too deep, too permanent; he had, in fact, to be thankful he was not blind as well. But the disfigurement was startling only at first. Everyone's initial reaction, meeting the young man for the first time, was shock; then pity; and then, as his gentleness and sensitivity touched them, people soon forgot the scars and saw after a while only a kind and poetic young man.

Together they made a remarkable pair.

Jennifer, nineteen, had blossomed into an uncannily beautiful young woman, whose beauty was enhanced by her silence, her mystique, and the special gaze in her eyes. Jennifer had a way of looking, a way of "listening" while one spoke, that gave the impression she was picking up more than words: it was as if she were tuned to finer communications. And standing next to Adam, her beauty seemed even more astounding. When they went around the city together, in the carriage or for long walks, they never failed to draw stares from passers-by. As they walked in their own world, speaking with their hands in their own language, Jenny and Adam were a freakish pair: his deformity next to her loveliness.

So many miracles these past seven years, Samantha reflected now. The discovery of a deep and profound feeling Jennifer trapped inside her speechless body. Young Adam, lonely and shunned, bitter and morose, learning to be gentle and loving. Samantha seeing her daughter emerge and seeing Jenny spell "mother" with her fingers for the first time.

Samantha gazed with misty eyes at the bay and laughed at a sweet memory. After the finger alphabet, Adam had taught Jenny to read. He taught her the word "draw," then demonstrated with a pencil and paper what it meant. But then Jenny read in her primer that "a horse draws a wagon." After Adam's explanation, she was baffled by a line in the *Chronicle* which read, "The concert drew a large audience." Her bafflement increased when she encountered, "Mr. Cole draws a mug of cider," "Miss Shaw draws a sigh," "A ship draws water," "A cook draws a fowl," and "Money draws interest." By the end of the evening, watching Jenny's puzzlement drive Adam to exasperation, Samantha had had to laugh.

So much joy, these past seven years . . .

Samantha sat on a bench among the flowers and her thoughts turned once again to Mark. He continued to walk with her, he had never left her side, now the only man in her life. Ever since sending Warren Dunwich away Samantha had come to an understanding with herself: she didn't want to marry, for Mark would always be her husband; and she didn't need babies of her own—besides Jennifer and Adam she had all the children at the Infirmary who, no matter how temporary, were hers for a while. And so she had gently put an end to Stanton Weatherby's earnest courtship (now he was a good friend and her attorney), an end to Hilary's matchmaking, and an end to any serious intentions a gentleman might exhibit.

From where she sat, down at the foot of the hillside garden, Samantha did not hear the ringing of the telephone up in the house. Miss Peoples had gone for a walk. It was the maids' night off and the other two inhabitants in the house could not hear it at all. And so the telephone went unanswered.

Samantha watched the running lights of a private yacht that was moored at the Marina and remembered that Darius was out on just such a vessel. Hilary had voiced fears to Samantha about this new sport, but there was no stopping Darius. If it was new and modern and fashionable he wanted it. Samantha recalled the day he had bought the new George Eastman hand-held camera and had forced everyone to stand in the garden in various unnatural poses to practice taking "snapshots." Samantha wondered where Darius got his energy and his imagination from. Now he was deeply involved in oranges—a venture which everyone predicted would fail, but which Darius felt certain could be made profitable if only a way of shipping them without spoilage could be found. He was dividing his time between Los Angeles where the crops were and Sacramento where he went over blueprints for an experimental refrigerated boxcar.

We're all so busy these days, Samantha thought as she rose from the bench. We hardly have time just to be people.

As she went back up the flagstone path to the house, Samantha's thoughts returned to the Infirmary. Again and always, money. That much-needed steam heating still remained maddeningly elusive; whenever funds came in, something else had priority. And now there was outside pressure to open a special Ophthalmic Ward.

Back in her study Samantha went straight to her desk, readjusted her glasses and read again the notes she had prepared for Willella Canby's defense. Stanton Weatherby had assured her that the plaintiff (the patient's irate father) would drop the charges as soon as he was apprised of all the circumstances (his daughter's deception). Now Samantha wanted to work on preventing future such mishaps.

She had read that faked miscarriages had become so common in urban hospitals that a physician at another hospital had recommended that, before automatically rushing the patient up to surgery, the blood should be inspected under a microscope, for that would prove conclusively whether or not the patient was indeed miscarrying: the red blood cell of a chicken has a nucleus, that of a human does not. Samantha picked up her pen and started to write.

-❦-

Hilary stared at the telephone and thought: You're never home anymore, Sam. The only way to get to see you is to be sick.

She rose from her writing desk and slipped into her nightgown. Her reflection moved with her, the body of a young woman who was no longer as slender as she had once been. She stared ruefully at the plumpish lines of her figure. She hadn't been horseback riding in years; archery maybe once every few months. She was turning into a cow; Hilary was disgusted with herself.

The dissatisfied see through biased eyes; Hilary's growing disillusionment with her life had distorted her vision, for she was no less lovely and attractive now than she had ever been. In fact, the added weight gave her a more girlish look; her cheeks dimpled when she smiled, and everyone said she looked wonderful. But it was no use—Hilary didn't like herself anymore.

She slumped down at her dresser and gazed at the little cardboard box.

She lifted the lid and glared at the odious object inside. Once she had been pleased and excited about the device; now she despised it. False security is worse than no security. She blamed the device for this unwanted pregnancy.

Anticonception was as old as womankind but in America it was also illegal. While European women enjoyed easy access to such popular and reliable devices as the diaphragm and cervical cap, American women had to resort to the blind sort of hit-and-miss contraception their mothers and grandmothers had used: sponges soaked in quinine, plugs of beeswax, garlic necklaces. Word of the European device had reached America and a great demand arose; the few diaphragms that were smuggled into the United States sold for high prices. The San Francisco Infirmary for Women heard hundreds of requests each month but there was nothing they could do; the law was clear: the dispensing of such items guaranteed immediate revocation of one's medical license.

It was a dilemma Samantha had wrestled with. Wanting on the one hand to help but on the other afraid of jeopardizing the Infirmary, she and her staff had on occasion managed to skirt the laws by dispensing tampons and syringes ostensibly for the treatment of vaginal infections. In fact they contained spermicides. It was a risky business and they all lived in fear of discovery, but the poor woman who presented her worn body at the Infirmary, promising that the next pregnancy would end in suicide, could not be turned away. And when Hilary approached Samantha for help, Samantha had not hesitated to equip her friend with a sponge and jelly.

The sponge had worked for six months, with Darius not even knowing it was there. Then one night it had failed and once was all that was needed: Cornelius was the result.

Hilary had then managed, through a friend, to gain possession of an illegal diaphragm. Samantha had fitted it and shown her how to use it, knowing all the while that both, if discovered, could have been arrested. The marvelous French device had worked for two blissful years—but now it had failed too. And Hilary felt she had come to the end of a line.

Wearily she put the lid back on the box, put it away in its secret drawer and got up. Her temples were still throbbing.

Returning to the bathroom, she took out the bottle of Farmer's.

TWO

*S*AMANTHA WAS ANGRY.

This was not the first such incident: the Infirmary saw more than she'd care to think about. As she gazed down at the pale blue lids and the peacefully sleeping face, Samantha thought: Damn them.

She straightened up from the bed. It appeared the girl was going to make it, although early this morning she had been close to death. Thank God for Willella Canby's quick thinking: her idea to pump the unconscious girl's stomach had saved her life. Now Samantha had to look forward to when the girl awoke, for then it would be her painful duty to inform her she was still pregnant. The "cycle restorer" she had bought at the local drugstore had not worked.

Samantha folded her stethoscope and slipped it into the large pocket of her skirt. Accidental overdoses from drugstore medicines were on the rise. More and more innocent girls and women were either becoming addicted or, worse, killing themselves on medicines that claimed to be healthful and harmless.

Samantha gazed thoughtfully down the rows of beds. At least twelve of these patients were here as a result of taking quack patent medicines. Another ten suffered from natural gynecological problems that, as yet, could not be cured. Four were hysterical cases: the causes of their afflictions were mental rather than physical. And two eluded diagnosis altogether. Of the forty, eight would die from their illnesses. Ten would have surgery, and of those ten only eight would survive. Fifteen would leave the hospital not totally healed, permanently impaired in some way, and the rest, through luck or medical intervention, would be restored.

Samantha didn't like those odds.

She went to her office, stopping along the way to exchange a few words with some of the patients, to consult with Dr. Lovejoy on the patient with massive fibroids, to go over Charity Ziegler's menu, and to hear once again that the downstairs porter had been found drunk and asleep on the post-mortem table. When she reached her office door, looking forward to a cup of tea, Nurse Constance told her a new patient was waiting in the examining room.

Samantha went in. The patient was a plump matronly lady wearing an outdated bustle and hat with ostrich plumes that seemed to fill the little room. She was cheery and robust and exhibited none of the shyness most new patients had. She didn't have a problem but a question: she was fifty-two years old and her monthly days had ceased a year ago, but she had started bleeding again and she wanted to know if she could get pregnant.

Samantha forced a professional smile. The woman's symptoms did not indicate a resuming of fertility but something quite the opposite. She helped her onto the examining table, did a gentle exploration, and her worst dread was confirmed. Cancer.

Samantha sat with Mrs. Paine for a while, offering smelling salts and a handkerchief, then she tugged the bell rope and asked Nurse Hampton to sit with Mrs. Paine in one of the private sitting rooms. After they had gone, Samantha remained seated on her stool.

It was impossible to remove a cancerous uterus without killing the patient. Other organs would be involved and malignant tissue bled profusely. Even hysterectomy for simple fibroids was risky—one in five women did not survive. Mrs. Paine had just received a death sentence.

There was a timid knock on the door. It was Nurse Constance. "Dr. Hargrave?"

"Yes, Constance."

"There's a Chinaman to see you. He says it's urgent."

Urgencies were not unusual, but the man's race was; few Celestials came to Samantha. He turned out to be the Gants' houseboy—and he was distraught. "Missy Gant very ill. Come now!"

Samantha shot to her feet. "Which Miss Gant?"

"Missy *Lady* Gant. Come quick now, please."

As she followed him down the hall, watching his long queue stay in a straight line down his back despite his brisk trot, Samantha grew alarmed. Leaving the care of the hospital to Dr. Canby, she climbed into the Gants' carriage and rode off into the dusk.

-⚜-

The housekeeper met her at the door. The habitually impeccable Mrs. Mainwaring was clearly upset and wringing her hands; she took Samantha through the hushed house, up the stairs and down the richly carpeted hall. She stopped at the end, knocked and murmured close to the door, "Dr. Hargrave is here."

Elsie opened the door. The paleness of her face shocked Samantha. "What's wrong, Elsie?" she asked, hastily shrugging off her coat. But before the maid could reply, Samantha saw Hilary stretched out on the bed. She was unconscious.

"Oh, Dr. Hargrave," squeaked Elsie, padding behind Samantha as she rushed to the bedside. "It was awful! She fell down the stairs!"

Samantha checked the vital signs: Hilary's pulse was feeble and slow; skin clammy; hands and feet like ice; lips bluish. Samantha lifted the eyelids and found pinpointed pupils. "How did it happen, Elsie?" she asked as she continued to check Hilary's body for broken bones.

Elsie looked as if she was trying to pull each of her fingers out of its joint. "Mrs. Gant wasn't acting right this morning. I had an awful time waking her, and then she seemed sort of . . . *hazy.* She stayed in her room all day. Then a little while ago we heard a crash, and there she was at the foot of the stairs!"

Samantha frowned. "What do you mean, hazy, Elsie? Can you describe her condition more precisely?"

"Well, she was drowsy. She said she had a terrible headache. And she was very thirsty. I couldn't keep her pitcher filled. Oh, Dr. Hargrave, is she going to die?"

"I need to know if she took anything. Pills, medicine—"

"She's been taking this." Elsie thrust an empty bottle under Samantha's nose. Farmer's Female Friend.

Samantha's brows came together as she read the finer print. "Guaranteed to relieve depression, counteract blues and dispel those feelings of dread that are common in the pregnant woman."

"How much of this did she drink, Elsie?"

"It was a full bottle last night, Doctor."

Samantha's eyes stared hard at the label. Female Friend. "Feelings of dread . . ."

"Do you know when she bought it?"

"That bottle? Yesterday, I think. When the other ran out."

Samantha brought her head up. "The other? You mean Mrs. Gant has taken this medicine before?"

"She's been taking it for a while now, Doctor. I believe she started when she was expecting Master Cornelius. Is she going to be all right?"

"Yes, Elsie," said Samantha calmly. "She'll be all right. We'll need lots of black coffee. Very strong." She looked up at the panicked maid. "Elsie?"

"Oh! Yes, Dr. Hargrave!" Elsie fled, glad of something to do, and Samantha looked again at the bottle. She had dealt with victims of Farmer's before. The medicine was heavily laced with opium, although there was no mention of that on the bottle; nor was there any warning as to limited intake.

She gazed at her friend's sleeping face and felt a sinking of her heart. Oh, Hilary . . .

Samantha and Elsie worked for an hour reviving Hilary, massaging her hands and feet, pumping her arms and legs, tapping her cheeks to waken her. Hilary emerged, then sank back; her lids fluttered; she groaned. Samantha stopped only to check her heart rate, which was starting to increase. Then Hilary's breathing became normal and the blueness disappeared from her lips.

When Hilary was groggily awake, Samantha cradled her in an arm and slowly fed her the strong coffee.

Hilary coughed and sputtered. "Oh, I feel awful. What happened?"

"You fell down the stairs."

"I did? I don't remember . . ."

"Luckily you were so doped you must have fallen like a rubber doll. You could have broken your neck."

"Doped?" Hilary tried to focus on Samantha's face. She felt vague, wooden. "Doped?" she said again.

"Farmer's. You must have drunk the entire bottle."

Hilary groaned. "I woke up with such a headache. I guess I lost track of how much I was taking . . ."

"Here, keep drinking the coffee. It will stimulate you. We have to counteract the opium."

"Opium? I didn't take any . . . oh no, I would never . . ."

"No, I know you wouldn't. Not on purpose. But Farmer's contains a large quantity of opium."

Hilary blinked in confusion. She sipped the coffee and licked her lips. "No, you're wrong. It's only a vegetable tonic. It says so . . . Samantha, I feel awful. Have I lost the baby?"

Samantha stared down at her friend. Hilary hadn't told her she was pregnant "No, the baby's fine, darling."

When Hilary's head lolled against Samantha's breast, she put the coffee cup down and stroked the auburn curls that were as soft as a child's. She held her friend for a very long time.

-❊-

The knock startled her. Samantha rose from the chair she had been sitting in for the past two hours and opened the door to Darius. He was wearing a sailing blazer, white slacks, and a commodore's hat. "Samantha! Mrs. Mainwaring told me—"

She put a finger to her lips. "Let's go downstairs."

"Is she all right? Mrs. Mainwaring said she fell down the stairs."

Samantha put a gentle hand on his arm. "We mustn't disturb her. Let's talk downstairs, Darius."

In the parlor Darius planted himself before the fireplace, his shadow filling the room and dancing with the flames. Samantha sat before him, hands clasped, and said quietly, "Hilary drank a medicine that made her disoriented. She lost her balance and fell."

"What sort of medicine?"

"It is supposedly for depression. Did you know that Hilary was depressed?"

"No, I didn't know . . ." Darius went to the easy chair. "I haven't been home much lately, but if she was depressed she would have told me, wouldn't she?"

Samantha sighed. "I'm her best friend, Darius, and *I* had no idea she was having problems. Darius, the medicine is specifically for pregnant women. Is Hilary unhappy about this pregnancy?"

He stared at her. "I didn't know she was pregnant."

Samantha thought a moment, and then she recalled the message she had received the other morning that Hilary had come by while she was in surgery. Samantha had meant to call Hilary that evening, but then the case with Dr. Canby had come up. Then Samantha started remembering other things: Hilary's unhappiness during her last pregnancy, the secretly purchased diaphragm, the declared hope that she was finished with all that. And suddenly Samantha understood everything.

She felt a pang. Hilary needed me and I wasn't there!

"Darius," she said softly, "we failed her. You have been busy with your oranges, and I have had the Infirmary."

"But Hilary is busy! She has her Ladies' Committee, six children, a house to look after!"

"Maybe that's not enough, Darius. Or maybe it's not what she wants. Hilary has been unhappy for a long time and we never noticed."

"I don't understand. How can she be unhappy? Especially if she's pregnant again. She should be overjoyed!"

"Maybe she doesn't want another baby, Darius."

"That's ridiculous."

"Did you know she was practicing anticonception?"

He gazed at her, looking dumfounded.

Then another, darker thought came to Samantha. Falling down the stairs. Just how accidental had it been?

"But why?" he said in a tight whisper. "Why shouldn't she want another baby?"

"Darius." Samantha reached for his hand. "Hilary is a good wife and mother, but she wants more than that. Since I first met her, she has spent half her life in confinement. Like a prisoner. She reached the end of it, Darius. She wants to be free."

"Free? Free from what?"

"From constant pregnancy."

"But that's a woman's purpose."

"She has six children, Darius. She's fulfilled that purpose."

"It's not fair." He swung his head from side to side. "To use anticonception without my knowledge. I have rights!"

"Hilary has rights too, Darius. To be a free woman. That's what anticonception is, why she resorted to it."

"I don't understand, Sam."

"Anticonception is a woman's ultimate act of independence, I suppose. As long as you can keep getting her pregnant, Hilary is subjugated by you. But, by depriving you of that tyranny, she is proclaiming her independence of you." And I suppose, thought Samantha sadly, by turning to a drugstore bottle for consolation, she was proclaiming her independence of me.

He gazed at her with a stricken look. "Then I've lost her?"

Samantha experienced a pain, for the same thought had occurred to her, but she said, "No, you haven't lost her. You still have, Darius, your marriage and the love you share with her."

"No, not if she doesn't want my children."

"Children aren't the issue here, Darius. It goes deeper. And it goes all the way back to the day she came so timidly to my office nine years ago, not telling you about the operation until it was over. She has been trying to make a bid for independence ever since, Darius. Hilary wants a little freedom, but she wants to come by it honestly."

"I don't understand. Does she want a divorce?"

"A woman can be married and still be free."

But Darius only frowned. That was like saying soup could be hot and cold at the same time. "She doesn't want me anymore."

"Talk to her, Darius. Hilary loves you no less just because she wants freedom. Talk to her, Darius, and *listen*."

He nodded uncertainly. "I'll do anything to make her happy."

Samantha smiled briefly, then pushed herself up from the chair. As she straightened her long skirt she thought: And I know what *I* have to do.

THREE

*S*HE PAUSED INSIDE THE DOORWAY TO LET HER EYES ADJUST TO stepping in out of the afternoon glare.

It was a drugstore like most others in the city, with shelves of bottles and tins reaching up to the ceiling, new glass counters containing health aids and colognes, a soda fountain with stools, and a large mirror behind it with signs advertising Coca-Cola, Bromo Seltzer and Moxie. In between displays of drugs on the counter tops were a stamp dispenser, a station for receiving film to be developed and cylinder phonograph records on a revolving rack. A few customers browsed and one was receiving a wrapped package from the druggist. Samantha decided to look around.

The products ranged in the hundreds and promised to cure everything from a split toenail to brain cancer. A bottle of Gono declared itself to be "an unequaled remedy for all unnatural discharges and inflammation; positively cures gonorrhea and gleet." A box of Dr. Rose's Obesity Powders addressed itself to "Fat Folks" and guaranteed weight loss in a "comparatively short time." Barry's Tricopherous promised to restore lost hair; Sozodont claimed to "harden and preserve teeth"; Brown's Iron Bitters promised to stop "decay in the liver, kidneys and bowels"; and Lydia Pinkham's Vegetable Compound guaranteed a "baby in every bottle." There were tubes of tartar emetic ointment for concerned parents to rub on the genitals of their sons to discourage masturbation; a bottle of The Unfortunate's Friend guaranteed a cure for syphilis; and there were vaginal tampons containing a "wonderful agent certain to restore the menstrual cycle that has been suppressed by nervous anxiety and other causes."

Samantha slowly moved along the counters, pausing to inspect displays of hypodermic syringes and needles; enema syringes accompanied by bottles of "soothing wine opiate"; and breast cups guaranteed to "enlarge and beautify the female bust." As she gradually worked her way to the cash register where the trout-faced druggist was giving advice to an elderly lady, Samantha lingered before a display of Sara Fenwick's Miracle Compound, stacked pyramid style on the counter; in front of it was a neat pile of pamphlets labeled, "Totally free. Take one."

She picked up a bottle and read the label. The herbal compound guaranteed to cure, restore, revitalize, rejuvenate, invigorate and remedy every possible complaint known to woman. There was no mention of the compound's ingredients.

Samantha picked up one of the pamphlets. "Every lady can be her own physician," declared the paragraph inside. "She can treat herself without having to reveal her intimate condition to anyone, or sacrifice her womanly modesty to an unnecessary examination by a physician. Do you want a strange man to hear all about your *intimate* ailments? Would you feel comfortable sitting down with this stranger and revealing to him all those sacred things which should only be known by woman? This is not natural for a woman; it is not in keeping with her acute sense of refinement and modesty. Every *real* woman experiences horror at the thought of revealing her *private* disorders to a man, be he physician or not. Mrs. Fenwick understands, for she is a woman herself. Write to Mrs. Fenwick yourself for Free and Personal advice. Men *never* see your letters. There are no boys in our office. All correspondence is handled by women, read by women and answered *by women only!*"

There followed a selection of letters from "our enormous correspondence from all over the country."

Mrs. G.V. of Scranton wrote: "For years I was a sufferer of constant womb trouble. I have had five tumors in four years and went to doctors but they did me no good: they were unsympathetic and put me on morphine. They said I would need surgery to have my womb removed, but then I heard of Mrs. Fenwick and wrote to her for advice. She said that I should take a tablespoon of the Miracle Compound after every meal and whenever I felt bilious. The tumors were expelled at once. I feel strong now and enjoy vigorous health. I am always cheerful and my husband comes home happily every night! I can sincerely say I might have died if it weren't for Sara Fenwick's Miracle Compound."

Samantha looked at the bottle again. The label on the back declared: "The shock of an operation is too great for most women. The Miracle Compound will dissolve tumors of the uterus cleanly and painlessly."

Glancing at the druggist, who was ringing up a sale, she quickly uncorked the bottle and sniffed. The alcohol was at least thirty percent.

She replaced the bottle and the pamphlet and gazed thoughtfully at them. *Dissolves tumors of the uterus . . .*

"May I help you, madam?"

She looked up at the druggist. "Yes. I'm looking for Farmer's Female Friend."

"Certainly, madam." He reached to a shelf behind and brought down a bottle.

Samantha took it, read the label and said, "Is it safe?"

"Guaranteed safe, madam."

"For a pregnant woman?"

"That's what it is specifically made for, madam."

Samantha said, "I'll take it."

As the druggist proceeded to wrap the bottle in a square of brown paper, Samantha casually scanned the shelves behind him. "Listerine," she murmured. "Coincidentally named for Dr. Lister, I suppose."

"It's no coincidence. Two sharp Missouri salesmen came up with the idea. Dr. Lister sold them his name, he gets royalties, and I have a product that's one of the fastest moving in the store."

"You're very well stocked here."

"I try to carry everything a body might need." He pulled a length of string from a spool and tied it around the package. "It's like this. Folks don't like to go to a doctor and shell out two bucks for him to tell them he can't help them. They come here, tell me their problem, and I recommend something. It's cheaper, quicker, less trouble and the cure is guaranteed. Now, what doctor can you say that of?"

She reached into her reticule and put a dollar bill on the counter. As the cash register rang, the druggist went on: "I sell people what they want. The Temperance ladies, for instance. They shout about beer and try to get it made illegal and then they come in here for Park's Vegetable Tonic. Beer is at most eight percent alcohol. Park's is forty-one." He counted out her change into her palm. "Hypocrites, know what I mean?"

She dropped the coins into her purse. "Perhaps they are not aware of it," she said, pointing to a bottle of the tonic, whose label emphatically declared: "Absolutely no alcohol." She reached for her package.

"There, that one," he went on. "The Balm of Gilead. Endorsed by clergymen. Seventy percent alcohol. The Temperance movement doesn't frighten me, I'm all for it. Close the saloons and folks'll flock to the drugstores!"

Samantha nodded in interest. "Do you stand behind everything you sell?"

"Absolutely. If I don't think it's good, then I won't stock it."

"Were you aware that this medicine I just bought is heavily laced with opium?"

His eyes flickered. "Howzat?"

"Farmer's Female Friend. It contains a great deal of opium. Don't you know that's harmful to a pregnant woman and her unborn child?"

The man's friendly manner evaporated. "Who says it contains opium?"

"I believe I just did."

"Doesn't say so on the label."

"Come now, sir. We both understand about labels. I'm just surprised that you would knowingly sell a harmful product."

"There's no opium in that compound, lady."

"I would like proof of that myself. Could you please provide me with the address of the manufacturer?"

"I can't tell you that."

"I have a right to know what I am drinking. Please give me the address of Farmer's."

He glared at her frostily. "Lady, if you don't like what's in the medicine, then don't buy it."

"How can I know what's in it when there is no mention on the label and when you yourself either don't know or won't tell a customer? I just happen to know that these bottles contain a dangerous narcotic. One of them nearly caused the death of a friend of mine. This so-called medicine makes addicts out of unsuspecting users. I think, sir, you have an obligation either to warn your customers or to remove the bottles from your shelves."

He continued to glare at her for a moment, then said in a low, angry tone, "My only obligation right now, lady, is to ask you to leave. I don't like what you're insinuating."

Samantha gazed coolly at him for a minute, then, looking around at the other customers, she clutched the bottle against her and calmly walked out.

"Then what did you do?"

"I ran an analysis here in the Infirmary. Farmer's Female Friend contains more opium than laudanum does."

"My dear, will you please stand still?"

Samantha was pacing the floor of her office, and Stanton Weatherby, her old friend, was watching. Samantha paused at the window to look out. The city was bundled in a cloak of evening fog and Kearny Street had taken on an eerie atmosphere—the street lamps glowed like suspended lanterns and carriages inched their way in and out of the mist like prehistoric beasts; the horn of an unseen motorcar blared in the silence.

"Please do continue your story, my dear," said Stanton.

She turned to look at him. "That's all. There is nothing else."

Stanton, as one of the trustees and also the attorney for the Infirmary, came by once a week to discuss business with Samantha. This afternoon, instead of their usual pleasant talk over tea, he had found an agitated Samantha and no tea.

She resumed pacing. "I was appalled, Stanton, to see such wholesale quackery in the drugstores! And the druggists either don't care or they are ignorant of what they are selling. Whichever, the customer has no protection."

"It's not illegal."

She stopped to look at him. "No, it's not illegal, but it should be. Anyone with a bit of colored water and a fancy label can cheat innocent people. And maybe even harm them."

"Colored water doesn't hurt."

"But it *does,* Stanton. Those quack medicines keep people from seeking proper medical treatment."

He studied her beautiful face and wished she hadn't rejected his courtship. "There's nothing you can do about it, Samantha."

"The public has a right to be informed, Stanton. They have a right to know what's in those bottles. And maybe, once the public *is* aware, they'll try to get some reforms put through, like a law requiring labels to list ingredients."

Stanton shook his head. He rose and went to the window where the white wall of fog cast back his reflection; he looked skeptical. "It's a hard fight, Samantha. The Proprietary Medicine Association has a powerful lobby. Every year bills are introduced into Congress and every year they quietly die."

"We can go to the newspapers for help."

"You'll get no help from them. A major portion of their revenue comes from drug company advertising."

"There must be a way!"

He turned around and rocked back on his heels. "Samantha, have you heard of Harvey Wiley?"

"Yes, I think so. Isn't he the chief of the Division of Chemistry in the Department of Agriculture?"

"Wiley is trying to stop food manufacturers and retailers from adulterating their foods to increase profits. Alum in bread to make it heavier, sand in sugar, dust mixed in with coffee, chalk in milk, embalmed beef in tin cans—the atrocities are endless. Grocers and suppliers, like drug manufacturers, are at liberty to do anything they want to food without informing the consumer. Harvey Wiley has been crusading to require such packagers to inform the customer if anything has been added, and so far all of his bills have died in Congress. And Harvey Wiley is a man of some influence."

"Stanton, we've got to do something."

Weatherby thought for a moment. "This is a free country, Samantha. A drug manufacturer has the right to put whatever it wants into its medicines. The government can't tell it what to do."

"I'm not saying that it should. I'm merely saying that, for the customer's protection, the manufacturer should be required to state what the medicine contains. The public has a right to know what is in the medicine it buys. The man who goes into the drugstore has the right to know what his dollar is paying for."

"You're talking about government intervention, Samantha."

"On the contrary, I'm talking about giving more freedom to the people. The freedom to know what they are buying. And the freedom from being defrauded."

She joined him at the window and looked out. "Stanton, I have felt this anger growing within me for years. Each time a victim of a quack medicine comes to this hospital I want to scream. Well, it's time I did something about it."

He studied her determined profile, a look he had seen many times before, and knew it was no use to argue. "What do you intend to do?"

"First, I'm going to educate the women who come to this hospital. Then I'm going to try to reach the American public. *Someone* will listen to me . . ."

FOUR

*M*AYBE OTHER PEOPLE GOT USED TO HIS UGLINESS, BUT ADAM never would. Every time he glimpsed his reflection he was repelled. That was why there was no mirror in his room, and therefore why his hair was never combed correctly. Still, there were times when it was unavoidable: there were mirrors all through the house, there were panes in the windows, there was a pond by the gazebo—all throwing back his reflection as if in mockery. And each time, with the stab of pain, twenty-nine-year-old Adam Wolff never failed to think: But *she* doesn't see it.

No, Jenny saw no ugliness in Adam. Just as she had once seen through the handsome façade of Warren Dunwich and into his heartless core, Jenny didn't see the scars on Adam's face: his soul shone through too beautifully and brightly.

Adam had believed long ago that the explosion on Telegraph Hill had done more than deafen and disfigure him, it had also hardened his heart. Holding a rag to his bleeding face and watching his father being dragged out from under the rubble, too shocked to realize he couldn't hear their shouts, young Adam had felt the dust from the blast go down his throat and settle around his heart, building up like a stone wall, sealing it forever. And in the months following, living in gutters, wretched and alone, at the mercy of any who wished to take advantage of him, the boy had believed most strongly that he had died with his dad.

And then the Franciscans at the Mission had found him, put him in a pauper home for children and then arranged for him to be taken in by the School for the Deaf. Later he learned from the principal of the school that if he had received proper medical attention at once he would not have been so badly disfigured. But it was too late now, the man had said sadly; Adam Wolff was fated to live out his life in a silent world, disturbing to any who looked upon him.

And so, when he completed his education, Adam had decided to stay on as a teacher, for within the protective walls of the Berkeley school he was guarded from the stares of normal people; his pupils, once they got used to him, accepted him as he was.

Adam didn't know for sure when the aloneness had set in. Loneliness he had known from the day he had run from the blasting site and hidden in the alleys of North Beach; but the *aloneness,* the awareness that he was truly different, apart, separated even from his fellow deaf mutes, *that* had come sometime during adolescence—during that painful time when Adam had looked at the pretty girls in the school and had longed for them, knowing they would never return his regard. So it was then that he had reinforced the stone wall around his heart: if they wouldn't have him, then he didn't need them. Or anybody. And when adolescence evolved into manhood, Adam Wolff became a quiet, reserved, and unreachable young man.

But he was a teacher of unsurpassed excellence. In his seclusion, cut off from friends and a social life, Adam had turned to developing his mind. He read and studied and inquired. He watched and learned and found better ways of teaching. Under him, students excelled in the finger alphabet. His acuity and devotion made achievers of the most reluctant of pupils. He began to be assigned to the difficult cases; soon he was teaching on an individual basis. So when Principal Wilkinson received a letter from Samantha

Hargrave, a woman he had met several times and whom he admired, requesting help for her daughter, who was a serious case, there was no question but that Adam Wolff was the person for the job.

Adam had resisted at first, fearing to go out into the world again, but after some thought he regarded it as a challenge, yet one more in a series of challenges, and he had decided to put it to the test. Or rather, himself, to see if he could succeed.

People had stared at him on the stagecoach, then on the ferry, then on the trolley, and then on the sidewalk of Kearny Street. By the time he reached the Hargrave address late Christmas Eve (two weeks early, he learned to his horror, due to a smudging of ink), drenched and resentful, Adam Wolff had decided that at the first look of shock or pity from whoever opened the door he would return at once to the school.

But the lovely lady who had opened the door had merely smiled, brought him inside, taken his wet bag and coat, and steered him toward a roaring fire.

And then, in the next instant, an incredible thing had happened.

There was a girl, eleven years old, standing in the glow of the dancing flames, and she had stared at him with big liquid eyes. The moment seemed to have gone on for an eternity, with Adam standing wet and awkward on the hearth, the girl gazing at him; then she had moved slowly toward him, as if in a trance, had come to a standstill before him, close, gazing up. She had raised an arm, touched her fingers to his pitted cheeks, and she had smiled.

Adam had felt a movement behind him. Turning, he saw the woman press her hands to her mouth, a look on her face that was a mixture of shock and joy, and when her hands came away, he saw that her lips were saying, "Jenny! You're smiling!"

He had looked back at the girl and experienced, in that moment, a miracle.

Adam felt a sudden melting away of all cynicism and bitterness; it was like a religious experience, looking down at the girl. Suddenly he was reminded of all the goodness in the world that still existed. He was Saul of Tarsus on the Damascus Road: the scales fell from his eyes; the wall crumbled away from his heart and he felt, for the first time in eleven years, *moved.*

It had all been so dreamlike, so fantastical after that: the warm, loving atmosphere of the house; Dr. Hargrave, a compassionate woman; Jenny, looking up at Adam as if he were a god descended from Olympus. He learned from Dr. Hargrave the closed, enigmatic little mystery Jenny was, and then Adam had proceeded to release her from that prison. It hadn't been easy at first: the finger alphabet was but a game. But finally the girl's own intelligence and desire to communicate had broken the code. *She understood.*

The days and weeks and seasons had rolled by, but Adam had barely been aware of them. Jenny's hunger to learn inspired him to new heights. Art, poetry, nature—there was nothing that did not amaze and delight her. And it was as though they were all gifts from *him.* Adam Wolff gave Jennifer the world, and in return she gave him adulation. It was all he could ever ask for.

Until now.

Walking down through the garden to where Jenny sat in the gazebo with a book by Elizabeth Browning, Adam Wolff felt his heart grow heavy. She was nineteen now. Self-sufficient, bright, educated, able to get along by herself. She didn't need him anymore. His usefulness was ending.

Adam paused by the rose arbor to watch her, unseen.

Jennifer's beauty had never failed to affect him, and he had marveled during her blossoming years to see the girl, whom he had regarded as a sister, transformed into something exquisite. However, of late, Adam had felt strange new yearnings invade his soul; feelings he had not had since his youth at the school. He found himself no longer thinking of her as a sister but as a woman. And the affection he bore for her was starting to turn into desire. Realizing what was happening, Adam felt sick at heart. He had no right to fall in love—not with someone like Jenny.

Sensing him, she looked up suddenly and smiled, laid aside her book and rose. Adam felt choked with love, and also sadness. It wasn't fair! He wanted her in a way she wouldn't understand. Adam had always been and always would be, he knew, just a brother to Jenny, nothing more. He wanted to turn away but couldn't. She was so slender, so ethereal in her gossamer dress stirring in the breeze, her thick black hair falling over her shoulders, her eyes, her lips—

He stepped out from behind the arbor and went to her. "Hello," he signed. "Do you like the poems?"

Jenny's slender fingers spoke fluidly. "Yes. Thank you. It was a lovely gift. Will you sit with me?"

He hesitated. There was the letter in his pocket, the one addressed to Principal Wilkinson, asking to come back to the school; he was anxious to mail it.

He sat next to her, facing her. The strong bay breezes made her hair dance off her shoulders and Adam was overcome with an urge to drive his hands into the curls. He forced himself to watch her rapidly moving fingers.

Jenny had taken to the manual alphabet as easily as others take to speech. And Adam was glad of it. The school also taught lip reading, but Adam shied away from Alexander Graham Bell's "visible speech" because it drew attention to his face.

"I haven't seen you smile today," she signed, then shook her finger at him as if lecturing a naughty boy.

He smiled thinly. It hadn't used to bother him whenever Jennifer looked at him, but of late he wished she wouldn't; he wished he could wear a sack over his head. Adam had become acutely aware of his face and thought that eyes as lovely as hers shouldn't behold ugliness.

Jennifer lightly touched his arm. "You're not happy today, Adam. Why?"

He thought long and hard. She had to be told. "I'm going back to Berkeley, Jenny."

Her face brightened. "May I come too?"

"No, it's not for a visit. It's for good."

Jenny's smile disappeared. Her eyes become grave. "Why?"

"It is time for me to go. I have been here almost eight years. I have taught you everything I know. My purpose here has ended. There is no reason for me to stay."

She regarded him for a moment, then, turning away, brought her hands up to her face.

It will only hurt for a little while, thought Adam. And then I'll just be a memory . . .

He clenched his fists, frustrated at his limited means of communication.

She turned back to him, tears streaking her cheeks. "Don't go," she signed.

"The school needs me."

"I need you."

He closed his eyes. Adam saw too well the future. He wouldn't be gone long before Jenny found herself surrounded by suitors. Adam had seen the way men looked at her; it was always with a mixture of hunger and awe. There was no reason Jenny couldn't marry and lead a normal life. Adam's usefulness as a translator had ended long ago when Dr. Hargrave and Mr. and Mrs. Gant and even Miss Peoples had mastered the finger alphabet. Any suitor could learn it.

"Adam, Adam," she signed over and over again.

He took hold of her wrists. "You don't need me anymore!" he cried. "I'm a hindrance to you. With me around as your constant companion, the suitors will stay away. I'm giving you your freedom, Jenny!"

Her eyes watched his lips intently, only barely understanding what he said. Then she pulled her wrists free. "Don't go," she signed frantically. "Don't go, don't go."

Adam saw the gazebo swim through rising tears. Fearful of breaking down in front of her, he shot to his feet, teetered uncertainly; then he turned and fled up the path.

Jennifer held her hands out, trying to shout with them, sobbing mutely, her fingers rapidly moving. Her thumb curled over the first three fingers: I. The index finger and thumb went up: L. She curved all the fingers to meet the thumb: O. Index finger and middle finger formed V. A fist: E.

But Adam saw none of her plea. He stumbled into the house, down the long hall past a startled Miss Peoples and out onto the street, turning toward Fillmore Avenue where, on the corner, stood a mailbox.

FIVE

*S*AMANTHA GLANCED AT HER WRISTWATCH. SHE WANTED TO BE
sure to have lunch before making rounds, but there was so much
paperwork on her desk, she hated to leave it. There was the order
for hemostats, new surgical instruments that were being widely reported
as revolutionizing abdominal operations; also an order for a pair of rubber gloves. A surgeon at Johns Hopkins, Dr. Halsted, out of concern for his
nurse's hands, which were being badly chapped by the carbolic, had given
her gloves to wear while operating, and he had discovered a sudden drop
in surgical infections. Samantha wanted to try them; she was sending her
glove size to the Goodyear Rubber Company. Then there was the request,
to be taken to the trustees, for one of the new Roentgen-ray machines that
allowed one to visualize bones beneath the flesh without surgery.

There was also an order for a shipment of diphtheria antitoxin, a new
wonder drug that was going to save thousands of children's lives. Eleven
years too late for little Clair buried on a San Francisco hillside.

And then there was correspondence to be answered. One letter was from a Scotsman named John Muir urging support for his recently formed Sierra Club; other letters came from grateful patients, a few contained donations, one was a request to adopt a Chinese baby. And finally there were the letters from newspapers and magazines Samantha had written to. Stanton Weatherby was right: the press wanted nothing to do with her urge for better drug control.

She shook her head over it all. And her desk at home was just as cluttered.

Samantha's face darkened. On that desk lay the letter she had received yesterday from Mr. Wilkinson at the Berkeley school. Adam Wolff, he said, had requested to come back.

Clearly, then, that had been the cause of Jenny's recent state. Three weeks ago Samantha had gone to work, leaving Jenny happily reading a book of poems in the gazebo, and had returned that night to find her sad, uncommunicative, and red-eyed. Adam had not joined them for supper, and the two had remained in this depressed mood ever since. No amount of coaxing had gotten either to confess what was wrong, and when the letter arrived, Samantha suddenly understood.

Tonight she was going to sit down and have a serious talk with them both.

A knock at her door preceded the appearance of Nurse Constance. "Dr. Hargrave? I'm sorry to disturb you but we have a bit of a problem. It's Dr. Canby's day to see new patients but she's still in surgery and I have a lady waiting in the examining room to see her."

"I'll take it, Constance."

When Samantha entered, the patient rose and extended her gloved hand as though receiving Samantha to tea. "How do you do, Doctor?"

"Hello. Please sit down." Samantha had developed the skill of studying a patient without being obvious about it. This woman was clearly a lady—every movement, every syllable, every hair of her perfect coiffure spoke refinement and an upbringing of class. In her late thirties, handsome, slender and self-possessed, and by appearance in excellent health. Samantha wondered what her problem could be.

"I am new to San Francisco, Doctor, for we have only just come from

St. Louis. I had been to specialists there who all gave me no hope, but your Infirmary has an excellent reputation and so I thought I would try you."

"What is your problem?"

"I want to have a child. I had one, six years ago, but immediately after the birth I came down with puerperal fever. I nearly died and my baby *did* die. Since then I have not been able to conceive. My husband and I so want a child!"

"I understand. I cannot say yet if I can do anything for you. I shall have to examine you. Does your husband know you've come to me?"

"Oh yes. In fact, I was ready to give up, having been to so many doctors, but he insisted I try the Infirmary. He has such faith in the medical profession." She smiled. "Of course, he is a doctor himself. On the staff of the University Medical College."

"From St. Louis? I wonder if I know of him . . ."

"Originally we are from New York. His name is Mark Rawlins."

Samantha stared. "What did you say?"

"My husband's name—he is Dr. Mark Rawlins."

"That's not possible. Mark Rawlins is dead."

"I beg your pardon? Did you know him? Oh—the tragedy at sea! That was a long time ago, before I met him. Mark was rescued by a fishing boat, along with eleven other passengers."

Samantha felt strangely numb. She looked down at her hands. "I thought he was dead, all these years."

"You knew him then?"

"Yes. Yes, a long time ago."

"I didn't know—When we discussed my coming here, Mark never mentioned you. Did you know him well?"

Samantha raised her head; her eyes had taken on a brittle, glasslike quality. "I knew his family," she said.

"I'm afraid I never knew Mark's parents. They both died before I went to New York."

"A fishing boat . . ."

"He and the other eleven were the only ones to survive the sinking of the *Excalibur.* They had been in a lifeboat for two weeks when they were picked up. They were exhausted, sick and mentally wasted. Mark had amnesia for months afterward; no one in the fishing village knew who he was or whom to contact. But then he regained his strength, and slowly most of his memory back. His return to New York received quite a bit of notice. I'm surprised it didn't make the San Francisco newspapers."

"It might have—I had only just gotten here and was so busy. But, in any case, I'm glad he's well. Most of his memory, you say?"

"There are blank spots still."

"Of course. It must have been a terrible ordeal."

"The others said he gave his food and water rations to the women and children. Did you know him well, Doctor?"

"Ours was a professional relationship. I had an opportunity to assist him once in surgery."

"I shall certainly tell him. And now my problem, Doctor?"

Samantha consulted her watch. "I'm afraid I've another appointment and your examination will take time. Can you come back tomorrow?"

"Yes, certainly."

Both women rose. "I hope to be able to tell you tomorrow what I think your chances are. Shall we say two o'clock?"

"Thank you very much, Doctor. Good day."

"You gave me such a scare! Standing at the door crying like that!"

Samantha shut out Hilary's sharp-edged voice. After Mrs. Rawlins left, Samantha had sat for a long time in the examining room, numb, transfixed; then she had jumped up, told Nurse Constance that she had an emergency, and rushed up California Street to Hilary's house. Mrs. Mainwaring had opened the door to the frantic knocking, startled by Dr. Hargrave's appearance, and when Hilary came down the stairs Samantha had said simply, "He's alive."

Now it was two hours later and the shock was subsiding.

"Mark," she whispered. "Here, in San Francisco. By now she's told him,

Hilary. He knows I'm here." Samantha looked at the parlor door as if expecting to hear a knock. "I mustn't see him, Hilary."

"Why not?"

"Because it's best to leave things as they are. He's married now and . . ." She bowed her head, trying not to cry. "I'm afraid."

"Of what?"

"In my mind Mark loves me still. At night, in bed, I close my eyes and we are together again as we once were. But if he becomes real, all that will change. Especially if . . . if I am part of his lost memory. Our love, the weeks we spent together, the nights—all gone . . ."

Hilary came to sit next to Samantha. She wanted to cry too. She also felt like taking a tablespoon of Farmer's but she had none in the house. After she had recovered from the fall, Hilary's first thought was: Thank God I didn't lose the baby! Then she had promised Samantha to give up the medicine. But, to her horror, it had not been as easy as she had expected. Each day the cravings came, and each day she had to fight them. But she would win, Hilary knew, because that incident had scared her, had scared them all. Especially Darius, who was now doting on her as if she were a bride.

"I'm afraid of two things, Hilary," said Samantha quietly. "I'm afraid that either he'll not remember me—that everything we once shared is lost forever—or that he will remember me and that his love is still strong. I don't think I could bear that, Hilary, Mark still being in love with me, feeling the same passion, the desire, but knowing we can never have one another again, not even touch . . ."

They sat for a while, each thinking private thoughts, then Hilary said, "You know you have to do what you can for her, Sam. She's Mark's wife, the woman he loves. And they want a baby."

Samantha screwed her eyes shut tight. *We had a baby once . . .*

"It was thirteen years ago, Sam. You are two different people now."

"But he has stayed with me. He has never left me."

"That's another Mark, Sam, not the one who's out there now. See her tomorrow. Face her. You know that if anyone can help her you can. You might be her only hope. Sam . . . make peace with the past."

❦

She braced herself. The woman was there, waiting for her—*Mrs. Rawlins*. Samantha hoped she had been able to cover up the dark circles under her eyes. Hilary was right—this was another world now, they were different people. Mark had his wife and his medical practice. Samantha had the Infirmary, Jenny and Adam, the reforms she strove for in medicine; so little remained of that interlude thirteen years ago. Not even baby Clair . . .

She entered smiling. "Hello," she said.

"Hello, Doctor," said Mrs. Rawlins.

"I'll explain to you every step of the way what I am doing. First, I must ask you to sit on this examining table. If you are wearing underthings please remove them."

Samantha turned her back to arrange her instruments and heard Mrs. Rawlins' refined voice say, "I told my husband about you last night, Doctor, about your knowing him back in New York. He says he doesn't remember you."

SIX

$\mathcal{S}$AMANTHA LOOKED OVER THE PAMPHLETS WITH satisfaction. After going through the Infirmary's records and gathering statistics on patients who had been addicted to or harmed in some way by patent medicines, Samantha had composed a diatribe against proprietary drugs, warning women of the hidden dangers, even naming certain brands, and had had it all printed up to be given out at the Infirmary. She set aside ten for mailing to various magazines and newspapers, then took off her glasses and rubbed the bridge of her nose.

The test Samantha had run on Lilian Rawlins that afternoon indicated she should still be able to become pregnant. Pelvic infections, such as the puerperal fever she had had six years before, often scarred the tubes, barring the path of the egg. Samantha had gently injected sterile saline into Mrs. Rawlins' uterus, carefully gauging when the uterus would be full and when, if the tubes were blocked, the water should run back. But it didn't. An entire syringeful went in and then Lilian complained of pelvic cramping, which meant the saline had gone clear through. Her tubes were open.

Afterward, Samantha had asked questions (painful ones for herself). "How often do you and your husband have intercourse?" ("Once a week.") "Do you get up right away or remain in bed?" ("I usually stay in bed.") "Do you douche afterward?" ("Mark told me not to.")

And then Lilian had asked if there was anything Samantha could do.

"It is possible," Samantha had said, "that the position you take during intercourse is causing the problem. Since deepest penetration is necessary, I recommend you lie on your back with a pillow under your hips. Do not use a lubricant, for it is thought that petroleum jelly weakens sperm. There is some research being done in this area, Mrs. Rawlins, and it is being thought now that the longer a man goes without intercourse the less sperm he generates. I recommend you and your husband have relations more often that once a week."

Samantha now rose from the desk and went to the french windows which opened onto the garden. It was a night early in December, redolent with decaying leaves and damp earth. Samantha supported herself against the doorframe and closed her eyes.

Mark, dear Mark . . .

The shock of his coming back to life after all these years having subsided, Samantha discovered that he was with her still, by her side, that nothing had changed. But whoever was the husband of Lilian Rawlins was another Mark. And in a way it was a Godsend he didn't remember Samantha, for now she could go on as before, still loving him, still reliving those days of long ago.

She opened her eyes and drew in a deep breath. Samantha truly hoped that, in a few months, Lilian Rawlins would return with happy news.

She heard a noise behind her and turned. "I've come to say good-bye, Dr. Hargrave."

Adam Wolff stood in the doorway holding the same carpetbag he'd brought with him eight years before. In the shadows he looked a tall, erect young man, handsome and well dressed, his voice careful and poised, not the speech of a deaf man. But then he stepped into the light and his face was illuminated and Samantha's heart went out to him.

She walked toward him and spoke slowly, carefully pronouncing each word. "I wish you wouldn't go, Adam."

"I have to, Doctor. It's time."

"Jenny is so unhappy."

"She will get over it."

"Adam." Samantha stepped up to him and placed a hand on his arm. "I don't think you really want to go."

He hesitated. "No, I don't. But you don't need me anymore and the school does."

"But we're your family, Adam."

Yes, he thought bleakly. And when Jenny gets married I shall be at her wedding as her brother, watching her go into the arms of another man.

Reluctantly, Samantha tugged the bellpull and, when Miss Peoples appeared, requested the carriage be brought out. Then Samantha went to her desk, unlocked a drawer and took out an envelope.

"I want you to have this, Adam. Please don't refuse it. If you don't want to use it for yourself, then give it to the school."

He slipped the envelope inside his jacket and then shifted awkwardly, as if this were his first night all over again, meeting Dr. Hargrave for the first time.

They didn't speak again, although both had so much to say, and when the driver knocked at the front door Adam moved toward it on wooden feet. He glanced at the staircase.

"Let me get Jenny," Samantha said.

"No."

"She doesn't understand, Adam. She thinks you're leaving because you want to. Tell her the truth, Adam."

But he said no more. Putting a clumsy arm around her, Adam buried his face in Samantha's neck with a suppressed sob, then he hurried out the door and down the steps.

Samantha stood on the sidewalk in the damp air watching the carriage go off into the night.

The next morning Jenny was missing.

"It's my fault!" cried Samantha, pacing before the fire. "I didn't handle it well! I knew she was unhappy but I thought that if I left her alone she'd work it out! But Jenny isn't like the rest of us. She's never had someone go out of her life before. Not like this, not someone she loves!"

The others in the room sat in silent sympathy. Darius leaned on the mantel studying the brandy in his glass; Hilary sat in an easy chair with her feet up, staring into the flames; Stanton Weatherby stood by the bay window watching the December rain fall like gold dust in the glow of the street lamps.

It was late and there was still no word from the police.

"She'll be all right, Sam," said Hilary quietly.

Samantha stopped, her face stricken. "How can she be? She's never been out of the house alone before, not once in her life, not even to the corner. She can't *hear*, Hilary. She wouldn't be able to hear a cable car or trolley. She could get run over. And she can't *speak*. How many people out there do you think understand sign language?"

"Hello," said Stanton. "Here's a cab pulling up."

Everyone rushed to the door.

When she saw Adam step down to the curb and then turn to help Jenny, Samantha ran down to the sidewalk. "Oh, thank God," she cried. "Where have you been? What happened?"

Adam and Jenny stood in the drizzle holding hands. "She brought me back, Dr. Hargrave," he said with a smile. "Jenny came all the way to the school by herself and she brought me back. We want to get married."

--- ⚜ ---

"It was truly the most beautiful wedding I have ever seen!" declared Dahlia Mason. "And such a wonderful touch, to have the minister perform the whole service with his hands. Why, it was so *moving*."

Samantha said, "Thank you," remembering Dahlia's initial reaction to the wedding: "You *aren't* going to let them marry, are you? Think how their children might turn out! And to do the service in sign language! Can it even be legal?"

But everyone had showed up, even Mr. Wilkinson and some of Adam's friends from the school, and the January day had showered them all with warmth and sunshine as the two stood beneath the rose arbor in the garden.

Samantha did not deny she harbored private concerns. Adam was determined to earn a living and support Jenny in their own house (and he was making a start by tutoring two deaf-mute pupils on Russian Hill), and there was no cause to worry about the health of their babies, should they have any, since Adam's deafness had been caused by an injury and Jenny's most likely by scarlet fever. Samantha worried about other things: how they would survive in a world that would regard them as freaks.

She was standing with Dahlia and LeGrand Mason, the Gants and Stanton Weatherby in the sumptuous lobby of the Opera House awaiting the rising of the curtain on Sarah Bernhardt in *Cyrano de Bergerae*. All six lifted their wine glasses in a toast to the bride and groom, who were not with them. Samantha was feeling happy about many things tonight: Jenny and Adam were settled and blissfully happy, things were going well at the Infirmary; and her pamphlets were being read by her patients, many of whom promised to distribute them to their friends.

"How are you feeling, Hilary darling?" Darius asked.

She squeezed his arm. Almost six months pregnant, Hilary was shocking her friends by being out in public in an Empire-style gown designed especially for her by Mr. Magnin. "I'm just fine, Darius. Don't fret so!" She sipped her wine; the craving for Farmer's had finally been overcome.

Darius drew Weatherby into a debate over Alfred Nobel's dynamite and whether or not it would put an end to all wars, as the Swedish scientist hoped. Hilary leaned close to Samantha and murmured, "Who is that man staring at you? Turn casually, to your right. He's standing by the wine table and he hasn't taken his eyes off you!"

Even before she turned, Samantha knew.

She turned, then froze, as their eyes met and locked across the crowded lobby.

She had known it was bound to happen; in a city forty-nine miles square, it was inevitable their paths should eventually meet. "It's Mark," she said quietly.

Hilary gently took hold of her arm. "He's coming toward us."

When Mark was a few feet away from her he stopped and stared. "Samantha?"

"Yes. Hello, Mark."

He frowned. "Is it truly you? Samantha Hargrave?"

"Then you remember."

"Remember? Of course I remember. I could never forget you. But I don't understand. What are you doing in San Francisco?"

"I thought your wife told you."

"Lilian? Are *you* the doctor she's been seeing?"

"She said she told you—told you about me. She said you had amnesia and that you didn't remember me."

"But she told me about a Dr. Canby!" he cried.

Dr. Canby! Samantha thought back. The day Lilian had first come to the Infirmary. Dr. Canby delayed in surgery. Good heavens, hadn't Constance told Mrs. Rawlins another doctor was to see her?

"There was a mix-up," Samantha said. "I'm afraid your wife was told she would see another doctor and I saw her instead. I never introduced myself. And when she came back the next day, why . . . the mistake was never . . ." He was staring down at her. It was the night of *Annabel Lee* again. "Dr. Rawlins, please permit me to introduce you to my friends. Mr. Darius Gant and his wife . . ."

He uttered a polite "How do you do," but his eyes never left Samantha's face.

Then Darius was starting to try to move them toward their seats as the bell rang, announcing that the curtain was about to go up. Stanton Weatherby gave the stranger's face a close look. He hadn't gotten to the grand age of sixty without learning something along the way. He sniffed and stirred his joints. So here it was, plain and simple, the reason why no man in San Francisco had been able to capture Samantha Hargrave's heart . . .

"I can't tell you what a surprise this is," Mark went on quietly. "When I looked over and saw you, I thought I was dreaming. You haven't changed a bit . . ."

"Nor have you," Samantha murmured. The crowd in the lobby seemed to vanish, then the lobby itself, and the floor beneath her feet and the chandeliers overhead, until all that existed in the universe were two intense brown eyes that Samantha had dreamt about every night for thirteen years. "I believed you were dead."

"I couldn't find you . . . no one knew . . ."

"Hello, Doctor," said Lilian Rawlins, materializing at her husband's side. Suddenly everything flooded back: the noise, the lights, the milling crowd.

"Good evening, Mrs. Rawlins."

"Lilian, it seems I do know this lady after all. She is Dr. Hargrave, not Dr. Canby."

Samantha explained the misunderstanding and Lilian said, "Then how nice! What a wonderful surprise it must be for both of you after all these years. You must have a great deal to talk about. Dr. Hargrave, could you and your friends dine with us after the performance?"

Samantha believed it to be the most awkward hour of her life.

Gradually they filled in the missing years, Samantha with her San Francisco adventures (although she said nothing of baby Clair), Mark with a remarkable account of his rescue and recovery. The talk was more superficial and polite than Samantha would have wished, and when Mark said he would like to see her hospital, Samantha's heart leapt. She invited him to come the next week for a tour, and Lilian, confessing an aversion to hospitals, begged off.

By the time the day came, and then the hour, and then the minute, Samantha was nearly fainting with tension and excitement. Aside from their initial episode of staring in the lobby, they had conducted themselves well, just like two old friends whose only common interests were microbes and stethoscopes. But *they* both knew, there was no hiding it from each other. She had felt an intense current and knew Mark could not mistake the yearning in her eyes. Their love thrived still; the thirteen years were erased in the wink of an eye: it was 1882 again.

Nurse Constance noticed Dr. Hargrave's crimson cheeks and wondered if she were coming down with an illness. She was also curious about her dress— Samantha wore a lovely afternoon gown of lavender silk edged with burgundy lace, which was quite unlike Dr. Hargrave, who always dressed somberly at the hospital. Finally Nurse Constance wondered about the special tea service and pastries, for Dr. Hargrave disliked displays of extravagance about the hospital. This surgeon from the East must be very special indeed.

Samantha paced and chided herself. This is nonsense; I'm nearly thirty-six years old, not a girl of sixteen. But when the door opened she started, and then Mark strode in.

"Dr. Rawlins," she said, turning.

"Hello, Samantha." They gazed at one another for a long moment, then, aware of Constance, Samantha said, "Please sit down, Dr. Rawlins. I've had tea brought up for us."

He sat in the chair and looked around the room. "You've come so far, Samantha," he said quietly.

She sat at her desk. "We're all proud of the Infirmary." She had to struggle to keep her hands from shaking as she poured tea into two cups. "Are you getting settled in San Francisco?"

"We've found a house in the Marina." His eyes watched her steadily.

The brief, awkward silence was disturbed by Nurse Constance clearing her throat, then she backed out of the office and closed the door.

Samantha raised her cup to her lips but held it there. "I cannot drink," she finally said.

"Nor can I."

The cup clattered into its saucer. "Mark, this is all a dream."

"Oh, Samantha! It's as though it were the Astor ball all over again. As if there have been no years in between, as if nothing else has happened. I feel as though I have come home. Samantha, I never for a day stopped thinking about you, wondering what had become of you, yearning for you."

"Nor I for you," she breathed. "It was unbearable at times . . ."

"Do you remember," he said softly, his voice as intense as it had been in the old days, "'I was a child and she was a child, In this kingdom by the sea, But we loved with a love that was more than love—'"

She closed her eyes. "Yes," she whispered. *"Annabel Lee."*

"I want you, Samantha. I ache for you."

"Oh, Mark! It can never be. We had our time and now it's gone. Please. This is so painful."

"I searched everywhere for you, Samantha," he said in a tight voice. "When I finally got to New York I was mad with longing to see you. No one knew where you had gone! You had simply vanished! Janelle told me of her last visit with you, that your bags had been packed. But you told no one where you were going. You simply vanished. I wrote to Landon Fremont in Europe but received no reply. I went looking for you myself. I thought you had gone back to England; I followed a false trail from London to Paris, they said a young lady doctor had bought passage—it was all a dead end. From there I went to see Fremont in Vienna only to be told he had died. I searched for four years, Samantha. Why? Why did you disappear?"

It was on her lips, to tell him about Clair, their baby. But now was not the moment; perhaps the time would never be right. "I thought you were dead," she said.

He nodded, unable to say any more. Samantha drew in a deep breath. "The past is gone, Mark. Today is now. I would like to show you my hospital, if I may."

He regarded her sadly, longingly, then he said, "And I should love to see it."

As he held the door open for her and Samantha passed close to him, Mark fought the impulse to reach out and draw her against him; and later, when they went up the stairs to the operating room and Mark had his hand on her elbow, it took all Samantha's strength to keep from turning into his arms. It was difficult at first, almost unbearable, but as they walked the wards and discussed patients, as Mark asked questions and Samantha explained, the pain started to subside; they were indeed two old friends sharing their mutual interest in medicine.

Mark was impressed but not surprised. "And what do you call this?" he asked, pausing before a large metal cupboard on wheels.

"It's one of our food carts. I should like to claim credit for it, but I cannot. I borrowed the idea from the Buffalo General Hospital. You see"—she opened the door—"the trays are kept on these shelves and at the bottom is a little stove for keeping food warm. The wheels are rubber and make little noise."

"You're extraordinarily well equipped."

"It's a constant struggle. If it weren't for the work of our diligent Ladies' Committee and their fund drives I don't know what we would have done."

Mark looked into the tiny nursery where they kept babies whose mothers had died or were too ill to care for them. A wet nurse was sitting in a rocking chair with a newborn at her breast. "The hand of Samantha Hargrave is everywhere," he murmured.

Mark gazed down at Samantha with a look that she had envisioned a hundred times in her fantasies, and the familiar ache returned. If you touch me, she thought. If you kiss me . . .

She found her voice. "Will you be practicing, Mark, or will all your time be devoted to the university?"

They began strolling again. "When the University of California asked me to come and teach at their medical college I saw it as an opportunity to turn my attention toward something I have wanted to do for some time."

They stepped to one side to allow a stretcher to go by.

"My practice in St. Louis kept me very busy, I had no time for anything else. But a professorship will give me some freedom."

"What is it you want to do?"

He stopped and looked down at her. "I want to do research."

"Research! In what area?"

"Cancer. You knew, didn't you? And Mother forbade you to tell me."

She raised her eyes to his and said softly, "I hope she didn't suffer at the end."

A look of sadness came over his face. "She was dead when I returned from the fishing village."

Suddenly the corridor felt hot and stifling. Samantha moved toward the window at the end. "Cancer research is a wonderful idea, Mark. So little is known, so little is being done."

She looked out, waiting for him to join her. The back of the Infirmary abutted what had once been an opium den. Contrary to everyone's warn-ings that the hospital would be in a bad neighborhood and therefore deter women from coming, the establishment of the Infirmary had had the opposite effect: it had changed the neighborhood. Slowly, the gambling houses had closed and respectable industries had taken their places. The opium den at the rear was now a bakery.

Mark came to stand close to her, looking up at the iron-gray February sky.

"I'm sorry about your mother, Mark. I wanted to tell you but . . ."

His hand sought hers; their fingers brushed, entwined, then clasped tightly.

"Where will you do your research?" she asked in a whisper.

"I'm looking for a laboratory to share. Unfortunately, there is little space, with so much work being done on antitoxins and vaccines."

Samantha looked up at him. Mark had changed little in thirteen years: he still wore his hair a little long and the gray at the temples added dignity rather than age; he still stood erect, his shoulders still broad, and the cut of his forest-green coat showed the well-kept athletic body beneath. "Mark," she said, "the state is giving us a grant for a pathology laboratory. We are going to start examining all surgical specimens instead of throwing them out. We shall be converting part of the basement and equipping it with standard laboratory apparatus, a microscope and an incubator. I am even hoping for a centrifuge. Our pathologist will only be working down there part-time. If you would like, Mark, you would certainly be welcome . . ." Her voice trailed off. He was staring down at her.

After a long moment Mark said, "Only if you allow me to contribute the centrifuge."

SEVEN

*L*ILIAN RAWLINS WAS LATE, WHICH WAS UNLIKE HER.

This would be her fifth visit with Samantha and they were go ing to attempt something new. After five months of trying, Lilian was still unable to get pregnant; Samantha wanted to try something she had read about recently in a medical journal.

She rose from her desk and went to the window. It was a beautiful April day: warm and sunny with the blustery winds so typical of San Francisco. The sidewalks were crowded with men and women hurrying along, holding on to their hats, and an automobile horn was blasting, demanding right of way through the carriages.

Samantha sighed. There was so much to be thankful for. Jenny and Adam were happy and managing nicely (they were looking for a small house of their own); Hilary, having had her baby the month before, was down in Los Angeles with Darius—a vacation away from the children; the Infirmary was prospering; and Mark Rawlins was down in the laboratory, right this minute, bent over a microscope.

There were days when Samantha never saw him, but knowing he was there, under the same roof, was enough. Tuesdays and Saturdays were his days; slicing, staining, examining and recording. It was Mark's theory that cancer cells were not unique but in fact normal cells that had gone awry. It was an unpopular theory but he stuck by it, determined to find the cause and then, hopefully, the cure for the killer disease.

Samantha looked at her watch and frowned. Lilian Rawlins was half an hour late for her appointment.

Samantha went to the door and looked out. Nurse Constance was hurrying by. "Nurse, have you seen Mrs. Rawlins?"

"Yes, Doctor. She's in the Accident Ward."

Samantha's eyebrows arched. "Is she hurt?"

"Oh no, Doctor! She's helping."

Samantha's surprise turned to puzzlement. Lilian Rawlins' aversion to hospitals was acute; it was all she could do to bring herself to see Samantha for treatment.

Samantha made her way through the busy corridors toward the Accident Ward, and was stopped twice to be told that Mrs. Jenkins' emphysema was worse and that Rosie Tubbs had not survived the varicose vein operation. The Accident Ward was crowded. Dr. Canby and the nurses were doing everything from painting throats to setting broken bones.

Samantha found Lilian Rawlins in the corner, sitting by a stretcher and talking to a little boy. When Samantha drew close she saw that the boy's right arm was freshly bandaged.

"Hello, Mrs. Rawlins."

Lilian looked up. "Hello, Doctor. I was just telling Jimmy here a story."

Samantha smiled down at the boy, noticing that his face was puffy from crying and that his pupils were pinpointed from a morphine injection. He was also extremely filthy and looked malnourished.

"Jimmy had an accident, didn't you?" Lilian said, patting the dirty little hand that emerged from the edge of the bandaging. "But he's going to be all right. Aren't you, Jimmy?"

He nodded and smiled shyly.

Lilian stood and said quietly, "I'm sorry I'm late for our appointment,

Doctor, but they were bringing him in just as I arrived. He was screaming and carrying on so, and so unhappy, the poor little thing. I've kept his mind off his arm with a story."

Dr. Canby came up, flush-faced, plumper than ever. "If it weren't for Mrs. Rawlins we would have had the dickens of a time getting the arm sutured. You have a magical touch with children, Mrs. Rawlins."

Two porters appeared and each took an end of the stretcher.

"Oh," said Lilian, "where are they taking him?"

"To the Children's Ward," said Samantha. "You may go along with him if you wish."

Lilian's face paled. "The Children's Ward . . ."

"He'll be there for several days," said Dr. Canby gently. "You can visit him any time you like."

"G'by, lady," came a small voice, and they all turned to see Jimmy waving his good arm.

❦

"I'm going to dilate your cervix, Mrs. Rawlins," said Samantha. "That is the opening into your uterus. Some recent studies have shown that a narrow cervix might be a cause of infertility. With a wider opening, the sperm have a better chance of getting in. Now, it shouldn't hurt and I shall go slowly. If you feel any discomfort, please tell me."

"I'm not afraid of pain, Doctor," said Lilian. Then, after a moment, she said, "Doctor, where will I find the Children's Ward?"

❦

At first she visited only Jimmy, then the boy in the next bed, then the little girl with an ear infection, and finally Lilian Rawlins was coming every day to see all the children. She never showed up empty-handed: there were fancy painted zoetropes, rag dolls, wooden soldiers, animals on wheels with strings to pull them. She brought licorice whips and peppermint sticks, rock candy, and chocolate. Those who could walk she gathered at her feet and read stories to; those confined to bed she visited individually. Lilian cried a lot at first, at the diseases and injuries, when a child died, when one was orphaned, and when Jimmy developed gangrene and died. But then she found her own inner strength and learned to keep her distress hidden. For the little girl tragically burned in a tenement fire, Lilian sat and combed her hair and told her she looked like a princess. To the little boy who was recovering from his seventh operation to correct a clubfoot she said that one day he would be a cavalry officer. She talked to them, listened to them, dispelled their fears, made them laugh and soon became known as Mother Rawlins. But when a pretty little girl put her arms around Lilian's neck and asked to go home with her, Lilian gently withdrew from the embrace and said that was not possible.

"Why?" asked Samantha when she visited the laboratory one afternoon.

Mark, his coat removed and his shirt sleeves rolled up, was preparing a slide. "Lilian and I discussed adoption once and she was so adamantly against it that I dropped it."

"But she loves children so, Mark. And she'd make a wonderful mother. Every morning now the children anxiously look for Mother Rawlins. She has done so much to help the children get well!"

Mark studied the slide he had just stained. "That's true. The Children's Ward has become her life now, Samantha. When we first came to San Francisco Lilian was terribly lonely. She missed her family back in St. Louis very much, and she wasn't interested in making friends with the ladies in our new neighborhood—they all have children and it is painful for her. And then when she started her treatments with you, Lilian was so certain they would work that she started converting an upstairs bedroom into a nursery. Now all of her time is taken up with either furnishing the nursery or making things to bring to the Children's Ward. Lilian has become obsessed with motherhood. To the point of—" He stopped. Mark was going to say, To the point of forgetting she has a husband. But he couldn't tell Samantha that. Nor could he tell her that Lilian's love-making had become mechanical and impersonal. To her the act had become a means to give her a baby and Mark often felt that the notion of "love" never entered into it.

Samantha knew a little of what he was going through. During her treatment sessions Lilian talked incessantly about her sisters' children in St. Louis, a total of eleven. She carried their photographs in her purse and was forever bringing them out. "Then all the more reason you should adopt, Mark."

He shook his head. "She wants a child from her own body. Maybe before the baby, maybe before she knew what it was like to have her own, she would have considered it. But having her own, and then having it die—Well, Lilian wants to replace the lost one, I suppose."

Samantha took a seat on the high stool before the workbench. Yes, to replace the one who died. How well she could sympathize with that! Baby Clair sleeping on a grassy hill . . .

Mark went to the sink and washed his hands. As he dried them he said, "I'm glad you came down here today, Sam. I want to discuss something with you."

"What is it?"

He rolled down his sleeves, buttoned his cuffs and strode to the roll-top desk. "This." He picked something up and held it out to her. It was one of her antidrug pamphlets.

"Yes?"

"Are these statistics accurate?"

"They're all from the Infirmary files."

Mark hefted the pamphlet up and down as if weighing it. "That's a lot of work, compiling all that data. And your claims about the medicines—Ellison's Elixir. Forty percent alcohol?"

"I ran the test myself."

He gazed at her for a long, thoughtful moment, then said, "I picked this up at the admitting desk on my way in this morning. It was mixed in with pamphlets on nursing bottles and proper house cleaning. It was buried, Sam."

"I know. The nurses try to keep the literature straight, but—"

"And it's lost," he said quietly. "It's lost out there on the counter. Information like this should be made public."

"I've tried that, Mark! I sent my pamphlets out to every publication I thought would be interested and had no results."

"I'm not surprised. Ellison's Elixir is a big advertiser. Magazines can't afford to lose them."

"Mark, I may not be publishing nationwide, but at least I am educating my patients."

"Is that enough?"

She hesitated. "No."

"Good." He walked to the coatrack and slipped the pamphlet into his coat pocket. "What is your schedule for the rest of the day?"

"I have rounds after lunch and then I cover the Accident Ward until supper."

"Can someone take over for you?"

"I believe so. Why?"

"Because," he said with a cryptic smile, "there is someone I want you to meet."

❈

The offices of *Woman's Companion* covered the top floor of the Wing Fah Imports Building on Battery Street, and when Samantha went through the door marked Editorial Offices she was a little bewildered. In the last few years *Woman's Companion* had been slowly failing until last year, she had heard, it had folded altogether. And yet here it was, apparently thriving amid the thunder of typewriters, bustling people and desks three rows deep. A natty young man approached them. "May I help you?"

"We would like to see Mr. Horace Chandler. Tell him it's Mark Rawlins."

A minute later they were going through a door marked private. On the other side of the office, against a backdrop of open windows and streaming sunlight, sat a man at an enormous desk. He jumped up. "Mark!"

"Hello, Horace." They shook hands. "Permit me to present Dr. Hargrave of the San Francisco Infirmary."

"How do you do, Dr. Hargrave? It is indeed a pleasure to meet you. You're famous in this city, you know." Horace Chandler was a very large man, especially around the middle, and when he stood he looked like a rearing grizzly bear. "Please have a seat. Mark, what a pleasant surprise! How is Lilian?"

"She's fine, Horace. And Gertrude?"

"Never better. Now, is this business or pleasure?"

"Business, Horace. We want your help with something."

During their carriage ride from the hospital Mark had explained to Samantha about his friend Horace Chandler. He had known the publisher back in St. Louis when Mr. Chandler had been working on a publication called *Gentleman's Weekly*. Horace Chandler, he had explained, made a career of buying magazines that were dying and resurrecting them. He had come to San Francisco the year before to pump some life into *Woman's Companion*.

Samantha had tried to remember when she had last read a copy of *Woman's Companion*. It had been years ago and she had dismissed it as a vapid publication, full of fashions, recipes, pale romances, and soon-to-be-forgotten poems. It had made her picture three old ladies running a printing press in their kitchen. But she hadn't read it since. "What kind of magazine is it now?" she had asked Mark.

"Still a woman's publication," he had explained in the carriage, "But one that gives women credit for having brains. They still have recipes and fashions, but they're on the exotic, daring side. They print news and opinions and aren't afraid of a healthy controversy. A recent issue had an overpopulation article that brought in a strong response because it dared to suggest virtues in anticonception."

Now, sitting in Mr. Chandler's office, Mark told his friend about Samantha's research on proprietary medicines and her futile efforts to publish the findings.

"And no one would touch it, right, Dr. Hargrave?" asked Mr. Chandler. "There's hardly a publication in this country that would dare risk losing its large drug advertising revenue by printing what you suggest. That's why the public will never know the truth. But it just happens that I established a policy right off when I purchased *Woman's Companion*. We print the truth no matter whom we offend, and you will notice that I have no ads for patent drugs in my magazine." He picked up a copy from his desk and handed it across to Samantha. She flipped through it, impressed.

"So, Mark," said Horace, leaning back and webbing his fingers over his generous stomach, "do I take it you want me to print this information of Dr. Hargrave's?"

Mark reached into his pocket and withdrew the pamphlet, tossing it on the desk. "Read it, Horace. Tell me what you think."

As the man went through it, pausing at various points, Mark looked at Samantha and winked. She felt her heart race. "Mr. Chandler," she said, "I want the public made aware of the danger of patent medicines. Labels claim the medicines are safe when in fact they are not. Pregnant women are taking 'tonics' that are harmful to their babies and don't know it. Cancer victims are drinking colored water instead of seeking medical help. The public has a right to know, Mr. Chandler, what they are buying and what they are putting into their bodies. And since the drug manufacturers will not tell them, then we must."

Horace Chandler put the pamphlet down and fixed a studious eye on Samantha. "Are you sure of these figures?"

"Yes."

"Can you get more? There isn't much here. Three manufacturers. It would give the article more weight if we could add others."

"I haven't had time," said Samantha, "but I've been thinking of analyzing Sara Fenwick's Miracle Compound."

His brows shot up. "The biggest in the country."

"I'll do it for you, Sam," said Mark. "All I need is a flask and a Bunsen burner."

Horace Chandler rubbed his chin. "Your pamphlet is good, Dr. Hargrave, but it reads like a medical journal. Would you object to my taking a little editorial license?"

"Not at all." Samantha felt herself growing more and more excited.

"Dr. Hargrave, I'll see to it that my readers think it's going to happen to them with the very next pill. Public indignation, doctors, that will be your weapon. You know, Dr. Hargrave, it's muckraking like this that gets laws changed."

"And increases magazine circulation," added Mark with a grin.

Horace rose. "I'm sorry, but I have an appointment now. Mark, my best to Lilian. Dr. Hargrave, it was a pleasure. Shall we meet again next week?"

As they stepped from the cool building into the hot August afternoon, Samantha felt her spirit expand and soar to the sky. Mark settled his Homburg on his head, squinted at the brilliant day, then grinned down at Samantha. "Dr. Hargrave," he said, "I do believe you and I are going to change the world!"

EIGHT

AMANTHA STARED AT THE WORDS SHE HAD JUST WRITTEN, not reading them, her head supported by one hand, the other hand holding the pen above the page as if waiting to be given life. This was going to be their second article for *Woman's Companion*. The first, published last month under the title "Don't Let This Happen to You," had generated such great public interest that Horace Chandler wanted to follow it right away with another; this one was going to include the laboratory analysis for ten popular drugstore medicines.

Samantha finally laid the pen down and sat back in her chair. Beyond her closed door the Infirmary was settled down for its night of semisleep (the hospital never really slept) and an atmosphere of quiet intimacy filled the air. Samantha drew in a deep breath and released it slowly in a long, melancholy sigh. She didn't know what was wrong with her tonight; she felt strangely out of touch.

Wearily she rose from her desk and went to the window. She drew back the heavy velvet drapes and looked out at the October night. The scene below appeared unreal; it was an eerie vista out of some supernatural play: The street was nearly deserted, the few pedestrians wrestled with the brisk wind for possession of their hats and seemed to hurry from one pool of gaslight to the next, as if being chased, or fearful of the October shadows. It was the Halloween season, the jack-o'-lantern season, the dying season . . .

Samantha gazed at her reflection and thought: Now, why did I think *that? The dying season.* Because it is. We start dying the instant we are conceived, we are born only to die, from swaddling clothes to shrouds, what is the purpose of it all?

Reflexively her hand went to her breast and she caressed the turquoise. Since the day (how many years ago?) she had had a chain made for it, the stone had rested against Samantha's heart. *My luck.* But is it? Am I lucky?

Samantha knew she was not normally a fantasizer, that she was not a true romantic in the sense Dr. Canby was (who played Caruso songs and surrounded herself with portraits of Edwin Booth and Napoleon Bonaparte); Samantha was pragmatic, a realist. Why, then, did she occasionally slip into these melodramatic moods? Particularly of late . . .

She knew why.

Turning away from the window, Samantha looked around her office and suddenly everything blurred. Good heavens, I'm on the verge of tears!

There was so much to be happy for, to rejoice about (the state had renewed their grant, the Crockers were going to finance a new operating room, and, best of all, Jenny was pregnant). There was no reason in the world for this sadness.

Samantha put her hand to her forehead as if to press back the tears. *I have no right. I gave him up long ago, he is no longer mine . . .*

She sighed again but it came out as a stifled sob. How much longer could she keep it up? Samantha knew she was a strong woman in all else, but in this . . . She wanted him, she *needed* him. *I shall perish if I cannot be in his arms once more.*

She had thought she would be able to do it, treat Mark as an old friend, work at his side, keep up the professional bearing, but it was becoming increasingly more difficult. With each passing day, each time he came into her office, every visit to Horace Chandler's, dinner at the Gants' house with Mark on one side and Lilian on the other—

Samantha suddenly felt claustrophobic. The walls were inching in. She went to her door and opened it. The dim corridor was deserted, hushed, like the autumn street outside; she wouldn't have been surprised to see red and orange leaves littering the floor . . .

I should go home. Why am I still here?

A grotesque shape emerged from the deep shadows at the end of the hall and came slowly toward her. It was a large, square hulk trundling on silent wheels, seemingly propelled of its own volition, clinking and rattling. As it drew near, Samantha saw the hands on either side, the head bobbing up and down, and finally the rhythmic rise and fall of the porter's back. "Evening, Doc," he muttered, pushing the food cart by.

Samantha opened her mouth but could not speak. She watched the porter and food cart disappear around the corner, then she looked back in the direction from which he had come.

The stairs.

The ache was becoming unbearable. Another night of lying in her bed and thinking about Mark, trying to recapture the feel of his body, the taste of his mouth, the smell of him . . .

Oh, Willella, is this what you go through every day of your life? I had no idea.

Samantha was suddenly overcome with a profound sadness, for poor Willella and her quiet desperation, for herself, and for all who yearn to be lovers but can never be.

She was barely aware that she moved; her feet were their own masters and they carried her, independent of her will, toward the stairs. She paused at the newel post, poised at the brink of the abyss, and she thought: *He's not there. He left hours ago.*

She took the stairs haltingly, as if to test each one for strength, uncertain that they would support her and the incredible burden she carried. Down, down, from darkness into darkness, in and out of weak ponds of electric light, a sleepwalker at the mercy of her feet, marching inexorably down while her mind said: *There's no one there.*

At the foot of the stairs she froze. The cavernous hall of the basement was illuminated by one bulb, revealing closed doors and locked cupboards. Cold, silent. And under the last door, the door at the faraway end, the laboratory door, *that* door, a seepage of light . . .

In the next instant she was standing before it. Of course, Dr. Mary Johns, the pathologist, was in there, working late.

Samantha knocked.

"Come in," said Mark on the other side.

She opened the door and stood framed in darkness and spectral light. As she stared at him, just straightening up from his microscope, Samantha thought: *It hasn't even been a year. How long shall I have to endure this? How many more Octobers to come?*

His handsome face was cast in shadow. Samantha couldn't tell if he was smiling or frowning; it looked like both. "Sam," he said softly. "You're working late."

"Yes. The article." She had difficulty finding breath. "You're working late too."

"Staining specimens . . ."

Again her body seemed to move on its own. Her hand closed the door behind her, her feet carried her to the workbench, and her voice, sounding strangely like another woman's, said, "I prefer to work on the article here at the hospital and then that way in case I'm needed I'm right here on hand and no one has to send for me at home . . ."

His eyes, not soft brown now but black and piercing, looked down at her, into her, through her. "You've been working late a lot recently."

"So have you."

His glance dropped down to her chest. A small furrow appeared between his brows. "What's this?" He reached out to take the stone; Samantha felt his hand brush her breast.

"Letitia gave it to me. Do you . . . remember her?"

"I remember."

"And Janelle?"

"Yes."

"And Landon Fremont," the words tumbled out in a rush, "and Dr.

Prince and Dr. Weston and Mrs. Knight . . . Oh, Mark! We've never talked about the past. We've kept it buried between us! I want it to live again!"

It happened so fast it startled her. His arms were enveloping her, drawing her against him, and then his mouth was covering hers, and suddenly they were back in that little room at St. Brigid's and Mark had just stormed in saying, "Damn it, Samantha, I love you!" and strains of laughter and banjo music came through the thin walls.

She clung to him, drowning; he devoured her, starving. When his hand slipped inside her blouse and cupped her breast, fourteen years disappeared in an instant: the *Excalibur,* his mother's death, the long, lonely journey across the country, baby Clair's birth and death, Jenny, Hilary, the Infirmary—none of it existed, it had never happened. It had all been a dream and Samantha was finally waking up.

"Oh God," Mark whispered into her hair. "I didn't think I could go on. Seeing you every day. Pretending to be just an old friend."

He took her by the shoulders and held her at arm's length, exploring her with his eyes, looking at her at last the way he had wanted to all these months, lingeringly, lovingly, drinking in the exquisite loveliness of her, the pearl-gray eyes, the raven hair now falling over her shoulders, a vision he had taken to bed with him every night for fourteen years. Then he gently slipped the blouse off her shoulders and then the straps of her camisole. He bent his head and kissed her breast. Samantha gasped.

When he raised his head he plunged his fingers into her hair, and whispered huskily, "'It was many and many a year ago, in a kingdom by the sea, that a maiden there lived whom you may know by the name of Annabel Lee—And this maiden she lived with no other thought than to love and be loved by me.'"

"Take me back, Mark," Samantha whispered. "Carry me into the past. Give us those days again before the *Excalibur*." She lifted the chain over her head and dropped the turquoise pendant onto the workbench. "Let's set aside, just this once, where we are and who we've become." Hot tears ran down her cheeks. Her hands reached out and, trembling, unbuttoned his shirt. "Talk to me of President Garfield. Complain to me about your father's bullheadedness. Tell me about your brothers, about Stephen's wasteful spending and your mother's constant lecturing. And I'll tell you about the fight at the hospital over the germ theory and Dr. Prince's stubborn refusal to let me into the operating room—"

The floor of the laboratory seemed to Mark and Samantha like a bed of eiderdown. He spread his coat and they began gently, but soon they held nothing back, all their passions and needs were met, the frustrations of the past indulged, for this one night.

Later, in the hour before dawn, as sounds of a stirring Infirmary drifted down to them, they would talk about it and come to grips with reality. They would agree that they were not free, that they could not indulge themselves again, that there were others to think of now, especially Lilian, and that the present was where they must live. Samantha told him about a baby named Clair and they tried, although it was painful, to accept that the past was in fact gone, that their day had gone. But for now, this one night belonged to them. And if tomorrow and all the other tomorrows would belong to others, this night was theirs, and they would try, with all their hearts and souls, to live a lifetime of loving in a few brief hours.

NINE

IT WAS THE END OF 1896 AND WORD OF GOLD IN ALASKA HAD started to spread. San Francisco soon found itself once again in the middle of a gold-rush boom. The Alaska gold hunter became a familiar sight, in his flannel shirt and wool parka, and newspapers started to give accounts of the hazards of the Yukon camps. Gold mania struck everyone, including Darius Gant, who grubstaked a couple of miners for half interest in their earnings, and for a while San Francisco was alive with the rowdiness of its former days.

As a result, Samantha's articles for *Woman's Companion* were competing with lots of other news for public attention.

The December issue carried an article called "There's Poison in That Medicine!" and in the January issue, "How Easily Are You Duped?" was presented in the form of a quiz to test the reader's knowledge of patent medicines. But neither created the response the very first article had—the public had been lured away by Yukon legends and the only way to get them back, Horace Chandler declared, was to write something truly sensational.

So when she was not in surgery or working on the wards, Samantha spent her spare time at home drafting a story called, "My Nightmare as a Dope Fiend." Although it was written in the first person under a fictitious name, the case history was based on one from Samantha's files. It drew a realistic and shocking picture of the typical patent medicine addict.

The days passed in an endless succession of patients, treatments, tragedies and victories; the wet San Francisco winter approached the threshold of spring, with the city's gold fever escalated.

Samantha and Mark saw a great deal of each other during those rainy months, but never did they re-create their night in the lab. Often they did little more than sit in her office and drink tea, listening to the food carts rumble by in the halls, the rain tap the windows. They didn't need to make physical love: They did it with their eyes, with an occasional touch, and with their thoughts, reaching out and joining. They worked on their drug articles—Mark in the laboratory analyzing tonics and elixirs, Samantha sketching outlines and statistics. But they never again spoke of what was really in their hearts, because it was unnecessary; they both knew. They were in love, and they wanted one another.

⁂

"Please relax, Mrs. Sargent, that's right." Samantha fixed her gaze on the wall opposite, visualizing the anatomy. "That's fine. You may get dressed now." She stepped away from the examining table and went to the sink to wash her hands.

On the utility table by the sink lay Mrs. Sargent's purse and gloves and the copy of the *Saturday Evening Post* she had been reading; it was open to an article about President McKinley, newly inaugurated. Samantha's eyes dropped to the advertisement box below. "Operations Avoided," the headline declared. "Do not neglect yourself and drag along until you are obliged to go to the hospital; build up your feminine system and cure those derangements which are danger signals. A daily dose of Sara Fenwick's Miracle Compound will restore and preserve the delicate female mechanism. Read below letters from women who have suffered and who turned to Mrs. Fenwick for help."

"Can you do anything for me, Doctor?"

"Mrs. Sargent, you have very large fibroids. They are the cause of the bleeding." Samantha dried her hands on a fresh towel and then turned around, buttoning her cuffs. "When did it start?"

Mrs. Sargent was a small woman and highly agitated. "About five years ago, after Timothy was born. It wasn't serious then, just spotting. And then about three years ago my monthly days lasted for two weeks."

"Did you do anything about it?"

"I would have lost my job at the bakery if I had taken time off to go to a doctor, so I wrote to Sara Fenwick. Her advertisements claim she can work wonders."

Samantha looked down reflexively at the ad. Sara Fenwick gazed benevolently from out of an oval portrait, her beautiful grandmotherly face set in a sublime smile. "And what did she recommend?"

"She sent me a bottle of her compound. Soon as I started taking it I felt better."

Samantha nodded; the high alcohol content would do that.

"But the bleeding continued. I wrote back and she told me to increase my daily dose of the compound. But it didn't work," said Mrs. Sargent with a bowed head. "I drank the compound every day until finally I could stand it no more. The bleeding got heavier and now I'm very weak."

Samantha drew up a chair and sat next to her. "Mrs. Sargent," she said in her easiest tone, "the fibroids are not cancerous but they must come out."

The little woman paled. "You mean surgery?"

"Yes."

"What kind of surgery?"

"Your womb will have to be removed."

Mrs. Sargent gave a cry of horror, then burst into tears.

Samantha patted her knee. "If you had gone to a doctor at the beginning something could have been done, but the condition is now beyond saving."

"We can't afford a doctor!" she wailed into the handkerchief. "We can barely afford to feed the kids!"

"Mrs. Sargent, the Infirmary is free to those who cannot pay."

"But oh, my womb removed! Dr. Hargrave, please try something else!"

Samantha experienced a brief pain.

"It's not me, it's how Harry will feel! He won't love me anymore!"

"Of course he will, Mrs. Sargent."

"But I'm not even forty! Please, Dr. Hargrave," Mrs. Sargent pleaded. "Don't do it! I'd rather die!"

Samantha rested a comforting hand on the woman's shoulder. "I truly wish there were an alternative."

"Wasn't the compound helping at all?"

"Sara Fenwick's is a tonic, Mrs. Sargent, something to make you feel good. It cannot correct structural defects."

"But my sister had a tumor on the womb and one bottle of Sara Fenwick's dissolved it clean away. And I have felt good otherwise. When I come home from the bakery after ten hours it's all I can do to drag myself up the steps. Then I drink my compound and right away I feel I can get through the cooking and cleaning." She reached for Samantha's hand. "Please, Doctor . . ."

Samantha felt tears start behind her eyes; the professional mask was not an easy one to wear. She spoke gently. "If we do not remove it, Mrs. Sargent, you will develop severe complications."

"But I don't want to get *old*."

"Old, Mrs. Sargent?"

She whispered, "*The menopause*. Hysterectomy does it."

"That's a myth, Mrs. Sargent. Only if the ovaries are removed does menopause come on. In your case we will remove only the uterus, which is just a muscle, nothing more."

"But I won't be a woman anymore . . ."

Samantha felt a lump in her throat. "Of *course* you will be!"

"Oh, Doctor, I'm so afraid . . ."

"Mark, may I have a word with you?"

He looked up from the microscope and the sudden joy on his face made Samantha's heart leap. "Of course, Sam! Come here, I want you to see something!"

She bent over the microscope, placing her eye against the lens while Mark adjusted the mirror for better light. "This is a sample of the breast tissue you removed yesterday. Can you see the normal cells around two o'clock?"

"Yes." He was standing close, almost touching her.

"They are well formed, typical, uniform in size and a few are undergoing division."

"Yes," she said softly. "I see that."

"Now look at the cells abutting them. Aberrant, distorted. And see how easily they break away. Sam, *those are all the same cells!*"

She straightened and found him beaming down at her. "I've never seen such a clear specimen," he went on. "That one slide almost proves my theory on the beginnings of cancer. And if I'm right, if malignant cells are simply renegades that were once normal, then we have a starting point for finding a cure!"

"It's wonderful, Mark." She glanced at the logbook in which he was describing and sketching his specimens. "But what does the university think of you spending all your time here?"

He turned away and busied himself at the work table. "I've asked for a sabbatical, Sam. My work here is too important. Both the cancer research and our drug campaign. And—"

"And?"

He turned to face her squarely; his smile was gone. "I'm worried about Lilian."

"What's wrong?"

"I don't know. She doesn't seem happy. Even though she's busy with the Children's Ward . . ." He shook his head. "I don't know. We hardly see each other anymore. And when we do, we don't seem to have anything to talk about."

"Do you think she suspects . . . about us?"

He turned away and walked to the sink. "I don't know, Sam. I don't think so. Lilian is a very straightforward person. If she suspected anything, she'd say something. It's something else. Her desire for a child, I suppose."

Mark washed his hands, dried them, then rolled down his sleeves. Turning around and leaning back against the sink, he said, "What did you want to talk about?"

Yes, let's get back to safe ground. "It's about our drug crusade, Mark. Mr. Chandler says the letters have dropped off. We aren't getting the public's attention."

"Maybe we should title the next one 'Drug Addiction on the Klondike.'"

"You're probably right. But I've been thinking. Maybe we are too diversified, spreading ourselves too thin, trying to alert the public to too many facts and figures."

"What's your idea?"

They heard the door open and turned to see Dr. Mary Johns, the pathologist, enter. "Good afternoon, Doctors," she said brightly, removing her coat.

"Hello, Mary," said Mark. "I was just leaving."

"No rush. I must have my cup of tea first!" Dr. Johns went straight to a workbench against one wall where, amid specimen jars, bottles of formaldehyde, flasks, test tubes and burners, there was a spirit lamp with a little kettle on it. "How is your daughter, Dr. Hargrave?"

"Jenny's fine, thank you. Big for six months. I'm thinking it might be twins."

Dr. Johns turned around. "Wouldn't that be nice!"

While Mark showed the pathologist the specimens that had come down from surgery, inviting also her opinion on the slide in the microscope, Samantha went to the door. "Mark, I'll be up on the General Ward."

"I would like to concentrate on one drug company," said Samantha when they were all settled in Horace Chandler's office. "I think we might catch the public's attention if we focus on one popular, well-known medicine."

Horace leaned back in his chair, clasping his hands over his belly. Behind him, March winds drove a heavy rain against the windows. "Have you one in mind?"

"A great number of my patients turned to Sara Fenwick's Miracle Compound before coming to the Infirmary. I think it is one patent drug that is found in almost every household."

Horace let out a long whistle. "Sara Fenwick is *the* biggest in the country, Doctor. And they are the major force behind the lobby in Washington. That's a mighty powerful opponent you're talking about."

"Are you afraid to pursue it?"

Horace gave a short laugh. "Not in the least! But I will tell you this." He rocked forward and spread his hands flat on the desk top. "If you want to take on Sara Fenwick you'll have to be *very* sure of your data." He turned to Mark. "Have you run an analysis yet?"

"Just for alcohol, which it has in abundance."

"Do you think it contains harmful ingredients, Dr. Hargrave?"

"That won't be my point of attack, Mr. Chandler, for I believe the Miracle Compound is basically harmless. What I protest is their practice of diagnosing and treating through correspondence. Every one of my patients who delayed coming to me because she was drinking the compound had written to the Fenwick company. And they were assured of a cure. That, Mr. Chandler, is what I protest."

Horace thought a moment. "This will require more than a bit of laboratory analysis and a few unhappy users." He rose out of his chair and strode to the bookcase that covered one wall. Sliding a panel to one side and exposing a shelf of bottles and glasses, Horace Chandler poured himself a drink. He didn't offer the doctors any, knowing they would refuse. Returning to his desk, but sitting on its edge rather than in his chair, Horace Chandler said, "It's a coincidence you came in today, Doctors, because I was going to pay a call on you this afternoon."

He swirled the whiskey around his glass, watching it but not drinking it, "For once, *I* have something to report to *you*. Have you ever heard of the 'red clause'?"

"No."

Chandler went on to explain about a little investigation he had been conducting on his own, something he hoped would give a boost to their articles and catch the public eye. A detective had been put on an assignment: to get hold of a copy of the contracts which drug companies used when arranging with magazines and newspapers for advertising. Posing as an ad man for a regional magazine, the Pinkerton agent had gone to the offices of the J. C. Ayer Company and obtained one of their advertising agreements. In it was the "red clause."

Horace opened a drawer and handed the document to Samantha and Mark. "Few people know about it," he said as they studied the clause in question, so named because it was printed in red ink. "It states that the contract will become void if any legislation is enacted against patent medicines or if any material detrimental to drug companies appears in the magazine. It's a universal clause found in all drug company contracts and it very effectively muzzles the press."

Samantha and Mark looked at one another, then at Horace. "I thought folks might like to know that the Bill of Rights is being violated. Freedom of the press, but only as long as it doesn't threaten profits."

Mark handed the contract back. "Are you going to print it?"

"The entire thing." Horace put down his untouched drink and went back to his chair. "What I now have in mind, Doctors, is using this same Pinkerton—Cy Jeffries his name is—to do a little snooping at the Sara Fenwick plant. He just might find out a few buried facts that would interest the public very much. And I have a hunch," he said, giving them a significant look, "that Mr. Jeffries is going to find something very interesting indeed."

TEN

*T*HIS WAS NOTHING LIKE THE OLD OPERATING THEATERS: Samantha and her team wore clean white smocks over their dresses and caps binding up their hair; the instruments were sterile, Mrs. Sargent slept beneath sterile sheets, and the anesthetist plotted her pulse and respiration on one of the new charts designed by Massachusetts General. This was going to be a routine abdominal operation: Samantha's daring experiments at St. Brigid's were becoming commonplace.

They worked in silence. Willella, standing opposite Samantha and holding retractors, thought Dr. Hargrave was in a distracted mood this morning: well, the directress had a lot of things on her mind.

One of the things occupying Samantha's thoughts on this sunny May morning was the party being held at the Masons' house that evening: a birthday party for Samantha, which she had protested, not wishing to be reminded that she was thirty-seven years old today. But there had been no dissuading her friends, especially Hilary, who, now that baby Winifred was over a year old, was free to start her new life.

Hilary was a lucky woman. After the accident on the stairs she had been able to sit down and talk with Darius, who, although still a little confused, had agreed to practice anticonception and to allow Hilary a little more freedom. He balked on the issue of her having her own checkbook, but in all else he was willing at least to try.

Samantha also thought of Jenny: Hilary had ended her long career of maternity and the other was just starting hers. While the imminent birth (she was due in two weeks) generated a great deal of excitement, Samantha could not help experiencing concern. Jenny was very large, and when Samantha examined her, she thought she had detected two heartbeats. Twins would be nice, but they also increased the risk of complications. Samantha wished now that she knew more about Jenny's family history.

⁂

Jenny herself was serene. As though all her purpose in life were being fulfilled, she waited in utter tranquillity, her hands resting on her large belly, Adam always by her side.

Samantha brought her thoughts back to the operation. The uterus was out now, and after rinsing the cavity for a clear view, she and Willella did an inspection of the surrounding organs; then they proceeded to close.

"Nurse, please tell Dr. Johns to do a gross examination of this uterus. And if Dr. Rawlins is down in the pathology lab, will you please tell him I'll be out in half an hour?"

As she started suturing, Samantha felt herself grow excited. After rounds, she and Mark were going to Horace Chandler's office to plan the final layout of the Sara Fenwick article.

There was no doubt now that what they planned—an exposé on the leading drug manufacturer in the United States—was going to cause a sensation. When Horace Chandler printed the Ayer contract under the heading, "Drug Manufacturer Laughs at Freedom of the Press," sales of Ayer's Bitters dropped sharply, *Woman's Companion* was swamped with letters, and the attorneys for Ayer's paid a visit to Mr. Chandler. Clearly, the public was reading what they were printing, and asking for more.

Well, Cy Jeffries had seen to it that the next article was going to be one of the hottest to come off the presses.

The Pinkerton man had done phenomenal work. Having gotten himself a job in the shipping room of the Fenwick company, the detective had uncovered more sensational material than had been hoped for: he had learned that many of the testimonial letters were paid for (twenty-five dollars to anyone who would write a letter claiming a cure) and had found unsanitary conditions in the bottling room. A major breakthrough had come when he gained entrance to the correspondence room where, Fenwick ads claimed, "No Man Ever Sets Foot." Jeffries counted several male employees and saw two youths sniggering in the corner over a letter that had just come in.

The biggest treasure of all, however, was the photograph.

Horace Chandler was going to run it on the first page of the September issue. It was a picture of Sara Fenwick's gravestone, the dates clearly seen—Sara Fenwick had died six years before the company was even started—and underneath, Horace was going to print a facsimile of one of their ads which read, "Mrs. Fenwick, in her parlor, is able to do more for the afflicted women of this country than any doctor."

Mark and Samantha had their contributions as well. In the lab Mark had run a thorough analysis of the compound and found it was not as harmless as they had thought: one ingredient was an abortifacient. For her part, Samantha had written a series of letters to Sara Fenwick, signing her name without the M.D. The first described a vague malaise and Sara Fenwick wrote back advising a tablespoon daily of the compound. Samantha sent a second letter, increasing her symptoms, and Sara Fenwick replied that she should double her dose. Samantha then wrote that her doctor recommended surgery and Sara Fenwick's response was that half a bottle of the compound a day would save Samantha from the scalpel.

There was so much material that Horace Chandler decided to devote almost the entire September issue of *Woman's Companion* to Sara Fenwick. Besides the Fenwick article he was going to run smaller, supplementary exposés. On Samantha's and Mark's advice, Horace was going to focus on Wertz's Bitters, Aunt Trudy's Kickapoo Cure, and the Sears Secret Liquor Cure. For this last, Horace planned a two-page spread reproducing the ad as it appeared in the Sears catalog: a picture of a woman surreptitiously pouring something into her unsuspecting husband's evening coffee, insinuating this would stop his drunken carousing at night. Horace's caption underneath was going to read: "It'll keep him home at night all right; the cure contains enough narcotic to put him out as soon as he has finished his coffee." And on the opposing page, with the caption, "This is in case the Liquor Cure works too well," a reproduction of the Sears Cure for the Opium and Morphine Habit. The entire edition was going to come out under one title, emblazoned on the cover in bright red letters: Caveat Emptor, *Buyer Beware!*

As Samantha applied dressings to Mrs. Sargent's incision, Nurse Constance came into the operating room. "Dr. Hargrave, Mrs. Rawlins asked if she could see you in your office."

"Certainly, Constance. Will you stay with Mrs. Sargent until she wakens, please?"

———❦———

"Hello, Lilian," she said, entering her office. "Can I offer you some tea?"

"No, thank you, Doctor."

Samantha came around her desk wondering what the reason was for this visit. Lilian's treatments had ended—there was nothing more Samantha could do; the rest was up to Lilian and Mark. And it was the hospital lunch hour; Lilian always helped feed the children at this time.

"What can I do for you, Lilian?" said Samantha, sitting and folding her hands on the desk.

"Dr. Hargrave, I want to thank you for everything you've tried to do for me. The treatments, the advice, the concern. It was more than the other doctors offered."

"Don't give up hope."

"But I have, Doctor. I've given up all hope."

Samantha stared at her. The declaration had come out calmly, quietly, and her posture was relaxed; the manner of a woman who is resigned. "Please don't give up yet," said Samantha.

Lilian held up a gloved hand. "No, Dr. Hargrave. When I gave up all hope in St. Louis, I was resigned to my fate. But then I came here and you gave me new hope and for that I am grateful. But I cannot hope a third time, Doctor. I would not be able to stand it."

"But there's no reason to give up hope yet."

"I shall be forty this year, Doctor. I married late. In fact, when I met Mark I was already resigned to being a spinster. I have no illusions anymore. I understand now it was never meant to be."

Samantha said gently, "Please don't think you have failed because you haven't been able to bear another child. To the boys and girls in the Children's Ward, you are their mother."

"It is not motherhood I am referring to, Doctor. What I speak of when I say it was never meant to be is my marriage to Mark."

The two women stared at one another.

"We were in love when we got married, Dr. Hargrave," came the quiet voice, "and we still love one another, but this year and a half in San Francisco has caused me to do a great deal of thinking and examination. I know now that I married Mark for the wrong reasons. I was lonely. I was past thirty and frightened of spinsterhood. And I desperately"—her voice dropped to a whisper—"*desperately* wanted a baby."

Lilian drew in a deep breath and shifted slightly. "Mark and I really had nothing in common. Oh, plays, poetry, that sort of thing. But nothing substantial or sustaining. I was in New York visiting cousins. I met Mark at a picnic. I believe he was drawn to me for the same reason I was to him: he wanted a family. And I suppose that, if we had been able to make a family, then we would have found that mutual interest. But after"—she looked down at her hands—"after our baby died, we started to grow apart. Mark became restless in St. Louis. He wanted to do more in life than have a neighborhood practice. When the university asked him to join their staff he saw it as a golden opportunity. Although I didn't want to leave my family, I wanted to do what was best for Mark's career, so I agreed to the move."

Lilian raised her head and gazed steadily at Samantha. "Mark did find what he wanted, here in San Francisco. He's happy now, involved, dedicated. And I am happy for him."

Samantha slowly unclasped her hands and eased herself back in her chair.

"Dr. Hargrave, I want to go home." For the first time, a flaw showed through Lilian's calm façade: her chin quivered. "I long for my family. I long to embrace my nieces and nephews. I feel such a hunger, such an emptiness. I know I have the children here in the Infirmary, but they are so fleeting. I grow attached to them and they leave. Now I am afraid to love them because of the pain that follows. Dr. Hargrave, I want permanent children, children who are in some way a part of me, my own flesh and blood. My sisters—" Her voice caught.

Samantha got up and yanked the bellpull. Then she went to sit next to Lilian.

"My sisters," she went on, "want me to come home, Dr. Hargrave." Lilian's hazel eyes misted. "That is where I belong."

Finally, the tears started to come. Samantha handed her a handkerchief; she could not yet find her own voice.

After a moment Lilian composed herself. "I love Mark, Dr. Hargrave, and I would not hurt him for the world. But I am not the woman he should be married to. I cannot give him what he needs—a sharing, an interest in his work. To be frank with you, Doctor, I find his laboratory work unpleasant. I admire him for what he is doing, but I do not like to hear about it. And I sense he finds my constant talk about my nieces and nephews tiresome."

There was a knock at the door and Nurse Hampton appeared. "Bring us some tea, please," said Samantha in a strained voice.

After the door closed, Lilian said, "This is not a rash decision, Doctor. I have thought about it for months. When Mrs. Gant had her baby last year I was beside myself with anxiety. Dr. Hargrave, I'm going home."

Samantha wanted to ask: Have you told Mark? What does he say? But she kept her silence.

However, as though reading her thoughts, Lilian said, "Mark is not happy about this. I told him last night. We had a long talk. It was our first really honest talk in a long time. He blames himself and I am not able to convince him otherwise."

Her voice grew stronger. "Mark and I belong in two separate worlds. Loving one another isn't enough. There is the need for fulfillment also. I need my sisters' children, and Mark needs his career. But I cannot achieve my desires here in San Francisco, and he cannot pursue his dream in St. Louis. We are holding each other back, preventing each other from attaining what we really want, and that is contrary to the purpose of a marriage. He must stay here and I must go back to St. Louis."

Lilian finally fell silent, as if she had ended a memorized speech, and Samantha thought: Why have you told me all this? But she knew why . . .

When Nurse Hampton returned with a tray, Samantha said, "Will you have tea with me, Lilian?"

Mrs. Rawlins managed a smile. "I should love to, Dr. Hargrave."

Samantha remained in her office for a long time afterward, requesting she not be disturbed, and when she was ready, got up and went out. She went down the stairs that led to the kitchens and laundry and morgue, and hesitated before the door marked Laboratory.

When she went in she found Mark at his microscope. He looked up.

ELEVEN

*J*ENNY STOOD FIRM. EVEN THOUGH SAMANTHA INSISTED SHE BE DE-
livered in the hospital, her daughter would not have it. Adam's baby
was to be born at home, with Adam at her side.

"But there could be complications," Samantha pleaded.

"No complications," signed Jenny. "Everything is fine."

Nonetheless, Samantha brought a complete obstetrical setup home and
asked Willella if she would mind standing by in case Samantha needed help.
Jenny scoffed at her mother's fears. She faced the coming hour with the same
serenity and calm she had faced everything else in her life.

"I don't know," said Samantha, wringing her hands. "It's too big. And I
don't hear two heartbeats anymore. And she's a week overdue."

"Dr. Hargrave," said Willella, "just listen to yourself. Jenny is not too big,
you did not definitely hear two heartbeats before, and it's common for the
first to be overdue."

It was a sultry June evening. They were all in Samantha's parlor drinking lemonade and trying to catch what breezes came through the open

windows. Willella fanned herself and wished she could loosen her corset; Hilary, who had slimmed down to the figure she had when she married Darius, was not uncomfortable in the heat—the glow on her forehead was from anxiety for Jenny; and the men had removed their coats and loosened their collars. Darius added a bit of "spike" to his lemonade and Stanton's, but Mark had declined. He leaned against the doorframe, hands in pockets, gazing out over the glittering city. Samantha knew what he was thinking about.

Miss Peoples appeared on the stairs.

"How is she?" asked Samantha, going to her.

"She's just fine, Doctor. She's resting. Mr. Wolff is watching her. I thought I'd make some more lemonade."

Samantha had fretted so around Jenny that the girl had finally asked her to leave. "You are tiring me, Mother. Please let me rest. I will call, I promise."

And downstairs, both Willella and Hilary had urged Samantha to give her daughter some peace. Samantha's motherly worries were only going to make the girl nervous.

"One would think," said Willella with a smile, "Dr. Hargrave hadn't delivered thousands of babies."

"I suppose it's different when it's your own daughter." Hilary thought of her own Merry Christmas, thirteen years old and on the threshold of womanhood. It wouldn't be long before Hilary was going through what Samantha was going through now.

"I really must go up," said Samantha.

But Willella rose from her chair. "Let me, Doctor. At least I won't scare the poor thing to death."

Samantha accompanied her to the doorway and murmured out of everyone's hearing, "Wait five minutes and feel for contractions. She was four centimeters an hour ago and insisting she still didn't feel anything."

Willella patted her hand. "I know what to do, Doctor."

Wringing her hands again, Samantha came back into the parlor and went to stand by Mark. The warm evening was heavily scented with the ripe fragrances of her garden: the flowers, the peach and apricot trees, the freshly cut grass. She caught an occasional whiff of savory smoke which meant that her neighbors were enjoying a California summer specialty—the barbecue.

Mark looked down at her and smiled. "How are you doing?"

"All right. And you?"

"I was just thinking."

"What about?"

He continued to gaze down at her. "I was thinking of Lilian. I wonder if she knew, if she sensed what you and I feel for each other. If she did, then she's a greater lady than I had thought."

"She's happy now, Mark. Her youngest sister is expecting again."

"Yes . . ." He returned to looking out over the garden.

Although Samantha and Mark had talked for many hours about Lilian, something vital always remained unsaid: their own plans after the divorce came through. Mark seemed not to want to talk about it and Samantha didn't want to press. But she wondered, hoped . . .

"All's well," announced Willella, coming back into the parlor. "Jenny is resting comfortably." She came up to Samantha and said quietly, "The contractions are five minutes apart and she's dilated to six centimeters."

"Has she any pain?"

"She says no. I felt the contraction and watched her face. I think it hurt me more than it did her!"

Now Samantha knew what the fathers went through in their special little sitting room at the Infirmary. It was the one room where smoking was allowed, and although liquor was forbidden, all the staff knew it was smuggled in.

Miss Peoples returned with a fresh pitcher of lemonade and a plate of Chinese almond cookies. While Darius refilled his and Stanton's glasses—adding a dash to each from his flask—Hilary picked up the deck of cards and invited Willella to a game. Samantha returned to the open doorway where she stood with Mark in a communicative silence.

Presently Willella looked up from her cards and said, "The cats are active tonight! There must be a lady in the neighborhood. Listen to that tom!"

Samantha smiled at the urgent meowing in the distance. Cats were lucky; they were so basic. When they wanted something they simply demanded it. No intricate games, no diplomacy, no manners or rules of etiquette—

"That's not a cat!" said Mark, pushing away from the doorframe.

"Oh, dear God!" cried Samantha.

She and Willella flew up the stairs, leaving everyone gathered at the parlor door looking anxious. Samantha didn't knock; she burst in.

Adam looked up, smiled, then went back to gently wiping the little body with a soft cloth.

"Jennifer!" said Samantha, rushing to the bed. She examined the baby first—he was just fine; then, with tears in her eyes, half laughing and half crying, she severely admonished her daughter and son-in-law with staccato gestures.

Adam laid the baby down long enough to sign, "There was no need to call you, Mother," then he picked him up and placed him in Jenny's waiting arms.

But Jenny was soon exhausted and finally let the two doctors take over. Samantha inspected the infant more closely. He was perfect in every way, and already, she thought, handsome. When he grew up they would all be able to see something of what Adam really looked like.

Samantha sat on the bed and signed, "What shall we call him?"

Adam spoke. "We've chosen Richard—for the king."

Samantha couldn't control her tears. They fell to the counterpane in big drops. "Richard Wolff. Such a noble little man."

When the news came down to the parlor, Stanton Weatherby muttered something about "headstrong Hargrave women" and refilled his glass, this time forgoing the lemonade altogether.

TWELVE

THE "CAVEAT" ISSUE HIT THE STANDS IN SEPTEMBER AND WAS sold out in three days. The offices of *Woman's Companion* were deluged with phone calls and letters, the presses could not keep up with demand. By the end of the week telegrams were coming in from all over the country—other publications requesting copies—and in another few days the Alaska gold rush found itself pushed off the front page of every newspaper in the country. Opinions ranged from a cry to burn the *Woman's Companion* headquarters to round praise from the *Saturday Evening Post*. Samantha's pamphlets rapidly disappeared from the admitting counter at the Infirmary and her printer couldn't keep the supply filled. San Francisco was suddenly abuzz with the scandal; *Woman's Companion* was seen rolled up under many an arm; druggists were swamped with questions and demands for the return of money; and within a month sales of the Sara Fenwick Miracle Compound plummeted.

"Now, this doesn't mean that people are swearing off proprietary medicines," said Horace behind his telegram-strewn desk. "It's just unfashionable right now to own a bottle of the Miracle Compound. My informers tell me that other drug company sales have risen. What we have to do now," he told Samantha and Mark, "is fan the flames. We've got to get the public incensed. We've got them worked up now, let's channel that energy into pushing for reform." His hand swept over the letters and telegrams. "This may be impressive, Doctors, but there is still a glaring silence from Washington. As the saying goes, shall we strike while the iron is hot?"

They next challenged the five most popular medicines in the country and got to work on a February issue, "to start 1898 with a bang."

On a rainy afternoon in November, Mark came up to Samantha's office. He had just received in the mail his copy of the divorce papers from Lilian's lawyer, and with them was a letter.

Samantha stood in the light of the window to read it.

"My dear Mark," Lilian's letter read. "I hope all goes well with you. I cannot tell you how happy I am. Dierdre is certain she will have twins this time, in which case my hands quite literally will be full! I am so content now, dear Mark, among my family. I have a feeling of belonging and of purpose. Isabel's house is constantly filled with noise and I never have a moment's peace to myself, for there is forever a little knock at my bedroom door! Everyone says I am spoiling the children, but it is myself I am spoiling, Mark. Sometimes I wonder what I have done to deserve such joy.

"We all read your marvelous magazine; and we are all so proud of you and Dr. Hargrave. It is a point of great pride to me to have known you.

"God keep you both."

Samantha remained by the window for a long minute, gazing down at Lilian's precise copperplate, then she found her voice and turned to Mark.

"I, too, received news today," she said in a tight voice. "Horace came by this morning." She picked up an envelope from the top of her desk and handed it across. "We're going to court, Mark. Sara Fenwick is suing us."

But he didn't open the envelope. He gazed across the desk at her, not hearing the distant street sounds or the trundle of a stretcher going past the closed door.

Samantha said, "Oh, Mark—"

He was around the desk in an instant, his arms gathering her up and Samantha pressing her face into his neck. When his mouth met hers it was in a long, unhurried kiss; now they knew they had all the time in the world.

THIRTEEN

*I*N A COINCIDENCE WHOSE IRONY WAS LOST ON NO ONE, THE February 1898 issue of *Woman's Companion*, titled *The Outrage Continues*, appeared on the stands the day the Sara Fenwick/*Woman's Companion* case was to be heard in court, and both were such sensational issues that the other news of the day—the sinking of the *Maine* in Havana Harbor—got little notice in San Francisco newspapers. The Sara Fenwick Company, it was rumored, was so incensed over the September issue that it was planning to put *Woman's Companion* out of business and bring Dr. Hargrave and her Infirmary into disrepute.

On the evening before the trial, Hilary had everyone over for dinner, as if to show the city they weren't afraid of the coming fight. Secretly, however, there was a great deal of trepidation in the air that evening.

Joining Samantha and Mark at the long table were their closest friends: the Masons, the Gants, Horace and Gertrude Chandler, Stanton Weatherby and Willella Canby, Merry Christmas, Jennifer and Adam. Baby Richard was upstairs in the same nursery his mother had once been sequestered in when the adults had parties, and with him were the other Gant children and the Masons' three rowdy boys. Hilary's menu consisted of roast beef with Yorkshire pudding and gravy, potatoes in their jackets, and for dessert a genuine six-layered English trifle. Darius brought wine up from his private stock which put everyone in a good mood, although the thought did cross Stanton Weatherby's mind that this was very like the meal of a man about to be hanged.

Yet dinner had an air of festivity despite a shared edginess.

"What I don't understand," said Darius, biting into a brussels sprout, "is why the fools insist on a trial! An out-of-court settlement would seem to be in their best interest. A trial can only be bad publicity for them."

"On the contrary," said Stanton, who had already prepared the defense. "The Fenwick Company thinks this will be *good* publicity for them. They believe they'll come out of the trial looking like martyrs. They are not imbeciles. Their lawyers are the best and sharpest money can buy. They'll see to it that everything you printed, Horace, is twisted to make you look like a liar. Then they'll find a way to sully Samantha's and Mark's reputations to cast doubt on their credibility. The press will pick up on every little crumb of dirt and smear it on every front page across the country."

Samantha shuddered at a thought: Could they possibly find out about an illegitimate child born fifteen years ago? She looked down the table at Mark and received from him a reassuring smile. Samantha wouldn't be afraid with Mark at her side.

Their defense was not going to be easy. Because of the extreme delicacy of the issue—women's intimate problems—it was going to be very hard on the witnesses for the defense. Samantha was concerned about the patients who had been damaged by taking the compound and who were now willing to take the stand.

"I still don't understand," said Darius, "how anyone, at this stage, can be on *their* side."

"It's no mystery," said Stanton. "First of all, Sara Fenwick is an old and familiar face around American households. She represents motherhood and female purity. I'll bet there isn't a cupboard in this country without a bottle of her compound in it. The Fenwick Company is a respected institution, as

American as baseball, and people don't like to have their idols attacked. And a lot of people believe we are trying to rob them of freedoms. Government control of drugs? What is the next step? How far before we have government control of our minds?"

"But that isn't the issue at all!" Darius boomed. "All we want is honest labeling on the bottles so people can decide for themselves if they want to be poisoned! We're not taking a freedom away, we're preserving it!"

"Darius dear," said Hilary, patting his arm, "we all agree with you. There's no need to shout."

"I'm afraid there'll be a lot of shouting at the trial," said Stanton. "And a whole lot of unpleasantness besides."

They all fell silent for a moment, then Stanton added quietly: "Ambrose Bierce once defined a lawsuit as a machine that you go into as a pig and come out as a sausage."

No one laughed.

❦

The courtroom was crowded to excess; people had lined up outside the courthouse an hour before the doors opened. There was a great deal of noise, a lot of spitting into the spittoons, the air was clogged with smoke and male voices, an occasional explosion from a photographer's hod, and the reporters at the press table were already scribbling the beginnings of their dramatic accounts. There were no women in attendance, for the courtroom was the province of men.

Isaac Venables was the judge and he was known to be a fair and open-minded man. The jurors (all men—women did not sit on juries) had already undergone the strenuous selection process and now filed into their box while the court fell silent and rose to its feet. Samantha was the only woman in the room, and when she stood, with Mark and Horace at the defense table, all eyes turned to her. "The beautiful Dr. Hargrave," noted one newsman on his pad, "was stunning and elegant in the very simplicity of her dress; she commands herself royally, as though she were a queen on trial, and the tilt of her proud head shows a defiance and courage rarely found in the gentler sex."

The three defendants—Samantha Hargrave, Mark Rawlins, Horace Chandler—were charged with having made "libelous and damaging remarks against an old and respected business," magnesium powder exploded in the photographers' hods, Judge Venables banged his gavel, and the trial began.

Mr. Cromwell, the chief counsel for the plaintiff John Fenwick, made his opening statement, a lengthy, purple speech intended to impress upon the twelve jurors the utter foulness of the deed these malicious three had committed, after which Mr. Berrigan, Stanton Weatherby's young partner, countered with opening remarks not only refuting Mr. Cromwell's charges but promising to prove beyond a doubt the criminal intentions of the Fenwick Company.

Mr. Cromwell called his first witness.

Dr. Smith was a pudgy little bespectacled man whom one creative reporter sketched as a mole in a white suit. He was the senior chemist at the Fenwick manufacturing plant.

"Dr. Smith, will you please tell us the ingredients in the Miracle Compound?"

"Yes, sir. It contains unicorn root, life root, black cohosh, pleurisy root, and fenugreek seed."

"Does the compound contain alcohol?"

"It does."

"What is its purpose?"

"To preserve the stability of the chemical balance."

"Has the Fenwick Company ever tried to keep its alcohol content a secret?"

"No, sir. We invite anyone to write for a detailed account of the making and composition of the compound."

"If a woman wishes to undergo the Fenwick cure, must she take in alcohol?"

"No, sir, for the compound also comes in pills and lozenges."

"Do you know of any cases of alcohol addiction due to Sara Fenwick's Miracle Compound?"

"No, sir, none that I know of."

"Now then, Dr. Smith." Mr. Cromwell, a towering giant with a shock of red beard spreading over his vest, filled the courtroom with his magnificent voice. "Under what circumstances is the compound manufactured?"

"What do you mean?"

"Is the laboratory clean or dirty?"

"Why, it is sterile, sir!"

"You are in charge of the laboratory?"

"I am."

"How much of the operation do you oversee?"

"Every step of it."

"Is it possible for impurities or harmful ingredients to get into the compound?"

"No, sir, it is not possible."

"Could harmful bacteria get into the compound?"

"No, sir. Every step of the process is executed under the most sterile conditions."

"One last question, Dr. Smith. Would you object to your wife or daughter taking Sara Fenwick's Miracle Compound?"

"I would not."

"Thank you. No further questions, your honor."

Mr. Berrigan, Stanton's earnest young partner, rose to a lanky height, looking like a blond Abe Lincoln, and Samantha could not help but feel doubts about him. He looked too young, too smooth-faced.

"Good morning, Dr. Smith," he said, smiling, shambling up. "I won't detain you for long. I know you'll be wanting to get back to your family. By the way, did Mrs. Smith and your daughter accompany you to San Francisco?"

The chemist pinked. "Er . . . I have no wife and daughter."

"Oh?" Mr. Berrigan's blond brows rose high and he looked around the courtroom. "My mistake, Dr. Smith! I could have *sworn* I heard Mr. Cromwell refer to a wife and daughter."

"I believe he was speaking hypothetically."

"I see. Now then, Dr. Smith, when you say the compound is manufactured under sterile conditions, what exactly do you mean?"

"I beg your pardon?"

"Would you please define the term 'sterile' for the jury. Owning, of course, that there is another definition other than the one we attach to oxen."

An appreciative chuckle ran through the room.

"Sterile means free from germs."

"And how do you test for those germs, Dr. Smith?"

"How's that?"

"In the Fenwick laboratory, how do you know if germs are present or not?"

"Why, uh . . ."

"Do you check under a microscope?"

"Yes, a microscope."

"Can you give us an example of a germ? Say, describe for us what a cholera vibrio looks like?"

"Ah well, you see, I usually refer to a text when I conduct my checks."

"Of course, most thorough of you, Doctor. Tell me, where did you receive your degree?"

"My degree?"

"In chemistry."

The little man's eyes flickered to the table where John Fenwick and his lawyers sat. "Ah, from the Jamestown College of Natural Sciences."

"Did you reside on campus while undergoing instruction, or did you live in town?"

"Objection, your honor, I see no point to this question."

"Your honor," said Mr. Berrigan, "my next question will make very clear the point I am getting at. If I may be permitted?"

"Objection overruled. Answer the question, Dr. Smith."

"No, I didn't live on campus."

"Why not?"

"Because the Jamestown College of—"

"Please speak up, Dr. Smith."

"Because the Jamestown College of Natural Sciences is a correspondence school."

"And how long a course of instruction did you receive?"

Dr. Smith's face brightened to tomato-red. "I don't recall."

"Is it not true, Doctor, that one can receive a diploma from that college simply by sending in one hundred dollars?"

Pause. "Yes."

"And is that how you received your degree in chemistry?"

"Yes."

"So it is a *hypothetical* degree!"

A murmur rippled through the courtroom and Judge Venables banged his gavel.

"And is the Fenwick Company aware of this hypothetical degree?"

"Yes."

"Thank you, *Doctor* Smith. No further questions."

Mr. Cromwell called the next witness, Dr. John Morgani, vice-president of the Fenwick Company.

Mr. Cromwell stroked his beard thoughtfully. "Can you tell this Court, Dr. Morgani, your position with the Fenwick Company?"

"I am in charge of production of the compound."

"I thought that was Dr. Smith's capacity."

"He is in charge of the laboratory. He works under me."

"Then Dr. Smith takes orders from you?"

"He does."

"Do you ever check the conditions of the laboratory?"

"Frequently."

At the press table, the reporter who had done Smith as a mole now sketched Dr. Morgani as a ferret.

"How do you check for the presence of germs in the lab?"

"Under a microscope."

"Can *you* describe for us, sir, what a cholera vibrio looks like?"

"Yes, it very much resembles a comma."

"Now, Dr. Morgani, will you tell the Court where you received your degree in chemistry?"

"Johns Hopkins University in Maryland."

"Did you reside on campus or live in town?"

The courtroom laughed, Judge Venables banged his gavel.

"I lived on campus."

"And how long a course of instruction did you receive?"

"Four years."

"Then, Dr. Morgani," rang Mr. Cromwell's theatrical voice, "yours is not a *hypothetical* degree!"

As the room erupted in laughter, Mark wrote a note and pushed it toward Stanton. "They did this on purpose." And Weatherby wrote back, "I know. But they won't get away with it. Watch."

Mr. Berrigan stood up for cross-examination, turned toward the audience and offered a self-effacing grin, then he strode to the witness box. "Johns Hopkins," he said pleasantly. "Most impressive. You know, Doctor, I'm a little confused on the recipe of the compound. Dr. Smith listed a few things that went right over my head. Maybe you could clarify those ingredients for the jury. Like, for example, he mentioned life root. Is that known by any other name?"

"It is also called squawweed."

"Now why do you suppose they call it that?"

"I have no idea," said the chemist frostily.

The lanky young attorney came back to his table and picked up a book. "I have here, Dr. Morgani, a copy of John King's *American Dispensary.* Are you familiar with it?"

"I am."

"Would you please tell the Court what this book contains?"

"It is a reference of all known botanical medical agents, their properties, effects, and uses."

"Is it a reliable book?"

"It is an excellent reference."

Mr. Berrigan strolled back to the stand, thumbing the pages. "I found a listing here for squawweed and it does say it is also called life root, but it says here it's also called 'The Female Regulator.' Now what do you suppose that means?"

"I believe the definition is there, sir. It means that it can cure cases of amenorrhea."

"Will you please define that term for the jury?"

"It means a stoppage of the menses, of the monthly days."

"Then squawweed, or life root as Sara Fenwick calls it, restores that cycle when it has stopped?"

"It does."

"And what are some likely causes of amenorrhea?"

"There are many."

"Is pregnancy one?"

"Of course."

"Then, in effect, life root, and therefore the compound, is an abortifacient."

The courtroom stirred, Judge Venables called for order.

"Dr. Morgani, is that true?"

"But it is not sold as such!"

"Yes or no, please, are the ingredients in the compound abortifacients?"

"Yes."

As Mr. Berrigan returned to his seat and an excited rustling traveled through the room, Mr. Cromwell rose from his table. "Dr. Morgani," he called, "does Sara Fenwick prescribe the compound for pregnant women?"

"She does not."

"What, in fact, is her practice in such a situation?"

"Sara Fenwick most emphatically advises against pregnant women ingesting the compound."

"Thank you, Dr. Morgani."

On the fourth day of the trial Mr. Cromwell called a Mrs. Mary Llewellyn to the stand. Stanton Weatherby ran his finger down a list and saw that she was one of the testimonials Cy Jeffries had been able to refute. Over a glass of lemonade one sultry August day the Omaha housewife had confided to the handsome "brush salesman" that she had written the testimonial for the money and had never even tasted the compound. But now she was a witness for the Fenwicks; Stanton looked back over his shoulder at Jeffries in the rear of the courtroom, who shrugged with a puzzled expression.

"Mrs. Llewellyn," said Mr. Cromwell, "did you on April 23, 1890, write a testimonial letter to Sara Fenwick?"

"I did."

"And what, basically, was the content of that letter?"

"I thanked her for saving my life and for restoring me to health and happiness and to my family."

"What prompted the writing of that letter?"

"For years I had been suffering terribly with female trouble, it drove me to near insanity, and my husband had to move out of the house. I neglected my children and stopped going to church. Someone recommended I write to Sara Fenwick. I did, and she wrote back with a free bottle of her compound, telling me to take it every day and that I would get better. Well, your honor, not only did I improve in health, but my husband came back to my loving arms, we are a happy family again and I attend church every Sunday."

Samantha chanced a glance over at the press table and saw the reporters taking down every word. One of them, a gentleman with a head of wild white hair and droopy mustache, caught her look and sent her a wink. Mark Twain had been away from San Francisco for years, but this sensational trial had lured him back.

Young Mr. Berrigan questioned the woman next. "Tell me, Mrs. Llewellyn, is this your first time in San Francisco?"

"Yes."

"What do you think of our city?"

"It's mighty wonderful, sir!"

"Where are you staying?"

"Objection!"

"Sustained."

"Mrs. Llewellyn, how is it you're here today, in San Francisco, I mean?"

"Why, Mr. Fenwick asked me to come."

"I see. And did he pay your train fare?"

"He did, and first class, too!"

"And your hotel?"

"That Mr. Fenwick is a generous one. I'm staying at the Palace!"

A ripple of laughter went through the courtroom.

"Mrs. Llewellyn, have you been promised anything for your testimony here today?"

She looked past him to the plaintiff's table. John Fenwick's expression was carved out of granite.

Judge Venables said, "Please answer the question, madam."

"Well, sirs." She shifted in her chair. "The house badly needs painting."

"Please answer directly, Mrs. Llewellyn. Did the Fenwick Company offer you anything for your testimony today?"

"Yes, sir. A hundred dollars."

Murmurs rose in the audience.

"Now, Mrs. Llewellyn. In August of last year, do you recall inviting a brush salesman into your kitchen for a glass of lemonade?"

Her face reddened. "I don't recall."

"You don't? He said his name was Peterson and you bought a hairbrush from him and then you gave him lemonade and pie. You don't recall?"

She fidgeted again. "No."

"Mrs. Llewellyn, may I remind you of your oath?"

"I don't remember no brush salesman!"

"No further questions, your honor."

Over the next five days a string of testimonial writers was marched up to the stand, every one of them on the list Cy Jeffries had given to Stanton, and every one of them, after Mrs. Llewellyn, declared emphatically that she was being given nothing for testifying.

Horace Chandler could barely contain his fury. He paced Samantha's carpet as if to stamp out the oriental design. "Hell and damnation!" he cried, not excusing himself. "I know what they're up to. One by one, they're taking each piece of evidence we printed and destroying it! How in featheration did they get the names of those women?"

Cy Jeffries, who looked like a Barbary Coast bouncer, could only shrug.

"I know how," said Mark, leaning on the mantel. "It's routine practice for the Fenwick Company, every now and then, to follow up on testimonial letter writers. Each one of those women, and others besides, heard from the Fenwick Company asking if anyone had inquired about their testimonials. I would imagine each of those women mentioned a certain dapper brush salesman." He smiled at Cy but the detective only scowled.

"So now what?" asked Darius.

Stanton twisted the onyx ring on his finger. "It's no use calling those women back. They've been bought. All we can do is bide our time. What

I'm curious to see is how they're going to handle the fact that Mrs. Fenwick doesn't exist. We should at least be able to nail them on false advertising and fraudulent mail. They show her face, declare that the compound recipe is hers, and claim she signs each letter that goes out."

"Maybe they do it through a medium," said Mark, but no one laughed.

Day ten of the trial finally saw women sitting in the audience. Hilary, despite Darius's objections, sat in the front row, and at her side was Jennifer, who caught the admiring eye of more than one news reporter. The sketch artist did not restrict himself to the participants of the trial: he picked a few out of the audience. Jenny emerged as a butterfly, Hilary Gant, in her fur coat, as a collie dog. Other women in the crowd represented the Women's Christian Temperance Union, the women's suffrage movement, a women authors' club, and several well-known feminists, brazenly smoking cigarettes. There were also a couple of illustrious lady physicians from back East.

Mr. Cromwell's next witness came as a surprise to the defense. In Cy's investigation, he had produced death certificates of women who had died but who were still used in Fenwick advertising as "miraculous cures." Three physicians were now called up to explain.

"Did you know Mrs. Saunders well, Doctor?"

"I did indeed."

"Were you with her at the end?"

"I was."

"Is this your handwriting on the death certificate?"

"It is."

"Will you tell the Court, please, what Mrs. Saunders died of?"

"A blood clot on the brain."

"Were you aware that Mrs. Saunders was taking Sara Fenwick's Miracle Compound every day?"

"I was."

"And what was it for?"

"Pelvic congestion."

"Did the compound cure that particular problem?"

"She claimed it did."

"Therefore, Doctor, would you say that, even though Mrs. Saunders is dead from one cause, the Miracle Compound could have cured her other, unrelated ailment?"

"Yes, sir."

Stanton drew angry triangles on his note pad. Then he scribbled, "They've gotten to everyone," and showed it to Samantha. She nodded, picked up the pen and wrote, "And at enormous expense. What now?"

The stony looks on the jurors' faces did not bode well. Samantha knew the Fenwicks had the upper hand. But only for now. When it was defense's turn, her witnesses would come forward, ladies who had been severely damaged by drinking the compound, and then Cy Jeffries would make his statement. All in all, she remained hopeful.

Mr. Cromwell's witness on day eleven was the supervisor of the correspondence room, who declared most religiously that *no men were allowed in the letter room,* which was a direct contradiction of Cy's observation.

"Our ads promise that no man sees the woman's letter, and we mean it. The correspondence room is strictly ladies only."

Stanton looked back at Cy, who shook his head.

On day twelve the bombastic Mr. Cromwell delivered his biggest surprise. "I call to the stand Jane Fenwick."

Everyone swiveled to watch the doors open, and Stanton muttered to Mark, "Who in blazes is Jane Fenwick?"

A prim lady in her mid-fifties came modestly down the aisle, took the stand, repeated the oath on the Bible, then seated herself. Upon Mr. Cromwell's request, she explained to the Court her relationship to the Fenwick family. "My husband's grandmother was Sara Fenwick."

"Then you are married?"

"I am."

"Then I shall address you as *Mrs.* Fenwick. Did you know Sara Fenwick during her life?"

"I did. I came to the Fenwick house when I was in my teens and I was companion to the ailing Sara Fenwick the last three years before her death."

"And during those years, what transpired between you two?"

"Mrs. Fenwick taught me all she knew about women's disorders, how to diagnose and advise, and before her death she voiced an old dream she had had to found a company, one devoted to the manufacture and sale of a medicine upon which she had relied for many years and which she used to brew on her own kitchen stove. Before she died, Sara Fenwick whispered the recipe of that medicine to me."

"Is that the compound?"

"It is."

"Then it is true that the compound is indeed Sara Fenwick's, and that the advice given in letters is in fact hers?"

"Yes."

"What is your position today with the Fenwick Company?"

"I work in the correspondence room."

The courtroom stirred (later, Cy Jeffries would insist that Jane Fenwick had never been seen around the plant in his six months of employment there).

"Tell me, Mrs. Fenwick, are you mentioned in any of the Fenwick advertisements?"

"I am."

"Would you please tell us in what context?"

"The ads promise that Mrs. Fenwick reads and answers all correspondence personally. *I* am that Mrs. Fenwick."

Four reporters jumped up and dashed out for the telephones and the courtroom was chaos over which the gavel could barely be heard. Samantha closed her eyes and took several deep breaths, and she thought: You were right, Horace, they've destroyed our whole case.

She opened her eyes and turned her head to the left. John Fenwick sat with arms across his barrel chest, utter satisfaction glowing in his eyes. And she mentally added: But we're not beaten yet . . .

❈

Life and *Saturday Evening Post* were on the side of the three defendants and ran satirical cartoons of a big cat that looked like John Fenwick trembling before three little mice with clubs; but the rest of the press coverage was unfavorable. Samantha's alabaster profile was a favorite front-page photo, and each little movement, each tiny stir she made, was dutifully recorded for the nation's eyes. "Dr. Samantha Hargrave is bearing up remarkably well, holding herself immobile, her aristocratic posture a veritable challenge to John Fenwick at the next table."

"What next, Stanton?"

The five were having a quiet dinner at the Gant house. It was drizzling outside and the air was gravid with the threat of a storm. "What next? Well, Cromwell might have a few more witnesses up his sleeve, but I'd say he's close to resting. He's fairly laid it on the jury with a trowel that everything the *Woman's Companion* printed was a lie." Stanton stopped there and didn't finish his thoughts. In fourteen days he had gotten a good reading of Cromwell's character and had a strong suspicion of what might come next; but he wouldn't voice it, at least not right now.

Day fourteen produced the maneuver Stanton had secretly feared. When Miss Hains, Chandler's secretary, was called, Stanton was the only one in the courtroom not surprised.

"Are you acquainted with Dr. Hargrave, Miss Hains?"

"Yes, sir." The poor woman turned big apologetic eyes toward her employer. Horace had to look away; he had guessed what Cromwell was up to and couldn't bear to watch his secretary's agony.

"Did Dr. Hargrave make frequent visits to Mr. Chandler's office?"

"I don't know what you mean by frequent."

"Once a week?"

"It was more like once every two weeks."

"And what went on during those visits?"

"Objection."

"Sustained."

"Did anyone else ever join them?"

"Yes, sir. Dr. Rawlins did."

"Did those sessions ever last into the evening?"

Mr. Berrigan flew to his feet. "Objection! Your honor, this line of questioning is not apropos of this trial."

Judge Venables said, "Mr. Cromwell, I presume your questioning is leading to something?"

"Your honor, we wish to establish the moral character of these people who have attacked my client. Mr. Fenwick has suffered loss of income, failing health, family upset, and his credibility in the business community. It is necessary therefore to determine the qualifications of those who have cast the stones!"

Samantha felt an icy tightening of her stomach and she could not help a quick glance at the "failing" John Fenwick. Every reporter in the room seized upon that glance. "She shot daggers at him," declared one newspaper. "If looks could annihilate," said another. The *Chronicle* described it as "righteous indignation."

"Objection overruled. Please answer the question, miss."

"Yes, their sessions sometimes went into the evening."

"Did you ever join them?"

"No, sir."

"So it was just Dr. Hargrave and the two gentlemen?"

"Yes, sir."

"Did you ever serve them refreshment?"

Miss Hains's hands worked on the strap of her purse. "Tea and biscuits."

"Did you ever serve them alcohol?"

When the purse handle snapped it sounded like a gunshot.

"Miss Hains?"

She bowed her head. "I once brought them brandy."

Stanton Weatherby looked over at the twelve in the jury box and, for the first time, saw real interest on their faces.

"Do you know what they talked about in Mr. Chandler's office?"

"It was all about drugs, sir."

"Any specific drugs?"

"Mostly Sara Fenwick's."

"In other words, a medicine for female problems."

"Yes."

"Did they ever use any materials, books perhaps?"

"Mr. Chandler's desk was always covered with pamphlets and letters and medical journals."

"What was the content of these materials?"

Her face was so crimson the poor woman looked as if she might pass out. "They were mostly about . . . women's problems."

"So!" Mr. Cromwell flung an oratorical finger ceilingward. "You are telling us that the three defendants, one woman and two men, kept late hours in Mr. Chandler's office, *alone*, drinking alcohol and discussing the very most intimate parts of a woman's body!"

When the reporters dashed for the telephones, Judge Venables rapped his gavel and then recessed the court so that "the gentlemen of the press might convene in chambers for a lesson on court deportment."

Miss Hains had to be helped from the room.

The next morning beneath a dark gray sky that was threatening to break into a major storm, a picket line marched before the courthouse steps, women carrying signs denouncing Mr. Cromwell's despicable tactics. The reporters had a heyday photographing this "army of formidable Amazons."

During that day's questioning the storm broke. Great cracks of thunder shook the courthouse, and Mr. Berrigan's voice was frequently drowned out.

That evening dinner was at Samantha's house. Now they all sat around the table spacing their conversation between gusts of howling wind that rattled the windows.

"I'm worried, Stanton," said Samantha, barely touching her dinner. "After seeing Mr. Cromwell in action, I am afraid for my patients. I don't know if they can stand up to his tactics."

Weatherby had no chance to reply, for just then the front-door chimes mingled with the cracks of thunder, and in the next instant a very soaked Mr. Berrigan burst in on them.

"What is it?" said Mark, rising.

"Cy Jeffries!" he blurted out, stumbling for a chair. "He's been in an accident!"

"What!"

"Darius, some whiskey, please, quickly!"

"Here, Berrigan. Sit here."

"Is he all right?"

"He's in County Hospital, barely alive."

"How—"

"What—"

The drenched young man looked up at the anxious faces circling him. "They say he slipped off the Hyde Street cable car"—there was a collective gasp—"and then was struck by a passing carriage."

Hilary sank into a chair, her eyes filling with tears, while the men mumbled strong oaths. Mark took the decanter from Darius and poured a large shot for Mr. Berrigan. Then he looked up at Samantha.

Her face was like a stone mask.

❈

She had two days to prepare, for the detective had met his accident on Friday and court wasn't reconvening until Monday. Samantha had a lot of thinking and planning to do.

The merciless downpour continued to hold San Francisco in a crippling grip, and as the heavy rain came down in unrelenting sheets Samantha sat alone in her office at home beside a warm fire with a glass of claret in her hand.

She heard Mark come through the front door, exchange a few words with Miss Peoples as he removed his wet coat, then he was kneeling next to Samantha, kissing her.

"How is he?" she asked.

"Not good, brain damage." Mark got up and went to the service cart.

"Mark," she said quietly.

"Yes, darling."

"I'm going to take the stand."

He turned around. "What?"

"Mr. Cromwell will attack my patients. I can't put them through it."

"No, Samantha."

She came to her feet, feeling unusually tired, and went into his arms. "We've sat and listened to their side long enough, Mark. Now I want to get up there and tell the world the truth."

"Leave it to Stanton, Sam. He knows best."

FOURTEEN

THE COURTROOM SMELLED OF DAMP CLOTHES. IT WAS A musty, chilly atmosphere and the inordinate number of bodies crammed into the room did little to warm it up. Last Friday the prosecution had rested, now it was the turn for the defense; Mr. Berrigan had to space his speech around the thunder. "It had been our intention at this time, your honor, to call our chief witness, Mr. Cy Jeffries, to the stand. However, Mr. Jeffries met with a serious accident and now lies critical in County Hospital. The man is not expected to live."

Samantha had to fight to keep herself from looking over at John Fenwick, who, she was certain, had arranged the "accident."

"The defense would like to call Mrs. Joan Sargent."

The door of the courtroom opened and everyone turned. A small woman stepped shyly into the room, and as she walked up to the stand, the artist reporter at the press table drew a mouse in a very large coat.

"Mrs. Sargent," said Mr. Berrigan, "will you please tell the Court when you first became Dr. Hargrave's patient?"

"It was one year ago."

"I'm sorry, Mrs. Sargent, but you're going to have to speak up."

"One year ago," she said more loudly.

"Now, Mrs. Sargent, would you please tell us why you went to Dr. Hargrave?"

Mrs. Sargent had frequently to be reminded to speak up, and every time the thunder clapped she jumped. "It all started after my Timmy was born, about six years ago . . ."

The room was eerily silent as everyone paid rapt attention to the quiet voice. Mrs. Sargent's story was interrupted only by the occasional *ping* of a tobacco quid flying into a spittoon or the distant grumble of thunder. She told of her letters to Sara Fenwick, the gradual increase of the doses of compound, Sara Fenwick's advice against surgery, and her final, desperate visit to Dr. Hargrave. When she reached the part about her hysterectomy, her voice started to quake. "I was scared my husband wouldn't love me anymore because I wasn't a whole woman."

Samantha kept a watchful eye on Mrs. Sargent, afraid she might break down.

"Now, Mrs. Sargent," said Mr. Berrigan, "will you please tell the Court the cause of all this tragedy?"

"Yes!" she cried sharply, startling everyone. "Dr. Hargrave told me if I'd gone to a doctor at the start instead of writing to Mrs. Fenwick I could have been saved a lot of grief. I wrote to Mrs. Fenwick that I was *awful* sick and she just wrote back and told me to drink more of the compound!" She raised an arm and leveled a shaking finger at John Fenwick. "You! I believed your lies!"

The courtroom stirred; Fenwick leaned over and murmured in Cromwell's ear. Berrigan looked at Stanton for a signal and, seeing it, said, "No further questions at this time."

When Cromwell rose, stroking his red beard, which was fanned across his checkered vest, Samantha whispered to Stanton, "Can this be stopped?"

"We've no choice."

"It was a mistake. He'll destroy her."

"Mrs. Sargent," boomed Cromwell, pacing back and forth before her as if to make her dizzy, "you told this Court that your condition was fibroids. Was this condition chronic, that is, did you have it all the time?"

"Nearly."

"How far had it progressed when you wrote to Mrs. Fenwick?"

"Not very."

Mr. Cromwell's eyes rounded. "You mean you wrote to her of a condition *you did not yet have?*"

"That's not what I meant. You're twisting my words."

"I'm confused, Mrs. Sargent. If you didn't know what your affliction was at that time, how could you possibly give Mrs. Fenwick enough information for her to make an accurate diagnosis?"

"I had the symptoms!"

"And what symptoms are those, madam?"

"You're a man, you wouldn't understand."

"Mrs. Sargent! Are you saying that the majority of the members of this Court, including his honor himself, and the gentlemen of the jury, all being men, cannot grasp the circumstances that led you to write that first letter? How then are we to determine if the letter was even legitimate?"

"It was legitimate!" she cried, and burst into tears.

"Mr. Cromwell," said Judge Venables, "you are bullying the witness. Mrs. Sargent, you may step down from the stand."

As a court officer helped the witness out of the room, there was a brief conference at the defense table, with four men shaking their heads and one woman nodding vigorously. Then Mr. Berrigan stood and, with great reluctance, said, "Your honor, the defense would like to call Dr. Samantha Hargrave."

❈

The reporter with the sketch pad was having difficulty settling upon a choice. The others had all been easy: Cromwell he depicted as a grizzly bear, Mr. Berrigan as a whooping crane, Stanton Weatherby as a bloodhound and Judge Venables as a St. Bernard. But Dr. Hargrave eluded him. He started with a long-necked Egyptian cat because of her peculiar eyes, then discarded it as a vain and selfish animal. He tried next a sleek horse, but it wasn't feminine enough; then a deer and decided that was too timid. At the last minute, on an inspiration, it came to him to create a whole new fantastical creature, complete with wings and fur, grace and power, and leaf-shaped eyes, and as he started sketching, and as Samantha started quietly to speak, in the distance could be heard from over the turbulent ocean the slow advance of thunder.

Right from the start she surprised them, and also disappointed them a little, for they had expected her to shout and emote and provide them all with a good show; but instead Samantha sat in an easy, self-assured way and spoke in a voice that was loud and yet curiously quiet at the same time. The silence that fell over the courtroom was an unearthly one, this time not even the spittoon disturbed the air, and the thunder, rather than compete with her, seemed to have been sent to help, punctuating her sentences.

"Your honor, esteemed gentlemen of the jury, dear friends and members of the press. This is indeed an unfortunate day in the history of our country, for our very presence here holds us up to all the world as a nation of self-interested money seekers who sacrifice honor and lives in the pursuit of the dollar. But I say that Mr. Fenwick's fight here today will bring him no gain, for there are no pockets in a shroud."

As Samantha turned her cold eyes to him, she felt overcome, once again, by an inexplicable fatigue which caused her to reach out for the rail. Mark, keeping a close eye on her, thought Samantha was unusually pale.

"I have many witnesses who wish to come forward and speak; but I would like to speak for them, if I may. One lady found herself one morning to have a small sore in her private area. A maiden lady who had all her life guarded her modesty from inspection, she believed the declaration in the Fenwick ads that a woman should not expose herself to anyone, not even a physician. She wrote to Mrs. Fenwick and received the reply that a tablespoon a day of the compound would alleviate her problem. There was no mention in that reply letter of the sore, nor any indication that Mrs. Fenwick had given any consideration to the woman's particular complaint. In time, the sore became larger and started to drain. The lady wrote again to Mrs. Fenwick and was again told that the compound would cure her. Trusting that mighty corporation, not knowing that their ads lied, and trusting the kindly face in the oval portrait, not knowing that it was the face of a woman long dead, my patient increased her daily intake of the Miracle Compound.

"The sore festered and soon became unbearable. She wrote a third time, utterly trusting and naive. A lotion was sent, with instructions to apply it daily, along with an order to increase her intake of the compound. By this time my patient was ingesting so much of the compound, which is twenty-five percent alcohol, that she had no appetite for food; she lost weight. The sore spread.

"It was on the insistence of her sister that I was finally brought in. I found the lady in such an advanced state of anemia, malnutrition, and depression that I feared there was little I could do. And when I examined her, it was my heartbreaking duty to inform the woman she had cancer."

Samantha paused, both for effect and to steady herself. In alarm she realized she was becoming lightheaded.

"Had that lady, who is in her forty-third year, come to me at the start, I could have excised that small sore and she would have gone on with her happy, productive life. Today I give her no more than a year to live, and those final months will be filled with agony beyond describing. Thanks to Sara Fenwick's Miracle Compound."

Samantha surveyed the faces in the courtroom, all fixed on her, all expressionless; even the men at the press table had forgotten the pencils in their hands.

"Another victim of the Fenwick Company is a young woman who was the sad prey, one night, of the advances of a drunken boarder in her mother's house. An innocent girl, ignorant of what had been done to her, she kept the awful incident a secret, and when her menses ceased, having no knowledge of these things and thus not connecting the cessation of her menses with that awful incident and thinking instead she had an illness, she wrote in fear and trembling to Mrs. Fenwick. That innocent child, barely out of girlhood, trustingly followed the advice of Mrs. Fenwick's letter to drink an entire bottle of the compound. As promised in the letter, a 'tumor on the uterus' was dislodged and expelled, with much pain and bleeding, and when the girl saw the features of that 'tumor,' she went into a form of hysteria that only the most drastic therapy has been able to cure. But she is today a shattered woman and can never hope for a normal life."

Samantha drew in a deep breath; the lightheadedness was worsening.

She shifted a little and settled her calm eyes on the twelve in the jury box. "Gentlemen, I have called drug manufacturers murderers. And I still do. In this courtroom today sits a man who has been left alone with eight children because his wife turned to Dr. Rupert Wells's Cancer Cure instead of going to a surgeon. How many of you, at this moment, have a wife or a daughter or a mother or a sister who is filling her poor afflicted body with the elixir of false hope and shameless deceit?

Mr. Cromwell, in his opening statement, spoke of rights and freedoms. He would have you believe that government regulation means slavery for all of you. But I will tell you whom you are slaves to—these drug manufacturers, they are your real lords and masters. For they have made you their puppets, with their lies. They make promises they cannot fulfill while they take your money, and they treat you like children and imbeciles, keeping secret the recipes of their compounds as though you hadn't the intelligence to understand them. And because there is no one to protect you, you trust them, like lambs going to the slaughter, handing over your hard-earned money while they feed you poison and addiction and death.

"Why should you be lied to, gentlemen? And why should you tolerate it? If you buy a bottle labeled rum, do you not expect rum to be in that bottle? And yet as many times as not, you have bought medicines that make claims to being what they are not! Mr. Cromwell has claimed I wish to rob you of your rights," she said in a loud, clear voice that belied the queer faintness that was coming over her. "I wish to *give* you rights! The right to know what is contained in the medicine you buy! For that, gentlemen, is the American way!"

Her voice rose; she started to tremble. When the room grew dim Samantha thought the electric lights were failing because of the storm, then she realized there was nothing wrong with the lights. *I'm going to pass out,* she thought.

Pushing herself up to her feet and holding on to the judge's bench for support, Samantha said in a ringing voice, "This inhuman exploitation must be stopped! And if you will not do it for yourselves, then do it for your wives and children. Do it for little Willie Jenkins who died in my arms after eating cough lozenges bought at the corner drugstore. Do it for an innocent laundress named Nellie who crushed an arm in a wringer after drinking a remedy so heavily laced with narcotic her senses were confused—"

Samantha's voice caught. Tears rose in her eyes. In a whisper that had the impact of a shout, she said, "Do it for the little babies who die in their sleep because Milikin's Soothing Syrup contains enough opium to knock out a man. And do it for the poor bereft mothers of those babies who must live out their lives knowing they had been the unwitting murderers of their children . . ."

Samantha closed her eyes and swayed. Thunder crashed directly overhead and the courthouse shook. Chaos erupted in the room, and as she dimly saw the reporters shoot out of their seats and dash for the telephones and heard the roar of a hundred people cheering, she thought absurdly: But I'm not finished yet . . .

And then the floor beneath the witness box suddenly gave way, like a trap door, and Samantha realized she was tumbling into the cold black basement below. But Mark caught her in time and the last thing she saw before unconsciousness swept over her were his gentle brown eyes, loving, and caring.

FIFTEEN

*F*LOATING.

The sky was red and she saw little white pinwheels. Her body felt like a feather. Then there was an awful nausea and she feared she was going to vomit in the witness stand. But then she realized she wasn't in the witness stand at all but sitting in the top tier of the operating theater at North London Hospital. Mr. Bomsie held his scalpel between his teeth and his apron was caked with the blood from a recent autopsy. He was about to remove a young woman's breast and Samantha tried to call out to tell him he had forgotten to sterilize his instruments and to give the patient ether to stop her screaming. And Freddy, next to her, was telling her that Mr. Bomsie didn't know better so she shouldn't get upset.

And then she was cold, freezing cold, and she was slipping and sliding on the ice and reaching into turbulent black water to get hold of the red hair just below the surface.

She rolled her head to the side, lifted her heavy lids and saw a dark gray rain washing down the windows, and she thought: The bay waters are rising, we'll all drown . . .

"How are you feeling?" came a deep voice.

Samantha blinked up at Mark. "What happened?"

"You fainted. How do you feel?"

She rolled her head to the side and moaned.

"I'm afraid you banged your head before I could catch you. Lie still, Sam. There's no hurry. Court's recessed for the day."

She looked around the room; it was Judge Venables' chamber. "How long have I been here?"

"Just a few minutes. As soon as you're up to it, I'll take you home." Mark brought a glass of brandy to her lips but she refused it. "What made you faint like that, Sam?"

She had to work to focus on his face, then, seeing the dark concern there, she smiled. "The doctor is the last to know! How stupid of me, Mark. I've been so wrapped up in the trial I didn't pay any attention to the signs."

"What signs?"

"The signs of pregnancy."

"Of preg—Oh, Sam! Is it true?"

Her smile widened. "I'm still under oath, aren't I?"

Mark's answer was to take her into his arms.

Judge Venables put his head into the room. "How is she?"

Samantha's patients took the stand and, as anticipated, Mr. Cromwell's theatrics discredited their testimonies; the jury was out for six days and came back with a judgment in favor of the Fenwick Company.

"They could go no other way," said Stanton Weatherby, putting another log on the fire. "The Fenwicks were able to substantiate all their advertising claims. But it's a pyrrhic victory for them."

Legally, the Fenwicks were in the right; morally and ethically, however, it was another question. The Fenwicks' victory was shortlived when the judge awarded a settlement of only fifty dollars and then proceeded to lecture Mr.

Fenwick very sternly on his future practices. And the press had so applauded Dr. Hargrave's cause that it appeared she had won the case.

"Now then," Samantha said, putting her feet up on a stool and smiling around at her friends. "We've started the movement. The *Chronicle* had to open a special office just to handle the mail that has come pouring in, all of it in favor of our crusade. But now I would like to broaden our interests. I think we should join with Harvey Wiley in his efforts to push for food reform as well, since we are basically aiming for the honest labeling of *everything* we put into our bodies, and—"

"Samantha dear," said Hilary, "when are you going to have time for all that? You are going to have to slow down now, you know."

"Whatever for? I'm pregnant, not sick! Horace, what are your thoughts on joining Mr. Wiley?"

"Well"—he pulled a toothpick out of his mouth—"I think we might be able to arouse some real public interest in that area. My readers would be very interested to know that the rum and brandy they buy is often nothing more than raw alcohol with food coloring."

"Our soldiers in the Philippines are being sent tins of embalmed beef," said Darius.

"And Mrs. Gossett in the kitchen," added Willella, "*swears* there is formaldehyde in our canned corn."

"Remember Toby Watson?" said Samantha. "Remember how sick he got on that molasses candy? We found sulfuric acid in it." Samantha's eyes brightened. "Yes, indeed, we must now turn our attention to everything we put into our bodies, drugs and food. And we must get started on it at once."

Mark came to sit on the arm of her chair, Samantha reached up for his hand. In the glow of the fire, with the rain coming down outside, and in the circle of her friends, Samantha had never felt happier. She thought of the crusade ahead, the courtroom fights, Mark's cancer research, and a bright future of medical progress; she envisioned a bigger Infirmary and thought of the new century, just a year and a half away. And she said quietly, "We may have lost the first battle but, by heavens, we'll continue the fight . . ."

FROM
THE DIVINING
A NOVEL BY BARBARA WOOD
NOW AVAILABLE

1

*S*HE CAME SEEKING ANSWERS.

Nineteen-year-old Ulrika had awoken that morning with the feeling that something was wrong. The feeling had grown while she had bathed and dressed, and her slaves had bound up her hair and tied sandals to her feet, and brought her a breakfast of wheat porridge and goat's milk. When the inexplicable uneasiness did not go away, she decided to visit the Street of Fortune-Tellers, where seers and mystics, astrologers and soothsayers promised solutions to life's mysteries.

Now, as she was carried through the noisy streets of Rome in a curtained chair, she wondered what had caused her uneasiness. Yesterday, everything had been fine. She had visited friends, browsed in bookshops, spent time at her loom—the typical day of a young woman of her class and breeding. But then she had had a strange dream . . .

Just past the midnight hour, Ulrika had dreamed that she gotten out of bed, crossed to her window, climbed out, and landed barefoot in snow. In the dream, tall pines grew all around her, instead of the fruit trees behind her villa, a forest instead of an orchard, and clouds whispered across the face of a winter moon. She saw tracks—big paw prints in the snow, leading into the woods. Ulrika followed them, feeling moonlight brush her bare shoulders. She came upon a large, shaggy wolf with golden eyes. She sat down in the snow and he came to lie beside her, putting his head in her lap. The night was pure, as pure as the wolf's eyes gazing up at her, and she could feel the steady beat of his mighty heart beneath his ribs. The golden eyes blinked and seemed to say: Here is trust, here is love, here is home.

Ulrika had awoken disoriented. And then she had wondered: Why did I dream of a wolf? Wulf was my father's name. He died long ago in faraway Persia.

Is the dream a sign? But a sign of what?

Her slaves brought the chair to a halt, and Ulrika stepped down, a tall girl wearing a long gown of pale pink silk, with a matching stole that draped over her head and shoulders in proper maidenly modesty, hiding tawny hair and a graceful neck. She carried herself with a poise and confidence that concealed a growing anxiety.

The Street of Fortune-Tellers was a narrow alley obscured by the shadow of crowded tenement buildings. The tents and stalls of the psychics, augers, seers, and soothsayers looked promising, painted in bright colors, festooned with glittering objects, each one brighter than the next. Business was booming for purveyors of good-luck charms, magic relics, and amulets.

As Ulrika entered the lane, desperate to know the meaning of the wolf dream, hawkers called to her from tents and booths, claiming to be "genuine Chaldeans," to have direct channels to the future, to possess the Third Eye. She went first to the bird-reader, who kept crates of pigeons whose entrails he read for a few pennies. His hands caked with blood, he assured Ulrika that she would find a husband before the year was out. She went next to the stall of the smoke-reader, who declared that the incense predicted five healthy children for Ulrika.

She continued on until, three quarters along the crowded lane, she came upon a person of humble appearance, sitting only on a frayed mat, with no shade or booth or tent. The seer sat cross-legged in a long white robe that had known better days, long bony hands resting on bony knees. The head was bowed, showing a crown of hair that was blacker than jet, parted in the middle and streaming over the shoulders and back. Ulrika did not know why she would choose so impoverished a soothsayer—perhaps on some level she felt this one might be more interested in truth than in money—but she came to a halt before the curious person, and waited.

After a moment, the fortune-teller lifted her head, and Ulrika was startled by the unusual aspect of the face, which was long and narrow, all bone and yellow skin, framed by the streaming black hair. Mournful black eyes beneath highly arched brows looked up at Ulrika. The woman almost did not look human, and she was ageless. Was she twenty or eighty? A brown and black spotted cat lay curled asleep next to the fortune-teller. Ulrika recognized the breed as an Egyptian Mau, said to be the most ancient of cat breeds, possibly even the progenitor from which all cats had sprung.

Ulrika brought her attention back to the fortune-teller's swimming black eyes filled with sadness and wisdom.

"You have a question," the fortune-teller said in perfect Latin, eyes peering steadily from deep sockets.

The sounds of the alley faded. Ulrika was captured by the black Egyptian eyes, while the brown cat snoozed obliviously.

"You want to ask me about a wolf," the Egyptian said in a voice that sounded older than the Nile.

"It was in a dream, Wise One. Was it a sign?"

"A sign of what? Tell me your question."

"I do not know where I belong, Wise One. My mother is Roman, my father German. I was born in Persia and have spent most of my life roaming with my mother, for she followed a quest. Everywhere we went, I felt like an outsider. I am worried, Wise One, that if I do not know where I belong, I will never know who I am. Was the wolf dream a sign that I belong in the Rhineland with my father's people? Is it time for me to leave Rome?"

"There are signs all about you, daughter. The gods guide us everywhere, every moment."

"You speak in riddles, Wise One. Can you at least tell me my future?"

"There will be a man," the fortune-teller said, "who will offer you a key. Take it."

"A key? To what?"

"You will know when the time comes . . ."

CPSIA information can be obtained at www.ICGtesting.com
Printed in the USA
LVOW12s1706270314

379216LV00006B/853/P